THEM OLD WAYS NEVER DIED

by

Joshua Cutchin

Them Old Ways Never Died © 2023 Joshua Cutchin

All rights reserved. No part of this book may be used or reproduced in any manner whatsoever without written permission, except in the case of brief quotations embodied in critical articles and reviews. For more information, please contact the author.

ISBN: 9798854608725

First edition in the United States, August 28, 2023
Author's website: JoshuaCutchin.com
Cover design and title page art by Miguel Romero
Edited by Barbara Fisher

This is a work of fiction. Names, characters, places, and incidents are the products of the author's imagination or are used fictitiously and are not to be construed as real.

Acknowledgments

The author wishes to thank Barbara Fisher, Mike Clelland, Miguel Romero, Wren Collier, Jack Hunter, Douglas Batchelor, Morgan Daimler, Neil Rushton, Greg Bishop, and his family.

With special gratitude to David Metcalfe. There, I finally did it. Happy now?

1

Monday, August 2, 1897

HAYSTORM

YEARS LATER, WHEN PEOPLE ASKED her to tell the story again, The Mother always said it was around six in the evening when her life fell apart.

Before everything took a turn for the worse, everyone on the farm held high hopes. Days of rain finally gave way to sunshine, the storm clouds breaking like an overlong fever. With it came a collective sigh of relief. So much was at stake.

Aided by their neighbors, The Family finished cutting the hay days earlier, just before the sky opened up, and once they realized it was here to stay, a mild undercurrent of dread set in. Any farmer in County Westmeath worth his salt knew that less than a week of showers could render all their backbreaking work useless.

The Father had watched the skies with a cautiously optimistic eye, consulting Old Lady Duffy daily on the condition of her knee, hoping for good news. "Ach, not yet," she'd say before returning to her knitting.

So he and The Family would trudge out to the fields once more, turn over the hay, and hope that tomorrow would be different. After three "Not yets," the weather shifted from pissin' to only spittin', and at last the pain in her knee relented.

"Might be tomorrow," she had grinned, patting her leg. "May be a good day for dryin'. Praise be. Pain was so awful, I was ready to dig a hole for myself."

Old Lady Duffy's knee was right—today was grand. The Mother knew it from daybreak. Dawn's golden light roused her with the warm caresses of a lover, heralding hard work ahead—but infinitely preferable to another day of toiling in the rain. The Father, having milked the cows before daybreak, burst into the bedroom.

"Good morning, love," he whispered, a grin lifting his bushy mustache. He sat on the bed, brushing strands of vermillion hair from her eyes. "Rain's gone. Air's fine today. Smells clean. No doubt it'll be splittin' stones by midday."

Right away, the neighbors descended upon the farm, all abuzz and eager to save the hay as soon as possible. Maybe a celebration was in the offing, should they finish early enough. Six men in total came to help, including the Brennan boys from over by Crookedwood. Riley Murphy even brought along his horse and newfangled hay turner to speed things up a bit.

To show The Family's gratitude, The Mother shared breakfast with everyone. Soon enough, a hefty helping of stirabout filled each man's belly.

Normally, they would have waited until around nine o'clock to let the dew evaporate off the top of the hay, but given how foul the weather had been, they set out early to maximize the time it could dry. Every person with two hands and a strong back grabbed a pitchfork, including The Mother.

The only person excused was Nan, who was taxed with even more laborious work: keeping tabs on The Family's three children. While everyone else took to the field, she and The Brother, The Sister, and The Child sat beneath the shade of a tall hawthorn tree along the southwest hedgerow.

The Mother was grateful. She trusted Nan implicitly. The Father may have been Nan's son, but she and The Mother claimed a special affinity. Nan never birthed a daughter herself, and when The Mother came into The Family five years ago, the bond between the two proved instantaneous.

How much changed in those five years. When The Mother first arrived, she had only seen twenty winters, and it was just her, The Father, and his parents, Nan and Big Liam. The forty-four acres of farmland were still rented back then, as were the barn and the sturdy, two story, gable-ended farmhouse in which they resided.

It did not stay that way for long. Soon after the wedding, the landlord passed away, God rest his soul. His son, thinking of Big Liam as something of a second father, parted with the property for a song. Combined with a government loan, owning the farm outright became feasible.

Too bad Big Liam can't be here to appreciate all this, The Mother thought as she began her work. He had survived The Famine alongside Nan, but couldn't survive the cruelty of chance. Two years, this September. At age thirty, The Father found himself sole proprietor of the farm, where he set about raising his own family.

The Mother knew Big Liam smiled upon his legacy. The property was a dream come true. Not only did they have enough acreage to raise chickens, a flock of sheep, and a pair of milk cows, but there was also ample room for gardening. For the children, it became Tír na nÓg, a playground where their imaginations ran amok.

There was much amok happening today. The Mother took a break from heaving hay to glance towards the hedgerow. Her heart skipped a beat when she only saw Nan and the cradle. Moments later, the sound of her son and daughter playing in the adjacent field wafted through the greenery from the other side. Dropping stones in the well, likely as not.

The Mother suffocated an uneasy twitch welling up in her gut. There was no reason to worry. The children knew not to wander any farther. They knew the stories about what lay beyond as well as anyone.

Still, she'd be beside herself, should anything happen. They were her reason for existing: The Brother, four, The Sister, two, and The Child, nearly one year old. He lay in his cradle beneath the tree, and even from this distance, The Mother could hear him giggling at Nan's teasing. Such sounds had become commonplace over the last year. Moreso than her other children, The Child seemed born with an especially good disposition, more prone to laugh than cry.

The Mother made a reminder to have him baptized, along with The Sister, before they got too far into the harvest. She intended to do so for a while, but things just always seemed too busy. Always something to do around the farm.

Having another child represented a short-term tradeoff, sacrificing immediate convenience for long-term joy and, frankly, help around the farm when they reached adolescence. For the time being, having an extra mouth to feed was a burden, if only briefly. Within years— sooner than you'd think—The Child would prove indispensable around the home, then around the farm. By that time, another sibling would likely be on the way. The Brother himself was already helping with routine chores.

But not today. Today, the children were granted free reign to play. The work of saving the hay was left to those "enjoying" years they would never actually enjoy, working sunup to sundown, only to ease into decrepitude, handing off the baton to the following generation.

But what would she rather do? The Mother's thoughts turned to those who lived in the Big Houses, who hardly needed to lift a finger to meet their needs. Was that such a better life, when all was tallied at the Final Judgement? Work was good and dignified, because it came from the Lord. Living in luxury meant an overabundance of free time, and free time inevitably filled itself with problems: infidelity, sloth, gluttony.

The Mother's own mother had always told her that those in Big Houses wore holes in their hearts that could never be filled, no matter how many vices they indulged. She said that, in their pursuit of wealth, the rich gained everything that money could buy, but lost everything that money couldn't. To the contrary, Nan was living proof that a humble life was a satisfying life, that living within your means meant that you always had less to lose and more to gain. The Family owned the farm, and the farm provided everything that they needed.

Tiny bits of hay wafted up to The Mother's nose, breaking her reverie with a sneeze. She sniffled and redoubled her efforts, slightly embarrassed by how far behind she had fallen.

Stab. Lift. Heave. Repeat. The sounds of her work were only interrupted by the chirping of birds, or whenever Riley's horse clopped by with the turner. The windrows were coming together nicely. Stab. Lift. Heave. Repeat.

After a time, one of the Brennan boys—she could never keep them straight—stopped to take a break, leaning on his pitchfork to steady himself. He pulled out a handkerchief, sopping the sweat from his brow.

"J'hear about the ruckus down at the Moran place?" he shouted to the big man whom the children called Prybar Bob.

"The Galmoylestown Morans or the ones by Multyfarnam?" he asked, continuing his work. "Don't traffic with them up north."

Brennan looked puzzled. "Weren't aware there were any Morans up there." He replaced his handkerchief. "The former."

Prybar Bob grunted.

"Heard tell last week—just afore the rains moved in—Seanáthair Moran found hoofprints all through their garden."

"So?" replied Prybar Bob, hoisting another load of hay onto a row.

"So," Brennan said, leaning forward on his pitchfork, "the Morans ain't got but one horse, and it was stabled up all night. Used to have two, but the other fell lame last month. And Biddy Nally told my sister that the Moran girl came to consumption this week." Brennan's expression darkened.

Prybar Bob finally stopped to stare at Brennan. The Mother noticed that his face had turned bright red, redder than it should have been from exertion alone.

"Tell me, boyo: j'ever pluck fowl, for to stuff their feathers in a pillow?" he asked.

"'Course."

"Best done on a calm day or when it's fierce windy?"

Brennan looked puzzled, as if he were stumbling into a trap. "Calm, I s'pose. Otherwise the feathers blow away."

"Aye."

"What's your point?"

"Point is, hold your whisht, boy," he scolded. "Rumors are like pluckin' on a windy day. The words leave your mouth and scatter. Can't reclaim 'em. T'aint proper to speak of such matters, and you know Biddy Nally isn't to be trifled with. Your mother learned you better." Prybar Bob began turning hay with renewed enthusiasm. "Aside, there's work to do."

The Brennan boy simply shrugged and pulled his pitchfork from the dirt. The Mother was suddenly grateful that she hadn't made a show of stopping to listen. Although she kept her green eyes focused squarely on the earth, she still sensed that she had overheard too much. Everyone fell quiet as work continued: Stab. Lift. Heave. Repeat.

For the next several hours, the only thing that she saw outside her shawl was the yellow and green tapestry of loose hay beneath her feet, watching it slowly gather into orderly rows under her guidance, all the while accompanied by the sound of children carousing in the hedgerow. Soon enough, the field was crisscrossed with a latticework of straight piles.

Now and again, Nan would fetch The Mother to feed her infant. "Between you focusing on the hay and how agreeable the little one is, I'm surprised we didn't forget," she chortled, hoisting The Child from its cradle. Her face was a weathered map of a hard life, but one well-lived. "Isn't the hunger at you, boy? You must ask for things in this life, or you won't get nowhere."

Nan looked to The Mother. "What about ye? Knackered, I'd wager."

"I'm well enough," she replied as she unbuttoned her linen blouse and lifted The Child to her breast. "Better when I earn a chance to see this one."

The little boy's face, already locked in a perpetual smile, brightened further when The Mother took him in her arms. Only then did he offer a slight whimper.

As the boy began nursing, Nan said, "Not a bother on him. Dead spit of his father. He was the sweetest babe, too. I sometimes forgot he was in the house."

At that moment, a small hand reached around Nan from behind and grabbed her left side. She looked to see who it was and, seeing no one, whipped her head to the opposite side, where her eldest grandson stood. He grinned, proudly displaying the gap where his eyetooth had sat the night before.

"Unlike *this* one, acting the maggot," Nan growled playfully as she reached out her frail hands to tickle The Brother. "You little scoundrel, I'll do you!"

The boy squeezed out of his grandmother's grasp, then hurtled back through the hedgerow to rejoin his sister. A short time later, the two women realized that The Child had fallen asleep while nursing, lulled by the warm August sun and that sweet security only infants know.

"I love you," The Mother whispered in The Child's ear as she swaddled him tighter. She handed the infant back over to Nan, who lowered him into his nest of sky blue blankets. Before The Mother even left the hawthorn tree, his grandmother was back to rocking the cradle, cooing, and singing lullabies.

At last, the sun dried the hayfield to a yellow hue. It now lay in stark contrast to its surroundings—not only the farm's neighboring parcels, but also the greener countryside beyond its borders. Although the rain proved detrimental to The Family's work, it sent the hills that gently rolled around the farm into an explosion of a thousand emerald shades.

Following a late dinner, the laborers returned to their work, heaping the last stragglers into the windrows. The Mother's back was aching, her mouth parched, by the time her husband arrived with a cup of water.

"A blessing, it is," The Father said as she finished. He doffed his cap, revealing long locks of dark hair soaked with sweat. "It's been so hot today, some of it's already dried out. I think we might be able to start making pikes."

The Mother swallowed, took a breath, and winced. "That's... grand."

"It's been a long day," he admitted, casting his brown eyes downward. "I'm spent, too. But the Lord has provided us this window of opportunity, and only He knows how long it'll last. We have to make the most of it."

"I know," The Mother said as she handed back the empty cup. "Even if you said otherwise, I'd keep at it."

The Father nodded. "I've already spoken to everyone else. Riley has a bit of a trake ahead of him, so he's heading back. But the rest of them are up for some handlin'." He gave his wife a hug, pressing his rail-thin body against her. The Mother enjoyed a brief respite, her head nestled beneath his chin, before he broke the embrace and turned towards the northeast, where the oldest windrows waited to be formed into the first pike.

The Mother wiped her hands on her skirt and took a moment to gather herself, glancing back at Nan and The Child. With a sigh, she followed her husband. Arriving at the worksite, she saw that the other laborers hadn't skipped a beat, and were well on their way towards forming the first mound of hay.

Soon enough, the sun dipped towards the horizon, casting shadows from the hay pikes that stretched like mountains across the field. A certain energy, or lack thereof, seized the workers: fatigue, coupled with the dawning realization that at least one more hard day's work lay before them.

One by one, they slowly left, until only Prybar Bob remained with The Mother and The Father. The day dragged on as they toiled in silence. The three of them, grimy and drenched in sweat, were putting the final touches on the last pike of the day when the wind picked up, gently lifting loose strands of hay off the unfinished windrows.

No one paid it any mind. After all, loose hay was bound to scatter. But gradually, the breeze picked up, accelerating exponentially until the windrows began eroding, piece by piece. Before she knew it, The Mother's skirt whipped around her legs, tugged by the unseen hand of a sudden low pressure front. Long strands of her hair hovered in front of her face, rendering work impossible.

The Father and The Mother paused, letting the tines of their pitchforks rest against the ground. Prybar Bob continued, absorbed in his work, before noticing that the couple had stopped. Only then did he lower his tool.

"Nothing what can be done," he sighed. As if in response, the wind doubled in force again, sending the nearest hedgerow dancing in a green and brown frenzy. The trees, once stoic, now took on a life of their own, struggling against their moorings in the earth like docked ships in a squall. Their limbs groaned under the stress, sending sharp cracks echoing through the stifling air. Prybar Bob said something else, but between the gale and the shouting leaves, it was impossible to hear.

Dozens of thoughts raced through The Mother's head. Despite the wind, the last light of the sun remained bright. Could Old Lady Duffy's knee have lied? Was there a storm coming, or at the very least, a sunshower? Here to ruin their hay once and for all?

That was when the pikes, which had withstood any damage up until this point, simply disintegrated into a swirling mess. Stems began flying in all directions, forming a bewildering crisscross, stinging everyone's faces and clinging to their clothing. In a matter of seconds, the hay cloud grew so dense that The Mother could barely see The Father or Prybar Bob.

She took a step towards her husband, but was immediately swept off her feet. Quick thinking afforded her a landing on one knee, from which she staggered upright. She wanted to take another step, but feared that if she yielded her secure footing, she might be swept into the tempest herself.

A golden haze swallowed the two men. Despite standing only a few feet away, they had vanished. The Mother felt alone. Through all the commotion, a singular thought, birthed from pure maternal will, surfaced above all others.

The children, she panicked. *I must reach the children.* Not even the Devil would stand in her way. Years working on the farm offered The Mother a general sense of their direction, even blind. She turned toward the far end of the field.

As she did so, the atmosphere cleared a bit. The wind refused to subside, yet the haphazard array of stalks suddenly changed direction. A vague sort of order emerged from the turmoil. Where a haphazard flurry of yellow stems previously blurred her vision, The Mother now realized that she was standing in the center of a whirlwind that was moving widdershins around her.

Such a sight might have struck her as marvelous if it hadn't been so terrifying. The Mother took a careful step forward, testing her ability to navigate the storm. Difficult, but not impossible. Slowly and deliberately, she abandoned the men in favor of reaching the far side of the field, where Nan and the children waited.

Wading into a river might have been less strenuous. Every step found the wind pressing back. Undaunted, The Mother called out to her offspring, hoping they could hear her voice above the tumultuous uproar.

It was a fool's errand. She couldn't even hear herself. Nothing could overpower the sound of the trees and the wind. Still, she continued to shout and press forward.

A new sound crept into her ears. After starting imperceptibly, it began to crescendo until superseding the storm itself. A horrid, ghastly buzzing, like being caught in the midst of an enormous swarm of bees. In a futile effort to block the incessant racket that now enveloped her, The Mother clasped her hands to her ears. She fell to her knees as another sensation emerged.

Make it stop, she thought. *It's like it's inside my head....*

Crouched in the middle of the storm, her eyes shut tight, she felt a throbbing pain blossom in her forehead. Her fingers burrowed deeper into her ears as the hay stems lashed her face and hands unrelentingly.

No human being should have to endure this, she thought through the pounding. *They must be terrified.*

The Mother's eyes welled up with tears, which were whisked away by the wind before they could fall down her cheeks. Simultaneously, something wet began trickling down her hands. Removing her fingers —*God, the buzzing is so much louder, now*—she held them in front of her face. Streaks of red blood coated her hands, clearly visible through the debris, standing in stark contrast to the amber frenzy surrounding her.

For a brief moment, The Mother's thoughts left her children. Might this be the Second Coming? Distantly, she remembered how, as a child, she had heard tales of visions to the west, where the Blessed Mother and Lamb of God appeared to a group of witnesses. Was some unspoken prophecy being fulfilled?

Just then, something changed. The storm's color shifted, brightening from the dull yellow of the hay into a dazzling golden glow. All the light intensified, drawing The Mother's eyes skyward. She could not say for certain—there was too much obscuring her vision—but it seemed to come from a series of points high above her, as many as ten, zig-zagging back and forth through the air.

For the first time since the storm began—if it could be called a storm, there was no rain—The Mother felt something other than fear. A religious wonder seized her, a momentary distraction from the overwhelming chaos. Nothing she had ever seen compared to what her eyes now beheld, a revelation solely reserved for ecstatics and saints. Reason, time, and will slipped beyond control.

Where is my body? The Mother asked herself. Her gaze widened. Bits of straw and dirt accepted the invitation to coat her eyes. Still, she did not blink. Instead, the vision paralyzed her, gazing into the sky, captive to the boundless majesty of eternity. A beautiful horror or a horrifying beauty.

My Lord, thought The Mother, *I submit*....

That was how Nan found her a few minutes later, once the storm passed: eyes and mouth agape, staring into an empty sky with an equally vacant expression. Nan's fingernails dug deep into her daughter-in-law's shoulders as she violently shook her and shouted her name. Yet the woman remained frozen in place.

Nan finally pulled back her hand and slapped The Mother hard across the jaw, all other attempts to rouse her exhausted. She recoiled onto the ground and blinked peacefully, as if she had just awoken from a long nap.

"Nan..." she mumbled, eyes now half-closed. "Nan, I..." An expression of alarm took hold as she stumbled back to her feet. "The children! Are the children well?!?"

"Come," Nan snapped, her mouth drawn up like a cinched purse string. She started dragging The Mother to the southwestern hedgerow by the hand. Every line of hay was obliterated, the pikes only barely intact. Now, the entirety of the day's work lay strewn about the field, covering the entire area in a layer of hay an inch thick.

The Mother's ears rang. Faintly, she recognized the voices of her husband and Prybar Bob. Both were shouting, their words overlapping, asking if she was injured. Their voices grew louder as they rushed across the field in her direction.

"She'll be fine!" Nan shot back, plowing across the field with a speed belying her age. "As will be your children!" She then added under her breath, "Eventually."

The Mother finally came to her senses and shook off Nan's grasp. "Nan, what happened? Where are my children?"

The wattles around Nan's neck jiggled as she gestured with her chin towards the hedgerow. "Neath the hawthorn yet."

The Mother blinked. She could scarcely see. Her vision remained blurry from the grime that had accumulated during the storm. After blinking again, she rubbed the grit out of her eyes and, when she opened them, found relief that The Brother and The Sister were both standing alongside the cradle. They were hysterical.

"Mama!" they wailed. "Mama, I'm frightened!" Hearing her children's voices sent a burst of adrenaline straight into The Mother, replacing the fatigue and fear that threatened to overwhelm her just moments earlier. Soon she had closed the distance.

"Wait!" shouted Nan. "Wait on me, you're not ready!" Her composure crumbled. "T'isn't my fault, child! I *brought* the milk, I *poured* it at the roots! Did *everything* I could to keep them safe!"

The Mother barely heard her as she stumbled into the arms of her children. Both were filthy, bits of hay clinging to their hair and clothing, their expressions blackened with dirt. The Sister, whom she had not seen all day, seemed especially distraught. Her running nose and sobbing eyes cut furrows through the filth now covering her face.

"All's well," The Mother cooed, kneeling down to cradle their heads. "Mama is here." She hugged them close, so tight it felt as though her heart might burst. "You're safe now," she whispered.

Whatever relief she enjoyed lasted but a heartbeat. "Your brother!" she exclaimed, turning her attention to the cradle.

Now Nan arrived, jabbering up a storm. "I'm so sorry, we can fix it," she begged repeatedly. "I went the field over to fetch water from the well for supper, I'm so sorry, I ran back as fast as I could, we can fix it." Now she, too, was fully in tears. "We can fix it."

The Mother stiffened mid-stride. She looked towards Nan, her face once again expressionless. A thousand sentences could have been exchanged; none were. The Mother's gaze sufficed.

She stepped forward cautiously, as one might approach a chasm. Everything fell deathly silent. The Brother and The Sister quit crying. Even the men, who had been running headlong towards them, now stopped halfway through the field, sensing that they wanted no part in what was unfolding underneath the hawthorn tree. The only sound was the soft crunch of hay beneath The Mother's feet.

When she reached the foot of the cradle, a giggle bubbled up from within. It was immediately obvious that something had changed. The noise from the cradle wasn't filled with childish mirth. What The Mother heard sounded brittle, terse, acerbic.

She took one final step forward, her eyes closed. Slowly, she opened them and looked inside.

The Child was no longer in the cradle.

But the cradle was not empty.

2

Saturday, November 16, 2019

A GOOD MAN

Rick Coulter's blue Toyota Corolla pulled up to his childhood home around noon, idling with a slight knock. Its driver looked outside and knew his misery would begin the moment he opened the door. The weather around the house looked cold and miserable, like the man who had just died inside.

"Childhood home" was a bit misleading. In a county where the median income stood around $27,000, it was a palace: a four-story mansion trimmed with Bedford limestone, imported from Indiana to North Carolina at great cost. Even during construction, the community found it to be something of an anachronism, a robber baron's estate pulled right out of the early twentieth century.

To the south and east, the structure shrank to a mere three stories, accommodating the gradual slope of the mountainside. Hipped and gabled roofs, layered in clay tiles, topped the entire building. From this sprouted a bevy of chimneys, each massive yet dwarfed by the imposing conical tower on the northwest side. Rick remembered gazing upon the surrounding Blue Ridge Mountains from that tower in his youth. He felt like a prince in those days, surveying his father's kingdom.

Certainly the residents below in Spruce Pine thought of his father as royalty. Most of them looked upon the mansion with envy. Not Rick. He always hated that place, from his teenage years onward, but now it seemed somehow worse. It loomed like something out of a Hammer film, its disapproving gaze glaring down at him from the dark windows encircling the upper stories.

Rick bit his lower lip and sighed. Should he park beside the fountain in the driveway roundabout? Today, of all days, he had every right to pull into the porte-cochere. But old habits die hard, and he had never been extended that right all those years ago. Instead, Rick circled in front of the house, stopping in the manicured lawn to the right hand side of the drive, facing the road for a quick getaway. The old man wouldn't have approved of that, either, but he wouldn't be complaining anytime soon.

About ten minutes passed before Rick mustered the courage to open the door of his car. He stepped outside, holding his garment bag, and immediately looked through the backseat window, cupping his hands over his eyes to fend off the glare. Everything was in its proper place.

Amp, cables, surge protector, stand, he thought. A beep issued from his key fob, unlatching the trunk. He swung it open. *Tele, Martin, pedals, mics,* he said, touching each item. Unzipping the side pockets on his gig bags, he fondled everything within. *Strings, picks, capo, tape, batteries.*

Closing the trunk, he briefly paused in the light drizzle, mentally repeating the items. *Amp, cables, surge protector, stand, Tele, Martin, pedals, mics, strings, picks, capo, tape, batteries.* Everything needed for later.

Rick set off towards the house. He made it to the fountain and stopped, pulling out a notebook and a pen, which he always kept on his person. A few moments passed as he jotted down some chord changes, adding them to reams of other good ideas that would likely never see the light of day. He replaced the notebook, clenched his fists, and mounted the stone steps. With trembling hands, he reached for the ornate handle on the heavy mahogany double doors.

Before he could touch it, a low groan set one of the entrances in motion. On the other side stood an old man, decked out in a three piece tweed suit. Perhaps the world's worst attempt at a combover sat atop his liver spotted head, accentuating the weakness held within his drawn, exhausted face. Rick still recognized his father's lawyer, despite his deterioration.

"Richard," the man's southern drawl wheezed. "Happy to see you."

Rick nodded and shook the man's hand, half worried that he might break it. "Randy Lael. How have you been?"

"Busy," Lael answered, opening the door wider. "But better than the alternative. I'm still on the right side of the dirt." Suddenly realizing how his commentary might seem macabre given the circumstances, he hastened to add, "My condolences."

Rick nodded. Any other son would have had plenty to say, but he didn't, and Lael knew it. All Rick could manage was a half-hearted thanks as he stepped onto the marble floor of the foyer.

Through the eyes of an adult, he anticipated that maybe the house would appear smaller. Yet now, fully aware of the financial responsibilities of adulthood, it somehow looked even bigger. To his left towered the staircase, tracing its way into the heavens past the Waterford crystal chandelier, while before him stretched the rambling hallway, with various doors on either side leading into the maze of the house.

The home was, in fact, no different than he remembered it. Remnants of his tricycle accident still scarred the newel post. Fading and general wear aside, the Persian rug covering the floor looked the same. Everything even smelled the same—an overwhelming reek of mothballs, which triggered memories of countless nights spent arguing, always ending in a feeling of helplessness. The only noticeable differences were a stack of medical supplies and equipment balanced precariously by the old grandfather clock and a chair lift tacked onto the stairs.

Lael allowed Rick a few moments to look around. He spent them sifting and winnowing his memory, trying to find nuggets of gold amidst the dross of despair. Idly, he found himself standing in front of his father's liquor cabinet, built into the wall alongside the stairs. Rows of the finest spirits money could buy sat inside, a fine layer of dust hugging each half-empty bottle.

Rick felt an excited tinge, then remembered that what he was seeing had sat in that state for seven years. While he wasn't above drinking spoiled liquor when things got desperate, he wasn't there today. Yet.

What a waste, thought Rick, his blue eyes shifting from the contents within to his own image on the glass. Nearly twenty-one years had passed since he saw himself reflected in that door. Some things remained the same. The high cheekbones, strong jawline, and broad shoulders remained, though they had receded slightly under thirty-nine years of wear and tear, as had his muscular physique, which, while still visible, carried a few extra pounds than it should.

Partying and junk food come for us all, Rick mused. Staring further, he felt a mild shock at how *tired* he looked. Flecks of salt and pepper streaked his light brown hair. Bags sat beneath his eyes, and an expression of utter defeat had taken root. *God, I wish you would take better care of yourself. Lazy bastard.*

Lael cleared his throat, sounding like a lawnmower engine trying to turn over after a long winter. "Richard—this is Mr. Worley; he's been handling all of the arrangements."

When Rick turned to look, a tall, lanky gentleman stood beside Lael. *Right out of central casting*, he thought after seeing the funeral director's cadaverous complexion.

"Nice to meet you," Rick said, extending a hand. "I really appreciate you working with Randy. I'm out-of-state, so having him as executor has been a lifesaver."

Worley opened his hands. "It's quite common," he said. "I'm sure, with the recent bereavement, you have enough to worry about." His voice changed from sympathetic to businesslike. "A few things I would like to discuss before we get started today. People will start arriving at two, yes?"

Rick nodded. "Very good, very good," Worley continued. "I was wondering if you'd like to extend the visitation. Ending at four seems a little early, and as a pillar of the community, I'm certain turnout for your father will prove substantial."

Rick made every effort to look like he gave a shit. "I understand. Only thing is, I have to go to work back in Georgia tonight. I'm heading there right after."

"Oh. On a Saturday?"

"I have a gig in Blue Ridge."

Worley scoffed so lightly, it might have gone unnoticed. "Oh, I thought you said you had to work? Surely, that could be postponed, given the circumstances—"

"Ah, I see," interrupted Rick. "You're one of *those*, aren't you?" A look of confusion apprehended Worley as Rick continued. "You don't get it. I bail and the show doesn't happen. I screw five friends out of a paycheck. It's not a hobby, it's a *job*."

"Mr. Coulter, my apologies—"

"Just... do your job, so I can do mine." Rick turned to Lael. "Is tomorrow all taken care of?"

Wisely, Lael had remained silent up until this point. "Of course," he answered. "I received your father's remains earlier this week. I'll be on site to oversee the proceedings."

Worley opened then closed his mouth. After a pause, he calmly spoke. "I see. So you will not attend the funeral."

"Nope," declared Rick, turning on his heel to head down the hallway. "I'm doing this today so I don't have to be there. Just talk to Randy, he'll handle everything." He stopped and turned. "Randy, is the caterer here yet?"

"Yes," Lael nodded. "They're in the kitchen." With that, Rick continued his departure, leaving both men in awkward silence.

For several reasons, Rick chose to set up shop in the Autumn Room—but not before pinching three cups of wine from the caterers. One of the workers shot him a sidelong glance, but it didn't bother Rick much. He was used to silent criticism. If only they knew... besides, who got drunk off three cups of wine?

As he settled into the guestroom and set the cups down on the dresser, he felt a mixture of pride and regret. Pride that he retained the decency to leave his flask at home, regret that he didn't have it. Probably for the best. Blue Ridge was four hours away, and if the drive was anything over a few miles, being half in the bag always proved more stressful than it was worth. Besides, getting drunk was for *after* the gig, maybe *during*, but never before.

Rick had always found the gold and crimson décor of the Autumn Room sickly, but it was the closest to the parlor, where the viewing was to be held. Plus, it held the fewest bad memories—not none, but the fewest. His father rarely punished him in the rooms closest to where they entertained. Otherwise, the company might hear Rick's anguished cries.

Have to keep up appearances, he mused. Like the other bedrooms, the walls of the Autumn Room were covered in lush wood paneling—not the tacky midcentury stuff, but deep, lush trappings befitting the dignified state of the Coulters. Like everything else, it cost a fortune to install.

A fortune, all thanks to a humble little rock, something once considered trash: feldspar. While the McKinney Mine over by Little Switzerland was by far the most famous—the largest in the world at one time, it was said—the Coulter holdings provided enough of the stuff to forge a small empire. Over the years, Rick's father made a killing offering feldspar to anyone who would buy it, the bounty from the Coulter mines finding its way into all sorts of products: glass, ceramics, rubber, paints, and plastics. And that was even before considering the sizable household cleaning market, which used the mineral as an abrasive.

At least his father possessed the wherewithal to diversify before the mine shut down, offloading his assets into various stocks and bonds. The end result erected an impregnable fortress of financial security around the Coulter family—or, at least, its patriarch.

Unlike some millionaires, Rick's father was no miser, and saw no shame in spending money on luxuries. Much of the family fortune had been spent on the very walls where Rick now stood, filling the pockets of artisans and architects from around the country.

Say whatever you want about Dad, Rick reflected as he pounded a cup of red. *He spared no expense on this place.* A picture of his father's bedroom, high up in the west wing, seeped into his mind unbidden. The heavy rolltop desk, where his most private correspondence was held; the window overlooking the garden and its hedge maze; the canopy bed, where he languished his final years.

Ugh. Rick started his second cup. The old man really did have a taste for Old World decadence. It was jarring, being immersed once more in luxury. Rick hadn't seen the bastard, nor a penny from his purse, since he left the house at age eighteen.

Well, except for the hospital visit. But that was only until he regained consciousness, just to let him know that his son still existed. Returning to Spruce Pine was something Rick had avoided for years, and it almost felt as if his father lurked around every corner, cigar and snifter of brandy in hand, a quick barb at the ready.

The third glass of wine disappeared, and with it a portion of the unease Rick felt since his arrival. He had dreaded this for ten days, and part of him didn't even know why he was here.

For one thing, there isn't anyone else, he reasoned, flopping on the bed and pulling out his phone. A handful of good years passed in his childhood before his mother succumbed to cancer. Maybe he was doing this for her. For the thousandth time, Rick considered whether or not she had been the stabilizing force in his father's life, the one who kept him civil to his family.

Over an hour later, Rick decided it was time to get dressed. Why did he arrive so early? He thought maybe he would need to be here to handle things, but Lael seemed to run a tight ship. That's what he was paid to do, of course, but Rick still found it comforting. For all his shortcomings, his father exhibited a knack for establishing loyalties and maintaining professional relationships. It was his family who always got the short end of the stick.

Rick slipped into his suit and tie. *The ol' liar's noose*, he thought as he smoothed the Windsor knot. No sooner had he finished than the faint chatter of the first visitors bobbed down the hallway. *Early. Might as well get this started.*

Stepping into the corridor, Rick found himself alone. Relieved that Lael had arrested the early birds, he meandered down the hall and through the open door of the parlor, where his father awaited him—all six pounds of him.

A gloomy, gray light filtered through the floor-to-ceiling windows, mixing with the orange glow of the fireplace that sent shadows dancing across the hardwood floor. From the back of the room, the face of Rick's father smiled back at him from within a simple wooden frame.

Rick approached the table arrangement, never taking his eyes off the portrait. He knew that look too well. Behind that mask lay the bitter, judgmental, cold, calculating mind of a man whose only true love was mining and the wealth it provided. A man born a century too late, always on the wrong side of history.

Today's visitors wouldn't see that. They'd see a warm, loving smile, and the son he left behind. What surprised (and upset) Rick the most was how much they now resembled each other—the only differences were that the man in the picture frame was old(er), bald(er), and fat(ter).

He couldn't hold that gaze for long. Instead, he turned his attention to the rest of the display. A forest of blooms crept in on all sides, threatening to eclipse not only the portrait but also the urn in which his father's remains sat adjacent.

Lael, outdoing himself again, Rick thought as he surveyed the floral arrangements, hands in his pockets. On the periphery, perched like a little teepee, was a simple placard, reading CONRAD ALLEN COULTER: MARCH 17, 1940 – NOVEMBER 7, 2019.

And not a day too soon, Rick thought, gritting his teeth.

"There he is," whispered a voice from behind. Turning, Rick saw an elderly couple crossing the room, with several people loitering in the hallway behind. He had no idea who they were.

"Richard," the wife pouted, opening her arms. "I'm so sorry." Rick stood in her embrace for a moment before reluctantly returning her hug. "He was such a fine man."

Rick pulled away and nodded solemnly. "I've heard that all my life," he replied. After decades onstage, acting the part of the grieving son was child's play.

"Spruce Pine will not be the same without him," the woman rambled on. "It *is* good to see you, though. Bless, it's been years. Are you still in Atlanta?"

Rick cleared his throat and glanced at the wedding band on his left hand. "Cassie and Jack are still in Alpharetta." The woman looked confused. Her husband, sensing the direction of the conversation, made a point of examining the flowers. "We're working some things out," Rick continued. "Right now, I'm actually living south of this little town called Ellijay. I see Jack every other weekend or so."

The woman nodded, unsure what to say. They were here for death, not marital trouble.

Her husband piped up. "Ellijay, I've heard of it," he boasted, coming to his wife's rescue. "In the foothills, I think." He put his arm around her, adding, "You remember? Ken and Janet always talk about that apple farm down there."

"There are certainly lots of those," Rick said through an uncomfortable smile. "Thanks for coming today. I know it would have meant a lot to him." The husband nodded and ushered his wife to the table holding the food, apparently as happy to end the conversation as Rick.

A line formed. Rick soon found himself shipwrecked amidst a sea of interactions. Waves of faces washed over him in a tide ranging from the unmistakable to the utterly foreign. Business associates and community members comprised the lion's share, all with tales about Conrad's generosity, or how he had been such a welcome sight around town.

A few extended relations from Tennessee and down the mountain appeared, but they told no such stories. They simply hugged Rick, a knowing look in their eyes.

The mood lightened when several of his cousins filtered through. From their faces, Rick could tell that they almost hated being there as much as he did. They talked abstractly about their childhood memories, as if they were scenes from old films. There was never a sense that these moments were actually shared. They happened a lifetime ago, and all of the players now felt as alien to their old selves as they did to each other.

By now, a low murmur filled the parlor, punctuated by the occasional chuckle, stifled for decorum's sake. The stream of visitors became exhausting, more than any three-hour gig. Around 3:15, Lael's trademark throat clearing brought the conversations to a halt.

"Thank you for gathering here today in Conrad's memory," he announced weakly. "I'm sure seeing everyone would have warmed his heart."

Shee-it, Rick thought. *A nuclear bomb wouldn't have done that.*

Lael continued. "As you know, we'll be wrapping up at four, but before any more of you leave, Conrad's friend and business partner Don Brotherton would like to say a few words." Everyone clapped as a bald man in his late fifties, short and squat, waddled from the crowd to stand by the table arrangement, next to Conrad's portrait. Rick vaguely recognized the name, but the man's appearance drew a blank.

"Thank you, Randy, for the introduction," he slurred. The man was clearly drunk—funny how spending time around Conrad had that effect on people. "And thank you for your help with my parking tickets." A chuckle went through the room. "Just to piggyback offa what Randy said… I knew Conrad Coulter for twenty-three years. I remember sitting down with him in his office the day I came onboard" —he gestured vaguely across the room, in the direction of the study— "and he said to me, he said, 'Don: I don't tolerate no freeloaders. You come to work at my company, you pull your weight. And it looks like you gotta lotta weight to pull.'"

Another chuckle, this one more uncomfortable. "But that was Con's way. He told it like he saw it, there never was any doubt he was sayin' what he meant. These past seven years, his voice has been sorely missed in Spruce Pine... Today, we celebrate his release from pain." A solemn nod rippled through the crowd.

"Takes a special person to accomplish what he accomplished," Don rambled on, gesturing to the house. "It's because of him that I am what I am today."

A ringing endorsement, Rick thought, gritting his teeth.

"He welcomed me into his business, into prosperity. All of you here saw some of that prosperity. He gave to this community, and without him, *we* wouldn't be who *we* are today."

He gave you scraps.

"So I raise a toast to Conrad Coulter," Don declared, hoisting his half-empty cup of wine. "A toast to a brave man. An intelligent man. A prosperous man. And, above all, a good man." He slammed the rest of his wine before chasing it with a second cup. Everyone in the crowd murmured in agreement and followed suit.

A trapdoor opened in Rick's stomach. Unconsciously, he found his fingers at his temples and immediately realized how he must look. He ran them through his hair and took a deep breath, trying to convey grief rather than resentment. Then, with as much purpose as he could discreetly gather, he wound his way through the throng of mourners and made a beeline for the Autumn Room, snatching another cup of wine on the way.

Fucking hell, he thought as he closed the door behind him and took a drink. It had been too much. Hearing so many accolades heaped upon his father—thinly veiled as they were—was more than he could bear. None of it tallied with his experience. Nor did it match the experience of anyone else in the family. He saw it in their eyes.

Rick was tearing up when a delicate knock came at the door. He wiped his eyes with his sleeves, sniffed his nose, and swallowed. After stacking the plastic cup within the empties on the dresser, he opened the door.

"Ricky? Are you okay?" It was his mother's sister. A sparkle of hope ignited in Rick. The two were not close but cordial, which was as much as could be said for any other surviving relative.

"Aunt Carol!" he exclaimed, reaching out. It was the first hug he had initiated all afternoon. "How are you? When did you get here?"

"A few minutes ago," the plump woman replied. Her smile stretched so wide, it nearly hid her eyes—beady, but kind. "Lord, boy, it's been ages. Last time I saw you was when your band played down in Gastonia. How long ago was that?"

"I remember, it was a Fourth of July thing." Rick counted on his fingers. "Nine years ago?"

"Must've been." She clasped her hands, then scrutinized his face. "Are you okay?" she repeated.

"Finer'n frog hair," Rick lied, opening the door wider. "Come on in." He sat down on the bed, and Carol joined him.

"I saw you leave," she said, putting her heavy arm around him. "I know it's a lot, honeypie. Bless his heart, he's drunk as a skunk. I'm sure he was just searchin' for kind things to say. I'd call Conrad a lot of things, but not 'good.'" She stopped smiling and looked down, feeling she had violated some sort of taboo. "That's not right to say on a day like today. To be fair, your father went through a lot. You all did. It'd make anyone miserable. Your mother, then your—"

"My dad was a sonofabitch, and you know it," Rick interjected before she could remind him. Carol flinched at the language. Both sat in silence for a few breaths.

"Well, it's over now," she offered, her mood brightening. "Inheritance should help."

"Ha," Rick snorted. "What inheritance? Hell with being 'good,' he wasn't even 'prosperous.' He never lived within his means. On top of that, do you know how much round-the-clock in-home care costs? Over seven years?" Carol shook her head. "Randy is selling this place. When all is said-and-done, I'll get about fifty grand. That's it."

Carol raised her eyebrows. "Better'n a kick in the drawers," she opined.

"Well… I got plenty of those while he was alive." Another silence.

"How about you and Cassie?"

"Uh…" answered Rick, unsure of what to say.

"She told me. I called the house when Conrad passed."

Rick nodded. "Better than we could be, not as good as I'd like."

Carol seemed to be searching for something to say. "I've been volunteering down at the library," she began, shifting her weight on the bed, throwing Rick off balance. "Just a few hours a day, reshelving and the like. Last week, they started training me on basic book repair. Lord, you wouldn't *believe* the shape some people leave these books in. But it ain't always their fault. We just found out the return bin has a leak in it, so every time it rains, our books get soaked. Do you know what happens when a book gets wet?"

"Uh, I guess," Rick replied, wondering where this was headed. "It's ruined, right?"

"Well," she continued, pronouncing the word like *whale*, "not necessarily. Only if you leave it *closed*, with the pages *together*. They showed me lots of tricks you can do. One of the best things is to shove a paper towel every twenty pages, soak up as much water as you can, and stand it on its end. Fan out the pages, separate them best you can… then you leave a fan blowing on it overnight."

Carol, sensing Rick's confusion, placed her chubby hands over his. "If there's any chance of saving the book, the pages need two things: *time* and *separation*. Relationships are the same way. Maybe you just need to dry out a little." She chuckled, embracing him one final time. "Okay. Gonna catch up with the kinfolk, then Darnell and I are heading over to Little Switzerland. Might as well make a weekend of it, we reckon."

She left Rick sitting on the bed, alone in his thoughts. By the time he emerged from the Autumn Room, the house was nearly empty. It seemed as if Don Brotherton's oration had offered a good excuse for everyone to escape. Rick retreated into the guest room, changed back into his jeans and t-shirt, and made his way toward the front door.

Lael was there to greet him, one final time. "Thanks for coming, Rick," he said sheepishly. "Don't worry about the funeral. I'll take care of everything. I presume you want the remains shipped to your house?"

"I guess so," Rick replied grudgingly, wondering where the hell he was going to put the urn. "You have my new address?"

"Yes, sir." With that, Lael wished Rick a safe trip and opened the door.

The weather was still foul, but at least the light showers were over. Rick trudged towards the Corolla. Even though he knew nothing had changed, he checked his gear one final time before getting in his car. He almost turned the ignition before getting back out and rechecking it again, cursing himself the entire time. *Amp, cables, surge protector, stand, Tele, Martin, pedals, mics, strings, picks, capo, tape, batteries.*

Rick slammed the trunk and walked to the driver's side, eager to hit the road. Four o'clock on the dot. Just barely enough time to get to Blue Ridge. Maybe they could even do a quick sound check.

As he reached to open the door, Rick spotted a figure reflected in the window, walking up behind him. It was short and stooped, but otherwise impossible to identify through the water coating the glass. Rick was frustrated. He needed to get going.

He sighed and turned. "Randy, I—"

The driveway was empty. The front door of the house was locked tight. The only sign of movement came from a clump of dead, wet leaves, which had met with a strong enough wind to push them across the cobblestones.

Rick stared at the house for another half minute before turning, hopping in the car, and peeling out of the driveway. As the house receded in his rearview mirror, he hoped that some old memories would stay behind, too.

He knew they wouldn't.

3

Saturday, November 16, 2019

FREE AS A BIRD

As much as Rick disliked driving to Spruce Pine, he didn't mind the drive itself. Unlike the monotony of the interstate, the highways offered no shortage of picturesque views, alternating between scenic mountain vistas and lush, claustrophobic valleys. It was entertaining, if a bit harrowing at points.

Around two hours in, his phone rang. He grabbed it. HOME, read the caller ID. Rick turned the radio down and answered.

"Hello?"

"Hey, Dad!" It was Jack.

"Jack Attack! What's up?"

"Uh, not much," he replied with the forced casualness of a typical eighth grader. "Mom and I wanted to call, see how Conrad's thing went."

"Fine," Rick sighed. "It's over, that's all that matters." He was eager to change topics. "You playing Mario Kart? Better be. You need a lot of practice."

Jack laughed. "Dad, we've been over this. You got lucky. You walked through a wall."

"Huh?"

"Like, yesterday, in physical science, Mrs. Sheldon said that since we're made up of atoms, and walls are made up of atoms, it's theoretically possible that if they lined up the right way, you could walk through a wall. She said it could happen, for real. That's what happened when you beat me. It was chance, like walking through a wall."

"Ah, I see," Rick chuckled. "Salty."

"Besides, there's, like, no way it can happen again. I'll show you next weekend."

Rick cringed. "Uh, I thought Mom told you... I've got a corporate hit that came through, I won't be there." Every second of silence on the phone was like a knife twisting in his gut.

"Oh, okay," finally came the response. "No big. The weekend after, though?"

Why can't it be through the week? reflected Rick as he negotiated a sharp switchback. Keeping a social life with people other than musicians was impossible. During your time off, everyone else was working. When you were free, they were in their nine-to-five.

Rick had a gig that Friday and Saturday night, but would try and find a substitute. "Absolutely. I'll ask Mom if maybe I can stay overnight at Thanksgiving. We'll make a long weekend of it."

"Awesome!" Jack exclaimed. "Hey, Mom says she wants to talk to you. Gonna bounce, love you!"

"Love you too," Rick smiled. There was a brief pause before Cassandra cleared her throat on the other end of the line.

"Hey," she began, "so it went okay?"

"Yeah. By which I mean, I'm an emotional wreck, but..."

"Sorry we weren't there."

Rick shook his head. "Don't be. I was only there because I had to be. We cut him out of our life for a good reason. Hell, I'm not even going to the funeral." Rick said this with more confidence than he felt. Despite his old man's objective cruelty, he still felt a little guilty for not being more involved here, at the end.

A brief pause. "We miss you."

Ball's in your court, he wanted to say. Instead, he mustered a simple, "Me too." They let that hang there for a while. "So, Jack wants to know if I can spend the night on Thanksgiving. I'll sleep in the spare room."

"Yeah, yeah, that's fine," she said slowly. "Can you behave yourself?"

Rick felt blood rushing to his ears. It was all he could do to withhold a sigh. "Of course."

"Okay... How far are you?"

"Just passed Bryson City."

"Are you okay to drive?"

Involuntarily, the sigh released itself. "Yes. I didn't drink at the visitation at all."

Another pause, the longest yet. "Mm-hmm." She knew all of his tells; it was stupid to hide it.

"Okay, one glass of wine," he said, unable to help himself. After so many lies between them, even a half truth felt more honest. "But, hand to God, I didn't bring anything with me. I've cut back."

"I'm proud of you. Have you gone to any meetings? I really wish you would at least try."

Rick had slowly been accelerating ever since Cassie took the phone. He forced himself to slow down. "I'm not going to lie to you, Cassie. No. You know what I'm going to say."

"Rick...."

"They don't work for me. And they're depressing as hell. Even if I did, what do you expect? That I'm just going to hand you my red chip and move back in again?"

"No," came the reply right away. Rick found it demoralizing. She used to get indignant. Now she was just resigned, which was all the more terrifying. If either of them gave up fighting for their marriage, it was over. "Well, I gotta go. Dinner's almost ready. Text me when you get to Blue Ridge. Let me know you're okay, will you?"

Rick felt defeated. "Yup." Reflexively, he added, "I love you."

"… love you, too," she said, then hung up. The car turned eerily quiet. Light rain began falling. Rick flicked on his headlights and windshield wipers. He left the radio off, just listening to the sound of the rubber blades and thinking.

Where did it all go wrong? How recently? Was it when he found himself at the liquor store every day? Was it when he started making up errands to get cash back, to launder into a bottle of bottom-shelf vodka? Was it when he started hiding his bottles around the house? Was it when he turned to drinking at the slightest sign of boredom?

Maybe it was earlier. Maybe the seeds of their separation were planted long before their marriage, when he refused to let the party end after graduating college. To make matters worse, it was hard to not drink in his line of work. The music scene was not exactly a paragon of sobriety.

Truth be known, Rick had long ago misplaced the "off" switch for his brain, and the noise within just grew too loud most days. Other men drank to fill themselves: full of passion, bravado, courage, mirth.

Rick, on the other hand, drank to *empty* himself... of thoughts, of self-doubt, of guilt, of pain.

Or, Richard Warren Coulter, maybe it's not you at all, he thought, squinting through the dirty smear of water thrown up by a passing semi-truck. There were two sides to every story. Rick and Cassandra Coulter's was no different. Yes, his drinking had gotten out of hand—but Cassie had not met his initial mistakes with empathy. Instead, resentment filled her, which she bottled up, only to release every few days during a completely unrelated, inconsequential argument. The dishes, the trash, his gigs: all served as excuses to release the pressure building inside her.

Even Jack, God bless him, became a catalyst. It may have taken fourteen years, but now they disagreed on every little thing about him, from how many after-school activities he should be involved in to his clothes to his circle of friends.

Rick's conversation with his family haunted him across state lines, still on his mind as he passed into Georgia an hour later. It was painful to admit, but, as Rick saw it, children were sometimes the worst thing you could introduce into a marriage. Not that he resented Jack's presence; on the contrary, he knew he'd collapse into a rudderless mess if he wasn't in his son's life.

No, the introduction of a child—seeing half of yourself incarnated with half of someone else—did one of two things: it either made you love the other parent more or it made you resent the other parent's existence. You either saw how your strengths amplified one another in the child or you saw in stark relief how incongruously the two of you fit into one body. From there, it was only natural to wonder whether you had any business getting together as a couple in the first place. Rick suspected that Cassie began to see some of his own compulsions in Jack.

Taken together, all of their disagreements thoroughly poisoned their relationship, giving Rick one more reason not only to drink but to drink *harder*. By the time they split up this past summer, Rick was no longer a functional alcoholic. He was a *professional* alcoholic, thank you, someone who had transcended vomiting, whose fridge was filled with Pedialyte and various other remedies to keep him alive during the pendulum swing from drunk to hungover back to drunk again.

It was ten till eight when the Corolla finally hit the outskirts of Blue Ridge. Rick was cutting it exceptionally close, but he had notified his band leader, who in turn passed it on to the club owner, that he was running a hair late. One of the benefits of a standing gig was that, having proven reliable, you could get away with little hiccups every now and again.

The bar was on the south side of the mountain town. *Just as good*, Rick thought as he jostled over the train tracks. *Some of the streets downtown are too narrow for loading in.* Rick drove faster than he was comfortable, past the boutiques and furniture stores, past the old drive-in movie theater, until the tourist district's congestion faded behind him.

At last, he reached the venue: the Valley Crossing strip mall, 1108 Baldwin Street, an older affair decked out in a cabin theme, complete with log siding and a green tin roof. Although other businesses occupied the adjacent storefronts, the bright neon sign reading "Terry Mac's" dominated the building, throwing shades of pink and purple on the patrons below as they filed inside.

It was an attractive façade, but not Rick's final destination. He cursed under his breath as an old, beaten, Chevrolet Suburban took its sweet time finding a parking space.

It's not a mortgage, just make a decision already, Rick grumbled to himself as the vehicle finally pulled away. Rick trailed around the back of the split-level building, down the hill to the lower, less glamorous entrance by the utility meters and dumpsters. He parked his car alongside his bandmates' and began hauling out his gear.

You can talk about endless hours in the practice room, you can talk about rehearsals, you can talk about networking—the real work of a musician is the load-in. Rick grabbed as much equipment as he could carry and approached the service entrance. Thankfully, one of the kitchen staff members on their smoke break had the kindness to hold the door open.

Rick mounted the stairs, mildly ungrateful but remembering how much worse it could be. *Beats the hell out of hauling shit up the back of Smith's Olde Bar in the rain*, he thought, recalling his early days when he mostly played in Atlanta. Arms aching, he popped out on the upper floor and mounted the stage, threading between the drum set and keyboard.

Rodney Beauregard leaned against his stool, tuning his Gibson J-185 amidst a flurry of last-minute preparation from the other band members. As Rick set down his first load, Rodney looked up from beneath his ten gallon Stetson.

"'Sup, Ricky," he rumbled. Rick hadn't known Rodney for long, but he knew he'd never get used to that deep, gravelly voice coming from a baby-faced twenty something with a pathetic wisp for a mustache. "Glad you got here alright."

"Me too," Rick said, turning immediately to head back downstairs. "Sorry I'm late."

"No worries, man, they know us here," Rodney said, returning to his guitar. He sat there fiddling with his setup, making idle chitchat with Travis, the dobro player. It wasn't until Rick was back onstage and setting up in front of the bass player that he spoke to the full band.

"Y'all ready to hit it?" he asked a little louder, above the dull rumble of the crowd.

Rick, preoccupied with his pedals, looked up at Rodney, then to the back of the bar where the sound man stood waiting, then back again. "I'm almost done. Wanna do a quick check?"

"Nah," Rodney drawled. "We'll do it on the fly. They got us dialed in pretty good here."

Rick nodded and wrapped up a few final things. At last he stood, adjusted his guitar strap, glanced at the setlist taped to the stage, and locked eyes with Rodney. The band leader nodded.

Rick launched into the opening riff of one of their originals, a simple blues called *Drowning Creek Road*. No matter how many times he did this, it never got old, even when he played the same tunes over and over again. The way an electric crackle filled the room; the way everyone on stage, regardless of what had happened earlier that day, immediately left all their troubles behind and locked into synch; the feeling of navigating breaks, labyrinthine forms, and slight changes in their return; the feeling when everyone remembered and executed their job perfectly. It was never the same twice.

Rick didn't need to get hammered onstage—the performance proved intoxicating enough. Being drunk only interfered with the ultimate high, replacing it with one significantly less rewarding that impacted his performance.

After two verses of Rodney's singing, the song opened up for solos. While the tune was straightforward enough, Rick used the spotlight as an opportunity to shine. He began simply, letting momentum build before unleashing a complex array of arpeggios and side stepping harmonies. Rick became vaguely aware of the crowd's growing enthusiasm as he navigated his way into the final changes.

He stared out into the hodgepodge of faces, keeping them in soft focus as he brought it home. The casual bar goers were in a frenzy, dazzled by the acrobatics of his left hand. He appreciated it, but they weren't who he was looking for. After a moment, he found them: the people remaining stock still, their eyes wide, their hands casually covering their mouths or supporting their chins. These, Rick knew, were connoisseurs in the audience, the ones who looked past the superficial spectacle and focused on his execution, on the refined technique of his right hand. They didn't *hear* the music; they *listened* to it.

These were the people for whom Rick played. They made him feel worthy of existing.

After effortlessly segueing into the second tune, the band's brief medley concluded, leaving the crowd an opportunity to erupt in applause. Rodney grabbed the mic.

"Thank you, thank you," he grinned. "We are Rodney Beauregard & the Rib Wrenches… Happy to be here at Terry Mac's Olde Irish Pub." Shouts of approval bubbled up from the crowd. "I'd like to thank Bob Knowles for havin' us out here, we are here every Saturday through December." Rodney squinted at the back of the room. "Soundin' good up here, Noah, if I could just get a little more keys in my monitor. Thanks." Then, without skipping a beat, he launched into the next song.

After about an hour, the first set finished, and the band broke for fifteen minutes. Rick grabbed a bottle of water, slammed it, and was ready to go again in five, but everyone else seemed to be enjoying their break. He wandered off the stage and into the crowd, pausing to acknowledge audience members as they expressed their enthusiasm.

"Linda," he asked the older lady behind the bar once he reached it, "PBR, please?" A couple to his left winced, causing Rick to chuckle. "Hey, it's a completely different beer on tap, okay?" he shot back in mock defense, to their delight. He turned to survey the room.

Terry Mac's had become something of a second home these past few months. The interior displayed none of the cutesy mountain décor seen outside, nor was there much to indicate its Irish branding. Instead, the bar was rather spartan, with gray indoor/outdoor carpet and generic high tops. Old, framed pictures of the owner's previous establishment littered the walls alongside Georgia Bulldogs paraphernalia and the occasional signed photo of a celebrity, few of which Rick thought were authentic.

Great crowd, decent enough pay... but, Rick mused, *it's still a dive bar*. He'd seen so many of these that they all started to look the same. The thought kindled a spark of inspiration in Rick, prompting him to take out his notebook and pen, which he used to scrawl lyrics until his beer arrived.

Linda handed Rick his drink, saying she would put it on the band's tab. Beverage in hand, he checked the time on his phone while slowly making his way back towards the stage. On the way, he happened to glance at one of the three lower tables reserved for larger parties.

Crowded around the scarred laminate tabletop were ten individuals, more or less an equal mixture of men and women. Although Rick certainly didn't recognize every person in the bar, standing gigs had a tendency to draw more or less the same crowd. All of these patrons, however, looked completely unfamiliar. Tourists, maybe?

Something about them left Rick deeply unsettled. Doing his best not to stare, he tried to place what it was. He felt like he knew them, but had no idea how. *Like a forgotten lyric in the middle of a verse you know by heart*, Rick thought.

Rick used furtive glances and his peripheral vision to scope out the party. He couldn't place a single face. None of them even seemed that remarkable. Their clothing was a potpourri ranging from t-shirts to casual evening wear, their ages equally diverse.

Rick stopped by their table, making a show of busying himself with his phone to seem inconspicuous. It took a few seconds for him to realize what was bothering him about the group: all of the people around the table were sitting stock still, their hands in their laps, stone silent, while everyone else in the room chattered away, laughing. Their gazes seemed split between random corners of the bar, their tablemates, and their drinks—all of which sat on the table in front of them completely full, a wet ring of condensation pooling around the bottom.

Seems like a fun crowd, Rick thought, noting the time on his phone. *Five minutes, better start herding cats.* As he put away his phone, one of the people at the table spoke to him.

"We're enjoying the music," the voice said, with the slightest hint of an unplaceable accent. Rick, a little alarmed, looked toward the head of the table, where an attractive woman—the kind his father would have called "handsome"—sat with the slightest smile on her lips. Her features were angular and statuesque. She wore a bob haircut so fair it was nearly white, blending into the pale complexion of her face. Her outfit—a pristine pantsuit—was also white.

No one else at the table looked in Rick's direction. "I'm glad," he said, forcing a smile in kind. "Thanks for coming out tonight."

The woman added nothing, instead choosing to stare at him. Her eyes were set deep within her face, large and blue. Judging from the faint hint of her sculpted, platinum eyebrows, she looked either concerned or expectant—Rick couldn't decide. After what seemed like forever, she raised an arm, long and thin, almost gangly, to extend a slender finger in the direction of the stage.

"Tick tock," she said with a slightly warmer tone. Rick nodded and mumbled something vaguely in agreement, then left as politely as he could. As he did so, he passed right beside the woman, noticing that her head, even though she was sitting, nearly reached as high as his chin.

I'm 6'1"... puzzled Rick as he ascended the stage's short steps. *Freaking Amazons up here.* He slung his Telecaster on and busied himself while the rest of the band trickled onstage.

The demands of the second set didn't allow Rick to dwell on the strange woman in white. He was on the clock and had a job to do. It went off mostly without a hitch until, around ten to ten, some drunk asshole yelled, "*Freebird!*" Chuckles and groans traced through the crowd and onto the stage in equal amounts.

"Well," said Travis from behind his dobro, pushing his glasses up his face. "At least it's not *Wagon Wheel*. Ten minutes from the end, that's gotta be some kind of record." The words barely escaped his mouth before a powerful G major chord droned from the Roland at the back of the stage.

Rick had heard this obnoxious request too many times over the years before arriving at a suitable solution. When he first joined the band back in August, he shared the antidote with the other Rib Wrenches: learn the damn song, so they could honor the request. Rodney was initially hesitant to reward poor audience behavior... until he discovered Rick's secret weapon and how it permanently silenced hecklers.

About five minutes into the song, Rick launched into Allen Collins's iconic solo, note for note—sixty clicks faster. The crowd quieted for a brief instant before devolving into a manic frenzy. Rick paid them no mind—he couldn't afford to—as his fingers danced across the strings. Finally, after several minutes of grueling work, he slid into the final chords like an airplane pilot making an emergency landing.

Everyone hit the stinger. Rick looked up. The applause was almost as loud as the music had been. Rick staggered back a bit, making a show of it, and raised a hand in gratitude.

"Rick Coulter, ladies and gentlemen!" shouted Rodney, grinning ear-to-ear. He let Rick bask in the glory before acknowledging everyone else in the band, then himself, followed by the usual call to action: "See you here next week, there's the tip jar, check us out on social media, blah blah blah." Like that, the gig was over. Everyone on stage began the protracted process of breaking down, while Rodney continued to work the members of the crowd who stepped forward to talk.

In those early moments, Rick happened to glance in the direction of where the woman in white once sat. She and her entire party were gone, although that meant nothing. Half the bar was empty by now. Rick was wrapping up his cables when Travis approached him.

"Killin', man, just killin'," he said as he offered a high-five that turned into a half-hug.

"Likewise," Rick responded.

"I know I keep saying it, but I'm so glad you moved to town," Travis said as Rick returned to his work. "We should hang out and jam sometime."

"Absolutely," Rick agreed, not meaning it. Idly, he wondered, as he had so often before: *Do fucking masons get together and build* walls with their buddies in their free time? Do doctors have their colleagues over for a little barbeque and surgery?

Rick hadn't spent any time getting to know the other musicians in north Georgia on a personal level. He just showed up to rehearsals and gigs and quietly retreated to the safety of home. Maybe he felt that, any day now, he'd get the invitation from Cassie to return home, and he'd be back among Atlanta's musician community. No sense in beginning friendships just to cut them short.

Sensing his own detachment, Rick added, "I'm just happy to be up here with y'all. You have no idea how much I appreciate the work. Band sounds great."

Travis nodded, then turned somber. "Sorry about your dad," he said.

Rick stopped, staring at Travis, deadly serious. "Why? Did you have something to do with his death?" He let the silence build between the two of them before slapping his bandmate on the arm. "I'm just fuckin' with you, dude. I appreciate it, but don't be sorry. We weren't close." The two of them laughed and Travis turned to start packing up.

Rick hoisted his first load before he spoke again, stopping the dobro player in his tracks. "Hey man, one thing: try to catch that 2/4 measure in *Cheatin' the Hangman*," he said. "I know I wrote it kind of weird, but it feels like someone different misses it every week."

Travis nodded, his face simultaneously admitting his mistake and betraying mild offense that it was brought up at all. "Sure thing, Rick. Will do. Safe drive home."

With that, Rick hauled both loads downstairs and back into the Corolla. He then returned to the stage, to make sure he hadn't missed anything, before checking the backseat and the trunk as he had in Spruce Pine: *amp, cables, surge protector, stand, Tele, Martin, pedals, mics, strings, picks, capo, tape, batteries.*

Rick pulled out from behind the bar. By 10:30, he was cruising through the darkness down US-76 West. Thankfully, there was no sign of the rain that had followed him all day. Within about twenty minutes he was parallel to Ellijay but, since he lived south of town, he stayed on the road as it merged with Georgia State Route 515. His mind was a blissful blank, all the pent up creative energy dispersed by his performance.

As he passed the exit for downtown, the Corolla's interior flooded with the technicolor bustle of fast food signs before returning once more to darkness, which only deepened as he turned off onto Old State Route 5, once a major thoroughfare between Atlanta and the mountains. It was like driving back in time. Gone were the trappings of modernity, replaced with empty shacks, plain mid-century houses, and vacant business properties sadly displaying faded FOR RENT signs. The heavily-wooded drive was quaintly enjoyable during the daytime, but in the darkness offered little to see.

Only now, with so few distractions, did Rick allow his mind to wander. Terry Mac's: a far cry from the conservatory where he cut his teeth. Even though Rick sometimes downplayed his classical training to his bandmates, he couldn't deny that it gave him the chops to pull off feats like tonight.

I may fuck up a lot of things, he thought, *and there's a lot of stuff I can't control. But my playing ain't one of 'em.*

Rick was fully aware that his college professors, looking at his career, would have perceived it as a downward slide of wasted potential. For Rick, that couldn't be further from the truth: he *loved* playing for people who weren't afraid to talk during a performance, to hang out, to actually *enjoy* the music. His only misgiving was how rarely he played jazz compared to his time in Atlanta. He never cared for Country.

Remember: a rock star plays five chords for ten thousand people, Rick thought as he focused on the blacktop darting through his high beams. *A jazz musician plays ten thousand chords for five people.* If you wanted to succeed in this corner of Georgia, it had to be commercial music, and Country music was king.

Country opened wallets, something Rick desperately needed after his separation from Cassie. He remembered how grateful he felt when he joined the Rib Wrenches, and his surprise when Rodney expressed enthusiasm to push the boundaries of the genre. It was delightful, watching the expressions from the rednecks in the crowd as they realized what they thought was a novelty act—"Lookee here, boys, a black cowboy!"—evolve into something legitimately challenging.

On some tunes, Rodney even permitted Rick to drag the band into outright spacy territory during his solos. "Acid Country," Travis had joked. While it didn't quite scratch Rick's jazz itch, it kept him sane.

That, and recording sessions in Atlanta, which he still booked from time to time.

Rick glanced at the clock. It read eleven. *Almost home*, he thought. *And there's a bottle with my name on it.* He rounded a curve, emerging onto one of the more precarious stretches of road. Here, a steep embankment rose on the passenger's side, while a precipitous drop from the opposite shoulder held a forested gully.

Rick noticed a pair of headlights coming his way in the distance. Although Old SR5 wasn't exactly lightly traveled, any traffic this late set him on edge. Best case scenario: it was just a random driver. A distant second, a cop. Any interaction, accident or otherwise, wouldn't end well—even on days like today, when he'd mostly abstained, his consistent blood alcohol level made him guilty until proven innocent. The worst scenario, the one he feared most this time of night on a weekend, was that another drunk driver was approaching, someone truly too intoxicated to drive.

As the lights drew nearer, Rick felt that something didn't look quite normal. Maybe it was the color—they looked bluish, like those xenon headlights found on some luxury cars. Rick slowed a bit, keenly aware of the narrowness of the road.

To Rick's horror, the headlights pivoted. Now they were straddling both lanes, coming directly towards him. Whatever endorphins the gig and his light buzz provided were dashed. He leaned forward on his horn and flashed his high beams wildly.

The other driver didn't react. Rick knew he had to act quickly to minimize damage. Slowing as much as he could, he pulled over into the oncoming lane, hoping that enough of a shoulder existed, unseen, to keep his car from tumbling into the gully below.

It was too late. By the time he reached the middle of the lane, the lights were no more than fifty feet away. Time slowed while a flipbook of images filled Rick's head: the Corolla, mangled beyond recognition; Jack and Cassie at his funeral; his bandmates, hearing the news, simply shaking their heads and saying, "Must've been his fault, guess it finally caught up to him."

A piercing squeal from his tires filled Rick's ears, accompanied by a cacophony of knocks and rumbles he had never heard the old car make. *This is it*, he thought, every muscle tense...

Then, without warning, the headlights split. One raced past his right side along the embankment, the other to his left. For a moment, Rick sat in shock, his heart racing.

"What the actual fuck?" he asked aloud. The calm in which he now sat contrasted sharply with the chaos of the past few seconds. The only sound was the Corolla, idling once more with its familiar knock.

Rick put the car in park, opened his door, and stepped outside into the cool fall air. There remained the tiniest sliver of blacktop between the driver's side and the foliage of the gully below. If he had swerved off here, his car would have hit the upper boughs of the trees reaching up from the bottom. But how did that light pass him on this side and avoid the same fate?

Motorcycles, Rick thought. *Gotta be bikers, probably drunk, heading up to the mountains for the weekend. Fuck me. They're lucky. We're* all *lucky.* He stood on the side of the road in utter shock, gazing into the pitch-black depths of the gully. He might as well have been staring into a cave.

Only a few seconds passed before Rick realized that he was still in danger. His car sat fully in the left hand lane, and another vehicle might come by any minute. *Time to get home and finish that bottle*, he thought, turning to open the door.

As he reached for the handle, Rick heard something: a scuffling in the bushes. He paused, listening, trying to hear over the idling Corolla. Slowly, he looked over his shoulder, back into the gully. There was no sign of movement—but then again, it was too dark to see anything.

God, I'm fucking shaking, he thought. *Pull yourself together, Rick. Probably a racoon or something.* No sooner had he finished this thought than a second sound drifted up from the darkness below. This time, the noise wasn't vegetal, nor was it animalistic.

It was a giggle, dainty and childlike.

Rick clambered into the driver's seat and threw the car in drive. Any doubt in his mind that he wouldn't get blackout drunk tonight vanished as he peeled out and down the highway.

The drive home should have taken about five minutes. Rick finished it in three.

Imagine his confusion when, pulling into his driveway, the car clock now read midnight.

4

Saturday, January 11, 2020

TOP OF THE WORLD

"Damn, you're good with your hands," Edna Durchdenwald croaked, rubbing a palm along the drywall. "If you were a bit older, or I was a bit younger, or if you had an elderly fetish, I'd put the moves on ya."

Rick stared at his landlady, trying not to laugh. "I'm, uh... flattered, Edna," he replied. "If any of those highly-specific criteria were met, I'd let you." The two stood in the unfinished addition of Edna's Ellijay property, surveying Rick's handiwork.

When he and Cassie decided to separate, Rick had immediately leapt into action looking for a new place to stay. On every gig, he asked the musicians if they knew of any opportunities opening up. It took a while before he found something suitable. Rent for most places in the metro area or Atlanta proper was exorbitantly high. Rick was about to give up when a saxophone player mentioned that his aunt was looking for a tenant in Ellijay. If one could endure her off-color wit, he said, it was a sweetheart deal.

"At this rate, you'll be outta here in no time," Edna said, passing from the first of two new bedrooms into the hallway adjoining them. She poked her head into the bathroom on her right. "Well, maybe not. A lot left to do in here."

"I know," Rick admitted. "But just think how it's going to look when it's done. Tourists are gonna love it."

For all her faults, Edna dreamed big. The tiny home that Rick rented had been in her family for generations. It mostly sat vacant, only used by friends and family, until the short-term homestay market boomed. Edna got an idea: expand the house to make it more appealing to folks flocking to Ellijay during the tourist season.

The only problem was, Edna was a self-professed cheapskate, and "didn't want to overpay no goddamn lazy contractor" to do the work. Thus, she found herself in the market for cheap labor in the summer of 2019—the same time, as luck would have it, that Rick found himself in the market for cheap rent.

It was a match made in heaven. Although the one-story, single bedroom home was quite old, its proximity to the mountains meant that Edna could have charged Rick much more than she did. He made up for the difference with his hands. Rick was more grateful than ever for the summers he spent working construction jobs during his college years.

Edna poked her head into the other bedroom, grunted, and shuffled out into the original part of the house opposite the bathroom door. "What about in here?" she asked, hands on her hips.

Rick still couldn't place Edna's age. She might have been a battle-worn fifty or a sprightly seventy. Her brown eyes were still clear and bright, her cheeks still round and rosy, her hair still clinging to the last vestiges of a youthful blond. At any rate, she could get around just fine, although she was shrunken with age, her heart-shaped face barely reaching Rick's chin.

Subjectively, she was an attractive older woman with plenty of life left in her years, if not years in her life. Objectively, she wore too much makeup, cursed like a sailor on shore leave, and smelled like the inside of a fumigated 1957 Chevy Bel Air.

"Well," Rick began, "I think we're pretty good. Knocking out the kitchen wall was a good decision, people are all about open floorplans nowadays." Rick went over and patted the short wall that now provided countertop space. It and an angled snack bar demarcated the kitchen. "I replaced most of the flooring in the dining room, just gotta finish the last little bit between the basement entrance and the patio door."

Another grunt. "What about that goddamn eyesore?" she asked, gesturing to the freestanding wall separating the living room from the dining room.

"I like it this way," Rick answered. Her ever-changing mindset provided a source of endless exasperation. *Maybe she likes having me around, and doesn't want the work to end*, he thought. Edna had made it clear that Rick needed to look for a new place as soon as everything was finished.

"You don't think we should close it off or knock it down?" she needled, wandering to the opposite end. She stood between the doors to the basement and the patio, her upturned nose bobbing to either side of the wall like the beak of a bird. "Nah, I guess not. Straight shot from the kitchen on this side. But lots of folks wanna watch TV while they eat. That's what I do. Only way I can catch up on *America's Got Talent*."

"That's not going to keep anyone from renting this place," Rick sighed. "A bigger problem is that the master bathroom doubles as a shared bath."

Edna scoffed and looked to the bathroom on the opposite side of the kitchen. "Well, it was fine for my cousin when he lived here. You can get to it from the bedroom, what difference does it make? It's the wall I'm talking about."

Rick pinched the bridge of his nose. So far, he had managed to power through his hangover, but now the landlady was pushing all his buttons. "Edna," he grumbled, "the time for this discussion has passed. We painted the place last week, you want to pay for that again?"

Edna stared at him for a beat, expressionless. "I need a smoke," she said, fishing into her blue jeans for a pack of Marlboro Reds. She pulled one out, shoved it into her mouth, and was about to light it when she stopped, noticing the expression on Rick's face. "Goddammit, can't even smoke in my own property."

She turned around. "*This* fucking thing," she grunted, lifting the wooden security stick that rested in the track of the sliding glass door. Rick stifled a smile as she fought the latch, stepped onto the covered patio, and lit up, leaving the door wide open.

Half to continue the conversation, half to close the door, Rick followed her outside, grabbing a Pedialyte from the refrigerator on the way. The morning had begun unseasonably warm, and he was perfectly comfortable in his jeans and t-shirt. "You know, the layout isn't going to keep people from booking," he said, flopping down on the back porch swing he installed last week. "It's the front yard."

"I know," Edna grumbled.

"They have people you can pay who will haul away your junk," Rick offered, idly swinging forward and back.

"Pay?" Edna's mouth hung open, her cigarette clinging to her lipstick. "Shee-it, boy, someone ought to pay *me* for that stuff. Good salvage."

Knowing the conversation was futile, Rick looked out over the thigh-high grass in the field that surrounded the entire house. Some people claimed Ellijay was in the mountains. Not Rick. Yes, the town sat only a stone's throw away from the Blue Ridge, with plenty of mountains nearby, but too much of the ground here was level, unlike his old stomping grounds. In some ways, this made the small peaks around Ellijay even more dramatic, rising above the placid meadows like arrested tsunamis of earth and rock.

Rick watched the wind send a cascading wave across the top of the grass, each stalk leaning in the same direction before pushing back in disagreement. The tree line beyond responded in kind, bits of undergrowth revealing remnants of a cattle fence, long in disrepair. Although he couldn't see it from this vantage point, a small brook bisected the middle distance, a few sparse trees lining its banks.

Watching over it all, unaffected by the gale, was Red Ear Mountain, dominating the southwestern half of the property. It wasn't a large mountain—only around two thousand feet—but at this proximity, it felt imposing. Somewhere up there the stream began, trickling downhill and into the field before disappearing into the woods on the other side in the direction of the highway.

The land had been in Edna's family for generations, and Rick still wasn't quite sure why she hadn't developed it. Maybe, since she lived on the other side of Red Ear, she actually felt a bit sentimental.

"Rick? Did you hear me?" asked Edna, breaking his daydream.

"Huh?"

"I said, 'How are you and Costanza?' Or whatever her name is."

"Cassandra," corrected Rick. "Um... okay. We're kind of in a holding pattern. She's bringing Jack up today, should be here soon. He hasn't been up here since before Thanksgiving, with the holidays and gigs and all. Plus his birthday was a few days ago, so we did that down in Alpharetta."

"Mm-hm," Edna nodded, lighting another cigarette to take a long drag. "Well, keep at it. And if it goes south, it's a big world out there. I got this app on my phone with a bunch of guys in town. I like one, I swipe right. He swipes right, we go on a date. Can you believe that? You see these?" She pointed to her eyes. "I ain't got crow's feet, I got ostrich toes. If I can get laid, you sure as hell can."

Rick just shook his head.

"How's work?" she asked.

"Okay," Rick said, unsure why she was asking. "You know how it is, money from club gigs has stayed the same for forty years. But I was busy around Christmas. Still playing some solo stuff in the wineries up the road." His mood, having turned dour, suddenly brightened. "The band has a lot of gigs booked out-of-state in the next couple of months," he added. "I've got a good feeling about this year."

At that moment, they both heard a car descending the gravel driveway at the front of the house. "They're early," Rick said, checking the clock on his phone. It read 11:08. Without another word to Edna, he stood, went inside, cut through the living room, padded across the tile foyer, and opened the front door.

Cassie's black Lexus ES pulled up outside, leaving Rick with the same mixture of pride and shame he felt every time she arrived. Pride, for not having booze on his breath, and for the picturesque surroundings in which he lived. The field sometimes felt magical, like an island in the woods. Even the approach to the house was scenic, a half mile drive from the highway through the forest until emerging into the vast field.

However, it was impossible to stand out front and not feel shame. The yard was home to that eclectic mixture of debris endemic to north Georgia properties: old gas station signs, half empty propane tanks, an old grill, a tractor drowning in weeds, blue fifty-five gallon barrels full of God-knows-what.

Rick pushed these thoughts from his mind as he approached the driver's side. Cassie already had her window down. A lump leapt into Rick's throat.

Even after all they had been through, these fleeting moments still made him whole. Some people, remembering how she looked in her twenties, would think she had aged poorly. Rick, on the other hand, saw in every line of her face a diary of their life together, all the hardships, the triumphs.

She brushed her glossy black hair behind her ear and looked at her husband, green eyes touching his soul. "Hello, sir," she smiled, using their old familiar greeting.

"Hey, lady," he responded. "I thought we said noon?"

Cassie sighed. "We said eleven, because I'm going to mom and dad's today. Remember?"

Rick nodded. Sometimes, it felt like reality constantly shifted beneath him, actively seeking to make him look the fool. *That, or you're constantly distracted*, Rick thought.

"How was the drive?" he asked after clearing his throat.

Cassie smiled, bringing her delicate features to life. "Not bad. Except I had to listen to Tom Waits the whole way."

"He's the greatest musical mind of our era!" came a voice from the passenger side.

"I blame *you* for this," Cassie joked to Rick as their son stepped out onto the driveway.

He looks taller every time I see him, Rick thought. Jack looked to his father and beamed. With his dark hair and blue eyes, he seemed a perfect synthesis of his parents, although Cassie always claimed he favored her side more.

Jack rounded the front of the car and embraced his father. "Hey there, string bean," Rick said, tousling his long hair, already disheveled. "Cassie, you gotta feed this kid!"

Cassie smiled, but didn't even offer a chuckle. Instead, she pulled a piece of paper from the console and handed it to Rick. His heart skipped a beat, thinking this might be the day he was finally served papers.

To his relief, Rick unfolded the sheet and saw a list of Jack's upcoming track meets. "Here's the spring schedule," Cassie said. "A few more might get added, but that's where it stands right now. I knew you'd want to have it."

"Yes, thanks."

"One of those is a little weird, it's early," she said. "March 13, the first one. Two o'clock. They're letting them out of school early. You don't have to come, though, it's all the way down in McDonough."

Rick shook his head. "Nowhere's too far." He looked up to see Edna waddling from the eastern side between the house and the shed.

Cassie smirked. "I didn't know you'd started seeing people."

"That's my landlady, and you know it," Rick said, rolling his eyes. In an uncharacteristic show of restraint, Edna Durchdenwald kept silent, merely waving to Rick and his family before hoisting herself into her pickup truck. She left in a plume of dust. "Anything else?" asked Rick.

Cassie hesitated. "Jack, can you give us a minute?" Once the boy was inside with his overnight bag, she finally spoke. "I went on a date."

Despite awaiting these words for months, they still landed like a blow to Rick's stomach. He took a deep breath.

"Before you say anything," Cassie hastened to add, "I didn't sleep with him. And I'm not going on a second date." She looked at her lap. "Getting back out there made me realize how much I miss you. And... I'm ready to try again. The next few months are busy at the firm, but after that, maybe this summer, I want to see you more. Maybe we can move you back in this fall. If you quit."

Ah yes, Rick thought. *The ever-present caveat.* He knew it needed to happen, but the time to act was always tomorrow. After a pause, he said, "Of course... Give me a couple of months to get there."

Cassie smiled, genuine but weak. "You can do it. Love you."

"Love you, too," Rick said, backing away. He stood in the driveway reflecting, twisting his wedding band around his finger. For the first time in ages, Rick Coulter felt hopeful.

"This thing gives me the damn creeps," echoed a voice from the front porch. Rick looked towards Jack. He was back outside, staring at a three-foot tall wooden statue sitting in the garden, immediately to the left of the front door below the kitchen window.

"Hey! Language," Rick scolded. "It's not mine. Edna says it's supposed to be a bear." He looked at the crudely-carved statue, standing upright amongst the dormant flowers Edna tended in the warmer months. The body was acceptable, but the face was all wrong, more like a dog than a bear, with bulging eyes and a lopsided smirk. "A friend of hers carved it with a chainsaw."

"Who gave a blind guy a chainsaw?" quipped Jack as he headed back inside. He stood in the foyer, taking in the renovations. "You've done a lot of work, Dad."

"Thanks, Jack Attack," Rick said as he shut the door behind him. "You hungry?"

"Sure. Whatcha got?"

"Uh... Hot Pockets."

Jack laughed. "I swear, Dad, seven months away from mom and you're already a bachelor meme."

Rick feigned offense. "That's a meme thing to say."

"Already with the dad jokes," Jack groaned. "That's it, I'm calling Mom, I wanna go back." The two laughed for a moment before Jack nodded to the urn sitting on the mantel above the fireplace. "Is that him?"

"Yeah," Rick answered, nodding. "I guess you haven't been up here since the visitation."

Jack nodded, sensing his father's mood. "Why are you keeping it?" he asked quietly.

Rick thought carefully before replying. "Did I ever tell you about my first guitar? I bought it myself, since *he*"—Rick nodded to the urn—"didn't want to. Cheap, but it was fine. It served its purpose. After I upgraded, I began to see it for what it was: an atrocious sounding block of wood. Yeah, I wouldn't be where I am without it, but there was no *reason* to keep it. It served no purpose. All it did was gather dust, get in the way, and remind me of how bad I used to be. Never could figure out why I held onto it. I just felt like I should, I guess."

"What'd you do with it?" asked Jack.

Rick looked his son squarely in the eye. "About the time you were born, I was still teaching lessons. One day, a new student came in who was involved in a 'rent to own' situation. Knew it would take him forever to pay it off. When he left that day, I sent my first guitar home with him. Today, I have no idea if he still has it or if it's in a landfill. I don't care. I did my part. Looking back, I would have thrown it in the trash if I had to look at it another day. Now, it kind of feels like the guitar told me what to do with it. But I had to wait."

Silence fell. Both of them were eager to change subjects. After Cassie's news, Rick was in the mood for a celebration, so they ordered pizza. Rick enlisted Jack in putting the pictures back on the walls and re-installing the spring door stops around the home, which had been removed for the painters.

It should have taken less than half an hour, but somehow Rick's screwdriver disappeared from right under his nose. One second, it was there, the next... gone. They turned the house upside down for fifteen minutes before finally locating it behind the door they were working on. Both Rick and Jack were certain they looked there a dozen times. Normally, Rick would have blamed his hangover, but with an objective observer present, the event left him puzzled.

The day's light work done, Jack sat on the couch doing homework at the coffee table while Rick busied himself with more chores: answering emails, fixing the garbage disposal, taking out the trash, and cleaning the kitchen. He finished by putting away the dishes, which had become something of a ritual: *knife, spoon, fork, knife, spoon, fork, knife, spoon, fork.* When he finished up with an extra spoon, Rick set it aside to put away later.

Around 3:30, the pair decided to go on a hike. Jack was ready before his father. "Meet you at the trailhead?" he asked.

"Yes," Rick said. "Remember where it is? By that hawthorn, all by itself?"

"Affirmative," Jack answered, halfway out the door. The moment it closed, Rick snuck to the kitchen, opened up the base cabinet, and reached inside, grabbing the plastic vodka bottle hidden underneath.

Thank God, he thought, squeezing the bottle into a pint glass. Next, he grabbed a soft drink out of the fridge to mix himself a 50/50 vodka and Coke. Walking over to the patio door, he watched Jack move towards the trailhead.

Over the teeth and past the gums, Rick thought, chugging the drink as fast as he could to avoid suspicion. He then dropped the glass in the sink, laced up his shoes, and fetched the hiking sticks from the shed. Within a few minutes Rick arrived at the tree, feeling himself again. Father and son headed into the woods, up the nearest slope of the mountain.

It wasn't necessarily scenic, hiking in the dead of winter. The surrounding vegetation had turned into a sea of brown and beige. It did, however, offer excellent visibility through the forest, revealing a diverse landscape of fallen logs and old stumps poking up from beneath a carpet of dead leaves, all visible between the thicker, older trees and scrawny younger specimens. Fern fronds and coils of ivy, clinging to existence through the long winter months, offered green blossoms of life here and there, promises of spring ahead.

Of the few hikers who climbed Red Ear, everyone—with the exception of Rick—did so without Edna's permission. The trail itself was one of several, but, being closed to the public, all were barely maintained. This made the otherwise gentle ascent far more strenuous, a constant struggle uphill through brambles and brush rendered all the more difficult by constant corrections in elevation.

After about half an hour, both Rick and Jack were covered in sweat. Rick became keenly aware that he could smell the booze seeping out of his pores.

"Watch out for that root," Rick said to his son, stepping over it.

Jack spit and sputtered. "Hell with the root, watch out for the spiderwebs."

I'll let that one slide, Rick thought as he stopped and turned around. He watched his son's feet, taking note of the sorry state of his shoes.

"Geez, boy, I bet you can feel every rock in those things," he remarked.

Jack stopped, huffing. "They're fine. I love these shoes."

Rick shook his head. "Yeah, but you've had those forever. You need new ones, especially with track coming up." Jack neither agreed nor disagreed. He simply pushed forward.

Rick made a mental note to start setting aside some money. Jack's birthday may have come and gone, but he still wanted to do something special.

Another five minutes passed before he spoke again. "We're about halfway up," Rick said. "There's an overlook just ahead. We'll stop there, then turn around and head back."

A few steps later they emerged, just as Rick promised, at a breathtaking view facing north. Ellijay could be seen in the distance, with lone peaks scattered all around, the stoic backdrop of the Blue Ridge Mountains lurking beyond. Bare, deciduous trunks clung to the slopes like a five o'clock shadow, the monotony broken here and there by patches of evergreens.

"Wow," Jack whispered. "You can see a lot better up here when the leaves are gone." He fell silent before adding, "It's hard to tell where the mountains end and the clouds begin."

Rick nodded. "I find myself thinking the same thing, sometimes." He loved it up north, far from the hustle and bustle of the metro. Maybe, if he was lucky, he could convince Cassie to relocate... if they got back together.

Father and son stood up there for several minutes, taking it all in before they sat down and talked: about life, about the separation, about school, about Jack's crushes. Rick's heart swelled with gratitude. Whenever their visits went poorly he always sulked for a week afterward, convinced of his failure as a father. But today he would leave the mountain confident in the strength of their relationship. In the face of all the trials over the past year, Rick felt blessed that he and Jack managed to remain close. He wasn't sure whether or not he believed in God, but he could be convinced by that alone.

At last, the sun dipped behind Red Ear, lengthening the shadows. Time to head back and clean up for dinner. Jack and Rick set off down the mountain, barely saying a word, fatigued from the ascent and spent from their mountaintop discussion. The day had been an inspiration, and Rick made regular stops along the way to scribble lyrics in his notebook, much to Jack's chagrin.

Once home, Rick let his son shower first. There was only one bathroom for the time being, with two doors, one leading to the master bedroom, the other to a short hallway joining the living room. Rick passed the time playing his guitar on his bed, picking away at a dozen tunes that he wasn't sure would ever be finished.

Eventually Jack appeared, plumes of steam swirling behind him. It was now Rick's turn. When he emerged freshly washed and dressed, he found Jack silently staring out the sliding glass door to the patio. He did not turn to look at his father, but was instead fixated on the darkness.

"What is it?" asked Rick. He had switched out his contacts for his glasses.

"I thought I saw a light on the mountain," Jack said slowly. "But it's gone now."

A long silence passed before Rick spoke. "Probably just hikers. We get them up there, sometimes."

Jack shook his head. "No, it was… there it is!" He pointed out the window, across the field, to the slopes of Red Ear. The moon lit the sky just enough to contrast with the blackened slope dominating their view. "See it?"

By now, Rick was standing behind him. Sure enough, there it was: a tiny dot shining through the barren branches on the northwestern slope—near the overlook, as a matter of fact. It did not seem to move, although it must have. Given the way it flickered from time to time, it looked as if it was passing between the trees. But there was none of the characteristic bobbing one would expect from a flashlight. Nor would one necessarily expect a hiker to carry a *blue* flashlight.

Rick thought back to November, his gut tensing. "Hikers," Rick said, more to himself than to Jack. "I'll have to let Edna know." At that moment, the light simply winked out of existence, leaving only the black, triangular void of Red Ear. Rick and Jack kept their gaze fixed on the mountain for about half a minute until the light reappeared—on the north*eastern* side.

No one could have traveled that fast. Even if they had an ATV. Besides, no trails up there were wide enough to accommodate an ATV.

"Yeah, Dad," Jack smirked. "Hikers."

Rick walked over to the refrigerator and pulled out the box of half-eaten pizza. "Not unheard of, getting two up there at once," he said, shoving a few slices into the microwave. *But never that color,* he added silently. "Maybe they're signaling to each other." Rick could no longer see out back. For some reason he found himself grateful that he couldn't.

Neither of them spoke about the light as they sat down to finish their leftovers. Instead, the conversation picked back up where they left it on the mountain, although there was much less to share, with long breaks of silence. Rick kept glancing back at the clock on the microwave, to make sure he didn't miraculously lose an hour again, like he had last fall.

The evening concluded with a little music lesson (at Jack's request) and listening to old records, followed by a rousing game of Scrabble where Rick got his ass thoroughly kicked. Around 10:30, Jack decided to turn in. Rick fetched some spare pillows and set his son up on the couch alongside the freestanding wall. He had offered his own bed to Jack, but the boy declined, saying that he thought the couch was comfier, and he might want to watch some television.

As Rick reached underneath the sink again, he felt a tinge of gratitude that Edna kept the wall up. Jack knew he drank, but walking back to your room with a fifth of rotgut did not paint a rosy picture. He slunk past the dining room, through the small hallway with the bathroom and laundry, and into the seclusion of his bedroom.

As had become habit, Rick drank himself to sleep that night, justifying it with the fact that he had only snuck one drink all day. He adored alcohol nearly as much as he loved Cassie. He didn't know how he would reconcile his two loves… although only one of them was asking him to abandon the other.

Within an hour, the bottle was finished and Rick was passed out. It was a deep, empty sleep, punctuated by only one dream: the sound of his guitar playing by itself in the middle of the night.

When Rick awoke the next day, he stayed in bed for half an hour, watching the room spin and trying to recall what he had dreamt. He only recovered fragments; bits and pieces of an angular melody, haunting and unexpected, yet somehow familiar. *Like a last-minute turn down a road you drove past all your life, but never traveled,* he thought.

Enough daydreaming. He pulled himself out of bed and stumbled into the living room. Jack was still asleep. As quietly as he could, Rick opened the fridge, pulled out some eggs, and began making breakfast, swilling Pedialyte and coffee, humming bits of the melody all the while.

Around ten, Jack walked into the dining room and sat down at the table, just as Rick was plating breakfast. He stared at the food as it was set down in front of him.

"Did you sleep good?" asked Rick. "Eat up, buddy."

Jack looked from his eggs to his father. "What are you humming?" he wondered.

"Oh, just something I heard in a dream last night," Rick answered, sitting down across from him. Jack looked confused.

"I heard it, too," he confessed.

5

Thursday, March 12, 2020

BEST LAID PLANS

THE FINAL CHORD ECHOED ACROSS DOWNTOWN, immediately followed by a swell of applause. "Yes!" Rodney shouted into the microphone. "Alright! That was *Cheatin' the Hangman* by our own Rick Coulter, over there on lead." Rick waved at the crowd gathered in the roundabout in front of the Gilmer County Courthouse.

"We are Rodney Beauregard & the Rib Wrenches," the singer continued. "Happy to be here at 'Spring into Spring' in beautiful downtown Ellijay. We're gonna take a quick fifteen, twenty minute break and see you right back here for some more fun. Don't go nowhere!" With that, he took off his guitar, and the rest of the band followed suit. None of them spoke a word, instead choosing to conserve their energy for their second set on the first day of the festival.

Not a bad crowd for a Thursday, Rick thought. These early festival slots were always tricky. People seemed hesitant to attend concerts on a weeknight. Luckily, the late afternoon slot that the Rib Wrenches had landed was only the first of several performances over the weekend, and the crowd was guaranteed to grow each day.

Rick descended the rickety stairs of the stage, landing in the middle of the crowd amassing between Dalton and Broad Streets. The entire roundabout was closed off to traffic for the weekend, allowing attendees to safely watch the stage nestled between the courthouse and the Downtown Welcome Center. Further down Broad a train of vendor booths, each covered with a white outdoor canopy, offered a variety of local arts, crafts, and food.

People swarmed in the roundabout like ants, crisscrossing the small, circular park in the center to dart in and out of the establishments surrounding it. There were a few empty storefronts sprinkled about, but they were easily lost amidst the thriving coffee shops, restaurants, and boutiques. Each building offered nearly two centuries' worth of stories to tell. These businesses represented another chapter.

Rick took a moment to appreciate how Ellijay, unlike so many other small towns in the south, had managed to reinvent itself into a vibrant tourist destination. Whether they treated it as a gateway to the mountains beyond or decided to stay longer, visitors found plenty to draw them there. Only winter calmed the streets. Otherwise, in the warmer months, people came for kayaking opportunities offered by the confluence of the Ellijay and Cartecay Rivers, while the fall saw thousands descend on Ellijay to visit the apple orchards, which sprung up around downtown like wild onions.

"Rick!" shouted a voice from the crowd. He turned and saw a tall woman in a yellow sundress approaching him.

"Bora!" he exclaimed, his face lighting up. Rick ran to embrace her. "You made it!"

"You're going to break my back," she coughed, wriggling out of his embrace. Rick looked into his old friend's face. In all the years they knew each other, only Rick seemed to age. Bora Choi's complexion remained as smooth as the day he had met her—no small feat given her constant smile—and the luxurious dark hair that cascaded down to the small of her back showed none of the flecks of gray seen in Rick's. She still managed to exude all the pluck and verve she exhibited in college, speaking so fast that Rick could hardly keep up.

"Of course I made it! I miss my old roommate," she pouted, her brown eyes sparkling. "Y'all sound so good! How long have you been with these guys?"

"About eight months," Rick answered, nodding. At that moment he noticed another woman looking on, eyebrows raised.

"Oh my goodness, I'm so rude," Bora apologized. "This is my girlfriend, Hope." A short, petite woman with a brush cut reached out an umber hand from behind Bora. Rick refused.

"Nah, come here," he said, opening his arms for an embrace. He stopped short. "Uh, sorry, I ripened a little onstage."

"It's no big deal," Hope laughed, giving Rick a big hug.

"Nice to meet you, Hope. What do you do?" he asked.

"Keep *this one* in line, mostly," she replied, chuckling and jabbing a thumb at Bora. "I'm a bartender at Elmyr."

Rick's eyes lit up. "Oh," he said to Bora, "right there by you. Is that how the two of you met?"

"Not the first time, no," Bora answered. "She came to an exhibition I had back in June in Roswell." She gestured towards the handful of trees, barely budding, in the roundabout's center park. "You must be so tired. Wanna sit down?"

"If we can find a spot," Rick said, passing through a break in the shrubbery. To his surprise, someone had just vacated one of the metal benches. "How the hell have you been?" he asked as the three of them sat down. Their newfound proximity allowed them to lower their voices.

"Busy, busy, busy," said Bora. "Still working at the pharmacy. I've been there long enough, though, that they've started being more flexible with my hours. I hardly had time to paint at all, for a minute there. I'm finishing up that new series I told you about."

"*Images of Inman*," Rick remembered.

Bora nodded. "I'm really pleased with how it's turning out. I feel it really captures snapshots of life in the neighborhood. I've just got a few more to complete before I'm ready to move on. If I can ever find the time, that is."

"Well, thanks for making the time to come see the band."

"Are you kidding me?" asked Bora, pulling her hair into a ponytail. "I'm just sad it took so long. We haven't seen each other since, what, when you left Alpharetta?" The question of Cassie hung in the air, unspoken. "It's beautiful up here, but I have to ask: why Ellijay?"

Rick shrugged. "Being nearer to the mountains just felt right. I was getting a little tired of Atlanta anyway. Big cities are like planets. They have this… gravitational pull. You've gotta work if you want to achieve escape velocity, get far enough out that they can't pull you back in."

"Yeah, but, like, how do you make a living?"

"Easy enough," Rick explained, shifting position. "You can make it work wherever you live. Just depends on how much you want to hustle. It's not so bad. Plenty of gigs between here and Blue Ridge, and I'm only, like, ninety minutes from downtown. Just an hour to Woodstock. Wouldn't be much better in town."

Hope nodded. "Yup. Atlanta is an hour from Atlanta," she joked.

Finally, the question which Rick had heard incessantly since last summer: "How are you holding up?" asked Bora.

"Cassie seems willing to give it another try," he said. "She's busy right now, and I was too, during Mardi Gras. Things should calm down for both of us in the next month or so. I'll start heading down to see her and Jack more often."

"I'm glad to hear that," Bora smiled, "but I didn't ask about Cassandra. I asked about *you*." Now she looked concerned. Hope was staring out into the crowd, obviously feeling awkward and trying to offer a modicum of privacy.

Rick rubbed his eyes. "I'm... okay," he whispered at last. "Started seeing a therapist here in town, she seems to help." He paused. Besides Cassie and Jack, he wasn't closer to anyone than Bora. Might as well tell her.

Hope began to stand. "Stay," Rick said, gently touching her arm. "Whatever I say to Bora, you'll hear about, anyway." He looked at his friend. "Remember Hideous Hideous?"

Bora rolled her eyes. "Will you *ever* let that go?" she sighed.

"Look, Bora, all I'm saying is the next time I want to get word out about a show, I'm going to share all the details with you, but tell you to keep it a secret," Rick joked. He snapped his fingers. "Instant Woodstock."

"Hideous Hideous... How was *I* supposed to know you hadn't told them you were leaving the band yet?" said Bora defensively. "It was junior year, I was high as a kite all the time. Ooh, that reminds me." She fished around in her clutch and pulled out a vape pen. "Want a hit?"

"No thanks," Rick declined as Bora took a long drag, filling the immediate area with the smell of weed. "Not my vice." Rick pulled out his flask, took a quick hit, and winced, ready to put the conversation back on track.

"It's okay," Hope interjected warmly. "I wanted to check out some of the vendors anyway. Y'all catch up."

"I like her," Rick said as Hope walked away. "Better not screw this one up." He continued. "My OCD has flared up something awful in the past few months. Not sure what's happening. I'm so meticulous about certain things, and yet... I keep finding stuff misplaced."

"Stuff? Like what?" asked Bora from the back of her throat, holding her breath. She coughed, sending a skunky cloud into Rick's face.

"Everything. Well, not everything. That's the weird part. Just the stuff that I'm OCD about: the silverware, tools, my gear. Picks and cables, especially. I religiously keep them on a shelf in my room. But last weekend, I was trying out a new mic for my solo gigs, and the XLR I was using finally died. No big deal—it was old, anyway—but I went to grab the spare, and it wasn't there. I looked for half an hour before I found it in the addition. No reason to be there. And my picks: I keep them in a mason jar on the same shelf. Just yesterday, I went to grab one, and the *entire mason jar* was gone. Know where I found it? In the fridge. The *fucking* fridge!"

Bora looked at the pocket where Rick had stowed his flask. "You sure it's not...?"

Rick nodded. "I'm never sure it's 'not,'" he confessed. "I thought that, too. Drunk Rick does a lot of stupid stuff, but this isn't his typical M.O. Besides, sometimes things pop up where I just looked a second ago." He passed a hand over his face. "I swear, Bora, I'm losing my grip. And it's all my fault." Rick didn't mention the lights or phantom guitar solo he heard in January, for fear that she'd truly disown him.

Bora put an arm around her friend. "Love you, bud," she said. "You've had a rough year. Cassie was bad enough, but your dad... I know you two never got along well, but it still must be tough. He held in there for a while after his accident, didn't he? Six years?"

"'Accident,' ha," Rick scoffed, restraining his resentment. "Seven." Now was not the time for bitterness.

"Do you know what my favorite Matisse is?" asked Bora abruptly.

"I can barely keep those guys straight."

"His *Blue Nudes*. Not the painting, the ones he made later. He underwent surgery for stomach cancer in the '40s, and afterwards had to use a wheelchair. He couldn't paint or sculpt anymore. So Matisse started making *decoupage*, using scissors to create these cutouts, and they're all fantastic. *Une seconde vie*, he called those last years. 'A second life.'"

She took another hit of her vape, then added, "Take it easy on yourself. We're all struggling. It's why we're artists, remember? We *use* that shit to make something better."

Rick took her hand. "Thanks, Bora. You're like the sister I never... *got* to have." His eyes lit up. "Artists!" he repeated. "I almost forgot. You know that new gallery near Little Five Points?"

"That swanky one that just opened up?"

"Yep. So it turns out, a buddy of mine's wife just got a job there as registrar. Seems there were some complications with another exhibition, and they have an opening in three weeks. I took the liberty of putting in a good word for you."

Bora looked shocked. "Rick, that's... that's so nice... but I'm not sure *Images of Inman* will be ready in time."

Rick smiled. "Of course it will be. Here's your chance. Remember what you told me about opportunities?"

"Say 'no' today, hear 'no' tomorrow," Bora sighed.

"Wise words," Rick said, rising from the bench. He could hear Travis noodling away on the dobro. "I should head back. Listen, let's get together more often. Like we used to. Okay?"

"I would *love* that," Bora beamed as he backed away. "Break a leg!"

Rick wound through the crowd. A half-hour had passed between sets. *Never trust a musician to keep their word about breaks*, he thought.

Before he could climb the steps, Rick paused for a large group to pass by. At first, they blended into the noise of the crowd, but Rick quickly realized that they were moving oddly, waddling away from him together in tandem. He stood there, perplexed, until the monotony of their single-file procession was broken by the final figure in line: a woman, shockingly tall, wearing a white pantsuit. Although Rick couldn't see her face, the back of her head displayed the same bob haircut as the woman from Terry Mac's back in November.

"Rick!" Rodney urgently shouted from the stage. "C'mon, man, we're running late!" Rick shook his head, trying his best to dismiss what he had seen. Maybe they were just budding fans of the band.

The second set commenced as second sets do: first with renewed exuberance, then relief that the end is within sight towards the middle, followed by mild sadness on the final tune. It all passed in a flash.

Joshua Cutchin

The bass player, ready to leave before anyone else, walked up to Rodney: "Hey, Rod, what's the deal with tomorrow?"

"Oh, good question," Rodney said. He abruptly quit glad-handing the crowd at the foot of the stage and turned. "Hey, guys," he announced a little louder, his deep voice booming over the din of music played between acts. "Before you load out, remember that we're back here tomorrow at 5:30." Mumbles of discontent spoken in the exhausted aftermath of the performance flitted across the stage.

Rodney turned to Rick. Speaking lower, he said, "That reminds me—I know you lined up a ringer to cover for you, but he texted me halfway through the set. Has some sort of bad flu or something. Are you *sure* you can't be here tomorrow afternoon?"

"Nah, man," Rick said, zipping his bag. He had been waiting for this conversation and was ready to stand his ground. "I'll be on the way home from Jack's track meet down in McDonough. Have you tried Grady Bishop? He's just down the road in Jasper." Rick looked to Travis.

"Grady's got chops," Travis nodded.

Rodney sighed. "Alright, I'll get his number from Travis. Thanks, man. Have fun tomorrow."

Rick smiled, left his gear, walked to the car, and brought it around backstage. After loading up and triple-checking that he had everything —*amp, cables, surge protector, stand, Tele, Martin, pedals, mics, strings, picks, capo, tape, batteries*—he hopped in the car and headed to Hilltop Beverage over by 515. A stop at the precarious package store had become a tradition after his downtown gigs.

The place was buzzing. People were stocking up, although Rick wasn't sure why. There was a line five people deep at checkout, while dozens of others milled about, trying to decide what to buy. Not Rick; even blindfolded, he could have walked to the vodka section, reached to the bottom rack, and grabbed a bottle of booze. He paused, turned, and grabbed a second, just to be safe.

As he stood in line to pay, Rick noticed that a few people sported paper face masks, the kind that doctors at urgent care always forced him to wear. *Weirdos*, Rick thought.

"That'll be $11.08," the man at the register declared. Rick reached into his pocket and pulled out a wad of tip money. Soon he was listening to music on his way home.

Once more, the post-gig cocktail of exhaustion and exhilaration kicked in, making the drive home pass quickly. The band kept sounding tighter with each performance, the mistakes fewer and farther between on each song. Rick rarely fumbled—he wrote a lot of the damn things—but when others missed the form or the changes, he always felt it reflected poorly on *him*. It either tarnished his performance by association or (even worse) suggested flaws in the songs he wrote.

Well, if it's the only thing I do well, I better do it right, he thought defensively. His mind turned to Bora. *It was great seeing her. I'm surprised she actually kept her promise and came all the way up here.* When it came to social commitments, her history painted a picture of a flighty friend, overpromising and underdelivering. *Too bad you were such a sad sack*, he silently scolded.

Rick really didn't have much to complain about. 2020 was off to a great start. The band pocketed a ton of money during Mardi Gras season. What Country music had to do with Mardi Gras, Rick couldn't explain for the life of him—but they did their due diligence and learned as much stuff as they could pull off, songs like *Jambalaya* and *Hey Pocky Way*.

Just another excuse for people to go out drinking, Rick thought, fully aware of his hypocrisy. *But without them, I'd be out of a job.* The February windfall provided enough spare change for Rick to buy Jack a brand new pair of running shoes. Half a dozen opportunities to give them to his son had presented themselves, but it always slipped Rick's mind. He was either too drunk to remember or too hungover to try.

So he instead kept the shoes in the small shed adjacent to the house, locked securely so the boy wouldn't spoil the surprise. Tomorrow was the first track meet of the season, and it seemed as good a time as any to hand them over. Rick couldn't wait to see Jack's face.

After parking at the house, Rick unloaded the car, making two trips. When everything was back in place he opened the cabinet above the sink, his hand hesitating over his collection of dusty shot glasses. Rick always felt a tinge of shame, seeing their state of neglect. *Who measures liquor, anyway?* he asked himself, grabbing his trusty pint glass.

By nine o'clock Rick was halfway through the bottle and ready to take in the night air. The temperature hovered in the sixties, so he tripped to his closet and grabbed a hoodie.

Slumped on the back porch swing, bottle at his feet, Rick continued drinking, staring out at the expansive field behind his temporary home. *I'll miss this place*, he thought vaguely. Once the motion-activated light on the porch finally switched off, his eyes adjusted to the darkness, allowing him to perceive, ever-so-slightly, the shape of Red Ear Mountain looming over the forest's edge. Maybe he could convince Edna to sell him this place. If he and Cassie got back together, that is.

Rick closed his eyes, listening to the chorus of crickets drifting up from the tall grass. In the coming months, the air would become thick, the night filled with the deafening chirps of an entire symphony of insects. These crickets were just the opening act.

Rick bent down, grabbing the bottle and draining it into his glass. He was past mixers, now. Raising the drink to his lips, he paused.

What was that? he wondered. He almost thought he heard another noise, faint, nearly drowned out by the crickets. The glass remained frozen, halfway to his mouth.

There it is, Rick thought. He stood and walked to the edge of the patio, thinking maybe the tall grass of the field was blocking some of the sound. For a few seconds, he stood there, straining to hear.

At long last it came again, clearer than ever. A melody, drifting over the field, low and mournful. *Like a last-minute turn down a road you drove past all your life*, Rick thought.

It was the same melody he and Jack had heard in their dreams. (*If they* were *dreams,* Rick thought.) What it was doing out here in the field was anyone's guess. From this distance, it was impossible to tell exactly where or what it was coming from other than the general direction of the forest around the mountain. Given how it shifted effortlessly from pitch to pitch, it could have been a voice, glissandi from a cello, or a trombone.

Or a goddamn theremin, for that matter, Rick added with a shiver. *Who the hell is making music out here at*—he glanced at his phone—*ten o'clock at night?*

Rick hiccupped. He had another reason to be grateful that he was drunk. Otherwise, he'd be terrified. Instead, he was seized with the intense urge to capture what he was hearing. Whether it was from a desire to turn it into a song or simply to remind himself of its reality when he was sober, he wasn't sure.

Opening the recording app on his phone, he held it high above his head, waiting patiently for the sound to return. There he stood, swaying gently like the grass in the field, the muscles in his arm starting to burn in protest. *C'mon, c'mon*, he thought.

As if in response to his thoughts, the melody sounded again, twice in succession. Rick dropped his arm and saved the recording, but stood there, still listening. Several minutes passed. Nothing.

Let's figure you out, you little fucker, he thought as he stumbled through the sliding glass door and into his bedroom once more. In one corner sat a cheap Casio keyboard, worthless for performing but indispensable for composition. He fumbled the power button, then played back the recording.

Rick must have stood there for the better part of forty-five minutes, replaying the melody and pecking away at the keys. The contour yielded itself soon enough. It was, frankly, brilliant. Rick would have been proud to write something so unique: a jagged collection of leaps and drops that should have sounded harsh and atonal. Yet played in succession, the aggregate intervals sounded perfectly satisfying, the phrase coming to a conclusion that reconciled the disparate parts into a cohesive whole.

Having decoded the melody, Rick sipped the remainder of his drink while playing with the harmony. It was time to figure out *how* it worked—yet nothing seemed to fit. Everything he tried failed, from a theoretical perspective. *I know I'm drunk*, he thought groggily, *but what the hell* is *this?*

Rick thumbed the recording once more. *Shit*, he thought, noticing the time. *I gotta get to bed. Big day for Jack tomorrow.* Staring at the screen, he saw that his phone was almost dead. Rick plugged it in, set the alarm for ten in the morning, and turned the volume up as loud as it would go.

He then collapsed onto his bed, still wearing his hoodie and jeans, and passed out.

6

Friday, March 13, 2020

DISINTEGRATION

THERE COMES A TIME in every alcoholic's descent when they realize there are worse things than hangovers. Yes, hangovers are horrific, but if you awoke with one, it meant you slept through part of it. A grimmer fate is waking up mildly drunk from the night before, knowing that you will get to experience the consequences of your actions fully conscious later that day.

This was the predicament Rick found himself in when he awoke the following morning. For a moment he lay there, eyes still shut, head spinning, before realizing that everything was wrong. It was freezing. Something rough and grainy had replaced the soft embrace of his pillow. Rick blinked and found himself on a cement floor, staring at a brightly-lit bag of drywall mud.

What in the world? he wondered, slowly sitting up. Seeing anything proved difficult at first. Blinding light spilled in through the windows. Rick reached for his glasses, just a few feet away on the floor, and slipped them on. Looking around, he came to realize that instead of the cluttered familiarity of his bedroom, he now sat half-naked in the addition. He only wore a t-shirt. His pants, underwear, and hoodie were nowhere to be seen, leaving him shivering.

Uh oh, Rick thought as he stiffly rose to his feet. *What the hell was I doing in here?* Bits of dust and dirt clung to every exposed part of his body—which, given his state, was most of it. He brushed off as much as he could before ambling out of the unfinished bedroom and into the living room.

Well, there's my clothes, Rick silently declared, seeing the pile on the floor of the kitchen. *And, I suppose, the perpetrator.* His second bottle of vodka sat half-emptied on the countertop, dominating the scene every bit as much as Red Ear dominated the backyard.

Confusion washed over Rick. He didn't remember drinking anything else after passing out.

Then again, that's why they call it "blacking out," isn't it? he mused. *Not the first time, won't be the last, I guess.* He paused, turning the bottle over in his shaking hands while adding, *Maybe it is….*

A glance at the microwave amplified Rick's bewilderment. *One o'clock?* he thought. *There's no way. The alarm on my phone didn't even go off. I would've heard it, even in the addition.* Perhaps a power failure had reset the clock. With newfound urgency, Rick stormed into his bedroom where his phone lay on the bedside table, screen black but still plugged in.

Rick picked up the phone and pressed the home button. An empty battery icon flashed onscreen. *Oh no,* Rick thought as he unplugged and replugged the power cord. *No, no, no.* A light chime accompanied by the picture of a lightning bolt appeared, and a few seconds later the phone booted up. Authoritative white letters declared the time: 1:02 p.m.

"Fuck!" shouted Rick, dropping the phone back on the table. "Goddamn piece of shit!"

A thousand questions raced through Rick's mind. Why had the phone failed to charge overnight—despite being plugged into the wall? It was charging just fine now. How did he sleep *so late*? What had he been doing in the addition? Why did he wake up dressed like Donald Duck? How did he manage to polish off half of a second bottle?

None of that mattered. What mattered was that Rick had Jack's track meet in an hour, and McDonough was at least two hours away. *Maybe three,* Rick panicked. Getting around or through Atlanta was always a roll of the dice on a Friday. *Fuck fuck FUCK!*

He needed to act quickly. Rick ripped off his shirt and jumped into the shower, not even bothering to wait for the water to warm. Once it did, he noticed that it caused a painful sensation whenever it struck the right side of his abdomen.

What now? wondered Rick. Lifting his arm, he looked down at where the pain originated. A neat little row of tiny blisters—maybe as many as twenty—traced up from his right hip to just below his nipple. Rick pivoted away from the water to stare at the injury. For the first time all morning, his mania subsided.

Rick Coulter, what did you get into last night? he asked for the hundredth time as he reached down to gingerly touch the string of welts. They were tender, but not excruciatingly so. The largest one was no bigger around than a pencil lead. They almost resembled burns. *But burns from what?*

No time for this, he scolded. After finishing his shower, Rick ran out to the kitchen, naked, and shoved a Hot Pocket into the microwave. While waiting for the food to finish, he slipped into fresh clothes, picking a new pair of jeans and a polo shirt.

The timer went off just as Rick stepped out of the bedroom, switching the microwave clock back to the correct time. *1:20... not bad*, thought Rick as he removed the Hot Pocket and took a bite. It burned his mouth. *No time to cool, I'll finish it later.* If he left now, he still might catch the end of Jack's meet.

Rick dashed outside and into the Corolla. He was about to turn the key when he remembered Jack's new shoes. Swearing under his breath, he left the car door open and headed over to the shed by the right-hand corner of the house.

The shed was a prefabricated affair, something Edna bought for some unknown purpose ages ago. While weathered and full of gaps, the simple wooden exterior provided ample shelter from the elements for the few possessions Rick kept inside. Edna had the decency to clear it out before Rick moved in, and said she was fine with him keeping a lock on the door as long as she knew the combination herself.

Rick grabbed the lock and tilted it upward, flicking his thumb across the four dials: 1-5-0-5. January 5, 2005. Jack's birthday. The door opened to reveal a hodgepodge of items waiting patiently: an extra music stand, some old sports equipment, a few of Rick's larger tools used more rarely. Above it all, on a shelf in the rear, sat the black-and-white Adidas box.

After wading through the mess, Rick retrieved the shoes from high on the shelf and made his way back outside, slamming the door behind him. He clasped the lock.

Rick shoved the shoebox under his left arm. Even in this moment of urgency, he couldn't help himself. Tribes had their totems, priests had their ceremonies, athletes had their good luck charms; Rick

Coulter had his own rituals. As he always did, he thumbed the dials back into their starting position: 0-0-0-0.

The blue Corolla tore out of the driveway, passing through the forest to the highway and beyond to I-575 south. The mountains faded into the distance, slowly supplanted by the familiar landscape Rick despised: fast food chains, apartment complexes, and high rises, clinging to the roadside like parasites on arteries, siphoning off the lifeblood of traffic.

Rick only vaguely noted the change. He was far too preoccupied with making good time and avoiding state troopers. Only when traffic became too heavy for him to speed did he finally allow his mind to wander. By now, the slightest hint of a hangover had crept into his head. It was going to be a long day—whatever was left of it.

Getting past Atlanta was always a tossup. Most of the time, I-285 was a lifesaver… unless there was a wreck. Rick remembered sitting on the road a few years ago, not budging an inch for three hours until an accident was cleared. After scanning through several traffic reports on the radio and discerning no difference between going around town versus straight through it, Rick opted for the latter.

It was a poor choice. Gridlock clogged I-75. Rick stifled a swell of rage, knowing that there was nothing he could do about it. Rather than give in to anger, he made the most of his time, using the stop-and-go traffic to jot some ideas in his notebook. Rick derived particular inspiration from fragments of a dream, barely remembered, that had occurred the night before: a young girl dancing in the forest, her face obscured by long, curly locks that reached past her shoulders.

Turns her face from the rest, he wrote, *Hair as red as cardinal's breast….*

Everything cleared up once again on the other side of downtown, as it often did. Rick resumed speed and put on a Weather Report album, the supercharged rhythms adding weight to his foot. Nearing his destination, he turned on his phone—barely charged enough to work—and plugged in 8011 Charlot Avenue, the address for the track meet.

The Corolla finally pulled into the high school parking lot at ten after four. For the first time since Jack began track, Rick was grateful that these events lasted as long as they did. *Might be able to catch the last little bit*, he thought, squeezing out of the driver's side door with the shoebox in hand. The assholes on either side, a gigantic F-150 and a dilapidated Suburban, provided just barely enough room for his tiny car to park.

Either the event was not ticketed or they had stopped charging attendees. In any case, Rick walked into the stadium unimpeded and mounted the bleachers. Turning to look at the crowd, he saw it was about a third of the way full. Oddly, Rick saw that some of the faces were masked, as they were yesterday in the liquor store. He shrugged this off and continued scanning the spectators, looking for Cassie and Jack. He found his son first.

Out on the field, Jack was finishing up his turn at shot put. His wiry frame twirled within the circle and released a dark globe that soared above the field, then landed with a dull thud.

"Thirty-two feet, ten inches," announced the official. Surprise and pride filled Rick's chest. When he heard that Jack was trying his hand at the event, he felt skeptical. The boy was tall, but seemed a little slight for shot put.

"Attaboy, Jack!" Rick yelled over the low, half-hearted applause filling the stadium. Only one other person, further down the row from where Rick stood, cheered louder than the rest: it was Cassie, shouting and encouraging her son. Rick slunk towards her, stowing the shoebox at his feet.

She only noticed him once he sat down. "Rick," she hissed in his ear, a stern expression contorting her face. "Where the hell have you been?"

"Traffic was horrendous," he answered sheepishly. To this half lie he added a full one: "When I went out the car, it was dead. I had to call Edna to give me a jump. She came all the way from Chattanooga."

Cassie looked disgusted. "What about the other guys in the band? Couldn't *they* have helped you out?"

"They have a gig today. I don't know what they're up to," Rick countered. "A gig that I'm *missing*, remember?"

Cassie started to snap back, but something restrained her. Rick wasn't sure what. Maybe she believed his lie. Maybe she remembered her part in the downward spiral of their marriage. Either way, she simply nodded and reached out to hold Rick's hand.

Eventually, Jack found his way to his parents, fingers still taped. After a brief embrace, the three of them sat in the bleachers quietly while the events wrapped up with the Girls Triple Jump. It almost felt like they were a family again. When the meet ended, everyone rose from their seats and began filing out of the stadium. Rick turned to Jack, having the first chance to properly greet him.

"I'm so proud of you, buddy," he said, wrapping an arm around his son. "Listen, I'm sorry I got here late. I had car trouble. Got to see the shot put, though! How did the other events go?"

Jack, clearly disappointed but happy to see his parents getting along, said, "They were fine. Didn't place, but the season is just starting. Just got to work harder for next time."

Rick beamed. Although Jack hadn't taken to music quite as much as Rick would have liked, he had still managed to internalize a musician's sense of work ethic into his other interests. Regardless of whether or not those interests were shared, Rick would be there to support his son.

"Speaking of next time," Rick began, "I have a surprise for you." He reached down and pulled the shoebox from its hiding place, handing it to Jack. The boy took it, looking surprised. As he opened the lid and shuffled the tissue paper aside, his expression turned to concern.

"Well?" asked Rick. "What do you think? Aren't those the ones you wanted? I thought Mom said they were."

"They're awesome, Dad," Jack mumbled tensely. "It's just..." He cast his eyes downward. On his feet sat the exact same Adidas running shoes.

"Oh, Rick," Cassie sighed, looking over her husband's shoulder. "I didn't say those were the ones he *wanted*, I said they were the ones I *got* for him. I texted you that, go back and check. Did you at least keep the receipt?"

Rick slowly closed his eyes. "Yes. I mean, I think so. Probably back at the house somewhere. I'm sorry."

Why didn't you read the text, Rick? he thought. *Why didn't you look at his shoes today?*

Cassie rubbed Rick's shoulders. "It was still really sweet of you," she said before turning to their son. "Jack, why don't you run and change? We'll meet you outside the front gate, okay?"

Jack nodded. "Thanks, Dad," he said with a look of pity, then trotted off. Once he was out of earshot, Rick finally spoke.

"Fuck me," he moaned. "I could've sworn that's not what you said." He pulled out his phone and began thumbing through his text messages. That was when he remembered how low the battery was and decided to postpone his search.

"It's... fine," Cassie said as he shoved the phone in his pocket. "It's just what you do."

"What does that mean?" asked Rick.

Cassie thought for a moment. "When Jack was little, I got him a book of Aesop's Fables. Do you remember the story of the astronomer, who was so focused on the stars that he never looked at his feet, and ended up falling into a well? That's you. You just... go off into your little hole, and get hyper-focused on one thing—or multiple things, or whatever the hell it is you're writing down in that little notebook of yours—but not *us*. When we were together, I never felt like I got more than thirty percent of your attention. Forty on a good day."

She and Rick slowly started towards the front gate, passing several spectators in cloth masks on the way. "I bet you have no idea what's even going on in the world right now, do you?" she wondered. "When you get home, turn on the TV."

Rick ignored the comment. "I can't help it," he apologized. "I thought it was getting better. I've been going to my therapist like you asked. Religiously. She says she's seen some improvement."

"How about the drinking?" prodded Cassie. When Rick remained silent, she stopped and turned towards him. "I swear to God, Rick, we have no hope of making this work unless you pull yourself together."

"I know," Rick nodded, holding back tears. "It's just... they're related. You think I *like* being distracted all the time? I'm trying to calm things down," he said, pointing to his head. "I don't drink to get *drunk*. I drink to feel *normal*."

"And that's *not* normal," added Cassie. As she said these words, Jack emerged from the field house at the edge of the stadium and trotted over to them. Her grim expression of pity immediately switched to one of parental pride. "Let's go get some dinner, how's that sound?" she asked.

The meal was predictably awkward. Rick tried his best to push past his failure, but the specter of the running shoes loomed over the conversation like a dark cloud. When they finished, the couple checked their schedules, with Rick making extra sure that he had all the details straight for the remainder of the month. He wished his wife and son goodbye and headed back up towards Ellijay.

The drive was uneventful. Rick tried putting on some music to distract him from his shortcomings, but it was no use. The shoebox sat in the opposite seat like a silent, judgmental passenger, constantly reminding him of yet another missed opportunity to be the father he never had.

Once he navigated the hazards of downtown and the metro, further doubts surfaced. Was he *ever* a good father? Or was he staying just drunk enough to *think* he was? What about his conversation with Jack on the mountain? Had that been as fulfilling as he thought, or just another memory clouded by alcoholic euphoria?

When he got home, only the bug-eyed wooden bear was there to greet him. "Yeah, fuck you too," he grumbled as he unlocked the front door. Then he slunk into the house, dropping the shoebox on the countertop alongside the vodka. Without a second thought, he swatted the plastic bottle into the trash.

As he did so, he stopped at the half-eaten Hot Pocket in front of the microwave. *Half-eaten...* thought Rick. *But I only took a bite....*

"To be fair," he said aloud to the empty room, "you *did* wake up drunk." A tiny noise echoed in the kitchen, eliding the final word. Rick froze. It sounded like a barely audible giggle, *sotto voce*. Was someone else in the house with—

Chee-reep. The sound made Rick jump, but he recognized it. It was his phone, finally on its last legs, alerting him that it needed to be plugged in. Shaking his head at how skittish he had become, Rick obliged, taking the phone back to his bedroom to charge. Reluctantly, he meandered back into the kitchen, retrieved the liquor bottle from the trash, and flopped onto the couch.

"When you get home, turn on the TV," Rick parroted in a snide imitation of his wife's voice. Why bother? Everything on there was either dumb or depressing, and there was enough of that in Rick's life as it was.

Still, curiosity got the best of him, and he reached for the remote. Just as Cassie asked, he turned on the television.

Then the world fell apart.

7

Sunday, August 15, 1897

LUS MÓR

"Ah, there you are," the old woman clucked, opening the door to her dingy cottage.

"*Dia duit*," The Mother whispered, a screaming infant clutched to her breast. "Sorry to arrive on top of you like this. Might I come in?"

"Of course, no trouble. I thought you'd be paying a visit earlier."

"Earlier? Why is that?"

"Mine own *bráthair* told me."

"Your... your brother? I'm so sorry, Biddy Nally. I thought you only had the one."

"Aye, that I do."

"Did he not drown as a child?"

"That he did. Still, Tom keeps me abreast of comings and goings. But he only shared news of your impending arrival, not your purpose... Husband has no inkling you came, hmmm? What ails you may not be my business."

"No, he doesn't. But I pray you show kindness in my time of need. You healed my father-in-law's thumb some fifteen winters ago. Nan—his widow—she bade him to see you, just as she instructed me today. Back then you said he might've lost his thumb entirely, were Nan not so quick to seek your advice."

"Ah, Big Liam? How fairs he?"

"He went to his reward two years ago."

"Tsk tsk. My condolences... that's a going Tom never disclosed. Always sins of omission from him. How did Big Liam pass? He was a good skin, that one."

"From what we gathered, something spooked his horse while returning from market. Threw him from the wagon. My husband found him the next day alongside the *boreen*. We never recovered the horse and wagon."

"Ach, poor girl. From one heartbreak to another. That's what brings you here today, isn't it? Another tragedy? Rarely do guests come for a little *craic*, it's usually something what ails 'em."

"... Yes. My boy. He's... different."

"Hmmm?"

"He once was so... happy. Peaceful, even. Now, his wailing never ceases."

"I have ears to hear, girl. Tell me: when you bring the babe up to your diddy, does he suck?"

"Yes. Constantly he begs for more to eat, but even his fill cannot sate him."

"And when did this begin?"

"Nearly a fortnight past. We were in the field and there was... a storm...."

"Ah, say no more. Let me see the child... oh dear. He's failed. His arms... there'd be more meat on a butcher's apron. Oh, hush you, hush!—Tell me, have his eyes always appeared as such?"

"No ma'am. Only these past few weeks."

"Ah, sound. Well, I've seen this before. Shush, wee one!—You know what you've got?"

"Yes, Biddy Nally. The things I have seen would take the night's sleep off of you. I hear... noises... coming from the cradle during the small hours. He always falls silent for them. Sounds like music... or whispers. More like something in between."

"Have you tried the eggshells?"

"That I have."

"And?"

"He... spoke. Well, not exactly. His mouth was shut. But I heard a voice. Inside my head."

"Hmmm. What did it say?"

"'The acorn afore the oak I knew'—"

"—'but never beer in eggshell brew.'"

"Well, not exactly. I used porridge, but... yes, that was the heart of the matter."

"*Ptooey!* Ach, *they*'re always changin', aren't *they*? Changin' how *they* look, how *they* act, the things *they* do... changin' people. But you can always tell, if your eye is keen. My, he causes such a racket!—What would you have me do?"

"I want my child back, of course."

"No doubt. Tell me, do you still count the farm your domicile?"

"Yes, Biddy Nally."

"Might there be a place, not a few miles from there, where a forth lies on a hill? The harm what came to your son came from there, likely as not that is where the true babe has gone. Were the father a courageous man, I might hazard he collect the babe hisself."

"… Would that be… safe?"

"'Course t'isnt *safe*. *Living* isn't safe. But it would work a charm."

"Isn't there some other way?"

"Wisha! If you balked at visiting the forth, no words of comfort can I offer! Wish to beat the child, do you? Hmmm? Burn 'im, stab 'im? Leave him by the river or on the rubbish heap overnight? Drown 'im? Any of those would put it out! But you mustn't be afeard, you must place trust in me!"

"Biddy Nally… I had no intention to offend. I just wondered…" The Mother trailed off. There was nothing left to say. She had clearly stated her intentions. If she was to watch The Child waste away, so be it. At least she would still have her husband, and would sleep well knowing that she hadn't directly contributed to her son's death.

The two sat across from each other, The Child's incessant cries echoing off the walls of the tiny cottage. Biddy Nally leaned forward in her old rocking chair and into the sunset shining through the window. One eye held The Mother's gaze while the other roved about beneath a white cataract. "If you'd like to see the boy again, there are ways," she said at last, her breath pushing the dust motes in an aerial ballet. "But the hour grows late."

The Mother nodded. Biddy Nally slowly stood upright. Since the beginning of their visit, the old woman, covered as she was in shawls and her blanket, seemed to have melded with the rocking chair. Now, the two separated once more, leaving the chair to pivot silently as Biddy Nally disappeared into a nearby door.

The Mother sat, rocking The Child, wishing desperately that he would stop crying. Moments later, the old woman reappeared, clutching something. She drew closer. Despite her shrunken form, Biddy Nally struck an intimidating figure as she stooped over The Mother and pressed the parcel in her palm.

"What is this?" asked The Mother, turning the small vial over in her hand. Through the glass, she could see it contained a light purple powder.

Biddy Nally shrugged. "Many things," she answered matter-of-factly. "*Lus mór*, mainly."

"Folk's Glove?"

"It has many names," the woman answered, waving a hand dismissively. "Mix it with milk and have the child take it. Odds are, he'll be better in no length." Biddy Nally ambled over to the hearth, where she started chopping vegetables and tossing them into a stewpot, signaling the end of their conversation. The Mother felt an inexorable tug towards the door, but remained seated.

"I have heard tell of this," she said at last. "Is this not what Michael Ward took for his heart last year?"

Biddy Nally shrugged again. "Don't know that man." Her disposition had shifted abruptly. No one would ever suspect how invested she had been mere minutes ago.

The Mother slowly nodded. "Well, I thank you for your time, Biddy Nally," she said, clutching the vial. "How might I repay you?"

The woman looked up from her work. "Not a thing. I only ask you heed my advice. *They* are about tonight. Don't take the road you planned to leave on. Avoid it. Enter no other buildings on the return home, lest you lose your chance. And take care; no matter what you do, by all means don't drop it." Biddy Nally paused, then looked in a completely different direction, as plainly as if someone had walked into the room. She stared for a time, listening and nodding, with the occasional whisper thrown in, inaudible over the cries of The Child. At last she looked back to The Mother.

"Tom apologizes for not letting me know about Big Liam," she finally explained. "Said he's been *there* for a while, it just slipped his mind. Forgetful eejit in life, forgetful eejit in death, I s'pose." She paused. "Tom says your husband's father offers a word."

The Mother, her hand on the door, raised her chin. "That is?"

"'Tell my son to bring the knife,'" Biddy Nally answered. "I've no idea what that means, although I speculate."

With that, The Mother left.

She felt no better than when she had arrived.

8

Friday, May 1, 2020

1-1-0-8

IT WAS ABOUT FIFTY DAYS INTO THE PANDEMIC when Rick woke up to find himself amidst a sea of empty bottles. As with the previous forty-nine mornings, he briefly considered consolidating them, straightening up the house, and making gestures towards acting like a functional human being… but what was the point?

Rick had weathered some bleak scenarios in his day. An abusive father, toxic relationships, financial catastrophes, a soured marriage. None of them compared to the current state of the world, however, which felt nigh-apocalyptic.

A degree of comfort this time around was the shared nature of it. Everyone was in the same boat, even if that boat was sinking. Still, it didn't make his daily existence any less tedious, nor did it make the developments spouted in the news any less depressing.

Rick lay on the couch where he passed out the night before, replaying what he knew for the thousandth time. It was overwhelming, and he never reached a conclusion. There were too many variables. No one seemed to know what the hell was going on.

The virus (God, there were so many names, SARS-CoV-2, Covid, the Coronavirus) had completely upended life, shuttering businesses and forcing everyone to stay at home. People debated the efficacy of face masks and "social distancing," how long (or if) the virus lingered on surfaces, hell, *whether or not there even was a virus at all.*

Rick didn't think that was the case. Clearly something was happening, but he couldn't get a grasp on its severity. Hospitals certainly seemed full of dying people. At the same time, Rick heard from several friends who had contracted the illness and, although they said it was the sickest they'd ever been, they pulled through just fine.

Yeah, and Rodney's parents died *from the damn thing,* he thought, ambling to the kitchen to pour himself a drink. *The truth is probably somewhere in between.* Each time the talking heads listed the risk factors for negative outcomes, Rick thanked his lucky stars that he was young and didn't have lung, heart, or immune system problems... and conveniently overlooked those pesky mentions of alcoholism and obesity.

Even these failed as accurate predictors, however. How Covid affected each individual seemed to unfold on a case-by-case basis. Some old folks handled it fine. Some young, healthy folks were laid out for weeks, even suffering lingering symptoms afterwards.

It's all random, he thought, returning to the couch and taking a long drink. *What's true, what's not, whether or not you'll get it, how bad it would be....*

There seemed no way to separate the truth from the nonsense. Rick—by no means a hypochondriac but taking the pandemic seriously—decided to play it safe and remain at home these past few months. He'd rather the threat be minimal and remain overly cautious than the threat be significant and put himself and others in danger.

In fact, uncertainty was the only thing Rick knew for certain. That, and the four walls that had morphed into something like a prison in the past few months. Life became monotonous, an endless cycle of worry punctuated by feeble attempts at productivity, only to drink himself to sleep and do it all over again. Hours passed completely unaccounted for; they might as well have not existed in the first place. Even the weather came and went unnoticed.

Rick realized he didn't even know what day it was. *May 1st,* he thought, looking at his phone. The day his childhood died. *Funny. I used to dread this day. How long has it been? Thirty-three, thirty-four years? How is that possible?*

He took another sip. To Rick, the most surprising thing about the pandemic was the fact that it had its own *taste*: the taste of stale air conditioning, of bile, of vodka and Grapefruit LeCroix at ten in the morning, the taste of hand sanitizer. God, *everything* tasted like hand sanitizer.

At least you can *taste... and smell*, Rick reasoned as he turned on his record player. People were starting to say that those were among the first signs that you had contracted the virus.

Pushing these intrusions from his head, Rick grabbed his copy of Peggy Lee's *Is That All There Is?* and played the title track. The song had become something of a pandemic anthem for him. Early on in lockdown, Rick tried to write a song capturing the desperation that pervaded every waking hour. After remembering the bleak fatalism of Leiber and Stoller's lyrics, he decided he could do no better.

"*... then let's keep dancing,*" Peggy crooned as Rick swayed side to side, drinking. He found himself trying to decide how he would differentiate this day from those before and the endless string of those yet to come.

Maybe I'll go on another hike later today, he decided. While Georgia was far less restrictive with lockdowns thus far than other states, many people in Atlanta had nowhere to go. Even if he remained in the comparative quiet of Alpharetta, Rick would have felt that the risks of doing *anything* far outweighed a momentary respite from cabin fever. Here, outside Ellijay, the mountains—free of people, free of sickness, untouched by the disarray in the human world—were always ready to welcome him.

Arguably, his access to the outdoors was the only thing keeping him sane. That, and the fact that liquor stores were deemed "essential businesses"; while he disagreed in principle, he had no idea what he would have done if they had closed.

Two things to be grateful for, Rick thought, *and a thousand to resent.* The past fifty days took so much from him. His birthday came and went, his only gifts an ill-advised online order from himself that he couldn't afford.

Don't forget the gigs, he thought, grabbing another drink before heading to the shower. 2020 was supposed to be the year that the Rib Wrenches blew up. Dates throughout the Southeast—one in the Midwest, even—fell like dominoes following the president's press conference. High-profile clubs, festivals, and private parties, any of which could have launched the band into a new phase, were all canceled with no hope of rescheduling.

Without gigs, Rick felt little reason to practice; without practice, he got rusty; and as his competence slipped, so did his own feelings of worth. Between the aimless days and his squandered talents, Rick felt like he was fading into nothingness.

Beyond the heartbreak of sidelining Rick's true passion, canceled gigs meant increased financial strain. Yes, there were government checks coming, and Edna was being charitable about rent, but things still remained difficult. *Thank God you drink the cheap stuff, Rick*, he thought as he stepped out of the shower and dried off.

Suffice to say, the possibility of quitting had been postponed for the time being. Not that it mattered. He hadn't seen his family since the track meet. Probably for the better, given the state he was in. Cassie told him that they would get together in June, although talk of repairing their marriage fell by the wayside. He had answered the phone drunk too many times.

Rick began unloading the dishwasher. *Knife, spoon, fork, knife, spoon, fork, fork...* He stopped, took all the silverware out, and began again. *Knife, spoon, spoon...* All the cutlery jumped as Rick slammed a fist on the countertop.

Any progress toward mental health had regressed. Rick's therapist offered to continue sessions online, but Rick used the change as an excuse to cut off her help entirely. Therapy was expensive. Drinking was cheap. *So is calling friends, and that's a lot healthier*, Rick chided himself, thinking for the hundredth time how he should call Bora. *You don't do that, either.*

Rick slowly and carefully began filing the silverware in the correct order. The ritual concluded with three spare knives. Rick started chuckling, eventually falling into a maniacal, full-throated laugh that echoed through the empty house before devolving into sobs.

Such anomalies had become commonplace. They represented another reason why Rick stopped seeing his therapist—his issues, he felt, were way above her paygrade, and if they weren't, she was doing a piss poor job of fixing them. In the past few months, the lights also began paying nightly visits to the mountain, so frequently that Rick installed a curtain rod just to circumvent any temptation to peek out back once darkness fell.

It's okay, thought Rick, wiping tears from his eyes. *It's okay. This will all be over soon. Like nothing happened. You'll see Jack again. Gigs will come back.* Setting the knives aside, he sniffled and stared up at the ceiling. Coming back better than ever was the only thing worth trying. Today, he would push through the malaise and work on his craft.

After a quick lunch, Rick passed the next several hours toiling away in the makeshift studio of his bedroom. He began combing through his notebook, finding which chord changes complemented which lyrics the best. From there, he tried to make the disparate parts come together into something whole. He largely failed, only winding up with two-thirds of one song and about half of another.

For a long while Rick sat perfectly still, staring through the side window at the lone hawthorn blooming by the trailhead, praying inspiration might strike. It didn't. When he spotted his phone on his desk, he opened up the recording app and replayed the melody he heard back in March. *Seems like a million years ago*, he lamented. Rick decided that the song had come from a neighbor, although he had no clue who it could have been; the only person nearby was Edna, and she lived on the other side of Red Ear Mountain. Still, the acoustics up here were peculiar. Maybe the other peaks batted the song around from some distant party, preserving just enough to reach Rick's ears in the field.

The last time he tried to transcribe the mysterious tune, Rick was drunk. Now he was only half drunk. He procured a sheet of staff paper and began pecking out the contours on the piano, writing them down as he went. When he finished, he replayed the recording, made a few amendments, and stared at the result.

"Yeah," he said. "That's it." Still, the harmony eluded him. *Maybe it's the keyboard*, he wondered. Only by the skin of his teeth had he passed class piano in college. Something about the instrument always remained foreign and unyielding. Playing guitar, on the other hand, was like breathing. He twirled around in his chair, grabbed his Martin, and looked for his music stand to hold the transcription.

It was nowhere to be found. A sinking feeling settled in Rick's gut. Silverware, picks, and cables were one thing; a music stand was altogether different. It was too big to simply vanish.

Rick replaced his guitar on its stand with a feeling of defeat and began searching the house. It obviously wasn't in the bedroom. After scouring the living room, dining room, and kitchen, Rick reluctantly investigated the bathroom and the addition, feeling like a fool the entire time.

Nothing, Rick cursed, rubbing his forehead. A second search of the entire house failed as well. *Hell with this. I'll grab the spare.* He slipped on his shoes and headed outside into the bright, warm sunshine toward the shed alongside the house. When he reached it, he took the lock in his hand, tilted it upward, and hesitated. His thumb hovered over the dials, which read 1-1-0-8.

The worst part about obsessive-compulsive disorder is that sometimes you realize the silliness of your quirks. Rick knew deep down that he wouldn't drop dead of a heart attack if the silverware was put up in the wrong order. He also knew that no robber would steal the contents of the shed if he didn't reset the lock to 0-0-0-0. But he still did these things because they gave him a degree of control in an otherwise chaotic existence.

Therefore, seeing the dials on the wrong numbers wasn't the end of the world for Rick—but it did make him wonder what other things would slip his mind. Would he leave the stove on someday, and come home to find the house burned down? Would he overlook routine maintenance on his car, only to breakdown en route to a gig?

Rick pursed his lips and slowly moved the dials back to 0-0-0-0, then to Jack's birthday. He tugged the lock. Nothing happened. He spun the dials randomly, set them to 1-5-0-5, and tugged again. Still the lock remained shut.

And the bolt cutters are in the shed, Rick giggled, reveling in the irony. *Maybe the lock is just old.* He tried the combination two more times, to no effect. *What if....*

He moved the dials back to their earlier configuration: 1-1-0-8. Gently, almost as if he wished it wouldn't work, Rick pulled the lock towards him. A soft click followed and the latch fell open as easily as it ever did.

Rick stared at the open lock in disbelief. For once, his mental fog lifted. The misplaced items might be his own fault. The lights on the mountain could still be hikers. But the lock—the same lock in his hands—suggested that something beyond his control had settled over the property.

Is somebody fucking with me? wondered Rick. *Edna is the only one with the combination, and she's been out of town for weeks.* When was the last time he opened the shed? For the life of him, he couldn't recall.

With great care, Rick swung open the door to the shed, the hinges creaking in protest. Warm spring sunlight filled the dim interior, casting its glow on the contents within. Everything he expected was there—and more. Both music stands sat in the middle of the mess, placed as neatly as if Rick had stored them there himself.

Rick's eyes bulged as he backed away from the shed. Something was happening. Sure, his quirks played a role in all this madness, but this was *not* solely the result of his constant stupor. Someone who knew the combination had reset the lock, taken his music stand from his bedroom, and placed it inside. But who? And when?

Was there something important about the number? 1-1-0-8? Rick racked his brain, trying to think of its significance as a value, a time, or a date. He came up with nothing until a thought suddenly entered his mind. *Wait!* he remembered, looking at the number on the lock. *Dad died on the eighth of November. Maybe it has something to... no, no, that's wrong. Dad died on the seventh. Besides, why would anyone change the number to the date of Dad's death, let alone the day after?*

Rick locked up the shed again, noting the new combination in his notebook. No more music today. He went inside to call Edna. When he picked up his phone from his bedroom desk, Rick found it dead again. The empty battery icon flashed.

"Piece of shit!" yelled Rick, throwing it across the room. The thing couldn't hold a charge worth a damn anymore. He obviously needed to replace it, but until he started working again, he could scarcely afford one. Seething with anger, Rick retrieved his phone from the floor and plugged it in. It started charging immediately, of course. A few minutes later, he dialed his landlady.

"Oh shit! Hey hon," Edna yelled, her voice barely audible over a chatter of laughter and music thrumming in the background. "Everything okay?"

"Hey Edna," Rick replied loudly, trying to make sure she could hear him. He stepped outside to stare at the shed. "Everything's fine. Um, where are you?"

"Miami, baby!" she exclaimed. "You should come on down. I tell ya, it's like nothing has changed down here—Eduardo! Can I get another Long Island? Thanks babe!—If everything's fine, why are you calling?"

Rick explained the situation as best he could, fiddling with the lock to check one last time that he hadn't gone completely insane. Edna had no idea what he was talking about.

"Just reset the fuckin' lock," she suggested. "Choose a completely different number. You can tell me later. Okay, kid, gotta go, Eduardo just got here with my drink. Toodles!"

She hung up, leaving Rick standing by the shed. "Toodles?" he repeated.

Rarely had Rick ever felt so alone. He stood there for several minutes, staring at the lock and listening to the wind as it picked up, carrying the scent of honeysuckle. Now that it was spring, the forest and the field it encompassed had become an orgy of life, a constantly shifting tapestry of green. Over the past few months, Rick often felt like the house had been dropped into an immense basin of emerald water, the instant of impact frozen in time. Like rebounding waves, the trees leaned in, threatening to engulf the field and everything in it —but they never did.

Instead, the trees remained rooted but were far from immobile. As the wind continued, the entire edge of the forest began shaking, the hiss of leaves combining with the incessant drone of insects to generate a dull white noise that smothered the field. To Rick, it sounded like a conversation between the two, a conspiratorial exchange dedicated to undermining his sanity.

Who did this? he wondered.

"*Shh, he can hear us.*" Rick spun around at the sound of the voice. He was sure he had heard it. It was as clear as if someone had whispered in his ear. But the side yard was empty. No one was there. He ran to the front of the house, where the deformed wooden bear stood watch. No one there, either. Next he circled around to the backyard, which was equally deserted. The only movement came from the rippling grass of the field and the trees bending back and forth in the distance below Red Ear Mountain.

"Hello?" he asked. "Is someone there?" The sole response he received was the porch swing, creaking in the breeze.

9

Monday, December 28, 1998

NOTHING

AFTER EIGHTEEN YEARS OF LIVING IN THE HOUSE, Rick knew the location of every creak in the massive staircase. Where most only saw wide slabs of oak descending to the bottom floor, he perceived a detailed map of quiet places to step, riskier spots dependent upon the weather outside, and points guaranteed to send groans throughout the large foyer downstairs. Holding his shoes, he deftly navigated the gauntlet from his second-story bedroom and landed on the marble below.

He was about to open the front door when, from far down the hallway, a voice bellowed: "Richard! Is that you, boy?"

Rick's heart sank. The old man's hearing bordered on the preternatural. "Yes, sir," he shouted back. "What is it?"

"Come here!" came the response, echoing through the cavernous corridor. "I wish to speak with you!"

Dejected, Rick slipped on his shoes and began the long walk towards the voice. The mansion did funny things with sound, throwing noises to other rooms. More than one guest had followed the laughter of dinner parties past the dining room only to wind up completely lost, missing several courses while awaiting rescue in the conservatory or the library.

At first, Rick thought his father might be in the parlor, but the sound of the fireplace and smell of cigar smoke invisibly drew him in the direction of the den. There, he found Conrad Coulter in repose, nursing his third brandy of the evening, the day's copy of *The New York Times* splayed across his lap. Portraits of his forefathers covered the walls, facing him like courtiers awaiting proclamations from a king.

Conrad was not a small man, but he appeared so slumped in the massive leather chair. He wore a crisp, white dress shirt, the top button threatening to pop under the strain of his double chin. Although only fifty-eight, the demands of working ceaselessly had twisted his features into those of a man a decade older. His hair suffered the most, with just a few snowy white wisps barely gripping the summit of his craggy forehead.

Conrad's baby-blue eyes immediately locked onto his son. "Have a seat," he croaked. It was not an invitation. It was a command.

Rick sat down in the opposite chair. His blue jeans, open flannel shirt, and tee underneath looked out-of-place amidst the opulence of his father's favorite room. Rick liked it that way. Nearly everything he did, from the way he behaved to the way he dressed, had become an act of rebellion. The consistent message: "I am an adult now, and I will never be you."

"Off somewhere?" his father asked, raising an eyebrow from behind his horn-rimmed glasses. The expression pulled his round, gin-blossomed face into a lopsided sneer. "Sneaking out, eh?"

"That wasn't my intention, sir." The one arena in which Rick knew better than to challenge his father was in their conversations. Any sign of disrespect, intentional or not, could result in a litany of punishments. Most of the time it meant taking away his car keys, although the old man was still not above giving him the belt. Rick took his punishment in stride, knowing that to resist would only escalate matters.

Although he knew the risks, Rick hastened to add, "I'm sorry. I thought you had said that once I turned eighteen, I could come and go as I please."

Conrad's eyebrows lifted higher. He puffed his cigar, the smoke obscuring his face for a brief moment. Once the clouds parted, Rick could see that he was nodding, his lips pursed in a smile. "You're right," he admitted. "You're a man now, and a man should be afforded a degree of autonomy."

This fissure in his father's icy demeanor took Rick completely by surprise. He cautiously wondered whether or not his passage into adulthood had served as some unseen threshold, beyond which respect and generosity might flourish between them.

Conrad tossed his newspaper beside his brandy on the cherry wood side table. "Well then, if I might ask," he continued, "where are you off to?"

"A date," Rick said, swallowing.

"Ah ha!" chuckled his father. "My young buck is in rut. What time?"

"I'm meeting her downtown at quarter till nine," Rick replied, fearing he had already shared too much.

Conrad pulled out his pocket watch. "I have the time as 8:11. Plenty of time to chit-chat, father to son. Who is she? How did you meet?"

Taking a deep breath, Rick said, "Her name is Cassandra. We met at that Charles Mingus tribute—the one you let me go to in Boone back in October."

"So she shares your... taste in music," Conrad elaborated, taking a sip of his drink. "Excellent. Tell me more."

"Well... she's two years older than me. She goes to App State."

"An older woman! And a Happy Appy to boot. So she's getting educated, good, good. Her family?"

Rick squirmed a bit. He wanted to lie. But his father had enough connections throughout western North Carolina that the truth would come out eventually. "It's just her and her mom, down in Hendersonville. Her father died a little while ago. They don't have much." Rick lit up, seizing upon something he knew his father would approve of. "She's paying her own way through college. Well, that and an academic scholarship. Wants to go to law school after she graduates."

Conrad clapped his hands together. "My goodness! Such drive, such dedication. That's not an easy thing to accomplish." He leaned forward, fingers digging into the leather armrests. "And she's pretty?"

"Yes, sir."

"... big tits, eh?"

Rick hung his head. "I don't... I guess."

"Well then. It seems like you've found a keeper. How serious is"—Conrad waved a finger—"all this?"

Rick straightened up. "Pretty serious, sir." The words hung in the air. Nothing else was said between them for what seemed like an eternity. The only sound came from the crackle of the dying fire and the loyal swing of the pendulum on the grandfather clock far away in the foyer.

"Richard," Conrad said at last, swirling his brandy under his nose and setting it back down. "I don't know what to say." When Rick remained silent, he continued. "I must confess, your display of maturity has taken me by surprise. When I was your age, I was out tomcatting around, not looking for the love of my life. But you... you seem to have found someone truly special."

Rick couldn't believe his ears. "Really?" he asked vulnerably.

Conrad guffawed. "Yes, my boy! Do you jest?" He steepled his fingers, separating them to gesticulate with each word. "An older lady. Beautiful. A hard worker. *Self-made*, I admire that greatly. And she wants to become an attorney. She sounds so fantastic, and you..." He finished off his brandy. "... you... are *nothing*."

Even after a lifetime of verbal and physical blows, the words cut Rick to the quick. He could feel his blood rushing to his ears, heating them with rage. Words couldn't express the anger he felt toward his father in that moment. Yet alongside this fury, a seed of fear germinated in Rick's belly, spreading across his entire being like vines of kudzu over an abandoned tractor: he knew that his father was completely right.

Conrad's face lost all its warmth, replaced by an emotionless mask. He leaned forward to swiftly enumerate Rick's shortcomings, plunging the knife ever-deeper: "A middling student, wasting his life on music. Lazy, unmotivated, selfish. Thickening around the waist with each passing day. An utter disgrace to the men hanging on the walls of this room." He collapsed in his seat, as if the attack spent every bit of his energy. "You'd *better* hold onto her with both hands, son. Otherwise you'll live your life in the gutter, spending the rest of your days playing minstrel shows."

Rick sat there, trying to get a handle on his emotions. "You withered old asshole," he whispered at last. "Is this what happens when everyone around you is gone? You push away the only person left? Or was it always going to be that way? Am I just the one with the fucking misfortune of being the last one to survive?" He bit his lower lip. "I'll tell you what I think. I think *you're* the reason they aren't here."

For a brief instant, Conrad Coulter looked wounded. The sight might have disarmed Rick if not for his father's immediate recovery. "Sniveling little shit," he sneered, suddenly unbothered. "You have no idea what I have done for this family. Things you will never be capable of. I got Mary back, didn't I? I spent a fortune on your mother, didn't I? I *fought* for them."

"You're wrong, Dad," Rick corrected. "Mom didn't die from cancer." He spun on his heel to make his exit, but stopped in the hall outside the den to turn his head. "She died from being around *you*. You're fucking malignant."

Rick passed down the corridor and up the staircase like a ghost. He had been wounded beyond tears, beyond emotion itself. He was done —done with his father, done with this house, done with pain.

When he reached his room, Rick hastily packed as many belongings as he could into a duffel bag. Then, guitar in one hand, his life in the other, he passed beyond the foyer's heavy double doors.

Over two decades later, he was still on the other side.

10

Wednesday, July 8, 2020

STRIGIFORM

"WELL DONE, CAYDEN," Rick lied to the screen after his student fumbled through the final measures of Tárrega's *Adelita*. "You've come a long way."

Cayden tossed his hair out of his face. "Yeah," he said from the other end.

"Yeah?" repeated Rick in his head. *What kind of a response is that to a generous compliment? This is exactly why I stopped teaching.* He sincerely hoped that none of his thoughts made their way onto his face. With all his gigs canceled, he couldn't afford to lose any online students.

At one point, Rick told himself he'd never go back to teaching—he lacked the patience—but now he had few excuses and every reason to start again, so in June he jumped back into the game. It came as something of a shock. Rick didn't dislike teaching, per se; his heart had been broken too many times by promising students who failed to apply themselves.

Now, staring at the computer, he wished for the simplicity of those days. In the thirteen or so years since he quit, young people had changed. Their attention spans shrank like overdried laundry, and the extra layer of removal imposed by online teaching made it nearly impossible to connect with any of them.

At least Rick knew it wasn't just him. In the past month, he had managed to power through his pride and call Bora. When he told her he planned to start teaching again, she warned him how the landscape had changed. "They've got so many distractions nowadays," Bora had cautioned. "Adjust your expectations, buddy." Now, staring at Cayden, all Rick could think of was how right she had been.

"I can tell you've been practicing," Rick said. He cleared his throat and adjusted the position of his laptop on the dining room table so it showed his hands. "One thing to remember—here, let me play the opening." Hoisting his guitar from its stand on the floor, Rick played the first few phrases from memory, modeling them for his student.

"Notice anything?" he asked.

"What? Huh?" the high schooler mumbled, looking up.

"Remember what we said about your phone, Cayden."

"Uh, sorry. Can you play it again?"

Rick grit his teeth and obliged. "Now—what did you see that I did that you didn't do?"

Cayden shrugged.

"When I play those E minor arpeggios, I'm making sure I alternate the fingers in my right hand. See?" Rick demonstrated the motion slowly. "You're normally pretty good about it, but when you played it just now, you were repeating fingers."

"I was?" Cayden looked confused. "I didn't realize it. Still sounds the same. Why does it matter?"

"Look, I'm going to level with you," Rick offered as charitably as he could. "If you can play guitar with your nose or your teeth and it still sounds good, no one's going to care. So you don't *have* to alternate fingers on your right hand for pieces this slow. It sounds fine on the easier stuff. But if you keep going this way, you're going to run into tension and tone issues with the more technically demanding rep."

Cayden stared back blankly. "Well, I have a hard time doing that. Besides, I don't *wanna* play that stuff," he huffed. "I wanna play rock and roll. When are we going to start playing real music?"

Rick returned his guitar, sat back in his chair, and folded his arms. "Tell me something, Cayden: Do you like video games?"

"Yeah," the boy said, his face lighting up.

"What do you play?"

"*Fortnight*, mostly. *Call of Duty*, some."

"Cool, cool. So, tell me—were you any good at *Fortnight* when it first came out?"

"Nah, man. I sucked."

"Are you any good now?"

"I'd say so. Had a killstreak of twelve last night."

"How did you get better?"

"Kept playing."

"How often do you play?"

"Every day."

"For how long?"

"Mom limits me to three hours." Cayden leaned in to whisper into the microphone. "Sometimes I come downstairs in the middle of the night. Keep that on the DL."

Rick smiled. "Of course."

"Mr. Coulter, why are you asking me about *Fortnight*?"

"Because, *Cayden*, you obviously aren't bad with your hands. If you spent a *fraction* of the time on guitar that you spend on goddamn *Fortnight*, you'd actually have no problem alternating fingers. But don't bother expending effort on anything tangible, just keep working on that killstreak, slugger. I'll email your mom and tell her I'm refunding today's lesson—but don't worry, your late night training is safe with me. Bye."

Cayden looked shocked. "No, Mr.—"

Rick closed his computer.

I'll regret that, he told himself, taking a sip from the drink he stashed off-camera. *But if I have to put up with this shit, I'll get even worse.*

Not that he was sure there was much further to go. Everything consistently degraded by the day. In his estimation, the pandemic was now an unmitigated shitshow. No one, civilian or official, handled it well. Everyone was caught with their pants down, managing to accomplish the remarkable: simultaneously doing too much and not enough to manage the crisis.

"We will rebuild," he quipped as he walked to the bathroom to take out his contacts. *If there's anything left*, he added. *Not that we deserve it.*

On top of everything else, now the country was wracked with civil strife. Covid, like an overdue rain shower, had washed away the country's thin veneer of civility like a fine layer of dust, revealing the rot underneath. Things more insidious than any virus were hurting people out there, and, while Rick always knew about them on an intellectual level, having them thrust in his face sickened him to his stomach.

Rick thought back to the Persian rug in the foyer of his childhood home, how years of neglect had left it tattered and faded, yet still intact. That was how the world felt to him: still functional, still in one piece, but only barely, its colors faded into a shadow of their former vibrancy. The fabric of stability was unraveling, the threads of hope and certainty fraying, coming undone with each passing day. If not repaired, the damage would soon expose the surface underneath for what it truly was—cold, hard, and unforgiving.

Defeated, Rick landed on the couch and flicked on the television. *I told myself I'd be so productive*, he thought, skimming through the programs. *All I've done is drink and watch Netflix.* He couldn't recall the last time he tried writing music. He kept telling himself that the strange, ethereal melody from the field could be turned into something outstanding, but it refused to cooperate. All harmonies failed. Any supporting structure he tried building around the melody only highlighted the shortcomings of his own writing.

Even if you could figure it out, what's the point? It'll never get played. This isolation will drag on forever. Faced with overwhelming defeat, Rick had even misplaced his trusty pen and notebook... although he wasn't sure whether their disappearance stemmed from depression or drunkenness.

Or The Boo-verly Hillbillies, he mused. *Say what you want about those phantom rednecks, at least they've injected something interesting into this monotony.*

Since discovering the reset lock, Rick had become convinced that someone was hanging around the property. Snippets of voices found their way to him on the wind. Each morning, the garbage strewn across the front lawn looked slightly rearranged in tiny, insignificant ways. Once or twice, he thought he glimpsed an old, brown SUV on the driveway as it passed the split towards Edna's house. The patio's automatic light flashed on nightly at odd hours, though Rick felt wildlife was at least occasionally to blame.

Rick tried capturing some of the intruders on video, but he never saw anything conclusive, just murky shadows lurking beyond the edge of the light. Even if someone *did* trespass, he wasn't sure he could rely on his phone—the damn thing kept dying, dropping from fully charged to empty in an instant.

One of those fancy doorbell cameras would do the trick, Rick grumbled. *But I can't afford that, either.* Utilities, booze, and streaming services left little disposable income. It wasn't like Edna would pitch in, either. She seemed completely disinterested in the developments, and was barely home long enough to care. Over the past few months, she had more or less toured the entire state of Florida, taking advantage of what she called the "freedom frontier." *Maybe I'll ask again when she gets back*, Rick decided as the movie began.

Tonight's schedule featured a three course meal of Chex mix, a banana, and a frozen burrito; a double feature of poorly-produced action films; and a quick listening party comprised of John Zorn, Casiopea, Ali Farka Touré, Cop Shoot Cop, and, of course, an obligatory spin with Peggy Lee. The afterparty consisted of a few drunken rants on social media, tirades he knew he would regret in the light of day. It was an early evening. He blacked out a little before nine o'clock, only for his own snoring to rouse him at ten thirty.

As he stood up from the couch, something stabbed his feet with a brittle snap. "Oh fuck," Rick said aloud. His glasses lay in a mangled heap of plastic on the floor. Maybe they were salvageable.

"Nope," Rick decided, turning them over in his hands. "Fuck it." He wasn't too concerned. Without them, his eyesight wasn't great, but it was passable. He wore his contacts almost exclusively. The glasses were reserved for early mornings or those brief minutes between taking out his contacts and going to bed, both of which had become nonexistent over the past few months.

Rick stumbled to the bathroom, tossed his ruined glasses on the vanity, and continued through the other door to his bedroom, where he collapsed in a dizzy heap on his bed. Before his head hit the pillow, he had passed out once more.

The only indication that Rick was walking on dead leaves came from the crunching sound beneath his feet. Whenever he looked down, he could only see from his knees upward. A thick fog settled below, turning the entire forest into a surrealist painting, an aerial arboretum in the clouds.

Despite not knowing how he arrived there, Rick remained unafraid. Somehow, he knew these woods better than any residence he had occupied. Where most would have seen a random array of tree trunks scattered along the gentle slope, he saw a precise arrangement of woodland features as familiar as the layout of his living room.

"Woot." Something soared low above him, so close that Rick thought he felt it brush the top of his head. When he cast his eyes skyward, Rick saw an enormous owl diving silently, then alighting in the branches of a nearby tree. It stared at him, its yellow eyes full of unspoken secrets.

Rick and the bird held one another's gaze until he heard his name whispered behind him. He knew that voice. Turning his head, he spotted a young girl, maybe eight years old, standing in the distant gloom, facing away from him. She wore a green dress, the bottom of which disappeared into the murk of the fog at her feet.

"Richard?" she repeated. Obviously she wanted his attention, but made no effort to turn in his direction. All Rick saw as he cautiously stepped toward her were crimson curls cascading down the back of her head, red as a cardinal's breast.

When he closed the distance to around fifteen feet, the girl slowly raised her arms. Rick stopped. From every direction, owls of various sizes began approaching, gliding through the air on wings as silent as prayers. Slowly, one by one, they landed on the female figure before him, finding perches on her arms and shoulders. Rick counted nine in total, although he had no idea how the little girl's frame could accommodate so many intimidating birds. Like cogs locking into place, they each rotated their heads to glare at Rick.

"Rickard!" The second voice startled Rick so abruptly that he tumbled to the ground. His fall cleared the fog enough to afford a moment of clarity before it rolled over him once more. In that brief instant, he saw a woman, freakishly tall with short hair, wearing a white pantsuit. He recognized it as the stranger from Terry Mac's, although her features were slightly different: she was even paler, her limbs thinner, her eyes larger and darker, tilted at a severe angle....

Rick gasped and sat up, his heart racing. It took him a while to remember where he was. Slowly, the physical sensations reminded him: the smell of stale air conditioning, the dim outline of his desk and guitars, the sheets, now wet with sweat. It was a dream. He was in bed at home. Checking his phone, he saw it was a little after one o'clock in the morning.

Touching his damp surroundings and sniffing his fingers, Rick felt a wave of shame. It wasn't just sweat soaking his bedsheets. He had pissed himself, too.

Goddammit, he scolded himself as he stood and stripped the bed. *What are you, three?* It had been a long time since he had been so drunk that he wet the bed. After changing shirts and underwear, he stepped into the bathroom to empty his bladder—*Talk about shutting the stable door after the horse has bolted*—and returned to the mattress. New sheets required too much energy this time of night.

Rick was about to lay back down when one of the bedroom windows brightened. Outside, the automatic light at the patio spilled its yellow beam across the field. Rick took three steps to the bathroom to fetch his glasses before stopping. *They're broken,* he remembered. Cursing his stupidity, Rick crept to the window, gently opened the curtains, and pressed his face to the glass.

Between the angle and his impaired vision, he could barely make out the left hand edge of the patio to his right. Everything seemed completely calm and still, with no sign of what triggered the sensor.

One patch of Rick's vision looked blurrier than the rest, however. Squinting, he saw that the haze was closer than he thought. It was condensation from his breath on the window pane. Rick passed his hand over the smudge, only to find that it stayed put.

It's... on the outside? Rick puzzled, rubbing the spot once more. *Yeah, it has to be. Maybe it's not condensation. Maybe it's some grime on the glass. Or maybe someone was looking inside...*

Rick turned his attention back to the patio. Nothing moved.

Whoomp! A flurry of white and beige filled Rick's vision. In those initial moments, he only saw flashes of whatever smacked the window inches from his face: something gangly, with a bulbous head and large, dark eyes. Screaming, Rick involuntarily threw a fist at the pane before pulling his punch, realizing what fluttered on the other side.

"What are the odds?" he asked aloud. There, in complete panic outside the window, hovered a barn owl. Apparently, it triggered the automatic light. Thumps and scratching noises filled the bedroom as its wings battered the glass. Surprisingly, it had not caused any cracks, despite hitting the window with tremendous force. If it injured itself, maybe Rick could step outside and rescue it, although he was clueless about how to nurse a raptor back to health.

There was no need. The bird quickly recovered and pulled away from the window, floating into the night. Its wings beat forcefully, lifting the owl from the ground and toward the roof. Rick craned his neck to watch its ascent.

"Where are you going, lil' fella?" he asked. When the owl reached the top of the gable above the bedroom, it disappeared not over, but rather *towards* the house. Rick stood back, wondering where it could have gone. Straightaway his adrenaline crashed, and the bed beckoned.

Hours passed as Rick lay there, awake, unable to sleep again. Despite his exhaustion, his circulatory system remained firing on all cylinders, his heart racing, new sweat covering the mattress—a feeling more and more common as of late.

Sometime around dawn, he took a long draw from the bottle, finally granting him a few hours' rest.

11

Thursday, July 9, 2020

SHELL SHOCK

AROUND NOON, Rick reawakened to another day indistinguishable from over a hundred previous ones. He washed the dried urine and sweat from his body, fixed some coffee and a light breakfast, and began chugging Pedialyte. By one o'clock, he started drinking again, and soon his thoughts returned to his early morning visitor.

I wonder where he went, Rick thought as he headed to the sliding glass door. It was another fine day, a good one for a hike, but Rick barely bothered anymore. Not only was the Georgia heat and humidity absolutely stifling in July, but Red Ear Mountain was now about as boring as the home he occupied.

Rick headed outside barefoot and stepped around to the bedroom window. Looking up at the gable, he easily found the answer to his question: the simple, circular vent that cooled the attic—it was barely an attic, more of a crawlspace—was dislodged. Sure enough, a large gap appeared between the vent and the siding, although he wasn't sure it was big enough to accommodate a good-sized barn owl. Rick had no idea how the vent became damaged or how long it had been loose, but he rarely paid the fixture any attention. Given the age of the house, any number of storms could have loosened its grip only to go unnoticed,.

At first, Rick simply added it to his mental checklist of things to fix. The more he thought, however, the more he realized that the attic warranted an inspection. For all he knew, the owl was up there, wounded. Even if it was okay, he didn't need its presence fouling the crawlspace with animal carcasses and droppings.

Better take a look, he thought, grabbing a pair of rubber gloves from the stockpile accumulated over the course of the pandemic. Next he found a flashlight and headed into the short hallway between the living room and his bedroom, where he tugged on the pull cord dangling from the ceiling between the bath and laundry.

Down came the ladder with a groan. As Rick unfolded the collapsed frame, he realized ages had passed since he ventured up there. *Probably just a good idea to check*, he chuckled, climbing the rungs. *Maybe Edna will want to turn it into a sauna or something.* He reached the top and looked inside. *Oh, thank God. It's smaller than I remembered. Sorry, Edna.*

The crawlspace was too low to fully stand. Rick hauled his sizable frame inside and shuffled through the rows of cardboard boxes and Christmas decorations on his hands and knees, flashlight in his mouth. Up ahead, the open vent was clearly visible, casting a welcome glow in the darkness. In the center of a pool of light sat a nest.

That's odd, Rick thought as he approached the cluster of twigs. *I didn't think owls made nests.* Somewhere, Rick vaguely remembered hearing that, if they nested at all, they preferred to move into homes already constructed by other birds. He approached the pile of debris, transferring the flashlight to his left hand. With his right, he reached out and pulled the nest closer.

Judging from the amount of trash he saw, Rick figured he was looking at the nest of another bird, or maybe a small mammal. There were discarded candy wrappers, cigarette butts, and even an old, empty mini-bottle of vodka. *Wonder where that came from,* he thought. He'd heard of birds using debris in their nests, but rarely had he seen such a motley collection.

One bit of refuse stood out from the rest, glinting golden and red in the sunlight. Sitting on his heels, Rick reached out and plucked it from the brambles, turning it over in the light. It was a shotgun shell. However, something looked peculiar. Rick brought the cylinder to his nose and sniffed it. The scent of gunpowder remained strong. Rick turned the shell around and looked at its brass base. Stamped on the bottom were the letters "WINCHESTER 16GA."

Sixteen gauge, Rick pondered as he examined the shell. It was a curious bore size—not exactly rare, but far from favored—although Rick had heard that its use was on the rise. *I don't know anyone who uses that. In fact, the last time I saw one of these was...*

All the color drained from Rick's face. He tossed the shotgun shell back into the nest and scrambled backward, hitting his head on rafters and scattering boxes as he went before half climbing, half falling down the ladder. Safely on solid ground, Rick slammed the attic access door and started sobbing.

"What the fuck is happening?" he asked himself. He scrambled for an answer. "It's just a random shotgun shell. You live in north Georgia, for Chrissake, there are hunters everywhere. People target practice year round. A bird just carried it into the house from somewhere out in the woods. A crow or something." None of this convinced him. The shell looked and smelled too fresh.

Regardless of how rational Rick wanted to be in that moment, he had crossed the Rubicon of anxiety. He knew *exactly* how the rest of today would unfold, and it ended with him in a bottle, just like all the others. Rick removed his gloves, stomped out of the hallway, and turned the corner into the kitchen, aching for another drink.

His eyes scanned the countertop for the clear, crisp outline of his trusty plastic container. It was nowhere to be found. Sitting in its place instead was something round, brown, and made of heavy glass. Rick instinctively retreated back around the corner. There he stood, wild eyed, as terrified as if he'd seen a ghost. He might as well have. He knew those contours all too well.

Rick had briefly glimpsed the distinctive shape of a Rémy Martin XO bottle. At well over $200 each, the bottle of brandy was about as out of place in his house as an elephant. The last time he saw that bottle—other than on a bar shelf—was back in Spruce Pine. At his father's home.

The same place I last saw that shell, too, he added, clutching his chest. *What am I going to do? Is he here?* Without moving, he cast an eye on his father's urn of ashes sitting on the mantle, visible from this angle.

Rick nearly jumped out of his skin as a loud chime broke the silence and his shorts began vibrating. He fumbled in his pocket and pulled out his phone. Jack's grin gazed back at him, full of carefree exuberance. He wanted to video chat.

Rick answered the phone, but not before peeking around the corner into the kitchen. The brandy was gone, replaced once again with the familiar vodka bottle. Rick rushed to it, took a shot, and winced, all before thumbing the button to accept the call.

Jack appeared onscreen and said, "Hey Dad... What's up?" His son looked tired, but a little happier than usual. Rick's only glimmer of hope in the last month was his visit with Jack, but he left Alpharetta more concerned than anything. Simply put, the endless isolation seemed to be taking its toll on the boy.

"Uh, just... um... nothing much," replied Rick, trying his best to stay casual. He moved over to the dining room table, where his laptop sat after teaching lessons the day before. "How are you?"

Jack nodded somberly, then forced a smile. "I'm... good. Mike and Chandler came over yesterday to spend the night, they just left."

"Oh... okay," Rick said slowly. "Your mom was fine with that?"

"Yeah," answered Jack, the camera tilting to show the underside of his chin as he walked to his room. "They quarantined beforehand, and we'll quarantine after."

Cassie was treating the pandemic even more seriously than Rick, restricting outside contact to the bare minimum. Rick felt like Cassie's withdrawal had taken Jack along with her. She adamantly limited Rick's visits to once per month until normalcy returned. As such, his next get together with his son wasn't for another two weeks.

Rick wanted to say, *"Tell your mother I've done nothing but quarantine, now can I see you more often?"* But what came out of his mouth was, "Oh, nice. Gotta be safe. Did you guys do anything fun?"

"We skated for a little bit, did some listening," Jack answered, settling onto his bed. "Mike introduced me to a new band. It's part of why I called you."

Rick raised his eyebrows. He was always eager for a new recommendation. When Jack offered them, they became extra special. The ordeals of the past twenty-four hours—the dream, the owl, the shotgun shell, the bottle—faded to Rick's periphery. He cleared his throat and said, "Cool, dude! What are they called?"

"The Shit Bees," Jack answered after a brief hesitation.

Rick chuckled. He needed some levity in his life. "It's okay to swear if it's the name of a band," he said, opening his laptop with his free hand. "'The Shit Bees,' huh? Lemme look them up. What song should I look for?"

"*Colon Response*," Jack offered. "Their Hollywood Bowl performance from 2018. I think that's a pretty good taste of their style."

"I'm not so sure I want to 'taste' the style of The Shit Bees' *Colon Response*," Rick joked, completing the search. "Okay, let's see... ah, here we go." He hit 'play' on the video. A swarm of five young men in brown- and yellow-striped jumpsuits swarmed the stage, middle fingers held aloft before launching into their opening song. Rick had heard a lot of strange, dissonant things in his time as a musician—being classically trained put you through the wringer—but *carefully executed* noise was different from *poorly executed* noise.

The band finished. Jack spoke up: "Well? What do you think?"

Rick hung his head, then looked back at his son. "Jack... this band is... *garbage*."

"Huh?"

"All they have to offer is shock value. Everything is out of tune, from the vocals to the rhythm section. The drummer speeds up, like, fifteen clicks by the end. Who the hell showed this to you? Mike, you said?"

Jack ignored the question, his expression darkening. Rick recognized it—he often made the same face. Jack was trying to get a handle on his emotions. "I thought you'd like them."

"I'm not going to lie to you, Jack, and say something is good when it isn't. They objectively have no redeeming qualities. There's no talent on display here."

"'Talent'—it's not always *about* talent, Dad," Jack huffed. "It's about showmanship. I thought you'd get that. I think they're fucking awesome."

"Jack, for the last time, stop swearing!" yelled Rick. "*You* don't know what you're talking about. *I* do. Maybe you'd recognize good music if you ever came to my shows!"

"*What* fucking shows, Dad?" shouted Jack. "You've barely played all year! Even if you had, just because you like what *you* play doesn't mean that I do!"

In that instant, Rick knew that the gulf that had appeared between them over the course of the past several months had widened into an uncrossable chasm. The boy was isolated and fragile and shouldn't be spoken to in such a way. Too much was said, egged on by stress and alcohol, and now Rick was losing the one thing in this world that mattered most to him.

"Jack, I'm... I'm sorry. I lied, I've not been good, it's been awful—"

His son's face disappeared as the screen shut off. The phone had powered down yet again, leaving Rick's haggard reflection staring back at him from the gleaming black screen. He wanted to recharge the phone and call back, but he knew it was too soon. If there was any chance of putting things right, it would happen on Jack's terms.

Rick dropped the dead phone on the table and began sobbing big, wet tears. Tears for his relationships, for his son, tears for his life. Tears for the world and what it had become. When he finally finished, he stared long and hard at his hands, imagining the last bits of sanity sieving through his fingers.

Jack had looked so wounded in those moments—wounded beyond tears, beyond emotion itself. *I'm becoming him*, Rick thought. *I'm becoming my father.* He took a deep breath and looked up... but immediately wished he hadn't.

Every cabinet door and kitchen drawer stood wide open. Rick blinked the remaining tears out of his eyes, and saw that it wasn't just the cabinets and drawers—the dishwasher and refrigerator were open too, as were the oven and microwave. Both their clocks displayed the same incorrect time: 11:08.

A deafening scream of primal terror filled the room. It frightened Rick even more until he realized it came from himself. When he finally mustered enough courage to investigate, he found that anything with a hinge sat in the same position—throughout the entire house. The toilet seat, the washer, the dryer, the coffeemaker, the front door, the doors to the rooms, hell, even his damn toolbox.

Most perplexing of all was the door to the patio. Even in the midst of such an inexplicable occurrence, the idea that anything could have removed the wooden security stick and silently slid open the glass door seemed utterly impossible. Yet not only did it obviously happen, it happened in the few minutes he spent crying. Rick gingerly closed the patio door and faced the living room, the dining room on the other side of the freestanding wall to his right.

Well, Rick, he thought wryly, surveying the rows of open doors, furniture, and appliances. *You had a nice go, but I think you've finally lost it. Funny, I thought insanity would feel a little more... ambiguous.* He thought back to everything in his life that had led to this point: his drinking, his split with Cassie, his father.

Just end it all, he thought. *Before you fully lose it and hurt someone. Before you turn into your father. You can't go on like this… and your existence just makes everything worse. It's not like anyone would miss you. After all…*

"You are nothing," he whispered. The words rang truer than ever.

Then, from somewhere deeper in the house came a gentle, feminine voice: *"Not to us."*

That instant, every framed picture on the walls began flying off in sequence, starting with those farthest from Rick. Instinctively, he leaped back and to the right, pressing himself against the basement door. Each frame launched forcefully from its hanger like a rivet escaping an overpressurized boiler, flying straight ahead before tumbling to the floor. The activity rapidly traced its way in Rick's direction until, at last, the final photograph jumped from the drywall to land at his feet. The glass lay in pieces on the carpet. It was a picture of him and Jack.

For months, Rick had fought the words. There were always prosaic explanations, always doubts, always some new way to blame himself for what was happening. Now he was forced to admit it.

The house was haunted.

12

Thursday, September 17, 2020

VULPE

A<small>NOTHER PUFF OF SMOKE</small> billowed from the cracked window, making the car look alive, like it was exhaling clouds of vapor. It served as the only indication that anyone was inside, waiting patiently to make an entrance.

The driver sat in complete darkness behind the wheel, his eyes closed, with a cigarette lodged between his lips. Only now and again did they purse, lighting up the tip before sending plumes of smoke from the man's nostrils and out the window. He never moved to flick the ash, which lengthened by the minute in a crooked, gray arch. When it got too heavy, it fell to his chest, leaving a charcoal smear on the Hawaiian shirt worn beneath his beige leisure suit.

Feeling this, the man finally opened his eyes, revealing a mismatched pair of piercing blue and dark, soulful brown. He lazily brushed the ash to the floor, only to grind it into the carpet with his tattered rattlesnake boots.

Finally, the man looked at his watch and spoke. "Showtime," he whispered, his thick southern drawl elongating the final syllable. From underneath his tousled brown hair, he extracted a single wireless earbud, filling the front seat with the tiny, tinny sound of Art Bell's voice. "*West of the Rockies, you're on—*"

Art's voice cut out of existence as he replaced the earbud in its case. After grabbing an oversized messenger bag from the passenger's seat, the man opened the door of the brown 2001 Chevrolet Suburban and stepped onto the driveway, revealing his full frame.

He was tall with a wiry runner's physique, the kind of person who never dieted or exercised a day in his life but happily reaped the benefits of a naturally overactive metabolism. A long neck sporting fiddler's calluses stretched from his bony shoulders. The house's dim exterior lighting only made his face more mysterious, sharpening the lines of his strong, angular features and aquiline nose. In another time, he might have made the quintessential cowboy, had he shown a propensity for waking at dawn and toiling under the sun.

No, the man standing in the driveway was a nocturnal creature, crepuscular at best—which, given his occupation, suited him just fine.

He finished his cigarette and dropped it onto the driveway, but only made it a few steps before whispering, "Aw, shee-it." He rushed back to the passenger's side of the car, opened the door, and rummaged around in the hefty pile of trash accumulated in the footwell. After a few seconds, he produced an empty glass mini-bottle, long since drained of liquor. He held it aloft as proudly as if he had discovered a diamond.

Quietly, the man crept over to the spigot on the side of the house and gently turned the handle, holding the open mini-bottle underneath. When it was full, he shut off the water and screwed the cap back on, then placed it in his jacket pocket. Now, fully prepared, he climbed the steps to the front door, his lanky frame skipping two at a time.

The man had never lived in such a fine house himself. Sugar Hill was full of the damn things. Yes, it was gaudy—a real McMansion affair, if on the small side—but it was a far cry from anywhere he ever called home. Not that he stayed in one place very much. Most of his days (not his nights, he worked those) were spent snoozing in his car, on clients' couches, in flop houses, or on the dirt floors of crude huts in faraway lands.

Home ain't where the heart is, he thought, ringing the doorbell. *It's where the head rests.* The lock unlatched and the door swung open, revealing a man and woman in their late thirties. The married couple looked anxious but greeted him warmly.

"Hi there, I'm Alex," said the woman, a short, petite thing. Her words overlapped with her husband's: "Come in, Mr. Fox, I'm Chad."

"Aw shucks," replied the visitor. "Please call me Devlin. Nice to meet y'all." He gestured toward his face. "Sorry, I ain't got no mask...."

"That's alright," Chad interjected. He was the picture of a suburban dad, the vestiges of a once-athletic frame drowning underneath the stress of a fifty-hour workweek and too many beers on weekends. "Damn things don't work, anyway."

Over the past half year, Devlin Fox had learned the hard way that the best answer to such comments was to simply nod and allow the other person to draw their own conclusions. "Lovely digs y'all got," he said. "How long have you lived here?"

"Four years this October," answered Alex. She gestured to the dining room, which lay past the staircase rising to the right. A large dent marred the wall at the bottom step. "Please, take a seat."

"Sure," said Devlin. He followed the couple to a modestly appointed dining room. In his time visiting such homes, Devlin found that half the people who could afford them barely had enough money leftover to furnish them. He pulled out a seat, retrieved a notebook from his messenger bag, and set it on the tabletop. The couple took their seats opposite. "So," he began, "sounds like something's been giving y'all the business."

"It's been… challenging," Alex replied, trying to act casual. Chad sat silently beside her, letting her do all the talking.

"I'm sorry to hear that. Happens, though, even in these newer places. Can you run through some of what y'all've experienced?"

Alex looked to her husband, saying, "Oh, gosh, where to begin? It started simple enough. Keys disappearing, only to be found where we'd left them a few hours later. Lights flicking on and off on their own. Everything electronic, malfunctioning."

"Sounds at night after everyone was in bed," Chad chimed in. "Footsteps. Voices."

Alex nodded. "Then it escalated. Our daughter Susan started telling us she would feel someone sit down on her bed while she was sleeping. When she looked up, there was no one there—well, until this last time, at least."

"How is she holding up?" asked Devlin after he finished taking notes.

"Not good," Alex confessed. "She told some of the kids at school what was going on. They said that back when this place was all wooded, there was a moonshine still on this property. Said a man was murdered back here, before the development."

"Mm-hmm. Age?"

"Fourteen."

"And now she's…?"

"With her grandmother," Alex said. "She refused to sleep in her room after what happened Saturday."

Chad interjected, "That's when we called you."

Devlin ignored the comment. "Any activity at grandma's?"

"No," answered Alex.

"Alright," Devlin continued. "You mentioned Saturday?"

"Right—on Saturday, she told us it had been the same as the other nights. Around three in the morning, she felt the weight of someone sitting on her bed. When she looked this time, she saw... how did she describe it, Chad?"

"Blacker than black, like a cutout of where a person was supposed to be," he explained. "I've seen it a few times, myself. Always upstairs in the hallway, always at night. Looks just like a head and shoulders peering out of the open doorway. Then it ducks back inside."

Devlin gestured to Chad's arm. "So you fell sometime between Saturday and tonight?" he asked.

Chad looked shocked. "How did you...?"

"Well, I spotted that dent by the stairs," Devlin clarified. "I saw plenty of them growing up. In my case, it usually meant my daddy was cork high and bottle deep, but since the Soloff household is a picture of domesticity"—he flashed a grin—"well, I can only assume something a little more... accidental. That, and you've been favoring your left hand since I darkened your doorstep."

Chad raised his eyebrows and winced while gently windmilling his right arm. "You're right," he said. "That was Tuesday. Still hurts like hell. I was surprised when the doc said I hadn't broken anything." He flexed his right hand. As he did so, Devlin noticed that one of his fingers bore the slightest hint of an indentation, as if a heavy ring had been recently removed. "I heard something up in Susie's room, so I went to check on her. She was fast asleep. When I got back to the stairs, something pushed me from behind. No one else was awake. I'm just glad I'm not any more banged up than I am."

"Me too," Devlin agreed. "My condolences. Feeling poorly on top of all this adds insult to injury. Or vice versa, I s'pose. Feller I helped in Sheboygan last year had the same thing happen." He looked down to his notebook, chewing on the tip of his pen. Finally, he looked back up, brown and blue eyes passing between the couple. "Personal life? Any new changes?"

His clients looked confused. "No..." said Chad. "What's that got to do with anything?"

"Everything," Devlin shot back. "So nothing? No renovations, no new relationships, new jobs... infidelity?"

"Certainly not," came Alex's immediate answer.

"Hmmm. What about your daughter? Any interest in the occult? Ouija boards, anything of that nature? They ain't just toys. You'd be surprised how often they invite things in."

"Susie's not into that," Chad declared emphatically. "No Ouija boards in this house."

"Okay, then," sighed Devlin, checking his watch. "I have the time as 11:30. I'll need a few hours to myself. Y'all got a place to post up?"

Alex nodded. "Yes—my mother's place with Susie. Although I doubt we'll sleep."

"Just as good," Devlin opined. "I might need a few days afterward to scrub through what I collect, but dimes to doughnuts I'll have an idea of what's going on, if anything, by four or five. My track record speaks for itself. I'll give y'all a ring so we can get together and debrief."

"What about paperwork?" asked Chad. "Anything we need to sign?"

Devlin shook his head. "No, sir. I operate on the honor system. We'll square up afterwards, depending on what I find and what I can do about it. If I find nothing, you owe me nothing. If I find something but can't do anything about it, I'll take a charitable donation in the amount you see fit. I find something and fix it—well, we'll cross that bridge when we come to it. I appreciate y'all reaching out to me. Other investigators, they won't charge you nothing, but they'd come in here with their fancy doodads and their matching black windbreakers, collect what they find, say, 'Gee whizz, seems like your house is haunted,' and not do much afterwards, except throw it all up on their website and hope they land a television deal out of it."

"You get what you pay for," Chad admitted.

Devlin stood and grabbed his bag. "Last thing's a tour of the house. Y'all mind giving me a quick lay of the land?"

The three of them walked through the entire house, beginning on the bottom floor, which included the master bedroom. Besides the odd misplaced item, little happened down there, the couple said. Devlin then followed Chad and Alex to the second floor, where the activity seemed strongest. It held all the remaining bedrooms, including two guest bedrooms, the daughter's room, and a fourth, used as an office. It was locked.

"Well, I guess we'll get out of your hair," said Alex, starting down the stairs.

"Um—hang on a sec," Devlin interrupted, pointing to the office. "What about this room?"

Chad shook his head and said, "It stays locked."

"Why?"

"I had to bring home a lot of sensitive documents from my job since I started working remotely. Corporate would have my head if they were out in the open."

"It's true," Alex admitted. "He won't let any of us in there. Not even me."

Chad continued downstairs. "No need to look," he said, passing the dent in the wall. "I've never seen anything in there, anyway."

"With all due respect, Mr. Soloff," began Devlin, his brow furrowed, "I need access to the entire house, if I'm to do this properly—"

"*No need*," Chad firmly replied, looking up from the foyer. "I appreciate your thoroughness, but whatever's happening in this house doesn't seem to care about my office." With that, he grabbed his coat, bid their visitor goodbye, and left with his wife through the front door.

"Fuller of shit than a Christmas goose," Devlin said to the empty stairway. The couple had left every light in the house on. He shrugged and began the tedious task of locating all the switches, dousing the lights, unplugging as many electronics as he could, and shutting off the HVAC before returning upstairs, flashlight in hand.

He then took a baseline for the property. He noted squeaky floorboards and ambient light, recorded temperatures, listened to what noises bled in from the outside, and identified anything else easily mistaken for paranormal activity. A short time later, the house became as familiar as if he lived there himself.

Devlin Fox much preferred his five (or six) senses to any fancy ghost hunting gadgetry. Hauntings were experienced by humans, so naturally the best evidence came from human experience, not the latest and greatest technology taking the field by storm.

Even still, over the course of the past decade or so, he had begrudgingly adopted a few of the simpler devices—not because they provided objective proof, but because they sometimes provided hints pointing in the right direction. To that end, he produced an EMF meter from his bag and checked the output from the remaining electronics and outlets as he swept from room to room upstairs. A noteworthy spike occurred in Susan's room.

Guess we start here, Devlin thought, dragging the chair from the girl's desk and setting up immediately outside the doorway. He pulled a camera mounted on a thin collapsible tripod from his bag and set it up at the end of the hall, facing the back of the chair.

Everything in its place, all measurements recorded, he finally sat down with his notebook, letting his eyes and ears adjust and forcing his heart rate to slow through deliberate, measured breaths. His long vigil had begun.

It was one of innumerable similar nights. After investigating cases across every inhabited continent over the years, Devlin came to realize something: there were no ghost stories. There were just architecture stories that happened to *include* ghosts. The layout of a building played as much of a role in these experiences as the spirits themselves. Floorplans facilitated or hindered sightings. Depending on their orientation, they could render otherwise mundane events impossible, or provide simple solutions to fantastic claims. That was before even getting to the history of the location, or how the spirits acted within a home. To tell a ghost story, you have to begin with a solid understanding of the building. Investigating them was no different.

Devlin had also discovered that, while only the bigger ones had wings, all buildings had arms. The newer ones—like where he was tonight—hung limp. They neither cared for nor rejected your presence.

The best ones boasted open arms, welcoming you in a warm embrace like an old friend. More often than not, these were older homes where the walls had absorbed multiple generations of love and affection.

Then there were the bad ones, buildings that greeted you with arms folded. They could be entered, but remained impenetrable. From the moment you crossed the threshold, you knew they resented your presence. Devlin had seen his share of those. No matter what unfolded tonight, at least this house was indifferent. Years of experience had honed his latent sensitivity—by no means inconsequential—allowing him to diagnose a property the moment he walked inside.

A flicker of movement caught Devlin's attention. A shape had ducked into one of the open bedrooms, just as Chad described. Devlin couldn't say how long it had watched him, as he only noticed its retreat. He stared at the doorway for another ten minutes before it slowly looked out again, the perfect shape of a human head, darker than the surrounding environment.

Many people would have shrieked or fled downstairs. For Devlin, this was simply a part of his job, as rote as data entry. Fear didn't fill his heart at that moment. Instead, he felt relief. Too many investigations came and went uneventfully. Even if this was the last thing he saw all night, at least it meant that *something* was going on. That meant a payday.

"Howdy," Devlin greeted the shape several minutes into their staring contest. It retreated again. *Hope that shows up on camera*, he thought.

A rustling in Susie's bedroom to his left caught his attention. These things sometimes did that—they drew your focus in one direction to distract you from whatever was happening in another. Peering through the darkness, he could see the girl's hairbrush lying on the floor. *Wasn't there before*, he noted, scratching the observation in his notebook. *Well, well, well, looks like it decided to put in an appearance.*

The next hour was shockingly active. Knocks sounded from the various bedrooms, objects moved here and there, and the shape continued playing peek-a-boo from various open doorways. Sometime around two o'clock, Devlin relocated to the room where it had initially appeared and began an EVP session, hoping to capture unheard responses to his questions.

Some ghost hunters invested in expensive digital equipment. Devlin discovered two things in his years of investigation: one, the more complex the tool, the greater likelihood of failure (or sabotage, at the hands of the phenomenon); and two, that he was incredibly impatient. The answer to both his quirks lay in an old, handheld cassette Dictaphone.

He asked a series of questions to the darkness, waiting fifteen seconds between each, making a verbal note each time his stomach grumbled or a car passed by outside. When he finished, he rewound and played the tape. As usual, most of his questions went unanswered.

"Is there anyone here?" Nothing. *"Can you say something, let me know you're here?"* Nothing. *"In one word, what do you want?"* Nothing. *"Is there a reason you chose this house?"* A faint whisper followed: "No choice." Devlin's monologue continued, unanswered, until the final seconds, when the voice spoke again: *"Fox."*

"So we're acquainted," Devlin spoke aloud, stopping playback. "Listen, if I done you dirty some time in the past, you gotta put that behind us. I've got a job to do here, and it'd really help if you opened up a bit."

Another two EVP sessions went by, with no more answers forthcoming. Frustrated and tired of rewinding and relistening, Devlin rummaged around in his bag and extracted two items: a packet of Flamin' Hot Cheetos and an old, battered Radio Shack pocket radio.

This was his "shack hack" spirit box. As with his recording equipment, it was a simple affair, bespoke rather than purchased off the shelf. Ages ago, Devlin removed the mute pin, allowing the radio to scan through AM and FM radio stations unimpeded. Ghost hunters held that supernatural forces could manipulate the frequency, choosing which words came through intelligibly to answer questions in real-time. Devlin was ambivalent as to its efficacy, but admitted that it occasionally offered some uncanny results.

He turned on the radio, popped open his bag of snacks, and stood up to pace the room. Devlin could scarcely stand still during his spirit box sessions. He pressed record on the Dictaphone and listened as the radio jumped from station to station, snippets of words emerging through the static.

"Okay," he said, licking Cheeto dust from his fingers. "What's going on?" Fragments of syllables answered, completely inconclusive. "Alright, have it your way. Is there anyone here?"

"... b... ve...we... ... ... OF COURSE... sh... m..."

"*That's* more like it," Devlin crunched. "I appreciate the cooperation. What should I call you?"

Static followed. Several moments passed before anything resembling an answer emerged: "... *rea... my... SAM...EYE...EEL... so... ... ... ho...*"

Devlin paused mid-bite, eyebrows raised. "Sam... *Samael?* Aw, shit, Sammie, how you doing, dude? Been a while. When did we cross paths last? İzmir?"

Nonsensical snippets filled the room. "Ah, not up to shootin' the shit. I get it. Probably a busy bee. Can you help me out here, though? I got this family..."

"*... va... THIRD... br...*"

At least, Devlin *thought* the word was *third*. Given his history with this spirit, it could well have been *turd*. "Listen—"

"*... UH... TONE... if... ha...*"

"... I know, Sammie. I'm working on it. Part of why I'm down here. But I need to know what you're doing kicking around suburbia."

"*... bi... IT'S... imp...*" Then, clear as day, the voice of Sean Hannity: "*... BUSH-GORE... sli...*"

"What the...?" Devlin closed his eyes, thinking. "Oh, you cheeky booger. Election of 2000. Hanging *chads*." No matter how often they happened, the playful tricks and inventiveness that spirits seemed so fond of never ceased to amaze him. "What are you doing here? Something to do with the father?"

"*... li... pa... WE... je*"

"Speaking French, now? So cultured. Listen, I just need one excuse to break down the door to that office. Can you gimme one?"

"*... tro... sh... HERE'S JOHNNY... so... bit... ... ...*"

"Say no more," Devlin smiled. "I appreciate your help. I promise to make an offering in the morning." With that, he turned off the spirit box, trading it for a simple lockpicking kit from his bag's side pocket. After marching down the hallway and flicking on the light—*Ah, that was a bad idea, gotta let my eyes adjust*—he started working on the doorknob. A few seconds later, a telltale click greeted Devlin's ears and the door swung open. He stepped inside.

At first glance, nothing appeared out of the ordinary. A large, colorful painting of a southwestern vista rendered in reds and purples hung on one wall. It was the only personal touch to be found. Atop a heavy desk sat a laptop and a second monitor, surrounded by piles of documents and a cheap desk lamp. The only other pieces of furniture were a chair, a filing cabinet, and an old, ratty loveseat holding a briefcase and boxes of papers.

For a few moments, Devlin shuffled through the documents, his eyes scanning the reams of numbers and names of people he would never meet. Seeing nothing of consequence, he dropped them on the desk.

"Gotta be *something* in here," he whispered. He scanned the room again, his eyes settling on the buttes and mesas of the painting. It was nice but rote, as if the artist—someone who cheekily signed it as "Art Amiss"—could have done it in his or her sleep. A moment later, Devlin lifted the frame from its hook for a look behind.

"Like I said, Sammie," Devlin whispered to his invisible companion. "Chad's a Christmas goose. And his goose is cooked." He pulled out his phone and dialed the Soloffs.

"Hello, Chad? I think I'm done. When can y'all be here? Aw, hell yeah. The one out by Peachtree Industrial? Say, would y'all mind grabbing me some hashbrowns? I'm fierce peckish. Scattered, smothered, and covered. Thanks."

13

Friday, September 18, 2020

THE MOST POWERFUL FORCE IN THE UNIVERSE

THIRTY MINUTES LATER, Devlin was wiping his mouth, Alex and Chad looking on half-disgusted, half-impatient. He finished his last bite and pushed the take-out container to the center of the dining room table. "Much obliged," he thanked them, stifling a burp. "We can do this now, or in the morning. Your call."

"It *is* the morning," Chad replied, looking at the time on his phone and rubbing his eyes. "We're awake, you're here, and we want to know. Is our house haunted?"

"Kinda."

"What do you mean, 'kinda'?" asked Chad.

Alex chimed in. "It's the bootlegger's ghost, right?"

Devlin shook his head. "Nope. I pulled the county records before I got here. This land was owned by a farmer in the twenties, real teetotaler type. Nor could I find anything in the newspaper archives about a murder hereabouts. Not a ghost what's in your house."

Alex and Chad stared at Devlin, waiting for him to answer. "What is it then?" inquired Alex. "A demon?"

Devlin shook his head. "'Fraid not. Worse. Y'all got yourselves an angel." He waited for their reaction. Chad's face lost all of its color, while Alex's turned into utter confusion.

"But… I thought…" she started.

"… that angels were all sweetness and light? It's a big spirit world, Mrs. Soloff. There's a lotta critters floating around out there. What we call angels, demons, ghosts… plus a lot more. And their reputations ain't always what they're cracked up to be. Angels *can* be good, I've run up against a lot in my day. But just as often they'll tear your life apart, little shitasses. You may wind up on the other side better or worse. All depends."

"Okay," Alex said slowly. "If you say so. But why would our house be haunted by an angel?"

Devlin jabbed a finger in her direction. "Ah ha—that's it. See, half the cases I take that turn out to be genuine, the building is haunted. The other half ain't the building. It's the *person*." He looked to Chad, now completely withdrawn and sullen. "And that person is *you*, Chad-a-rino."

The husband made a show of being offended. "Mr. Fox, I don't know what you're—"

Holding up his hand, Devlin continued. "So that Ensign of Mars hiding behind that painting in your office is just a... mural you're working on?"

Chad opened his mouth, searching for words. He finally found them, his face turning beet red. "I *told* you that was off limits—"

"Spare me. You hired me to do a job. I did it."

Alex looked at her husband, confused and wounded. "Chadwick, what is he talking about?"

"Let me fill you in, Alex," offered Devlin, his voice turning to genuine concern. "There's lots of reasons a place might attract activity. No one's pinned it down, though they've tried. 'Oh, it's an Indian burial ground, oh, there was a murder here, oh, there's an underground stream.' Back in the eighties, 'devil worship'—mostly your garden-variety occultism—was the culprit. Most accusations were bullshit. But sometimes—*sometimes*—they're right. Sometimes, people mess with stuff they shouldn't. Your daughter is, what, thirteen?"

"Fourteen," Alex corrected.

"My apologies—fourteen. So I'm running through the possibilities. Pubescent girl? Might be a poltergeist, there are tons of cases in the literature suggesting that recurrent spontaneous psychokinesis manifests around that demographic. But see, I'm *enlightened*; I don't believe that no more. My colleagues are starting to doubt it, too. So I run through the other possibilities. I think, 'Maybe this kid is playing with the occult.' I know you said there were no Ouija boards in the house, but teenagers are good at hiding things. But then I wonder—if *she's* the center of activity, why is this stuff persisting *here*? Why ain't grandma's place popped off? Maybe she opened a doorway... Maybe not. Maybe the perpetrator is still in the building."

Devlin looked directly at Chad. "What I found in your office, Mr. Soloff, confirms it."

Chad started to speak. Alex smacked him on the shoulder, never breaking Devlin's gaze. "What did you find, Mr. Fox?"

"The writing on the wall. Literally. Ensign of Mars, signifying the angel Samael. Tasked by Michael with revealing the outer circumference of the Seal of the True God. I found *that* up there, too, but it ain't the one you should be using. Yours is from *The Sworn Book of Honorius*. If you want results, you should be using John Dee's Sigillum Dei Aemeth, which don't even include Samael. Dee didn't really work with our boy Sammie too much... but he sure as shit seems to have taken a shine to Chad fucking Soloff."

Seeing the confusion on Alex's face, Devlin waved a hand dismissively while bringing out his cigarettes. "Neither here nor there, really. Enochian magic. Point is, your husband here caught the attention of one of the big boys."

Chad, his composure slightly regained, said in a calm monotone: "I don't know what you're talking about."

"Really?" Devlin looked to Alex. "Lemme guess—has he been complainin' about headaches, like someone nailed him 'twixt the eyes with a ball-peen hammer?"

Alex said nothing. The only sign that Devlin was correct was the look of astonishment on her face. He continued.

"You ever notice how it looks like your husband's been wearing a ring on his right hand? I'd bet the farm it's his Enochian 'PELE' ring. You should get your hands on it, Alex, take it to the pawn shop—no way he could've gotten as far as he has without it being made of pure gold." He returned his eyes to her husband. "Where'd you stash that, Chad? Up your ass?" Devlin pressed on before he could defend himself. "Now, here's the thing that bothers me—mind if I smoke?"

"Yes, actually—"

Devlin lit up and took a long drag, his first in hours. "... Alex, your husband's playing with fire. Not the trendy bullshit, no, no, no. I'd not even bring it up if his office was full of edgelord shit like Marilyn Manson posters—I mean, he ain't had an album I've liked since *Pale*

Emperor, and Christ knows he's a scumbag"—Devlin turned to Chad— "No, *you're* dabbling in some legit magic. Now, look… man-to-man, I can't condemn this. I'm well versed in this stuff myself. Hell, I used it a few years ago to smooth over some problems in Turkey. Truth be told, it ain't even inherently dangerous, so long as you know what you're doing. Like using a corn picker. But *I* know what I'm doing. *You* are in way over your head, sir."

"What makes you say that?" challenged Chad. "Maybe I know exactly what I'm doing."

Devlin took another long drag before flicking his ashes into the Styrofoam box. "Tell you what. As much as all this Enochian ephemera bothers me, the thing I *really* found concerning was what I *didn't* see. No New Age stuff like crystals or sage. No library, which to me is a red flag for any occultist. Suggests one of two things. Either you're *really* good at this stuff and have it all memorized, which I doubt, because otherwise, why call me? Or… you decided to jump into the deep end of the pool without knowing how to swim. Didn't you?"

"I… could have ebooks," Chad replied sheepishly.

"Shee-it, I'd believe y'all had a demon before I'd believe that," Devlin countered with a smile. "Lemme guess: you got *hungry*. Some aspect of life didn't seem like enough. Work, job, wife, finances, it's always the same things. So you hopped online, took a look around, and stumbled on the most powerful magical practice in existence. The most powerful, and the most *volatile*. Maybe you did buy an ebook or two. But what you didn't do is *take the time to learn what the hell you were doing*." Devlin dropped his cigarette butt into the remnants of the hashbrowns. "What was it Samael promised you? Crushin' a competitor? Money? That sweet little piece down in accounting?... Don't matter. You're fixin' to be in a *world* of hurt, you keep dabblin'. And so is your family. That fall you took is going to look like a love tap."

Silence settled over the dining room. The wife was staring at the table, the husband at Devlin. When at last Chad spoke, his voice cracked. "Tell me what to do," he whispered. "I can't control it anymore. Just tell me what to do, and I'll do it. For them."

Devlin chuckled. "'Anymore'? Hate to break it to you, pal, but it was *never* in your control. As to what you do next, it depends on whether or not you're man enough. If I was you, I'd get my ass to a hotel and deal with it on my own. Call me in a few weeks, we'll hash it out. After you cut the check, that is."

Chad nodded. "How much?"

"Five hunnerd, which includes some dragon's blood incense I want y'all to burn," Devlin answered. "Although…" He reached into his jacket pocket and pulled out the mini-bottle he had filled with tap water a few hours ago. "I'd advise getting this too. Holy water, blessed by a priest when I was down in Buenos Aires. Been looking for someone who genuinely needs it." He turned to Alex. "It's yours for one-fifty."

Chad scoffed, soliciting a series of blows from his wife. "Mother*fucker*!" she shouted. "We're going to have a long talk after he leaves!" She looked at the bottle of ordinary tap water. "Couldn't I just have a priest bless some water here for free?"

"You have a home church?"

"Well… no. Does Holy water protect against angels, though?"

"Ain't necessarily about angels. I'll take care of Sammie—already finished the License to Depart afore y'all got back. No, it's about the door your husband left open. No telling what varmints might creep in."

Alex nodded. "Cut the goddamn check, asshole," she said to Chad. "Six-fifty." Chad stood up and went to fetch his checkbook, tail between his legs. Devlin handed over the mini-bottle. "Will this really work?" asked Alex.

Devlin slung the messenger bag over his shoulder before quietly accepting his check from Chad. "All depends."

"Depends?" Alex repeated. "On what?"

"Whether or not you *believe* it will work. Do you believe it will?"

Alex turned the bottle over in her hands. Without looking at Devlin, she replied, "From you?... Yes. Yes, I do."

"Then that's all you need," Devlin assured her, heading for the door. "Belief is the most powerful force in the universe."

14

Wednesday, September 30, 2020

CAPREOLINAE

FOR THE FIRST TIME since the pandemic began, peace had settled over the small house at the foot of Red Ear Mountain. Not happiness, mind you, nor even contentment—but peace.

Rick stared at the ceiling in the gray morning light, listening to the white noise of the sound machine. He bought it in August, a last ditch effort to control the panic that every sound in the house elicited. When it was off, the silence transformed every little creak and knock into the footsteps of a bloodthirsty specter waiting to pounce. When it was on, Rick stood a better chance of sleeping through the night—although only marginally. Between his alcohol-induced insomnia and knowing that *something* unnatural was going on, he rarely slept more than a few hours at a time.

The only relief Rick found was when he drank until he passed out. Last night was another one of those evenings. So, while aggressively hungover (yet again), he was nonetheless grateful to awaken halfway refreshed.

It wasn't just the sound machine and the bottle that brought Rick peace. After cleaning up the house in July, he spent a week scouring the Internet for someone to help with his situation. (As a professed agnostic, Rick still hated the word "haunting," but three hours of closing doors, cleaning broken glass, and re-hanging picture frames cured him of that aversion.) Every ghost hunting organization he found either refused to help due to the pandemic or their website looked like it hadn't been updated since the early 2000s. Finally, at his wit's end, he did the only thing that made sense: he moved his father's urn from the mantle into the shed.

A parting of the clouds could not have wrought a more dramatic shift. The strange noises stopped. So did the missing items. Everything seemed as it was before the pandemic. The end result left him no happier—his life remained a wreck—but Rick's anxious mania had subsided into a calm, uneventful depression.

Rick rolled onto his side, unsure of what time it was. His phone, sitting dead on the nightstand, remained as unreliable as ever. Since the sun was barely up, Rick guessed it was sometime between seven and eight o'clock. The weather matched his mood: muggy and gray.

He swung out of bed, plugged in his phone, and turned down the sound machine on his desk. Its white noise decrescendoed into silence, then switched off with a click. Judging by the waves of nausea crashing against him as he put in his contacts, Rick thought it best to forego breakfast and coffee. Instead, he wandered into the kitchen and opened the fridge for a Pedialyte. There were none.

Great, Rick thought, dropping some ice in a glass before heading to the sink. *Water it is*. He drank it all, refilled it, and walked over to the sliding glass door, opening the curtains.

Rick did a double take. Something was moving through the backyard in the far distance, just alongside the creek. Looking closer, he made out the telltale shape of a deer, a doe, daintily tip-toeing (tip-hoofing?) through the tall grass before lowering its head. Rick took another sip, realizing that the deer was probably taking a drink herself.

As Rick stood there watching, something resembling joy flickered within him. The feeling was so foreign, he didn't even recognize it, other than noting a slight alleviation in his constant despair. He always enjoyed watching the parade of wildlife across the field. Wild turkeys, raccoons, foxes, coyotes, even the occasional bobcat and black bear put in an appearance throughout the changing seasons. He saw deer most often, although that made this sighting no less special.

The doe raised her head, affording Rick a good look for the first time. He immediately noticed something wrong. Her ears were fringed in vibrant red. The color was so striking that, for a moment, Rick wondered if she suffered from some sort of disease. That was when he realized that the ears weren't the only thing out of place—her coat, while not completely white, was several shades too light.

Could be a special condition, Rick thought, remembering an aquarium visit several years ago with Jack and Cassie. An exhibition had just moved in featuring a white alligator—not albino, but *white*. Leucism, they called it, a rare condition easily distinguishable from albinism because the alligator's eyes were not pink, but rather a bright cobalt color. *Maybe it's something like that*, he decided, draining his glass.

As he arrived at this conclusion, the grass around the doe's legs erupted in movement, yet she remained still. From out of the vegetation came a fawn, tiny and frail, with the exact same coloration. *That answers that question*, Rick deduced. *A genetic condition, for sure.* Another fawn, identical, came out to join its sibling, batting its hooves playfully against the other's back.

"Wow," Rick said aloud. "Mother of twins! My condolences." That was when a third baby emerged... followed by several others. Rick felt his jaw drop. "Three, four... eight, *nine*? Are you kidding me?"

Never before had Rick seen so many fawns with one mother. Although he was far from an outdoorsman, he could state with relative confidence that deer had no more than two or three offspring at a time, and even that was a rarity. *Now that I think of it, aren't they usually born in the spring?* he pondered. *These look* really *young*. Rick continued watching the group of fawns as they played under the watchful eye of their mother. She remained calm but alert, taking regular breaks from chewing grass to pop up her head and survey the field at the foot of the mountain.

Rick was about to walk away when the clouds momentarily broke, bathing the field in golden light. The abrupt change seemed to spook the doe, who immediately raised her tail and bolted for the tree line. Her nine wards reflexively fell in line, following her into the forest and out of sight. By the time they disappeared, so had the sun.

"Goodbye, lady," Rick said. "Tell the bucks to pull out every now and then." He turned back towards the kitchen to put his glass in the sink... but realized his hands were empty. For a moment, he simply stared at them. Then he whispered, "That's... impossible."

Looking towards the countertop, he saw the glass perched precariously atop a heap of dirty dishes in the basin. At any moment, it looked as if it might topple over. A faint print from his lips lingered on the rim above the fresh ice in the bottom of the glass, confirming it as the one held in his hands just moments ago.

Hesitantly, Rick allowed his gaze to leave the sink and trace toward the microwave sitting on the counter to the left. To his horror, the clock read shockingly late: 11:08, an innocuous number that had become the bane of his existence. He still had no idea what it meant, but he hated it.

"Don't you start," Rick demanded, pushing that old familiar feeling from his head. In an effort to quell the encroaching mania, he carefully explained the situation to himself. "You were distracted by the deer. *You* put the glass in the sink." His eyes darted back to the microwave. "You never saw what time it was when you woke up. You slept later than you thought. Nothing to see, here... Besides, your father is in the shed." With that, he headed to the shower to clear his head.

After washing up, Rick fixed himself lunch and tried to busy himself with chores until his first online lesson. By the time the last one rolled around at six o'clock, he was both mentally and physically spent, and decided now was the time to indulge his Netflix obsession.

As Rick settled in on the couch with his vodka and Coke, his phone rang, sending his heart into a somersault. Maybe it was Jack, finally calling him. A quick glance at the caller ID dashed his hopes.

Another telemarketer, Rick grumbled, tossing the phone on the coffee table. He hadn't been in touch with Jack for weeks. Every attempt to reach out went straight to voicemail.

Nor had they met much in person. Rick's outburst in July prompted Cassie to conveniently schedule their son for a doctor's appointment on the predetermined day, indefinitely postponing that month's meeting.

September's visit came and went too, after Jack and Cassie caught Covid. Rick spoke to them briefly over the course of their illness—they both sounded terrible. It was the worst sickness they ever had, they said, but luckily they pulled through, and, some prolonged fatigue notwithstanding, both seemed well on the road to recovery.

Now that he thought of it, the only time Rick saw Jack recently was for two hours in August, at a park halfway between Ellijay and Alpharetta. Most of it involved Rick watching his son practice his skateboard.

Still, Rick knew that his relationship with Jack was salvageable. The boy just needed more time. Cassie, on the other hand, was gone for good. On the rare occasions they conversed, the exchange was terse and businesslike.

Rick looked at his wedding band, wondering why he refused to take it off. The superstitious side of him thought that his marriage would actually end if he ever removed it. Rick's rational side figured that the only reason he hadn't seen divorce papers yet was that Cassie was waiting for the pandemic to officially end before serving him.

Even in the face of all I've done, she still has sympathy for me—or maybe it's pity, Rick thought, selecting a new series on television. Either way, he appreciated the mercy. For Rick, the impending divorce was a bit like death; he knew it was inevitable, but was in no rush to see it happen.

That isn't true, he corrected himself as the opening credits rolled. *You've come pretty close these past few months.* Sometimes, Rick wondered why he hadn't committed suicide. When the house was at its most active, it felt like the only suitable escape: from the madness, from the despair, from the incessant internal monologue. If he had to pinpoint a reason why he withheld, though, it was the lingering fear that he would fail.

He had seen firsthand the aftermath of a botched suicide attempt. It wasn't pretty.

The phone rang again. Rick almost didn't look, but was glad he did. It was Rodney Beauregard.

"Hello?" asked Rick after pausing the episode and clearing his throat.

"Hey there, slim," Rodney rumbled. "Just wanted to give you the heads up. I sent a few new dates to your email. Give 'em a look as soon as you can and let me know if you're free or if I need to find someone else."

"Uh... will do. Are these club dates, or private parties, or...?"

"Festivals. In the spring. Got the Atlanta Dogwood Festival interested."

"Wow, awesome." Rick paused before asking the obvious question that neither of them knew the answer to: "Think these will happen? Or will they fall through like all the others?"

"I hear you," Rodney chuckled grimly. "Remember where we were supposed to be this weekend?"

Asking Rick to pick out one cancellation from a sea of disappointments felt impossible. "Uh... Savannah?"

"Naw, that was supposed to be last weekend. This weekend was supposed to be that Chattanooga apple festival." Rodney sighed. "I dunno, man. I'm trying to keep positive. I ever tell you the story of my first drummer?"

"I don't think so."

"This cat's name was Louis. Could play anything you put in his hands, but the thing he was best at was percussion. Fantastic player, kept time like a Swiss watch. Well, we were doing a December residency at this club in Houston—must've been around three years ago—and Christmas Eve rolls around. We're supposed to play. Who the hell wants to do that? And all of us just ain't feelin' it. Except Louis. He calls me, I tell him I'm feeling under the weather. He finally convinces me to come out, but man, did it suck. No one in the club all damn night. We have about twenty minutes left, and everyone is ready to bag. We're playing for, like, four people. But Louis stays the course. He tells us to finish the drill.

"We're two songs from the end and this guy walks in with an entourage. And Louis, he's just going hell bent for leather, you know? Acting like he's playing the AstroDome or something. That fellow who walked in at the end? Worked for UMG Nashville. Before we even loaded out, he had Louis ready to relocate. By the end of the next year, he'd played and toured with everyone under the sun. Has two houses now, one in Nashville, the other in Malibu."

Rick didn't believe this story for a minute. Thousands of variations had made their way to him over the years.

"Look," Rodney concluded. "Things gotta open up at some point. Or at least we gotta keep acting like they will." He waited for a positive affirmation from Rick and, receiving none, brought the conversation to a close. "Just let me know about those spring dates, okay?"

"Sure thing," Rick managed. After hanging up, he sat motionless on the couch, watching the screensaver dance across the television. Inside, he teetered on an emotional seesaw. While nothing could fully extinguish his love of music, the truth of the matter was that Rick didn't hold much hope for his future as a musician.

Venues had cautiously started hosting live music again, though the experience had taken on an alien aspect. Some of his friends, like Travis, were back grinding away as if nothing ever happened. Not

Rick. What few gigs he played the last two months—solo affairs at the local wineries—turned out disastrous. Something was different. It wasn't the mask he had to wear while performing, although that was obnoxious enough. It wasn't even the crowds, which seemed decent, despite the pandemic lingering on.

No, if Rick had to put a finger on it, it was *himself.* Something had broken inside him in the past six months. Where he once felt joy, his emotions before and during gigs had devolved into a constant panic. He wanted to think it was Covid anxiety. While that certainly played a role, he was equally aware that his dependence on alcohol probably manifested the trembling hands, sweating brow, and rapid heartbeat that took control during sets. Whenever he loaded up and hopped in the car to return home, the only thing he now felt was relief that his performance was over. He would come home, embrace the depression for what it was, and drink himself to sleep.

Part of him was anxious about the upcoming festivals that Rodney had booked for the Rib Wrenches. Another part of him felt like they would never happen. If they weren't canceled due to Covid fears, Rodney might preempt the decision himself. Rick doubted his enthusiasm. He had already canned another residency at Terry Mac's. After the passing of his parents, Rodney seemed hesitant to start performing again.

Let Rodney do his thing—what about you? wondered Rick. *If you can't play, who* are *you? If you gave up music, what would you do?* He glanced at the entrance to the unfinished addition. With Edna out-of-town so often, little had progressed—but he enjoyed the work whenever he managed to push past his depression-induced procrastination. *Maybe I should contract full-time,* he pondered. *Wouldn't be as fulfilling as music, but at least it would pay the bills, and I'm not half bad.*

Immediately, a voice echoed in his head: *You're not half good, either.*

Rick closed his eyes for a few seconds to quiet his mind. Over the course of three episodes, he polished off the vodka. He had skipped dinner again, as he often did nowadays. Soon he opened a new bottle and took a long pull. The alcohol simultaneously burned his stomach and fanned the flames of emotion, reigniting that small ember of musical passion that refused to die.

No, he said to himself. *You're a musician, goddammit.* Half-deluded, half-motivated, and all drunk, he went to his bedroom, grabbed his guitar, and headed out to the patio.

It had been months since he had sat under the stars at night. He was too afraid of the lights on the mountain. Tonight, however, he walked straight past the porch swing and sat cross-legged at the edge of the patio, guitar in his lap, new drink at his side. Sitting there, looking across the backyard, Rick half expected the field to lap up onto the cement, like waves breaking against the shore. Past the sea of grass, Red Ear Mountain stood as faithfully as it always had, its slopes a cloak of shadows draped across the canvas of the night sky. The smell of a bonfire somewhere far off in the distance was the only sign of human habitation. On evenings like tonight, Rick felt truly isolated—in a good way.

He took a long drink and strummed a few chords, playing whatever entered his head. The crickets' ostinato provided the perfect atmosphere, rendering even the most familiar tunes magical. Something about tonight had freed him, in a way. Regardless of whether or not his father's ghost was responsible, knowing that the madness of the past six months was behind him liberated Rick.

His eyes drifted to the sky, where a break in the clouds allowed the ashen face of the moon to peep through, a clutch of stars surrounding her like ladies in waiting. For whatever reason, Rick began playing the introduction to *Stairway to Heaven*, humming the bass recorder part, harmonizing on the fly.

If I could just write something half as brilliant… he thought, abruptly stopping. *Maybe if I could figure out how to use that fuckin' melody…*

Rick began picking through the tune he had recorded at this very spot back in May. His fingers were heavy, leaden, thickened by alcohol. Each time, he stumbled as he approached the cadence. It took him six attempts before he completed the phrase accurately. *So haunting… Too bad it can't be harmonized—*

Ding. The sound of a bell interrupted his thoughts. For a split second, he assumed it was his phone. He then realized that not only was his phone still inside, but this noise was completely different from any notification sound he ever assigned. It resembled a hotel call bell more than anything else, right down to the heavy metallic attack and long, resonating decay. From its volume, it couldn't have come from more than a few feet away.

Rick wasn't about to let himself be spooked. The issue was resolved. He glanced to his right, towards the side of the house where his father's urn sat securely in the shed. Everything looked normal. Casting his eyes left—toward the lonely hawthorn guarding the trailhead leading up the northeast side of the mountain—offered no further clues.

Ding. The bell sounded again, more faintly... higher. Above Rick's head, even. His eyes were on their way to the approximate location when he spotted a bright, blue-tinted star above Red Ear.

Was that there before? Rick asked himself, knowing damn well it hadn't been. The sight should have alarmed him. But rather than panicking, Rick's inebriation revealed the humor in the moment. He struck up the chorus of *We Three Kings*.

"... westward leading, still proceeding, guide us to thy perfect light!" he half shouted, half sang. "There, lil' star! A gift! For you!" As he said this, several other points gradually ignited in the sky. The change began imperceptibly, but soon enough, eight other lights had appeared, just as bright as the first, forming a circular pattern in the night like a halo over the top of the mountain. There was nothing threatening about the vision at all; in another context, it might have seemed divine, even holy.

The lights in the sky cut through the cloud of intoxication surrounding Rick, searing into his mind a message with abject clarity: *It is not over.*

Rick didn't know whose voice it was, but it wasn't his own. *Could be God,* he thought. He'd resisted the notion for four decades, but now that he knew ghosts were real, who could say whether or not those bedtime stories were true? He staggered to his feet, almost losing his balance. *Fuck, I'm plastered,* he realized. Feeling seen, he held up a hand to the halo above the mountain.

"Okay, okay, I hear ya, I hear ya," he said. "I'll call it a night." He turned and headed inside, resisting the urge to look behind him as he closed the sliding glass door. After laying his guitar on the couch, he meandered over to the sink for a glass of water.

Tonight was a first. In all of his years of drinking, he had never experienced a full-fledged hallucination. Maybe this was a good opportunity to get his act together.

Rick finished his water, dropped the glass in the sink, and turned out the light. The kitchen dimmed, but remained brighter than it should.

"What the hell?" whispered Rick. Bright light streamed in through the kitchen window from the front lawn. Rick rushed towards it, fully expecting to see a car pulling into the driveway. Maybe Edna was finally back from Florida. Rick envied her ability to just up and leave her house for half a year at a time.

It was not Edna. What Rick saw was indeed about the same size and shape as a car headlight. It was about the same height off the ground, and about the same distance as an automobile just emerging onto the driveway from the woods. However, there were three groups of three, bobbing along, following the contours of the landscape in single file. As he watched, the globes of light shifted from blue, to white, to a sickly yellow. The procession continued into the field and past the house, in the direction of the hawthorn.

Despite half a year of avoiding the backyard at night, a morbid curiosity overtook Rick. He rushed to the sliding glass door, cupping his hands alongside his eyes to better see out into the darkness. He arrived just as the parade of lights snaked its way into the backyard, where they dropped low, partially obscured by the tall grass, as if half-heartedly trying to avoid detection.

When they reached the few trees dotting the banks by the stream, all nine lights shot straight into the air as rapidly as if they had been yanked up by an invisible pulley. Rick's mouth hung agape as he watched the ensuing aerial ballet, the orbs traveling around, over, and beneath one another. Then, just as they had less than ten minutes earlier, they all took their pre-determined places in the circular formation above Red Ear Mountain before dropping back to Earth, descending in a zig-zag pattern like a handful of falling leaves. Each settled onto the slopes in various positions, flaring bright blue before winking out of sight.

It was a long time before Rick closed the curtains. It took everything within his power to step away from the sliding glass door. That surprised him. Given all that he had endured in 2020, he thought he would have felt more fear than he did, watching those lights.

It wasn't like that at all, Rick thought, heading to the bathroom and taking out his contacts. *It was... what's the word... 'Majestic'? 'Powerful'?*

Something inside Rick told him that he now better—if not fully—understood the nature of the lights. Yet identifying that understanding proved elusive. The closest point of comparison was seeing a pride of lions at the zoo, safely behind bars. What you saw carried all the indications of danger. You felt that on a deep, evolutionary level, if nothing else. But at the same time there was a respect for what they represented: pure, unbridled force, stripped of quaint human concepts like morality, cruelty, or mercy. Whatever he had just seen, like lions, simply *were.* They didn't hate you. They didn't love you, either.

And if you get in their way, don't be surprised when your interests fail to align, Rick thought as he splashed water on his face. Even with all the booze he had consumed tonight, he only felt slightly buzzed now, rather than fully drunk. The excitement clarified his cognition, bringing the world into focus like the sharpness dial on an old television set. He clicked on the sound machine and hopped in bed, though he doubted he would fall asleep for a while.

After a few minutes of lying there, he began to notice another sound layered over the white noise. A light *tap-tap-tapping* coming from somewhere in the room. Initially, he wrote it off as a trick of his ear, something that often happened since he started using his sound machine. Some nights, he even thought he could hear voices in the noise.

However, he always managed to warp those voices, thinking of new phrases to which his ear adapted. This was different. The sound persisted at irregular intervals, always a series of three taps. After realizing this mystery would prevent any chance of sleeping, Rick stood up, turned on the light, and flicked off the sound machine. Immediately, the noise came once more: *tap-tap-tap.*

He waited for it to happen again, so he could triangulate the location. Finally: *tap-tap-tap.*

The sound came from the window.

All of the wonder and respect Rick had felt for the lights vanished as he stared at the curtains, imagining what lay on the other side. *Should I put my contacts back in?* he asked himself. *If it's nothing, it'll be such a pain in the ass to take them back out...* Deciding against it, Rick cautiously crept over to the window and gently pulled back the curtain.

From what his blurry vision revealed, the lights were back, far in the distance. This time, however, there were only two. They remained perfectly still, hovering out there in the darkness. Rick squinted, leaning closer to the glass. They looked different, somehow. Never before had they appeared in this exact position, shape, or color...

Rick came within six inches of the glass before his brain grasped what he was seeing. Those little specks were not distant points of illumination. They were the lights of his own bedroom glinting off two enormous eyes not a foot away, sad and wet, set within the barest hint of a wizened face a little larger than a toddler's.

Rick stifled a scream. He staggered, catching a glimpse of silent commotion outside before falling backwards to the floor. There he lay frozen, staring at the blackened square, hoping to see the face again, praying he wouldn't. After a moment, he realized that he was no longer still. His pounding heart made his chest pulse, repeatedly raising his back from the carpet ever so slightly.

Rick listened for the tapping. The only sound he could discern was the wash of blood in his ears.

A few seconds passed before, from this low vantage point, he spotted a series of shapes parading past the window with the telltale bob of someone—some*thing*—walking on two feet. Though his vision remained blurred, Rick concluded that he was seeing nothing less than a procession of some sort from left to right towards the back patio, only the uppermost portion of the participants' heads visible.

Rick sprung to his feet, yanking the curtains closed as the patio light came on. Moving urgently, he locked his bedroom door and the door to the bathroom, shoving his desk chair and nightstand against the former. Fueled by adrenaline, he clumsily walked his dresser over to the window, shoving it as close against the curtains as he could. He tried to move his heavy desk in front of the bathroom door, but it refused to budge. Instead, he piled all the belongings he could up against the entrance, then collapsed onto his bed in a nervous wreck.

When he rose the next morning, Rick found himself unsure of how long he had remained there awake before falling asleep with the lights on. All he knew was that one thought repeated itself over and over in his head, and even persisted into his dreams. It was on his lips the moment he opened his eyes.

"It's not ghosts," he whispered. "It was never ghosts."

15

Wednesday, August 18, 1897

FORTH

IF NOT FOR THE CHILD'S INCESSANT CATERWAULING from the next room, the house would have been deathly quiet. The Brother and Sister were asleep upstairs, insulated from their sibling's cries, while The Mother, The Father, and Nan silently sat by the hearth watching the fire. None of them moved. Teacups sat undrunk in their hands, the steam long since dissipated. Gradually, the fire began dying away too, its fading light rendering the grim tableau somehow even more somber.

At length, Nan spoke. "Wee one is fierce angry tonight," she muttered, rising from her rocking chair to prod the flames. "Having a good old cry for himself." It was the kind of inane observation that only someone in their advanced age would feel comfortable verbalizing. Nan returned to her position, her feet making a sweeping sound as they padded back across the flagstones.

Both parents held their tongues. There was nothing else to say. For over two weeks, they played out every scenario, enacted every dramatic confrontation, blamed everyone there was to blame. None of it could remedy what had befallen their youngest child.

Nor was there anything to *do*. Not acting was infinitely more difficult than not speaking, however. The Mother wanted nothing more than to take The Child into her arms, to shush and coo until he slipped into the relief of sleep, but now she knew the futility of these maternal instincts. The two would only find themselves more upset.

As if unsure the couple had heard her, Nan piped again: "All ends up, we have to do *something*."

Her plea prompted The Mother to reply at last. "What would you have of me?" she asked over her wailing son.

"The *lus mór*, of course! Why drop in on Biddy Nally if not to heed her advice?"

The Mother looked to her husband, whose face remained unreadable. "Nan, we've walked this path before," she explained, trying to keep her voice steady. "Do you not remember Michael Ward?" Nan stared back, her face either stubborn or forgetful. "I heard tell this same potion was given him, for to help his heart. He passed shortly thereafter. Do you know what that means?" Nan grunted.

"It means at best it doesn't work," continued The Mother. "And at worst, it's what did him in. Would you have me inflict that same risk upon my son?"

"That *thing* in the cradle," Nan croaked, lifting a crooked finger in the direction of the crying infant, "is not your son. You *know* that."

The Mother shot up from her chair, drawing closer to the fire. Flames reflected off the tears streaming down her cheeks, making it look as though her face might split in two.

"And what of it?" asked The Mother. "Were it the child of my sworn enemy, I would not condemn it to such a fate." She placed a hand on the fireplace to steady herself, then, finding it too hot, retreated back to her own chair. Silence descended once again, only broken by the occasional pop from the burning logs. Surprisingly, it was The Father who spoke at last.

"My Da told me a tale once," he said, leaning forward and smoothing his mustache. "He was nearly a boy at the time, barely older'n fifteen. *Seanathair* tasked him with watching the sheep back in those days. Whenever the sun began dipping below the hills, he knew it was wise to return home. Always brought them back, he did, locked up tight by nightfall."

At this point, The Father paused and produced some tobacco, his pipe, and a matchbox from some unseen pocket as effortlessly as if they had materialized from thin air. Packing the bowl, he lit the pipe and puffed, sending aromatic coils snaking through the room. The Child continued crying. After another puff, The Father proceeded.

"One night a storm swept in, terrible violent, worse than what's set in tonight. Da gathered the flock handy enough, but when he reached the *boreen*, he found the entire way flooded. At first, he didn't care. There were plenty handholds for him to steady himself, what with trees and fenceposts and the like. But then he realized that losing part of the flock was a certainty. He didn't know what to do. Soon, the flock would be riled into full-fledged panic.

"So Da thinks. He stands there and recalls a path *Seanathair* warned him against ever taking, a path over the hill. That journey was too rocky, too uneven, too steep, fierce treacherous for a man—but not so for a surefooted sheep. They would be fine. So Da made a choice. Rather than put the flock at risk, he risked himself. Got a tongue lashing from his father, but he and the flock made it home, safe and sound." The Father puffed again. For a while he sat there, the lesson hanging in the air alongside the pipe smoke.

"I'm able for it," he said at last, rising and heading to the door. Nan's eyes widened as he donned his cap and coat, then grabbed the knob.

"Wait!" exclaimed The Mother. She ran to him, grabbing his arm. "Please no. I won't lose you as well! You cannot go."

"Full well I can," The Father retorted, shaking off her grip. He swung the door open, sending a cool blast of air rolling into the room, erasing the vestiges of smoke.

As his boots crossed the threshold, The Mother yelled one final time. "Wait!" she sobbed. "If you must…" She looked around the room, finally spotting the knife Nan had used to cut vegetables earlier in the day. "… take this with you." The Father's eyebrows furrowed. For a moment, it looked as if he would ignore her. Without a word, he reached out his hand, took the knife, and was out the door, closing it fast behind himself.

It was a foul night, but it could have been much worse. The rain that had settled in had diminished substantially into a light drizzle that could easily be ignored. Even if the precipitation had been heavier, The Father would scarcely have noticed. A task was set before him, and any chance of returning—with or without The Child—depended upon a clear head as much as it did a stout heart.

His boots caked with muck, The Father passed onto the main road, then circled around the edge of his property until he reached the corner of the southwestern field. The hedgerows of the farm lay behind him, clearly demarcating the order of his pastures from the wild, untamed wilderness beyond. Fingers of brambles and thorns interlocked each other, barring his passage.

It looked impenetrable. But The Father knew that things nonetheless trod here, even if human beings were not among their number. For him, the only way through the unyielding tangle was a narrow, poorly marked footpath heading downhill in the direction of the river.

When he reached its swollen banks and emerged onto the road running parallel, The Father could barely hear anything over the water. The rain had barely let up in the past fortnight, and the inky blackness of the river far exceeded its usual level, traveling swiftly down stream in a foamy boil. When he first left home, The Father had hoped that he might ford those waters, as his destination lay on the other side. Now he knew he had no choice but to head further, towards the small bridge about a half mile away that crossed at the nearest bend.

Reaching it, The Father found it just as he remembered, though he had not crossed it in some time. He knew what lay on the other side, and refused to set eyes on it until he was forced to. Now safely on the opposite bank, he departed the shoulder of the road and began the long journey uphill.

Ascending the green slopes proved even more treacherous than he had feared. It seemed to take forever to only reach the halfway point. What little could be discerned of the sky looked black as Ballingarry coal, marbled with wisps of gray clouds. In that moment, with his feet slipping and the moon nowhere to be seen, The Father cursed himself for being in too much of a rush to fetch a lantern. Still, he pressed on, until at last the terrain leveled out.

There, cloaked in darkness, lay the forth.

A lifetime had transpired since he gazed upon those stones, last seen in the foolishness of youth. Now he realized it was not a place to tarry. Slowly and cautiously, The Father approached. In response, the ancient structure slowly came into focus, as if inviting him closer.

The Father knew not whose hands had built the old ringfort. All he knew was that it was no place for any sane person to venture, especially at night. Even if *they* didn't call it home, it would have sent shivers up anyone's spine: the copse of lonely trees standing high on the mound of Earth, swaying in the wind like the beckoning fingers of some buried giant; the rubble of twenty generations, scattered across the hilltop; bits of thorny gorse thrusting up between mismatched stonework; the vast, circular depression surrounding it all, the remnants of a long-forgotten moat.

This was the boundary that The Father would not cross under any circumstances. It wasn't that he feared for his life; there were things worse than that. Seeing it for the first time in so many decades, The Father vaguely recalled when some learned men came up from Trinity College to survey the forth. He had heard that they determined it was some ancient dwelling, where perhaps The Father's own ancestors once lived. The moat, the professors said, was for defense.

But The Father knew differently. It wasn't to keep anyone out. It was to keep things *in*.

The Father gripped his knife, wishing it was larger and sharper. He realized that if he stood any chance of retrieving The Child, he had to capitalize on the element of surprise. Looking across the hilltop, he barely perceived a cluster of bushes a few yards away. It would have to suffice. He made his way over to the hiding spot and climbed inside, not caring at all about the branches scraping his hands and face. Once securely concealed, he tossed a few soggy clumps of wet leaves over his body to complete the deception. And there he waited.

It was several hours before he returned home, bloodied and filthy. The rain had stopped. He found his mother pacing back and forth in front of the house, fretting nervously, unable to take The Child's crying any longer. When she finally saw her son, she started, convinced she had seen a ghost.

"My son!" exclaimed Nan after regaining her composure. She rushed to The Father and embraced him, unbothered by the grime covering his body. "You returned! Heavens, the state of you! Come, warm yourself by the fire. But first, you must tell me—what about the boy? Did you see the boy?"

The Father simply stood there, looking completely broken. He didn't say a word. Only when Nan tried to drag him inside did he speak: "Stop." His voice contained no hint of emotion. "I failed, Mother."

Nan's expression tightened as she gazed up at her son. "Come again?"

"You heard me," he mumbled, pulling a twig from his hair. "My son stays with *them* yet."

"No, no," began Nan, wiping tears from her eyes. "We still have Biddy Nally's remedy, we can—"

"Mother—*he is lost to us*. I saw him myself." He started crying. "I cannot face my wife…"

"She sleeps, son," Nan said, trying her best to show strength. "You say you saw The Child? Tell me."

The Father took a deep breath. "I waited there. By the forth. I waited through all of it—through the lashing rain, through the cold, through my muscles as they ached and begged to move. I watched and watched, and nothing happened. Not till this past hour. That was when I saw *them*."

Nan gasped and spat on the ground. "God bless all here! You kept your sight, it seems."

The Father nodded. "Aye, but… I wish I hadn't. It began as a glow below the hill. A light. I suspected mine own eyes were playing tricks, but no… it was *them*. *They* were bet in against each other. *They* came as lights, Mother. *They* came as things that flew, as things that crawled, as beasts from the forest and as birds from the sky. As things… things we haven't any name for. Things moving like poppets. Some gigantic, some small, some tiny. Some invisible, perceived only by their movement through the heather. Men and women astride black and grizzled steeds, some riders handsome, some with goggling eyes, or single eyes, or no eyes, or the feet of a cockerel, or bodies hairy… Such a motley procession I have never beheld. The top of the hill was falling down with *them*." He stared into the distance beyond his mother with a look that conveyed what words could not.

Nan reached up to place her hands on The Father's face. "*The boy, son*," she demanded, trying to lock eyes. "*Tell me about the boy*."

The Father returned his gaze to his mother. "*They* looked like some class of people, so many I thought the procession would never stop. Just cogging along up the mountain and *poof!* into the forth, without so much as a doorway to accommodate *them*. At last, it all slowed to a trickle, only a few at a time. I thought all was lost… then I saw *her*."

"Who? Who did you see?"

"The woman in white, across a snow-white mare. Mother, she was… fair, so fair… a more elegant lady there never lived. I stopped breathing. My heart seized in my throat… and then I spotted, in her lap, my son. Just as I—" The Father stopped to break out into a violent sob that turned into a bittersweet smile. "Just as I remembered him. All joy and laughter and smiles. *She held him*, Mother. And… it seemed she *loved* him, and he her. He looked so happy, he looked like... like maybe he should stay with her. Like she could bring him all the joy we never could."

"What did you do?" whispered Nan.

The Father cleared his throat and began pantomiming. "I jumped from the bushes and rushed forward. I grabbed her steed by its reins and pulled back my knife"—he looked to his hands, now empty—"and I plunged it towards her heart. And do you know what, Mother? She didn't even look surprised. She looked like... like she was expecting it. Like this had already happened to her, even. Instead of being afeared, she just held up a long, slender hand, and my own—the one holding the knife—it stopped at her breast. I couldn't move it, no matter how I tried. It seized up, somehow. You couldn't have slipped the page of a book betwixt the tip and the lady, but there it stayed, despite how hard I pushed.

"All this time, the horse was bucking, trying to get away. I stumbled, I, I slipped at my wrist... it wrenched towards The Child. The blade of the knife touched him and..." The Father paused, exhaling in what may have been a chuckle, may have been a forceful sigh. "... and didn't it all just vanish, like that. The lady, the horse, the knife... my son."

With these last words, The Father wailed, tears falling from his face. He collapsed to his knees, cradled his head in his hands, and wept big, wet tears. Tears for his relationships, for his son, tears for his life. Tears for his world and what it had become.

Nan stood there, unsure what to do. She had weathered so much heartache—The Famine, the loss of her husband, now her grandson and her own child, whom she feared might never recover from his grief. Instead, she offered what only parents could: she was *there*. Not saying a word of comfort, not busying herself with cleaning him, or pampering him, or embracing him. She simply stood there, cried with him, and hoped that, as in all the years past, her mere presence would be enough to pull him from despondency.

A sound at the door interrupted their grieving. It was The Mother, weeping as well. Neither Nan nor The Father knew how they were going to break the news.

"You pair!" shouted The Mother, stepping into the night. "Where have you been?!?" She rushed towards them, tears streaming down her face, a bundle of clothes in her arms.

The Father looked up from his kneeling position. "I am so sorry, my love. I failed."

"Is that so?" she asked. "Perhaps you should tell *him*." With that, she knelt down to meet her husband. "The crying—the crying stopped! It was that which roused me."

The Mother passed the bundle of clothes to The Father as a gentle giggle bubbled between them. He immediately recognized that heft and warmth, despite not having held it for weeks. In his hands, tightly swaddled, lay The Child—smiling, calm as ever, with only the slightest flicker of confusion across his pudgy face.

The Family was whole again.

16

Friday, October 2, 2020

VISITORS

ANY SANE PERSON would have relocated after the face in the window.

Rick was not only unsure of his sanity; he also had no place to go. He couldn't afford a hotel room. Cassie wouldn't take him. Perhaps he could have crashed at Edna's place, but she wouldn't be back in town permanently until later in the month. Besides, if her property had indeed become a UFO hotspot, Rick was sure that they would find him just as easily on the other side of the mountain.

First I thought it was me, then trespassers, then ghosts, now flying fucking saucers, thought Rick as he turned off the main road, his headlights transforming the forested driveway into a tunnel of brown. Under less isolated circumstances, with someone to verify what he had seen, Rick might have found his slow descent into madness mildly amusing.

Not tonight. Tonight, he had plans. The agenda turned his mind somber and reflective.

Rick reached over to the passenger seat to steady the gigantic bottle of 190-proof liquor as the Corolla jostled down the dirt driveway. Every war could be ended with the nuclear option; his war, he hoped, could be ended with the *Ever*clear option.

Although fully admitting his own alcoholism, Rick had never purchased the highly potent spirit. It frightened him. Too many late night college parties involving Everclear ground to a halt after an attendee was carted away to the hospital. Rick still remembered how the lights of the ambulance glinted off the red Solo cup in his hand, and the accompanying vow to never touch the stuff.

However, the events of the past year converted the dangers of Everclear into a selling point. Rick didn't care if he ended up needing an ambulance tonight, nor did it bother him that no one would be there to call 911. To the contrary. He wanted nothing more than a way out of this mess.

Rick had thought long and hard about the best way to do it. A fear that he might survive precluded the use of firearms. Equally, Rick knew he lacked the discipline to successfully slit his wrists. Nooses were too much work, and he didn't trust his own craftsmanship. Pills were always a possibility, but he wasn't sure that he could keep them down.

So at last he settled on what he did best: he would drink himself to death. Rick wasn't sure how much it would take, but he was certain to cross the point of no return eventually, and the path there would at least alleviate some of the pain he now constantly carried with him.

Rick parked the car and stepped outside. It was a quarter after seven o'clock. Before he retrieved the bottle, Rick took a moment to appreciate how the sunset painted the field he had called home for over a year.

Not content to confine themselves to the sky, the amber, garnet, and slightly amethyst hues spilled down over the trees, casting the entire area in a dim twilight, rendering even the most familiar nearby objects foreign and alien. With a little imagination, the garbage littering the front lawn became a diorama depicting some long-lost civilization's cyclopean ruins, choked in weeds rather than vines. Behind the house, the shadows obscuring the nearest side of Red Ear Mountain turned the landmark into an enormous triangular hollow, like a generous serving cut from some aerial pie.

Rick watched as the field inevitably succumbed to the fading light. *Everything ends in darkness*, he thought fatalistically as he grabbed the Everclear from the passenger's seat. *Entropy comes for us all. Even the trees*, he added, looking at the surrounding forest, whose leaves had only barely begun to turn. Other parts of the world were well on their way into autumn. Not in Georgia. Here, summer lingered on like an oblivious houseguest outstaying his welcome. It only delayed the inevitable.

With heavy feet, Rick trudged to the front door. Now only the barest hint of the sunset lingered, stripping all mystery from his surroundings. His peripheral vision took in the detritus strewn across the front lawn and the vague outline of that stupid chainsawed bear statue beneath the kitchen window.

Won't miss that thing, Rick thought as he turned to enter the house...

He froze. Something stood on the doorstep, blocking his way. It took Rick a moment to realize what it was. Staring back at him was the exact same bug-eyed statue he had barely registered just seconds earlier in the garden. Rick stepped forward and touched the wooden bear, as if to prove its reality.

If this is here, he thought, rubbing the roughly hewn surface, *then what did I just see standing below the kitchen window?* Taking several hesitant steps backward, Rick peered around to the left, towards the wooden effigy's usual spot.

Nothing. Just a depression in the mulch where the bear was supposed to be. *I could have sworn I saw it standing there,* Rick marveled, rubbing his eyes. *It was dark, though, and I've been wearing my contacts nonstop since I saw that face in the window. Maybe it was nothing.* Deep in the back of his mind, Rick knew this wasn't true. *Something* had stood there just moments before, the approximate size and shape of the statue... but where it was now remained a mystery.

Setting down the liquor bottle, Rick walked the heavy statue back into place below the window. Doing so, he spied a second curious indentation alongside the first, a little closer to the house. In reality, it wasn't an indentation—it was a tunnel, maybe eighteen inches wide, cutting down at a forty-five degree angle in the direction of the house.

In the direction of the basement, Rick corrected himself. *Better take a look.* As he retrieved the Everclear and brought out his keys, Rick wondered why he even cared. *With luck, you'll be gone in the morning. This isn't your problem. Let Edna worry about it.*

The truth of the matter was—despite his plans for the evening—Rick was too curious to let go of the incident. Besides, if he was going to shuffle off this mortal coil tonight, it would be on his terms, not at the hands of a ghost, or an alien, or whatever the fuck he had seen.

Rick placed his car keys and the Everclear on the countertop separating the kitchen from the living room. The clink of glass against granite was shockingly unfamiliar, louder than his usual plastic bottle. Next, he cut through the dining room and towards the basement entrance, which lay to the left of the patio door.

For all of its tininess, the house that Edna rented to Rick boasted a sizable finished basement beneath. The space was a rarity in Georgia since basements were non-essential given the higher frost line in the south. Early on, Edna expressed to Rick an interest in turning the basement into a second living room or another bedroom. He had agreed to help under one condition: that he wouldn't be the one in charge of cleaning it out. Thus, the matter was dropped, leaving the exercise equipment, suitcases, kitchen supplies, clothes, and innumerable old magazines to molder underground.

When Rick reached the bottom of the stairs, he flicked on the light switch. *Glad it's on the wall*, he chuckled, surveying the array of boxes. *I'd feel like I was in a cheesy horror novel if it was one of those damn pull cords.* Rather than a sole lightbulb, overhead fluorescents illuminated the space, although there wasn't much to see past a few feet. The basement was an absolute mess, with things stacked higher than Rick's head.

Rather than wading into that labyrinth, Rick did his best to survey the room from the bottom stair. He was about to return to the living room when something caught his eye on the opposite wall. Past an old treadmill, one brick looked loose, the surrounding mortar crumbled. After bushwhacking his way through Edna's trash, Rick found that in reality it was several bricks, all sitting within the wall but easily pulled out.

He removed one and peered inside. It was difficult to tell, but it seemed as if the backfill behind the basement wall was carved out. Suddenly, it dawned on him: this spot in the wall was directly beneath the kitchen window. Something had tunneled from the garden towards the basement and managed to exert enough force—*How?*—to separate the bricks from their mortar.

I don't have time for this shit, Rick silently complained. There was a bag of Quikrete in the addition, but spending his final hours patching a hole in a wall struck him as absurd. *Maybe I can just...* He replaced the bricks as firmly as he could, wedging whatever was at hand into the margins between them: an April 1983 *Newsweek*, some yellowed women's shoulder pads, a bit of bubble wrap. Hopefully, it would keep anything out long enough to afford him some peace.

Back upstairs, Rick mixed the Everclear with orange juice and started sipping. Even for an ironclad stomach like his, the spirit proved challenging. He sat there, listening to old records, trying to hasten his end. For his third drink, he put on Cannonball Adderley's *Somethin' Else*. Before Miles's solo in *Autumn Leaves* concluded, he was vomiting into the sink.

"Well, Rick," he said, wiping a few chunks from his lips with the sleeve of his shirt. "Lesson learned. Dance with the one who brung you." He snatched up his trusty plastic bottle—it was about a quarter full—and squeezed the remaining vodka into a new glass. Returning to the couch, he cued up *Is That All There Is?* and started drinking.

Rick didn't remember passing out. The next thing he knew, the title track was skipping. "... *end it all?—end it all?—end it all?....*" He groggily hoisted himself to his feet, shut off the record player, and stumbled to the bedroom. Somehow, he possessed the presence of mind to flick on the sound machine. He collapsed onto the bed, fully clothed, reeking of vomit and stale booze, as the white noise washed through the room.

He slept deeply, at least at first, with the alcohol tamping down his insomnia. Eventually, though, sobriety crept in and Rick became more agitated, tossing and turning. A stream of faces fluttered through his dreams: Jack, Cassie, Bora, Edna, the red-haired girl, his father. All of them shared the same message: "*You're worthless. A failure. You're so incompetent, you can't even kill yourself. You're destined to linger on, and make everyone around you worse off just by existing.*"

From time to time, he would awaken, hear the sound machine, then drift back off to sleep. Inevitably, the faces would return to hurl their insults, lurching him back to consciousness. After repeating this enough times, Rick forced himself to remain awake, staring at the ceiling. He might have lain there, eyes half-lidded, for minutes or hours. He wasn't sure. But after a time, he noticed something peculiar.

The white noise that filled his bedroom slowly got quieter and quieter. It was impossible to notice at first, but soon it became undeniable: the sound was receding, bit by bit. Rick suspected that he had accidentally unplugged the sound machine when he came to bed. Four batteries inside allowed it to be used without electricity—most likely, they were dying, causing the sound to fade. It trickled to the barest murmur until...

Click. The simple noise sent an icy shiver down Rick's spine. Any speculation regarding dying batteries or a malfunction died in that instant. Someone had manually turned down the sound machine, steadily decreasing the volume until shutting it off completely. That unassuming little click meant that whoever it was remained in the bedroom, watching him in newfound silence.

Rick closed his eyes tightly. Before reopening them, he said a quick, vague prayer that it was all a dream—but the scene was the same. The sound machine remained off. Rick ever-so-slightly turned his head towards the sound machine on his desk, fully aware that he might be unable to handle what awaited him there.

Even though he wore his contacts, the hours spent sleeping had blurred Rick's vision. He blinked, trying to get a handle on whatever was perched atop his desk. There, silhouetted against the window, crouched a figure. It looked vaguely like a person, but its head was far too large and its stature far too small. Rick estimated that, if it were upright, it might have stood three feet tall at the most. It might have been sitting, hugging its knees, or squatting, ready to pounce... it was simply too dark to tell. No other details were apparent. Whatever it was, it completely lacked facial features, save for two eyes—sad and wet, like the ones seen two nights earlier—that glistened in the ambient light of the bedroom.

When people discuss the fear responses of "fight or flight," they rarely address another natural reaction: "freeze." Rick involuntarily chose this option, lying there with his eyes locked onto those of the intruder. It was impossible to tell where it was looking, if anywhere; all Rick could see were highlights glinting back from the glassy surface of each eye. Whether they were all black, darkened by the night, or possessed any pupils was anyone's guess.

As he lay there, Rick slowly became aware that the room was not actually silent. Shallow, ragged breathing, like someone suffering an asthma attack, quietly drifted from the desk. The respiration followed a noticeable pattern: a two second inhale, followed by a brief pause and an equally long exhale. Rick also noticed a strange odor in the room, like the lingering scent of a fireworks display. Underneath that wafted something else, like someone had scooped up a pile of wet, rotting flowers and dropped them onto his desk—not a foul aroma per se, but simply one carrying the telltale whiff of decay as a natural, necessary process.

Eventually, Rick pushed past his fear and tried to figure out how he should act. His paralysis was voluntary, now. Thinking back to how the lights had reminded him of a pride of lions, the safest course of action seemed to dictate lying in bed, perfectly still. Maybe it would move on if it thought he was asleep. Maybe it wouldn't notice him.

But what if it just sits there? wondered Rick, trying not to panic. He knew he needed to get away from the house, back to civilization, back to the city, where the endless bustle and business pushed such monstrosities to the fringes of imagination where they belonged. *I could jump out the window*, he decided, then quickly scrapped the idea. For all he knew, there were more of those things waiting outside. That could be the entire point: to flush him out into the open.

Besides, he added, staring at the motionless figure, *if I'm leaving, I need the car keys.* He recalled setting them down on the countertop near the front door. *If I can get to the kitchen, get the keys, and rush outside, I might be able to reach the Corolla.* He had no idea where he would go after that, but he didn't care, so long as it was away from Red Ear Mountain. *But how do I sneak past this thing?*

As if responding to his thoughts, the figure dropped to all fours, scuttled off the desk, and bolted out the open bedroom door into the house, all within the blink of an eye. Rick laid there for a moment, afraid to move, waiting to see if it would come back. When it failed to return, he gingerly lifted the covers and tiptoed to the doorway.

The short hallway with the second bathroom entrance and laundry was completely empty. Beyond lay the kitchen, softly illuminated by the bulb in the range hood above the stove. The intruder didn't seem to be there, either, though Rick couldn't see much from this perspective. Rick could barely spot the microwave, which he fully expected to read 11:08. Actually, it was 1:18 in the morning.

Cheeky bastard, he thought, smirking. *We doing remixes, now?* Rick hazarded a glance around the corner to his left, towards the rear of the house. Just as he suspected, the basement door was ajar, a single shoulder pad sitting amidst a trail of dirt. His effort to seal the tunnel had clearly failed.

Rick ducked back into his bedroom. As quickly and quietly as possible, he threw on a spare shirt and a dirty pair of jeans, laced up a pair of sneakers, and crept out into the kitchen, half-crouched. He couldn't decide whether he should move quickly and get it all over with, or if he should take his time and pray he remained hidden. He chose the latter option, dropping to his hands and knees.

As he hoped, the kitchen was empty. However, his visitor clearly spent some time in there earlier. The refrigerator door stood wide open, the automatic light long since shut off. A milk carton, open and resting on its side, spilled across the linoleum below. A set of wet, ill-defined footprints traced out of the kitchen between the snack bar and the half-wall supporting the countertop, disappearing into the living room. Rather than navigate the mess, Rick simply forged ahead, wincing as the cold milk soaked into his jeans and coated the palms of his hands. Passing the gap between the bar and the countertop, he saw that the living room, too, remained empty, thank God.

Rick reached the end of the countertop nearest the door. Although he could not see them from this low angle, he knew that his keys sat above him alongside the Everclear bottle. There he stopped, his back against the half-wall's base cabinets. The plastic trash can, overflowing with refuse and old bottles, sat at the wall's end to his left. Rick listened for the ragged breathing he heard in his bedroom, but noticed nothing—although he doubted he could have heard anything over the sound of his heart hammering in his ears.

Now or never, he encouraged himself, cautiously reaching a hand above and behind him. His fingers scrambled over the granite, searching for his keys. At last, he touched cold metal. Rick pivoted his wrist as best he could for a better grip—

—and instantly withdrew, abandoning the keys on the countertop. The breathing had returned, louder than in his bedroom. Rick closed his eyes and pulled his legs to his chest, trying to compress himself as small as possible against the cabinets. Another sound arose, wet and tacky, like a wad of biscuit dough slapping a pan, then lifting. As the noise repeated, it slowly dawned on Rick that these were most likely footsteps crossing the tile of the foyer toward the front door.

That means it's right here, he thought, biting into his lower lip. *It's just on the other side of this wall...*

The deadbolt *thunked* open, followed by a clatter at the doorknob—clumsy, as if the technology were foreign, or being turned with fingers too large or too small to manipulate it properly. Once or twice, the operator became frustrated, grunting under their breath while smacking the door. Then, at long last, Rick heard the telltale creak of the front door swinging wide open, followed by more footsteps, some bare, others shod, still others clattering on the tile like claws or hooves.

Rick opened his eyes and leaned forward, trying to catch a glimpse of what was happening. All he could see was the upper half of the door. It should have been enough to see whoever was walking inside... unless they, like the figure in the bedroom, were incredibly short. Then the door slammed shut—but, Rick noticed gratefully, remained unlocked.

The intruders began chattering among themselves in small whispers of utter gibberish that Rick doubted he would have understood even if they had been more audible. What sounded like an argument ensued, with multiple voices overlapping before falling apart into terse snippets and giggles. From there, it sounded like the group dispersed into the living room. Rick allowed himself a slight sigh of relief. Although they might eventually find their way to the kitchen, they seemed distracted for now.

Rick could tell that there were several presences in the house, though it was impossible to know how many. More than five but less than a dozen. He listened as they raised all sorts of commotion in the living room: turning on lamps, jumping on the couch, rocking in the old recliner Rick barely used, rummaging through the open bag of chips on the coffee table. Eventually, Rick heard his record collection tumble onto the floor, followed by chirps of excitement.

Everything fell silent. Then, from the living room, Rick heard the halting piano figure that had become so familiar this year, followed by Peggy Lee's voice: "*I remember, when I was a little girl...*" An image flooded Rick's mind: nine or ten little aliens, crowded around his record player, listening closely, enraptured by Peggy Lee singing about the underwhelming experience of a house fire.

Rick allowed the surreal image to play out in his head until the first chorus began. "*Is that all there is?*" Peggy crooned as he reached upward once more. He found the keys immediately, quickly withdrawing his arm back to safety behind the wall. As he did so, his left shoulder bumped the trash can. It was just enough to send one of the many plastic vodka bottles careening to the floor, where it landed with a clatter clearly audible over the record player.

Oh, fuck. Rick sat there in complete shock at his utter foolishness. *I always knew the bottle would kill me, but... not like this.* For a split second, he thought about trying to escape, but he never had time to react.

The moment the bottle finished bouncing, a figure poked its head into the kitchen from the corner nearest the door. The dim light from the range hood, while much brighter than the bedroom, only offered the briefest impression before Rick reflexively clamped his eyes shut: a leather cap and jerkin; skeletally thin arms and legs; an oversized head; a pair of gigantic, black, blank, unblinking, almond-shaped eyes.

Rick clenched his fists and pressed them against his own eyes. He could hear the thing creeping closer. Rick noticed a warm feeling trickling down his wrists. It was his own blood. He was clutching the car keys so tightly that they pierced his palms. The ragged breathing was closer than ever, until Rick felt the thing wheezing against his face. The smell of dead flowers and fireworks returned, stronger than ever, overwhelming even.

A new noise supplanted both the breathing and the record player, an incessant buzzing that rose to such a volume it felt as if it might burrow into Rick's brain. As it increased, Rick lost all sense of time. The creature should have fallen upon him at any moment, but instead the drone dragged on for what felt like minutes. Rick began beating his own head furiously, trying to drive the noise from his mind...

It abruptly stopped. Rick opened one eye as the strings and flute ushered in the final cadence of the last track, *Don't Smoke in Bed*—the end of an album half an hour long. He had no idea what transpired during that period, other than that it felt like a fraction of the time. Hesitantly, he opened his other eye and saw that the kitchen was now completely empty. The only sound was the record player running out across the dead wax, sending pops through the empty house.

Get the fuck out, Rick told himself. He struggled to his feet—and immediately toppled over, catching himself on the opposite countertop. A chorus of belly laughs echoed from another room, most likely the addition. Looking to his feet, Rick saw that the laces on his sneakers had been tangled into an intractable knot. It was such a bizarre development that he couldn't help but shake his head.

Before he could reach down and untie them, the cabinet immediately above Rick exploded open. Something cold and wet thrust toward his scalp, securing a fistful of hair by the roots and tugging upward, as if trying to lift him off his feet.

"Fuck!" shouted Rick, his hands slapping the countertop in a mad search for the knife block. It sat just out of reach. With no other option, he began batting his fists above his head. They connected with something spongy, but still, the grip held fast.

As before, Rick failed to get a decent look at his assailant. Instead, he only caught snippets. It seemed entirely different from what had approached him on the floor, or even from what he had seen in his bedroom, for that matter. Its skin sported the same color and texture as an olive. Rick thought he glimpsed a head in the shape of a perfect sphere with two yellow, froglike eyes slung low on either side. He failed to see any mouth. Although it was difficult to make any sense of what he saw as he struggled to escape, Rick clearly recognized a pair of swept back ears extending far above the crown of its head, green and veiny like a tree leaf. The body seemed muscular, the arms overlong.

"Get off me you *fucking shitass!*" Rick shouted as he pummeled his attacker. Finally, for no apparent reason, the thing released him, shutting the cabinet door behind itself. Rick had been struggling so forcefully that he careened back into the opposite cabinet, knocking the Everclear bottle to the floor. More laughter ensued.

"Hell with this," Rick muttered as he stepped on his heels and slipped out of his shoes. He started towards the front door when two more small shapes—different yet, moving too quickly to comprehend —rushed from the opposite side of the half wall into the foyer, blocking his path.

Rick immediately reversed direction, his socks hitting the spilled milk and sending him skidding out of control. His first instinct was to flee to the patio, but he knew it would take far too long to lift the security stick, unlock the door, and slide the glass open. He needed a secure place to buy time.

He bolted from the kitchen and darted back into the short hall connecting the bedroom to the rest of the house. Half running, half tumbling, Rick careened through the open door of the bathroom. Once inside, he locked both doors—the one to the hall and the one to his bedroom—and leaned against the vanity, catching his breath.

"Fuck me," he whispered, staring at the ceiling. "First I thought it was me, then dad's ghost, then aliens... You're telling me it was goddamn *goblins* all along?" He started chuckling. A knock at both doors sharply interrupted this moment of levity.

Gotta get outta here, he thought. He looked to the other end of the bathroom and spotted the window positioned between the shower bath and the toilet. *Squeeze out here, circle around the side of the house, get to the car out front,* he thought as he ran over and began unlatching the folding locks. The window slid open without a hitch, sending a blast of cool air into the confined bathroom.

He was about to punch out the screen when he heard another knock. This time, the sound was hollower and deeper.

It came from the bathtub.

Rick watched in horror as several small, pale, bone white fingers slipped around the edge of the shower curtain. For a split second, Rick's brain refused to make sense of what he was seeing; it looked like they took far too long to emerge. That was when he realized that each finger held an extra joint at the end, totaling four knuckles. The sight was rendered even more uncanny when he noticed that none of them sported fingernails. The digits slowly wrapped around the curtain's edge, tightening, preparing to fling the shower open...

Rick bashed at the screen as hard as he could, sending the covering flying into the night. A sudden surge of upper body strength pulled his bulky frame through the tight space, catapulting him with a splat onto the mud below. It was cold. Rick immediately wished he was wearing a coat—and shoes, for that matter—but there was no time for comfort. He needed to reach the Corolla.

Racing counterclockwise around the house, Rick made his way through the yard, sliding in the mud and early morning dew. Just before he reached the field of garbage out front, he stumbled and fell flat on his face. He sprung back to his feet, weaving between the old tractor and the blue barrels, lurching headlong towards the safety of his car.

A chirp from the fob unlocked the Corolla. At last, he threw open the door, hurled himself inside, and slammed the lock button.

Jamming the key in the ignition, he over cranked, causing the engine to grate in protest.

He was about to throw the transmission in reverse when he spotted movement from the house. *If they see me leave, they might follow me*, Rick thought. To hide his presence, he quickly turned off the headlights.

Rick watched as the front door opened once more. A moment later, a sphere of light, no more than knee-high above the ground and no bigger than a tennis ball, bobbed across the threshold and into the front yard. It traced its way underneath the kitchen window, past the side of the house with the bathroom, and then towards the lone hawthorn standing far off to the left of the field. When it reached the tree, it circled the trunk while a procession of seven more lights emerged, tracing the same pathway to join the first.

Finally, something different appeared in the doorway: a small figure roughly proportioned like a toddler. The darkness and the distance made it impossible to make out any details. The only thing Rick could say for certain was that the figure waved at him before skipping twice in the direction of the hawthorn. On the third bounce, it transformed into another ball of light, making nine total, and joined the others dancing around the tree. After several rotations, the lights dispersed back in the direction of Red Ear Mountain, where they settled onto the forested slopes, just as they did two nights ago.

Rick sat in the car for several minutes, waiting to see if the lights would return. They did not. Then, at last, he turned off the car. He needed to go inside, pack, and close up.

"Fuck the virus," he said aloud. "Fuck the pandemic. Fuck staying at home."

17

Saturday, October 3, 2020

A FRIEND IN NEED

Gzzzt. The call box to the Inman Park apartment building fell silent. Several more attempts brought the same result. After the third try, the other end of the intercom finally crackled to life. A woman's voice, sluggish with sleep, rose from the wall: "Hello? Who is it?"

"Yeah, uh… hey, Bora. It's me, Rick." Another pause followed, longer than Rick would have liked.

"… Rick? What?… Hey buddy. It's, like, four o'clock in the morning. Are you okay?"

Rick chewed on the right words for a moment. "I will be. But right now I'm kind of in a bind. I was hoping I might be able to crash with you for a little while." His plea received no response until, maybe thirty seconds later, the door to the lobby unlatched with another resounding buzz.

He shifted the shoulder strap on his duffel bag, grabbed his guitar case, and headed inside towards the elevators. Before pressing any buttons, he stopped briefly in the lobby to rummage through his luggage as he had half a dozen times before, making sure he brought everything he planned to.

When Rick reached Bora Choi's apartment on the third floor, he stood at the door for a long time, hesitating. Rick felt like such a burden. He knew it was rude to drop in uninvited in the middle of the night, but he *had* to escape Ellijay, and there was simply nowhere else to go.

At last, he knocked. Bora answered the door, wearing a tank top and pajama pants, her eyes barely open. "Hey, man," she groaned. "Fuck, you look rough."

"Been hearing that a lot," Rick replied. "Apparently, this is just the way I look now."

Bora forced a smile. "What's going on? Is everything okay?"

"Yeah, yeah," he said, stepping forward to walk through the door. Bora hesitated and backed up. "Bora... what's wrong?"

"C'mon, Rick," Bora replied apologetically. "You know how it is. Covid and all. I'm not sure..."

Rick's heart sank. "Bora, *please*. I love you, but believe me when I say that if I had anywhere else I could go, I would. Cassie's at her wit's end with me. Like I said, I just need a few days to get my bearings."

Bora stood there, her face betraying every emotion as she weighed the situation. At last, she widened the door and gestured him inside. "I've had it already," she said. "It's probably fine. Sorry to hear about you and Cassie. That bad, huh?"

"Unfortunately," Rick reiterated, looking around the apartment. He had never been here, though he knew the address from some care packages the two sent each other from time to time. Rick wasn't sure exactly what he was expecting—maybe something a little more eclectic, a little funkier, a little more "Bora." This place didn't look like her at all. Aside from the dining room that had been repurposed as a makeshift art studio, he would have never guessed that his best friend lived in the nondescript one-bedroom unit.

"How are you and Hope?" he asked, sitting down on her couch. Bora winced. "That bad, huh?" he added.

"Unfortunately," she parroted back. "Lucky at cards, unlucky in love, I guess." She rubbed her eyes. "Look, let's catch up tomorrow. Make yourself at home on the couch; help yourself to anything in the fridge. Ooh, except the Topo Chico, that's for me. I've got to be at work by 8:30, but it's just around the corner. If you're up to it, I'll fix us some breakfast in"—she looked at the clock on the wall—"ugh, three hours."

Rick nodded. Bora retreated to her bedroom. Before she even closed the door, he had fallen asleep on the couch.

The smell of bacon—an aroma he had not enjoyed in months—awoke Rick around 7:30. Usually, the grease sent his hangover-addled stomach into cartwheels, but something about the smell seemed appealing today. Although he was still exhausted, there would be plenty of time to catch up on sleep while Bora was at the pharmacy. He dragged himself off the couch and sat down at the small bar at the edge of the kitchen.

"It lives," Bora quipped, setting a plate of hashbrowns and bacon in front of him. For a moment, Rick wondered why only the top half of her face was made up. Then he realized that a pharmacist in Atlanta was probably wearing a facemask full-time nowadays.

"Barely," he said. "Couch doesn't sleep bad, though."

Bora didn't bother sitting, instead choosing to stand in the kitchen, drinking her coffee and nibbling a little bacon. "Got it at The Dump. You know those commercials?"

Together, they both chimed in, then fell into chuckles: "Shop *The Dump!*" After their laughter subsided, Bora looked square at Rick.

"First thing's first: where'd you park?" she asked. "They will boot your ass in the blink of an eye out here, so we need to move your car ASAP if—"

"I took MARTA in, then an Uber to here. Figured parking was probably a nightmare."

"Tells you how bad parking is, that MARTA is preferable." Bora sipped her coffee before adding, "It's fine that you're here, Rick, but you've got to tell me what's going on."

Rick didn't answer. Instead, he picked up a painting sitting on the bar to his right. It was an impressionist watercolor of patrons milling about Krog Street Market. "God, I haven't been there in years. Bora, this is fantastic! I love this!"

Bora sighed. "Thanks," she said, washing her hands before taking the painting from Rick. "I was taking a picture of that to send to Dad. The gallery had to delay *Images of Inman* indefinitely after the pandemic set in, so I've taken the last few months to just bank some stuff for a follow-up exhibition once things settle down. *If* they settle down." She walked over to the dining room, slipped the painting onto an art drying rack with several others, and wheeled the entire affair into a small closet in the short hallway between her bedroom and the single bath.

"I'm sorry to hear that," Rick offered, his voice showing genuine concern. He finally picked up a piece of bacon, testing his stomach.

"Rick," Bora chided. "You're not getting out of it that easy. You *never* drop in on me. What have you gotten into? Is it…" She paused, tilting her head down. "… is it drugs? It's drugs, isn't it? I tell ya, you've gotta look out for those Dixie Mafia thugs up there in the mountains, you should have just asked me, you don't have to deal with anyone shady, I've got—"

"No, Bora, it's not drugs," Rick interrupted, shutting off the stream of words hitting him full blast like a firehose. "I wish it was that simple."

"Well, I'm listening. I've got a minute to hear it."

"Not everyone talks as quickly as you do."

"You sound like Hope," she said, chuckling and rolling her eyes. "Okay, have it your way. It's just the morning shift today, so I should be home around 2:30. We'll get takeout and drink our faces off while you tell me all about it. But you're spilling the beans tonight, mister."

Rick splayed his fingers, holding his hands up vulnerably. "Bring home some Gas-X from the pharmacy, girl, 'cause I've got more beans than you can handle." With that, Bora laughed, hugged him goodbye, and left for work.

Rick slumped in his chair. All the isolation of the pandemic had made even the simplest social interactions exhausting. That, coupled with his late night and his depression—he hoped he was hiding it well enough—left Rick completely spent. After picking through his bacon and hash browns, he rummaged around in his duffel bag for the Everclear bottle. He barely choked through a shot, just enough to return him to sleep, and spent the remainder of the morning and early afternoon dozing on the couch.

Bora's arrival roused Rick a little before three o'clock, just as she promised. She took a long, steady drag on her vape pen, sending smoke coiling through the apartment, before even setting down her purse. After the usual pleasantries—how was your day, one customer did this, the boss did that—Bora took a long shower. By the time she emerged, it was 4:30. The two of them settled on barbeque, which both of them fell upon ravenously once it arrived.

As they sat together eating on the couch, Rick recounted all that had happened to him as best he was able between bites. Over the past few months, he had only shared a few of the tamest oddities with her over the phone. To her credit, Bora refused to pass judgment, at least until he outlined the events of the night prior.

"*Goblins?*" asked Bora, wiping her mouth and pushing her tray aside.

"I don't know, Bora," Rick admitted, feeling foolish. "That's the best word I can find. I know it sounds absolutely absurd."

"What did they look like?"

"They all looked... different. No two alike. I only got flashes. Small. Big eyes. Fast. Shitty sense of humor."

"You sure it wasn't tweakers?" suggested Bora. When he didn't laugh, she stared at Rick for a prolonged period, scrutinizing his face, wondering if she was being pranked. Finally, she said, "I believe you, Rick."

He scoffed. "Why would you?"

"I didn't say I believed in goblins," she explained carefully. As frustrating as he sometimes found Bora's rapid fire speech, it allowed Rick to clearly identify her honesty whenever it slowed. "But whether or not these things actually happened the way that you feel that they did... how they *affected you* is real. Sounds traumatic. If it's supernatural, you deserve sympathy. If it's all in your head, if you're..."

"... crazy?"

"Not my words, Rick, not my words. But... yeah. If it's that, too—you still deserve sympathy."

Rick began tearing up. "Thanks, Bora. I feel safe here. Good to be away from the mountain."

Bora leaned over to give Rick a long, hard hug. "You should feel safe," she affirmed after releasing him. "I don't know if I believe in this spooky shit—what little I've learned has come to me through, like, cultural osmosis—but unless you're demonically possessed, I think it should stay back at the house in Ellijay." She chuckled. "If you find goblins popping out of *my* cabinets, *then* we've got a problem."

"Or *I* have a problem," Rick said. "If I start seeing things here, you'll be the first to know. That would be a pretty good indication that it's all in my head, right? Ghosts haunt specific houses. No one sees UFOs in big cities. Isn't that how it goes?"

Bora nodded. "And goblins are just in 1980s fantasy films starring David Bowie's dick." The two of them burst into laughter.

When they recovered, Rick asked, "Bora... do you think I'm crazy?"

"I don't think I've ever seen you more agitated," she admitted. "Honestly, Rick? I don't know. If I saw what you say you've seen, I know that I would doubt *my* sanity."

"Well, it's not like I *don't*. But so much of this has been *real*. Things that either something else did or I did but don't remember doing. Like the lock, or the picture frames. I mean, look at my hands, where I gripped the keys." He showed Bora his scabbed palms. She said nothing, so he reached into his duffel bag and hoisted out the bottle of Everclear.

"No doubt about it now. You *are* crazy," remarked Bora, hitting her vape. "Shit, dude, you don't fuck around these days."

"It's a long story," Rick said, pouring a little into his Styrofoam cup of sweet tea. "It's like part of me—part of me is depressed, right? We're all a little depressed after this fucking year. So I'm not in the best shape mentally, I realize that. But another part of me *knows* that these things happened. So am I crazy or not? Where is that threshold?" He took a sip, then gazed out the sliding glass window, past the balcony, to the traffic moving like molasses on the street below. "I had a professor once—economics, or ethics, or somesuch—put forth a question to the class." He turned to Bora. "Would you sell a kidney for a billion dollars?"

"Of course," Bora scoffed. "Got two. I could get by with one for that sort of bank."

"What about one dollar?"

"Hell no."

"See? That's the trick. Where is that line? So you start whittling it down on both ends. Would you sell a kidney for two dollars? No. But you'd probably sell one for five hundred million. How big is that window in the middle, right on the cusp of where you will and won't sell? Is there a single dollar that tips your decision in one direction or another? Probably not. That line in the middle is vague, ill defined. It could go either way." He took another drink, this one longer. "That's how I feel with my sanity, Bora. Right there in the middle, like I could go either way. Not that it matters. Even if it's *all* real, it still doesn't fix anything else in my life."

Bora grabbed the Everclear and poured some into her own cup. "You're... resilient. You know that, Rick?" she asked. "You just keep going. I think a lot about what you've been through. Seems you keep getting dealt a shit hand, even as a kid. I remember what you said about your sister. You barely talk about her now, but I remember sitting in the lounge of the art building late one night, freshman year, you telling me what happened. I can't imagine going through that, thinking the worst was behind you, only to weather everything since then. From the outside, it looks like just one unbroken string of heartbreak." She took a sip and immediately coughed. "Sweet Christmas, how do you drink this stuff?"

"I don't," Rick said as he took another sip. The two of them laughed and forced the conversation in a different direction. Slowly, Rick began feeling a bit better, if only temporarily. He realized that the alcohol had likely begun to numb his depression, distracting him from how difficult his life had become. At the same time, he realized how much he had missed Bora's friendship—anyone's friendship, for that matter. For a few hours, at least, the isolation of the pandemic seemed a distant memory.

By nine o'clock, the two of them were utterly plastered. "I'm about to turn into a pumpkin," Bora groaned through her hiccups.

Rick guffawed and took a long drink. "Pumkins? W-whatchu talking about pumkins?"

"Y'know, like *Cinnerella*," Bora said, swatting Rick as she snickered. "Stroke of midnight, *poof!* her car turns into a pumpkin. We used to go all night, me n' you. Now we're *old*, Rick. We are *old. Old old old old old.*"

"Hey, to be fair, to be fair—this is strong shit," Rick responded. It was the last thing he remembered before passing out.

Rick and Bora spent the following day recovering from the night before. Rick, an old pro in such matters, walked down to the bodega for a few Pedialytes before Bora woke up—easy enough, since she didn't pull herself out of bed until around noon. At first she found Rick's offer confusing, but (after several trips to the bathroom) she soon became a true believer in the remedy, which managed to keep her hydrated and alleviate the pounding headache that settled over them both.

After Rick taught a handful of lessons online, the day concluded with Bora painting a bit in the dining room while he fixed dinner, a simple casserole that had served as a staple during his college days. Rick rarely felt the need to cook since he had moved out of the house in Alpharetta, but as he prepared dinner for Bora, he remembered how much he enjoyed it. Cooking was just another expression of art—unlike baking, which was more of a science. It was probably why Rick never got the hang of it. But cooking? He could cook.

Just as he was plating dinner, Bora finished painting, sliding her completed watercolors onto the drying rack and back into the closet. After eating, the two of them continued catching up. While fun, the inebriation of last night's conversation impeded anything beyond carousing and small talk. The only thing they had discussed in any depth were the trials Rick suffered back in Ellijay.

As Rick readied himself for bed that night, he experienced something he had not felt in a long time: he felt loved. He felt safe and secure here in the tiny apartment. Though he always thought himself more at home in the country, he couldn't deny the sense of security brought by knowing another person was just one room away, with hundreds of other tenants above, below, and to the sides. Their proximity seemed enough to keep the horrors of the past year at bay.

Rick closed his eyes and fell asleep. Ignorance is bliss.

18

Monday, October 5, 2020

TAKEN

THE FOLLOWING MORNING, Rick busied himself as best he could between naps. Although his depression still lingered, the change in scenery carried with it the implication that things might improve. He walked around the neighborhood, taking comfort in seeing that other people were carrying on with their lives. In isolation, it was so easy to forget how big and beautiful the outside world could be, how many possibilities yet existed. On top of that, Rick was relieved to see the effects of the pandemic waning significantly. While it varied from establishment to establishment, some places were completely open, barely enforcing mask mandates. Rick wasn't convinced of the wisdom in that, but had to admit the development was reassuring.

Encouraged by his stroll, he returned to Bora's apartment and took the time to complete some light housekeeping. He called all the venues up north—wineries, mostly—and canceled his performances, claiming that he was ill. One benefit of the pandemic was that no one pushed back whenever you called in sick.

Next, he scrolled through the contacts in his phone, calling the musicians whom he knew were still playing in town. A few hours and a couple of kind rejections later, he had a handful of jazz gigs lined up. Some of his friends even thought they could scrounge together a little extra money to allow him to sit in. Rick hoped that a return to his primary passion might further dispel the clouds of depression.

He dutifully struggled through his afternoon lessons, and by the time Bora returned from work around five o'clock, he already had dinner ready. "I could get used to having you around, Mr. Coulter," Bora said as she sat down to eat.

"Don't worry, Ms. Choi—I'm not being nice," Rick countered. "I'm just trying to make myself as helpful as possible so you don't throw me out." Over the course of their meal, their conversation turned to art.

"That reminds me," Rick said, standing from his empty plate. "You've got to hear this." He fetched his guitar and sat on the couch while Bora cleaned the dishes. When she was finished, she sat alongside him and listened while he plucked out the mysterious melody, reveling in its sublime angularity.

"That's... *incredible*," Bora said after he finished. "When did you write that?"

"I didn't," corrected Rick. "It's the melody I told you about Saturday night. I first heard it the last time I saw you, when I got back from the gig at the festival."

"Wow. I mean, I've never heard anything like it." Bora's eyes widened. "You should turn that into a metal power ballad or some shit. It rocks."

"I wish," Rick moaned. "I've been trying to do something with it for months. But I can't make it work. Even if I did, what does it matter? It'll never get played."

"Don't say that. You see it around here. Things are starting to open up."

"Or so people keep saying. But sometimes I wonder if anyone even wants to listen to my stuff. You should hear this godawful band Jack loves." Rick reached into his pocket and brought out his phone. "This fucking thing! It's been on the fritz for months now." He showed her the flashing battery icon.

"No worries," Bora reassured him, producing her own phone. "I'll just... huh. That's funny. Mine's dead, too. Let me go plug it in and I'll get my laptop." When she returned, she looked quizzically at Rick. "What are they called?"

"The Shit Bees."

Bora's face lit up. "What?!?" she exclaimed. "Are you kidding me? They're awesome."

"We've got to be talking about a different band."

"No way," she said, looking up one of their videos. "I mean, they started out a little rough, but don't a lot of bands? Besides"—she swung the laptop around—"look who that is on keys."

Rick couldn't believe his eyes. "Is that... Matt?"

Bora nodded. "Yup! He started playing for them last year."

"I haven't seen him since school," remarked Rick, leaning in closer. He wasn't sure when the video was taken, but the band seemed much tighter than in the recording he watched back in July. The sophomoric scatological content remained, but there was at least some decent playing on display. Rick's eyebrows raised as his friend took a dazzling keyboard solo. "Wow, not bad, Matt," he said, immediately feeling ashamed for having so quickly dismissed the band.

His emotions must have made their way to his face, because Bora immediately asked Rick what was wrong. "I, uh…" he began. "Jack told me to look them up a few months ago. I told him they were awful, and… we've barely spoken since."

Now it was Bora's turn to look uncomfortable. "Yikes," she whispered, closing the laptop as the final notes rang out. "Maybe you can give him a call, explain that you've had a change of heart. Now that you're back in town, getting together should be easier, right?" She glanced at the clock, then said, "Listen, man, I enjoy you being here, but we can't party tonight. I've got to get back into my normal routine. Stay up as long as you like… see you in the morning." She gave him a quick hug and wandered back towards the bathroom, where she started preparing for bed.

Rick sat there for a while, waiting until Bora was in her bedroom before pounding down a few drinks. He tried to sleep, head toward the balcony window, feet toward the kitchen, but could not get comfortable. Part of him regretted leaving the sound machine back in Ellijay, but the memories associated with it were too terrifying. Besides, here in town, the traffic was heavy enough to fill the apartment with comparable noise, even in the middle of the night.

Rick lay on the couch, staring at the headlights as they came through the balcony window and reflected off the ceiling with each passing motorist. Over the past few days with Bora, he had managed to push away all of his shortcomings. Their discussion of Jack brought them rushing back. He watched the play of light and shadow on the ceiling, thinking how the rise and fall of illumination mirrored the highs and lows of his life. The only difference was that his life held more darkness and the brief flashes were fewer and farther between. Most of the time, he felt choked by the shadow of failure: as a father, as a husband, as a musician.

Failures to fall asleep even, although he realized that he must have dozed off several times. At some undisclosed hour, he found himself staring once more at the lights on the ceiling as some late night cab driver or poor worker on their way to the graveyard shift passed the apartment. They came and went with just a few seconds of respite between each one.

Eventually, one of the lights splashed across the ceiling and refused to budge. Rick grew increasingly impatient in the brightened room. *An Uber driver or delivery man*, he thought, tossing about on the cushions. *C'mon, dude. Just drop off your pad thai, or your bachelor party, or whatever, and move on. Please?*

The light refused to budge for several more minutes. When it did, it did not slink off past the window, as the others had. Rather, it slowly shrank, coalescing into a tiny, focused spotlight on the ceiling.

No, Rick thought, the first tinge of anxiety sweeping over him. *No, it can't be. I left you back in Ellijay. Fuck off.* No matter how Rick protested, however, the spotlight refused to depart. To the contrary, it began sweeping across the ceiling in a broad arc, then—Rick didn't know exactly how to describe it—it *popped off the wall*, changing from a two-dimensional spotlight into a three dimensional, glowing yellow sphere that descended into the kitchen. It should have illuminated the cabinets but failed to do so. Rather than anything physical, it looked more like a hole cut in reality.

Rick wanted to launch off the couch, rush into the bedroom, and rouse Bora. When he tried to move, however, he found himself completely incapable. Every part of him had become heavy, immobile. It felt as though he were sinking into the couch. The sensation of paralysis, coupled with the surging adrenaline in his limbs, became excruciating. Inside, every fiber of his being wanted to move, yet outwardly he remained still. He could not even yell for help. The only thing he could control were his eyes.

He watched the orb drift from the kitchen towards the couch. Each passing foot made the surroundings change and warp in strange ways: as the orb grew larger, the apartment above, below, and to the sides shrank, almost as if Rick was looking through a fisheye lens. The effect became so pronounced that before long the light dominated his vision, the surroundings turning to the barest hint of pale blue on all sides.

The only thing Rick could do was press his eyes shut. However, the orb either grew so bright or drew so near that his vision became a field of red, the illumination piercing his eyelids. Pressing his eyes tighter, a familiar sound filled the room: the incessant buzzing heard just days earlier, when the creature had approached him in the kitchen.

Rick refused to open his eyes. As before, he lost all sense of time. Eventually, he became vaguely aware of a drop in pressure, primarily along the back of his body. Although he knew it was impossible, Rick felt as though he were flying, like he had levitated from the couch as effortlessly as a gust of wind might lift a feather. There was the sensation of an ever-increasing distance between himself—or a *part* of himself—and the cushions, a feeling that persisted long after he should have reached the ceiling.

An image flashed in his mind's eye. It was a third person perspective above his own body on the couch, as if his point of view had somehow separated from the rest of him. Looking down, Rick was surprised to find himself looking peaceful if rigid. His arms lay straight by his sides, his face wearing a calm expression, his eyes shut gently.

Oh God, oh God, what the fuck is happening? he panicked. *Am I dead? Is that me, dead, on the couch? I am so sorry, Bora, you don't deserve to find me like this. Oh, fuck...*

The resulting dissociation made it feel as if the very fabric of reality had been ripped asunder. There was the impression of being stuck between the like poles of two gigantic magnets repelling each other, a kind of frictionless, invisible force barely held in check. Rick sensed his consciousness—the very essence of his being—slipping over the edge of reality, like a seafarer's ship tumbling off the map, over the threshold of a flat earth. *Hic sunt dracones.*

A peculiar thought entered Rick's mind, if he even had one at this point. It was a voice, completely alien, the same he had heard back in September when he saw the lights in the sky: *Everything is a construct. Your life is a story, Rickard Coulter. You are in Chapter 18, page 172. Your destiny has been plotted out for you. You cannot resist the inevitable.*

The voice abruptly cut off as a burning hot pain lanced through Rick's entire body. Involuntarily, he opened his eyes to the blinding light—

—the late morning sun poured in through the balcony window. Rick felt atrocious. His head pounded, his mouth was bone dry, and his contacts might as well have been strips of sandpaper. Squinting and shielding his eyes from the sunlight, he barely perceived a bird flutter away from its perch on the metal railing and off into the clear October sky.

Another day, another hangover, Rick thought as he swung his legs to the floor. *I didn't think I had that much last night.* He looked at the half-empty bottle of Everclear. *Not much less than I remembered. Doesn't take a lot of that stuff, though.*

Bora was long gone. As he walked into the kitchen, he noticed that, thankfully, she had left behind half a pot of coffee. He rooted around in the cabinet, searching for a mug, only to withdraw his hand after touching the sharp blade of a blender lying loose from its pitcher.

"Ow," Rick said aloud. "For Chrissake, Bora, put your shit away—"

As he looked at the cut on his thumb, memories began flooding back. He instantly recalled the light, the buzzing, the levitation, and seeing his own body. Along with these came new images: a flat, metallic surface beneath him, a dimly lit dome above; spindly bodies topped by long, teardrop-shaped faces, ashy gray, with bottomless black pools for eyes; a needle, pausing millimeters from his eyeball before thrusting forward.

Below it all lingered snippets of an unremembered message. Rick only retained two words: "life" and "death."

Rick had to brace himself on the countertop to keep from collapsing. He found himself retching. "It was a dream," he whispered through the gags. "You left all that in Ellijay. It was..." Rick looked to the couch and remembered that he had fallen asleep in a completely different direction. When he awoke, his feet were towards the window. "You got up," he continued. "You got up to use the bathroom and laid back down differently. That's all."

Rick stomped to the bathroom and promptly vomited into the toilet. When he finished, he flushed and turned on the faucet, cleaning his face with cold water. It refreshed and calmed him a bit. Grasping both sides of the sink, he looked up at his dripping reflection in the mirror. He had lost weight. It would have been a welcome sight under other circumstances, but Rick realized that, prior to visiting Bora, he hadn't been eating like he should. Most of his diet was liquid.

His eyes drifted to his clothes. Something was wrong. He remembered falling asleep in one of his Rib Wrenches tee shirts, but the logo was nowhere to be seen, just a solid swathe of black fabric. Rick looked over his shoulder. His shirt was reversed. A quick inspection revealed that the gym shorts he wore to bed were the same. Cautiously pulling the elastic waistband from his body, Rick saw not the fly but rather the seat of his boxers. His socks were also inverted.

Rick steadied himself in the bathroom doorway, clutching the frame with white knuckles. It had followed him here. Whatever it was —he was more confused than ever— was not confined to Red Ear Mountain, nor Ellijay, nor Gilmer County. It had followed him all the way to Atlanta, to the big city, the heart of modernity. It was inescapable.

"*Rickard Coulter....*" Rick flinched as a faint whisper barely reached his ears before fading into oblivion.

"Why did you follow me?!?" he shouted at the empty apartment. "What do you want? Can you just come out and say it, once and for all? You can't just expect me to know. Otherwise, I am *beyond done* with this shit." He listened intently for a reply, but only heard the clock.

Returning to the couch, Rick searched his mind for any hint that might explain what was going on. Edna's property itself didn't seem to be haunted, that was apparent enough. Was he possessed? Rick didn't believe in demons, but his beliefs didn't seem to matter much anymore. Was that it? Demons? What else could appear as a goblin one minute and an extraterrestrial the next?

Fuck, Rick realized. *Am I an alien abductee now?* Years prior, he had openly scoffed at the inbred hillbillies and burned-out hippies who seriously entertained such things. But he couldn't deny his inverted clothing nor the incredibly vivid memories—*No, Rick, it was a dream*—playing out through his head.

Hours later, Bora arrived to find Rick sleeping on the couch. Although she made no effort to wake him, her presence still slowly brought him back to consciousness. He sat up, rubbed his eyes, and simply sat there without acknowledging her.

"Hey, sleepyhead," she said, busily shuffling around the apartment from the kitchen to the bedroom and back again, smoking her vape all the way. "You would not *believe* what happened at work today. This older dude—I guess he was maybe in his seventies?—he walks in, without a mask, mind you, and asks where all the hand sanitizer is. And I, like, can't *even* right now, because I'm trying to fill out these nine prescriptions that people are waiting for, and he comes up to the counter and is just asking over and over again. Finally, he—get this—he tries to leap across the counter, because he says that we're *hoarding* the hand sanitizer. Can you believe that? Seven months into this thing, and people still—"

At last she noticed her friend's expression. "Rick," she asked, "are you okay?"

Rick stared out the balcony window. "Bora," he managed at last, his voice sounding dry and brittle. "It's here."

"What's here?"

"The... the things. I heard a voice again today. Have you heard anything strange? Or... have you noticed anything is missing? Earlier today I went to charge my phone, I couldn't find my charger, I *know* I brought it because I've been using it, but now it's nowhere, not in my bag, not anywhere out here, and I didn't want to go into your bedroom but I had to, I borrowed an extra cord of yours—"

"Rick," Bora said, holding up her hands. "I just got way too high way too fast for you to start talking like me. I can't believe I'm the one saying this, but *slow down.* I haven't heard anything, and everything of mine is just where I left it. Whatever was bothering you in Ellijay is not here, understand?"

"They were here last night."

Bora's eyebrows steepled in concern. "Rick... nothing happened last night, buddy."

"They were *here*, Bora."

"I was too, and I didn't see or hear anything," she said, stepping towards the couch. "It was just a nightmare. That's all."

"*No*," Rick said emphatically, finally looking to his friend. "They were here. Last night. They took me."

"*Took* you?" she repeated, puffing away.

Rick rubbed his face. "I know this is going to sound crazy but... but I think I was abducted."

Bora laughed, a puff of marijuana smoke escaping her lungs. When Rick's expression remained the same, she stopped and said, "Wait—you're fucking with me, right?"

"A light came into the apartment and lifted me off the couch," Rick explained, standing up and pacing. "There was light, light everywhere, so bright I couldn't even look at it. I was taken somewhere, experimented on."

"And you... remember all this?"

"Yes. No. Well, snippets, really." He stopped pacing to look at Bora. "I remember the light. I remember floating. I remember seeing my body—"

"Wait," Bora interjected. "You had an *out-of-body experience*?" Rick stayed silent. "I mean, what, did you get into my ketamine? If you want to get high, Rick, just ask me—"

"No, I didn't 'get into your fucking ketamine.' I'm telling you, something took me last night."

Bora's eyes drifted to the Everclear bottle. "Look, man... I didn't want to say anything but... maybe you should start taking it easy."

"Take what easy?"

"What do you think? The *booze*, Rick. As long as I've known you, you've been a partier, but it's never been like this. You're going to kill yourself."

"Thanks, Bora, I really appreciate that," Rick sniped sarcastically. "I've already got one woman nagging me about my fucking drinking, I don't need another."

"Did it ever occur to you that Cassie might be right, Rick?" asked Bora. "Either you'll stop drinking, or it'll stop you. It's going to catch up with you sooner or later. It catches up with everybody."

"Bull*shit*. I've got good genetics. My father drank all his life. It never caught up with *him*."

Bora's mouth dropped open. "Your *father?*" she shouted. "*That's* who you want to compare yourself to? That monster who beat you so hard he broke your fucking arm?"

"Bora," Rick started, his face turning red, "that's not the point—"

"Oh no, Rick, it *is* the point. Can you really say it didn't catch up to him? Did I miss something? Did we just suddenly erase the events of the past eight years from history? Do you not remember what he did to himself?"

She allowed the question to hang there for a moment before continuing. "How can you sleep on *my* couch, out of work, your family estranged, and say it hasn't *already* caught up with you? For years, I've put up with your perfectionist, judgmental bullshit, but this is new. Now you can't even control *yourself!*"

"Everything I care about is out of my control!" he shot back. "My whole life has been that way. My whole life, there have only been two things I *can* control: how well I play and how drunk I get. So *that's* what I do."

Bora headed for her bedroom. "Stellar fucking résumé," she said. "No wonder you don't have a real job."

"You want to talk character flaws, Bora?" asked Rick, following her to the short hallway. "Wanna play this game? How about you? Every time a relationship shows the slightest bit of trouble, you head for the hills. Is that what happened to Hope? Did she not get along with Daddy, like Claudio? Or was it like Sofia, she showed too many signs of commitment? Sometimes I wonder: if our friendship ever hit the slightest speedbump, would you even make time for *me?* Hell, that's the reason I didn't call ahead when I came over here. You would have found a reason to bail."

Bora, who had her back to him this whole time, turned around in her bedroom doorway, tears in her eyes. "Fuck you, Rick," she whispered, then slammed the door behind her.

Rick stood there for a moment, looking at the door, immediately regretting everything he had said, hoping she would open it again. When she didn't, he meandered back to the couch and sat down, wallowing in a mixture of pity and righteous indignation. The only sound was the clock on the wall, ticking down the minutes.

After about forty-five of those passed, Bora emerged, eyes red. She flopped down beside him. "Ordered pizza," she muttered. "You dick."

"I'm sorry, Bora," he offered. "I'm just… scared. And frustrated. I don't know who I'd be if I quit drinking."

Bora reached out and squeezed his hand. "You'd be Rick Coulter. The most talented guy I've ever met." She smiled. "Also the biggest asshole I ever met, but those two usually go hand in hand."

"Birds of a feather, huh?" Rick smiled, giving her a light punch on the shoulder. "Bora, I may be an asshole. I may be a drunk. But I'm not crazy." When she remained silent, he asked: "How's your phone?"

"What?"

"I said, 'your phone.' Take it out." Rick watched as Bora walked over to the bar and dug into her pocketbook.

"What about it?" she asked, holding it aloft.

"Tell me what percentage your battery is at."

Bora rolled her eyes and thumbed the power button. "It's… twenty percent?" She looked at Rick, then back at the screen. "That's impossible, I charged it all day at work, I…"

Rick leaned back on the couch, slightly smirking in pyrrhic victory. "Probably dropped the moment you walked through the door," he declared. "I'm telling you, Bora. *Something* is happening. It's *not* all just in my head."

Bora gently placed her phone on the bar. "You getting drunk tonight?" she asked.

"No. Don't want to prove you right. You going to throw me out?"

"No," she sighed, heading to the bedroom to charge her phone. "For the same reason."

19

Wednesday, October 11, 1922

A CHANCE TO CHANGE

"It worked," John O'Flanagan cried, stepping inside the run-down farmhouse. The owner wordlessly stepped aside and gestured for John to come and warm himself by the fire. "Scarce can I believe it, but it worked, sir."

The Man remained silent. He sat down in an old, rickety chair opposite his visitor, who waited expectantly for acknowledgement. John always felt anxious in his company. The Man could not have been more than twenty-five, and looked appropriately healthy and young: thin, muscular, with piercing brown eyes and a shock of hair to match. But he had the demeanor of a person three times his age. He moved slowly. He knew secrets no one else remembered nor cared to know. He was quick to listen yet slow to speak, and he rarely entertained company except on official business.

John took in his surroundings as his host silently packed and lit his pipe. Like its owner, the house was much newer than it appeared. A layer of grime coated everything, and various cooking implements and clothes littered the floor. A few spare chickens came and went as they pleased through the open back door, squawking, pecking, and shitting as if they owned the place.

It was sad to see the house in such a state. John remembered this building in its heyday, though he never called on its owners. Everyone in County Westmeath had always spoken well of The Family, who seemed for the longest time to be the model of Christian living. Kind, generous, and hard workers to boot. For neither the first nor the last time, John wondered what calamity could have befallen them.

The only tidy spot on the ground floor was the corner furthest from the fireplace, which The Man kept immaculate. Even the chickens knew better than to tread there. Instead, the space was occupied by a table heaped with herbs, supporting a large mortar and pestle and a stack of crockery. Pushed against the table was a chair supporting a tall walking stick. A large cabinet served as the tableau's centerpiece. John only knew a little of what it contained: remedies, potions, and unassuming baubles with varying degrees of occult potency. He always wondered what other arcane ephemera might lurk in its furthest recesses.

After three puffs, The Man finally spoke. "Which method?" he asked, his bristly mustache twitching with the words. His voice, like the rest of him, was deep and weathered with unearned age.

John cleared his throat. "I tried the first. Seemed simplest. I wrote the alphabet on a scrap of paper, all twenty-six, held it underneath Caoimhe's nose, and lit it aflame."

"And?" asked The Man.

"Not a thing, sir. That's when I knew it had to be that shifty character what arrived from out Trismore way. You recall I mentioned him? All dark and swarthy, that one. If t'weren't him, I didn't know who was to blame for the evil eye. For luck, my neighbors held a dance last night. And would you believe it? *He* was there. So I wait until he's in line for punch, and I creep up behind him, all shnakey like, and snip off a bit of his coattail. Right proud of my subterfuge. I rushed straight home, ran into the barn, and held it beneath Caoimhe's nose. The moment the smoke reached her she changed."

The Man nodded. "No longer listless, I take it? Her milk has returned?"

"Oh she's grand, sir, in the whole of her health. I could not be happier for her. This last week she's been like a tree over a blessed well. Now she's jolly as the day she was calved."

"Then our business has concluded," The Man proclaimed, rising from his chair. "I'm pleased I could assist." With that, he ushered his client to the door, though not before pocketing a steep fee. John didn't mind.

Before The Man shut the door behind him, John took a chance and hesitantly spoke once more. His curiosity demanded it. "Thank you again," he stammered. "I don't know what I would have done without your intercession." The Man mumbled something and began closing the door. John stopped it with a swift hand. "If I might ask... how might I come by this knowledge myself?"

Even though the day was fair and crisp, John thought for a moment that a cloud had drifted over the sun. He then realized that it was only The Man's demeanor which had darkened. The two stared at each other for a few moments before The Man answered. "You don't want it," he replied.

"But... say I did?"

By now, The Man's face bore a curious expression, a mix of frustration and sadness with the germ of anger. "When I was but a child, I lived in this very house," he said at last, gazing up at the weather-beaten walls. "I was not a year old when *they* took me." John's eyes grew wide as The Man continued. "I remember little before then, nor do I know much of what transpired during my time among *them*. My mother always said I returned... different. Knew things no one else did. Secrets kept hidden to all others. The song of birds became like conversation. I knew when it would rain, when someone was going to die... when my kin died."

"Forgive me, sir, for pressing the matter: how did your family pass?" John hazarded. "I remember them all healthy and hale."

The Man, once The Child, began closing the door. "*They* don't take kindly to interference. I have other business to attend to. Good day, O'Flanagan. Give my regards to Caoimhe." The final words were muffled as the door shut tightly, leaving the poor farmer to wander home, deep in thought.

The Man waited until he was sure John had passed beyond the borders of the property before returning to his day. Next, he busied himself in the small garden alongside the house, gathering vegetables to support him through the long winter he knew would come. The garden was a source of shame for The Man. This land was meant for so much more. From time to time, he would stand up from his work, wipe his brow, and gaze out upon the overgrown fields surrounding the house. Where once there had been a vibrant farm, now the fields lay fallow, congested by snarls of tall, thick grass and brambles. The only patch of earth retaining its original purpose was this tiny subsistence garden. The rest belonged to *them*.

It was well enough. Much of The Man's work relied on staying in *their* good graces.

As the day progressed, other visitors dropped by seeking advice and assistance. Some he gave for free, others he charged (the ones he knew could afford it). The entire country felt troubled, nowadays—not just the civil unrest but the citizenry as well. A wife came to alleviate her husband's dropsy. A father came for a remedy to soothe his daughter's fever. Yet another, explaining his predicament, revealed a bigger project: he had foolishly failed to consult The Man about where to build his home, and now it stood over one of *their* pathways. The Man agreed to help, but it was a greater endeavor than he could attend to today. Come back tomorrow.

At last, arms weak and knees sore, The Man retired inside as night fell across the farm. Because of his sensitivity, the days leading up to Samhain became too potent to be caught outside after dark. It was best to simply stay in front of the fire and smoke his pipe, remembering how much joy and laughter once echoed across the hearth.

After a time, a knock came at the door, weak and pathetic. The Man had made it known far and wide that he preferred visitors in the light of day unless it was an emergency. Grumbling to himself, he went and opened the door.

A large, bulbous figure of a middle-aged man stood at the doorstep, his balding head and beady eyes both glinting in the moonlight, the former enhanced by a sheen of sweat. Barely visible under his thick neck was the white trim of a clerical collar. "Father Cormick," The Man said without subsequent greeting.

"My apologies for calling upon you at this hour," he wheezed, his face contorted with anxiety. "I have committed a grave sin."

"Sins are your domain," countered The Man. "I only remedy ailments and mistakes."

Father Cormick looked at the ground, wringing his hands. "I pray we can put our past differences aside to assist a poor soul in need. Might I come in? The subject is"—he looked around the house for anyone eavesdropping—"right dire."

Long ago, The Man had sworn a private oath to himself to never let the lecherous priest darken his doorstep. "If it's said within these walls, it's heard outside as well," he slowly intoned. "Get on with it."

Before explaining his predicament, Cormick fretted for a second, as if he might insist on entering. "We are only human, you know. Even myself. I had a moment of weakness. Who can resist when the enemy comes for you in such a beguiling form? Even you, in your solitude, must comprehend these... failings. Two months past, one of my flock, this, this *Jezebel*, she lingered after Mass and—"

The Man doubled over in ribbons. When at last he recovered from laughing, he exclaimed, "Up the frock of the flock, is it? 'The enemy!'" He spat at Cormick's feet. "You'd know the enemy better if you'd have a chat with him now and again. I'm sure he misses you. How old?"

Cormick squirmed for a few moments before finally speaking. "Sixteen," he said, hanging his head in shame. "She is sixteen." The Man said nothing. "Please understand that I have no one else to turn to," begged Cormick, his face turning purple. "If anyone besides the three of us finds out—yourself, myself, herself—it shall be the end of me."

"Three turns to four soon enough," The Man riposted. "How far along, you say? Two months?"

"Yes, sir," Cormick replied. He waited, obviously hoping his meaning would be understood. Instead, The Man forced him to speak the words aloud. "You apprenticed with Biddy Nally, did you not? I understand she had methods—"

"Oh, so now you approve of her?" snapped The Man. "Years of lobbing condemnation from the pulpit, and only after she's in the grave do you see her wisdom. I've every reason to slam my door, Father."

"Please!" the portly priest wailed. "Please. I humble myself before you. There is no other way! Won't you help me? Won't you help *her?*"

The Man allowed Cormick to wallow in self pity for a few moments longer before answering. "Fine, then," he conceded. "Under one condition: I speak to the girl myself."

"*Her?!?*" spat Cormick, his face turning from purple to crimson. "What's the point in that?"

"Well *you've* got a great welcome for yourself! And here I thought you had ears. I offer my services only after I speak to the girl. Your mickey's had its say; now she gets hers." The Man then slammed the door in Cormick's face and returned to the fireside, not caring if the matter developed any further.

The following day, The Man was back in his garden when a slender form came striding up the road. He was no stranger to seeing spirits, and for the longest time he simply leaned against his hoe and stared, convinced that his mother had revisited him. It had been years since she had reached out from the great beyond, and never in broad daylight. She was just as he remembered her—slightly built, with a torrent of red hair cascading around her shoulders in an unruly mess. As the girl drew nearer, The Man saw that, despite the remarkable resemblance, it was not his mother, but rather a young girl in the flesh.

"*Dia duit*," The Man finally mustered the courage to say. "How are you today, miss?"

Even beneath her white dress, she was showing. In a departure from his mother, the girl's eyes were an icy blue that perfectly complemented the autumnal sky. They flitted down to the ground as she squeaked a quiet, "Pleased to meet you. I understand Father Cormick paid a visit to you?"

"Aye," The Man said. "That one's thick as bottled shite." The girl recoiled at the words. "I'm sorry, miss. Forgive my language. I failed to catch your name."

"Kathleen," she said, looking up at last.

The Man was so arrested by her gaze that he struggled to find the words to reply. "Kathleen? I'm... I'm Cillian," he said at last. His own name felt so foreign in his mouth. He rarely took the time for pleasantries. "Please, won't you step inside? I'll fetch some water, you must be parched."

In no time, Cillian and Kathleen were both sitting by the cold fireplace. It took the girl a while to emerge from her shell, but eventually she warmed enough to share the barest details of her encounter with Cormick, all of which roughly corresponded to the priest's retelling. When she finished, Cillian asked: "Is that you speaking, or Cormick? Has he put the guilts on you?"

Kathleen pursed her lips, hung her head, and slowly shook it. "No... no, sir. That's just as it happened."

Cillian leaned forward and did his best to catch her gaze. "Kathleen, listen to me. You see that door? All manner of folk come to that door. Very few are calm and collected. When I look at you, I see the same look on your face. You look scared sideways. Is that because you're with child... or are you afraid of Cormick?"

Kathleen held her eyes on the floor. "I'm not afraid of the child. I have no desire to besmirch Father Cormick's name."

Cillian scoffed, sitting back in his chair. "Not to downplay the severity of your situation, miss, but I've heard far worse from holier men." Kathleen looked up, pools of tears clinging to the bottoms of her eyelids. "Do you want to tell me what really happened, Kathleen?" he asked.

She took a deep breath and began. "I live with my mother near Monilea. She's poorly, so I go to Mass without her each week. I'll never forget that day, much as I'd like. It was the thirteenth of August, and halfway there, it started to rain. My dress—this dress—was soaking wet by the time I reached church. I sat in the back, shivering the whole time. When Mass ended, I tarried. It was still coming down, and I wanted to wait until the rain passed. Eventually, I was the last person there. Well, me and Father Cormick, that is."

Cillian closed his eyes, not wanting to hear what came next. "He saw me there," Kathleen slowly continued. "He came up, said he would... let me dry off in the sacristy. Said he had some rags back there I could use. It was there that it happened." When Cillian opened his eyes, Kathleen's were staring directly into his. "I didn't want it," she said, increasing the pace of her speech. "No matter what he told you, it wasn't me. It was him. He's not a sound man, Cillian, he's a beast." She broke into full fledged sobs. "I didn't want it. But..." She touched a hand to her belly. "It isn't the fault of the babe."

"Kathleen," Cillian whispered, his voice small in the vacant house. "This child will be many things. Many good things, aye. But it shall be a burden as well. To raise it will require all your love and what little coin you and your mother have. Always, the child shall remind you of that day."

"I'll live with it regardless," she said, wiping the tears from her eyes. "If I do what Father Cormick wants, then that day in the sacristy... it'll just be another day for him when he got his way. His life won't change. But for me, it'll always remain the worst day of my life. Forever. If I keep it... maybe I'll just be heaping regret on top of the pain. But maybe, just *maybe*, that day will take on a different meaning. Not *good*, mind you, but... This way, that day has a chance to change."

Cillian reached out his hand. Kathleen took it. "It may not change," he countered.

"Yet it may."

Cillian sighed. "I will ask you this one time what you would have of me," he whispered. "I ask not for Father Cormick—he should be shamed from a height." Cillian glanced at his cupboard. "I have something for him later, regardless. No, I'm not asking for his sake. I'm asking for *yours*. This is *your* decision. Cormick made his. Don't be afraid of becoming a phantom washerwoman, or burning in eternal damnation, or any of that rubbish. I don't hold with such nonsense, and neither should you. This is a decision for this life, not the next. If you choose to part with the child, it will not be comfortable, but I can give you something for that as well. I ask: *Do you want this child?*"

For the first time since they met, Kathleen's face broke into the barest hint of a smile. "Yes. Yes, I do."

Cillian winced. Although part of him hoped otherwise, he expected no less from an avid churchgoer. Coupled with the naïveté of youth, it was a recipe for disaster.

In that moment, Cillian wanted to say so many things. He wanted to tell her that, even if it meant aligning with Father Cormick's wishes, he could make her life immeasurably easier, could allow her to *have* a life. He wanted to remind her of how fallen women were treated, of the conditions in the Magdalene asylums. They might be run by the church she so loved, but none of their mercy found its way there.

Nor would it extend to the broader community. He wanted to tell her that, judging her as a harlot, no man in the village would have her. That the women would judge her even worse.

He wanted to tell her how many times he had helped others in similar predicaments in the past, that there was nothing to fear. He wanted her to *thrive*, and this was not the path.

But it was her decision.

"Very well then," he sighed, standing and heading over to the cabinet.

"But," Kathleen began, "but I said I wish to keep it…"

"I heard you," Cillian said, pulling a small jar from deep within a drawer and pouring its powdery contents into a small envelope. "This is for your sickness." He added a bit more of something else. "And this," he declared, handing over the parcel, "is for the health of the child. I caution you, Kathleen: do not return to Mass. Father Cormick will know of your choice, and there will be repercussions. For both of us. He'll discover the truth eventually, but the further along you get, the better for everyone."

Kathleen held the envelope gingerly, as if it were made of glass. "I don't know what to say, Mr. Cillian. Thank you. Thank you so very much." Her diffident façade melted away, replaced with determined hope.

"You are most welcome, Kathleen," he smiled, feeling a pang of sadness as he walked her to the door. "I shall drop by Monilea soon. When I do, we'll discuss getting someone a little closer to home to help you as your condition progresses."

Kathleen flashed him a smile as she set off back down the road, looking more like his mother than ever. "Thank you," she said one final time before pausing. "Cillian... I like that." She rubbed her stomach, repeated the name, then continued on her way. Cillian remained in the doorway, watching her until she disappeared over the hill.

He was out of sorts for the remainder of the day. Several nights later, he was thinking of Kathleen, staring into the fire, when a forceful knock sounded at the door. It was Father Cormick. Cillian knew this day was coming and did his best to repeat the responses he had rehearsed in his head.

"Good evening," Cormick said, boldly squeezing past Cillian and into the house. No longer did he seem timid. "Having a nice smoke by the fireside? Got any water of life on you? Maybe some of that poteen you culchies always yammer on about?"

Cillian ignored the slur. Now was not the time to press his luck. "I'm afraid not, Father Cormick," he said, standing his ground between the entryway and the fireplace. "Might I assist you?"

The priest grinned, his teeth appearing yellower than usual in the firelight. Of all the horrendous spirits Cillian had encountered in his life, none were as horrible as that grimace on a living man. "Come now, *Cillian*. You can't be serious. I'm checking on the welfare of the girl. Katherine."

"*Kathleen*," Cillian corrected, clenching his fists. "Yes, what of her?"

"Don't be a fool. Did you take care of her?"

Cillian took a deep breath. "Aye. She wanted rid of it as well. I sent her home with a remedy. Powerful strong, I'd expect her to be bedridden for some time."

"Is that so? Good, good. When might you anticipate her recovery?"

"It depends on her constitution," he lied. "As long as half a year."

"Half the year! Well, I suppose I won't be seeing her at Mass any time soon. All for the best, I suppose." Cormick folded his arms and looked around the house. "My my, it is fit for a swine in here. Do you happen to have a Bible in the house?"

Cillian swallowed. "Somewhere. Do you wish me to fetch it?"

"No, that's alright," Cormick replied, shaking his head. "Do you ever read it? I've always found great utility in Proverbs. Are you familiar with that book?" Cillian remained silent. "19:9 says, 'A false witness shall not be unpunished, and he that speaketh lies shall perish.' That doesn't bode right well for you, does it? On top of congress with spirits, a disseminator of falsehoods as well?"

"I'm afraid I don't follow, sir," Cillian muttered. His knees were growing weak.

"'Sir'? I've never heard you call me *that*," the priest hissed. "All these years, I have tolerated your meddling with this community. Offering remedies to my congregation, all so they can be healed by false gods. By the devil. That time has passed. No longer shall you lead my flock astray." He jabbed a finger in Cillian's face. "I know what you did. Or rather, what you *didn't* do. You see, last night I visited some of my parishioners. As just so happens, I found myself down Monilea way."

Cormick swung a massive fist. Cillian took it squarely on the jaw, sending him sprawling into the refuse on the floor.

"You thought I wouldn't find out?!?" the priest asked, his bulky form towering over him. "You'll pay for this, you know!"

"I doubt you'll be in good standing either, *Father*," Cillian said before sending a gob of crimson spittle to the floor. "Tell me, how does the Church look upon bastards these days?"

Cormick crouched down low until he was inches from Cillian's face. His eyebrows raised, lifting the wrinkles of his barren scalp. "They will never know," he chuckled, his breath smelling of whisky. "I finished the task I assigned you. That girl's poor mother was too feeble to help. She didn't even get out of bed. Kathleen put up a fight, though."

The priest smiled wider. "*I beat it out of her*," he snarled.

Cillian closed his eyes and searched for words, but none sufficed. He only managed to mutter, "Monster...."

"More lies," Cormick chuckled. "I should never have sought your help in the first place. 'Be ye not unequally yoked together with unbelievers: for what fellowship hath righteousness with unrighteousness? And what communion hath light with darkness?'" With great effort, Father Cormick raised his body and plodded toward the door. Before leaving, he turned and offered one final word.

"My congregation always thought so highly of that girl. They will be horrified to learn what you did to her. Unsurprised, but horrified nonetheless. Disposing of the child *and* assaulting her? *Tsk tsk.* Hopefully some upstanding citizens report it to the authorities...."

20

Saturday, October 10, 2020

PILOT LIGHT

RICK AND JACK slipped off their facemasks and took places opposite one another at their table in the dingy diner. The worn wooden seat of the booth felt welcoming, but not because it was especially comfortable. Rather, it was pure nostalgia. The diner wasn't more than a few minutes' drive from their home in Alpharetta. Once upon a time, this crummy establishment hosted a regular Saturday morning ritual where Rick's family got together to discuss their week and plan the remainder of the weekend.

Almost feels like old times, Rick thought, taking the greasy menu from the server. He looked at the empty space beside Jack. *Minus one.*

"Seeing you twice in one week?" he said to his son, not taking his eyes off the menu. "This has got to be some sort of record, huh?" Cassie had finally eased up on her self-imposed quarantine restrictions and was surprisingly receptive to allowing more visits with Jack, now that Rick was in town.

It's probably because I am *in town,* Rick decided. *Easier to keep tabs on me.* The cynicism of the thought felt oddly out-of-place. Ever since arriving at Bora's, things had still seemed bleak—*Don't get me wrong*—but carried with them the slightest hint of hope, alien abduction be damned. Something about being in Atlanta brought clarity. Even his OCD, which raged unbound in Ellijay, found reason to subside in the barely controlled chaos of the city. Since the hustle and bustle of daily life and everything else was out of his control here, there was no urge to force anything *into* his control.

Miraculously, even Bora had proven a stabilizing influence, something Rick never expected. Knowing she would return each day kept him grounded even as whispers and giggles continued filling the apartment when she was away. As a result, he leaned on the bottle a little less these days, though still far more than he should.

Don't sell yourself short, Rick advised himself. *You've kinda sorta been behaving yourself. At least you don't answer Cassie's calls drunk anymore. That's got to count for something.*

"Dad?" said Jack. The sound of his voice brought Rick back into the moment, where he realized the server hovered patiently over them. "Dad, I said, 'What are you gonna get?'"

"Oh," Rick mumbled. The actual act of ordering hadn't even crossed his mind yet. His eyes scanned the menu. "Coffee, definitely… thinking steak and eggs. You?"

"The usual," Jack said, then looked at the server. "Country Special and a water." The combination had everything a ravenous teen desired: eggs, toast, grits, a waffle, and a choice of breakfast meat. Rick scanned the prices to make sure he had enough cash on him… Jack's meal would be eleven dollars, his own eight…

Feeling a flush of superstition, Rick cleared his throat. "Um, miss?" he asked the server before she turned to the kitchen. "On second thought, maybe I'll just get an omelet. Sorry about that." She nodded, took the menus, amended their order, and went about her business.

"I'd ask if there's anything new, but I just saw you," Rick began. "It's kind of nice for a change, right? To not have a ton to catch up on?" He glanced down at the place setting and, seeing the *fork, knife, spoon* arrangement, reordered them to *knife, spoon, fork.*

"Yeah," Jack replied at last, listlessly. He didn't seem to be any better now than he was a few days ago. After their last get together, Rick hoped that the boy's mood had been a fluke. Now, looking across the table at Jack, he recognized what he was seeing—because he saw it in himself.

His son was lethargic, and looked like he hadn't showered in days. The skin on the left side of his right thumbnail was a mangled mess of proud flesh, anxiously chewed on over the past seven months. Cassie called it Jack's "pandemic thumb," just one of countless signs that their son was slipping. Although he had never been a straight-A student, Cassie was also concerned about Jack's grades, which had steadily slipped over the past year of distance learning.

Rick completely understood Jack's despair, and even felt partially responsible. Alongside the unending isolation and the shortened track season—which included a canceled championship—Jack was left vulnerable to his father's own shortcomings. There was the debacle with the shoes and their argument back in July; hell, the separation alone could have been enough to set him on this path. Rick glanced at the backpack he borrowed from Bora, hoping that what he brought might lift the boy's spirits a bit.

"Jack," Rick said as their drinks arrived. "Are you okay, dude? You seem a little under the weather."

Jack raised his thumb and set to biting. "I guess," he said, admiring his handiwork before hiding his hand under the table. "I'm just kind of 'blah,' I guess."

"Anything I can do to help?"

"No."

"Well... can you tell me what's causing it?"

Jack shrugged. "I'm just ready for things to be normal. You and mom... my friends. I think I'd like high school, but class keeps getting canceled every time a teacher or a student gets Covid."

"I never thought I'd see you, of all kids, complaining about school getting canceled," chuckled Rick, trying to force some levity into their conversation.

Next came honesty: "I can't make any promises about me and Mom. Truth is, you probably have a better idea of where that's headed than I do, at this point. But I will stay in your life as long as I'm breathing."

Then came lies, words he knew his son needed to hear—words he didn't believe himself, though he desperately wished he did: "As for everything else... Things will get back to normal at some point, Jack. They have to. You've just got to be patient. In the meantime, you know that Mom and Dad are here for you. You can *always* talk to us."

Jack said nothing. *Probably remembering our argument*, Rick realized. If he had any idea how that exchange would have affected his son, he would have bitten his tongue clean in half.

Once their food arrived, Rick was pleased to see that Jack retained his appetite. It represented an encouraging sign that maybe he hadn't fallen into full-fledged depression yet. Their conversation included only the barest amount of small talk. As they finished up, Rick hauled the backpack onto the table.

"Before we get going," he began, unzipping the bag, "I want you to have something." Reaching inside, he pulled out a series of items, placing them on the vacant spaces of the table as quickly as possible. Within seconds, a baseball cap, t-shirt, glossy photograph, and flash drive all lay in an orderly row between the empty plates.

Jack stared at the lineup of Shit Bees swag. "Dad, I... what? How did you get all this?"

"See this guy?" asked Rick, pointing out the keyboard player in the press photograph, which was signed by the entire band. "Matt Mrozinski. Went to school with him. I think you'd call us 'frenemies.' Talented as all get out. He joined the band late last year. When I heard he was playing with them, I reached out immediately, and he just sent me all this." Rick waved his hands over the array of items. "So I lied when I told you the Shit Bees had no redeeming qualities. If they've got Matt on board, they have exactly *one* redeeming quality."

Jack laughed—a more welcome sight Rick had never seen—and smacked his father from across the table. "In all seriousness," Rick proceeded, "I gave them another listen. I spoke too soon. They're actually not bad. In fact"—he held up the flash drive—"some of the stuff on *this* is stellar."

"What is it?" Jack beamed with wonder.

"Took me a minute to figure out," explained Rick. "When you plug it in, it's just a bunch of audio files. Turns out it's a bunch of Shit Bees rehearsal recordings, including some stuff that I couldn't find on any of their track listings."

Jack's eyes gleamed like his father was holding a hundred-dollar bill. He went to snatch the flash drive, but Rick withdrew his hand. "Uh uh uh. There are conditions for this. First, don't share it with *anyone*." Jack nodded. "Next, just... try to ignore some of the language you hear." Jack chuckled. "And finally, I'm giving this to Mom. We've agreed you can have this when you get a B in Biology. Okay?" Jack looked down in disappointment, then looked back with renewed determination.

Rick pocketed the flash drive as Jack reached out his arms and swept the remaining merchandise to his side of the table. After donning his cap, his expression changed to one of regret. "Sorry I got so upset with you over a stupid band," he muttered.

"No, Jack—I was the one who overreacted," Rick offered. "I made a snap judgment because… because I haven't been doing so well."

Jack nodded gently. "Mom told me that. What's wrong?"

What do I tell him? wondered Rick. *That I'm an alcoholic? That I've spent the last year drowning in self-pity? That I'm experiencing the same thing that he is, and I'm flirting with suicide?... That his father is under attack by goblins, or an alien abductee?*

Finally, Rick said, "… a lot… of things. I can't talk about them— I'm not in trouble with the law or anything, it's just complicated adult stuff. It's part of why I snapped at you that day." He stopped to take the check from the server. "Let me see… do you know what a pilot light is, Jack?"

Jack shook his head, so Rick explained. "Furnaces and water heaters, especially the older ones, they have a flame that stays lit all the time. When you turn up the heat, gas hits the pilot light, and the water gets heated. This one, tiny flame keeps everything warm and cozy throughout the entire house."

"What if it goes out?" his son asked.

Rick chuckled, handing over his money. "You've got to relight it and pray that the gas hasn't been leaking the whole time. Lost plenty of arm hair that way."

"… okay. Why are we talking about this?"

"Being an adult… being a *parent*… you're kind of like the pilot light. You're responsible for bringing warmth to the rest of the family. But sometimes that little light, it goes out. And because of that, you fail to do the one thing you were meant to do. You leave everyone else huddled in the dark. Shivering. Alone."

Jack nodded. "So… what's your pilot light, Dad? And why is it out?"

"It's probably something different for everyone," Rick pondered, taking the change back from the server. "Probably *a couple of* things for most people. For me, it was—it *is*—music. And you. I haven't had a lot of that in my life this year, and that's made everything else worse."

The two of them stood from the table and wandered out to the parking lot towards the Corolla, Rick with the empty backpack,

Jack clutching the band swag. At long last, the trees were starting to lose their luster, the barest tint of autumnal color bleeding into each leaf like a slow-developing bruise. When they reached the car, the boy spoke up.

"Do you think it'll come back on?"

"What?"

"Your pilot light."

"It's starting to," Rick said, making a point to smile at his son. He hopped inside and turned the ignition. "Days like today? It's starting to."

21

Tuesday, April 15, 1986

FANTOCCINI

ONCE UPON A TIME, there was a young girl who loved playing in the woods.

When she arrived that first morning, she bolted out of her father's car like a bird dog on the opening day of hunting season. Months of energy, pent up after a long, snowy winter, propelled her straight towards the forest's edge. Her father yelled after her: "Not too far, Mary. I'm just checking on the boys, I won't be long."

"Yes, Daddy!" she replied, disappearing into the tree line. The last thing her father saw was a streak of hair, red as a cardinal's breast, darting between two blooming dogwoods. Although her father harbored mild apprehension at her wandering in the woods alone, it was far safer than playing near the craggy cliffs of the quarry or along the road, where dump trucks full of ore rolled by every few minutes. Besides, she always returned soaking wet and caked in mud, so he knew exactly where she would be: a small creek no more than two hundred yards uphill.

Mary made her way deeper into the woods, clambering over small boulders jutting out from the mountainside. For her, the forest was like a playground nestled at the bottom of some secret garden, full of inviting paths to explore and new things to see with every change of season.

Everything was alive. March may have come in like a lion and out like a lamb, but that designation was too meek to describe April in Spruce Pine. Like Mary, everything displayed renewed vigor, from the trees and flowers to the birds and animals, sending an almost electric charge into the air as thick as the pollen itself. Mary listened to how her own footfalls added to the aural tapestry of the forest: the birds belting like opera divas, the rustle of trees overhead, the nearby babble of water, and the deep rumble of distant mining equipment undergirding it all.

At last she reached the creek. It was deeply eroded, with high banks towering on either side. The waters flowed gently downhill, always in a hurry to reach their destination but never arriving, instead stuck in perpetual movement. Although the green canopy above had darkened most of the surface, here and there renegade sunrays evaded the leaves to make their way to the ground, transmuting both the creek and the surrounding underbrush into a lace doily of warm spring sunlight.

It was a serene scene—perfect for an eight-year-old tomboy to wreck. Mary leapt into the stream from the high embankment, sending a curtain of cold water in all directions. When the ripples at last subsided, so did she. Mary was on a mission. Her eyes scanned the surface, looking for the slightest sign of movement. From the corner of her eye, she spotted a slight ripple under the water.

Mary pounced with the dexterity of a wildcat, burying her paw in the stream. When it emerged, it held the back of a crawdad, waving its claws in futile protest, as if conducting some silent symphony. Fully soaked, Mary tromped a bit further downstream where the banks lowered, and sat down upon an inviting rock.

There she stayed, examining the creature. She picked up a twig and allowed it to take hold, testing the strength of its claws. When her curiosity was satisfied, Mary replaced the crawdad close to where she found it. As she watched it scuttle beneath a rock, Mary thought how much her little brother would enjoy this. She couldn't wait to bring him here. In a few years, Mommy and Daddy told her, they would let her supersize—*What was the word?*—supervise him.

Mary was searching for more wildlife when something broke her concentration. She was not alone in the forest. Someone was beyond the bank above, whistling an awkward tune unlike anything Mary had ever heard. She realized it was probably a worker taking a stroll on an early lunch break, but in her mind she decided it was the huntsman, escorting Snow White. Carefully, she peered over the bank and into the forest.

In a stark contrast to the vibrancy experienced minutes earlier, the forest was now quiet and still. Not even a breeze tickled the trees. As Mary watched, the whistling stopped. She looked from tree to tree, hoping to catch a glimpse of whoever it was. As the moments stretched on with no one in sight, Mary became slightly uneasy.

A bit of movement alongside a tree maybe fifty yards away caught her attention. Eyes glued to the trunk, she watched the right side of a face peep out from four feet above the ground, then withdraw again. She watched. It did not reappear.

Then, from a tree half that distance, another face—*The same face?*—reappeared in the same motion. Mary's unease blossomed into mild anxiety. Was someone spying on her?

"Hello?" she called. No answer. "Is somebody there?"

From behind the tree, a figure rushed at Mary, its legs rapidly pinwheeling. At first, she thought it was running. But Mary instantly realized two bizarre details: it traveled far too slowly for how fast its legs moved, and its feet did not touch the ground. Instead, it floated towards her until it stopped at the creekside, looking down at her.

At first, Mary wanted to run and scream, but the thing simply looked too silly to be frightening. For all the world, it resembled a marionette, down to the thick joints that allowed its clunky arms and legs to pivot. Mary looked beyond the figure and up into the canopy, hoping to find a puppeteer clinging to a branch. Seeing no one, she returned to the figure.

It was dressed in long-sleeved motley from its feet to its neck. Above this multicolored patchwork hung a white, androgynous, porcelain face, bearing a slight smile and a pair of large eyes frozen in perpetual surprise. The eyes themselves were completely black, like a doll's. A jester's hat topped the whole affair, though it lacked any bells to jingle.

"Are—are you a puppet?" asked Mary.

The thing replied in a thin, singsong voice, although its lips did not move. They remained locked in their beatific position. "I know I am a sight to see, but please forgive the state of me. I'm not a liar—if you desire, a puppet for you I shall be."

The rhyming was so silly, so convoluted, it sent Mary into giggles. "You talk funny," she laughed. "Do you live out here? What's your name?"

"Folks come through, they never see me. No one would ever choose to be me. I'm filled with fear, it's lonely here... You can call me 'Fantoccini.'"

Mary smiled, revealing a missing tooth. "Hi, Mr. Fantoccini," she greeted, hauling herself out of the creek. She stood and extended a hand. "My name is Mary. I'm eight."

Fantoccini cocked its head and reached out. The hand was cold to the touch, without the slightest hint of strength behind it.

At that moment, Mary's father called for her. "Mary! Time to head home for lunch!"

"That's Daddy," Mary sighed, releasing the hand. "I have to go home."

The marionette drooped and hung its head, but its expression remained unchanged. "I saw you in the riverbend. I do so hope you come again. Go get your snack, and hurry back. Won't you, Mary, be my friend?"

"Don't worry, Fantoccini," Mary called as she skipped away. "I'll be back!"

When she reached the road, Mary's father scolded her for being so filthy. Luckily, he had the foresight to bring a towel. He cleaned and dried her off enough to ride home. The whole way back, Mary talked about her new friend, though her father paid the rantings of a child little mind. Besides, he was too preoccupied with work at the mine.

Several days later, Mary begged to accompany her father as he made his rounds at work once again. When she arrived at the forest, she found Fantoccini sitting on a fallen log across the stream.

"Fantoccini!" she exclaimed as she crawled past the ferns and down onto the creek bed. "What are you doing up *there*, silly goose?"

Her friend looked to either side, then recited: "I must look silly, it is true. But rarely I meet someone new. When you left, I was bereft, so here I sat to wait for you!" With that, Fantoccini's hands tinkled as they came together in a limp pantomime of clapping.

"Well, you can't stay up there all day," Mary scolded, rooting around in the silt. "I'm on a quest for salamanders today. Want to help?"

Fantoccini nodded. The gesture pitched the weight of its body, however, throwing the puppet head over heels, splashing into the water. Mary rushed to Fantoccini's side, pulling it from the mud.

"Are you okay?" she asked. Her friend nodded, and the two of them laughed as it shakily rose to its feet.

Mary then began sharing all the telltale signs she had learned over the years of searching for critters in the creek, like how salamanders preferred resting underneath debris where the water pooled up most. She had read that it wasn't good to handle them, but she saw no problem with Fantoccini holding them, since its hands were fashioned of porcelain. The puppet accepted its mission with alacrity, singing questions as they went. It proved an apt pupil, fishing salamanders out of the water for Mary to inspect closer than she ever had been able to before.

After around an hour, Mary's father called from the road once again. "Bye, Fantoccini!" she said, tumbling downhill. "See you later!"

Mary was back the following day, with Fantoccini waiting in its appointed position along the log. "Do you want to look for more critters?" she asked, heading down into the creek. "I thought maybe we could find frogs today."

The puppet stretched a wobbly arm to the forest. "Though creeks are full of treasures rare, to what I have they can't compare. Meet me up here, my Mary dear—I have a special gift to share!"

Mary stopped her descent and grabbed an exposed root to haul herself back onto the embankment. Then Fantoccini shuffled to the opposite side of the creek, waving for the girl to follow it. After carefully navigating the log, Mary paraded behind the puppet deeper into the sea of greenery, though still within eyesight of the creek. She was glad Fantoccini didn't run; whenever it ran, it lifted off the ground, and Mary had never quite gotten used to that.

Eventually, Fantoccini abruptly lurched to a halt, then flopped down onto a stump. When Mary neared, she noticed eight piles of flat stones surrounding her friend in a perfect circle, each stacked no more than two feet high. It looked almost like a little village. "What is this?" the girl asked.

"Homes and houses you have got. The likes of me? Well, I have not. Unlike you, I must make do; this place here's my *special* spot."

"Is it where you live?"

"I live far, too far to roam. When I'm out here, I'm all alone. While out this way, so you could say, this is my home away from home."

Mary nodded. "Is this what you wanted to show me?"

Fantoccini shook its head mechanically, sunlight glinting off its gleaming face. With great purpose, it raised its left hand. As it did so, the cairns began glowing, coalescing until a luminous sphere of pure light surmounted each rock pile.

Mary's eyes widened. She had never seen something so fantastic—even an animated marionette. Fantoccini then raised its other hand, at which the eight lights began traversing the circle counterclockwise. Bringing its hands together, the lights followed suit, combining their intensity into one massive ball of fire that shrank until it was the size of a golf ball, though its brightness never diminished. Next, the orb danced over to Mary. She reached out an open hand, letting the light playfully outline the contours of her fingers.

Fantoccini lowered its arms. "A gift for you, of five and three. Don't ever let your parents see. Take this today, to light your way, whenever you might visit me."

Mary watched the little light wink out of existence. Then came the sound which always heralded an end to their visits. "Mary!" her father bellowed.

Before leaving, she ran up and gave the puppet a hug. It smelled peculiar, like how the flowers started smelling towards the end of her mother's hospital stays. "Thank you, Fantoccini. I will see you soon!"

Mary didn't realize it at the time, but she lied. A business trip had taken her father out of town for the better part of a week. During that time, Mary fretted endlessly about her promise to Fantoccini, hoping that her friend wouldn't forget about her while she was away. Her concerns were only slightly alleviated by the little light, which appeared every evening as she lay in bed to dance around the ceiling until she fell asleep.

When at last her father returned on the first of May, Mary begged him to take her to the quarry. He was in a sour mood, and forbade her to go. At last he relented, but the concession came with a price: this was to be her last visit. The quarry was no place for a girl, he said, cursing himself for being foolish enough to let her come in the first place. He had tolerated her woodland roving for far too long.

The ride over to the quarry ended in a full-fledged shouting match that sent Mary into hysterics. The moment the car was parked, she was out the door, fleeing into the forest.

Soon, Fantoccini noticed her climbing the hill in tears, her long, red hair covering her face. The little light bobbed before her, guiding her towards the puppet's location. In its floating fashion, Fantoccini ran to her, brushing her hair from her eyes.

"For your friendship, I feel blessed. My dear, you're different from the rest. I don't know why, but when you cry, I begin to feel distressed."

Mary sniffled and managed a smile. Although its face was perpetually locked in the same expression, she felt in that moment Fantoccini did as well. Her friend continued: "Usually, you laugh and leap! Any secret, I can keep. Tell me now—who, what, or how—why, my dear, does Mary weep?"

"Daddy," she began. "He yelled at me. He told me that I can't come see you anymore." She threw her arms around the puppet, which ineptly patted her back with short, halting movements. "Fantoccini, I don't know what to do. I don't want to say goodbye."

A long moment passed. Fantoccini spoke, still with its characteristic lilt, but its cadence was slower, more measured. "I know a place dads never yell. Its quite nearby, just up the dell. My mum's there too, she knows 'bout you, and loves to meet my friends as well."

"Really?" Mary sniffed. "Can I come visit for a while? That sounds nice." As if taking a command, Fantoccini whirled about on its heel and began tromping through the dead leaves. Mary wavered a moment before falling in line behind it. Maybe if she was gone for a while, her father would experience a change of heart. Realize that he shouldn't take her for granted, that these visits into the woods by the quarry meant everything to her.

The pair wandered through the woods away from the creek, the tiny ball of light hovering between them like a faithful dog. After about ten minutes, they reached the tiny dell, an old, dry stream channel tracing its way through a series of moderate hillocks on the mountainside. The further they traveled uphill, the more it seemed to Mary as if the trees on either side began leaning in, narrowing their path into a claustrophobic tunnel. The green of spring gave way to the russet hues of autumn, making the entire journey feel like a trek through the seasons until, at last, the trees were completely barren and so close to one another that they formed an impenetrable wall on both sides.

After a long time, the path terminated in a sheer wall of rock. Mary knew it had to be the face of the mountain. There was the slightest cleft where the old spring must have seeped up years ago before running down through the dell.

"Where do we go now?" asked Mary, looking at her guide. "It's just a rock." Fantoccini said nothing. It simply waved a hand over the girl's face. Immediately, Mary perceived a low, soft rumbling beneath her feet, like the very roots of the mountain were twisting and shifting in the bedrock. Looking back to the stone wall, she watched in amazement as the cleft widened, shaking and trembling, until it became an open doorway only slightly taller than Mary and her companion. She could perceive very little within, only the slightest hint of torchlight in the black chasm beyond.

Mary hesitated. All of a sudden, she had a deep desire to return home. Sensing this, Fantoccini sang: "There sits the household of my kin. A grander place, there's never been. We've food and drink, enough I think, if Mary would but step within."

"I probably shouldn't stay too long," she admitted, taking a step inside. "Do you think I will be home for supper?" She waited for Fantoccini's singsong response as it followed behind her. When it failed to speak, Mary turned and looked at her friend, its black eyes appearing cavernous in the dim light. "I asked if you think I'll be home for supper?"

"*No*," Fantoccini replied, its voice deeper, completely stripped of all levity. "*No, you will not.*"

22

Saturday, October 17, 2020

DEVLIN AT THE CROSSROADS

WHEN THE LITTLE CIRCLE FLASHED BLOOD RED, Rick half expected it to issue a somber, *"Good morning, Dave."* Given all he had experienced this year, it wouldn't have been surprising. Instead, the only sound that greeted his ears was the dull thrum of the elevator ascending from beneath his feet, chiming as it passed every level below.

As he stood alone in the skybridge connecting the parking garage to the building in which he had just performed, Rick realized that he wanted nothing more than to hop in Bora's car, get back to the apartment, climb into a bottle, and forget tonight. The first three goals were achievable; the final one, not so much. He had, quite frankly, made an ass of himself.

When he first booked tonight's quartet gig through an old friend, he detected a surge of enthusiasm he hadn't felt in months. The restaurant wasn't prestigious by any stretch of the imagination, but it *was* downtown, and he *was* playing jazz again. Perhaps, he dreamed, a return to the genre would reignite his pilot light.

Rick was halfway through the first set around 7:30 when he realized his performance anxiety, like his strange visitors, had followed him from Ellijay. Until then, he had managed to keep his unease in check, and hoped that the laid back nature of the gig would keep the technical demands low enough to hide in the background. That was when the band leader called *Giant Steps*.

Seriously, who calls Giant Steps *on a restaurant gig?* he asked as he watched the glowing numbers above the door slowly approach his level. *On the first set, no less?* The results were nothing short of disastrous. When it came time to take a solo, Rick fought through his racing heartbeat until halfway through the chorus, when his fingers simply stopped responding. An attentive rescue from the trumpet player saved him, but for the rest of the night, Rick refused to take a solo on anything except the slowest ballads.

So it looks like guitar is gone, along with Cassie, he thought. *At least I still have Jack.* In the handful of visits since the diner date, the boy's mood had done nothing but improve. Rick even detected a thaw in Cassie's demeanor. *Maybe I'm too pessimistic*, he thought as the elevator arrived at last. *Could be there's something still there…*

"Dear Excelsior Parking Atlanta," he mumbled to himself, stepping inside and taking care not to strike the doorway with his gig bag. "Please replace your elevators. I missed several birthdays while waiting for one. Signed, Richard Coulter, Winner, 2020's Worst Guitarist of the Year."

The interior smelled like your typical downtown parking garage elevator, like piss and weed. Rick pressed the button for the ground floor where he had parked, wishing he had brought his flask from Ellijay. *I'd finish it by the time the ride is over*, he ruminated.

As predicted, the ride down was long… but not uneventful. The elevator descended one level, then lurched to a stop. When it refused to budge, Rick started punching the button for the ground floor.

"Listen," he said at last. "I don't know what you are. I really don't care. I just need this nonsense to stop. Please?" Immediately, the elevator resumed its descent, only to shudder once again when it hit the next floor.

"Ha ha, very funny," Rick sneered. "C'mon let's get this over with." The elevator resumed. "Well, at least you're responsive, now." The numbers illuminated uninterrupted until finally settling on the ground floor.

Is this the rest of my life now? wondered Rick. *Flinching at every little glitch, yelling in elevators like a madman? Being terrified of audience members?* Rick thought he had seen the tall woman from Terry Mac's at tonight's gig. Luckily, he had been mistaken, but the sight rattled him all the same. It didn't help that the voices continued apace wherever he went—he even heard them in the bathroom tonight, whispering his name incorrectly as they always did.

The doors opened with a sharp, clear ding. Rick moved to step off the elevator, but stopped mid-stride.

An odor of mothballs assailed his nostrils. Beyond the doorway was not the drab concrete of the parking garage. There were no automobiles, no flickering fluorescent lights.

Instead, a dark, wooden staircase stretched before him, dimly lit by ornate wall sconces, tracing up to a landing about a story above. From somewhere beyond the open doorway, the piercing clarinet of Artie Shaw's *Nightmare* echoed across the scene.

Rick took a step backwards and began frantically pressing the button to close the elevator doors. He knew that ascent all too well. It was the final few stairs before Conrad Coulter's bedroom, somehow transplanted to a grimy parking garage in downtown Atlanta. For him, it might as well have been the threshold of a lion's den.

No matter how hard he pressed the button in the elevator, the doors refused to shut. In desperation, he began mashing every floor, but nothing could compel the metal box to do anything other than stubbornly sit there. At last, Rick kicked the panel, shouting a stream of curses.

Nightmare ended, making way for the opening trumpet of *Stardust*. Rick was fully aware that it made zero sense to leave the safety of the elevator, but to him it seemed he had little choice. He could stand there, waiting for God knows how long—or he could accept the only option presented to him. Maybe his compliance would take the bastards by surprise.

Rick hesitated. There was the issue of his guitar. If his encounter at the house in Ellijay was any indication, he might get knocked around a bit and need to move quickly. Reluctantly, Rick slipped off his instrument and dropped it at the foot of the stairs, not abandoning it in the elevator should it choose to move, but unencumbering him for the journey upstairs. Then, grasping the long, smooth handrail jutting from the wall, he climbed up towards his father's bedroom.

Every creak, he thought as the string section took over. *Every creak is* exactly *where I remember it...* With ponderous steps, he drew closer to the landing, each footfall sending the ancient wood groaning in protest. When he reached the top, there it was, just as he remembered it—or, at the very least, an immaculate recreation.

Rick stood at the top of the stairs and surveyed the opulent room. To his left, embers lay dying in the fireplace, which rose like a tower of stone before disappearing into the ceiling; to his right, the massive, hunchbacked rolltop desk, a fortress filled with old letters and business papers. Rick's eyes followed the wooden floor across the area rug and to the ornate chaise at the foot of his father's bed. At last his gaze landed on the tasseled, oxblood canopy covering where his father slept his entire life. The curtains were closed. No signs of life could be seen.

Nor could they be heard. The music continued, masking all other noises in the room. Realizing he would have no warning prior to an ambush, Rick carefully approached the record player, glancing at the tall window adjacent to the bed. He had no plans to look outside. If he did, he fully expected to see the hedge maze looming below; from this perspective, the exterior simply looked like a black sheet hanging over the glass.

Just as the trombone solo kicked in, Rick gingerly lifted the needle, leaving the bedroom as quiet as the grave. The silence unnerved him, but Rick was afraid to speak. *Why are you doing this?* he wanted to ask. *Does this serve a greater purpose, or is it just nonsense? Or am I still back in the elevator, having a seizure or something?*

The briefest snippet of a giggle broke the silence. Before Rick could speak, another noise followed immediately in its wake: the sound of a shotgun shell being fumbled into its chamber with a snap. Rick was only able to identify it by the sharp, telltale sound of the weapon racking that followed.

Even though Rick knew he was not the intended target, he spun on his heel to head for the staircase. His haphazard departure caused the area rug to slip beneath his feet, turning his escape into a frantic stumble. He reached the head of the stairs with too much momentum, missed the top step, and began crashing down towards the open elevator doors as the shotgun discharged. The deafening sound reverberated through the enclosed space of the bedroom, filling Rick's ears with a high-pitched, whining drone as he landed on each stair. The stiff, unyielding wood beneath him battered Rick like a punching bag, knocking the wind out of him with each blow.

When he finally landed beside his guitar at the bottom of the staircase, Rick groaned loudly, an animalistic wail of pain and anguish. To his shock, the moan trailed on after he thought he had stopped. That was when he realized another voice had raised itself at the top of the stairs, a pathetic, weak whimper accompanied by a series of loud, measured thumps.

Rick stared upwards as the thumping drew nearer. The voice upstairs coughed, layering a wet, sticky gurgle beneath the whimper. At last, the thumping reached the open doorway at the top of the stairs, revealing its source: the bloodied hand of an old man, clawing its way towards Rick.

There was no need to wait and see its owner. Rick knew what lay just beyond the doorframe. Hauling himself to his feet, Rick grabbed his guitar and limped into the elevator, where he began frenetically pushing every button he could reach. None responded. Finally, he began jabbing the button for the ground floor, his desperation mounting as the doorway above revealed a forearm, then an elbow...

The man's head was just beginning to appear when the elevator doors started drawing together. Rick continued jamming the button in encouragement. At last they shut, the elevator shivered, and a sense of downward momentum ensued.

Rick crumpled in the nearest corner alongside the panel, crying tears of terror and pain. He was so overcome with emotion that he failed to notice when the elevator opened on the ground floor of the parking garage, revealing a man dressed in tatters and a beanie, awaiting his ride up.

"We all been there, brother," the homeless man said, taking a long pull on his brown paper bag. "We all been there."

Rick found his way home that night in Bora's borrowed Nissan Sentra, but not before stopping at the liquor store. Because he had polished off the Everclear earlier that week, he stocked up on vodka and bought a new flask, filling it up before finishing his trip. His last stop was at Target to buy some new socks, since the ones he had brought with him had all vanished, the latest casualty of the phenomenon's kleptomania.

For the next day and most of the week, Rick became a ghost in Bora's apartment, watching television when she was at work, finding reasons to slip out whenever she returned home. The last thing he wanted was for her to see the bruises he had earned on the staircase. Those would lead to questions, and Rick knew she would never accept the answers.

So—with the exception of having a place to lay his head—Rick lived like a vagrant. He barely ate. Instead, he would wander the streets for hours in a desperate attempt to escape the voices that followed wherever he went, sipping his flask the entire time. After a few days of draining it without the slightest buzz, he simply grabbed one of the plastic bottles and hid it in his hoodie's kangaroo pocket, then resumed his rambling. Luckily, it was small enough to conceal, only brought out whenever he found a moment of privacy in public restrooms or alleyways.

On Thursday afternoon, he wandered farther than ever before and found himself gazing into the smudged windows of a local pawnshop. For the better part of an hour he stood there, gazing past the bars and into the store beyond. Although he never entered, he could see the rows and rows of firearms waiting inside. The affair in the parking garage left him reevaluating everything, including his stance on killing himself and whether or not the quickest way was the best way. He wasn't sure he could go on like this. If the remainder of his life was to be filled with torturous visions, then it was no life at all. Not even Jack's improved demeanor could heal that wound.

Rick was about to step inside and seriously consider purchasing a gun when he became aware of a melody lilting towards him across the intersection. He had no idea why he hadn't noticed the busker earlier. Perhaps the thin strains of fiddle music failed to overcome the whizz of passing traffic, or perhaps Rick's mind had simply added it to the rest of the intersection's soundscape. Either way, now he took careful notice. Most of the time, buskers in Atlanta played guitar, maybe the occasional saxophone or trumpet. Fiddlers were a rarer sort.

He turned as the fiddler took up a new tune. After several bars, Rick recognized it as *Carrickfergus*, an Irish folk song he had played at Saint Patrick's Day gigs in past years. The fiddler didn't sound half bad—he was pitchy, yes, but there was a great deal of warmth to his sound. Looking across the street, Rick spotted a gangly, middle-aged fellow in a loud Hawaiian shirt swaying with a fiddle clasped under his chin.

The melancholy song concluded, leaving Rick with a feeling of satisfaction. He didn't know if it was the last song he would ever hear, but if it was, he wasn't sure he could have come up with anything better. He turned back to the glass door of the pawnshop and grabbed the handle. As he swung it open, the fiddler played another tune.

"C'mon, buddy," groused the owner, a pudgy fellow with a thick northern accent. "In or out, I got customers here." Rick, who had stopped for several seconds with the door wide open, mumbled an apology and released the handle. The pawn shop door closed as he turned to stare intently at the fiddler.

Rick could not believe what he was hearing. For the last year, he had lived and breathed that melody. It had burrowed into his brain like a parasite, refusing to leave, draining his attention while offering nothing in return. It was angular and elegant, foreign and familiar, uplifting and dismal. And this man, standing across the street with a sharp nose and unruly brown hair covering his ears, was playing it on his fiddle. *Like a last-minute turn down a road you drove past all your life, but never traveled....*

A car whizzed by, its driver laying on the horn as Rick almost stepped into traffic. He was grateful for the wakeup call. Rick patiently waited for the traffic lights to afford him safe passage, then loped across the intersection. Within seconds, he stood alongside the busker, who had abandoned the mysterious melody in favor of a new song. He stood patiently until the musician completed the final cadence.

The strings hadn't even stopped resonating when Rick spoke. "That last song—you *have* to tell me what that last song was."

The fiddler flashed the grin of a used car salesman, then said in a thick Appalachian drawl, "*The Virginia Reel*, my man."

"No, the one before that."

The fiddler's smile faded, his mismatched eyes darting to the intersection. "Ah, that old thing? Just foolin' around, ain't got no name."

"Bullshit it doesn't," Rick said as he pulled out his wallet, extracted a wad of bills, and began counting. "Look, I've got fifty... fifty-three bucks here, and I'll go to the ATM and make it an even hundred if you tell me what that melody is called and where you heard it."

"Why you so interested, if I might pry?"

Rick hesitated. "Because... because it's been stuck in my head all year."

The fiddler's grin returned. He considered the offer for a few moments, then countered, "Tell you what: you keep your money. Buy me a couple rounds, tell me where *you* know it from, and we've got a deal."

"Man after my own heart," Rick said, replacing his wallet. "There's a place I passed just a while ago. Follow me. My name's Rick. I'm a musician, too."

"Mine's Devlin," the fiddler replied, pocketing his tips and putting away his instrument. "Pleased to make your acquaintance, Ricky."

23

Thursday, October 22, 2020

THE F-WORD

"Quite a story you got there, hoss," Devlin Fox said after draining his beer. He stifled a belch, then waved across the pitted wood of the bar. "Ma'am, can I get another? Thankee."

Rick gawked at the busker. He didn't seem the slightest bit surprised, though Rick admittedly omitted the strangest parts of his tale. He only painted a broad picture of the past year, of things disappearing and the melody he first heard in May. "You... don't think I'm crazy?" he hazarded after a few moments, lowering his voice so other patrons in the dive bar couldn't hear.

"My personal threshold for 'crazy' is *way* above that."

"Do you run a *lunatic* asylum?"

"Whole world's a lunatic asylum these days."

"... listen, you're two beers in. I kept my end of the bargain. Your turn. Where did you learn that melody?"

"Been in the family for generations."

"Where did they learn it, then?"

"Same as you, more or less. Tune just sorta... drifted outta the woods."

"There's got to be more to it than that."

"'Course there is. But you're asking the wrong questions. You don't care where I learned it. What you really wanna know is where it comes from, who wrote it in the first place... what's in the woods."

"Well?"

"Well, my family learned it from them."

"Them? Them who?"

"Tell me: you seen them lights, too?"

"... how did you—"

"How about them lil' fellers?"

"… um… uh… maybe. Yeah, okay, I might have seen something like that."

"You'd make a great politician, Ricky."

"Okay, say I did. Do you know anything about 'them'?"

"More'n I should. People of the Hills."

"Huh?"

"The Living Host. Y'know? The Gentry, the Good Folk, the *Aos Sidhe*. The Other Crowd. The *Little* People… Don't look at me like that. Aw, you're gonna make me say it. Really? The f-word? They fuckin' *hate* that."

"Dammit, Devlin, *who?*"

"… the Fae Folk. *Fairies.*"

"The f…? You've got to be fucking joking. Here I thought *I* was the headcase—Miss? I'll take the tab, we're done here."

"Suit yourself."

"Look, Devlin, I appreciate your—what you *think* is—help, but this isn't anything to laugh about. *I'm* the one suffering a nervous breakdown, here, I don't need someone putting more nonsense in my head."

"Fair 'nuff. Probably ain't nothing to worry about. So long as they ain't taken you yet."

"… Taken… *taken?*… What if… what if they had?"

"That would constitute escalation. But since it ain't come to that, nothing to worry about. You have a nice life, Ricky."

"Escalation?"

"Somethin' beyond a passing interest. They wouldn't leave you alone until they got what they wanted. But you said that ain't happened, so it'll likely pass. Been seeing a lot of low-level stuff lately, what with everyone cooped up in their houses all year."

"I… um… I'm pretty sure they've taken me. At least twice."

"Hoo boy. Then you got a problem. Reckoned as much, you look worn slap out. If they're hasslin' you, not a lot of folks who can help you through that. Now are you ready to have a conversation like two grown-ass men?… Thought so. Miss, another one for me and my friend. My treat this time… So… what do you remember?"

"Just flashes. Images. This last time, there was a bright light… I was lifted off the couch, I remember surgical tools. That's what I'm saying: whatever took me wasn't fairies. Not unless Disney started making snuff films."

"Not fairies, huh? What makes you so sure?"

"I just told you. It was an *alien abduction*, man, not a trip to Neverland."

"Aliens?"

"That's what I remember, at least. From a couple nights ago. They looked like aliens: big heads, big eyes, the whole nine yards. And I saw lights in the sky back in Ellijay. That's UFO stuff."

"So you're the expert now, that it?"

"No. I'm just saying that aliens are more likely than Tinker Bell."

"*Shee-it.* You're gonna be a tough nut to crack. So... extraterrestrials, is it? Area 51? You put stock in all that?"

"It's more believable than what *you're* suggesting. It's a big universe, right? There's got to be intelligent life *somewhere*."

"Of course there is. Sure as hell ain't *here*. But people don't grasp the size of the universe. If aliens did abduct you, they came an awful long way."

"It's aliens. They've got... I dunno. Warp engines."

"You ever looked into that possibility? I mean, *really* looked into it? Even if they could travel at the speed of light, they'd have to have left their planet sometime around the crucifixion to get here in time to visit lil' ol' you."

"It's the only thing that explains what I'm experiencing. There have to be other civilizations out there."

"Not arguing against that. The question is, 'Are aliens visiting *here*?'"

"Seems that way."

"So you believe in bug-eyed space freaks kidnapping people for a bit of the ol' in and out?"

"I wouldn't put it like that, but nowadays? Yeah."

"Hate to break it to you, Ricky, but you believe in fairies."

"You keep saying that word, like anyone over the age of five would believe it."

"The beings our culture calls 'aliens' are fairies."

"Fairies are from other planets?"

"No, no, no. Not what I mean... I get so tired of having this conversation."

"Make your case, then."

"Dunno if we got the time to cover seven decades of Ufology and Parapsychology tonight."

"I don't have anywhere to be."

"Not gonna waste my breath if you ain't gonna listen, Ricky."

"If you genuinely think you can help, I'm listening."

"Okay... Bear with me. What I'm saying is that there is an unbroken chain of consistency stretching back from myths about the Fae Folk all the way into the modern UFO experience. Everything you've been through, people have been going through since time began: small beings, bright lights, abductions, missing time, cattle mutilations, implants, *all* that shit. And *they* are always to blame. Wasn't until recently that we neutered 'em, made 'em little sprites at the bottom of the garden helping flowers grow and protecting the forest. That's wrong. They ain't protectors. They're *possessors.*"

"Look, I didn't go skipping into the forest with them. They *took* me. To a metal table on a spaceship. They didn't wave a magic wand over me. They stabbed me in the eye with a syringe. A fucking *syringe*, Devlin."

"How about the other stuff? It don't *all* correspond to aliens, does it? The poltergeist effects, the missing tools? Lemme guess—you thought you had a ghost at one point, didn't you? That sound like technology or something supernatural?"

"Didn't Isaac Asimov say something about that? Technology can look like magic?"

"Arthur C. Clarke, actually. 'Any sufficiently advanced technology would be indistinguishable from magic.' But Art, that ol' fart, he missed a trick. The reverse holds true, too: magic is indistinguishable from tech, if you do it right."

"You think magic is real?"

"I think there's only so much you can handle in one day, Ricky."

"Let's say you're right about all this. Then how do you explain what people are seeing? They don't see nymphs and fairies. They see spaceships made out of metal. I saw a TV show one time where people were taken into outer space, for Chrissake. And these things... Granted, I didn't get a great look myself, but none of them had any wings or tutus."

"Still ain't gettin' it, are ya? The map ain't the territory. We've been trying to describe 'em since the beginning, but we always fail. Used to call 'em 'fairies,' but that ain't quite right. Nor is 'extraterrestrials.'"

"But they looked—"

"*They change how they look.* Blend into the cultural tapestry. Accommodate our expectations. It takes two to tango… Question is, Ricky: what are you bringing to the dance? Sounds to me like you've got space invaders on the brain."

"I don't think that's the case."

"'Course it is. It's the culture you're embedded in. '*Paradigm*,' if you wanna get fancy. You see them as aliens—at least you've started to—because *you* find that more palatable."

"'Palatable'?"

"You can *believe* that easier. You just told me. And they thrive on belief. If you were fresh off the boat, or Cherokee, or Creek, they'd probably look a lot different to you. Hell, they might even change between now and the next time you see 'em. For the time being, your little men *wearing* green have become *little green men*. It's that way for most folks. We don't believe in 'em, at least not like we used to. But they've stuck around."

"I don't think I understand, Devlin."

"Don't matter if you understand. Just the way it is. Somehow, they figure out what you've got in your noggin, meet you halfway between their true form and what you expect 'em to be."

"What's their 'true form,' then?"

"No one knows. Them lights you seen, maybe. Sometimes I think that's how they look when you strip away all expectations."

"Meaning they're from…?"

"Here. Out there. Everywhere. Wherever you want them to be. *What*ever you want them to be."

"… I think I follow… Okay, maybe you're onto something. Maybe. But I still don't see how they do it."

"Do what?"

"How they change, how they… make me experience things. I've been hearing noises. Voices, chimes, laughter. And seeing things. Really strange things. Weird animals. Sometimes I… sometimes, it looks like I'm places I shouldn't be. Places I *couldn't* be. And I've been having these dreams... How are they doing *that*?"

"You not listening? Don't you remember how I said they can kick around inside your head? Old folks used to call it 'glamour,' the way they could make themselves and things appear different than they really are, shapeshifting and the like. Nowadays, all the UFO geeks call it 'screen memories,' but they never bother to say how those get implanted. Tech, tech, tech, it's always tech with them chuckleheads. I think all these things have a direct line right into our brains, make us see whatever they goddamn well please."

"This wasn't a hallucination, Devlin. This seemed real."

"Then maybe it was. Maybe they literally change reality. However they do it, they can bend anything to their will... except *our* will. Which begs the question you so desperately need answered: why they got a bee in their bonnet about *you?* What do they *want* from you?"

"You tell me."

"Well, they all want *somethin'*. Maybe it's simple. Maybe they want Rick Coulter."

"That makes no sense, especially after what happened two weeks ago. If they wanted me, why didn't they keep me when they had me?"

"What, your abduction? Eh, that's a different kind of taking, without much keeping. Think of it as a rental. They want ownership, and that has to be *given* to 'em. Naw, I think that's it, Ricky: they want you. We just gotta figure out *why*."

"Is there any chance they'll just... go away? Leave me alone?"

"*Highly* doubtful. They're determined and contractually minded boogers. If I didn't know any better, I'd say you owed 'em something. Y'ain't been dabbling, have you?"

"Dabbling?"

"In the occult."

"Don't know the first thing about it."

"Smart feller. I deal with a lot of spooky stuff, and *these* things scare the pants off me. I've tangled with 'em more than I'd care to. Rarely ends well."

Rick let the gravity of Devlin's statement sink in. "Maybe they want... I, um..." Rick stuttered, lowering his voice to a whisper. "My clothes were on backwards when I woke up. Y'know, after the abduction? Does that mean I...?"

"Got cornholed?" Devlin laughed. "Man, you're *deep* in the space invader shit, ain't you? Think you got probed? Nah. Don't get me wrong, sometimes they do that. But the clothes thing? Hear it a lot. Flipping clothes inside out was one way to escape in the older stories. Probably has something to do with that, the transition between worlds."

A protracted silence fell over their corner of the bar before Devlin spoke once more. "Honestly, a lot of what you're experiencing seems pretty typical, but until you determine what their interest is, I don't know what to tell you," he said. "Anything else worth mentioning? Things that might seem mundane, but feel like they ain't? Repetitions of people, places, things?"

"Funny you should ask. I keep seeing this number, 1-1-0-8, or variations on it. Everywhere. Clocks, addresses, bills. I even had a combination lock changed from my son's birthday to 1108."

"Hmmm. Any significance to you?"

"Not really. Closest thing is the day my father died, but that was November 7, not November 8."

"Eleven seven, eleven eight... A year and a day. Interesting... Well, I tell you what, Ricky, that's a real head-scratcher. Best of luck." Without another word, Devlin shoved some tip money across the bar, grabbed his fiddle case, and headed for the door. Rick scrambled to catch up.

"Wait!" he shouted, stepping outside. Night had since fallen, just barely cold enough for his breath to form thin curls. Somewhere in the distance, a bevy of sirens rushed to some undisclosed emergency. "Wait a minute—that's it? You're just going to drop all this on me and walk away?"

Devlin took out his phone, scrolling through the apps. "I've got appointments tonight, Ricky. Appreciate the beers, though."

"Hang on—appointments?" Rick stood there until Devlin looked up from his phone. "What is it you do, exactly? I thought you were a busker?"

"Oh this ol' thing?" asked Devlin, hoisting his fiddle case. "Nah, it's a secondary source of income."

"What's your primary source?"

Devlin thought for a moment, looked right into Rick's eyes with his own mismatched pair, then asked, "What's your airplane answer?"

"My what?" replied Rick.

"Y'know, your airplane answer. You get crammed into a metal tube, ass to elbows with someone you don't know from Adam, and they ask you what you do for a living. What do you tell 'em? That you're a heavy drinking, dirt poor, guitar playin' hillbilly?"

Whatever anger momentarily flushed through Rick was quickly replaced by begrudging appreciation for Devlin's assessment. Even if uncharitable, it was not entirely incorrect. "Atlanta recording artist," he admitted, somewhat ashamedly.

Devlin nodded. "See, I start off gentle. I say I'm an author, maybe a researcher, depending on the vibe I get from 'em. If they press, I tell 'em I write 'speculative nonfiction.' If they ain't left me alone, or I wanna shut down the conversation, well, I just come right out and say, 'Weird shit: ghosts and goblins, UFOs and monsters.' Usually ends the chit-chat pretty quick."

"So you write books?" asked Rick.

"Sometimes. Pen name, don't bother looking me up. But I also make money from fixing people's problems. With this sort of thing."

"Are you a psychic?"

"Wouldn't say that. Mildly sensitive at best, runs in the family. Lot of them old ways never died, 'specially where I grew up."

"So you're a paranormal investigator, then?"

"I'm not an 'investigator,'" countered Devlin, mildly annoyed. "Investigators go in agnostic, try to determine the truth. I've moved beyond that. I'm a *fixer*. I solve problems after hoaxes and misidentifications are ruled out."

"There's money in that?"

"A little," Devlin stated. "Government contracts, even, if you know the right people. Although half the time I take whatever people barter with. Depends on the country. I've been paid in cowries, francs, chickens, grave goods, rubles, even got offered a manservant, once. Don't worry, I declined. When people *really* need my services, when they *believe* in what I have to offer...? I sell that shit faster'n a carrot in a convent. But... I don't think you have much to offer me, Rick Coulter."

Rick looked dejected. Over the course of the last hour or so, he had been convinced that this strange character, this Devlin Fox, might hold the key to setting his life back on track. Everything had gone so haywire in the past seven months that it made the previous years—the ones he had thought were so awful, the ones he had spent drinking in self-pity—pale by comparison. If he could get his life straightened out, Rick was certain the shift in perspective would bring with it newfound gratitude, which he might parlay into reconnecting with Cassie or even (dare it be said) sobriety.

"Cheer up, buttercup," smirked Devlin, returning to his phone to set up a ride. "Didn't say I was gonna abandon you. What, you thought I was gonna leave you hanging, so some New Ager full of Blavatsky dreck could come take advantage of you?" He replaced his phone. "Nah."

The emotional whiplash sent Rick reeling: first hope, then disappointment, now skepticism. "For free?"

"Didn't say that," Devlin chuckled as he lit a cigarette. "You got nothing I *need*, but you do got something I *want*. Yours seems like a special case. Might move a few books. If I help you, I want exclusive rights."

"That's it?" asked Rick. "Done. When do we start?"

"Tonight. Ish," Devlin answered. Lips clutching his smoke, he crouched, opened up his fiddle case, and lifted the lid of a compartment on one end. From there, amidst a container of rosin and a few loose coins, he produced something hanging from a leather loop.

"Iron and steel used to work," he explained, "but since that stuff's all over the city, maybe not so much for these fellers. But it's worth a try." He held out his hand. Rick reached forward and accepted a necklace from the mysterious stranger. Dangling from the end was a small replica of a horseshoe.

"Double trouble," Devlin said. "Cornish iron, cast in one of the most effective shapes. If it works, it'll work a charm, pardon the pun. Heard tell of keeping them at bay with nothing more'n a sewing needle, so this oughta do the trick. Won't keep 'em from harassin' you—hell, they might even still *hurt* you—but likely as not they won't *take* you again, so long as you wear it."

"Thanks, Devlin," Rick said, sliding the necklace over his head. "Is that it?"

"Far from it," Devlin replied as his ride arrived. Grinding out his cigarette beneath his bootheel, he handed Rick a card showing a phone number and nothing else.

"Call me in a week and we'll talk."

24

Wednesday, October 28, 2020

FOLIE À DEUX

THE EVENING BEGAN AS SO MANY OTHERS HAD the past several weeks. Bora burst into the apartment with the momentum of a freight train, smoking almost as much, then started narrating her day at work, knowing full well that Rick would have little to share in return. She tried stretching her monologue as long as she could, hoping to forestall the inevitable moment when her friend would rise from the couch, mumbling a few requisite words of acknowledgement before drifting off to wander the streets.

She never liked seeing that happen, but she liked it even less tonight, when an important conversation loomed. To Bora, it felt like a roiling thunderhead mustering its strength on the horizon, destined to strike the apartment before the night finished.

Aware of this inevitability, Bora began her rain dance. "Rick, I've been thinking," she said, sitting on the couch beside him. "It's been great getting to see you these past few weeks, but—"

"Way ahead of you," Rick interrupted with a broad grin.

The sight took Bora completely off guard. She had become so used to her old friend's sulking that she wondered whether or not he had finally snapped. "Okay," she ventured cautiously, "what do you think I'm trying to say?"

"It's obvious, isn't it?" asked Rick between sips of water. "I've been here most of October. It's time I headed home."

"Listen: I'm here for you as much as you need me," Bora offered. "If you want to stick around longer, that's fine. But you're right—it might be nice for us to return to some normalcy. Only if you're ready."

"Decision's not up to me at this point," Rick said proudly. "I called all the wineries and told them I'd be able to play this weekend. I'm heading out in the morning. I regretfully declare an end to my stay at Casa de Choi. Try not to cry."

"Are you kidding me? I'm so happy," Bora squeaked. "Hang on, that came out wrong—not happy that you're leaving, just happy that you feel good enough *to* leave. Can I ask what happened? Did something change?"

"I feel better, for one thing."

"But the voices?" asked Bora, cautiously optimistic. "The disappearing stuff...?"

"Nothing this past week, believe it or not," Rick confessed. "You could've heard a pin drop while you were away."

"Why do you think that is?"

Rick gently touched his chest. Bora had noticed that he had started wearing some sort of necklace, though she had no clue what hung from it. "I have an idea," he mumbled at last with a cryptic reverence. "Maybe I'll tell you later. But it isn't because I was crazy, I can tell you that much."

Bora shook her head, smiling. Perhaps Rick had gotten religion. Not her cup of tea—she considered herself spiritual, not religious—but whatever helped him, she enthusiastically endorsed. After all, he seemed to be drinking less. Not by a lot, but a noticeable improvement. In the past week, she had only seen two empty vodka bottles in the trash.

"I don't know what to say," she marveled eventually. "Whatever it is, I'm happy for you."

"Me too," Rick smiled. He reached out and gave his friend a gigantic bear hug. "Thanks for helping me out," he added, his voice cracking. "I couldn't have done it without you."

"Not too sure exactly what I did," Bora said once she extracted herself from his embrace. "But I'd gladly do it again." A mischievous look flashed across her face. "Takeout?"

Rick agreed. After placing their order, she headed to the balcony to paint some watercolors, taking advantage of the dying light. When dinner arrived and night had fully fallen, she moved her easel back into the dining room, where her drying rack waited. The remainder of their evening became a modest celebration of the last month, full of quiet conversation and light intoxication. Bora, having long ago abandoned Rick's poison for her usual glass of wine, was pleased to see that her friend only pounded back one of his signature half-and-half vodka and Cokes rather than an entire bottle's worth.

Sometime around eleven o'clock, it was time to call it a night. "It's been great having you here, Rick," she said, heading to the bathroom. "Bora will miss you, but her liver and kidneys will not."

Rick swallowed the last bit of his drink as she disappeared. "Hey!" he called. "Your paintings!" When she poked her head around the corner, toothbrush in her mouth, Rick pointed to the art in the dining room sitting on the rack and easel.

"Eh," Bora said, dismissively waving a hand in the air. She vanished once again to spit and rinse. Then, from around the corner, Rick heard her mumble a farewell: "I'll get it in the morning, after I see you off. G'night, Rick."

"Goodnight, Bora," he said as her bedroom door closed. Rick then headed to the bathroom, showered, brushed his teeth, and slipped into his pajamas before snuggling in on the couch in his usual position: head to the window, feet to the kitchen.

Rick lay there for a time, enjoying his light buzz and thinking of how dramatically his fortunes had improved since meeting Devlin Fox. He fingered the small iron horseshoe hanging around his neck. *Who would have thought something so small could bring about so much change?* he wondered. Ever since he had left the bar, Rick had worn the necklace nonstop.

Rick thought back to Devlin's words: "Won't keep 'em from harassing you," he had warned, "but they likely as not won't take you again...." From what Rick could tell, Devlin had been completely wrong.

It was just as he had told Bora: in the past six nights, absolutely nothing had happened. No voices, no missing items, no visions, and certainly no visitors. While Rick had experienced similar periods of inactivity over the previous months, something felt different this time. It was this sense of peace that allowed him to drift off less drunk than usual, and soon he fell into a deep sleep.

Rick shuffled through the forest once again, his feet carving deep furrows in the thick layer of dead leaves. He had no idea how he arrived there or how long he had been staring at the ground. Drawing his eyes up, he looked around and recognized the forest for the first time. It was his father's land.

Instantly, he was seized by an awareness of the dreamscape's geography. The main road to the quarry snaked away uphill somewhere behind him. Up ahead sat the stream running the length of the mountainside, looking like a miniature canyon amidst the leaf cover, its depths obscured by a thick layer of fog.

Rick had only visited here a handful of times following Mary's disappearance. His parents rarely allowed their only surviving child to venture into those woods after the tragedy. Once Rick's mother died, Conrad Coulter strictly forbade any future visits to the worksite.

"Rick," a voice called from further upstream. Looking ahead, he saw something moving in the chasm, barely breaking the cloudy layer that had settled above it. It was the barest hint of hair, red as a cardinal's breast, peeping up from the creek bed.

Rick had never seen this exact scenario, but had played it out hundreds of times in his head over the years: his sister playing in the stream, held in rapt fascination for hours on end by the creatures hidden within. According to his mother, it had been her favorite pastime. Cautiously, he approached his sister and, within moments, reached the embankment above where she stood. There, the barest bit of red surfaced above an impenetrable soup of fog at his feet.

"Mary?" he whispered. "Mary, is that you?"

"Yes," she giggled back. "I want to show you something."

"What is it?" asked Rick, dropping to his knees.

"I've caught something. Take a look."

Rick reached out a hand, trying his best to wave away the fog for a better look. It stubbornly refused, behaving more like a thick vapor than anything else. "I can't see," he said at last. "What is it?"

With that, a tiny hand like a porcelain puppet's palm, clumsy and inarticulate, emerged from the fog alongside his own. Rick recoiled as the ghastly appendage pawed at the top of the red hair, which slipped away like a wig into the murk, revealing a shiny, bald scalp. As it rose above the fog, Rick's voice caught in his throat. It was the face of a puppet, frozen in the slightest smile, its eyes large and dark, blacker than black, ever-widening. Rick felt himself tugged forward into those eyes, which grew so large they threatened to swallow him whole....

Rick opened his eyes with a slight whimper. He was relieved to find himself lying on his side on Bora's couch, the empty darkness of the apartment enveloping him. As he stared at the room, some headlights passed onto the ceiling, then mercifully filed out once more. Rick closed his eyes again, repeating to himself that what he had experienced had only been a dream.

He lay there for a while, lingering on the cusp of sleep, until he felt someone jostle him. "Bora," he mumbled, half-conscious. "What is it?"

Another jostle. "Bora," he moaned, cracking his eyelids. "I'm trying to—"

Rick was now on his back, his head to the side. When he opened his eyes this time, however, a face stared back at him, not five inches away. It was so close, in fact, that the only thing he noticed at first were its eyes: large, dark, blacker than black...

Rick panicked. He tried lashing out but, as before, found himself completely immobile. *It's happening again,* his mind raced. *No, it can't be. It's over, it's behind me...* Rick tried closing his eyes. He could not. *Oh God, no. No. That's the only thing that saved me last time....*

He lay there, trying his best to avert his eyes from the small figure standing alongside the couch, to no avail. Its teardrop-shaped head, swollen larger than his own, occupied his entire field of vision. Everywhere he looked, a new, horrifying detail met his gaze: the gigantic, pitch-black eyes; the barest hint of two nostrils; a slit forming a vestigial mouth; all set within a face so smooth and rigid, it might as well have been carved of marble. Below that dangled a skeletal torso with arms and legs so impossibly frail that it looked like it could barely stand.

The body doesn't have a head, Rick realized. *The head has a body.*

Thankfully, Rick didn't have to look for long. With the characteristic wobbliness of a marionette, the being lifted its left hand from its resting place on Rick's shoulder, then floated backwards into the apartment. There, it joined eight others of various sizes, none much taller than the knob of Bora's front door. All appeared nude, yet Rick could not see any genitals, only their smooth, shining skin glinting in the dim light, the color of dishwater.

You little fuckers! Rick silently cursed at the row of figures standing in front of the television. *You have no right to do this! You can't just do this to people!* Amidst the escalating terror, a more pragmatic thought emerged: *If I survive this, I am going to wring that scrawny hillbilly's fucking neck.*

As a multitude of epithets raced through his mind, Rick watched the nine intruders sluggishly turn their heads in unison toward the short hallway leading to the rest of the apartment. With great effort, Rick found himself able to follow their gaze. Whether he turned his neck by sheer will or he was simply *allowed* to, he couldn't say.

A pale blue light filled the room. Its intensity was unparalleled, yet Rick somehow had no trouble keeping his eyes open. He could not pinpoint its origin; it seemed to come from everywhere and nowhere at once. Simultaneously, a deep thrum took up residence in Rick's ears, lower in pitch than ever before. One by one, the smallest items throughout the apartment began lifting of their own accord: utensils, papers, remotes, tissue boxes, empty bottles, the salt and pepper shakers, fruit, mugs, even Bora's watercolors. They hovered above the surfaces where they once sat, forming a debris field suspended in midair.

Movement from the hallway caught Rick's eye. Something stood just around the corner, casting an immense shadow that stretched all the way to the front door. Whatever it was, it stood far taller than the other visitors. A pair of immense, three-fingered hands clasped the frame of the hallway toward the top, near the ceiling. Each snow-white digit stretched a knuckle too far, and none bore fingernails.

For a split second, wonder overwhelmed fear. Judging by the shadows it cast, something taller than the apartment was bending down to enter the room. To Rick, it gave the impression of a collapsible ladder folding on its own just out of sight. The hands on either side of the entryway strained, struggling to pull their owner beyond the threshold. The first thing that Rick saw was a gigantic head the size of his torso entering the living room slowly and purposefully. A hideous form followed, looking like little more than skin stretched over bare bone. Beyond its size and blinding white coloration, it was practically identical to its nine companions.

The thing pushed forward, spiderlike, all four limbs touching the floor, its head held lower than the rest of its body. Whenever it connected with a bit of floating debris, it sent the errant object lazily spiraling away, freed from the constraints of gravity. After what felt like an eternity, it reached Rick's position, towering over the couch.

Rick felt something warm spreading across his shorts. It took him a moment to realize that he had pissed himself.

The giant steadied its lanky frame by delicately resting one hand on the armrest above Rick's head and the other on the back of the couch. Its massive skull lowered until it was inches from his face, its large, emotionless eyes gazing into the depths of Rick's soul. In his mind, he heard the same voice that had plagued him for months: "*Rickard Coulter*," it hissed, drawing out the vowels. "*Life... death....*"

The entire form moved with a shudder, freeing a hand to trace the outline of Rick's body. One of its massive fingers hovered millimeters away from his bare flesh and wet clothes, beginning at his feet, moving upwards with no apparent sense of urgency. It followed the contours of his body, moving steadily until, at last, it reached Rick's chest.

Although the giant's face betrayed no emotion, its finger hesitated just above Rick's tee shirt. The other digits lifted, opening the hand with the same ponderous effort that one might use to swing open the door to an ancient crypt. Though he thought it impossible, the thrum in Rick's ears deepened to a low bass frequency that threatened to burst his eardrums at any moment.

Rick felt a tickle at his neck. The leather strap connected to his pendant was moving on its own, sliding backward, pulling the tiny horseshoe closer to his chin. Even though its protection seemed to be failing spectacularly, Rick still desperately hoped that the necklace would remain in place rather than slip over his head. After a few moments of dragging up his chest in fits and starts, the barest bit of iron popped above Rick's collar.

What happened next unfolded in a single second. The giant's face, until now an unreadable mask, took on a different aspect. Its massive eyes somehow managed to widen further, its thin lips slightly pursing. The frequency in his ears rapidly ascended from the deepest bass to the highest soprano shriek, passing beyond the threshold of human hearing. The moment it faded, the light in the room snapped off as abruptly as a switch being thrown. With it, all the intruders disappeared, including the gigantic figure glowering above the couch. All the household items instantly succumbed to gravity and tumbled to the floor, the most fragile among them shattering into dozens of tiny fragments.

Rick, able to move once more, gripped the frame of the couch and gasped for breath. He hadn't felt this way since he was a child. It was the exact same sensation as being at the bottom of a swimming pool, holding your breath until the last possible minute, then surfacing rapidly in self-rescue.

He sat up, looking at the mess surrounding him. Bora would be furious. *How am I going to explain this to her?* he wondered through the adrenaline crash. Then a second thought arrived, one that could not be silenced.

"Holy shit," Rick whispered to the darkness. "It worked. The pendant... it worked."

In the hour that followed, Rick wanted to do many things. He wanted to rush to Bora's bedroom, wake her, and share what had happened. He wanted to clean up the apartment. He wanted to scrounge through his duffel bag for Devlin Fox's number, dial up the bastard, and offer to pay any price the man asked.

However, Rick did none of these things because, above all, he simply wanted to sleep. To quiet his racing mind, he drank straight from the bottle, pummeling his thoughts into submission until, at last, they subsided in an alcoholic haze, then succumbed to the familiar release of blacking out.

When he finally regained consciousness, the first thing Rick saw was the clock on the wall. It read half past eleven. The second thing he saw was Bora. She had pulled up a stool from the bar and placed it in front of the couch, sitting exactly where the small shapes had stood only hours earlier. The morning sunlight on her face revealed a look of intense concern; her hands were folded across a piece of paper in her lap.

"Bora," Rick managed through his headache. "You're... you're supposed to be at work." She said nothing. "I'm so sorry... I've made your life a living hell. I was drunk again. As soon as I clean up—"

"I've already done it," Bora snapped.

Rick glanced around the tidy room, trying to lick his parched lips. His tongue felt like a dried-out sponge. "I was going to—"

"Don't get me wrong," she said, ignoring his protests. "I was super pissed at first. I figured you'd gotten shitfaced again, and trashed the apartment. Honestly, Rick, there are very few things you could do that would ruin our relationship. Fucking with my art is one of them."

"Bora, listen—"

"That's when I noticed this." Rick's host held up the paper in her hands. It was a painting, one that she had completed last night. It showed an African American family laughing together at a picnic, their teenage daughter looking sullen in the background. It was a moment frozen in time only the way Bora could, telling an entire story in a single image.

However, something looked wrong. The colors appeared less vibrant. They looked aged, like the painting had hung on a wall for a lifetime.

"All of them are like this," explained Bora. "Even the ones that I had on the drying rack. They look like they sat in direct sunlight for months. Years, even. How the fuck does that happen overnight?"

Rick had no idea what to say. "Anything I tell you, you won't believe."

Bora dropped the painting to the floor and lowered her head. "I'm not so sure about that, Rick," she said quietly. "Once I started cleaning up, I remembered a dream I had last night. It's funny; I had completely forgotten about it until I picked up the paintings. In this dream, I was wide awake in my bed. But I couldn't move. There was a light, barely coming in underneath the bedroom door. Then I heard something. Something heavy. Moving on the other side. Making the floorboards creak." She broke into a weak laugh. "I don't even know if this fucking apartment *has* wooden floorboards."

She looked up, a single tear spilling down her cheek. "I love you, Rick, but I think your life is a mess. You drink too much. I'm worried that you might be crazy. And now... now I'm worried that I might be crazy, too. Is 'crazy' contagious? Can that happen?"

Rick closed his eyes. "I think they call it, uh... *folie à deux*."

Bora nodded. "Of course it's fucking French," she chuckled. "Rick, what the fuck is happening?" Quiet settled over the apartment.

"I... I don't know," Rick said at last. "But I can call someone who does."

25

Thursday, October 29, 2020

SEEING THINGS THROUGH

Devlin arrived within an hour of Rick's call. At first, the self-proclaimed paranormal fixer had bridled at being called "so early"—the ungodly hour of noon—but, after hearing Rick's story, he headed over to Bora's apartment the moment the call concluded.

In the time between hanging up and Devlin's arrival, Rick explained to Bora his conversation in the bar and the charm he had received. He could not have done a worse job if he had tried and simply ended up sounding like a lunatic. Before long, the pair found themselves in a low-key argument.

"Wait," Bora hesitated, trying to grasp the entire picture. "How did you meet this guy again?"

"He was busking outside a pawn shop," answered Rick, fully aware that he was not making the strongest case for his own sanity.

"Rick! Are you kidding me?!? This is *my* apartment. Are you telling me you just invited a street person over here?!? During a pandemic?!? I can't—"

"He's *not* a street person," Rick argued. "At least, I don't think so. Besides, I'm a musician and you're an artist, we're one degree removed from being street people ourselves."

"Okay, fine," she pouted. "If you say so. But what about Covid?"

"I'm locked in a life-or-death struggle with extraterrestrial elves, and you're worried about Covid?" As soon as Rick finished the words, a knock came at the door. "That's him," Rick whispered, nodding for Bora to answer. It was her apartment, after all.

Bora swung open the door, revealing Devlin Fox in all his glory: a battered leisure suit over yet another Hawaiian shirt, this one patterned with tiny images of Bigfoot riding a surfboard and smoking a blunt.

Devlin grunted and extended a hand. "Pleased to make your acquaintance," he drawled. Name's Devlin Fox, I'm heading up investigation on your friend Ricky's case."

Wide-eyed, Bora glanced at Rick, who offered a *"Well, don't just stand there!"* look from behind the door. Realizing how rude she must seem, she gestured for Devlin to come inside. "Mr. Fox," she greeted. "I'm Bora Choi. Rick was just telling me about you."

Devlin peered around the corner and lifted his chin at Rick. Another grunt. He sidestepped over the threshold, the maneuver necessitated by a large messenger bag slung across one shoulder. Dropping it on the bar, he immediately began rummaging through the bag before extracting a necklace identical to the one Rick wore.

"Ms. Choi, is it? Wear this. You'll need it if you're going to be spending so much time around Ricky." Devlin tapped his chest. "I'll be wearing mine for the duration of my engagement as well."

"Um, thanks," Bora managed, taking the leather loop and iron horseshoe from the stranger.

As she examined it, Devlin said, "Out of the goodness of my heart, I ain't chargin' you for it. *Put it on.*"

Bora nodded, shocked speechless by the visitor's brusque demand. She draped the necklace over her head, then gestured for Devlin and Rick to sit on the couch while she took up her post on the lone barstool.

"Is this a job interview?" grumbled Devlin as he settled in. "I'm allergic to such formalities. I assure you, Ms. Choi, my services have already been procured."

"Nothing of the sort," Bora replied. "And please, just 'Bora' is fine. Rick filled me in on how y'all met."

"Fated, I'spose," Devlin said, glancing at Rick. "Usually the way these things go. If I hadn't taken up to buskin' at that intersection, y'all'd be shit outta luck. You said the charm worked?" Rick nodded. "Knew it would. Gonna make life a helluva lot easier moving forward. How you holdin' up, Rickaroonie? Last night aside, I mean?"

Rick cleared his throat. "I'm, uh, I'm good. Great, even. For a minute there, I thought all this stuff was gone completely. No voices or anything."

Devlin nodded. "Odds are they were probably taken aback when I gave you that necklace outside the bar," he speculated. "If I had to guess, last night was reconnaissance, a little fact-finding mission to see if you were really wearing it."

"I'm sorry," Bora said, confused. "Someone else was with you at the bar?"

"Naw," Devlin explained. "But they're always watching, inches from your nose, invisible. Probably in this room right now." He looked around the apartment.

Bora smiled broadly, but her eyes told another story. Rick recognized that look: it always preceded those rare moments when she shed her playful exterior. Cynicism usually followed. "Mm-hmm," she mused. "And 'they' are…?"

"Fairies," Rick offered, leaping in to smooth over whatever was about to follow. "But they're not like the ones from fairy tales, they're different. Sometimes they look like aliens, it's all mixed up."

Bora nodded, looked at her lap, then stared directly at Devlin. "Mr. Fox—"

"Devlin," he interjected.

"Devlin, you realize that none of this sounds very… reasonable?"

"'Reasonable'?" he repeated. "It's the sleep of reason what produces monsters, Bora."

Bora sighed, searching for another way to delicately phrase her concerns. She failed. "Why are you filling my friend's head with this… this *bullshit*?" she asked venomously. "I don't know what's going on here. If he thinks that wearing a magic necklace keeps him safe, that's one thing. Drawing him into your fantasy is something else entirely. He might see you as some sort of guru, but do you know who I see on my couch? A conman and his mark." She looked to Rick with pity. "Sorry, buddy. No offense to you. Just calling it like I see it."

Rick rushed to the defense. "But the *paintings*, Bora, you said yourself—" He abruptly stopped as Devlin held up a hand. Looking across the couch, Rick saw that the man appeared completely calm. His gaze had never left Bora.

Devlin slowly closed his eyes. Following a deep breath and exhalation, he opened them once more and said, "Stage Four colorectal cancer."

Bora turned her head, eyeing Devlin sideways. "Beg your pardon?"

"You heard me. 'Stage Four colorectal cancer.' Helluva thing for a nine year old to hear. I can't imagine. Did you even understand the words? How long after the diagnosis did you realize she was going to pass?"

Bora was speechless. Several times she opened her mouth to try to speak, but nothing came out. "How do you...?" she managed to say at last.

"Oh. Did Ricky not tell you? I hear things. Sometimes see 'em, too, though it ain't as much as the movies would have you believe. Listen, Bora... she loved you more than anything, you know that? Still does." Devlin paused. To Rick, it looked as if he was debating whether or not to press the matter. "I have to ask... I'm getting something else. Is that... is that why you split up with Hope? Her mama's diagnosis hit a little too close to home?"

For a moment, it looked like Bora might fall off the barstool. She gripped the seat with all her might. Rick jumped off the couch and rushed to Bora's side, embracing her as she let loose a series of sobs that quaked her entire body. There he stood for minutes on end, cradling his crying friend as she teetered on the stool. When she eventually recovered, Bora wiped her eyes, took a deep breath, and glared at Devlin.

"You asshole," she whispered.

Devlin nodded. "Been called worse. Getting results in this field can be tricky, Bora. Folks don't always agree with my methods. I'm a lot of things, but I ain't no conman. So—for the sake of our mutual friend—can you push past your skepticism, so we can get him some help?"

Bora nodded begrudgingly. "What do we need to do?"

Devlin rose from the couch and went to the balcony window. "Good question," he admitted, shoving his hands into his pockets and rocking on his heels. "When first we met, Ricky, what'd I say?"

"That they want something," he replied, releasing Bora.

"And what is that 'something'?"

"*Me.*"

"Right. If that's our working hypothesis, we gotta figure out *why.*"

"How do we do that?"

Devlin pivoted back towards the living room. "Same way you find out what anybody wants," he shrugged. "Ask 'em."

"*Ask* them?"

"There are lots of methods. First thing is to establish a viable channel of communication, a way we can easily raise 'em on the horn." Devlin looked around the apartment. "Not the best space, but it'll do."

Rick thought for a moment, then asked haltingly, "Devlin... This thing... *These things*... I thought they were just *my* problem. But obviously they're starting to affect Bora."

"That happens," Devlin acknowledged with a nod. "There's a contagious quality."

"Contagious," Rick repeated. "We're in an *apartment building*, for Chrissake. Could what we do here put others in danger?"

Devlin chuckled. "Y'ever hear of *koro*?"

"Is that an anime or something?"

"There's an outbreak every now and then. Last one was in the Democratic Republic of the Congo. 2008, I think. I was there when it happened, helping some folks with this real nasty *Emela-Ntouka* that set up shop outside their village. Didn't hear about the outbreak until I got back to Kinshasa, though."

"What are we talking about?" asked Bora, rubbing her forehead.

"Koro's a belief that your penis is withdrawing into your body," Devlin explained. "Not just like, 'Oh, the pool is too cold,' I mean a full-on penile disappearing act. Despite no evidence for its existence, men become convinced that their peckers are retreating into their bodies. And when one feller gets it, you can bet others will follow. One year in the '80s, koro afflicted about three thousand men in China. All because they *believed* it was possible."

"What does this have to do with anything?" asked Rick.

"Belief is the most powerful force in the universe," Devlin declared. "Mass hysteria is genuine, before you even get to the *reality* of these other things. Their attention seems... equally transmissible. So yes, what we do here could spread to others in the building. Easily."

"You know, you could have led with that," Bora scolded. Devlin simply shrugged.

"That settles it, then," Rick decided.

"Settles what?" asked Devlin.

"We're going back to Ellijay," Rick declared, rubbing his face with both hands. When he finished, he looked at his left hand with its glinting wedding band, then toward the bottle of vodka sitting on the bar. "Other people shouldn't get pulled into my problems."

"I don't know about that," Bora responded. "Your problems are my problems. I'm coming with you."

"Really, Bora? You want to follow me up there? After all I've put you through?"

Bora looked pointedly at Devlin. "This time, I'm seeing things through to the end," she said. Her glimmer of belief made the man smile for the first time since he had arrived.

In fact, Devlin's entire demeanor had abruptly shifted. Rick diagnosed it as relief and renewal, like a once-onerous task had been suddenly rendered achievable. He sometimes felt that same shift himself, long ago, back when he still gave a damn about teaching guitar. Rick would become disinterested in a student until they themselves demonstrated an eagerness to learn. Then, and only then, would his attitude adjust in turn.

"*Sehr gut*," Devlin said, clapping his hands together. "Bora, why don't you pack a bag? Everything I own is still in the car." He looked at his watch. "Just in time, too. My meter's runnin' out. Ricky, why don't you text your address to that number I gave you? I'll meet y'all there."

Rick pulled out his phone, gratefully noting that it was still partially charged. As he did so, determination blossomed in his chest. He had no idea what lay before him... but whatever it was, he wouldn't face it alone.

26

Saturday, October 4, 1941

LAGOMORPH

"Should just about do it," Cillian grunted as he and the boy hauled the last bushel of corn from the bed of the beaten blue pickup truck. Together, they dragged their load until it sat beneath one of the three tables they had parked behind. Their next task was to frantically sort as many ears as possible into baskets beside the other produce before buyers came flooding into the market.

"That's it," Cillian said, surveying the autumnal tableau the two had created. In addition to the corn, several trips back-and-forth to the farm had left their tables overflowing with a few pumpkins, a sizable stack of zucchini and squash, several baskets of turnips, a pile of potatoes, and a barrel of apples sitting on the ground.

Cillian wiped his brow with a handkerchief, then returned it to his shirt pocket. "Hoof it to your Ma, ask if she needs any assistance," he told his son. "While you're at it, see if you can't find your sister and get her to help, too. She's likely down by the chickens." Ever since the family had sold their own, the girl always spent market days down by the livestock across the field.

"Yes, Pa," the youth smiled. He darted off, weaving between other farmers readying themselves for a long day hawking their goods. Any minute now, locals and people from down the mountain would join them, spending hard-earned cash on everything from foodstuffs to homespun clothing and crafts.

Cillian looked across his own spread with a thankful heart. The morning was clear and sunny, bringing with it the telltale crispness that accompanied the harvest season. These fleeting months were his family's busiest, but they were also their most lucrative. The entire season left everyone in the family absolutely exhausted, especially Cillian. Now forty-four, he began feeling the first tinge of old age setting in. Things he once did without a second thought were simply not as easily accomplished now.

But the hardships and duration of his life also brought him wisdom. The word so often carried weight, as if it was only useful for determining the big picture, like one's path in life. For Cillian, there were different kinds of wisdom: it led to the most prudent decisions, yes, but it also guided innumerable smaller ones. Today, wisdom dictated that he rest as long as he could on the tailgate of his pickup truck for the lengthy day ahead.

He was about to settle down when the first customer arrived. *No rest for the wicked*, he thought as he snatched his money box from the back of the truck. "Good morning, miss," he said with a smile.

The customer, a plump older lady, touched one glove to her chest. "Well, good mornin' to you, too, honey-pie," she gasped in a voice thicker than molasses. "I do declare, you don't quite sound like you're from around these parts!"

"Aye," Cillian confirmed. The people hereabouts were kind enough—quite like those he grew up around—but he never stopped feeling like an outsider.

"Well, inquiring minds want to know! Might you be English, mister...?"

"*Irish*, actually," he responded, giving her the benefit of the doubt. "My name is Cillian."

"Doesn't that beat all?!?" she exclaimed. "Tell me, Cillian, have you got any four-leafed clovers for sale?" She laughed, quite pleased with her joke. Cillian only responded with a tired grin. The woman introduced herself as Beula Mae Lineberger.

"What does your stewpot want, Ms. Lineberger?" asked Cillian. "Got a whole press of squash, if that's to your taste."

Beula Mae ignored the question. "My goodness, I don't know if I have ever met someone from *Ira-land*," she rattled on. "How long have you been in America?"

Cillian sighed. He wasn't good at this. Never was. Deep down inside, he was a reclusive homebody and, although overwhelmed with appreciation for his new life and family, secretly yearned to be back in his farmhouse thousands of miles away, brusquely dispensing remedies to people who knew when they should get down to business rather than engage in idle banter. Still, this was part of his job now. He had mouths to feed.

"Oh, let me think," he ruminated, waving a fly from his face. "We left home early in '23, spent a few weeks in Liverpool, then headed over after that."

"You said, 'We'," Beula Mae pried. "You got a family?"

"Yes, ma'am. My wife Kathleen came with me. Though she weren't my wife at the time, we wed several years afterward." When he saw the barely concealed shock on his customer's face, Cillian rushed to explain. "No, no, Miss Lineberger. Nothing scandalous. I helped her escape some family trouble, is all."

Although he had no desire to revisit them, Cillian thought back to those anxious months after rescuing Kathleen from Monilea. There were ample reasons to leave the country: the blossoming civil war, the threat of church and state persecution, and her mother's fatal heart attack, an aftershock of Father Cormick's cruelty. Until they reached the United States, they had cowered like churchmice in Belfast dosshouses until she recovered, the two of them sleeping in shifts to assuage the ever-present threat posed by authorities and thieves alike.

Cillian never had designs on the girl—he thought of her more like a wounded bird and treated her as a ward until she turned twenty—but affinity bred affection, so the two came together to start a new life. Neither of them had any love for the city, so shortly thereafter they left New York with what little they had earned. By the time Black Thursday hit, they were isolated and as happy as could be on a mountain farm far, far to the south in their adopted homeland. Though the work was hard, Cillian found pride in returning to the vocation of his forefathers.

It would have been easier to tell Beula Mae the whole story, but Cillian disliked reliving those years. He doubted she would have appreciated the tale, anyway. The woman's expression remained frozen in revulsion.

"Ah, I've made a pig's mickey of it," Cillian added under his breath, grateful that she didn't understand the idiom. "We've been married fifteen years, now," he declared more confidently. "Got three children, two boys and a girl. Youngest nineteen months, oldest eleven years. My pride and joy, they are."

The narrative now rectified, Beula Mae broke into a smile. "Bless your heart," she said. "Well, I, for one, would like to support the American dream. I'll take these here squash." She plucked a trio of yellow vegetables from their crate. After paying, she slipped them into her poke along with her other goods and turned to leave.

"I'll be, a real-life leprechaun," she chuckled. She wound through the other customers, whistling *When Irish Eyes Are Shining*.

Wouldn't wish for that if I were you, Cillian thought as she disappeared into the crowd. Even though he had literally dealt with *them* his entire life, he never got used to how he felt in *their* presence. Everything felt lighter when *they* were around—not in a positive, uplifting sense, but rather like the slightest breeze might sweep all of reality away in a heartbeat.

Yet it was this exact quality that allowed *them* to be so helpful. If there was anything *they* couldn't do, Cillian had yet to come across it. All you had to do was ask the right questions and offer appropriate compensation. Otherwise, you'd float away on the wind, never heard from again.

In the old country, *their* presence was unnerving. Here in America, with so much land yet untamed, the sensation was downright panic-inducing. Sometimes it seemed like *they* were everywhere, thick as the grass. From the day he arrived, Cillian could never quite decide whether *they* had followed him to these shores or whether *they* already awaited him here. He suspected it was a little of both, that such distinctions mattered little to *them*. *They* were, *they* always would be, and paid little mind to such human constructs as time or geography.

Either way, the ones in these mountains were queer. The first few of *them* he met at night, coming in the opposite direction down the road on foot. On each occasion, he mistook *them* for one of the natives hereabouts, descendants of those allowed to remain after their tribes' removal. It was only after they passed by that he comprehended their anachronistic appearance, as stereotypical as if they had stepped out of a dime novel: muscular braves covered in war paint, bare-chested, wearing loincloths, with feathers in their long, dark hair. Whenever he looked behind himself or glanced in his rearview mirror, the Indians were inevitably nowhere to be found.

Cillian didn't realize the error of his ways until he actually befriended some of the tribespeople and saw their traditional clothing, which looked very little like what he had seen. When these new friends shared the myths of their people with Cillian, it left him startled. Their own stories were remarkably consistent with his interactions growing up. He concluded that these tribes must have interacted with the same presence that had defined his own life all those years ago across the Atlantic.

After that, *they* appeared to him in more familiar guises: lights, little people, animals, movement caught out of the corner of his eye. Contact firmly reestablished, Cillian rekindled his relationship with the Other Crowd. Soon his old livelihood, once his primary source of income, had become a thriving secondary occupation. Most of the time, he didn't need *their* help. When he did, however, it proved invaluable... though it always came with the same steep price it carried back home.

Kathleen didn't seem to mind him taking up the old ways again. After all, she and Cillian wouldn't have a family without *their* intercession. Her only condition was that her husband keep his actions relatively quiet. Neither of them wished to face the scorn of the Church again, and the people in this part of the country were convinced that the devil himself lurked around every corner. Therefore, none of Cillian's folk cures were offered for sale today at the market, only the very boring, wholesome yield from the farm.

The morning soon shifted to midday. Whenever there was a lull, Cillian would take out his diary and work on today's entry. For years, he had fastidiously documented the passing of each day.

It was early afternoon when Cillian noticed a familiar sensation. It occurred in another one of those long stretches between customers, when he rearranged his produce. Although his back was to the market, there was the sense of the crowd thinning behind him, paired with the approach of two presences. The hair on his neck stood on end. A slight ring rose in his ears, barely perceptible but present nonetheless. Worst of all, everything around him—to his utter dismay—began feeling *lighter.*

"Daddy!" a small voice behind him exclaimed. "My new friend wanted to meet you." Turning, Cillian saw two vastly disproportionate figures. His middle child, five-year-old Siobhán, was looking up at a woman a few inches taller than her father. The lady was dressed in a white skirt suit that matched her Castle bob. She looked expectantly at

Cillian with deep-set blue eyes. Behind her, the market appeared mostly empty. The few farmers who remained at their stalls wore blank expressions, staring off into the distance.

Cillian knew those angular features as well as he knew his own mother's face. Instinctively, he placed a hand atop Siobhán's dark head, drawing her closer. As he did so, the woman feigned an expression like she was wounded.

"Cillian," the lady offered, her light voice lilting with the same brogue as the man she addressed. "I must confess, I'm a bit hurt. I was just catching up with an old friend. I haven't seen Siobhán in years. She's grown so!"

"Stay away from her," Cillian growled. "You agreed to as much."

The woman in white clucked her tongue, then started examining the produce, running her long fingers down the length of a zucchini. "Where are the rabbits?" she asked.

"Don't breed rabbits no more," responded Cillian.

"But you still hunt, don't you? I remember a time when it seemed like you brought coneys to market every day." The lady smiled, her immaculate white teeth gleaming in the sunlight. "I do so *love* a good rabbit stew," she added with a jagged breath.

"Plenty in the forests hereabouts. You're welcome to hunt them yourself, ma'am."

"Oh, but you always bagged the *best* ones," she cried, shaking a fist. Her enthusiasm startled Siobhán, who fell behind her father.

Cillian chose his words carefully. "That's because I only brought the *right* ones," he explained. "Some are too young, others too wily. Today, whenever I go hunting for the *market*, many a time… I cannot pull the trigger."

The lady's eyebrows, immaculately sculpted, raised in surprise. "Come now, Cillian. Do you not appreciate the virtues of capitalism? Supply and demand? I stand before you, an eager buyer, willing to pay any price." She thrust out her lower lip in a pout. "And you have no rabbits for me."

Cillian stood up straighter, doing his best to meet the woman's eyes. "I seem to recall a time long ago, far away, when you took more than your fair share. Never was duly compensated for that."

"Were you not?!?" the lady cackled. She waved a hand, either gesturing at the tables of produce, Siobhán, or both—Cillian wasn't sure. Her laughter continued much longer than it should have, until she was fully doubled over. Despite making a complete fool of herself, none of the other farmers reacted, nor did the few customers who meandered by.

When the woman stopped, she arched her back. Whatever few inches Cillian had gained, she reclaimed, towering above him.

"Have it your way," she announced. "You have to go hunting *eventually*. My advice? Best done before the frost sets in." Her eyes wandered to the little girl cowering behind her father.

The woman in white uttered one final statement: "Wouldn't want the little ones to suffer, would we?" With that, she clasped her hands together and backed into the crowd, which had somehow thickened without Cillian noticing. In the blink of an eye, she was gone.

"Daddy?" chirped Siobhán.

Cillian kept his eyes locked on the spot where the woman in white had disappeared. "Yes, love?"

"I was wrong. I don't think she's my friend."

"I don't think so either," Cillian agreed.

The day resumed as if nothing had ever happened. In fact, it was a resounding success. The family had very little produce left over to take home. Kathleen arrived shortly before the market closed. She brought with her the few items of clothing she had not sold during her time at her own booth across the market, but those treasures were far less valuable than the warm, calming presence that accompanied her.

As he loaded the pickup truck with his wife in the late afternoon sun, Cillian wondered not for the first time whether his mother would have looked so happy had she lived a bit longer. Time had been kind to neither of them, but Cillian cared little for such superficialities. Rather than the superficial dross of Kathleen's outward appearance—the laugh lines, the sun spots, the stretch marks evident as she crawled into bed beside him each night—he saw the resiliency of her spirit. Every challenge she ever faced, she surmounted through determination and sheer will. Kathleen's ability to turn the worst situations for the better was a magic far more powerful and mysterious than anything Cillian ever learned during his lifetime of sorcery.

After they finished packing, their eldest hopped in the bed of the truck while the rest of the family crammed into the cab for the long ride home. The family rode in silence most of the way, listening to the gravel scrape and bump beneath the tires. Not even the toddler clutching Kathleen's breast uttered a sound. Siobhán fell asleep somewhere along the way.

It wasn't until the car turned off the main road that Kathleen spoke. "Did you meet Siobhán's 'friend'?" she asked. "She came by my table to 'introduce' me before she ran off to find you."

"That I did," Cillian quietly replied. "You met her, too?"

Kathleen chuckled. "Cillian, you never cease to amaze me."

"How's that?"

"You're such a good father, even after all these years. I don't have the patience anymore. I told her she was getting too old for imaginary friends."

27

Thursday, October 29, 2020

HOMECOMING

Around ten minutes until three o'clock, the trio of cars began their bumpy descent down the last leg of the dirt driveway: Rick's blue Corolla, Bora's black Sentra, and Devlin's rusting, brown Suburban. A figure in a purple tank top and jeans, small and stooped, awaited them by the front door of Rick's house, chain smoking. She may have appeared tiny, but she asserted her ownership and presence no less authoritatively than the Colossus of Rhodes.

Rick was the first to greet her after everyone had parked. "Hey, stranger," he said, slamming the door and stepping out into the sunlight. Immediately, he started sweating through his black tee shirt. The temperature was approaching eighty degrees again—one of those revolting days of summer that somehow infiltrated autumn in Georgia.

Edna Durchdenwald finished her cigarette, ground it on the cement doorstep, and lit another. "I've been gone half a year, and you ain't got shit done around here, Rick," she said, her voice rattling. "Starting to make me think I should've forked out the money for a professional. Who the fuck are all these people?"

Rick retrieved his duffel bag and guitar from the trunk. "I tried calling every other week," he sighed. "You never answered. When you did, you were always too preoccupied to talk. Don't you check your voicemail?" Edna only grunted. "How was Florida? Looks like you got a tan."

"You mean my great Freedom Tour?" she asked. "Fan-fucking-tastic. Gotta show you pictures." She pulled out her cellphone and began swiping through a montage of palm trees, nightclubs, and an abundance of bronzed, wrinkled flesh. "Ooh, this is the hunk I told you about, Eduardo, I think he's sweet on me. Won't stop texting—" Edna stopped abruptly, just now noticing Bora's approach. Devlin had yet to exit his car.

"Hi," Bora said, extending a hand. She wore a red blouse and blue jeans. "I'm Bora, Rick's friend."

"Well ain't you just cute as a speckled pup?" said Edna, her cigarette bouncing with every word. "I like her, Rick." Edna then held the back of her hand to her mouth, adding loud enough for them both to hear: "I never liked that Credenza, anyhow."

"For the last time, *Cassandra*," corrected Rick.

"I'm just a friend," Bora rushed to explain. For the first time today she was all smiles, back to her chit-chatty self. "This place is amazing. What an incredible view! And I love that shirt—oh, I'm sorry. I'm so rude. Do you want me to put on my mask, Ms. Durchdenwald?"

Edna scoffed. "I ain't afraid of no 'kai-rona virus.' If you're fine with me not wearing one, I don't give two shits what you do. Hate the goddamn things. Tell you what, I ain't worn a mask since 1996. Ended up $200 short and sore for a week."

"... oh... okay..."

"Well, if y'ain't fuckin', how do y'all know each other?"

"Old college buddies," Rick said.

Bora added, "Rick's been staying at my place until he can get back on his feet."

Edna's face contorted into a dramatic expression, so popeyed that Rick half wondered whether or not she was a goblin herself. "Back on your feet? Rick, what the fuck is going on? All these people... the house has been turned upside down... you on drugs? I don't mind weed, but anything else—"

"Nothing like that, Edna," Rick interjected. He was growing weary of wading through the skepticism of others, but his story had to be retold. "You're not going to believe me, but—"

His voice was drowned out by a sudden blare of music. A pair of rattlesnake boots dropped to the dust, accompanied by the final chorus of The Band's *The Night They Drove Old Dixie Down*. Devlin Fox swung from the cracked driver's seat of the Suburban like a gunslinger dismounting his horse, cutting through the humidity and heat with a lopsided swagger on his way to the showdown. Without breaking Edna's gaze, he casually flicked the butt of his cigarette into the garden, sending it bouncing off the head of the wooden bear and tumbling to the ground.

"Ricky never told me you were such a looker, Ms. Durchdenwald," he grinned, charisma dripping from his teeth. "My name is Devlin Fox. This must be the henhouse."

Rick was confused. He didn't recall ever mentioning Edna to Devlin, but it seemed possible that such a minor detail had slipped over the past week of intoxicated terror. Edna, on the other hand, was enraptured.

"*Enchanté*," she said, eyes gleaming.

"*Une belle langue d'une belle dame*," Devlin continued. "*Je ne devrais pas être surpris. Quand y avez-vous vécu?*"

Edna giggled and blushed. "Oh my *goodness*. Rick, how long will your friends be staying?"

"Just until I finish my job, madam," Devlin replied.

"Job? What job?"

"Seems like the Little People have taken an interest in your tenant, here. They've been harassing him—misplaced objects, disembodied voices, things moving around the house, poltergeist activity, plus all that UFO pageantry like missing time, unexplained aerial phenomena... seems our boy here even got himself abducted a few weeks back. Don't you worry your pretty lil' head, though, I'm gonna get to the bottom of it, Lord willing and the creek don't rise. I'll be using your basic suite of detection equipment. Nothin' too fancy, just your usual stuff, trying to catch EVPs, anomalous EMF readings, and the like. That don't work, I've got some esoteric skills I can try. Shouldn't be more'n a week, I reckon."

There was a long pause while Rick and Bora looked expectantly at Edna, fully prepared to spend the rest of the afternoon on the doorstep trying to convince her to let a madman into her rental property. The old lady took a long drag on her cigarette, eyeing him suspiciously, then let her arm fall loosely to her side as she shifted her weight from foot to foot.

"Shitfire, boy, come on in!" she exclaimed, whirling about and opening the door. "I *love* this shit. I never miss an episode of *Ghost Adventures*. Tell me, you know Zak Bagans?"

Devlin followed her inside, smiling. From the looks of it, he never doubted whether or not Edna would receive him warmly. "Funny you should ask," he began, his voice trailing off as the pair disappeared inside. "First time I…"

Bora looked at Rick. The two of them were too astonished to move. This was not the same taciturn misanthrope who had visited her apartment earlier that day. "Remind me where you found this guy again?" she asked.

"I told you," said Rick. "Crossroads in front of a pawn shop."

Bora took a long drag on her vape as she headed back to the car to grab her bag. "You sure he's not the devil?" she wondered.

Everyone settled into the Ellijay property. Rick and Bora soon began to feel like they were eavesdropping on a private date between Devlin and Edna, who spent the next few hours inseparable. They giggled and laughed, Devlin regaling her with war stories from Yakutsk, Auckland, São Paulo, Vienna, Kuala Lumpur, Nepal, Nairobi, and a dozen other locales Edna would never visit, only to be interrupted from time to time to listen to her own (perceived) brushes with the paranormal. When he produced another horseshoe pendant for her to wear, Edna accepted it from him like it was an engagement ring. They even took a trip to the supermarket together to pick up ingredients for dinner, which Edna enthusiastically offered to cook.

In the meantime, Rick did his best to get everyone set up in their makeshift accommodations, sipping from his flask all the while. Bora would sleep on the couch. Rick was worried about her taking time off from work, but Bora assured him that it wasn't an issue. She had extra vacation days to use up before the end of the year anyway, she said, and had taken hardly any because the pandemic kept the pharmacy so busy.

When it came time to find Devlin a place to stay, he chose the unfinished addition. Rick offered an air mattress, but the peculiar man said he'd be just as comfortable on the cold, hard cement floor.

Afterwards, Rick set in on the strenuous task of getting the house into some semblance of normalcy, cleaning up the mess his visitors had left at the start of the month. He cursed himself for not taking the time to do the bare minimum before fleeing to Atlanta. Plates were scattered about, some broken; clods of dirt lay strewn across the carpet and tile foyer; and worst of all, the entire house smelled like sour milk and old trash. Amidst his floor scrubbing and Febreze spraying, Rick found a moment to thank himself for closing the refrigerator prior to leaving.

He had just finished ordering the silverware—thankfully, the *knife, spoon, fork* ritual went smoothly—when Devlin and Edna returned from the grocery store. Rushing out to help, Rick found the two carrying in the first load, chattering like old friends.

"I forgot to remark on the lovely state of your garden," Devlin commented, hoisting a paper bag in his arms. "Is that cowslip, perchance?"

"Absolutely is," Edna answered, rattling off the other things she grew. She slipped past Rick as he held the door open, barely acknowledging his presence. After everything was unloaded, the happy couple began chopping vegetables and singing old showtunes while Rick hauled material down to the basement to patch the hole in the wall.

Everything was just as he left it, with a few notable exceptions. The loose bricks had fallen to the floor alongside the magazine and bubble wrap. With a sigh, he began his work, made less tedious by the nascent buzz brought on by his flask. Eventually, Rick replaced the bricks and headed upstairs, leaving the mortar to dry. Hopefully it would set by the time his intruders paid another visit.

Rick paused halfway to listen to an unfamiliar sound floating down the steps. It was laughter, something this house had not heard in a long, long time. Although he had grown to resent this place since March, it had nothing to do with the residence itself. A house is but a mirror. It reflects the emotions of those within. As he closed the basement door behind him, Rick realized that he didn't hate the building at all. What he felt was resentment toward *himself*. Each room was a character defect made material. The kitchen—always full of empty bottles—was his gluttony, the makeshift studio of his bedroom his pride, the unfinished addition his sloth. The laughter of friends, old and new, washed all that away, feeling like nothing less than expiation.

Everyone settled into dinner a little after seven o'clock. Rick threw on Dave Alvin's *Ashgrove*, a little music to dine by. Once they gathered, the conversation naturally gravitated toward Rick's situation. Part of him felt awkward being the topic of discussion. Another part of him, the part that loved being the center of attention onstage, kind of enjoyed it.

"Tell me, Edna," Devlin asked after swallowing a big bite of fried chicken. "Ricky says he's been seeing lights on the mountain. All this time, your family has owned this land. Ever hear about that growing up?"

Edna thought for a second, then said, "Not really. But you know how it is. Those kinds of stories are a dime a dozen up here. Indian women looking for their lost lovers after they die, headless train conductors, all that stuff. Don't surprise me to hear something like that happening on Red Ear. Never saw none of it myself, though." Devlin nodded. He looked mildly concerned.

"So what's the plan?" wondered Rick, wiping his mouth. "We going to set up cameras and stuff? I was thinking we could focus on my bedroom. Use me as bait."

"I do *not* want footage of your bedroom," quipped Bora, poking at her green beans.

"We shall pick up an existence from its frogs, Ricky," Devlin said. Everyone looked confused. "Nothing so fancy as all that. We watch and we wait. Keep an eye out for the little things."

"Seems pretty quiet so far," Rick observed. "I've stayed pretty busy, though. Not sure I'd notice otherwise."

"Looks like we might get our first chance soon. Take a gander at the clock." Following Devlin's instruction, Rick looked at the microwave. It was 8:10. He grabbed the remote and paused the album.

"What about it?" asked Bora.

Devlin tapped the table thoughtfully as the clock advanced a minute. For sixty seconds, everyone remained quiet, waiting for something to happen. Once the clock showed 8:12, Devlin spoke. "Dang. Guess we gotta wait for, what? 10:18? You wanna get 'em up to speed, Ricardo?"

"I've been seeing these numbers, over and over," Rick clarified, turning the music back on. "Usually it's 1-1-0-8, but sometimes it's rearranged. Seems like it's important somehow."

"The fuck is all that about?" asked Edna, pausing halfway to burp.

"Theater," Devlin replied. "It's their language, the easiest way for them to communicate. This 1108 thing… they're trying to tell us somethin', tell *Ricky* somethin'. Part of what we have to figure out."

"They speak in numbers?" probed Bora.

"Ain't just numbers. Synchronicities more generally—you know, them lil' blips you experience from time to time. 'Turkey tracks in red snow.' You read a story about Djibouti, then the rest of the day you hear it over and over again—on the news, in conversation, in a movie, in your dreams. Or you think of someone you ain't thought about in years, and they call you up on the phone."

"That happens to me!" piped up Edna. "I was flipping through the channels the other day and Disney was showing *Lilo & Stitch*. Get this: the day before, *I bought a Lelo Soraya*. It's even blue, like that little alien." She looked expectantly around the table, sure that everyone would grasp the connection.

"What's that?" inquired Rick.

"A rabbit," Edna revealed.

"Huh?"

"A *vibrator*, Rick, she's talking about a vibrator," Bora shouted, mildly disgusted by the image Edna's story conjured. "Look—I'm having trouble with this whole 'fairy' thing." Devlin flinched at the word. "For the sake of the argument, let's say you're right. Why are they *here*? Aren't fairies just in, like, Ireland and Scotland?"

"That's a bit like asking, 'Ain't Christ just in Israel?'" retorted Devlin, leaning back from the table, his hands behind his head. "Ones we're dealing with might've come over with the immigrants. Might've been here already—most of the tribes on this continent believed in Little People, too. You'll find the same legends repeated all across the globe. In Iceland, for example, there are elves practically identical to the *Aos Sidhe*. They call 'em the *Huldufólk*."

"Who the fuck?" asked Edna.

"Never mind. Main takeaway is that these things are everywhere and nowhere."

"And they're *fairies*," Bora added skeptically. "Or are they goblins? Gnomes? I think I saw one guarding a lawn down the highway, maybe you should start there."

Devlin chose to take Bora's jab seriously. "You can even call 'em aliens if you like, Bora," he drawled. "I don't split hairs much on taxonomy. Sometimes, I call 'em 'faeliens.' Get it?"

"Oh, I get it," she shot back. "They're anything and everything to you, so you can never be wrong."

Devlin shook his head. "Everyone's a con artist to you, ain't they? I'm just being honest. All I can say for certain is that they're older than we can comprehend. Older than comprehension itself, probably. Beyond that, it's all just guesses. Maybe they're spirits. Maybe they're us. As for me, I suspect that they're—y'ever read Jung?—they're the flora and fauna of the Collective Unconscious. Where all our myths, old and new, even imagination itself, originate."

"'Spirits'?" asked Rick, knotting his brow. "'Us'? You think they could be... dead people?" He thought of his father's urn in the shed.

"Some folks used to equate 'em with the dead, for sure," Devlin replied. "I don't adhere to that myself, though there's something to it. After all, plenty of dead folk seem to find their way to 'em. But sortin' it all out... where you draw those lines? Ain't important." He looked around the dining room. "The sort of stuff you've experienced here—things disappearing, doors opening, pictures flying off the walls—you'll find a little of it in everything. Encounters with ghosts? Yeah. But also fairies and UFOs. Hell, even some Bigfoot sightings."

Bora nearly spit out her drink. Rick said what she was thinking. "Bigfoot, Devlin? Really?"

"You're having an existential crisis involving fairies and you're gonna scoff when I mention Bigfoot?" countered Devlin. "Is that your new line in the sand?"

"Fair enough," Rick admitted.

Devlin leaned forward, looking intently across the table at Bora with his blue and brown eyes. "So, to answer your original question, Bora: yes, *fairies*. And I'll tell you right now... y'all better dissuade yourselves of the notion that they look like little vixens with wings. Whatever happens the next few days, be prepared for anything. They're shapeshifters."

"Like Pennywise," Rick offered.

Devlin rolled his eyes. "Yes, Ricky, like Pennywise."

"Shapeshifters," Bora interjected, keeping her eyes locked on Devlin's. "Like I said: anything and everything."

"Not so," grumbled Devlin, fending off defeat. "At their core, they're probably the same thing. Let's see... Tell me, Ricky: what style music you play?"

"A little bit of everything," Rick explained. "A lot of country these days. I'd like to play more jazz. But I can show up to the gig and play whatever."

"But regardless of whether or not you're playing country or classical or funk, it's still you behind the guitar, right?"

"Of course. I just... change the style to match the setting."

"See, Bora?" sniped Devlin. "*He* gets it. Now let's reverse the scenario, Ricky: if you're one of three guitarists, all playing—shit, I dunno, Bach or something—Bora here, listening to a recording, might be forgiven for thinking it's all the same player on the same instrument, right?"

"Yeah, I guess," Rick admitted, looking at his friend. "Sometimes it takes a trained ear to hear differences between performances of the same composition."

"*A trained ear can tell the difference.* Hear that, Bora? Otherwise, you assume it's all the same person when it ain't, or you assume it's all different people when it ain't. Same thing with this stuff. Situation like you got here? Ain't worth saying whether it's classical, or jazz, or country. There are bits of this, bits of that. When all is said and done, it's all guitar music. That's how you gotta approach it: focus less on *what* it is, and more on the fact that it *just is*. At the end of the day, it's all *them*."

With that, Devlin rose from the table and began collecting everyone's empty plates. Once the dishes were washed, everyone gathered in the living room. Devlin was the last to enter, and commanded everyone to their feet.

"We need to make sure we're protected moving forward," he said. "Not just the physical body, but the etheric body as well. Now, I want everyone to close your eyes. Inhale through your nose. Relax. I want you to picture a bright, white light, like a wall in front of you... imagine that light envelopin' you like a blanket ... surroundin' your body... surroundin' this house...."

All told, Devlin's guided meditation lasted about half an hour. Rick tried his best to stay focused. He could sense Bora's frustration at what he was sure she thought was just a load of hocus pocus; while Devlin's psychic revelation from her mother had proven convincing, Bora still had a long way to go, and the lingering resentment certainly didn't help. Devlin concluded his protections by smudging everyone with sage, trailing the smoke down their bodies, leaving the pleasant odor to diffuse throughout the house.

"Now what?" asked Edna. "Are you going to break out your ghost hunting equipment? I'll take the tape recorder. I wanna catch an EVP. I've got so many questions."

Devlin looked to the windows around the room. None of the curtains were drawn. "No gadgets tonight. In fact, that reminds me: phones off. Not silent, *off.* We take our posts. Edna, you get the storm door up front; Bora, the kitchen window. I'll set up looking out over the patio at the mountain."

"What about me?" wondered Rick.

"You're the center of it all, so you take the center," Devlin directed. "Patrol the living room and dining room. Poke your head into the other rooms every now and then, but don't linger alone. Look and listen for anything out of the ordinary. Watch our backs for us."

Edna and Devlin took one last smoke break. After they pulled up their chairs to the appointed positions, Devlin turned off all the lights and the HVAC. Everyone then sat quietly in the darkness, facing the moonlit landscape outside.

28

Thursday, October 29, 2020

THE GREAT KABBALAH
OF THE GREEN BUTTERFLY

Rarely had Rick done anything so tedious as wandering the house over and over in the dark. The urge to throw on an album to make it pass more quickly became irresistible.

Thank God I have this flask, he thought, taking another drink to push back the boredom. *I've been in louder libraries.* Absolutely nothing happened. The irony that their first attempt to make contact would be so uneventful—when for months Rick had suffered abundant activity unsolicited—was not lost on him.

After about an hour, however, he noticed that the energy in the room changed. Rick realized that everyone was bracing for 10:18, but the time came and went without incident. In the minutes that followed, all four observers managed to remain silent and still, saying very little in anticipation of 11:08's dreaded approach. It, too, fell into the past without the barest hint of fulfilling its threat.

At last, their discipline gave way to light conversation. It was Bora who broke protocol. "Ugh," she groaned. "Remind me why we're doing this again?"

"Waitin' to see what happens," Devlin answered flatly, staring into the darkness.

"How long is it supposed to take?"

"Look, I never said this stuff shows rhyme or reason. It's repeatable, but not on demand."

"See, I have trouble buying that," snapped Bora. "My whole life, I've never seen one convincing bit of evidence for *any* of this stuff. It's always a bunch of blurry photos of lights in the sky or tree stumps with red circles around them that are supposed to be Bigfoot."

"Not always," Edna countered, taking her phone from her pocket and booting it up. The splash of light underneath her face made her look like a late-night public-access horror host. "I've got this app on my phone, *GhostSnapp*. It lets you take pictures of spirits."

"Edna!" hissed Rick. "We're not supposed to—"

"Nah, that's alright," Devlin interrupted, rubbing his eyes. "While we're at it, Bora, boot up your phone, too."

There was a bit of fumbling in the dark before Bora sheepishly admitted, "I can't. It's dead. Again."

A chortle rose in front of the sliding glass window. "What was that about photographic evidence, again?" teased Devlin. "How can you rely on pictures when these things sap your battery? Whatever they are, *they* control the narrative, up to and includin' how often they're caught on camera."

"Mine's working fine," croaked Edna as she pecked away at her screen.

"Well," Devlin pointed out, "you ain't been around Ricky as much, have you?"

Edna ignored the question. "Let's see… *GhostSnapp*. I've got lots of pictures you need to see, Devlin. Oh, this one's good." She left her post and wobbled through the darkened living room to share the slideshow of photos with her new friend. "See?" she said, reaching her arm around Devlin's shoulder, cramming her phone in his face. "This one looks just like the ghost of a little dog. Oh, and I think this one's a dead Confederate soldier. I took that in my bedroom."

Devlin squinted at the bright screen, looking pained as the parade of nonsense scrolled by. From what Rick could see, Edna mostly had a collection of overlit dust particles, digital artifacts, and lens malfunctions. She stopped to point out one in particular. "Couldn't figure this one out," she puzzled. "Looks like a winged beaver-man eating a corndog."

Devlin's face pulled closer to Edna's phone. "Now *that* looks legit," he stated. "Others, not so much."

"Gimme a fucking break," Bora moaned in exasperation.

"Don't be so quick to throw out the odd stuff," Devlin admonished her. "Nine times out of ten, that stuff's the real deal."

"That's not the way these things work," argued Bora, spinning around in her chair to face the back of Devlin's head. "I've seen the movies. There are rules."

"Rules?" asked Rick, taking another sip from his flask.

"Yeah, you know. Like, a demon can possess a person, but it can't possess a toaster."

"I know a feller in Bozeman who would disagree with that," Devlin drawled. "*Rules*? There ain't no *rules*, Bora. Only guidelines at best. Whatever these are—and look, after thirty-odd years of doin' this, I ain't so certain what they are myself—but whatever they are, they skirt the boundaries between reality and unreality. I've seen things… One-in-a-million odds flip to a million-in-one. Impossibilities become certainties. Some folks call it 'High Strangeness.' I call it 'The Wake.' When you're caught up in the same space as them, nonsense starts bubblin' up."

Rick struggled to comprehend Devlin's point. "Wait, are you saying that's why our phones keep dying?"

"I think that's different. No one can say for sure, though. Some folks think it's how these phenomena gather energy to manifest in our world. Edna's phone will probably start drainin' soon enough."

"What about clocks, then? Is that why they keep going haywire around me? Sometimes I look, and I can't account for where the time went." Rick paused. "I mean, when I'm not drunk," he added.

"Well, used to be they said missing time was just amnesia, that the aliens had somehow 'wiped your memory' in the interim before returning you to Earth. I suspect it's stranger. Something to do with time bendin' in their presence." Devlin took a deep breath, then exhaled wearily. "Or it could be both. All just theories."

By now, Edna had returned to her seat. "You said these things want Rick," she declared, changing the subject. "That don't sound too good to me. They wanna fuck 'im?"

"Seems like they could've done that already," mumbled Rick.

"I dunno, I've been trying for over a year," Edna joked. "If not that, then what? They want his soul? Are they evil?"

"Maybe," admitted Devlin. "Maybe not. Too soon to tell. Part of what I wanna suss out."

Bora finally posed the million dollar question. Rick might have been offended had he not fretted over it countless times himself: "You think they might kill him?"

"Certainly on the table," Devlin acknowledged. "But I wouldn't fret too much over that. There are worse things, after all."

"*Worse* things?"

Devlin rose from his position, looking like a southern fried skeleton stretching in the darkness. His face slipped from the moonlight back into shadow as he faced Bora, who was still turned around in her chair. "You tell me," he prodded. "Can you think of anything worse?"

Bora hesitated. After a moment, she suggested, "Hell?"

"Nope. Close."

"... not existing at all?"

"Lookit that, she *can* be taught! What do you think, Bora? Is that a fate worse than death? We used to believe in the possibility. As one among many, consider Ammit, the Egyptian soul devourer. A demoness with the head of a crocodile, the mane of a lion, and the body of a hippopotamus."

"Sounds like Noah needed some chaperones," Edna remarked.

Devlin continued. "If you died and your heart was weighed heavier than a feather, she'd devour it whole. Then you're gone." He snapped his fingers. "Just like that. No reincarnation, no afterlife, just... nothing. Worse than eternal damnation, don'tcha think?"

"Bummer," Bora wisecracked, taking a drag on her vape.

Rick rubbed his eyes, pondering the possibility. Somehow, after all he'd been through, it actually sounded kind of pleasant. "I'd take it," he challenged, looking at his flask flashing in the moonlight. "It's not the worst thing."

"You kidding me?" countered Devlin. He looked incredulous.

"Absolutely. I can think of a lot of worse things than that."

"Like *what?*"

"Like seeing the world crumble around you with no way of fixing it. Like a lifetime of wasted potential. Like disappointing your friends and family. Hurting them. Pushing them away... Not existing? I'd take that in a heartbeat." With these final words, he drained his flask and headed to the kitchen to refill it.

Edna watched as he went. "Is that it?" she exclaimed. "We done here?"

"Not quite," Devlin corrected, looking at his watch. "Coming up on 1:18 soon. Wanna try one last thing before we call it a night."

"What's that?" inquired Rick.

"Poke the bear," Devlin responded, acting like it explained everything. With feline grace, he followed Rick into the kitchen and began rummaging through the cabinets.

"Uh, can I help you?" asked Rick mid-pour.

"Need a copper pan."

"Should be a saucepan below the microwave…"

Devlin thanked Rick as he dove into the base cabinet. He popped back up holding the saucepan and a Tupperware container, then pointed to the flask. "That brandy?"

"Hardly," Rick chuckled. "Bottom shelf vodka."

"Eh, it'll do in a pinch," Devlin conceded as he darted back into the living room. "After all, ain't noon or the summer, neither. Bring that flask with ya, if you don't mind." He opened the sliding glass door and disappeared, leaving Rick, Bora, and Edna half-illuminated by the patio light. The trio looked at each other, shrugged, and filed out into the darkness, Edna eagerly lighting a cigarette as they crossed the threshold.

While the day had proven unseasonably hot, the night felt more like fall. It even smelled like it too. A breeze had cleansed the air of any lingering summer humidity, ushering in the scent of decaying leaves. It made the night crisp, allowing the nearly full moon to shine down upon them unimpeded, outlining Red Ear Mountain in a buttery gilt. Devlin was nowhere to be seen.

"Over here!" a voice shouted. When everyone looked in its direction, they found Devlin standing far to their left beneath the hawthorn tree. Rick and Edna stepped off the patio, cutting a path through the field.

"Rick!" whispered Bora as she caught up to them in the side yard. "What the *hell* is going on?"

"Just as clueless as you," he admitted. Upon reaching the tree, they found Devlin holding the kitchenware, impatiently tapping his foot on the ground—not out of any apparent frustration with them but rather with the situation. Standing to his right side, Rick could barely discern a manic look spreading across Devlin's profile in the dim light.

"What y'all think?" he asked, staring at the tree. "Salamanders? Hmm? Salamanders?" He bobbled his head back and forth. "Balls of light, salamanders—makes sense to me." Bora and Rick exchanged glances, confirming their shared confusion.

Edna's eyes never left Devlin. She watched intently as he handed Rick the saucepan and Tupperware, then produced something from his jacket pocket. It looked like a short stick. With intense focus, he began walking a clockwise circle around the tree, wide enough to enclose the group, his stick aimed ominously at the ground.

Bora spoke up. "Is that a—"

"Wand?" snapped Devlin. "Yes. Hush." He then faced east, proclaimed to the darkness, *"Hekas, Hekas, Este Bebeloi!"* and began tracing his wand through the air, gurgling words from his gut in some unknown language. When he finished, he faced south and shouted, *"Oip Teaa Pedoce!* In the names and letters of the Great Southern Quadrangle, I invoke ye, ye Angels of the Watchtower of the South!"

The sound of the words echoing off the mountain made Rick feel uneasy. Somewhere deep inside, he realized that he was in way over his head and slowly began backing away. Before he could break the circle, Devlin paused his invocation to grab Rick's shirt.

"Wouldn't do that if I were you, Richard," he warned, tugging him back. "I know you might not feel comfortable right now, but I promise you that, at this moment, the safest place on the planet for you is inside this circle. You break that invisible line, there ain't nothing I can do to protect you." Releasing Rick's collar, he looked at Bora and Edna. They remained frozen in place. "Same goes for y'all, too."

Devlin continued chanting and waving his arms, but Rick was a thousand miles away. He stood there in a daze while the magician rambled on, proclaiming words to the west and north. The sound of Rick's *actual* name coming from Devlin's mouth, rather than the usual jovial nicknames, conveyed Devlin's sincerity more than any physical assault ever could. By the time the opening invocation finished, Rick finally came to his wits.

"Holy art thou, Lord of the Universe," the magician proclaimed. "Holy art thou, whom Nature hath not formed. Holy art thou, the Vast and the Mighty One. Lord of the Light and the Darkness... The circle is cast."

Replacing his wand, Devlin began a mad scramble up the hawthorn tree, cursing whenever his hands came into contact with the thorniest bits. It ended with him sprawled across the largest of the lower branches, lounging like a leopard. The limb, no higher than Rick's head, creaked under his weight.

He gestured for Rick to pass up both pieces of kitchenware. The moment he did, Devlin began banging the copper saucepan on the limb.

Given the stillness of the night, the development took everyone completely by surprise, forcing them to cover their ears. The sound was deafening and continued far longer than anyone wanted. Rick lost track after fifteen blows, but it seemed like Devlin must have struck the tree twenty-five or thirty times.

Everyone was on the verge of a nervous chuckle when Devlin began shouting, his voice authoritatively ringing out above the trailhead and bouncing off the nearby face of Red Ear Mountain. Rick, his ears still ringing, only caught bits and pieces.

"Immortal, eternal, ineffable and Holy Father of all the things, you who are carried on the chariot that turns the world continuously, dominating the ethereal countries where the throne of your power is raised... O sparkling fire which ignites itself with your own splendor, and comes from your essence inexhaustible streams of light... you created in the elements a third quality of monarchs; and our continuous exercise is to praise you and adore your will...."

Eventually Devlin finished, hands trembling, eyes manic. Everyone waited patiently. As absurd as the last several minutes had proven, Devlin finished the ritual with such conviction that everyone was momentarily seized by a quasi-religious fear.

For a few brief moments, it felt as if revelation was imminent. In those fleeting breaths, Rick, Bora, and Edna joined countless others across time: those standing before the empty tomb, those waiting in the Parthenon, those in Tenochtitlan anticipating the drop of the knife, those interring the Pharaoh in his final resting place. Every star looked like a spaceship waiting to descend, every shadow a demon waiting to congeal out of the darkness. The moments stretched on and on for an eternity... until it became apparent that nothing of import was scheduled for tonight.

"Y'all see any butterflies?" asked Devlin at last.

Rick looked at Bora and Edna. Their faces said everything. Now that the gravity of the moment had passed, everyone simply felt silly, standing there in the field watching a lunatic in a tree with kitchenware in his hands. "Devlin," Rick sighed. "Of course not. It's one in the morning."

"True!" he exclaimed, jabbing a finger at Rick in recognition. "Moths, then?!?"

Trying hard to take him seriously, everyone dutifully surveyed their surroundings. "Some over by the patio light...?" offered Edna.

Devlin squinted from his perch. "Nah. Lookin' for a swarm with green wings."

As he unscrewed the cap of his flask to take a drink, Rick asked, "Still need my booze?"

Devlin shook his head, completely dejected. "Nope," he answered quietly, hoisting the Tupperware. "If I don't need this, I certainly don't need that." He tossed it and the saucepan onto the ground, grumbling. He landed not long afterward, sending up a spray of dew and looking more confused than ever.

"After all that rigamarole," he complained, scratching his head. "I tell you what, sometimes this shit is more interesting when it *don't* work. Turns into a puzzle you have to reverse engineer. Was it 'salamanders'? Was that the wrong choice? Maybe I shoulda tried sylphs. Or was it the timing?" He turned to the others. "What do y'all think?" Everyone shook their heads, eyes wide as saucers.

"Could be I went too far with the sage..." he reasoned, pacing back and forth as much as the circle's confines permitted. "That, or our pendants made these things gun shy. We can't go around wearing 'em the rest of our lives, though. We need *answers*." He ran his fingers through his hair with a sigh, then began moving counterclockwise around the tree, mumbling all the way. "Circle's broken. Y'all are free to go. Get some sleep."

One by one, the participants wordlessly shuffled back into the house. Edna returned home to the other side of the mountain, decidedly less enthusiastic about the paranormal than she had been earlier. As for Rick and Bora, they shared only one short exchange before turning in for the night.

"The fuck was that?" she asked, more concerned than ever.

"I dunno, Bora," Rick answered quietly.

"Rick, we're spending the night with a madman. Promise me he's the harmless kind, rather than the cut-you-into-pieces-while-you-sleep kind."

"I can't," he admitted. "But Devlin's the only hope I've got. The pendants work, don't they?" Bora didn't answer. She simply turned and took her place on the couch.

For several hours afterward, Devlin remained on the patio, frustrated and alone, the automatic light flickering on and off whenever it pleased. As he gazed out on the empty field, it occurred to Devlin that whatever afflicted Rick Coulter seemed to behave in much the same way. Most of the time it festered in the shadows, hiding its secrets in the gaps of Devlin's knowledge. Only now and again did momentary flashes of insight permeate the darkness of ignorance.

Sometime around four in the morning, Devlin crept to the edge of the patio and lit his final cigarette. After his initial drag, he stood there, watching the smoke cling to the awning, then the eaves, then drift into the night sky. His eyes stayed on the house for a long time.

"I'll be damned," he murmured, lips barely moving. "Your arms are folded tight as a drum, ain't they?"

29

Friday, October 30, 2020

PRIMING THE PUMP

DAWN DIDN'T BREAK THE FOLLOWING DAY. It chose instead to dissolve into an overcast mess, peppering the field and forest with a steady downpour. This was fine with Devlin, who, having fallen asleep in the addition only eight or so hours earlier, finally rose at one o'clock in the afternoon. Too often, the sunshine cut his slumber short.

That's a good floor, he thought, peeling off the suit jacket that he had hastily repurposed as a blanket. *Top ten, at least.* He only wore his undershirt and found the room's poor insulation far worse than the lack of a mattress. Rubbing his bare arms, Devlin began rummaging around in his suitcase for a new set of clothes to wear after he took his shower.

Rarely did Devlin consciously sneak up on people, but it happened often nonetheless. The reason why eluded him for years until, on a visit to Myanmar, a Naga shaman matter-of-factly explained to him that he shared their affinity for big cats. Devlin's body, the shaman proclaimed, held within it a leopard that left his body nightly to prowl the astral plane. Rather than file such an assertion under "true" or "false," Devlin chose a third path, accepting it as a metaphorical truth rather than a literal one.

However, moments like this one made him reassess that position. Despite no attempt at subterfuge, Devlin still found himself on the verge of the doorway, with neither Rick nor Bora exhibiting any awareness that he was awake. Instead, they were whispering to each other in the dining room.

"… we going to do about it?" asked Bora from behind the freestanding wall.

"Can't we just wait and see what happens today?" quietly begged Rick.

"But what if this escalates? I'm not half as afraid of these 'fairies' as I am of him. He's a goddamn lunatic, can't you see that?"

"He's harmless."

"For now. Are you sure you don't want to head back to Atlanta with me? You can stay as long as you'd like."

"And let him hex a whole apartment building?"

"He'd stay here."

"Then I stay here."

There was a long silence. Finally, Bora responded. "Fuck. I guess that means I'm stuck."

Devlin made it a point to stomp into the living room, hoping to save the pair from any embarrassment. Rounding the half wall, he leaned a shoulder against it and put on a show of looking groggy, rubbing his eyes. "Mornin' glory," he yawned. "What's your story?"

Bora forced a smile. "Morning? It's ten after one, dude," she said. "I envy you; you're actually living the life everyone *thinks* artists do."

"My lifestyle dictates an unconventional sleep schedule," Devlin explained. "I stay awake so you don't have to."

"Thank you for your service," joked Rick, grabbing his empty lunch plate along with Bora's and taking it to the sink. "Deli meat's in the fridge. Help yourself. Got a little bit of coffee too, if you want me to throw it in the microwave." Devlin nodded, and Rick obliged. "See anything else last night after we turned in?"

"Not a peep. How about y'all, anything odd this morning?"

"Bora saw an owl at 11:08," Rick answered, handing Devlin the coffee. As for himself, Devlin saw that Rick had already moved onto something stronger.

Devlin's eyebrows raised as he took a sip. "Really?"

"It was just an owl, Devlin," argued Bora. "It flew from the house out over the field and into the woods."

"Situations like this, Bora, it's rarely *just* an owl. Had the rain set in yet?"

"Been like this since we got up."

"You know what's interesting about Strigiformes?" asked Devlin as he opened the fridge to rummage around. "Owls' wings sacrificed waterproofing for silence. Don't like flying in the rain." He grabbed a packet of ham and some cheese and began assembling a sandwich with the bread left on the countertop.

"Listen," he continued, smearing mayonnaise over a slice. "I was thinkin', after y'all went to bed... My little Zacchaeus act last night might've been a bit much." Though he didn't make eye contact with them, Devlin could sense Rick and Bora exchanging glances. "In fact, I violated some of my own protocols. Should've filled y'all in on what was going down."

"Well, is there something you'd like to share with the class now?" solicited Rick.

"After the Oration of the Salamanders, a flock of butterflies with green wings was supposed to appear."

"Salamanders?"

"Not the amphibians," Devlin mumbled through a bite, firing crumbs from his mouth. "Fire elementals. You ask for their help, they send the butterflies, you catch one in a snuff box—"

"—the Tupperware—"

"—right. You come inside, make a fire of alder wood, and keep it going with brandy. Or rotgut vodka, in our case. When the fire dies, you put the snuff box in the ashes, and..." Devlin took another bite and waved his hand. "Long story short, Astaroth appears to answer your questions. Of which we have many."

"Astaroth?" asked Bora from the couch, looking for clarification.

"A spirit," Devlin replied tersely. Best not to overshare since everyone seemed jumpy enough as it was. The ironic thing was that the Goetic "demons" were far tamer and more predictable than the things coming after Rick.

"Devlin, this sounds a little too... elaborate for my taste," Rick admitted. "I think there might be simpler ways of drawing this stuff in. Like playing that melody."

"Must confess that didn't occur to me. That work?"

"Seems to sometimes."

"Why didn't you suggest it?"

"What, you want me to be the ringmaster of your little circus now? I was following your lead. By the time I knew you were actively seeking to coax these things out, you were halfway up a tree banging pots and pans. After that, well... we were all ready to call it a night."

Devlin nodded, swallowing the last bite of his sandwich. "Okay, we'll try that this evening," he said, licking his fingers.

"Why not now?"

"How often you see these things in the day?"

Rick tried to think back to all the madness he had experienced. "I mean, I've seen things during the day…"

"That's just The Wake, Ricky. I'm talking about the lil' fellers themselves."

Rick shrugged, leaving an opening for Bora to challenge Devlin's reasoning. "Admit it, man," she criticized, flipping through a magazine. "You just like doing this stuff at night because it's spooky."

Devlin shook his head. "You ask me, this stuff is photophobic. Somethin' about daylight interferes with their ability to manifest." When no one raised any objections, he added, "With that in mind, y'all rest up. Got a big night ahead of us."

Everyone followed his advice for the remainder of the day, killing time in a variety of ways. After showering, Devlin kept mostly to himself in the dining room, buried in a stack of musty books whose titles and authors had long since faded from their covers. Rick and Bora held a mini Scrabble tournament in the living room. After she emerged victorious, Rick tried busying himself in his bedroom, drinking and tinkering with several compositions he had abandoned months ago. Sometime around 4:30, he started picking at the infamous melody, but Devlin seemed to be onto something. Nothing noteworthy happened.

An hour later, Devlin spoke up at last, raising his voice so it could be heard throughout the small home. "That Chinese place up on 515 any good?"

"You mean China One?" shouted Rick from the bedroom. "I mean, it's takeout Chinese food in north Georgia so… your mileage may vary. Fine for what it is, I guess."

"Gonna get everyone something before our shenanigans start tonight," Devlin offered, rising from his chair. "My treat."

After calling in their order, Devlin hopped in his Suburban and started up the driveway. When he emerged onto the main road, he was pleased to find that the foul weather had moved on, leaving a clear canvas of sky for the sun to spill her pigment.

Twenty minutes later, he had paid for their order at China One and was heading back—but not before one final request. In Cantonese, Devlin asked for a few extra plastic bags, the largest they had. When he found himself on the forested portion of Rick's driveway, he brought the car to a stop, shut off the ignition, and hopped out.

Devlin paced back and forth into the forest on either side of the dirt road, head craned directly above. He was searching for an opening in the trees. After locating one of suitable dimensions, he returned to the car, grabbed the extra bags from the passenger's seat, and popped the trunk. He slunk around to the rear of the Suburban and fumbled through the pile of junk until he found what he was looking for: a pair of scissors, a spool of wire, and three tea lights. He then set to work.

As he snipped the bags, Devlin thought back to his missteps from the night before. After months of meticulous work, how had he allowed himself to behave so rashly? It threatened to upend everything he hoped to accomplish. Any more mistakes like that, and Rick would be lost forever—as would Devlin's only shot at redemption.

Devlin should have known that everyone would find The Great Kabbalah of the Green Butterfly silly. Ritual magic often looked that way to the uninitiated. For every intimidating ritual like the Headless Rite there existed several dozen absurd folk spells—and, although they often worked just as well (or better), they relied on something this group sorely lacked.

Why the ritual had failed seemed so obvious in hindsight. Devlin had grossly miscalculated everyone's belief, both in the phenomenon and in himself. What little they held, he had squandered. The absurdity of climbing the tree and banging the pot even caused him to lose Edna—a damning development, as her belief alone could have easily carried them through. It was a critical miscalculation, going too deep too fast.

Probably for the better, he thought, twisting a length of wire into a circle. *Not sure Astaroth was the right person for the job, anyway.* A few minutes later, he admired his handiwork. Before him sat a trio of crudely fashioned sky lanterns. Hopefully they would prove enough to rekindle everyone's belief. He wasn't worried about Edna—she'd be easy to fool—and Rick seemed open enough to anything, after what he'd been through. Bora, on the other hand....

"Time to prime the pump," Devlin said, grabbing the lanterns and heading back to the open space in the forest. One by one, he lit their candles, gently supporting each until it began ascending on its own like an oversized artificial firefly. They floated into the uppermost branches, then out through the opening in the canopy, where a gentle breeze caught them at last. The lanterns were swept up on a flight path over the forest, perpendicular to the house in the field beyond.

His work done, Devlin hopped back in his car and raced to the front door. He found Rick and Bora sitting at the dining room table expectantly, with silverware, napkins, and drinks laid out for the three of them.

"Sorry I'm late," Devlin apologized, dropping the food on the table. "They got my order wrong, so I had to wait. Yours might be a little cold."

"No worries," Bora assured him as she took her Hunan chicken from the bag. "Mine feels fine."

Devlin had just sat down to eat when a knock came at the door. It was Edna. "Holy shit, y'all!" she exclaimed, pushing past Rick into the house. "Did you see 'em?"

"See what?" asked Bora.

Without saying anything else, Edna simply dragged Rick back out the storm door. Moments later, Bora and Devlin joined them outside.

"Spotted 'em and headed over fast as I could," Edna huffed, engaging in the contradictory act of lighting a cigarette while out of breath. She then pointed out above the trees, where three yellowish white dots could clearly be seen bobbing along off to the south in the fading sunlight. The sky had darkened just enough to provide the requisite contrast as they danced with one another, their formation expanding and contracting with the wind. Even though Devlin knew exactly where they came from, the illusion still appeared sufficiently eerie to the untrained eye.

"What *are* those?" wondered Rick, taking a sip. Like any good alcoholic, he had brought his drink with him. Devlin refused to answer, instead waiting to assess the potency of his ruse.

"You kiddin' me? Fuckin' UFOs," came Edna's evaluation. She held her phone aloft, busily taking a series of photographs. "What do you think, Bora?"

Bora squinted. "Hard to tell," she admitted. "Sky lanterns, maybe? That's kind of how they're moving..."

"Of course *you* think they're Chinese lanterns," Edna retorted.

Bora stared her down. "You know I'm Korean, right?"

"Simmer down, not what I meant," Edna explained, "I mean you're the resident skeptic."

"I'd say lanterns, too," Devlin jumped in, "but what's the occasion? Diwali? Ain't for another two weeks, at least. There a lot of Hindi folk in these parts, Edna?"

"Halloween's tomorrow," Bora argued.

"Yeah, but I ain't never seen nothing like this at Halloween," Edna said. She widened her thumb and index finger across the screen of her phone, zooming in. "Oh! I think I see the pilot!"

Or a yellow smiley face with 'Thank You' written underneath, Devlin thought as Edna snapped a picture. *At least she's back on board.* He watched Rick's landlady share what she captured with her tenant. Luckily, it was completely ambiguous, like so many UFO photos.

"Odd, for sure," Rick answered, eyes darting between Edna's phone and the lanterns. *That's two*, Devlin thought. *Even if they just widen the door a little for everyone, that might suffice—*

"Look!" shouted Edna. "Up there, see it?!?" Following the crooked trajectory of her finger, everyone watched a fourth light that had just appeared, identical to the others but traveling in the opposite direction.

"Can't be lanterns, then," Rick reasoned. "It's moving against the wind." As if responding to his words, the light dipped below the others, zigzagging downward before shooting straight up with an unearthly grace. Once it came to a halt, the lanterns floated beyond it like ships passing a lighthouse into treacherous seas.

It's working, Devlin thought. *I'll be damned if it ain't working.* For decades, he had studied all sides of the debate, whether such things came from the phenomenon itself or from the spectators—a psychic projection into physical reality from their subconscious, perhaps. In moments like this, however, all the academic fart-sniffing in the world didn't matter. Something had taken up residence in the sky over Ellijay, something that could not be explained by conventional standards.

"Hey, Bora," Devlin solicited with relish, "how's that lantern theory holdin' up?" Turning to look at the group's most rational thinker, he immediately regretted his sarcasm. The woman looked white as a ghost, mouth agape, her eyes staring off into the sky. Her expression wasn't altogether different from when he shared her mother's diagnosis.

Devlin cleared his throat. "Seems like, uh, we're back in the game," he announced. "Y'all wanna head inside and eat? We can discuss what's on the docket for tonight."

30

Friday, October 30, 2020

SÉANCE

RICK NOTICED THAT BORA barely touched her food. She only stared at it, hitting her vape as Devlin explained last night to Edna, apologizing all the way.

"... but saying you're afraid of the occult is like saying you're afraid of politics," Devlin reasoned, taking a sip of wine the two of them had purchased the night before. "Y'ain't afraid of politics, you're afraid of *bad* politics and idiots who don't know what the fuck they're doing. But look, here I am, making excuses. I really screwed the pooch on my first impression. I'm sorry."

Edna, who had already eaten, drained her glass and set it back down with an air of superiority. "S'alright," she said, rolling her eyes. She leaned forward and offered a forgiving smile. "I thought it was goofy, more'n anything."

Devlin returned her expression. "I appreciate that, ma'am," he said, leaning back in his chair. "I'd like to offer everyone present an ultimatum. I wanna try something tonight. It don't work, y'all can run me outta town on a rail."

Even though he feared the answer, Rick had to ask. "What's that?"

Devlin held Rick's gaze for several seconds before answering. "A séance," he announced.

Edna and Bora immediately shifted uncomfortably in their seats. Devlin never looked away from his client. "Don't get your feathers ruffled," he soothed. "Bora, Edna, you can tap out if you wanna. But them lights in the sky"—he pointed a finger toward the front yard—"they're a greeting. The lines of communication are back open. I'm willing to bet my reputation that this'll work."

"I'm in," Bora said, looking up from her takeout container for the first time. "Anything that gets all this over faster, I'll do it."

"Me too," Edna chimed in. "Only no devil stuff."

Devlin held up his hands. "No devil stuff. Just some good, ol' fashioned Spiritualism like Mama used to make."

"Aren't séances all about contacting the dead?" asked Rick.

"Good for contacting anything on the other side of the veil," explained Devlin. "As I've tried to learn you, such distinctions ain't really useful at this point." He took stock of everyone else. "Any questions?... Alright, I'm gonna head out to the car, grab some supplies. Y'all mind clearing all this off?"

Forty-five minutes later, the stage was set. All the blinds were closed, the curtains tightly drawn. On a black tablecloth sat a row of lit candles, the only source of light. In the table's center, a séance trumpet stood upright on its wide end, nothing more than a cone of aluminum with a few strips of glow-in-the-dark tape affixed to the surface. Atop a piece of paper hastily scrawled with YES and NO lay a cloudy crystal affixed to a chain.

Glancing around the room, Rick wondered if this was what the inside of Devlin's head looked like. Bora probably thought the same.

"How's this going to work?" he asked. "Are they going to talk through you?"

"Naw," admitted Devlin, admiring the setup. The candlelight rendered his face sphinxlike. "I may be sensitive, but I'm a piss poor medium. Still—you got any zip ties?"

"I, uh… maybe in the shed."

"Fetch 'em, if you don't mind."

After Rick stepped out the front door, Devlin looked at Bora. "Listen, Bora… I sense some animosity between us. Not a good thing to have going into a situation like this. I want to apologize. Having your paradigm shattered… learning that the world don't work the way it's s'posed to… it ain't an easy thing. I've lived with this stuff for so long, I forget that sometimes."

It was difficult to tell whether Bora's shock lingered from the UFO sighting or whether Devlin's candor had renewed it. Either way, she just stood there, the tiny flames reflecting off her widening eyes.

Before she could speak, Edna emerged from the bathroom with a flush. Bora simply nodded and muttered her thanks. Rick entered and shut the front door, zip ties in hand.

"Devlin," he said, wrinkling his nose and handing them over, "you've got to warn us before breaking out the incense. That's awful."

"It was me," admitted Edna, scuffing over the linoleum towards the sink for a glass of water. "Had collards for supper."

Devlin sat down at the spot he had occupied at dinner. "Okay, Ricky," he began, "I want you to tie me to the chair."

"Huh?"

"Use the zip ties and bind my wrists and ankles to the arms and legs of the chair," explained Devlin. "Helps show I'm not a fraud. In my experience, the spirits seem to like removing that possibility, too." Rick did as instructed, the zip ties buzzing as he wrenched them as tightly as he dared.

"These spirits seem to know how to spend a Friday night," Edna remarked.

"Devlin..." ventured Bora quietly. "What if I get afraid?"

"Simple," he responded, tugging on the bindings to ensure their security. "Just find that part of yourself and kill it afore it gets any worse. Suffocate it in its cradle. Like baby Hitler."

An expression flew across Bora's face, like she had tasted something bitter. "That's disgusting. And terrible advice."

"You could always try my way," Rick suggested, hoisting his flask for a long drink. Bora considered this a moment, then reached out a hand. She accepted the flask, took a drink almost as long as Rick's, and handed it back over.

"Thanks," she coughed. She then offered her vape. "Want a little flower, maybe take the edge off?"

"I'm fine," declined Rick.

"Suit yourself." Bora puffed awhile, then turned to Devlin. "Okay," she declared, newfound determination in her eyes. "Let's do this."

Devlin nodded, testing the zip ties. "That's good. Might help if we held hands, but this table's a little too large... Just keep 'em up top, if you don't mind. Remember, y'all, no sudden movements, if you please. Be polite. You see something, don't say nothing. Remain calm. Try not to react too strongly. Bora—you want to pick out some music for us? I'm afraid if I ask Ricky he'll turn on some noodly jazz bullshit. Something soothing to listen to, get us relaxed."

Bora nodded. While Rick and Edna took their seats, she retrieved her phone, which was perpetually plugged into an outlet in the kitchen. Bora hemmed and hawed before finally tapping the screen. A series of pizzicato synthesizer chords filled the room.

Rick recognized it instantly. "Really?" he asked in disgust. "*Orinoco Flow?*"

"Yeah," Bora admitted innocently. "What's wrong with that?"

"I just thought you had better taste, is all."

"Don't let him get to you, Bora," Devlin said from the darkness. "Just find a playlist of spa music online."

"On it," Bora declared. A few seconds later, an advertisement for vitamin supplements began blaring. "Sorry, sorry—let me skip this." The bodybuilder's nasally voice gave way to soothing pentatonic flute melodies over the sound of a babbling brook. Bora then took her place at the table, each of them occupying their own side: Devlin's back to the freestanding wall, Bora's toward the kitchen, Rick's against the wall of the bedroom, Edna in front of the patio and basement door. There they sat for a long time, letting the music lull them into a more relaxed state.

"Alright, sitters. I want y'all to imagine a column of light, emerging from the tops of your heads," Devlin slowly instructed. "Imagine all that energy, reaching out... connecting with you... with me..." He paused for several minutes before proceeding. "That energy gathers together and reaches out above this house, above this field, into the night sky... past the atmosphere... into deep space. Imagine yourself weightless, nothing but disembodied consciousness travelin' between stars, between planets, between nebulae...."

Devlin continued in this fashion for a while longer, then slipped into silence once more. Rick was on the verge of nodding off when Devlin spoke again twenty minutes later.

"Okay," he whispered, barely audible above the music. "When I count down, y'all gently draw your consciousness back into this room, retreating all the way from outer space into your deepest, most personal inner space. Here we go... Five... Four... Three... Two... One. Welcome back. Bora, would you mind shutting off the music?"

She obliged, then returned to her seat. "Thank you," said Devlin. "Richard, if you will, take the pendulum in your right hand and hold it above the paper." Rick did as instructed, elbow on the table, crystal dangling between YES and NO.

Everyone except Devlin was visibly nervous. To Rick, it seemed like they were all lost at sea, clinging to the table for dear life like survivors to a raft lost amidst an endless expanse of darkness. Only the candles served as beacons, keeping them tethered to reality. The tension in the room amplified, becoming taut like a sail, waiting for winds from another world to usher them into whatever lay beyond the horizon of the psyche.

When Devlin spoke again, it was obvious that he was not addressing anyone in the house—at least, not anyone who could be seen. "Is there anyone here with us?" he asked the empty room. He took a breath and held it, eyes fixed on the pendulum. It did not move.

"Are you there yet?" he asked. Nothing. "If there is someone with us, would you kindly move that pendulum in my friend's hand?" The crystal hanging between the words refused to budge.

Edna shifted in her seat. Sensing her frustration, Devlin ever-so-slightly shook his head. "Stay put," he said. "Richard, set down the pendulum—*gentle, gentle*—and calmly go get your guitar."

Rick tried his best to remain reverent. In spite of the effort, he still managed to feel like a kid walking in front of a congregation to use the bathroom mid-sermon. When he returned from his bedroom, he needed no instruction regarding what to do next. He simply waited for Devlin to nod.

Although he had been drinking steadily all day, Rick's heart leapt to his throat as he began playing the melody, fighting the worst case of stage fright he could remember. Somehow, he persevered and managed to pluck the strings, sending the song through the house. Never before had it sounded so simultaneously jagged and elegant as it did then, rising above the candles and into the darkness. It only took a few moments to perform, but lingered in the air like smoke. Time stopped.

Everyone turned their heads in Edna's direction. The patio light had come on behind her, slipping a faint glow over the edges of the drawn curtain. While it had been temperamental over the past few months, everyone was well aware of the implication. Rick let his guitar slip to the floor, then grabbed the pendulum's chain once more.

"Thank you for that," Devlin said. Rick was certain he wasn't speaking to him. "I take it that was you?"

The pendulum twitched in Rick's hand so firmly that for a split second he was certain Edna had reached across the table to tug on it. He looked, only to find her sitting there, shocked, hands laying flat on the table, clearly visible. The point of the crystal had indeed moved of its own volition, hovering in the direction of YES with a magnetic intensity. It strained in that direction momentarily before the tension on the chain loosened, sending it swinging back over the paper to settle between the words.

Rick looked up from the paper at everyone else, a huge grin on his face. Edna looked surprised. Bora looked terrified. Devlin's face betrayed all the enthusiasm of a successful trip to the post office. "We appreciate your participation," he drawled. "May we ask a few questions?"

The pendulum swung to YES then released, its crystal sending fragments of candlelight playing over their faces. Devlin began his interrogation.

"Are you attached to this land?" NO. "Are you attached to a person?" YES. "Is that person in the room with us right now?" YES. "Is that person me?" NO. Devlin nodded for Bora to repeat the same question.

"Is it me?" she asked meekly. The pendulum swung to NO.

"Are you interested in me?" came Edna's voice through the firelight. The crystal remained affixed in the direction of NO.

Rick swallowed. "So it is me," he whispered. More forcefully than ever, the pendulum yanked towards YES. Rick had to consciously pull in the opposite direction to keep it from flying out of his grasp.

Devlin nodded. "Thankee," he said. "We understand." Once more, the invisible force relinquished the crystal, letting it drop to the center.

"Do you want something from him?" speculated Devlin. Again, a tug in the affirmative, accompanied by a gasp from Edna.

"Is it a material possession?" NO.

Then, the question Rick dreaded: "Is it his life?" inquired Devlin emotionlessly. Everyone's eyes were fixed on the pendulum. Beyond a few jumps from Rick's trembling hand, it remained immobile.

Rick looked up from the crystal to Devlin. For the first time since the séance began, his face showed a hint of frustration. His lips were barely parted; there was a slight sign of movement on his cheeks, giving the impression that he was running his tongue along his molars. Each passing second ratcheted up the tension rising in the room. "Is it his soul?" he asked at last. Still, the pendulum refused to budge.

Devlin cleared his throat. "Sorry if we're barkin' up the wrong tree," he apologized. "Let's go back to basics. Are you a living entity?" At last, the pendulum moved, but it refused to confirm or deny the issue. Instead, it chose to swing back and forth over both answers, spiraling out into an ever-widening parabola.

"So you're dead, then?" interjected Edna. Devlin shot her a glare, but her interference seemed to make little difference. The crystal continued tracing a broad arc over the paper, refusing to cooperate. The force pulling the other end increased with each rotation, and Rick soon felt the chain sliding from his hand, no matter how tightly he gripped.

Rick was concentrating so hard on restraining the pendulum that he barely noticed the spirit trumpet in the center of the table, which began rocking back and forth on its own, threatening to tip over at any moment. The sound of aluminum on wood filled the dining room, despite the thick tablecloth separating them. At last it toppled over with a clang, the same instant that the pendulum flew from Rick's hands. It launched out into the kitchen and struck the floor, shattering the crystal, leaving behind a miniature starburst across the linoleum.

Rather than sending everyone running, the simultaneous crashes froze all three sitters in place. They glanced at each other in the darkness, trying to comprehend what had just occurred. Eventually, this search for answers guided their gaze to Devlin. He only stared at the spirit trumpet, looking like he was on the receiving end of a mildly confusing insult.

Before Rick could speak, a noise undermined their silent awe. It sounded like someone banging on the walls of another room—the bedroom perhaps. He instinctively looked over his shoulder and, of course, saw nothing. That was when another sound above his head drew his attention.

"Y'all hear footsteps?" whispered Edna. "In the attic?"

Devlin nodded, then reflexively placed a finger to his lips to quiet her down. Everyone, including Devlin, realized the impossibility of this gesture. He stared at his wrists, miraculously free, before leaning back to check his ankles under the table. From his expression, they had been released from the chair as well.

Rick tried looking at his own feet but stopped when he found all the zip ties in a pile on his thighs. They looked good as new, as if they had never been cinched. "They're... in my lap," he explained, holding one above the table.

Suddenly, the raps throughout the house increased in both frequency and volume, although it was unclear whether they were actually getting louder or simply drawing closer. Raps became knocks, knocks became booms, and the booms finally culminated in an ear-splitting bang that sounded like a small firework had exploded directly above their heads.

Rick's ears were still ringing when the spirit trumpet began spinning on the tablecloth. Rather than starting slowly, it instantly took off in a whirlwind fashion, rotating so quickly that the glow-in-the-dark tape became a mere smudge of neon green in Rick's vision. The breeze it threw off caused the candles to flicker and wink out. Then, like a miniature propeller, it whirled high above the table, stopping just short of the ceiling to twirl above them in the darkness.

Except, Rick noticed, it didn't seem so dark anymore. That was when he realized that, while the spinning trumpet had snuffed the candles on the table, it heralded the arrival of a new light source: nine luminescent spheres, none larger than a Ping-Pong ball, had somehow entered the room. Each had a different color, varying in pastel shades of pink, green, blue, and yellow. Rather than floating aimlessly like dust motes, they seemed to move by bouncing on invisible platforms in midair, imparting the cluster of orbs with a playful demeanor not unlike a group of frisky rabbits.

Rick took his eyes off the luminous choreography to briefly gauge everyone's reaction. Bora had moved on from terror into awe, Edna from awe into childlike glee. Devlin remained indifferent. As for Rick, he wasn't sure precisely how he felt; it was one thing to witness this as a third party, another thing to be aware that *you* were the reason for their presence.

Life... death... Rick heard the voice as clearly as if one of his friends had spoken it. Yet he saw none of their mouths move, nor did anyone's face suggest they had noticed it themselves. The voice came again, cold and sharp as an icicle in his mind: *Life... death... Rickard Coulter....*

The scene overhead mesmerized Bora and Edna. Their faces passed in and out of shadow as each glowing sphere threw its light upon them. Now and again, one would bob closer to the observers, coming within inches before darting out of the way like a startled animal.

After around a minute of this behavior, each orb took its position surrounding the trumpet, still spinning by the ceiling. When the last one was in place, the cone of aluminum dropped to the table with a loud bang, making everyone jump. Beyond that, they barely had time to react as all the lights shrank towards one another, collapsing the circle like a contracting pupil until, at last, they became one single blue orb. Now the size of a basketball, it descended along the same trajectory as the trumpet, stopping about a foot above the table.

Although he knew Devlin wouldn't like it, Rick dug his flask out of his jeans and finished it off. He then stared long and hard into the center of the sphere, watching the fire swirl within. It looked neither like light nor like liquid but shared attributes of both. Rick thought back to some of the bigger shows he had played, how the fog machines would pump the room full of vapor to make the stage lights seem thicker, like something lived within the beams. The effect was similar, if less remarkable, to whatever the luminous orb before him contained.

From out of this soupy mixture, a shape began to form. The swirls condensed until they created a pure, white center within the blue confines. From this emerged tendrils, seven total, which slowly grew more and more distinct: an arm, then another arm, then two legs, and a head. The final two tendrils coalesced into appendages jutting from the tiny figure's back. Once the basic proportions were finalized, bits of definition and texture began popping up here and there across its surface: tiny fingers, miniscule toes, the lacy lattice of insect wings, and, finally, long, flowing locks.

To Rick's astonishment, the orb of light now contained, at its center, the classic image of a fairy—the very thing Devlin insisted these things were not. Although it faced away from Rick, he could clearly discern the shape of a nude, winged woman, stretching its arms and legs as if emerging from a deep slumber.

Without acknowledging anyone, it turned to the right and glided straight toward Bora. As the orb and pixie drifted away, Rick caught a glimpse of Devlin, who still cast a jaundiced eye over the proceedings, looking thoroughly unimpressed.

Bora, on the other hand, appeared enchanted by the tiny figure as it drew closer. It stopped inches from her nose, imparting her expression with a blue pallor.

Rick watched as the little sprite looked over its shoulder in his direction. Only now did he manage to see its face—*her face*, he corrected himself. The being's features were attractive, if vaguely caprine, with a long distance separating her eyes from her nose. She winked at Rick mischievously, then turned her attention back to his friend.

The figure leaned towards Bora with an exaggerated gesture, half-bowing, wings fluttering against her sculpted buttocks. From what Rick could tell, the little creature planted a dainty kiss on Bora's nose, then—without warning—simply vanished from existence, taking the orb with it.

Darkness flooded the room. The fireball's abrupt disappearance made the change even more disorienting. When Rick's eyes finally adjusted, only one source of light remained: the microwave clock, which impossibly read 11:08. Even if the séance had taken a full hour —and there was no way it had—it couldn't have brought them so deep into the evening.

From the inky blackness to Rick's right came Bora's voice. "Rick?" she asked.

"Yes, Bora?"

"I think someone laced my weed."

"No one laced your weed. We all saw it. I've been seeing this stuff for months."

For a few seconds, no one said anything. Then, from the patio end of the table, came Edna's response.

"Goddamn, boy. No wonder you stay drunk."

31

Wednesday, September 5, 2012

INTO THE BLACK

THERE WERE FEW THINGS Conrad Coulter hated more than unfulfilled potential. On nights like tonight, few things exemplified unfulfilled potential more than an empty brandy snifter. He rectified the problem by emptying the remainder of the Rémy Martin bottle, which barely contained enough to qualify as a pour, and walked over to his bedroom window overlooking the garden.

When he initially contemplated his plight earlier in the evening, Conrad was all sophistication and ceremony, swirling each new glass before taking his first sip. Now, having demolished the rest of the bottle, he gave no thought to such pleasantries. He took a long drink, finishing half of the pour in a single swallow.

Afterwards, he leaned an arm along the right hand side of the window frame, taking stock of the hedge maze one final time. Part of him wondered why he kept the damn thing. He hadn't taken the time to walk it in years. None of his visitors ever bothered, either. The only people who had truly enjoyed it were Richard and Mary.

As he looked, he noticed that the once-immaculate bushes now sported rebellious branches thrusting here and there beyond their orderly comrades. They made the entire garden resemble an unruly youth after resisting a haircut.

When you pay good money, you expect good work, he grimaced. *I bet those bastards didn't think I'd notice. I'll have to give them a piece of my—*

Conrad caught his error and staggered, steadying himself on one of the posts of his canopy bed. He wouldn't need to give them a piece of anything. It would all end tonight. He wasn't sure whose problem it would be—likely his son's if he didn't sell the estate—but it certainly wasn't *his* concern any longer.

The thought was both unnerving and comforting. He had borne many burdens over the years, but the one accrued over the past twenty-six was by far the worst. Living each day with the knowledge of how things would end (how they *had* to end) made all the other joys of life turn to ash.

A byproduct of the agreement created two Conrad Coulters: one, the strong, iron-willed businessman he had always been; the other, a shadow of his former self, pitiful and sniveling, kneeling before the inevitable. Since he could scarcely afford to let his colleagues see the latter, he doubled down on the former, allowing it to take over his entire life. Instead of meeting with warmth, every relationship since faced this steely façade; his demeanor became indistinguishable whether in the nursery or the office, the bedroom or the boardroom.

Come now, he thought, finishing his drink and shuffling over to his desk on the opposite side of the room. *You never were a sentimental man.* For as long as he could remember, he had surveyed his existence with a certain icy detachment, thinking primarily of those around him as means to an end. If a relationship didn't serve a purpose, it didn't last long. With practice, he eventually managed to feign a believable level of empathy—*You don't get far in business without it*—but, with the exception of a few fleeting moments with his wife and children, he rarely felt anything genuine.

The blood in most folks' veins ran red. Conrad's ran black. He hated red. Red meant debt.

He settled down at his desk, sliding the rolltop upwards like the stone door of a tomb, revealing paperwork piled like perfectly balanced cairns. He pushed these to the sides and back, leaving the once-cluttered desktop largely empty.

Some debts I'm willing to pass along, he thought. *They are unavoidable.* This wasn't one of them. Today, he would pay in full, taking his lineage out of the red and into the black. In a life defined by financial success, it was a noble gesture—in fact, any objective outside observer apprised of the agreement's stipulations would see it as Conrad Coulter's ultimate act of compassion.

With groans and creaks coming from both him and the desk, he began pulling out drawers, looking for what he needed. Regardless of whether or not he found what he sought, he left each one open before moving on to the next, and soon the desk looked less like furniture and more like a fully unfolded Swiss Army knife. One by one, he located each document: the power of attorney, living trust, insurance policies, bank account information, loan documents, and, most importantly, his will.

The only thing missing were his deeds and titles, which, having been discovered nowhere else, must lie in the final drawer. He bent over, hauling it out by the brass handle, and was greeted by a crowd of faces staring up at him.

Conrad stared at the photographs for a few moments before fishing them out of the drawer. He couldn't recall the last time he had seen them or who had taken them. Dimly, Conrad realized it must have been himself, as he was absent from all of them. There were pictures of his wife, long before her interminable hospital stay. In one, she wore a yellow dress and was looking up from her book as she sat reading under a tree in the garden. There were pictures of Mary, all innocence and light, her red hair full of twigs and brambles after one of her sylvan excursions. Finally, more than anyone else, there were photographs of Richard as a child: riding his tricycle, playing guitar, swimming with his sister, and other snapshots of daily life.

Not for the first time, Conrad wondered how his son fared. He had learned only little through sparse correspondence over the years, rarely from his son and mostly through extended relations. There was a marriage, presumably to the girl he had left town with. There was also a grandson, apparently, though Conrad didn't even know the boy's name. As time inexorably drifted by, Conrad often considered reaching out to Richard and his family, but the barriers of pride and egotism always barred his path.

As he stared at the pictures, Conrad felt something welling up inside of him. This time, he refused to fight the emotions kept at bay since his son left. If he didn't let them out now, then when?

Only too late did he realize the error of his ways. He kept expecting Richard to come back to him. When he failed to do so year after year, Conrad realized something: he left his potential as a father unfulfilled. He expected too much of the boy too early, and, like an underperforming stock destined to eventually skyrocket, he had foolishly ended their relationship far too soon.

Richard had been an opportunity to invest in the future. In him, Conrad's legacy could have lived on. Instead, like a fool, he had failed to capitalize on that. It was not the most compassionate way to look at their estrangement, but it reframed their relationship in a way that made sense to him.

Conrad noticed that some of the photographs were wet. It was then that he realized, for the first time in his memory, he was crying.

"I'm sorry," he whispered aloud. "I'm sorry, Richard. But I will set things right. You will never know... but I will set things right." The floodgates were open, and Conrad Coulter let loose with big, wet tears. Tears for his relationships, for his son, tears for his life. Tears for their world and what it had become.

He finally finished, not because the wound had closed but simply because he had no more tears to cry. Gathering his resolve, he replaced the pictures in the drawer and continued to rummage around until, at last, he found the property deed and car titles. Setting everything in order, Conrad wearily rose from his chair and made his way downstairs, past the sconces, which provided only the bare minimum of illumination. When he reached the second floor, he stopped by Rick's room. The door was closed.

Opening it, he found the air not stale and musty, but rather clean and refreshed. *The gardeners might be falling behind on their duties*, Conrad observed wryly, *but I hired damn good housekeepers.*

They had kept the room clean and dust-free, even though they hadn't moved a thing since Richard's departure. There on the wall, yellowed and curled, still clung an old Herbie Hancock poster. An outdated Casio keyboard, dormant for nearly a decade and a half, sat just as it had the night he left.

Conrad never allowed any guests to stay in the room. It was a memorial to the living, a mausoleum whose resident yet breathed. Having someone else occupy the space would have felt like closing the door on the possibility of his son's return for good.

He closed the door and slowly climbed downstairs, completely alone. With his bloated torso and frail appendages, his descent through the empty mansion looked a bit like a languid beetle, movements dulled deep into winter, scuttling over a carcass long stripped of flesh.

Conrad sighed. For decades, he had turned the conditions of the pact over and over in his mind, searching for some sort of loophole. He never found any. What had to be done was clear as day. *If it must end this way, let it end tonight*, he thought, continuing his journey downstairs. *Contracts must be honored, even if one dislikes the outcome.*

In some regards, it was refreshing. Only a handful of times in his long history of business had he been successfully outflanked. Being backed into a contractual corner felt like a fitting end, the sole time in his life of negotiation that he met defeat. What an end it would be.

At last he arrived on the ground floor. Save for the ticking of the grandfather clock, everything was silent. Conrad traced a path past the Autumn Room, beyond the parlor, before finally arriving at the gun room. After locating the correct key, he opened the door and stepped inside.

It was a sight to behold. Conrad's collection was far from the most robust, but the manner in which it was displayed—rows of long guns, pistols, and bird decoys sheltered behind gleaming glass built into the oaken walls—was impressive. He stood for a moment, considering his options, before unlocking the cabinet and fetching his sixteen gauge. After placing the firearm on the green felt tabletop behind him, he turned back around and grabbed a box of Winchester shells from the top shelf. He started to pull out several, then realized he would only need one, and replaced the box before locking the cabinet.

As he loaded the shotgun, Conrad briefly considered switching it out with a more powerful weapon. He decided against it, however, for two reasons: one, he didn't want to make more of a mess than necessary; and two, the sixteen gauge had been the first he ever held. It seemed fitting to end things the way they had begun.

Conrad Coulter returned to the hallway, shotgun in hand. After a few moments of quiet debate, he snatched another bottle of brandy from the liquor cabinet, then continued his ascent up the staircase, deep in contemplation. Once he reached the bedroom, he put an old Artie Shaw album on the record player, pulled back the oxblood curtains of his canopy bed, and slipped inside. There he lay, listening and drinking straight from the bottle, cradling his firearm, until it was time to settle his debt.

32

Saturday, October 31, 2020

SAMHAIN

Following the séance, everyone adopted Devlin's sleep pattern. With late nights ahead of them and the likelihood of losing a few hours unexpectedly, it seemed the prudent thing to do to prepare for the coming day. Thus, Rick, Bora, and Edna ended up sleeping until late the following morning.

Devlin, however, was up earlier than usual. Bora was surprised to find him already awake when she rose to use the bathroom around eight o'clock. He was facing the sliding glass door of the patio, not moving a muscle, and said nothing to her as she slunk away. When she returned, grinding the sleep out of her eyes, she padded up beside him. Neither of them greeted the other. Eager to see what held Devlin's attention, Bora looked out in the direction of Red Ear Mountain, across the field, which had begun to yellow with the deepening autumn.

"Is that...?" asked Bora when she spotted it.

"Mm-hmm," he replied.

"And is it... is that... coloration... normal?"

"Believe not. But it depends on what you mean by 'normal.' Heard tell of a three-foot tall plaid rabbit what showed up in a witness's driveway the day after their UFO sighting in Arizona. Bodes well."

"For what?"

"Tonight."

"What's happening tonight?"

"Think that's best discussed when we have a quorum."

"... Okay. What does it mean?"

"What, that? You mean the *purpose*? *Yo no sé.* Your guess is as good as mine. But it *does* mean we're caught up in The Wake. They're here, they'll probably be around tonight, and we have their attention." He paused. "This kinda goofy shit is actually pretty routine, but still...

Doors slammin', lights in the sky, elves dancin' at the tree line, you get used to all that. This stuff? Don't never get old. Wonders never cease."

Bora rubbed her face, then turned back towards the couch. "... Dev? Do me a favor?... Don't tell Rick you saw a polka-dotted kangaroo in the field today. It'll break his brain."

"Okay..." As she fell back to sleep, Devlin frowned. "Could be a wallaby."

As for Rick, he finally pulled himself out of bed around one o'clock. When he reached the dining room, his guests barely acknowledged him. They were engaged in an animated discussion, gesticulating broadly above empty plates.

"Look, I'm not saying I don't see the talent there," argued Bora. "I acknowledge that his paintings are masterpieces. They just don't resonate with me."

"And that's fine," Devlin conceded. "A wise friend of mine said that there are bad things you don't like, and bad things you do like. Same thing with good stuff. You can acknowledge it's good. It doesn't have to speak to you."

"I'm the same way with Radiohead," Rick interjected, sitting down with a Pedialyte and a granola bar. He had tied one off in spectacular fashion following the séance, and his head was splitting. "What are we talking about?"

"Debating the finer points of Goya," said Devlin.

"Not a debate," Bora countered.

"Oh, *him*," realized Rick. "I like his chickpeas." Catching looks from both his friends, he burst into laughter. "I'm kidding, I'm kidding... How long y'all been awake?"

Devlin and Bora exchanged glances. Rick thought he saw her head twitch in the slightest indication of a shake. "I just got up half an hour ago," she answered.

"Same time," volunteered Devlin. "Sandman was a stingy bastard between seven and nine. Gave me some time to plan for this evening, though."

Rick took his last bite and washed it down. "What's that?"

"Teddybear's picnic," Devlin answered cryptically.

"Huh?" asked Rick, looking at Bora. She shrugged.

"We're going out into the woods."

Rick almost spit his Pedialyte across the room. "You've got to be kidding."

Devlin looked confused. "We've got a golden opportunity here. You know what day it is?"

"Ugh," Bora groaned. "Careful what you say, Dev. I'm just beginning to like you."

Devlin ignored the jab. "Samhain."

"I'm sorry, man, I've wrecked my ears at concerts," apologized Rick. "Saw what?"

"Samhain. Halloween. The timing is perfect. It's *their* night."

"I thought Halloween was just for kids."

"I swear, pop culture's going to be the death of me. Samhain, its *true* name, is an old, old holiday. All that horror movie stuff about the veil bein' thin tonight? S'true. Great time of year to get work like this done. Why, last Halloween I helped a woman rid herself of some polt activity she picked up following a UFO sighting. Year before that, a family with a *wechuge* on their property in Alberta. Year before that, this poor fishing village in Phú Yên. This *con rit* kept ruining their catch—"

Rick put his fingers to his temples. "This sounds like a horrible idea."

"—why's that?"

"Good ol' boys, for one. I dunno where you're from, Devlin, but around here, it's hunting season. People are always shooting something. Even if that wasn't the case, I'm not so sure looking for these things in the woods after dark is entirely safe."

"They seemed nice enough last night," Bora smiled, remembering the tiny pixie that planted a kiss on her nose.

Rick smirked. "Easy for *you* to say," he grumbled. "Do I need to remind you what the pendulum said? They're interested in *me*."

Devlin rolled his eyes. "That could mean a whole heap 'o things, Ricky."

"Did y'all hear the voice last night?" asked Rick. Both Bora and Devlin shook their heads. "I sure as hell did. Even if it was in my head, it didn't come from me."

"What'd it say?" pried Bora.

Rick shrugged. "I dunno. I only remember my name and two words. 'Life' and 'death.'"

Sensing his client's concern, Devlin nodded, reached across the table, and put a hand on his shoulder. "Precisely the kind of vagaries we need to shine light on. Don't worry, Richard. We all have the necklaces, remember?" He stared at Rick with his mismatched eyes. "Do you believe they work?" Rick nodded reluctantly.

"Then they can't take you again," Devlin reassured him.

"I don't know if that makes them any less dangerous."

"Careful there, tiger," Devlin cautioned. "With that attitude, you might be right. Sometimes ya get whatcha give. Set n' setting, and all that." Seeing that this made Rick no more comfortable, he continued pitching the idea.

"Look, man, I ain't tellin' you what to do. Last night was fun 'n all, but it weren't exactly elucidating. If our goal is to get answers, that's best accomplished by *assuring contact*. Out there, on their turf, on the one night of the year when the veil is thinnest? That's a sure thing. Like gettin' laid on your honeymoon. Last night was the royal court dropping by your hovel on a whim. If we go into the forest tonight, we're envoys at the palace. They *have* to listen to our questions."

At last, Rick yielded. "If you say so. What is it, then? Another séance on the mountain?"

Devlin stood from his seat and loped into the kitchen to refill his coffee. "Not quite," he said, filling his cup. "I wanna—"

He paused as the front door opened. It was Edna, bursting through with the predictability of a guest star on a sitcom, chewing the scenery with gusto.

"A-hoy, a-holes," she shouted from behind a pair of oversized sunglasses. In one hand she held a large, red-lidded Tupperware container. "I baked y'all ingrates some muffins." She popped off the lid, pulled one out, and took a bite. "Although you probably shouldn't take one if you need to pass a piss test," she added, spraying crumbs everywhere. "They're poppyseed. Sent my last boyfriend back to prison that way."

Devlin thanked Edna and took the container for Rick and Bora to grab their muffins. "As you were saying," Bora encouraged Devlin before enjoying hers.

"Right," said Devlin, picking up the thread. "So, Edna, just to fill you in—we're heading out to the woods tonight."

Even though the landlady's eyes remained obscured, everyone could tell they widened. "Like *Finding Bigfoot?*"

Devlin pushed on. "Do you think it's safe to go out at night?" he asked. He gestured toward Rick. "Some have expressed misgivings."

"It's safe if I come along," Edna replied. "I know those woods like the back of my hand. Been roaming 'em since I was knee high to a lightnin' bug. Shee-it, over the years? Bet I've leaned up against every tree on this property while getting railed in a sundress." Bora snickered. "What're we doing out there? I mean, I wouldn't be opposed to *that*, but I imagine y'all have somethin' else in mind."

Devlin drained his coffee mug, then replied, "Estes."

"Oh, I seen that!" exclaimed Edna.

"Mind filling the rest of us in?" asked Rick.

"The Estes Method," Devlin began. "A relatively new approach. Sort of a double blind way to—"

"Ooh, let me," Edna interrupted. "First, they hook you up to a spirit box with headphones—"

Bora waved her hands. "Stop—spirit box?"

"It's a radio that scans through all the frequencies," continued Edna. "Ghosts pick and choose what words come through the static. But here's the thing: you're blindfolded, and the headphones got that noise-silencing stuff, so you can't hear what's going on around you."

"Yes," Devlin confirmed, asserting control over the conversation. "You have the noise-canceling headphones, and you can't see. Meantime, a sitter asks the spirits questions."

"But if you can't hear the questions, how do you answer them?" asked Rick.

"*You* don't. The spirits do. Or 'noncorporeal presences,' however you wanna define 'em. They choose answers, which go through the spirit box to the listener—in our case, *you*. You repeat whatever you hear, regardless of whether or not it makes any sense. When I get a clear answer from you, despite your inability to hear my questions or read my lips... well, that's somethin' special."

"So it's like..." Bora searched for the words. When she grasped the comparison, she was visibly unsettled to speak them. "Channeling with technology?"

"Yup," said Devlin. "Even more reliable, in my opinion, since the listener can't be contaminated by outside stimuli."

"Sounds fun," Rick decided sarcastically. "When do we start?"

Devlin looked at his watch. "Comin' up on two now," he observed. "I wanna make sure we get a lay of the land in daylight. Sun should set just before seven, so let's head out from here in… four hours?" He looked around the room. "For now, take it easy and rest up. Start gettin' ready around five. Wanna begin the Estes session as close as we can to 11:08, so we'll be out there a while. Pack accordingly: water, snacks, flashlights, spare batteries, anything else you might need. Everybody got a backpack?"

Rick, Bora, and Edna all nodded. "Good," Devlin said. "Like last night… last chance if anyone wants to opt out." No one said anything. "Alrighty, then," he concluded before disappearing back into the addition.

Edna returned home, agreeing to meet out front around six o'clock. Everyone else then went their separate ways, occupying themselves much as they had the day before. Rick noted that Devlin spent most of the afternoon napping—either he had been up longer than he claimed, or he truly was trying to preserve all of his energy for tonight.

Sometime in the middle of the afternoon, Rick's phone went off. It was Jack.

"Hey, Dad," the boy said after he answered.

"Hey, buddy," said Rick. "Good to hear your voice! What's up?"

"I was just wondering… You're still in town, right?"

Rick, who had been in the living room, retreated to his bedroom, hastening to explain his predicament in the vaguest terms. "Actually, no… some, uh, things had to be done up here in Ellijay. Landlady's getting impatient with the addition, so I thought I'd get some work done. Why? Are you okay?"

"Yeah, yeah, I'm fine," Jack answered. "If you're up there, never mind, then."

"No, Jack… what is it?"

"I was just wondering if you wanted to hang out tomorrow. I know it's kinda last minute. Mom offered to pay for us to go to the aquarium. I was just saying to her how I hadn't been in forever."

Rick took the phone from his ear, pressed the edge against his forehead, and closed his eyes, cursing his luck. He had *way* too much going on to traipse down to Atlanta, look at fish for three hours, then come all the way back up here. At the same time, he had tried so hard to rebuild his relationship with Jack. He didn't want to waste a single opportunity with him.

Can I swing this? he asked himself. *I mean, it's not like we're doing a lot through the day...*

"Dad?" asked Jack, his voice tiny and tinny.

Rick cleared his throat. "Yeah, bud, I'd love to," he replied at last. "What time were you thinking?"

Rick agreed to pick up his son at eleven o'clock the next morning. It would make for a long day—driving there on only a few hours' sleep, wading through crowds fully masked, driving back—but he wasn't about to reject such a warm invitation.

Everyone found dinner on their own, picking at leftovers or raiding the meager contents of the refrigerator. At a quarter to five, Rick began drinking in earnest (he was proud of the restraint he showed) and slowly started filling his backpack. Bora retrieved hers from her car and did the same. They stuffed in as much as they could without making them too heavy. The last thing that Rick shoved inside was a vodka bottle, a necessary addition since he would drain the flask well before the night was through. Depending on what happened, he might be glad he had more.

Rick checked and re-checked everything several times: *Water, granola bars, extra shirt, flashlight, batteries, power stick, spare phone charger, rewetting drops, booze.* Outwardly, it looked like another OCD flare-up, a simple quirk; inwardly, Rick knew that it was because of the intense amount of anxiety he held about going into the woods.

Devlin could talk all he wanted to about protective talismans, Bora how the presence seemed kind... but Rick couldn't shake the vague feeling that he was walking into a trap. *If these things are benevolent, why have they been making my life a living hell?* he wondered.

Rick dropped his backpack off by the front door and started back for the bedroom to get dressed. He turned around in the kitchen to check one last time: *Water, granola bars, extra shirt, flashlight, batteries, power stick, phone charger, rewetting drops, booze.* Everything appeared in order.

Counterpoint, Rick said to himself. *If these things are malevolent, then why haven't they been more aggressive?* While it was true that one of them had grabbed his hair in the kitchen back in September, that wasn't especially violent, all things considered. Plus, he was vulnerable countless nights, with no sign of attack.

Maybe they're just trying to communicate, he decided, slipping on a buffalo plaid flannel shirt. *Something about life and death. But what?* He had to admit that, as much apprehension as he felt, the possibility of getting answers at long last appealed immensely to him.

Rick emerged into the living room just before six, wearing a baseball cap and jeans. Bora looked slightly absurd, decked out in an ensemble better suited for a night on the town than an evening in the forest: a grey puffy vest with a brown fur collar, black yoga pants, a pair of Uggs, and, most incongruously, an old Soviet ushanka-hat.

"You look like a Siberian sorority sister," Rick chuckled. "You sure your head will be warm enough?"

"I packed what I packed," snapped Bora, hoisting her bag. "Cut me some slack. How was I supposed to know we were going full *Blair Witch*? This isn't even my hat. Dev got it for me out of his trunk."

Rick wrinkled his nose. "Smells like borscht and motor oil," he remarked. "You know, you could've asked me. I've got plenty of caps you could borrow."

Bora shook her head, ear flaps pirouetting like wings. "It's actually kinda cozy," she decided. "Plus... Dev was so excited to help, I don't want to offend him." Rick was surprised at how far the two of them had come in the past forty-eight hours.

"Well, let me know if you need me to pick up lice shampoo," joked Rick after putting on his own backpack. "Or maybe you can ask Edna. Sounds like something she would have used recently." The two of them laughed as Devlin came out of the addition.

He didn't look like he had prepared much for their outing at all. He still wore the pants of his leisure suit, though he had swapped out the jacket for a tattered leather blazer that bore bits of paint here and there. Rick was surprised to see that Devlin had abandoned his garish Hawaiian shirts in favor of a plain, black tee shirt. Instead of a backpack, he carried his massive messenger bag.

"Lookit you, Ranger Rick," Devlin said. "Y'all two ready to go?" They nodded, and the three of them headed out the front door, Rick pausing a moment to lock up behind them. As they waited, a pickup truck pulled up, and out popped Edna, dressed in sweatpants, a heavy winter jacket, and a baseball cap emblazoned with GAS, GRASS, OR ASS: NOBODY RIDES FOR FREE. A series of logos depicted each commodity, in case there was any confusion.

"Ain't we a motley fucking crew?" she croaked, grabbing her backpack and a walking stick from the bed. "Rick, Devlin, y'all wanna help me grab those chairs?" She gestured to four camping chairs in the passenger's seat, collapsed into their carry bags. Each of the men grabbed a pair. "Alright, kids," Edna said, lighting a cigarette. "Where y'all wanna go?"

Everyone cast their eyes into the field around the house. Like all landscapes clinging to mountains' northeastern sides, the Ellijay property enjoyed two sunsets: one when the sun slipped behind the peak, and another around half an hour later, when the earth swallowed the last loitering rays. The interim transformed the marigold sky into a cycloptic Jack-o-lantern, the unpaired eye of Red Ear Mountain peeking over the trees, casting its hollow gaze over the fields below, before fading like a memory against the bleak expanse of night.

Devlin stood in the last bit of light before the pseudo-sunset, eyes scanning the tall grass waving back and forth. His tongue flicked across his lips. To Rick, Devlin's gaze seemed predatory, like a large cat surveying the savannah for its next meal. "To be frank, Edna, I ain't sure," he admitted. "Ricky's seen lights up on the mountain, so maybe there?"

"I don't rightly recommend going up and down Red Ear at night," Edna advised. "Slope's more gradual on the eastern side, though, kinda catty-cornered here off the kitchen." She pointed in the direction where, nestled somewhere within the trees, the driveway forked to lead to her house. "There's a couple gaps in the fence we can pass through over yonder."

Without looking for confirmation, she set off into the meadow, her footing as sure as someone a third her age. Everyone fell in behind her. Soon enough, they had crossed the amber expanse and stood on the forest's edge, a pair of kudzu-wrapped tree trunks serving as a postern into the gloom beyond. While the field was still well-lit, the spaces between the trees ahead were already succumbing to shadow, harboring a thousand darkened corners for the unspoken to seek refuge.

Before stepping inside, Devlin asked everyone to check their horseshoe talismans one final time. With precautions confirmed, they set off into the unknown.

None of them would return the same.

33

Saturday, October 31, 2020

CAMPFIRE TALES

Rick, Bora, Edna, and Devlin pressed through the forest, roughly staying together but navigating the terrain of each unique path as they saw fit. The forest floor was a patchwork of light and shadow, a quilt of leaves obscuring numerous obstacles, from stumps to roots to the occasional rock and small sink hole. It was far from hazardous terrain, but still demanded everyone's attention, lest they suffer a twisted ankle.

For the longest time, nothing could be heard except the telltale shamble of eight feet across dead leaves. Like the humans below, the branches of the canopy were themselves on the march, slowly but surely progressing toward peak color for one final celebration before dropping their leaves. On the forest floor, they would rejoin their fallen comrades, only to desiccate and brown as one.

Rick relished being back in nature, and scolded himself for cowering indoors all summer. It was invigorating. Even in the season of death, the forest remained alive. Nowhere was this contradiction better illustrated than when he stepped over a mushroom-encrusted log, only to have his footfall release a rich aroma of decay, the smell that would fuel growth several months hence. In the woods, autumn wasn't the end; it was *potential*, every bit as vibrant and full of promise as the noisy flamboyance of springtime.

To Rick, it seemed to be full of other things as well, though no one else acknowledged them. Every now and again, he would catch a slight glimmer out of the corner of his eye—a light, low to the ground, off at an angle, flashing for but a second before disappearing. Rick was sure some of them were nothing more than a trick of the fading day, perhaps a patch of sunlight revealed for only a moment before being obscured by vegetation. As for the others….

Edna had fallen to second place, allowing Devlin to take the lead. From time to time he would stop, glance around, and sniff the air, almost like tracking some unseen quarry. In these instances, his narrow physique, coupled with his beige pants and brown jacket, momentarily caused him to fade into the background of the forest, looking perfectly at home amidst the pattern of thin, young trunks and thicker, older growth. Then, as abruptly as he stopped, he would start moving once more, emerging from the mosaic of bark to gracefully negotiate the next obstacle, be it a cluster of brambles or a pile of limbs jutting above the leaf litter like jagged bones.

Bit by bit, the terrain began sloping upwards, leaving everyone a little sweatier, a little more winded than when they started. After about thirty minutes of tromping ever-deeper, sunset officially commenced. They found themselves standing before a dense thicket of mountain laurel. The impenetrable tangle dominated the gradual slope of the mountainside, choking out the taller trees and prying open the canopy to reveal the reddening sky above.

"Here," said Devlin, setting down his bag and two chairs. Rick followed suit.

"I was wondering when you'd let us take a break," Bora huffed. She turned to Rick. "You live in a beautiful place, dude. I can see why you love it up here."

"Let's revisit that claim after the sun goes down," advised Rick. He turned to their leader. "What now?" he asked.

Devlin was already gathering wood, examining each bit before keeping or tossing it aside. "Spread out, but stay within sight," he directed, not looking up from his task. "Wanna build a fire."

The rest of the group pitched in, slight whisps of vapor from their breath hinting at a colder night ahead. Within twenty minutes, everyone's hard work left them with a ring of stones surrounding a pile of kindling and small logs. When he went to light it, Devlin discovered that his lighter had died, but Edna was ready with a backup. Soon enough, everyone was set up in their camping chairs, warming themselves around the dancing flames. Rick found himself especially toasty, the burning in his gut augmenting the fire's heat with each furtive sip.

"Bora," said Edna, dragging on a Marlboro Red. "Third night together, and I still don't know too much about you."

Bora leaned forward on her elbows toward the fire, warming her hands. Only the crackling blaze and chirping crickets answered. "Not much to say," she said at length from beneath her gigantic hat. "I work in a pharmacy. I'm an artist... at least I try to be. Still not making a living from it. But something'll pop someday." Bora could see from Edna's expression that she wanted to know more. "Born in Buford, second generation Korean. Straight-A student until I discovered this." She held up her vape, then took a puff and gestured in Rick's direction. "Still somehow managed to get into college, where I met this numbskull."

The tip of Edna's cigarette flared, then dimmed. "Folks still around?" she asked from behind a veil of smoke.

"Dad is," answered Bora, watching the flames.

"A great guy," Rick leapt in. "Super generous. Helped me out a couple of times... In fact, I probably wouldn't have graduated without him."

"Enough about me," Bora said to Edna. "Tell me about you."

Edna waved a hand dismissively. "Same as anyone else with a lick of sense my age," she replied. "I like to eat, drink, and watch TV. Like to fuck, too, but don't happen too often no more."

Bora nodded slowly, eyes wide, aware that this was not comfortable territory to tread. "Well, what about our man of the hour?" she inquired, looking at Devlin. "We know all about your exploits, Mr. Fox, but not a lot about your history. Where are you from, exactly?"

The question took Devlin by surprise. It was obvious he had not been listening. He was instead too engrossed with every little sound of the forest, his head roving around the campfire like an attentive watchdog. "Who, me?" he said once he realized the question. "I like to say I'm from everywhere. Citizen of the world, as it is."

"Everyone's born someplace," countered Bora. She took a drink from her water bottle.

"I'm from here... abouts," Devlin finally offered. "Son of Appalachian dirt farmers. Didn't have two pennies to rub together, growing up. Couple brothers, one deceased, one sister, alive."

"When did you start"—Bora waved a hand in his direction—"all this?"

Devlin sighed, puffing out his cheeks. "Seen my first ghost when I was… I dunno? Three? Never *not* seen 'em. Helped my first client when I was ten, if you can believe it. Thought their house was haunted, turned out to be leaky pipes. First exorcism at sixteen, been on the road ever since." Bora nodded, not feeling like she knew much more than when they began.

"Is there a… school for that?" asked Rick.

"Some people might tell you as much," admitted Devlin, pulling out a cigarette. Edna offered her lighter. "But naw. Me, I'm an autodidact. Self taught. Read every chance I can get. Everything I know came out of a book or someone else. That and more trial n' error than I care to remember." He took a break and inhaled. "Still don't know enough."

"Surely, after all these years, you've got a good idea?" pressed Rick.

Devlin rolled his cigarette between his fingers, examining it. "Did you know that you can't measure a shoreline?" he mused, looking up at the smoke trailing into the sky. Darkness had fallen at last, enticing the stars out to play. "It's so simple, yet we just can't do it. Oh, yeah, we got satellite imagery and all that, but the actual length of the coast? It's a compromise. Always will be." He finished his cigarette, flicked it into the fire, and leaned forward, the flames casting an ever-changing pattern of light and shadow across his features.

"Y'see, coastlines are fractals," he continued. "Beaches are straightforward enough, but harbors have inlets, inlets have coves, and coves have dozens of miniscule nooks and crannies. The more you zoom in, the more they multiply. They become infinite. Millimeters heading inland, then doubling back on themselves. Those add up, if you measure 'em all. That means even the smallest pond has an immeasurable shoreline." He took out another cigarette and lit it directly on the campfire. "We, as a species, don't know jack shit. And if eight billion people can't measure a shoreline, how can one person, all alone in this cold, dark universe, know a damn thing for certain?"

Everyone sat, trying to comprehend both the concept and what Devlin was driving at. Finally, Bora stood up. "I have to pee," she announced, heading away from the campfire. "If I didn't know any better, Dev, I'd think *you* were the stoner."

Bora cautiously headed into the forest, threading between the trees and keeping a close eye on how much the campfire illuminated her surroundings. She had no desire to venture too far, but fear and modesty were playing chicken within her, and the latter was winning. Watching the layer of pine needles and leaves beneath her feet slowly grow more indistinct, she stopped the moment she found herself completely enveloped in darkness, maybe fifty feet away. She realized this distance was probably overkill, but knew that if she didn't feel completely hidden, her bashful bladder meant she'd likely crouch there forever, trying and failing to relieve herself.

Here, just beyond the edge of the light, she experienced no such difficulty. Her business completed, she pulled up her jeans, zipped them, and turned back towards the campfire. Doing so, she fully appreciated just how far she had wandered from everyone else.

To her surprise, the flames were but a dim speck in the distance, completely unrecognizable through the trees, which now seemed as densely woven as a wicker basket. Somehow, the campfire looked at least three times farther than she thought she had wandered.

Bora took a cautious step forward before realizing that, like a fool, she had traipsed into the forest without her flashlight. She chalked it up to spending too much time in the city; she had forgotten how truly *dark* it could be out here in the middle of nowhere.

The thought brought a swell of panic, which she quickly tamped down. There was nothing to fear. After all, the moon was bright and the light of the campfire was obvious. Bora decided it shouldn't be too much trouble finding her way back. In fact, she was surprised at how quickly one acclimated to the woods at night once the initial unfamiliarity waned.

With halting strides, she crept forward, testing each step for holes and roots before setting her foot down. The mountain sloping up to her left, she slowly made her way closer, using her hands to stabilize her approach against the sturdier trees. Once or twice she became entangled in a knot of vines and branches, but she still managed to keep the light of the campfire squarely in view.

A few minutes later, Bora drew within fifty feet of her destination —the distance she initially thought she had traveled. She immediately recognized that something was dreadfully wrong.

Only three figures should have reclined around the flames. Yet here were many, all of them circumnavigating the fire, their movements frenzied and erratic. Instinctively, Bora crouched behind the nearest trunk, her heart threatening to pound straight from her chest.

Eventually, she gathered enough nerve to peek around the pine tree. Having caught her breath, Bora was able to make out more details, although they remained little more than impressions. The clearest observation was that none of the figures dancing around the fire would have reached her waist. Beyond that, everything else remained speculative. The ones nearest her were simple silhouettes.

Every time their procession reached the far side of the campfire, however, another vague detail revealed itself. From the light they reflected, it appeared as if each figure was shirtless. Their sex remained indeterminate, but all sported long, flowing manes of jet black hair that flung to and fro as they gamboled about the flames. Every now and then one of them would stop, leaving the hair to settle in place past the small of its back, where a hint of buckskin pants or a loincloth could be barely discerned in the fading light. It would then pick up the dance with renewed vigor.

To Bora, the strangest thing of all was the *silence*. Beyond the sound of her breath and her heart in her ears, nothing could be heard. There was no recognizable speech, no crackling bonfire, and no footfalls as the figures cartwheeled about. Even the other sounds of the forest seemed temporarily stifled.

Bora watched this enthusiastic fireside display until, to her horror, one of the figures stopped on the side nearest her position. It faced the forest, scanning its surroundings until a pair of black eyes—only discernible because of how much darker they were than the rest of its face—locked with her own. A flurry of movement below them followed, suggesting a grimace or sneer…

Realizing she had been spotted, Bora released her grip on the bark. She immediately began backpedaling, dried leaves and brittle twigs causing an absolute racket beneath her feet. The commotion caught the attention of the rest of the group. Each figure, perhaps as many as nine, all froze in place… then pivoted, slowly facing her…

Bora's heel caught on a stump, sending her head over heels. Her hands barely kept her from breaking her back on the jagged wood thrusting up from the ground. She tried to stand but only flailed, her arms sending up a curtain of dead leaves in the process. When at last she rose to her feet, heart pounding, she was prepared to fight. However, there was nothing to be seen—only a dark expanse of forest before her, barely illuminated by the full moon. There was not even a trace of smoke.

"*Bora?!?*" Her name echoed up the mountainside. From far downhill to her right, she saw another light in the distance. "*Bora?!? Where are you?!?*"

"Here!" she exclaimed, scrambling as fast as she safely could in the direction of Rick's voice. "I'm here! I'm coming!" Thankfully, the journey proved far clearer than her approach to the other campfire. It was a good thing, too, because, with gravity on her side, she found herself careening through the bush with a headlong momentum that left her almost as terrified as the phantom fire. In no time, she had fallen into Rick's arms.

"Good Lord, Bora," he said, reacting either to her return or how firmly she gripped him. Dried leaves clung to the collar of her vest. "What took so long? Did you take a dump instead?"

Bora collapsed in her chair, chugging water until she regained her composure. When at last she felt settled enough, she took a long drag on her vape and explained the entire situation, lapsing into the trademark rapid-fire style she always employed when agitated: why she had wandered so far, how it seemed further than she had thought, the decoy campfire, the small figures. Her doppelgänger mimicked the delivery in a shadowy pantomime across the maze of laurel behind her.

"I fucking *hate* Halloween," she grumbled when she was finished. Edna and Rick looked horrified. Devlin, on the other hand, grabbed his flashlight and bolted into the forest in the approximate direction Bora had indicated. All she managed to get out before he disappeared was, "Dev, I don't think that's a good—"

Ten long minutes later, Devlin returned, breathing heavily. "Boy, them fellers really led you down the garden path, didn't they?" he remarked. "Gotta be, what, a hunnerd yards away, at least?"

"Find anything?" asked Rick.

"Not really. A big ol' clearing, some small scuff marks on the ground, a few bits of burned wood. They were cold to the touch, no telling how long they've been up there... But this is good news."

"Good news?"

"For one, Bora's still with us," Devlin elaborated. "Charms are doing their job. But there's something else. Y'all notice the time? It's almost 8:30 now, so I put Bora's little encounter around, eh, 8:10, 8:11. They're not only here; they're sticking to a *schedule*." He kneeled down to his messenger bag and fished around inside for a minute until he produced a pair of walkie-talkies. He stood, handing one to Bora.

"What's this for?" she asked warily. "Don't tell me we're separating."

"We're separating," responded Devlin, grabbing two chairs and hoisting the bag on his shoulder.

"Why?" retorted Bora.

"Probably not best to have a crowd for the Estes session. No worries, we're still on the buddy system. You and Edna stay here. Me and Ricky are gonna post up on that ridge we passed on the way in." He nodded into the darkness. "Keep an eye out for anything odd. Ear out, too. I recommend sittin' y'all's chairs back-to-back, so nothing sneaks up on you. No matter what, keep your necklaces on. You see anything, call us on the walkie. You hear anything, call us on the walkie. You need anything—"

"—call you on the walkie," Bora finished with a nod. "Meet back in...?"

Devlin's form had already started fading into the trees. "No sense settin' a deadline," he yelled back. "We're done when we're done... but I imagine 11:08 will be quite memorable." With that, he and Rick slipped beyond the campfire's edge, leaving the two women alone.

Bora began rearranging the campsite, trying to fend off the encroaching anxiety with small talk. "So," Bora remarked, "Durchdenwald... That's German, right?"

"Yes ma'am," replied Edna, settling in for a smoke. "And proud of it. Y'ever get to Helen? You know, that lil' town over in White County they made to look like an Alpine village?"

An image of herself doing the *Chicken Dance,* completely plastered, flashed in Bora's mind, followed by a memory of her worst hangover. "No, don't think I have," she lied.

"Well, it's right neat, should you ever get the chance to visit. Lots of fun. My kinfolk helped with the revamp back in the late '60s."

"Wow," said Bora. "What an... enduring cultural contribution." A bit of silence passed, then she spoke again. "Your property is really beautiful, Edna."

"Thanks, Bora. Been here so long, I sometimes forget that. Wanna move up here? I'd love to sell at least *some* of it, retire to Miami."

"What's keeping you?"

"Ah, never can get the right price," Edna scoffed. "I keep tellin' myself to wait. Ain't nobody making more land, right? Price is bound to go up." She took a long drag on her cigarette. "Though I'll always hang on to some of it. Got no choice. Government won't let me sell the far side of the mountain. Goddamn Indian burial mounds, or somesuch nonsense." She paused before asking, "Think you can get kai-rona virus from elves? Not that I'm scared...."

34

Saturday, October 31, 2020

ONCORHYNCHUS

DEVLIN AND RICK set themselves up on the ridge a few minutes later. It was neither uphill nor downhill, but rather a hundred or so yards further across the slope from Bora and Edna, at the same elevation. As Rick unfolded his camping chair to face down the mountain, he took comfort in the fact that he could easily see the campfire and his friends to his right. Should an emergency arise, they wouldn't exactly get there quickly—Rick was still winded from navigating the steep gully separating them—but there was no chance of anyone getting lost.

Before settling in, Rick took one last opportunity to check his bag. He fully realized that, should he find something missing, he couldn't do anything about it... but the ritual seemed to calm his nerves. *Water, granola bars, extra shirt, flashlight, batteries, power stick, phone charger, rewetting drops, booze.*

Devlin took his own advice and set up with his back against Rick's chair, taking the upslope watch. For a long time, they simply sat there, catching their breath and adjusting to their new surroundings. Rick didn't realize how much the campfire ruined his night vision. Now, without a constant light source battering his retinas, the forest took on a new life. Where once sat nothing but a black matte beyond the flames, now stood an entire landscape of depth and contrast. The difference was profound, like exchanging a photograph for a diorama.

Or, Rick remarked, *a stage*. It took little imagination to turn the largest trees into a makeshift proscenium, their trunks stretching, columnlike, towards the arch of the canopy. Instead of a curtain, the forest had the darkness itself, obscuring the action more dramatically than any theater could hope for. There was even an audience. The leaves rustling overhead sounded like nothing less than the excited whispers of a crowd eager for entertainment.

Let's hope it's not a tragedy, thought Rick. *Or even a comedy.* Long ago, he had heard that comedy was simply tragedy plus distance. On a night like tonight, he was far too close to the action to appreciate it. The notion left him unsettled. Whatever was scheduled for this evening remained unclear, from the plot to the players themselves.

Ruminating on this, Rick asked, "Are they all bad?"

Devlin's signature drawl drifted over his shoulder. "Shitfire, man. I have trouble saying *any* are bad. Most times, even the bad ones make something good out of it. Life's like that, too. Sometimes a controlled burn has to come through, make way for new growth."

Rick sighed. It wasn't an easy thing to hear. "Yeah, I'm not so sure about that," he said, sipping his flask. When he noticed it was almost empty, he opened his backpack and reached for the bottle.

"Hmm?"

"Look at me," lamented Rick as the vodka gurgled into his flask. "My marriage is done. I can't play music without getting hit with panic attacks. I'm drinking myself to death. And to top everything off, I've got... goblin problems." He sighed, screwed on the lid, and tossed the bottle back inside his bag with a huff. "What good can come from all *this*? Even when things were going great, I just felt so... so *unfulfilled*. Like there was an empty hole inside of me. Only now I realize that it was never a hole. It was my entire self. I'm empty. I'm... *I am nothing.*"

A dog barked somewhere far away. Devlin took so long to formulate a response that Rick started to wonder whether he had been heard.

"Now hang on," Devlin disagreed at last. "Everybody's *somethin'*. I mean, you're clearly important to *them*. Besides, ain't you got, like, a bunch of record credits? People come to see you play music. Don't they love it?"

"Never feels like enough," grumbled Rick. When he said the words aloud, he realized how petulant they sounded.

"Well, that's part of your problem, Bubba. Sure, you can keep chasing that. Maybe you'll be validated from time to time. But it won't last. You'll just need more and more praise to feel the same way, and the crash will get worse and worse... Just like that flask of yours."

Rick looked at the canister in his hands, realizing that Devlin was right but unwilling to admit it. "What's the solution, then?" he wondered, earnestly hoping that he might find some insight. "What's the point?"

"The point? The point is... well... What do you know about salmons?"

It took Rick a moment to comprehend the word. "Um... they're delicious? They swim upstream?"

"Attaboy. Yup. They swim upstream to breed and die. You know what's funny about a salmon? I seen 'em once in Bristol Bay, and the entire time I'm lookin' at 'em, I'm thinking to myself: this ain't no *river* fish. Hell, naw. Sometimes the cricks they wind up in are barely deep enough to accommodate 'em. No, what you see is a fuckin' streamlined oceanic predator that, for some reason—I know, I know, to breed, but bear with me—for some reason, they go where they can't even fit and *die*, piled up one on top of another'n. An ignominious end for such a majestic creature. Why not just breed in the ocean?"

Devlin craned his neck to look over his shoulder, his leather jacket squeaking like a trapped mouse. "So I'm watching these fellers," he continued, waving his hands, "and it dawns on me: they're bringing all them nutrients from the ocean miles upon miles inland, upstream, up mountains, to be shared in an entirely new ecosystem. It ain't a tragic end; it's one filled with *purpose*. Not because the salmons accomplished anything. Even if they fail to breed, they still redistribute nutrients. Simply by merit of existing. Existing and *struggling*. The struggle, all that effort and exertion and exhaustion... it's the entire point of their lives. Every one of them fish dies without realizing its greatest contribution was simply... existing."

When Rick said nothing, Devlin added, "You've got a leg up on the salmons, Ricky. Well, I mean, two legs up, technically, but you know what I mean. You've got an advantage. *You can realize your intrinsic value before your struggle is over.*"

"I didn't know you were a therapist, too," Rick snarked at last. "And how do I accomplish that, pray tell?"

"You've known me for a while," replied Devlin, folding his arms and sliding down in his chair to stretch his legs. "What do you think I'll say?"

For some reason, Rick found himself staring long and hard at a dead leaf trapped on the ground, moving slightly in the wind, not ten feet away. It batted up and down as if it were on a hinge before breaking free and tumbling over the forest floor. "Belief?" suggested Rick as the leaf vanished from view.

"Apt pupil. You and Bora both."

"Learning something is different from applying it. Hard to believe anything when your face is in the mud all the time."

"Faith don't thrive in plenty, Rico. It thrives in scarcity."

"Spare me the sermon. Wish in one hand—*'believe'* in one hand—and shit in the other. See which one fills up first."

"Yeah, well, I dunno 'bout you, but most of the time I *decide* to pinch a loaf. Don't just fall out."

Rick managed a halfhearted chuckle. "Yeah, but you can feel it, right? I don't *feel* anything... I don't *hear* anything. Just more empty promises."

"Empty?!?" bellowed Devlin. "I mean what I said, Ricky: Belief is the most powerful force in the universe. Civilizations are *built* on the back of belief. It's belief what causes empires to rise and fall. Belief is conquest, liberation, peace, war, victory, defeat. Belief can heal, it can wound. Belief can literally change reality... To a degree, belief is what these lil' fellers are always after. They want to be *believed* in... but not *too* much, it seems. Most of the time, they prefer to remain in the shadows, in that zone between belief and disbelief. You want to come through whatever this is in one piece? Then you gotta *believe*, Ricky: in them... in me... in yourself. Draw 'em out into the sunlight, where you can fight on your own terms."

Before Rick could offer a rational counterargument (he thought of at least a dozen), Devlin pointed skyward. "See that?" he added. "Moon's vibratin'."

"Devlin," Rick whined, "you want me to believe you, then you go and say—" When his eyes reached the sky, his words caught in his throat. He saw exactly what Devlin meant, if only for a split second. Ever-so-slightly, the full moon trembled back and forth incredibly fast, then stilled. It reminded Rick of catching the final oscillations of a guitar string long after it had been plucked, just before falling silent. "What does it mean?" he asked.

"Wouldn't get too hung up on it," Devlin replied with a yawn. "Probably just part of The Wake." These were the last words either of them said for a long time. For the next few hours, they simply sat and listened. Every now and then, Devlin would check in on Edna and Bora over the walkie-talkie. They had nothing to report.

Otherwise, the only dialogue shared between the two men was spoken in the aftermath of something seen or heard. Usually it had a mundane explanation: animals, the wind, tricks of the light. Only a handful of times did anything seem truly anomalous. Even then, these consisted of little more than glimpses of light or shadow from the corner of their vision.

It wasn't much, but it still proved disconcerting for Rick. He slowly began to suspect that he and Devlin were sitting in the center of an ever-tightening circle: a flock of vultures overhead; a trash compactor pressing down; a pack of wolves pacing the perimeter; a hangman's noose slowly contracting.

The moment that Devlin announced the arrival of eleven o'clock, something struck Rick on his chest. It didn't hurt at all, but, with his nerves on high alert, it absolutely terrified him. He started, releasing a string of curses. When it became evident that nothing else was going to happen, he quickly settled down.

"What was that?" inquired Devlin.

"I dunno..." Rick replied. He flicked on his flashlight, half-concealing the brightness with his fingers, and shone it onto his lap. There, atop his jeans, sat a small, brown rock, presumably what had hit him moments earlier. "A pebble, looks like," he explained.

The instant he said this, the walkie-talkie flared to life, too loud for comfort. Even Devlin, seasoned as he was, jumped at the sound. "Jesus, forgot I even had this thing," he exclaimed, pressing the talk button. "This is Devlin, over," he announced. A quick chirp followed.

Another chirp. "Hey sexy," Edna said on the other end. "Wanted y'all to know that a rock just hit my shoe, over." Rick looked over his shoulder, exchanging a knowing glance with Devlin. Things finally appeared to be heating up.

"Ten four," Devlin answered. "Same thing just happened to—" He stopped mid-sentence. Rick turned and found him stock still, eyes fixed on something further up the mountain. There, far up the slope, scintillating in the distance, was a light—though other than that, little else could be determined. It was clearly not from the campfire, however, which sat a full ninety degrees away. "Y'all see that?" whispered Devlin into the walkie-talkie.

"No... yeah, yeah we do," Edna corrected herself. Before she cut off her transmission, Rick heard Bora say from the background, "Same color as that campfire—"

Devlin and Rick stared at the light for a while, though Rick could not guess how long. It might have been thirty seconds; it might have been ninety. Either way, the sight was short-lived, persisting long enough to catch their attention but short enough to prevent any closer examination. It was hard to tell whether or not it moved. In any case, as lights so often did along Red Ear Mountain, the mysterious pinpoint simply extinguished, leaving the landscape looking as if it had never existed at all.

Devlin stood, picked up his messenger bag, and dropped it onto his chair. "That, Nature Boy," he said, unzipping the largest compartment, "is our cue."

35

Saturday, October 31, 2020

ESTES

RICK WATCHED DEVLIN remove several items from his bag: first, a large pair of headphones, followed by a pocket radio and a small tape recorder. He moved quickly and efficiently, but there was a hint of freneticism simmering just below the surface. Devlin plugged the headphones into the radio, handed them over to Rick, and slipped the recorder into his jacket pocket.

"We're just going to jump right in?" fretted Rick, looking at the headphones. Of all Devlin's possessions, they were by far the most sophisticated thing Rick had seen, a high-end affair with noise-canceling capability. "Aren't you going to do some protections? Set up a circle?"

"Did that the first night and absolutely nothing happened," Devlin said, shaking his head. "C'mon, it's almost 11:08. We gotta move quick."

Rick started to slip on the headphones, then remembered they were missing something. "Blindfold?" he asked.

"Shit!" Devlin started rummaging through his bag. "Almost forgot." From some hidden compartment, he extracted a simple sleep mask. Before handing it over, he offered one final word of comfort. "You're gonna feel real isolated, Richard. Don't let it spook you. I'm your eyes and ears to the real world. The minute I feel like we're in danger, I'm pullin' you out and we're hightailin' back home. Okay?" Rick nodded. "You ain't gonna hear any of my prompts. The moment I start this radio up, it's going to scan through the stations. You'll hear a lot of static. Repeat any words clear enough to recognize. We shouldn't need long—just a few minutes. *Capisce?*"

Rick nodded again, then dutifully slipped the blindfold over his eyes. It brought with it a fleeting twinge of panic. Pushing through, he secured the headphones over his ears and immediately felt far removed from everything around him. The only thing that indicated he was still in the forest was the chilly breeze against his exposed skin and the gradual slope of the mountainside beneath his shoes.

In many respects, Rick felt like he had just plunged underwater, although instead of reaching the lowest point and resurfacing, that moment was suspended indefinitely. He now stood at the bottom of an unfathomable, dark pool, weights tied to his feet, pinning him down. A few seconds passed before Rick realized he was holding his breath. With great intention, he forced his respiration into a slow, steady rhythm.

Somewhere out in the darkness, he imagined Devlin still holding the radio. It flickered on. There was no warning, just an endless stream of noise that picked up *in media res*, leaving Rick scrambling to catch up with the flurry of words already assaulting his ears. He listened closely through the collage of static and late-night radio programs, repeating whatever seemed to surface above the hissing ostinato. Now and then, what felt like interminable stretches of nonsense or white noise were the only thing he heard, leaving him feeling like he was missing something or failing the experiment entirely.

"Okay, first thing I heard was 'Mount,'" he whispered, his voice booming in his own head. "If... it...." He kept listening and repeating:

... ih... tr... ab... ... ... NUMEROUS... ... ter... ... ... SHE... ah... enk... leh... ze... cr...fi... ... ... YOU... er...bi... FOE... ... ... COULD... anel... mun... th... vi... SOMETIMES... ALSO... YOU... ... ... PERSON WHO... cu...pr... ya... jo... mi... nk... ni... OUTSTANDING... sh... bu... A... COUNT... tr... ... ... un... ing... ... ... s... DETT... ... ...

The middle portion of a long, ringing tone broke through before the static swallowed it once again. "Uh, I just heard a bell chime," Rick rapidly explained. "Dunno if I need to say that—" He was already missing more words...

... co... il... min... ar... ... ... cath... im... gr... s... BARD... v... HER... ree... ers... COUNSEL... BOLD... bon... de... be... pa... rr... ATTEMPT... ... ... ral... fic... tr... ris... RED... sh... WALL... ... ... SPAGHETTI... VERY...

FALCONS ... ing... gr... da... igh... pi... SELF... shr... ENDING... ... ... mon... ur... k... ji... cuh... ... ... DRESS... APPEAR... qui... ANTS... ... ...

Rick strained to listen, trying to pick out more words. Only fragments met his ears, the barest bones of vowels and consonants. Soon, even these became scarce, leaving him listening to snippets of static, fluctuating in pitch yet constant in rhythm, spaced about a second apart. He stood there in the darkness, feeling like an astronaut unloosed from his tether, drifting further and further out into deep space....

... d... v... ly... ... ... ex... z... b... n... ... ... u... h... ... ... ch... ... ... ea... ... ... g... ... ... j... ... ... s... ... ...

"*Fucking hell, move!*" Devlin's voice interrupted the static. With one hand, he batted off Rick's headphones, while the other wrenched the eye mask away, snapping its elastic straps. Both fell to the ground, tossing up leaves. As loud as Devlin had shouted, his voice was only barely perceptible above a deep, abiding hum that permeated the forest. Even the rock below Rick's feet seemed to vibrate with each rising pulse.

At first, Rick could not see anything. Having his eyes closed for so long left them overly sensitive, and the light stabbing through the trees could not have appeared any brighter. When his vision at last adjusted enough, Rick's first thought was that a helicopter had descended into the forest.

Every tree felt alive, pitching wildly, caught in the grip of a gale thick with dried leaves. As they did so, their branches darted in and out of an intense light far down the mountainside, sending shadows groping uphill towards Rick and Devlin. Even at this distance, the glare penetrated between the trunks with blinding strength. It was as if the sun, somehow turning blue, had joined forces with a hurricane to descend beneath the canopy, settling on the forest floor.

After spending hours in darkness, the commotion was startling. Yet it was far from the most disturbing thing that Rick saw.

Down toward the light—but drawing inexorably closer with each passing moment—came a series of short figures, heads like melons, bodies emaciated, appearing as no more than silhouettes against the sea of flaring blue. Their ascent uphill was unhurried yet obviously filled with purpose. It was the approach of a hunting party taking its time, reveling in the glory of successfully downing their quarry.

Somehow, Rick managed to pull his gaze from this macabre incursion long enough to glance to his right. Across the gully, the campfire in front of the laurel thicket was extinguished, victim of the ferocious wind. Edna and Bora's chairs lay scattered on the ground, surrounded by a whirlwind of pine needles. There was no sign of either of them, though it was impossible to see much through the frenzy of debris that choked the air between the trees.

"*Richard!*" shouted Devlin as he grabbed him by the sleeve. "*We have to get the fuck out of here!*" For the first time since they had met, Rick saw Devlin's face seized by true terror. The two of them began scrambling away from the gully, toward the safety of the field somewhere down the mountain below. They made it only a few feet before Rick began tugging in the opposite direction.

"*The fuck you doing?*" yelled Devlin above the din.

"*Bora and Edna!*" Rick shouted back as the wind blew off his ballcap. "*I'm not leaving them!*"

Before Devlin could object, Rick was slipping down into the gully. Briars snagged his shirt and scratched his face as he descended in something halfway between a stumble and a slide. Branches whipped his eyes, momentarily blinding him just long enough for a misstep. The few leaves not taken up by the wind slipped beneath him, catapulting Rick onto his stomach.

As he staggered to his feet at the bottom of the gulch, wet and filthy, he risked a glance toward the light. The figures had already closed half the distance, reoriented on a trajectory with his position.

For a moment, Rick panicked. One of them was already upon him. He quickly realized the presence tumbling to his rear was actually Devlin, following reluctantly, swearing all the way.

Hands bleeding, Rick started grasping anything he could to ascend the other side: moss-covered rocks, rotten stumps, ferns, saplings. Most of them dislodged or uprooted under the strain. A few remained put, affording him purchase uphill. The last few feet he covered through sheer will on his hands and knees, fingers digging deep into the damp soil as he clawed his way atop the opposite rise.

At last, the ground leveled out. Rick noticed a new series of shadows playing over his face. Out of the corner of his eye, he gathered that the figures were almost upon them, close enough to block a substantial portion of the light filtering up from below. They had drawn so close that he might have been able to make out more features, but he had no desire to linger. The largest obstacle had been conquered. Nothing more than the usual hazards of the forest floor stood between him and where the campfire once blazed.

Rick heaved himself upright, then began a mad dash toward the laurel thicket. At one point, he nearly twisted his ankle on a hole but quickly recovered, using his momentum to bounce against the trunk of an oak. The bark scraped his hands, leaving them further bloodied.

Rick kept on running until he slid to a stop before the stone circle that once held the fire. Only a few spare embers, barely clinging to life, glowed as they took to the sky amidst the tempest. Edna and

Bora's chairs were still abandoned, covered with dead leaves that clung here and there before being swept away on the wind.

It was just as Rick feared—his friends were nowhere to be seen. He circled the fire pit in desperation, hoping that some clue might still remain. Even with the light pouring in from downhill, it remained impossible to tell. The only noticeable detail was the absence of their backpacks.

Completely at a loss, Rick shouted and started for the shaking cluster of laurel, ready to burst through. He made it shoulder-deep before realizing that the undergrowth was too thick for anyone to have entered. Wherever his friends had fled, it was not through there.

Rick stood for a moment, watching the shadows shimmer across the trembling thicket. His back was against the proverbial wall. Resigned to whatever happened next, he turned and saw Devlin clamoring over to the firepit, a wild look in his eyes. Just behind him the figures advanced, no more than thirty yards away. They maintained the same measured approach as before, but had fallen into single file. Within moments, they would be close enough to touch...

"Rick, they're not here!" begged Devlin. "We have got *to go!*" As his sentence finished, the thrumming ascended in pitch, turning into a whining suction sound. Rick became aware of a nearly imperceptible sensation of pressure leaving his feet, as if he had become lighter somehow. The chairs shuddered and lifted off the ground, no more than half an inch. As quickly as this feeling took hold, it released. With it, the light and the wind vanished, plunging the scene into a darkness whose depth was only outmatched by its stillness.

The two men stood, bodies rigid, ready for the intruders' arrival. Since his eyes could not keep up with the abrupt change, Rick relied on his ears to locate their position. There were no clues. The forest seemed quieter than ever. The only sound was Rick's breath, which, despite being held, still escaped in tiny puffs forced out by his rapid heartbeat.

About thirty seconds passed before he realized that he still had his flashlight crammed in his back pocket. Rick reached around, freed the device, and flicked it on. It first landed on Devlin, who instinctively drew a hand over his face. Rick then played the light across the abandoned campsite and the surrounding forest. Everything looked exactly as it had moments before, with the exception of the light, wind, and figures, all of which had disappeared.

"Richard," said Devlin, "this is just a stay of execution. From what you told me back there, I can't imagine they won't be back—"

"*Rick?!?*" Devlin stopped at the sound of Bora's voice, farther up the mountain. "*Dev?!?*"

"Bora!" Rick shouted back, dancing in front of the laurel. *"Stay where you are! We're coming for you!"* There was no reply from Bora. Rick shined his light across the mountainside, scrambling to formulate a plan. It didn't sound like she had wandered too far.

Finally, Rick shouted, *"Keep yelling! Keep your light on! Gonna find you!"* He trained his flashlight on Devlin's chest, casting a reflection off his brown and blue eyes. "Listen, maybe we can triangulate—"

"Richard, *listen to me*, I ain't pulling your leg," Devlin interjected above Bora as she began shouting their names over and over. "For your own sake, we have to—" Again, he was cut off. This time, however, it was not a distant yell but the sound of something much closer that caught his attention. Both of them heard it: the snap of a twig, followed by the characteristic tromp of a quadruped hesitantly navigating the underbrush.

Devlin drew a finger to his mouth. A slight wobble of his head indicated the direction in which he thought Rick should shine his flashlight.

Rick gradually pivoted the cone of illumination away from Devlin. The nearest tree trunk lapsed into the light and passed beyond its borders, sending the beam deeper into the forest. The image repeated itself several times, with the nearest trees jumping into view before Rick passed the light onward. Nothing noteworthy appeared until, at last, the flashlight landed upon an animal.

It was a deer. It simply stood there, head held low, obscured behind some brush. Rick was surprised that the animal had drawn so close. In fact, it seemed odd that it would have remained in this section of the woods at all. If nothing else, he thought that it surely would have fled the moment the forest filled with light. Relieved, Rick prepared to shoo it away.

He never had the chance. The animal moved. With one swift motion, its neck tensed, drawing its head up from behind the bush.

When it stopped, fully raised, Rick was staring at nothing more than the doe's skull. Its exposed teeth, arranged in a blood-flecked rictus, cowered beneath the pointed, fleshless taper of its snout. Bits of fur hung here and there from the jawbone, dangling in the yellow beam of the flashlight. Further back, one ear, fringed in red, remained attached with the barest bit of sinew, leaving it to droop lifelessly. The doe's eye sockets, empty and dark, seemed too deep to penetrate. They simply gazed back pitilessly like a pair of bottomless pits.

Only now did Rick notice the sorry state of the rest of its body. A giant gash in its side exposed several ribs and an empty cavity beyond, around which maggots coiled and burrowed into decaying muscle. The rest of its white hide lay in tatters, as if ripped asunder by a voracious predator or having fallen from a great height.

As he stared down the length of the beast, Rick noticed movement deeper in the forest. It was nine fawns, wobbling weakly behind their mother, all in similar states of decay, their skulls devoid of flesh. The one nearest Rick stumbled, then fell to its front knees with a sickening, wet crack. One leg, now broken, lay splayed at a ninety-degree angle.

Rick and Devlin remained completely frozen in revulsion. The doe lowered her skull once again, just above the brush. The jaw swung open on its hinge. A voice, clearly coming from the deer, billowed out amidst a cloud of vapor. It sounded almost as if spoken with an inhalation rather than an exhalation, and it drew out every vowel: *"Riiickaaard Coooulteeer...."*

The sound was enough to snap Rick out of his trance. Without saying a word, he took off as quickly as he could along the edge of the mountain laurel, flashlight bobbing the whole way. Reaching the edge of the thicket, he pivoted and ran up the mountainside in the approximate direction of Bora, who had never stopped calling for help. The entire time, the deer continued to wail, its voice carried on the breeze by nonexistent lungs and spoken by an invisible tongue: *"Riiickaaard Coooulteeer...."*

Rick began climbing the mountain with plenty of momentum on his side, but soon that wasn't enough. He was running out of steam, and the terrain became more treacherous with each step, forcing him to shine his flashlight before him. Though he still maintained an arduous pace, his speed slowed considerably. He was covered in sweat, his muscles ached, and his heart felt like it might explode at any moment.

The only thing worse than the agony was the terror. Every tree was a hidden face, every sound a prelude to an ambush, every stump a tiny, malevolent figure waiting to pounce. The entire time, the deer down the slope refused to stop howling.

After several minutes, Rick was completely spent. However, he took comfort in the fact that Bora's voice steadily grew louder, while the shrieks of the deer consistently diminished. Onward he pressed, until at last the ground leveled out a bit and the trees thinned. Bora's voice was closer than ever. It seemed to be coming from a clearing up ahead, as evidenced by the ease with which the moonlight illuminated the ground. With an abundance of caution, Rick took his first steps into what appeared to be a cemetery.

It took him a moment to realize there weren't headstones dotting the clearing but rather boulders, ranging in size from as small as a basketball to as large as a small car. In the moonlight, the boulder field almost looked like the aftermath of some mythic battle, its combatants frozen in time. Giant slabs lay on their sides, bleeding pebbles onto the tall grass. Smaller bits sat separated from these, scattered like hastily amputated limbs or discarded helmets.

In all his hikes up and down Red Ear Mountain, Rick had never been here before. He was surprised he had missed it. The entire area must have encompassed an acre or two. His observations were interrupted by another call from Bora. Somewhere deep inside the maze of monoliths, her voice rang out. It bounced against the rocks in a series of echoes that made pinpointing her exact position impossible.

"*Bora!*" cried Rick. He was so exhausted that he barely summoned enough breath to shout, leaving his voice weak and raspy. "*Bora!*... I'm here... Can... can you turn... turn on your flashlight? Can't... figure out where... where you are!" The moment he said this, a light blossomed to his right, illuminating the far edge of the field.

Rick warily picked his way across the clearing, more frightened at the prospect of injuring himself than any supernatural threat. After a minute or two of delicate tiptoeing, he found Bora and Edna huddled in the shelter of one of the larger boulders. Their faces lit up with joyful relief when they saw him.

"Rick! Glad you're okay," Edna croaked from the ground. She seemed nonplussed, cigarette in hand, a pile of butts beside her in the dirt. "Although at this point I'm inclined to say you're the worst tenant I ever had."

"Rick!" exclaimed Bora, tears in her eyes. Her hat was missing, leaving her dark hair decorated with bits of leaves and twigs. She jumped to her feet and gave Rick a hug. "Holy shit, I thought I'd never see you again!"

"Me too," Rick sighed. He pulled her away and held her shoulders, examining her face by the light of the moon. Other than a few scratches, she looked mostly fine. "Are you okay?" he asked at last.

She shook her head. "I guess so… when the forest lit up, the campfire blew out, and I ran. Didn't care where or how far, I just… ran. Found this place pretty quick. Edna, God bless her"—she gestured to the landlady—"she never stopped looking for me."

"Took a while," mused Edna, grinding her smoke out on the boulder behind her. "What the hell took you so long, Rick? We been waitin' on you for a couple hours, seems like. I'm almost done with my second pack."

Rick pursed his lips. "I don't know the exact time," he answered slowly, "but I can guarantee you it's been less than an hour since that light appeared." Bora and Edna looked at each other in disbelief.

"No way," Bora objected, confused. "It's been two hours, at *least*."

"What does your phone say?"

"Both dead."

"Ten till midnight," a tired voice declared from the other side of the rock. A moment of panic seized everyone before they realized it was Devlin. He peeked over the top of the boulder, looking completely drained. His face was paler than usual, and his hair had transformed into a rat's nest of sweaty tangles. After leaping over to the other side, he collapsed on the ground with Edna, who immediately handed him a cigarette.

"Sweet baby Jesus, I don't think I've ever needed this more in my life," he said as she lit it for him. "Thank you." He took a long puff, closed his eyes, and rested his head against the boulder. "Began the Estes session at 11:08 on the dot," he exhaled, "so I'm afraid we can't account for your missing time. Or *found* time, such as it is. Welcome to The Wake." He took another drag, eyes darting from boulder to boulder. "Edna—any clue where we are?"

Edna shrugged. "Kinda. Seem to recall playin' up here as a kid, though that was ages ago. Got a pretty good idea which direction to head," she chuckled. "I'd start with 'downhill.'"

"If you know the way home, Edna, why'd you wait on us?" asked Rick.

Edna tugged on her sweatpants, revealing her ankle. It looked ghastly, swollen, and was beginning to take on hues of yellow and purple. "Twisted it somethin' fierce on the way up here," she explained. "Thought Bora could use the help of some strapping young lads to get my fat ass back home." She rolled the leg of her pants back down, wincing all the way.

"Sounds good," Rick said with a nod. "'Edna is my co-pilot.' Devlin and I will support you while you tell us which way to head. Get us all back home, put some ice on that, grab a drink... and he can fill us in on what the fuck happened down there."

Without protesting, Devlin wearily stood, throwing on Edna's backpack before reaching a hand out to her. She accepted, and soon enough everyone began carefully finding their way down the mountain. Rick and Devlin stood on either side of Edna as she limped along between them, while Bora scouted with her flashlight just a few feet ahead, pointing out any obstacles in their way. Once in a while, they would all stop and wait for Edna to take a look around, gather her bearings, and bark directions on how to adjust course.

Before long, they passed directly by the laurel thicket and the campsite. "Sorry, Edna," apologized Rick. "I don't think I can carry you *and* the chairs."

"No nevermind," she wheezed. "They're cheap. Got 'em at a yardsale." She glanced at Devlin. "Where's y'all's bags?"

Devlin looked far to the left, in the direction of the gully, where he knew his bag, Rick's backpack, and their chairs lay strewn across the ridge. "Nothing I can't replace," he decided. "Might look for it tomorrow. You okay leaving your stuff, Ricky?"

The only thing Rick wanted was his vodka. "Yeah," he said. "I've got my flask, and another bottle at home. Rest of it can wait, far as I'm concerned."

They all continued down the mountain. Twenty minutes later, the incline was barely noticeable, allowing their pace to quicken. A few times, someone other than Edna would recognize a landmark from earlier in the afternoon and shout a grateful affirmation.

"Look, guys," Bora said eventually, pointing up towards the canopy. "You can see the moon a little better. Bet the field is just up ahead." She stopped and turned towards the group. "Hell, even *I* could get us home from…"

She trailed off, looking past them, a confused expression clouding her face. Suddenly, her entire body flashed red, as if she were standing behind a car pumping its brakes. Her mouth hung open. One word followed: "*Run.*"

Devlin and Rick shared the same idea. Acting as one, they summoned every last bit of strength to lift Edna off the ground. For her part, she tried to make her rescuers' job easier by lifting her feet so they would not catch on any passing debris. The three of them rushed headlong downhill, determined to let no obstacle stand in their way. There was no time to pick through vines, no time to brush spiderwebs from faces, no time to do anything but *run* as Bora instructed, to escape whatever she had glimpsed creeping up behind them.

As they tumbled over the final yards, everyone's shadows reached ahead, carving long, dark holes from the red light flooding the forest behind them. Bora was nearly at the tree line. Trunks whizzed past. Branches reached out to retard their progress, but were ignored. They were almost there… just a little further….

For reasons known only to her, Edna craned her neck to look over her shoulder. The movement instantly solicited a warning from Devlin. With everyone careening out of control, Rick had no idea what he said. The only thing he knew was that the next instant, the light behind them exploded in a white flash accompanied by a loud snapping sound, as if an electrical transformer had just discharged. Something resembling a miniature, concussive wave erupted behind them, just forceful enough to knock everyone off balance and send them flying into the field.

Bora dropped to her stomach, the wind knocked out of her. Rick's knee took the brunt of his landing. Devlin managed to keep himself from falling fully, one hand on the ground underneath him, the other holding Edna upright. While she never hit the ground, she still staggered and collapsed against Devlin as he rose up.

"Everyone okay?" asked Rick, receiving muttered reassurances in response. When no one disclosed any serious injuries, he turned his attention to the field. It was dark—but better to wander in darkness out in the open than to endure any more of that hideous light in the forest.

For the first time all night, they saw the full moon shining down in all its glory, unabated, outlining the small oasis that Rick called home. Amidst the dim lighting stood his house, tiny yet welcoming in the distance, its windows shining with the same promise of warmth and security once held by the campfire. Never before had Rick been so happy to see it. Within moments, they would all be sharing a drink, warming themselves. Rick might even grab some firewood from the front yard on his way in to make everything a bit cozier.

"If that ain't a sight for sore eyes," Rick said in satisfaction.

"Ain't what?" asked Edna. Everyone turned to look at her. To their shock, the light of the moon revealed that her eyes, once clear and lucid, now looked cloudy, as if a milky veil had been draped over each. She blinked.

"Rick? Devlin? Bora?" Edna searched, panic rising in her voice. "We almost to the field?"

36

Sunday, November 1, 2020

PLAYBACK

No matter where Rick looked, the house was a mess. A broad trail of leaves, twigs, and mud, remnants of their arrival, stretched from the front door. At the edge of the foyer, the path splintered into three separate directions, a visual embodiment of the chaos that unfolded the moment they opened the door.

In an admirable attempt to clean up and patch up his friends, Rick had run to the linen closet, bathroom, and kitchen, returning with towels, the first aid kit, and soap. Devlin cut a direct path across the living room into the addition, where he still remained, doing God knows what. Bora left a trail of footprints behind when she tromped to the coffee table to get the keys to her car. Only poor Edna, plunged into perpetual darkness, remained in the foyer, listening helplessly to the havoc around her.

After Rick attended to everyone's cuts and scrapes, Bora grabbed the spare key to the house, dragged Edna out to her Nissan, and headed straight to the emergency room. At the time, it felt like the proper course of action given Edna's condition. Now, sitting in his recliner, alone with a fresh drink, Rick wasn't as certain.

As far as medical achievements go, I doubt we have a cure for sudden onset elf blindness, he thought, taking a long drink. The past three hours had pulled him to the edge of sobriety, from which he was just now managing to claw away. *Devlin should draft up some fine print on the limitations of his horseshoe charms. "Offer not valid for ranged attacks."*

Besides his rapid descent into inebriation—*Re-nebriation*, he quipped—Rick found himself searching for other ways to calm his nerves. He should have thought to ask Bora for a few hits of her vape, but she left long ago, so he tried seeking solace in his rituals. It struck him as a good idea at first. After all, they now seemed like the only thing within his control. But after emptying the dishwasher and—for the first time—emptying the entire silverware drawer, the ceremony of *knife, spoon, fork* failed to help. It brought no sense of calm or control. Instead, it left him empty and, halfway through filing the flatware a second time, feeling like a complete madman. Only out of a sense of obligation did he finish his task before settling in with another drink.

There Rick sat in the living room, staring at the couch along the freestanding wall, waiting for... something. *Answers?* he wondered. *Solace? A chance to process the abject disaster we just went through?*

At that moment, Devlin popped out of the addition behind Rick, as if summoned by his thoughts like some eldritch horror. At this point, he wouldn't be surprised if that turned out to be the case. The man now appeared completely nonplussed by the evening's trials. He wore a pair of camouflage pants and a white undershirt, and was casually stuffing a bag of Swedish Fish into his mouth.

"Heya, slugger," he greeted, chewing away. "Got somethin' you ought to hear."

Rick nodded, a pained expression on his face. On top of everything else, the extreme exertion of tonight was finally beginning to catch up with his muscles. Everything ached. "Lay it on me," he mumbled distantly. He tried to clear his head with a good shake and mustered his remaining energy to pay attention.

"Alright," Devlin acknowledged. He traipsed to the dining room, pulled a chair into the living room, and straddled it backwards like a cowboy mounting a horse. Finishing the last piece of candy, he crumpled the bag and shoved it into one pocket of his pants. With his other hand, he reached into the opposite pocket to produce the small handheld Dictaphone that Rick noticed just before the Estes session.

"Been reviewing this since we got back," he explained, holding up the recorder. "You were only privy to one side of our conversation. This captured what I heard. I'm gonna play it back. I'll try to let it run uninterrupted, but I might have to explain things from time to time." Without further ado, he depressed the play button and sat the tape recorder on the coffee table to his left. The quiet, warbly sound of their own voices, recorded three hours prior, began issuing from the tiny speaker.

"*Estes session ten-thirty-one-twenty-twenty,*" came Devlin's voice. "*Red Ear Mountain, Georgia. Time is 11:08 p.m. My name is Devlin Fox, this is Richard Coulter... Hoping to make contact with the presence that has attached itself to my client... Is there anyone else here with us?*"

In the pause that followed, crickets came to the forefront of the recording, then cordially receded for Rick's response. "'... Mount. If it...'" his voice repeated.

"*What do you call yourselves?*" Devlin asked on the tape. There was no response until the following question. "*What do* we *call you?* '... Numerous. She...' *The sidhe?* '... You. Foe...' *I ain't your enem—oh, wait. You mean UFOs?* '... Could...' *Do you remember when the people here called you Yunwi Tsunsdi? Are you Nûññë'hï?* '... Sometimes. Also. You...'"

At this point, Devlin paused the tape to offer commentary. "Seems like they're at least *partially* human," he explained. He restarted the recording.

"*We need clarification on something you indicated last night. Are you willing to help?* '... Person who?...' *Our friend Richard, here. Last night, you told us you want something from him. Can you tell us what that is?* '... Outstanding...' *Outstanding what?* '... A... Count...'"

Devlin paused the tape once more. "I heard 'account.' You?" Rick nodded, and playback resumed.

"*I don't understand.* '... Debt...' *Debt—wait a minute. Is that what you've been telling him all along? Not 'life' and 'death,' but 'life' and 'debt'?* '... Uh, I just heard a bell chime, dunno if I need to say that...'"

"Winner, winner, chicken dinner!" interjected Devlin as the tape rolled on.

"*Okay, okay... gotcha. So... this debt is related to Richard's life?*" No response. "*What was the nature of this agreement?* '... Bart... her...'"

It was Rick's turn to comment. "I hear 'barter,'" he suggested. Devlin agreed.

"*Did Richard incur this debt?* '... Counsel. Bold...' *I'm afraid I don't follow. How can this debt be paid?* '... Attempt...' *How can he attempt payment?*" On the tape, Rick said nothing. "*Has payment been attempted already?"* continued Devlin's voice. *"'... Red. Wall...'"* Another long silence took hold, followed by a string of nonsense. *"'... Spaghetti. Very. Falcons. Self. Ending...'"*

Devlin rewound the tape, saying, "Okay, clearly some noise amidst the signal, but pay attention to those last two words." He hit play.

"'... Self. Ending...' What service was offered in exchange for this debt?" The question was met with silence. Then, Devlin asked the final question before all hell broke loose: *"What issue was resolved? '... Dress... Appear... Ants...' A disappearance?"*

Devlin pressed the stop button for the final time. The living room seemed quiet as a tomb. "There you have it," said Devlin, resting his forearms across the back of the chair. "Any insights?"

Rick folded his arms and began gently rocking in the recliner. He found it uncanny how these random words took on new meaning in this context. While he had some ideas, he wasn't eager to share them just yet. It might prove more elucidating to get Devlin's impression. "Maybe," he offered at last. "Still pretty confused by some of it."

"I told you," Devlin reminded him, "the Spaghetti-Falcons word salad is likely just interference."

"No, not that. The thing about—what did I say?—'counsel brave'?"

"'Counsel bold.' Gotta admit, that had me plum stumped for a while, too. Been racking my brain ever since I heard you say that. Still not a hunnerd percent sure what to make of it. Are *we* this 'bold counsel'? Asking too many questions? But then I got to thinking... if this was indeed an answer to my question, maybe it indicated an event. Still got nothin'. But what if... what if it's a *person*? Tell me, Ricky, you ever looked into the meanings of names?"

"Can't say I have," he replied, staring at the silent tape recorder. "Or if I ever did, it was a long time ago."

"Well, take us, for example. *Richard* means 'mighty' or 'brave ruler,' depending on who you ask. As for me, my name means 'unlucky.' Go fig. But if you look up the words 'counsel' and 'bold,' you get the name *Conrad*. That mean anything to you?"

Rick's face turned white as a sheet. The room began spinning around him like a thousand gears had just slipped into place and been set in motion. In his mind's eye, he watched their teeth push and pull against each other, the cogs driving some vast machine toward an unfathomable goal. He had no idea what the machine was or its purpose for existing, but he at least glimpsed a fraction of its inner workings. Grasping the armrests of the recliner, knuckles white, Rick tried to find the words.

"My father," he summoned at last, "was named Conrad."

Devlin rubbed a hand over his mouth, leaving it agape as he tugged at his bottom lip. "Ho-lee shee-it," he whispered. "And he died last year, you said?"

Rick's head slowly bobbed up and down. "What did he die from?" asked Devlin.

"Complications from an event seven years before."

"And this 'event' was…?"

"He tried to kill himself. September 5, 2012. Put a sixteen gauge shotgun under his chin and pulled the trigger with his toe. His skin and bones were so brittle, the recoil ripped it right off his foot. Took off a good portion of his face, too. Left a mess all over his bedroom."

"'Red wall,'" marveled Devlin with a look of realization. "'Self ending.'"

Rick continued. "The housekeeper found him just a couple minutes later. She had come back because she had forgotten her purse. I got a call from her and headed straight up to Blue Ridge Regional. My relationship with my father was… difficult. To say the least. Not even sure why I came to see him, to tell you the truth. I guess I wanted to see if I was finally rid of him. I stayed until he was out of surgery, all through the first bit of his recovery… The minute he regained consciousness and recognized me, I left."

Rick involuntarily let out a dry chuckle. "It's funny, you know?" he mused. "Everyone thought he'd work himself to death. Except me. I knew he was too mean to die. They say that hope can keep you alive… seems like bitterness can, too. Hospital staff kept using the word 'miracle.' Not me." Rick wiped a tear from his eye. "All the children who die from cancer, all the college kids in traffic accidents… and this fucker, of all people, got to survive. It wasn't a miracle. It was a… testimony to the persistence of hate. You know that surviving a self-inflicted gunshot wound only represents one percent of failed suicide attempts? And here this spiteful old man pulls through. He was seventy-two, Devlin. *Seventy-two!* His surgeon said the odds of him making it out alive were one-in-a-million."

"Flipped to a million-in-one," observed Devlin with a sigh. "Musta been caught up in The Wake."

"He stayed bedridden until about a year ago," Rick added. "A vegetable, more or less, until the day he died. I hope it was torture. I've got him out in the shed. His ashes."

Devlin looked at the coffee table, tracing his fingers along the grain of the faux wood before speaking again. "Any idea why he did it?" he asked at last.

"If I were him, I'd have a thousand reasons," Rick said with a shrug. "His finances were always fine, but he didn't have any family anymore. Mom died when I was young. Last time I spoke to him was the night I left at eighteen." He took a deep breath. "Which brings me to something else that might have some bearing on our session. I had a sister. She disappeared when I was six."

Devlin rested his elbows on the back of the chair to bury his face in his hands. "What was her name?" he inquired from behind his fingers.

"Mary," replied Rick.

"How old was Mary?"

"Eight."

"Did they find her body?"

"They found her *alive*."

"Lost or kidnapped?"

"Still don't know. Mary went into the woods near my father's mining operation on the first of May, 1986, and simply vanished. The whole community came out to help. They must've walked that property a thousand times. Never found a thing. No clothes, no hair, nothing. We all gave up hope. Then, about three weeks later, Conrad came home with her. The thing I remember most is her hair. It was always so red, Devlin. Like a cardinal. But when she came back, it was filthy. Black. I hardly recognized her." Rick steepled his fingers, letting his forehead rest on the tips. "My father said he went up to the quarry to look one last time, and there she was, naked in the mud of the creek she always played around. I still find that hard to believe. That was the *first* place everyone looked, the one place they kept coming back to, and Mary was *never* there. Where she was between when she disappeared and when she was found was a mystery."

"You mention she was nude. Signs of sexual abuse?"

"Not that anyone could tell, thank God. Clothes were folded neatly alongside her shoes on the bank of the creek."

"And this was in Spruce Pine?"

Rick started to answer but hesitated. He never remembered telling Devlin where he grew up. It never seemed important until now. "How did you know?"

Devlin took a breath and held it for a moment before answering. "I did a little research between the time we met and when you called me over to Bora's apartment," he explained. "Standard operating procedure for all new clients: make sure they're on the up-and-up." He looked like he was in a hurry to move on. "This about your sister is all new to me. So what about Mary? What did she remember?"

"Not a goddamn thing."

"Where is she now?"

Rick refused to answer or even make eye contact for the better part of half a minute. His eyes wandered to everything in the room besides the man with whom he was conversing: the light fixtures, the patio door, the tape recorder, the coffee table, the kitchen. When he was ready, he looked into Devlin's mismatched eyes and declared, "She's dead."

Devlin's eyebrows raised. "Jesus, I'm sorry," he said. "How long?"

"Years. Decades, actually. Mary was so weak when she got home… I still remember how pale she looked. I was just a little kid, but I remember thinking how I could've looked right through her. Like a ghost. We were all so happy to have her back that we didn't realize how sick she was until a few weeks later. We just thought she needed to recover. But the days dragged on, and she only got worse. She just laid in bed, sweating, shivering, barely eating. Then the coughing started. Mary died within a month of coming back to us."

"How was the cause of death listed?"

"Tuberculosis, of all things," Rick grimaced. It was as if the very word left a revolting taste in his mouth, salty and copperish. "I didn't even know we still *had* tuberculosis in this country. By the time we realized what was wrong… it was too late."

Devlin looked pensive, then rose and headed towards the patio door. After opening the curtains, he began to speak, more to himself than to Rick. "So haunt thy days and chill thy dreaming nights, that thou would wish thine own heart dry of blood, so in my veins red life might stream again, and thou be conscience-calmed—see here it is—I hold it towards you..." When his recitation was finished, he spoke a little louder.

"We're no longer in The Wake, Ricky. We're in the goddamn *path* of this thing, and it's headed straight for you. We're closer to figuring this out, but some pieces are still missing. Seems to me all this is related—your father's attempted suicide, your sister's disappearance, what you've been going through this year—though the particulars escape me. Still not sure what all this has to do with *you*, specifically, or what they want. Maybe you got a bloodline they're interested in, or something to that effect?" Devlin paused, looking as though he stood on the cusp of answering the entire riddle, but for some reason, he restrained himself.

"I'm headin' outta town tonight," he proclaimed after clearing his throat. "Something about all this rings a bell. Like I heard it or read it somewhere before. I got a colleague up in Asheville, a real Renaissance man, who might be able to shed some light on this. I'll be back tomorrow afternoon."

Apprehension slammed into Rick like a wave crashing against the shore. "You're leaving me alone?" he asked, his voice cracking.

"To be honest, bud, me being here probably wouldn't make you any safer. I ain't sure what you've got circling you, Ricky, but it seems hell-bent for leather. We gotta go old school with this. Still got your pendant?" Rick nodded. "Good. Didya grow up religious? 'Cause that sure as shit would help right about now."

"No," Rick admitted sheepishly.

"You never need it 'til you *need* it, do you?" griped Devlin, running his fingers through his hair. "Alright. Next best thing is protecting the property. I don't think they'll be back again tonight, they really seem to dig this 11:08 thing, plus it probably took a lot of energy to put on tonight's little performance. In the morning, I want you to go to the local tack store and get your hands on as many horseshoes as you can. Nail 'em over every entrance—the doors, the windows, everything. Next you're gonna wanna pick up a bag of salt. Don't matter if it's table salt or road salt. Just get enough to encircle the entire outside of the house, 'bout six inches wide. Can you do that for me?"

"Um, of course," Rick agreed. "Whatever you think will help. But... they tunneled in the first time. Can't I just make sure that's fixed and, I dunno, batten the hatches?"

Devlin shook his head. "You know that person at the party who has to make sure everyone knows they've arrived?" he asked. "That's them. That stuff with the tunnel was all just theater, to ramp up your anxiety. Hate to break it to you, but they go wherever they damn well please, walls and doors be damned. You see them open any doors during the séance?"

"Okay, if you say so," conceded Rick. "What if I went somewhere else? Like a hotel? Think it would be any safer away from the mountain?"

"You want to *leave*?" scoffed Devlin. "Won't do shit." He then spoke slowly and carefully. "Remember, Richard, they're attached to *you*. And to keep them out, I am telling you: we *need* horseshoes and salt. Understand?"

Knowing that there was no sense in pressing the matter, Rick yielded. He simply muttered an agreement as Devlin headed to the door, taking comfort in the fact that no effort was made to retrieve his belongings from the addition. It seemed like, true to his word, Devlin had every intention of returning from his research trip as soon as he was able.

Locking the door behind his last guest, Rick found himself alone for the first time all month. The realization left him uneasy, harkening back to the earliest days of the pandemic, when it felt as though the isolation would stretch on into eternity. To quell the growing anxiety, he returned to the recliner and swallowed the final half of his drink, welcoming the burning liquor down his throat.

Hopefully, it would help dampen the emotions conjured over the last hour. He hadn't directly spoken about Mary in a decade. In fact, prior to her recent intrusions into his dreams, he barely tried to think of her. Conrad's suicide attempt was treated with the same detachment over the years, perhaps because he nursed lingering doubts that he somehow should have shown more compassion afterward.

Approaching the bottle for a refill, he disabused himself of that notion. So long as he lived, his father's last words to him would never go away fully: *You are nothing.*

Rick had already started to squeeze the plastic when he remembered the commitment he had made to Jack. *Fuck,* he thought, looking at the clock on the microwave. *It's already three. I have to pick him up in eight hours.* He looked at the bottle in his hands, weighing the temptation of oblivion against his responsibility as a father.

Maybe just a little more, he rationalized. But the bottle didn't move. Something else inside him, long dormant, stayed his hand. *No,* a voice inside of him objected. *Remember the track meet, how you overslept? Do you want that to happen again? That was a choice. This is another. In this moment, make it the right one. Take the chance to change.*

Rick knew what he was signing up for. A night of sweating, of a racing heart, of tossing and turning. Hours of sobriety stretching into the following day, his entire nervous system no longer numbed, bucking at a deluge of amplified stimuli.

Part of him hoped it would be worth it. The other knew that it would.

37

Sunday, November 1, 2020

EVERY WALL HAS TWO SIDES

AS SCHEDULED, RICK MET JACK AT THEIR OLD HOUSE at eleven o'clock. The exuberance with which his son greeted him after jumping in the Corolla alleviated some of the misery Rick had fought all morning. He caught a little shuteye between three and six, which, thanks to the switch over to daylight savings, meant he managed to sleep for four hours. The next three, however, became an absolute nightmare, a half-awake battle against wave after wave of anxiety attacks and relentless hypnic jerks that batted him fully alert whenever he began drifting off.

However, not only did he make it away from the house right on time, but traffic cooperated. By noon, Rick and Jack were filing into the aquarium along with hundreds of other patrons, fully masked and pressed shoulder-to-shoulder. For Rick, it was a trying experience. Even if he hadn't been hungover, exhausted, and trembling, he now hated crowds… and the throngs inside the aquarium were by far the largest gathering he had participated in since the start of the pandemic. The shock of such close proximity, after avoiding unnecessary contact for the better part of a year, left him a jangled bundle of nerves.

Luckily, the crowd dispersed significantly once inside, with each group choosing different exhibits to head towards first. Jack tugged his father into the Ocean Voyager section. Soon they were bathed in the dim blue twilight of an underwater tunnel that stretched over a hundred feet through a massive tank filled with the largest specimens, including a few whale sharks. They glided by lazily like submerged semi-trailers, completely unperturbed by the smaller fish, sharks, and rays.

Rick stared in wonder as one of the massive animals coasted by, momentarily forgetting his troubles. He leaned down behind Jack and whispered in his ear, "Do you ever wonder if they think *we're* the ones held captive?"

"Eh," Jack shrugged, peering through the thick acrylic. "Every wall has two sides, right? And after this year, who's to say they're wrong?"

Shortly thereafter, they wound up in the River Scout exhibit ("presented by Southern Company," the signage incessantly reminded them). The cobalt maritime mood was replaced by the deep ambers and lush greens of freshwater habitats. It was a refreshing change that brought with it a variety of life besides fish, including otters, alligators, and turtles basking lazily in displays filled with artfully constructed waterfalls and logjams.

Rounding a corner, Rick found himself confronted by a large group clotting the walkway. Up ahead, an aquarium employee droned on with a prepared spiel that, bless her heart, she must have delivered a dozen times each day.

"... we have our temporary salmon exhibit, thanks to a generous grant from Southern Company," the young lady explained into her microphone. Rick followed her hand as it indicated a tank to her right, brimming with large fish. Collectively, they fought against an artificial current coursing through the tank, each member jockeying for position toward a goal they would never reach.

"These are actually coho salmon," she carried on, her sentences running together in a slurry of boredom. "Like all six species of Pacific salmon, they spend years in the ocean before returning to the streams where they were born. Once they arrive at their destination, they spawn and die, sacrificing their own lives for the sake of their offspring, ensuring that the next generation of salmon has a chance to thrive...."

Rick stared into the tank with such focus that he didn't notice Jack until he tugged on his sleeve the third or fourth time. "Dad?" he repeated emphatically. Rick finally acknowledged his son.

"Uh, sorry, Jack Attack," he apologized. "My mind was wandering. You okay?"

"Yeah," he replied. "Just wanted to see if we could grab a bite to eat."

After paying far too much for a pair of underwhelming sandwiches, Rick and Jack finished touring the other exhibits. To cap it all off, they took in a dolphin show, though Rick hardly enjoyed it. He was still thinking about salmon, his mind repeating both the tour guide's speech and Devlin's soliloquy from the night before. At a quarter until three, they were back in the car.

When they arrived at Cassie's place—Rick didn't think of it as his, anymore—they sat in the driveway for a moment, making small talk and catching up on life. For the first time, Rick noticed that the "pandemic thumb" Jack had been gnawing at had started to heal.

"Really enjoyed today, Dad," the boy smiled. "Almost felt like old times." He didn't elaborate on whether or not "old times" meant pre-pandemic or pre-separation.

"I know, right?" said Rick, turning in his seat to face his son. "What was your favorite part?"

"You know—" Together they answered, "The penguins!" before falling apart into light laughter.

"Every single time," Rick chuckled. "I take you there, and I keep expecting you to change, but you never do. Ever since you were a little kid, it's always the penguins."

Jack managed a lopsided grin. "Well, I'm not a little kid anymore," he countered. "But I guess some things never change." He suddenly looked somber. "That's what mom says. 'People don't change.'"

Rick cast his eyes to his legs to prevent Jack from seeing his pained expression. "That's… often the case," he confessed. "But not always. Sometimes people surprise you. I've been trying myself, but it isn't easy. I'm not sure if Mom has noticed."

"When you showed up on time, she said she was happy," managed Jack with a slight smile.

"Really? 'Happy'?"

"Well… surprised," Jack corrected. "That's something, though, right?"

Rick nodded. "Not much," he agreed, "but something." With that, he reached out, embraced his son, and bid him goodbye. "Love you, kid," he said out the open car window as he turned around in the driveway. "Taking care of some things up at the house this week. After they're done, we'll get together again, okay?"

"Sounds good," Jack replied with a smile and a wave. "Love you too, Dad!"

Rick pulled out onto the road. After a few miles, he was on 572 heading toward 515. All things considered, his time at the aquarium with Jack was a great visit, the kind Rick would have killed for earlier in the year.

I just wish I wasn't so distracted, he thought. *Goddamn salmon.* He began wondering what other seeds Devlin had planted in his head to germinate in the future.

"Devlin!" he exclaimed to the empty car. "Dammit!" Rick was halfway home and had completely forgotten to pick up horseshoes and salt.

Probably doesn't matter, he thought, turning down the radio and pulling onto the shoulder of the road. *There's got to be a tack store open closer to home.* The only reason he planned on looking for supplies in Atlanta was that the city afforded more options. Grabbing his phone by its car charging cord, he opened the web browser and started studying his options.

Other cars continued onward to their destinations, rocking the Corolla back and forth on the shoulder as they whizzed past. Rick sat inside, becoming increasingly frustrated. All of the nearby tack stores were closed today. He briefly considered turning around and heading back to the city, but by the time he arrived, he doubted that anywhere would be open so late on a Sunday afternoon.

There's always the chance that their websites aren't up-to-date, Rick thought as he pulled back onto the road. He charted a course for the tack store nearest his house, closer to downtown Ellijay. About half an hour later, he spotted the sign, complete with model horse, towering above the road. He pulled into the gravel parking lot with high hopes, only to have them dashed once he saw the darkened interior through the glass door. Closed.

Rick sat in the car, massaging his temples and trying to figure out where in the hell he might find horseshoes on a Sunday afternoon in north Georgia. His eyes drifted to a sign on the store's red, wooden exterior: "HATE THE LINE? ORDER ONLINE!"

Picking up his phone once more, Rick began scouring the Internet. He easily found a box of twenty horseshoes for sale on Amazon. He wasn't sure if they were steed-worthy, but he didn't think they had to be. They were cast iron, which Rick remembered Devlin mentioning as protective in its own right. After selecting the fastest delivery option, Rick received an email notifying him that his order should arrive by midday tomorrow.

Better late than never, Rick rationalized as he put the car in drive. *Now for salt.* He pulled back onto the road, letting his intuition guide him.

"And where do we go when we need lots of generic shit for cheap, kids?" he asked no one as he exited the highway and wheeled over a gigantic expanse of asphalt. "That's right! Walmart!" He parked the car as close as he could and blew a raspberry, disappointed that he was forced to support two corporate empires in one day.

Show yourself some grace, he thought as he stepped inside. *You've kinda got a lot on your plate.*

After a few minutes of searching, he had to admit that he couldn't have made a better choice. To his delight, a plethora of options awaited him, spread across the entire store. There was plenty of salt in the grocery section, of course, but none of the containers were large enough. More could be found in the automotive and outdoor sections, but Rick held off on committing just a little longer.

He eventually steered his shopping cart into a section crammed full of pool supplies, where massive, forty-pound bags of dirt-cheap salt waited on the shelves. He emptied them, taking every bag he could find, and wound up with nearly a dozen sacks of the stuff.

Finally, around five o'clock, he pulled up in front of the house in Ellijay. When he spotted Bora's car sitting in the driveway, he was pleasantly surprised. Not only could she help him salt the property, but he was eager to hear about Edna.

When he entered, he found her half asleep on the couch with the curtains drawn and the blinds closed. "Hey," she mumbled feebly.

"Sorry," he said, setting down the first bag of salt and heading towards the partially empty bottle. He had a lot of catching up to do. "Didn't mean to wake you."

"No, it's fine," yawned Bora. "I've been here for a while. I was already up."

Rick took a long swig. His splitting headache and simmering anxiety immediately began evaporating. "How's Edna?" he asked.

Bora stood and shook her head. "Still in the hospital. Doctors couldn't figure out what happened." She began opening the blinds. "I wonder why," she added sarcastically.

"What did you tell them?"

"I didn't say anything. Edna did all the talking. Told them she just woke up in the middle of the night and couldn't see. Said it's how she twisted her ankle. They're putting her through a battery of tests."

"How's she feel about what happened?"

"Honestly? I think she's kind of enjoying all the attention," Bora laughed. "She's handling it like a champ. I asked her how she felt about the possibility of never seeing again. What did she say? 'Shit, Bora, half of what I wanna do is sleep anyway, and I haven't gotten lucky with the lights on since the Bush administration.' She clarified that she meant Bush *One*, not Bush Two."

Rick chuckled as he refilled his drink. "I can't help but imagine she'll miss television."

"I thought the same thing," Bora responded. "She had an answer for that, too. Something about not caring, because she just discovered paranormal podcasts. That, and, 'You'd be surprised how much disability checks are nowadays.' She's a trooper." A serious look fell over Bora. "She's also a good person, Rick. Underneath all the crust, of course. When we were separated last night—I know you said it wasn't that long, but it felt like forever to us—I had no clue where I was once I reached the boulder field. Edna could have easily ... She *should* have headed back here. But she didn't. She kept looking until she found me, twisting her ankle in the process. Now she's blind and I... I can't help but feel partially responsible."

"Don't go down that road, Bora," warned Rick. "I've been traveling ones like it all my life, and it leads nowhere. It's just one big circle back to where you started."

"It's not that," Bora explained. "She... *headed toward trouble,* when she had every reason to run away. Not something I'm used to seeing. Or doing." She sighed. "In other news, where's Devlin? Did y'all learn anything from last night? I told work that I had Covid, so I can stay here as long as you need me."

Over the next half hour, Rick tried his best to fill Bora in on everything she had missed. As he did, they began laying down salt, encircling the entire exterior according to Devlin's directions. What should have been a straightforward task became torturous as now and then the salt would make contact with their cuts and scrapes inflicted the night before, sending both of them dancing around, flailing their hands in an effort to flush the pain.

In a flash of insight, Bora stopped halfway through the process to pour a little extra salt inside, over the threshold of the basement and across the hearth in front of the fireplace, just in case there was some technicality that might grant the intruders entry through those passages.

After rejoining outside, they completed their circuit around the exterior. When their separate lines of salt met at the front door, Bora rekindled their conversation about the disturbing details surrounding Rick's family.

"So what's he think?" asked Bora. She looked tired and sweaty as she pulled her hair out of her face into a ponytail. "That your dad's suicide attempt was a… failed payment of some kind?"

"Why don't you ask him yourself?" suggested Rick. The brown Suburban had just emerged from the woods and was tumbling down the driveway. The moment it parked, Devlin leapt from the driver's seat, a cigarette hanging from his mouth, wearing the same clothes he had left in early that morning. Rick found it baffling that, despite sleeping less—or so he presumed—he looked far more energized than either of them.

Devlin offered nothing in the way of a greeting. He simply stomped to the front door.

"Good," he grunted after surveying the salt. "Horseshoes?"

"Well, 'Hello' to you, too," Rick remarked wryly. "I wasn't able to find any today, but they'll be here tomorrow."

"Guess it'll have to do," Devlin granted, pushing past them into the house. As he did so, Rick noticed he held something in his hand. "Follow me."

"What's that?" asked Bora, pointing to whatever he held. It looked like a small book of some sort, battered with age, the leather cover stained, splitting, and torn.

Devlin reached the dining room, tossed the book on the table, and put his hands on his hips. The stance, combined with his lanky frame, made him look like a living pentagram. He stood there, a peculiar mixture of pride and concern on his face.

"Devlin?" urged Rick. "Did you hear what Bora said? What is it?"

Devlin bit his lower lip and nodded in the direction of the table. "Answers," he offered cryptically. Then, without another word of preamble, he snatched up the notebook, opened it to a yellowed page toward the end, and began reading aloud.

38

Sunday, May 18, 1986

THE DIVIL HISSELF

The day I've had today! Awoke afore the dawn, as is my wont after nearly ninety years. Ever since the foreclosure, I find myself lying abed in the dark, running through a list of duties to which I no longer answer. Old habits and all that.

Fixed a little breakfast—'country ham,' they call it in these parts. Not a proper fry, but it suffices. Kathleen could never abide it. Always found it too salty for her liking, God love her. Her absence only adds to the emptiness of my days. Realised it will be three years next month. Had a good run of it, Kat. Always ~~thought~~ hoped I'd go first.

Settled in with a bit of coffee on the front porch. This part of my day is the only that doesn't outstay its welcome. Everything seems fresh and new. Like something interesting might happen. By nightfall, there is no potential left. Only thing to do is get some kip and hope that tomorrow lives up to the promise.

I must say I despise this arrangement. God be with the days when folks realised you ~~couldn't~~ shouldn't spread out a family. Three generations under one roof, helping one another. Now everyone is spread out. Someday we'll understand our error. Generations are like rows of crops. Sew them too far apart, and they're left vulnerable to the harsh winds of life. Unless you have a windbreak, of course. My family was not blessed with any such fortune. The farm was our windbreak. Now it is gone, and we are scattered.

I should count my blessings, however. Today was full of import. Siobhán came by with her boys again. Good to see them as always. Her youngest has taken to calling me "Cillian" in my advanced age. Seems he thinks me a peer. Boy, if you only knew...

I worry about them. Think they get by on the clippings of tin, which is something you can't have this day and age. Everything is awful complicated. In my day, you had to pay only a handful of folk to exist. Now, everyone comes to you with an open palm.

Can you believe she had the ~~timer~~ *temerity to ask again about moving me into one of those homes with the other auldfellas? Told her she knew damn well none of us could afford it, and I was happy with my bockety rocking chair out the country. Better than wasting away in front of the teevee, anyhow.*

I try to go easy on her. Sometimes my aches and pains get the best of me. But she always sends me money, sees my needs met. She's so like her mother. Like mine own. At least she had enough kindness to stay close by down in Marion. Haven't seen Liam and John since they moved up north. They phone and write often enough, but haven't visited since Kat. I suspect her passing, coupled with the way they handled the farm, left them embarrassed. Hope they'll come round soon enough.

Siobhán and the boys left early afternoon. Tended to a few chores. Mostly alone with my thoughts. Times were, I was out the door with people seeking my aid. Remained that way the first few years I moved. I healed wounds. Broke fevers. Mended hearts. Turned bad luck to good. But now... I have trouble finding ways of putting in the day. Thought for a time maybe folks found Little Switzerland too isolated. But everyone has a car these days, so that can't be it. In my darkest hours, I wonder if the old ways are dying. There's no room for them *in the age of* ~~compyu~~ *computers and fax machines.*

But tonight! Tonight made a fool of me in this regard. They *seem alive enough.*

Just finished supper and was packing my pipe when, to my surprise, a knock came at the cabin door. Thought maybe one of Siobhán's boys forgot something.

When I opened the door... I would have thought it the divil hisself, had I not already made that acquaintance long ago. Here is a man I never met but knew much from the moment I laid eyes. Looks like a boiled shite, but beneath his weariness a fiery rage holds fast. Seems in bits about something.

The big man clasps his flask shut and asks if I am Cillian. Years amongst the Bible thumpers hereabouts have left me circumspect. 'Who wants to know?' says I.

The man introduces hisself as Conrad Colder, or something to that effect. Says he is in a bad way. Searched far and wide for me. Needs my help. When I finally admit I am who he thinks I am, he asks to come inside.

Don't know what made me consent. ~~Loneliness, I s'pose. The promise of a little jingle in my pocket might offset some of the burden on Siobhán.~~ *Maybe it was just that him asking for my assistance reminded me of the old days. When I was needed.*

Me and him sit by the fireplace. I light my pipe while he launches into his story. Seems as though his daughter, Mary, disappeared some weeks back at a quarry where she used to play. Just vanished into the woods. It's only at this point that I realise who he is. This Conrad character runs the fellsbar mines down around Spruce Pine.

He seems utterly wrecked. Despondent. Hopeless. Despite my unease in his presence, my heart goes out to him. I cannot conceive of my reaction if I had lost one of my own. But I know my limitations. I also know that life has gotten more complicated. Last thing I want is to run ~~afow~~ *afoul of the law. Best I can reckon is that, somewhere within me, fears still linger from when me and Kat were on the lam.*

I ask him, 'Why seek my council? Certainly this is a matter for policemen.'

'I doubt that,' he says. Seems as though their investigation has dragged on for weeks. Everyone is exhausted. Can't find hide nor hair of Mary. I suppose if I had a teevee or cared a whit for this world, I might have gleaned these details myself.

At any rate, he tells me he long ago lost faith in the police. Started looking around for other ways to find the girl. He tried some psychics—those phony ones you ring on the telephone—but they told him nothing, of course.

'How did you come across me?' I wondered. He says his miners heard tell from another man who heard tell from his nan... you know how it goes. Flattered, of course. But I still fail to see why I am the man he seeks.

Conrad then shares something he never told anyone else. Says he has seen some things he can't quite explain. His workers got spooked a month or two ago. Knocks and voices in the mines, lights and ~~them~~ *strange people hanging about. Suffice to say, I'm interested. Can count on one hand the number of times I've dealt with the Other Crowd since Kat passed.*

At first, Conrad believed not a word of it. They never do. But he started seeing the lights hisself. Called out some group I've never heard tell of, the USGS or something to that effect, to investigate. Said they thought it was gas—ha!—can you believe that? When there's gas, there's shite, and these folk seem full of it. Plain as the nose on my face, what's going on.

Ill news for his fellsbar operation, though. Seems like the government might shut it down. Safety concerns. Back at the end of April, Conrad says he flew up to New York City—bless him, I can't abide the place—to do what he called 'diversifying.' Take it this means investing. Never had a head for that malarkey myself.

Once he got back, he forbade Mary from playing at the mines. Being a father, he consented to one final visit. That was when she disappeared. Says he can't help but wonder if it's connected to everything his employees spoke of.

'Ah, here, of course it is! What a fool for thinking otherwise!' Conrad seems confused. Tell him all I know—at least, all I have permission to share. He doesn't believe it. Says even if they did exist, it would be unnatural.

'Unnatural!' Can you fathom the arrogance? 'Sure,' I tell him, 'they're unnatural if you consider the wind unnatural, the sun, the tides. They are but one of a thousand thousand invisible forces dictating our existence.'

Didn't seem to convince him, but desperation makes for strange bedfellows. Says he'll do anything. 'Anything?' asks I. 'Anything,' he confirms. Then he says it directly: 'Can you get me back my Mary?'

At first, I didn't want a bar of this business. Missing girl or no, this world has forgotten me. Why should I help anyone it favors? We used to revile people like him in their big houses. Still do. Little did I know that this same resentment would lead to me helping him... in a fashion.

We sit in silence. I give him enough rope to hang hisself. Soon enough, he's awful worked up. Starts trying every angle to convince me. ~~I think~~ *Never did I doubt that he genuinely loves his daughter, in whatever form or fashion that takes. But this is one of many* motivations for him to resolve the issue. And didn't he just let his true colors shine through?

'I'm a suspect!' he cries. 'The police are starting to think I was involved somehow!' Poor little man. Think of his standing in the community, he begs. Worst of all, his friends up north are starting to get cold feet. Can't ~~be~~ do business with a murderer, can they?

I never met Conrad Colder before today. But I know him, yes, I do. Dealt with his equals a hundred times. Men who put their own well being, their own reputations, their own standing in the community over those of young people—young women—in true danger. They want to put their mistakes behind them at any cost. Make it just another day. Only the lives of their victims change. Their own lives don't change.

But this Conrad Colder... his *life will change*. I'll see to that. I watch him fall into silence, drain his flask.

He looks like a frightened hare. He is.

'Anything?' I ask one final time. He nods.

'Very well then,' I tell him. 'Full well you can have your daughter back. I enjoy what you might call a working relationship with these people. Allow me to consult their *leader.*'

Conrad looks shocked. Perhaps he knows what he is asking of me.

~~I've made this mistake in the pa~~ These matters rely on clarity. I ask, 'Are you prepared to accept whatever terms I broker?' He starts to nod. Hesitates. Asks if I have any idea what these might entail.

'You get what you want,' I explain. 'They get something they want in return.' He nods fully this time.

'Very well,' says I. 'Give me several days to make contact. Soon, you'll meet with them. After that, the agreement will be binding. For now, I'll leave you to the door.'

He is about to step outside when he asks one final question. How, he wonders, will he know the appointed time and place?

I slap an arm on his shoulder. Look him square in the eyes. Tell him what I have come to learn over a lifetime: 'They'll *find* you.

39

Sunday, November 1, 2020

THREE HUNNERD SIXTY-SIX

DEVLIN ALLOWED A MOMENT OF SILENCE after reading the passage. Rick was grateful for the opportunity. His head was swimming. The entire thing sounded far too fantastic to believe… but, then again, he had been confronted with equally unbelievable things over the past several months. It made too much sense to disregard.

When Devlin failed to continue reading, Rick demanded, "Where the hell did you *find* that?" It beggared belief that something so specific would have just fallen into his lap.

"Told you this story rang a bell," explained Devlin. It sounded like he anticipated the question. "Turns out I read this diary years ago. It was in the private collection of a colleague in Asheville, just as I remembered. He collects anything like this he can get his mitts on. Just goes from estate sale to estate sale, buying everything in bulk. Most of it he junks, but whenever he comes across something pertaining to the occult, he holds onto it. Me and him worked on a case up in Blowing Rock a while back. Spent about a week in that pigsty he calls a house. This diary had just come into his possession. He was chompin' at the bit to share it with me back then." Devlin's mismatched eyes gazed into the distance. "Had no idea how important it would become. Hardly believe I remembered it."

"Well, don't leave us hanging," Bora said excitedly. A cloud of smoke from her vape hovered over her head. "What does it say next?"

"The author then goes on to enumerate the… conditions… of the agreement," replied Devlin cautiously.

"And those are?"

Devlin disregarded Bora's demands and turned his attention to Rick instead. "Tell me Richard, and be honest. We're all friends here. You been having any… invasive thoughts this past year?"

For a while, Rick didn't answer. He needed to refill his drink. Only after doing so and taking a sip did he acknowledge the question. "A few times, yeah," he admitted.

Bora grasped the back of the nearest chair to steady herself, looking shocked. "Rick—are you saying that you actually thought about...?"

"Who wouldn't, Bora?" he shot back. "Think of everything I've been through. Then you add whatever *this* mess is on top of it?" He walked back to the table and dropped down into his usual chair. As he did, he noticed Bora's eyes filling with water.

"Rick, you *know* you could have reached out to me at any point," she said, sliding into her seat opposite him. She reached out her hand. Rick took it, joining in her tears.

Devlin gave them a moment, but otherwise looked indifferent. "Well, take heart," he reassured them. "I ain't saying these things caused all your problems, but they clearly didn't help. Proud of you for holding out this long. You need to realize somethin', though: as bad as your life has been, it will continue to get worse."

Rick wiped his eyes and cleared his throat as Devlin joined them at the table. "There's a lot to unpack here," Devlin said, picking at a callus on his palm. "Not sure where to begin... Judgin' from that entry and what I read later in the diary, this Cillian feller negotiated some pretty harsh stipulations. A life for a life. Seems like your daddy agreed to Mary's return in exchange for his own death. Well, not exactly. His *suicide*. *Very* different. I imagine Conrad didn't mind too much, just figured he'd do it toward the end of his life. Which he did. Or tried to, at least. But since he survived, his end of the bargain was never fulfilled. I suspect that, upon his death... that obligation passed along to you."

For the second time in twenty-four hours, a gulf opened up beneath Rick's feet, leaving him to reconsider everything he thought he knew. He tried processing what he was hearing. As alarmed as Devlin's story had left him, he was more shocked at his father's actions. The nature of the pact offered a whole new interpretation of his behavior, a seismic shift profoundly reframing their relationship.

All this time, I thought there wasn't a kind bone in that man's body, Rick realized. *I thought his suicide attempt was the most selfish thing that he could have ever done. The capstone on a life in which he thought of no one but himself. Yet... he did it for Mary. Even if he was worried about his reputation, there was something else inside him that found the terms of this agreement acceptable. And he tried to honor it...*

"I'm... cursed?" asked Rick slowly after clearing his head.

"One way to put it," Devlin admitted.

Rick nodded. "So if he had managed to kill himself," he deduced, "then none of this would have ever happened to me?"

"That's my best guess," responded Devlin.

"But he didn't do it just for Mary," Rick thought aloud. "He did it for *me*, too. To keep me from having to go through this. His one act of compassion toward his son."

It seemed to Rick that, although his father had always been a bitter man, carrying this burden must have weighed heavily on his conscience. Conrad Coulter had been a wounded wild animal; yes, it was wise to avoid him under the best of circumstances, but the pain he suffered partially explained his aggression.

Another thought occurred to Rick. "Hang on," he urged. "Back up. Why did these things take Mary in the first place? What did they want from her?"

"Been doing it to people forever. Lotsa reasons. Y'ever hear tell of 'The Scorpion and the Frog'? Sometimes I wonder if it's just that way with them. They take people 'cause it's in their nature to. No greater purpose. If I had to put a reason on it, I think maybe their numbers deplete over time unless they bring in some new blood." He stopped and cobbled together a halfhearted smile. "They didn't keep Mary, though. Your daddy seen to that. She was returned."

"Only to die," Bora scoffed. "You said, 'A life for a life,' right? Well, Mary died. These things swindled Rick's dad."

"Not the way they see it," argued Devlin, shaking his head. "Ain't the way these things work. To them, they kept their end of the bargain. She was returned. That's all they agreed to. Good news is, a contract *honored* on technicalities can be *broken* on technicalities."

"Okay—technicalities," Bora countered forcefully. "Conrad Coulter died last year. Debt settled."

"Nope," disagreed Devlin. "Had to be at his own hand."

"That's absurd. It makes no difference, he's dead."

"Tell me, Bora… is there a difference between something you buy yourself and a *gift*? How about a gift and something you just find lying by the side of the road?" Devlin looked at Rick. "I imagine they got pretty impatient after Conrad died. This is their entire motivation: to drive you to suicide. Not to wait until you die of cirrhosis, or cancer, or old age. They are going to make every day a *living hell* for you until you fulfill your father's debt."

For the first time since their conversation began, Rick realized the irony. All year, he had flirted with killing himself. Now it was presented as the only solution, mere days after he had begun to fully appreciate life once more. Even if Cassie was out of the picture, he still had Jack. He had Bora and Edna, and—*I can't believe I'm thinking this*—Devlin, too.

Rick began proposing scenarios that might offer an escape. "There's got to be some fine print or something in that diary," he demanded. "What if I just hold out?"

"You gonna live in a protected house forever?" retorted Devlin. "Even if you could, it'd pass on down the lineage." His eyebrows raised. "That an option?"

"Fuck no. And make Jack go through all this? And his son, maybe? No way in hell."

"What I thought."

"Then… how about I just off myself when I'm an old man?"

"Like your daddy tried to, and failed? What if you get hit by a bus before then, Ricky? Asides, the way *they're* acting? I doubt you'd make it that long."

"Can we somehow… *substitute* Rick's suicide?" suggested Bora.

Devlin puffed his cheeks in a dramatic exhale. "Y'all really wanna go that route? It'd have to be big. Comparable. Death of another, maybe. Y'all up to that?" His question hovered on a knife's edge between rhetorical and serious.

"Jesus, Dev," objected Bora.

"Didn't think so. Just as good, I ain't too sure how to transfer the obligation." Devlin paused, then looked directly at Rick again. "Maybe you could sacrifice your identity?"

Rick didn't know what to make of the idea. "What the hell does that even look like?" he wondered aloud. "A fake passport? Going off the grid?"

"Naw, those are just constructs. I mean something in the fabric of your soul."

Rick thought for a moment. Only one thing came to mind. "Quit playing music?"

"Might be enough," Devlin considered. "Might not. Not sure how you'd be able to prove your commitment."

Bora started chewing her thumbnail. "You're not giving us a lot of options here, Dev," she groaned. "What can we do about this?"

"Maybe we're gettin' ahead of ourselves," Devlin replied. "First question ain't *what;* it's *when*. A lot of them old stories emphasize how these spells could be broken after a year and a day. For example, people would take to dancin' in a circle with the Good Folk, only to disappear. But if you came back three hunnerd and sixty-six days later, they'd reappear and you could pull 'em out. Seems like that might be our opportunity to rescind this agreement… Ricky, when did your daddy pass away?"

"November 7, 2019," Rick answered without hesitation.

"And what number you keep seeing?"

"1-1-0-8."

Devlin held up his hands as if he had just wowed an audience with a magic trick. "Mystery solved," he proclaimed. "Told you their language was synchronicity. That's what they were trying to convey. Something in their nature is so goddamn contractually-minded that they just *had* to share it with you. The pact was transferred after your father's death. A year and a day later, it can be broken. No more, no less. That's our window, when whatever we do stands the best chance of working."

"That's… that's in a *week*," Bora quivered. "You're telling me that we have one week to figure this out, or Rick has to either kill himself or pass this on to Jack?"

"Afraid so," apologized Devlin as he rose to his feet. "Lemme mull this over a bit. Figure out the *whys* and the *wheres*. I'll go through my books, call some friends. A week should be plenty time to pull a plan together. Tonight, we have to hold them off." After extracting his pack of cigarettes, he disappeared out the patio door.

Normally, Rick and Bora would have discussed the ramifications of what Devlin had just revealed. Instead, both were too dumbfounded to react. They went their separate ways in silence. Bora returned to her nest on the couch to bury herself in her phone, while Rick followed Devlin to the patio door. He did not go outside. Instead, he watched his friend face the field, chain smoking.

The sun had already taken over the sky. It drew up the last light from the ground to set the air ablaze, leaving the earth to languish in ever-lengthening shadows. There was a time when sunsets lit an artistic spark within Rick, filling him with hope, wonder, and a sense of magic. Transition was a marvelous thing, full of unspoken potential.

Now, he was simply filled with dread. All his life, he had felt that daylight, goodness, and warmth were the defaults under which the planet existed. Night was just a silly carnival mask that Day slipped on to hide her face.

Watching the last rays dip over the top of Red Ear Mountain, Rick now feared the opposite: Night was the true nature of things. Day was the deception. It didn't dispel the shadows; it only obscured them. It fooled you into believing that shadows don't exist.

Something caught his eye far in the distance, out along the tree line. While Devlin didn't seem to notice, Rick spied the barest glimpse of a figure, small and childlike, ducking back into the vegetation.

A sickening feeling arose in his gut. It was going to be a long night.

40

Sunday, November 1, 2020

ANURA

EVEN BEFORE THE DARKNESS TOOK HOLD, a heavy, leaden quality fell over the evening, both indoors and out. Inside, everyone remained silent. Outside, a low pressure system was mounting.

After some light discussion, everyone settled on a basic plan: remain awake until 11:08 came and went, then keep watch in shifts until morning. Bora would take the first, giving Devlin a chance to catch up on the sleep he had missed during his trip to Asheville; Rick would take the second; Devlin the third. Once Devlin walked them through another set of protections—positive visualizations, meditation, and rituals—the three of them preoccupied themselves with separate tasks, trying to ignore the anxiety caused by the approaching hour. Since it seemed prudent to retain the ability to see outside, the only light came from a lamp or two and the range hood in the kitchen.

It was around a quarter to eleven when, somewhere in the distance, thunder rolled across the north Georgia mountains. Each time it reached the house in Ellijay, Rick noticed that Devlin winced, as though he thought it signified something more ominous than mere lightning.

I wonder if it was like this way back when, reflected Rick. *When you were in a castle under siege. Just waiting for the attack. The pounding of enemy armies marching closer. The sound of catapults and trebuchets opening fire on the battlements...*

"Devlin," Rick said from the recliner, hoping to break his pensive demeanor, "this guy who owned the diary—what was his name again?"

"Cillian," answered Devlin. He was staring out the kitchen window, barely paying attention to the conversation.

"What do you know about him?"

"Didn't have time to read much. Irish immigrant. Dealt with this stuff all his life. He's real vague about his time in the old country."

"Was he... like you?" asked Bora from the couch. "A magician?"

"Cunning man, seer, magician, call him what you will," Devlin suggested.

"What happened to him?"

"Kicked the bucket a short while after he met Conrad. Well, I say that. Seems as if he just... wandered into the woods. Never came back."

"And that's in the diary?" asked Bora.

"Uh-huh," he replied.

"Can I read it?"

"Maybe later," Devlin mumbled noncommittally. His eyes were focused on something outside. Just then a peal of thunder, louder than before, rocked the house, vibrating the fixtures and sending everyone jumping except for Devlin.

A nervous silence followed. It stretched on interminably until Devlin began whispering once more. "'Twas brillig, and the slithy toves did gyre and gimble in the wabe," he said to himself. "All mimsy were the borogoves, and the mome raths outgrabe...."

Rick exchanged a quick look with Bora. Both of them recognized the poem, and while they had no idea how it related to their current situation, it didn't exactly bode well. Rick rose from his chair and cautiously tiptoed into the kitchen, approaching Devlin like a cornered wildcat. When he drew near enough, he peered through the kitchen window over Devlin's shoulder.

For a few moments, he saw very little. There was the slightest indication of the plants in the garden whipping in the wind, but beyond that lay utter darkness. Rick stepped from behind Devlin to his side, affording a wider view of the landscape. Then he saw them: a cluster of yellow lights—*Nine, always nine*—coasting through the sky in their direction, in the same approximate location they had appeared on the night of the séance. They looked less playful than in previous sightings, refraining from their usual loops and twirls.

In fact, their simple, straightforward passage allowed Rick to hope, if only for a moment, that they might be airplanes. *Could be a military flight of three planes*, he thought to himself. *In close forma—*

At that moment, the sky turned a murky gray, illuminated by another distant lightning strike. It was as if a failing lightbulb had been flicked on then immediately off. In that flash, another shape appeared behind the lights: vast, triangular, and pitch black. Rick's first thought was that it was Red Ear, towering in the distance. He then realized that not only did the mountain lie in a completely different direction, but he could also perceive the slightest bit of sky below the bottom edge. It was just as it appeared: a gigantic wedge suspended in the air, blacker than black, behind the lights. It also seemed to be moving on a dead heading toward the house, its uppermost tip penetrating past the tree line and into the field.

"Y'all see that?" asked Bora, startling him. She had quietly taken a post behind them.

"Unfortunately," Rick answered.

"What was it, Dev?" she wondered. "A mothership?"

Devlin's blue and brown eyes never left the window. "No," he declared.

"No? Then what was it?"

Devlin didn't speak until another flash of lightning lit up the sky. The gigantic triangle was now missing. When the scene darkened, so were the smaller lights. Over the booming thunder that followed, Devlin offered one word in response: "Royalty."

A pitter-patter of white noise began filling the house. "Starting to rain," Bora observed.

Rick listened. The sound was too heavy. "Not rain," Rick countered. "Raindrops don't bounce like that. Hail maybe?" He looked out the kitchen window. Something was falling to the ground, but he couldn't tell what. "Bora, take a look out back," he requested.

Bora did as instructed, while Rick and Devlin remained glued to the window. When she arrived, she stood there a moment, then spoke haltingly. "Um… guys… you'd… you'd better take a look."

Rick raced to her side, skidding to a halt in front of the glass patio door. The automatic light had been triggered, casting a yellow circle across the field. Within its confines, the ground wriggled with life. Tiny, greenish-brown objects, none much bigger than a penny, were falling into the light from the sky above. After landing, each one began bouncing up and down like popcorn in a kettle. It took Rick a few seconds to speak.

"Frogs?" he managed at last. Bora nodded.

"Typical," snorted Devlin. He had remained in the kitchen, and sounded completely disinterested in the bizarre development.

"What you got over there?" asked Rick. He looked back at the microwave. It was coming up on eleven o'clock.

"Shapes," Devlin answered. "Moving between the trash in the front yard."

As he spoke, another, more familiar sound arose. Returning his focus to the light in the backyard, Rick saw streaks of rain caught in the beam along with the larger, rounder frogs. It looked like a shower of Morse code.

Devlin moved for the first time. He walked quickly toward the front door and threw it open, leaving the storm door locked. "We got a problem," he said after flicking on the porch light. His voice was louder than ever, carrying a hint of alarm.

Rick and Bora met him at the front of the house. There was no need to ask what Devlin meant. They could see it themselves. There, cast in pale yellow outside, the once-thick band of salt crossing the cement had begun to erode.

"That barrier breaks, ain't nothing keeping 'em out," warned Devlin. "Hope y'all're still wearing them necklaces."

Even as they watched, the wind and rain washed the salt further away. It was already half as thick as it had begun. A few frogs crossed the white line here and there, kicking up clods of wet grains as they went. The situation was likely the same all around the outside of the house.

Rick searched for a solution. He could only find one. "We have to lay the salt again," he declared.

"They're already here," explained Devlin. "You really wanna go outside?"

Rick fell silent and stared out at the salt, which vanished with the slow consistency of a draining hourglass. *Think, think, think,* he commanded himself. *There's got to be a way...*

Suddenly, his interaction with Jack at the aquarium forced itself into his mind. "Every wall has two sides," he whispered. "Devlin—is there a reason we can't salt the *inside* perimeter?"

Devlin's eyebrows moved from a steepled expression of concern to one of relief. "Not a goddamn reason in the world," he shouted enthusiastically. "Good thinking, Ricky! Where'd y'all put it?"

Bora said what Rick didn't want to admit. "In the shed," she groaned.

"Well, shee-it," Devlin muttered, suddenly defeated. The line of salt was thinner than ever. "Who wants to be the one to fetch it? Can't send Rick. He's the one they're after."

"I'll go," Bora volunteered.

"Can't ask you to do that—" began Devlin.

"Spare me the chivalry, Dev," Bora interjected. "It's my choice. Besides, if these things thrive on belief, then maybe the fact that I believe in them the least of any of us counts for something."

Rick nodded. He had no desire to put his best friend at risk, but it made the most sense. "Closest window is over here," he said, heading toward the addition. Bora followed him into the new bedroom closest to the front, where Devlin's suitcase lay on the floor amidst a wasteland of dirty clothes scattered across the cement.

"He knows I have a washing machine, right?" asked Rick.

"Not the time," Bora scolded. She stepped toward the window. The faint glow of the front porch light barely highlighted the edge of the shed, not fifteen feet away.

As she placed her hands on the latches, she asked, "What's the combination again?"

"Hang on," Rick said, taking her hands off the window. "Don't you want to take a knife or something?"

Bora shook her head. "I can work the lock faster if I don't," she replied. "Besides, those bags are pretty heavy, I'll need both hands free. Now—the combination?"

"1-5-0-5," answered Rick. "If not that, try 1-1-0-8. Don't bother closing up." He faced the window and placed his hands on the latches. "You ready?" He looked back as another flash of lightning lit the room, casting Bora in an eerie luster.

"Ready as I'll ever be," she said with a sigh. She shook her hands and, after a moment of high-stepping to warm up her legs, nodded. "Now."

"Wait," Devlin announced, entering the room. "Put this in your pocket." He handed her a wadded-up slice of what appeared to be bread.

"Huh?" asked Bora.

"Don't worry about why, just take it," he demanded. "More witchy stuff."

Bora shrugged and took it, then turned to face the window once more. She nodded.

Rick flipped the latches and flung up the pane. A wash of water and sound filled the room, bouncing against all of its hard, unfinished surfaces. None of them spoke a word as Bora clambered over the sill and disappeared out of sight into the night. Rick shut the window but kept his hands in place.

They waited in silence. It seemed to take forever. The two men peered outside, but between the water on the glass and the lack of light, little could be discerned. Rick kept hoping for another lightning strike, so he could get some sense of Bora's safety or success. *C'mon, c'mon, c'mon...* prayed Rick. *I know you can do this, Bora... Please...*

At last, she shambled out of the darkness, soaking wet, dragging two full bags of salt behind her. Even though the shed was close, the weight of her load slowed her progress. Rick opened the window again. With all her might, Bora hoisted the first bag up to the windowsill, at which point Devlin grabbed it, flung it to the floor, and reached out for the second. Taking it in one hand, he reached with the other for Bora to steady herself as she reentered the house. Rick grabbed her arm as well, and the pair began dragging her inside.

"See?" she chuckled, wiping a strand of wet hair from her face. "Not so bad."

Bora was halfway through the window when a lightning bolt hit closer than ever, somewhere in the field on the edge of the forest. The sound was deafening, and the sudden fright caused Rick and Devlin's grip to slip on Bora's wet flesh.

The field filled with a white light that lingered longer than any lightning strike. It allowed Rick to see the entire landscape: the darkened edge of the forest far away, stretching up like jagged teeth; the vast expanse of tall grass, battered down by the rain; and a row of tiny figures standing halfway between the house and the shed.

Bora's body lurched back out the window. Devlin dropped the salt and used both hands to grab her clothing, pulling back with all his might, as did Rick. Two new sounds joined the rain and thunder: Bora's screams and maniacal laughter from outside, just below the window's edge.

Bora continued slipping out the window, the frame riding up her shirt and rubbing her abdomen raw. Devlin and Rick pitched forward. They were losing the struggle. It felt as if ten bodybuilders were on the other end of Bora, dead set on either winning this grim tug-of-war or tearing her in two. Rick tried clutching her arm up near her shoulder, but his grasp continued to slip, first to her elbow… then her forearm… then her hands…

The moment it slipped to her fingers, Rick launched himself out the window and reached past Bora's shirt, toward her pants. As he hoped, she was wearing a belt, and he seized the leather as tightly as he could. Doing so, he spotted an army of small hands further down her body, tugging at the legs of her pants. One pair let go and reached toward Rick's hands, pawing at his fingers, trying to loosen his grip. They felt cold and rubbery.

Devlin saw Rick's strategy and followed suit. He grabbed her belt as well, but not before knocking away the tiny hands of their enemy. Devlin placed a booted foot on the wall below the window and, with one final exertion, yanked Bora back inside. The two of them tumbled to the floor as Rick slammed the window shut and latched it. Somewhere outside, the laughter turned to wails of rage.

"You okay?!?" asked Rick, kneeling down to check on his friend. She was soaked and scraped, but otherwise seemed unharmed.

"Don't worry about me," she implored, rising to her feet. "Get going!"

41

Sunday, November 1, 2020

ROYALTY

AFTER GRABBING BOTH BAGS OF SALT, Devlin escaped out of the unfinished bedroom. Rick and Bora staggered behind him. To their surprise, they found the living room no longer warmly lit by the lamps but instead plunged into a darkness rivaling the addition. Apparently, the house had lost power following the last lightning strike.

Devlin had already torn open one bag and was starting to trace a broad circle in the center of the living room, trying to strike a balance between using enough and not being wasteful. Seeing the size of the space he was creating, Rick and Bora began moving everything out of the way, including the recliner and coffee table. When they finished, Rick noticed that Devlin had stopped. Only a quarter of the circle was complete.

"For Chrissake, keep going!" shouted Rick. No sooner had the words left his mouth than he realized what was going on. He heard it, too: a parade of feet tramping across the roof. Even though Rick knew the intruders were small, their footfalls felt immeasurably heavy. The steps progressed from a steady march to a chaotic clamor that sounded as if the sky had just unleashed a violent hailstorm.

Then something truly peculiar happened. Although it sounded exactly the same, the noise on the roof shifted. To Rick, it resembled the way one might alter the balance or fade in a car's audio system. In fact, if he didn't know any better, he would have thought that someone shifted a knob from "outside" to "inside." To his horror, Rick recognized that the sound was now concentrated in the addition.

"Fuck!" exclaimed Devlin, dropping the salt. "Perimeter's breached!" He bolted for the part of the house they had just left. "Whatever you do, don't stop!" he shouted as he disappeared around the corner.

Both of them scrambled to grab the salt, Bora taking the open bag and Rick going for the new one. Hands shaking, they continued outlining the circle. From the addition, a series of disconcerting noises arose: shrieks, both human and inhuman; shouts and commandments from Devlin in a variety of tongues; the sound of objects being tossed about the room.

The circle was halfway finished when Bora screamed. She pointed toward the doorway, where two short, shadowy shapes stood in the darkness. They had somehow made their way past Devlin. Both silhouettes raised their hands, crouched, then sprinted toward them.

Rick froze. His only thought was that he needed a weapon. Dodging between the two attackers, he slipped past the bar and into the kitchen. There, he slid into the countertop by the stove, fumbling for the chef's knife. It slipped from the wooden block with a metallic zing. Rick spun on his heels, but it was too late—both assailants were upon him.

One wrapped its arms around his left leg. The other grabbed the opposite arm that was wielding the knife. Rick attempted to switch hands, but each time he tried, the one on his arm would tug forcefully in the opposite direction with a strength that belied its size. Meanwhile, his other attacker was viciously biting and clawing at his leg. The pain became so intense that Rick thought his knee might buckle any minute.

Although all of Rick's senses were overwhelmed, his hearing might have suffered the most. His own cries of terror mingled with cackling from the intruders. Devlin was still struggling with something in the addition, bellowing all sorts of arcane threats. The thunder had developed into a near-constant rumble.

Rick flailed wildly, trying to shake the shapes from his body, which in the dim light looked like little more than a flurry of glinting fangs and thrashing limbs. Somehow, he found enough strength and determination to limp his way back into the living room. There he saw Bora on her back, pummeling another shape that had her pinned to the floor. The space between them was a blur of motion, both of their hands vying for control amidst a deluge of fists and claws.

Amidst all the confusion, Rick spotted an open bag of salt spilling across the floor just a few inches away. With his free foot, he managed to kick it in Bora's direction, spraying a white arc directly into her adversary. The shape reeled, squealing as if it had been set aflame. Pushing hard against it, Bora sent the figure to the floor, kicked it square in the head, and struggled to her feet.

Only now did she notice Rick. Thinking quickly, Bora reached back down to the salt, grabbed a wad in each hand, and stomped toward him. When an opening in Rick's struggle presented itself, she thrust her hands towards his attackers. Both fistfuls hit their marks. For a moment, Bora wore an expression of gleeful revenge as she rubbed the salt in their faces. Like their counterpart, the assailants relinquished their grip, recoiling with wails of pain.

Even through the fear, Rick felt a wave of pride. He didn't allow himself long to gloat, however. Their attackers might have been writhing on the floor in agony, but the circle was still unfinished. Tossing the knife inside, Rick grabbed the other bag and resumed work with Bora. The time for moderation had passed. They hastily emptied the contents of each bag onto the floor, and before the intruders recovered, they were nearly finished.

The timing was perfect. Devlin launched out of the doorway to the addition moments before the circle was joined. He jumped inside, landing in a roll. Rick was surprised by what he saw. While he and Bora suffered their own injuries, Devlin looked like he had easily experienced the worst. His hair was even more disheveled than usual, his white shirt was in tatters, and a gash above his eye had sent a curtain of red down the left side of his face.

"Sometimes I hate this gig," he rasped. Everyone indulged in a nervous chuckle. Whether or not they were, they felt safe at last. Around them, the ring of salt shone in the darkness like a halo of protective light.

Rick reached out a hand and pulled Devlin upright. "You okay?" he asked.

"Nothin' a little Bactine won't fix," he answered, gingerly touching his wound. "More upset about my shirt. How about you, Bora?"

Bora joined the huddle. "Seen better days," she wheezed between breaths. They all faced each other. "Think this circle will hold?"

"Take a look yourself," said Devlin, nodding over her shoulder. Their huddle loosened like a tense muscle finally allowed to relax. As Rick examined the area beyond the border of salt, he found his living room transformed into a disaster area. Lamps lay on the floor, their bulbs shattered. Furniture was overturned. A variety of belongings, including his records, sat strewn across the floor. Amidst it all, perched here and there, lurked a grotesque menagerie of nine.

What surprised Rick the most was their diversity. Beyond their size, no two were alike. Some seemed feral, bestial, caprine, or birdlike, while others simply looked like small people. Among those who wore any, their clothing appeared equally varied, from robes to vests to jumpsuits to little more than loincloths. All of them remained silent and still, glowering with the futility of caged animals in a zoo.

Rick's only opportunity to study them came during the sporadic lightning flashes, and those had diminished significantly. Even then, these moments were brief. One he recognized as the individual who had grabbed his hair. Another retained the same form as when they had appeared in Bora's apartment. A third was the ghastly puppet from his nightmare that same night. Behind these, over by his upturned recliner, crouched a short human with horns and the bottom half of a goat.

The closest one resembled an elderly man decked out in old-fashioned pantaloons and a jerkin. A tight-fitting leather cap topped a deeply wrinkled, large-nosed face. A pair of sharply pointed ears jutted out from either side.

The farthest, standing in the foyer, was by far the tallest. It resembled nothing so much as a small, dark-furred ape, although the face looked perhaps the most human of the bunch, its hooded nose the proper size and shape.

It was all too much to take in, frankly. Rick dropped his eyes to the floor, having no desire to look upon them any more than required. He noticed that Bora did the same. Even with their eyes averted, neither of them could escape the distinctive aroma of gunpowder and decaying flowers. Only Devlin kept his head up.

"How long do we stay here?" whispered Bora.

"All night if we have to," Devlin advised, glancing around the room. "They'll probably leave by daybreak... Damn, Ricardo. You got the fuckin' Village People up your ass, don't y—"

Everyone ducked reflexively. A sharp noise, brittle and deafening, had interrupted Devlin. The sound of the thunderstorm now permeated the entire house.

When everyone dared to look back up, they saw that all the commotion came from the foyer, where the front door remained open. The storm door had shattered from the outside with a force overwhelming enough to scatter glass across the carpet. A few shards even reached the salt circle, where they clung to everyone's hair. A gust of chilly, damp air now coursed through the house, covering everything with a fine spray of mist and sending bits of paper whirling about. Notably, none of their visitors reacted to this development in the slightest.

"What the f—" began Rick. His voice caught in his throat as a shadow appeared in the doorway. With ponderous purpose, it oozed across the threshold, the vanguard of something far more threatening. Into the porchlight stepped a feminine figure, tall and lithe. She was entirely backlit, so her facial features were unrecognizable—but Rick didn't need to see them. He knew exactly who she was. She had plagued his dreams ever since he first laid eyes on her in a smoky old bar one year ago.

Her outline froze in the empty door frame, nearly reaching the top. Only her head moved. Otherwise, she was motionless. By contrast, her white dress was an animated mass with a life of its own, a long train billowing in the wind of the storm. When her gaze met the group cowering in the circle, her head stopped.

The woman in white began her approach. Even though she was barefoot, she didn't seem to notice the sharp splinters littering the carpet. Her gait was measured and steady, unbothered. The only sounds came from the rain, the rushing wind, and the occasional tinkle of her dress across the broken glass. One by one, her retinue parted, making way for her passage until, finally, she stood within a foot of the circle of salt, close enough to reveal her face.

She looks just like she did back then, Rick thought. For an entire year, that face had haunted him. In the back of his mind, he always knew that she must somehow be connected to all the trials he experienced. He just didn't know how she fit in. Only now did he venture a guess: *Royalty....*

The woman cast her eyes toward the circle of salt. No one inside said a word. She paced the outside perimeter like a tiger, her eyes never leaving the white line, as if probing for a gap. At last, she circumnavigated the entire ring and stopped directly in front of Rick to stare at him.

Rick couldn't help himself. His eyes met hers. Even in the darkness, they shone with an unnatural blue brilliance, like two large whirlpools set in alabaster. The pull was intoxicating and irresistible—neither amorous nor sexual, but rather filled with the promise of liberation or release, like jumping into a void without fretting over the consequences. A freedom from responsibility, from gravity, from life. Rick felt himself lean forward, coming to the very edge of the salt circle...

Rick vaguely heard Devlin shout something about not looking at her. His voice seemed muffled, like it came from across the house. Even if it had been more present, Rick didn't care what Devlin had to say. All he wanted now was freedom, and all he heard was a deep, low hum.

The woman in white lifted her hand toward Rick's face. Extending a single finger—far too long for any human being—she aimed it at a point directly between his eyes. Darkness swelled before Rick, growing larger until it crowded his vision. When it became too much for the confines of his eyes, it burst and enveloped him, reaching out, dragging him lower and lower, deeper into those eyes, deeper into the whirlpools, deeper into the abyss where light no longer penetrated...

Time slipped away. Language slipped away, as did any sense of meaning, of logic, of right or wrong. Rick might have been in that place for thirty seconds or thirty centuries. All he knew was that everything around him was pitch black. At first, there was only the humming. Then there were voices. Each sentence came slowly at first, as clearly as if it were whispered in his ear.

However, he recognized neither the voices nor the words. He had forgotten how to speak. Only after three hundred years of repetition did he come to understand them. First the syllables registered, then each word, then the sentences, and finally the meaning held within each.

"Just end it all... your existence just makes everything worse... You are nothing... Everything ends in darkness... Entropy comes for us all... You're worthless... A failure... You're so incompetent, you can't even kill yourself... You're destined to linger on, and make everyone around you worse off just by existing...."

Suddenly, Rick found himself sitting alone in a darkened movie theater. The action had already started. It looked as if there was some sort of struggle between three individuals in a darkened living room. While the movie wasn't familiar, he vaguely recognized the actors. It looked as if two people—a lanky white fellow and a Korean woman—were fighting with a middle-aged man. All three of them stood inside a white circle. The man held a chef's knife in his hands and was pulling it toward his body, tip-first. It looked like he was trying to commit suicide. No matter how hard they fought, the blade kept drawing closer to his chest. To one side stood a fourth individual: a tall woman, dressed in white, watching detachedly. There was no soundtrack, only the sentences, repeating on a loop…

The voices were impossible to silence. "You are nothing," they droned. "Everything ends in darkness…."

Something about this felt wrong. "No," Rick fought. "No, no, no. That's not true. I remember… someone. I remember a boy… A boy full of love and hope and talent and kindness. I remember a son….

Rick felt a sharp pain in his wrist, pulling him instantly back into his body. First came memory. He remembered the lifetime he had abandoned. It came crashing back to him with absolute clarity. He remembered Jack. He remembered who he was, where he was, and what was happening.

Then came vision. He saw the knife in his hands, only half an inch from his chest. He was trying to kill himself. Bora and Devlin were pulling in the opposite direction with all their might, but his own muscles were bolstered by a supernatural strength. Each passing moment brought the blade closer.

Then came control, and with it the capacity to surrender. Rick quit trying to stab himself. His muscles relaxed, instantly giving his friends the power to pull his hand away. The pent-up momentum of the struggle sent everyone flying to the floor along with the knife.

For just a breath, everything was still. Even the freakish audience surrounding them refused to budge, turning the living room into a tableau that would make Hieronymus Bosch blush.

Rick blinked. Every muscle in his body ached. Rolling onto his side, he watched Devlin snatch up the blade and scramble to his feet. He looked furious. Rick had never seen him with that exact expression, and it looked as terrifying as any of the monstrosities that watched from the living room. He looked like a man with a score to settle.

Thankfully, his ire was not directed at Rick. It was focused on the woman in white. Glancing in her direction, Rick saw she stood exactly where he remembered. Her face was neither angry nor surprised. She simply looked disappointed. Her hands were held at her sides, palms upward, in a saintly display of mock innocence.

Devlin obviously didn't buy it. His hand clutching the chef's knife tightened, whitening at the knuckles. After slowly shaking his head, he summoned a massive gob of spit and blood from his throat and launched it over his right shoulder onto the carpet. Next, without the slightest hesitation, he shifted his grip to the blade, pulled back his arm, and launched the knife at the woman.

It all happened too fast to keep track of. One second, the knife was in Devlin's hand; the next, it was embedded in the drywall. Somewhere between those two moments, the woman in white had vanished, as had her unholy host. The only sign that they had ever been there was the room, which still lay in shambles.

Rick looked at Bora, who lay on her side across the circle from him. She was crying, and continued long after the power came back on.

42

Monday, November 2, 2020

THAT LITTLE SHITE

When Bora awoke late the following morning, Rick had already disappeared into the rain. She knew where he was: the liquor store. She really couldn't blame him this time. Last night had proven even more exhausting than the night before. If she had different tastes, she might have crawled into a bottle herself. By the time Rick returned, brown bag in hand, Bora had filled the house with a thick haze of marijuana smoke.

Rick was pleased to see the work they had done. It was also obvious from his demeanor that he felt ashamed that they had started without him. Bora and Devlin had already cleaned up half of the mess in the living room. Between the glass and the salt, the vacuum had to be emptied seven times. Rick joined in and they continued, the recovery effort eating up what little was left of the morning.

After that, Rick helped put the furniture back in place, and they began re-salting the interior of the house. Rather than the emergency circle formed last night, they deposited a thick band all along the interior walls, right up against the baseboards. It offered a sense of security no matter where they went. Rick assisted as much as he could, but by three o'clock he was too drunk to stand, and Bora forced him to retire to the couch. He passed out right away.

Shortly thereafter, the doorbell rang. Devlin was pleased to discover it was Rick's order of horseshoes. He opened the box and dumped the contents onto the counter with an abrasive clang.

"Our boy spared no expense," said Devlin, picking one off the top of the pile to examine it. In his other hand, he held the packing slip. "Twenty!" he quietly exclaimed. It prompted an admiring glance in Rick's direction. Although he was snoring loudly, Devlin still offered a quick, "Attaboy."

Bora picked up one of the horseshoes herself. Finding it much heavier than she anticipated, it occurred to her that she might not have held one since she was a kid. "Great," she sighed, hoisting the curved metal. "Now what do we do?"

Devlin looked around the room. "This place has, what, maybe thirteen windows, couple of doors to the outside? We hang one of these bad boys above each of 'em. Maybe toss one in the fireplace for good measure. Any we have leftover, we mount on all the doorways inside. As insurance."

Bora nodded. "I really don't want to try and get answers out of him in this state," she said, eyes on Rick. "Any idea where his toolbox is?"

"Sure," said Devlin, waltzing out of the room. "It's in the bathroom of the addition." He returned with a hammer and a handful of nails.

"I saw a ladder in the shed last night," Bora remembered. "You hammer, I spot. Sound good?"

"Sounds good," agreed Devlin, and they stepped out the front door.

Thankfully, the rain had slowed to a drizzle about half an hour earlier, although the day remained overcast. Devlin vocally appreciated Bora's presence, as the spray left each step of the aluminum ladder dangerously slick. As it turned out, mounting the horseshoes proved quick and easy. It also proved quiet, as both of them were exhausted from last night's invasion and the morning cleanup. Finally afforded some time to reflect, Bora was shocked to see how much she had changed in the past few days.

Once upon a time, she spoke without thinking, incessantly rattling on to fill the silence, lest it become awkward. That, and a deep-seated insecurity that others might mistake an immobile mouth for a simple mind. But here, she knew how wrong she had been. The mountains were quiet but far from empty. They were brimming with life—seen and unseen. The past few days illustrated that they were also filled with a power and strength beyond Bora's comprehension. She took a lesson from that. If such a magnificent place could stay silent, then it seemed profane not to respect and reflect it. It was too precious a gift to reject mindlessly.

Still, there was one question on her mind. "That woman last night," she began, handing a horseshoe up to Devlin. "Who was she?"

After plucking a nail from his lips, threading it through one of the holes, and hammering the horseshoe above the window, Devlin finally answered. "The phrase 'principalities and powers' mean anything to you?" he inquired, stepping to the ground.

"Not really," she admitted. They each picked up a side of the ladder and began clumsily walking it to the next spot.

Devlin wiped the mist from his brow, wincing as his hand passed over his fresh wound. It wasn't nearly as large as it had looked last night. Until they cleaned it up, Bora was worried he might need stitches.

"A leader," he explained. It was the only word he uttered as he started back up the ladder. He got halfway, reached into his pocket for a new nail, and cursed. "Plumb out," he declared. "You mind grabbing s'more? Need a smoke break."

"Sure thing, Dev," Bora said, tracing her way around to the front door. "Already on it." She walked inside, past Rick, who was still asleep, and found the toolbox in the unfinished bathroom. She pocketed another fistful of nails and turned to head back outside, but stopped short.

The absolute disarray in the bedroom to her left, where Devlin had been sleeping, caught her eye. Last night, it served as the infiltration point for their visitors. She was curious to see what kind of damage they had inflicted.

Everything was a mess. Rick had a lot of work ahead of him. If someone had told her that a miniature earthquake had struck this one room, Bora wouldn't have doubted the claim. What little drywall Rick had hung now sat in crumbled piles. The window was now cracked, although Bora couldn't say for certain whether it had happened during Devlin's wizard battle or during her struggle to get back inside. Thinking back to those terrifying moments, she gently put one hand on her belly to judge its sensitivity and winced. It still ached from the incident.

As for Devlin's personal effects, all of them were scattered across the floor. Last night when she was in here, there was just a messy pile of clothes. Now *everything* he brought lay in a chaotic jumble: his toothbrush, his comb, his cassette player, his fiddle case, his books…

One of the volumes sitting alone in the far corner drew Bora's attention. It was small, with a weathered leather cover: the diary that Devlin Fox had brought home, the one that held the key to unraveling the whole mystery surrounding Rick Coulter.

Bora couldn't help herself. She was intrigued by the fate of this "Cillian" character. Walking forward, she glanced out the window and spotted Devlin out there in the damp, appearing completely unhurried and lost in thought as he gazed out across the field. He didn't look like he was planning on resuming work any time soon. In fact, he had just lit another cigarette.

Bora crept across the room, unsure why she was behaving so secretively. She stooped, picked up the diary, and began rifling through the pages. Each sheet felt so brittle, it almost threatened to crumble to dust. Sure enough, some had chunks missing, while others had fallen out entirely.

Most of it was boring. Tallies of turnips and seeds sown, heads of horses and the cost of cattle. The bits that weren't boring were downright sad.

Thursday, July 7, 1938, Bora read. *Clarksons came over this morning. Seems as if their boy has the consumption. Promised to do what I can, but I fear it may be too late....*

She skimmed ahead, stopping at the entry for Saturday, October 4, 1941: *Glad to be out of today. Market was fine, but that almighty wagon showed up. Been so long, I foolishly thought I'd seen the last of her. Seems she's still after a few more. Will do what I must, of course. Should find a way to distance myself, for the family's sake....*

Nested between the bleak and ominous entries were snapshots of a happy life—births of children and grandchildren, anniversaries, weddings, the sense of accomplishment brought about by a hard day's work. Bora found herself starting to envy the simplicity of this man's life.

She flipped to the very back, hoping to pinpoint where Devlin read about Cillian's disappearance. The final pages were blank. Before those, the last entry in the diary told no such story either. It was a grocery list. The one before that was written in late 1988:

She's finally done. Siobhán says she wants no more of him. Drawing up papers now. Says that the minute he signs them and it all goes through, she's going down to the courthouse with the children.

*Wants them to have her maiden name—*our *name. Couldn't approve of it more myself. Never cared for the eejit.*

The writing was thin and frail, a dramatic contrast to the elegant pen strokes of his earlier years. It was fascinating to see, but not what she was looking for. Bora kept flipping the pages backward, hoping to find some clue about why the man wandered off into the forest, but there was nothing remotely of the sort.

At last, she found herself in 1986, staring at the entry that Devlin had read. She turned the page to the next entry, skimmed it, and kept going until she landed on Saturday, May 24, 1986. After casting another glance beyond the cracked glass to assure herself that Devlin was in no rush, she read the entire page.

Only a few matters of import. Growing tired, so I shall keep this to the pertinents. Conrad Colder returned today.

Seems he found the girl in the nip last night. Right where she disappeared. Poorly, he says, but high hopes for recovery. Can't believe it worked. Lots of feelings in that fella. Wrecked out, for certain. Cheerful to have his girl back. Then he was in a fouler.

'These people of yours drive a hard bargain,' he whinged. All I could do is nod. Tried not to smile. Knew full well what they *asked of him, I* ~~brock~~ *brokered the bloody thing.*

Couldn't help myself. Asked what happened. Told me they *met him in his fellsbar mine two days after we met. Scared him sideways,* they *did. Told me he consented to a life for a life, just as I suspected. Not a bother on him in that regard. I was taken aback.*

'Ain't one of your fancy business contracts,' I warned him. 'Can't shimmy your way out with them. *If you do, it'll haunt your lineage till the Second Coming.' Said he knows, he knows. Then he told me* they *demanded one more stipulation.*

They want him to close the mine! Nearly broke my arse laughing. Tried to contain myself. The mine will be flooded by the end of the decade. Must admit, I found it funnier than he found it distressing. Didn't take a feather out of him. But I'd be hard pressed to author a more fitting end to his legacy.

No matter. He found no humor in the subject. Wanted to get down to brass tacks, compensate me for my services. 'Couldn't be happier,' says I. Waited for him to pull out some coin, and he pulls out a checkbook. Can't believe it. I protested.

~~I told him to fu~~ 'Are you joking me? I didn't come down in the last shower!'

Conrad Colder just gives me the eyes. Says it's the check or naught. Can't have that, can we?

'Fine, no use getting in a heap about it.' Asks me my name. The auld clod can't even spell 'Cillian.' So I spells it out for him: 'C-I-L-L-I-A-N.'

'Last name?' he asks. 'F-O-X'—

Bora dropped the diary like it was a hot frying pan. It landed on the cement floor, kicking up a cloud of drywall dust. Bora watched the particles drifting through the air, trying to comprehend what she had just read.

It could be a coincidence. It had to be a coincidence.

It *couldn't* be a coincidence. Snatching up the diary once more, she began speeding through the pages, searching for something to confirm her suspicions. She kept an eye out for names, for proper nouns, for—

She stopped. The answer was staring right back at her. There, toward the end of an entry from early 1987, were words that she simply could not believe.

Siobhán and her boys dropped in just as promised. Nice visit. Saw my new granddaughter again. Shaping up to be a fine family, that lot.

Only wish that little shite Devlin would stop calling me 'Cillian.'

43

Monday, November 2, 2020

REVELATION

Devlin never had a chance to react. He had just slipped inside when Bora came storming out of the addition, carrying the diary. "Came in to check on you," he said when he saw her, his wet boots squeaking across the foyer. "Everything alright? Thought it was taking a while—"

Bora planted a right hook across his jaw. The punch wasn't especially forceful, but it took him off guard. The only thing that kept him upright on the slippery tile was the front door. He steadied himself on the doorknob, looking betrayed and confused. His reaction was lost on Bora, however. She had already doubled back to the couch.

"Rick!" she shouted, shaking her friend from his stupor. "Rick! Wake the hell up! Now!"

By the time Rick finally sat up, Devlin had joined them in the living room. They all took a moment. Rick teetered back and forth, still intoxicated. Devlin rubbed his jaw, his eyes locked on the diary. Bora fumed and paced a tight, two-step line back and forth across the carpet.

"What's the going rate, Bora?" asked Devlin when no one else spoke. "Still thirty pieces of silver?"

Bora's eyes narrowed. "You lying sack of *shit*," she hissed, stabbing a finger in his face with the last word.

"B-Bora," Rick stammered, steadying himself on the cushions with one hand and cradling his head with the other. "I'm still pretty drunk. W-what's happening?"

She didn't take her eyes off Devlin. "He's known all along," she spat. "This entire time, he has known *exactly* what has been happening to you." She held the diary aloft. Devlin made a weak attempt to snatch it from her hands, but she pulled it back. "It's all in here. Everything."

Even without the better part of a bottle in him, Rick would have been no less confused. "What are you talking about?" he groaned.

Bora knelt down to the couch, pressing the diary into Rick's hands. "The *seer*, Rick. The one your dad met with? He's Devlin's fucking *grandfather. He* is the reason you're going through all this."

Rick stared at the diary like it was an overdue time bomb, ready to detonate if jostled in the slightest. "Devlin," he whispered, "is—is that true…?"

Devlin had managed to recover his composure. He stood there silently, sucking his swelling lower lip, until at last he sighed, wiped his mouth on his arm, and tried to explain with one of his anecdotes. "This one time in Shreveport, I had the rare honor of—"

"Quit with the bullshit!" erupted Bora. "He asked you a simple fucking question! 'Yes' or 'no'?!?"

"Yes," Devlin said without hesitation. The word came quietly but clearly. Both of them turned their attention to Rick to gauge his reaction. Instead of looking angry, he simply appeared confused and wounded.

"I still don't understand," Rick mumbled. He didn't bother opening the book in his hands. "Your friend in Asheville just so happened to have your grandfather's diary?"

"Naw," replied Devlin, lowering his head. For the first time since he had entered their lives, the man looked timid. His shoulders slumped. The shift in body language transformed his sizable frame into something tiny and defeated. "I had it all along," he added.

"Then where did you go yesterday?" wondered Rick. While the magnitude of the revelation seemed to sober him up a bit, his words still slipped and slid into each other.

"Collecting supplies," Devlin explained. "Replacing what I left in my bag in the woods. Books, too. Trying to find a way to get you out of this mess." When he looked back up, he was on the verge of tears, though everyone knew it wouldn't progress to that. "Ricky, you ain't just a case. You're… you're my *responsibility*."

"How long have you known?"

Devlin shook his head as if trying to recall. "A couple years, maybe? Mama died... When we cleaned out the house, I found Cillian's diary tucked way back in her Chester drawers. Wasn't surprised by most of it. We all got the sight from Granpap. He taught me most of what I know... Never told me 'bout your daddy, though." He paused to rub his eyes. "Conrad Coulter ain't the only one in them pages who got a raw deal, you know. I'm not certain how Granpap was mixed up in these things... but it seems he had some debts to pay himself. Had to *deliver* folks to them every now and then."

"'Deliver' them?" puzzled Rick.

"Whatever it was, Cillian Fox was wrapped up in some bad mojo," Devlin said with a shrug. "The kinda thing what could put a hurtin' on *me* if it ain't amended... 'cause I sure as shit ain't harvestin' *no one*. When I first read that, I knew right away I needed to find Conrad. Looked into him, found out he was still alive, so I knew the pact was unfulfilled. Been waitin' for his obituary to drop ever since, hoping he'd do the right thing and honor the terms. Had no idea he'd tried to eight years ago."

Devlin sighed. "So... flashforward a year or two to last November. Finally seen your daddy's obit pop up. Thought maybe he'd done it... Still remember that sinking feeling I got when I read that he had 'died peacefully in his sleep.' So I rolled up my sleeves and got to work. Made my way back down south, started learnin' as much as I could about the Coulters."

"When were you planning on sharing this?" asked Rick.

"Ain't sure," Devlin mumbled. "Sometime. Soon. Would have earlier, but I was afraid of all"—Devlin waved his hands around the room—"*this*. I'm sorry, Richard. I haven't been entirely... transparent."

Devlin's sudden remorse did little to tamp down Bora's fury. "That's it?" she shouted. "'Sorry'? You sat on this for *years*, Devlin. And here we are, with less than a week left, and all you can say is 'sorry'? Why didn't you come to us right away? Why lie to us? You could have come to Rick last month—hell, *six* months ago—and we could've hit the ground running. Now we're out of time!"

The atmosphere in the room crackled. Devlin's demeanor changed along with it. His nostrils flared. He was in the bucking chute, raring to go.

"Oh *really?!?*" he scoffed, answering her indignation in kind. "Lil' Miss Skeptic over here, sayin' I should've come to y'all earlier this year!" He chuckled dryly and propped his hands on his hips. "Y'all would've thought I was a goddamn lunatic if I came to you with this story six months ago! I had to gain Ricky's trust. Y'all had to *believe* our meeting was fated."

"Yeah, yeah, I know," Bora said, rolling her eyes and raising her voice. "'Belief is the most powerful-blah-blah-blah.' Blow it out your ass."

That seemed to genuinely hurt Devlin. "I stand by that," he countered. He let his mouth hang open for a second before further justifying his actions. "But you know what? Let's say I'm full of shit. Say I should've approached Ricky sooner. What then? I needed more information from y'all. Things that ain't in the public record. Things you don't just volunteer to strangers. The particulars of Ricky's daddy's life, of his sister's disappearance, hell, *whether or not the situation was as bad as I feared.* If these little bastards were just misplacing your car keys or leaving circles of mushrooms in your backyard, then coming in here guns blazing would've turned this house into a supernatural Waco."

Bora refused to see his point. "Edna is *blind* because of you!" she yelled, her entire body trembling with rage.

"No," objected Devlin, wagging his finger. "No, no, no, no, no. You don't get to put that shit on me. I gave her the chance to opt out, just like I gave you and him. *I* didn't do that. *They* did that. I can't control what these things do, or *you* do, or *she* does, or *he* does, or *anyone* does. I'm only responsible for *myself,* righting the wrongs in *my* past. I've been living for *years* knowing what I needed to do. To break the cycle Cillian set in motion. *He* didn't do jack shit. *My uncles* didn't do jack shit. *Mama* didn't do jack shit. But *I* am. This ends with *me.* Ricky has one life, and I have one chance. A chance to change this. I'll be *damned* if I don't, or die trying."

"You selfish asshole," she sniped.

"'Selfish'?" repeated Devlin, incredulous. "'*Selfish*'? You got any idea what I normally charge for this kinda work?!?" He pointed to Rick, who remained silent. "I'm trying to *save* his drunk ass!"

No one said a word. The house filled with the sound of the newly-rejoined rain lightly dancing on the rooftop. For a heartbeat, it seemed like Bora might launch herself at Devlin. She clenched her hands into fists... then slowly released them. When they finally opened, the only sign of tension remained on her lips, which were tightly pursed.

"Rick, I've seen you kick out band members just for missing a downbeat," she said, looking down at him. "Tell him he's got to leave."

Despite his lingering intoxication, Rick had managed to completely follow the conversation. He tried to speak clearly and slowly, but his tongue stubbornly refused to cooperate. "Bora, you're... you're..." he slurred. "It's not your call. Quit speaking for me. I can speak for myself." He looked at Devlin. "I can't believe you didn't tell us."

Devlin offered a simple, deep nod, like a drinking bird. "Fair," he admitted. "Didn't know any other way to handle it. I've done lotsa things in my time... Most of 'em probably ain't been done before. But this time? I'm in *completely* uncharted territory. That scares the piss outta me."

His confession only reignited Bora's anger. "Rick, you can't tell me—"

Rick held up a hand. "You're upset... I am, too. But you don't fire the lead trumpet the night before your Maynard tribute. Devlin is the only person who can help me right now. My only chance. He leaves, and I might as well kill myself right now." He slid the diary onto the coffee table beside his half-empty bottle. "You said you've seen me kick guys out of bands... that's music. This is life. It's not some... immaculately composed chorale with right and wrong notes. We're all just... improvising over the changes. Yeah, some choices are better than others, but, at the end of the day, we're all just feeling around in the dark."

He grabbed the bottle, took a long pull, followed by another, and reclined back on the couch. "You know what's interesting about improvisation?" he continued, sounding drowsier and more distant with each word. "Whenever you play a wrong note, you're only a half step away from a resolution. The slightest correction—literally the smallest interval—can fix your mistake. It's not how you begin the phrase, or even what happens in the middle… It's how you end it." Rick closed his eyes. "Let Devlin finish…." His sentence concluded with a massive snore.

Devlin and Bora looked back at each other. They held the gaze for a while, listening to Rick's snorts punctuate the droning rainfall, before Devlin looked at his watch. It was approaching five o'clock.

"If we're done here, I'm gonna finish puttin' up these horseshoes," Devlin said quietly to Bora. "Don't want a spotter no more. Need someone to watch my back, not stab it."

44

Tuesday, November 3, 2020

ANGEL BAND

WITH THE EXCEPTION OF THIRTY MINUTES when he drank himself back to sleep in the middle of the night, Rick slept straight through to the next day. He had no clue how Bora and Devlin's conflict resolved itself. Part of him wished he had stayed sober enough to mediate, while another was relieved that he didn't have to endure what must have been a long, awkward evening.

Rick awoke in his bed sometime around two o'clock in the afternoon. Whether he found his way there himself or had been guided, he couldn't say. In any event, he greeted the day relatively rested, if hungover. Rick didn't mind—the headache and nausea were a small price to pay compared to a night of tossing and turning. Bad sleep is better than no sleep.

Stiffly and unsteadily, Rick rose and turned off his sound machine. His leg still ached from the attack two nights earlier. It could have been much worse. While the creatures had left him bruised and sore, they had not managed to break through his pants.

After glancing at the rain outside, Rick made his way to the bathroom and wrenched on the shower. The house was so quiet that it turned the sound into a thundering cataract. When he emerged, Rick expected the silence to return, but instead his ears were met by the faint strains of a fiddle.

From far away in the addition, Devlin began singing. Rick listened to the lyrics as he dressed himself. "My latest sun is sinking fast, my race is nearly run," Devlin crooned gently. "My strongest trials now are past, my triumph hath begun…"

There are lots of songs. Songs of love, songs of loss; thoughtful songs, nonsensical songs; songs of hedonism, songs of reflection. They come to us on their own terms, but can only meet us halfway.

The performer provides one part, the listener the other. The liminal territory in between the two is what imbues songs with meaning.

Sometimes the song picks up the listener and carries them far, far away. Sometimes it fails to connect. No fault of the song or even the composer. Other times, it does neither. It simply sits there in a state of potential, waiting for the right moment to mean something. The moment might come, or it might not. That's because a song isn't just harmony, melody, rhythm, or lyrics. A song is a time and a place.

Rick had heard *Angel Band* dozens of times, but never in that moment. Listening to it waft plaintively from deeper in the house, it spoke to him in a way it never had before. All of Rick's longing, his exhaustion, his hopes for peace, seemed wrapped up in those words—words he had heard on countless occasions, but words that had never *connected*.

He grabbed his guitar and entered the addition just in time to join the final refrain. Devlin sat beneath the cracked bedroom window amidst his scattered belongings and the crumbled drywall, looking like the last busker on Earth, trying to raise survivors' spirits in the aftermath of a nuclear holocaust. He sawed away, singing with his eyes closed, and did not react when Rick began strumming. "Oh, bear me away on your snow-white wings to my immortal home," the two finished.

Rick kicked some debris out of the way and sat down beside Devlin on the concrete. The final cadence was still reverberating off the exposed surfaces when he asked, "Where's Bora?"

Devlin sniffed, coughed, and rested his fiddle on his lap. "Left a note," he explained, idly plucking the strings. "Gone to pick up Edna."

Rick nodded, and the two of them sat in silence. "You sound good," he said at last.

"Thankee," Devlin mumbled. He brought the fiddle upright, resting it on his knee. "It was his, y'know? Cillian's. He taught me how to play, too." Devlin rubbed his nose. "He wasn't a bad man, Ricky. Least not that I knew. He saved more lives than he ruined, I promise. Just doing what he thought he had to for his family."

"Tell me more," Rick requested.

Devlin obliged. "Grew up in Ireland," he elaborated. "Came over in the twenties with Grannie, eventually settled down in western North Carolina. Had a farm near the mountains."

"You telling me we grew up in the same town?"

"Practically. Grew up with Mama down outside Marion. Never heard of your kinfolk until I read the diary, though."

"Wonder if we ever ran into each other…"

"Doubt it. Didn't leave town until I left it for good."

"I know what you mean. Why'd you leave?"

"Felt like I had work to do. Daddy left when I was pretty young, so I spent a lotta time around Cillian. When it became obvious I had his gift, he drummed it into my head that I needed to use it to help folks." He looked squarely at Rick. "You don't use it, it makes your life hell."

Rick looked at Devlin skeptically. "You still want me to believe you're psychic, Devlin?" he criticized. "After yesterday?"

Devlin nodded, though Rick wasn't certain whether he was addressing his own authenticity or acknowledging his transgressions. "Lord strike me dead. Seems to come and go, nowadays. Have to rely a lot more on conventional methods."

"So that stuff with Bora's mom…?"

"Ain't nobody's life private no more," Devlin admitted sheepishly. "No such thing as a secret, just things people ain't made the effort to learn. You take enough time and enough money, you can find out anything you want about anybody. Full disclosure? I got a file on you two inches thick in my trunk. You, your family, your bandmates, your closest friends… including Bora."

"That's invasive."

"Ain't saying it's *pretty*," Devlin countered. "I'm saying it *works*. Once was a time the spirits would have told me everything I wanted. Past few years… seems like I'm losing touch. Used to be, they wouldn't stop bugging me. Now it's… spottier. Like bad cellphone coverage. They don't trust me no more. Can't help but think it's blowback from Cillian's dealings."

"Is that how he got his gifts in the first place?" inquired Rick. "By harvesting people?"

Devlin set his fiddle back down on his lap and stared at the empty wall across the room. "He spent some time among them," he said. "Never told me much. From what I gather, he was real young. When something like that touches you at that age, it sticks with you, whether you want it to or not. As far as *why* he was up to *what* he was up to, I didn't learn about his pacts with folks like your daddy until I read the diary. Been wondering ever since. Near as I can reckon, these things felt slighted when Cillian came back to our world. Felt like they'd been robbed. Made him repay his debt with interest. Just a guess, though. S'pose it was the price he had to pay for all they taught him."

Devlin suddenly grinned. "Speaking of which… remember that melody? The one what's been bugging you all year?"

"Of course," said Rick. "Couldn't forget it if I tried."

"They taught him that, too," Devlin declared, positioning his fiddle underneath his chin and bowing a few quick double stops. "Can I show you something?"

"Sure."

"Alright. Start playing it."

Rick hesitated. He had grown to hate that melody. It heralded the hardest year of his life and, artistically speaking, had frustrated him to his breaking point. Still, curiosity got the better of him, and he wondered where Devlin was going. Reluctantly, he cradled his guitar in his lap and began picking at the awkward tune.

Once the first measure passed, Devlin joined in confidently, starting at the beginning. The fiddle and guitar intertwined with the synchronistic transcendence that only music can deliver. Within moments, it was obvious what was happening: it was a round. The answer was so obvious that Rick might have kicked himself, had he not been so enraptured by the result. The mysterious melody was finally yielding its innermost secrets—secrets hiding all along in plain sight.

Every awkward leap found support beneath, every descent a complimentary rise. Each measure bolstered the incomprehensible harmonic shifts of the next in a perfect setup and payoff. As the tune folded in on itself, it made sense of the unreasonable and imparted meaning to the meaningless, like looking back over a lifetime with the hindsight of old age.

This, Rick realized, was what he had failed to understand. The melody *never* needed any ostentatious accompaniment. Everything it needed was there from the start. All it needed was *itself*.

Rick's mouth hung open as Devlin concluded his contribution. All he could do was laugh. His mind began racing with all the ways he could use this in his work. *Maybe I can finally perform this*, he thought. *There's so much there to build upon—*

"Um... Devlin," he said, suddenly somber after realizing how much he was planning for an uncertain future. "If this doesn't work... If we can't figure something out and I have to... kill myself... what will happen?"

Devlin, who had been grinning the entire time, let his expression fall. "Y'know what's funny?" he asked. "Much as me and my colleagues like to think we've got a good handle on the supernatural, we really don't know *shit* about the afterlife. Most of that stuff we think we know, from Dante and the like? All that Medieval writing? Basically early church fan fiction."

"That's not what I mean," Rick clarified, setting his guitar aside. "I made peace with all that stuff as best I could in college. I mean, what happens *if they get to keep me?*"

Devlin slowly shook his head. Never before had Rick seen him so vulnerable, so unsure. In the past, even when he didn't claim an answer instantly, there was always the sense that he would find one. This was no longer the case.

Before Devlin could speak, there was the sound of someone at the door. Leaving his guitar on the floor along with his concerns, Rick leapt to his feet and ran out to the living room. Bora stood in the foyer, wearing jeans and a new hoodie that she had apparently bought on her errands earlier in the day.

"Hey," she greeted, managing a feeble smile. Her eyes and nose were red, as if she had been crying. The gray light seeping in through the windows made her look even more ill. "How you feeling?"

"Splitting headache, on the verge of vomiting," answered Rick. "Y'know, the usual."

"When all this is said and done, we're having a talk," Bora warned, setting her keys on the countertop. "You, me, and Edna."

Rick ignored the threat of an intervention. "How's she doing?" he asked.

"All things considered? Great," replied Bora. "Just set her up over at her house. Got a Life Alert bracelet and everything. She's been living there so long, I don't think she'll have too much trouble adjusting."

"Anything new from the doctors?"

"Still at a loss," she sighed, making her way to the fridge. She grabbed a soft drink, opened it, and downed a big gulp. "Said her vision may come back, may not. Just have to wait and see."

Rick nodded solemnly. "How about you?" he asked. "How are you feeling?"

Bora was about to answer when Devlin stepped into the room. The two of them stared at each other. Rick, caught in the middle, knew he was about to be overwhelmed by a barrage of friendly fire. He backed out of no man's land to seek shelter in the living room.

Both Bora and Devlin opened fire, trying to speak at once, their words mixing in an impenetrable flurry that clouded the air like artillery. Only after they started shouting each other's names did Rick make any sense of what was being said. Devlin was the first to relent and hold up his hands in defeat

"Dev, Dev—Dev," urged Bora, setting down her can. "Please, let me speak. I... I'm still mad at you. You should have told us earlier. Even if it was just a few days." Devlin tried to interject. Bora cut him off. "But—*but*... I understand it."

She stepped around the bar and leaned back against it, as if signaling her vulnerability. "Last week, when you asked about my mom—how it was to hear her diagnosis—I never answered you. Truth is... I never felt anything. I never allowed myself to. It was the first thing that I ever ran away from. Been running ever since. I mean, I have to forgive myself—I was only nine—but I didn't... *engage* with the idea, you know? I spent every minute I could away from that house. With friends, with relatives, anywhere but *there,* with *her.* I should have spent every waking moment with her in those last months, and I didn't. I've regretted that ever since.

"That's why I left Hope. At least, that's what I told myself. When I heard about her mom, I knew what I would be: a distraction. A distraction, when the *only* thing she should be doing is spending every last minute she can with her mother. And I *know* she would have clung to me, I just *know* it, and... I didn't want that for her.

"The things she said when we broke up... the names she called me... made me feel like a monster. And I was, honestly. I *had* to be.

THEM OLD WAYS NEVER DIED

But I didn't explain why. She would have found a reason to stay, and I would have caved. Instead, I just kept everything as simple and straightforward as I could. I had my reasons for doing what I did. I might be able to tell her that someday. Might not."

Bora wiped her eyes. "I did what I thought was best based on my experience. You did what you thought was best based on yours. Again, I wish you would have said something about your grandfather sooner, but… I understand. It made sense to you at the time."

Devlin folded his arms, nodded, and looked toward the foyer. "I'm sorry," he apologized, without looking toward her. "You're right. I should have just spilled the beans earlier. After the séance, maybe." He finally met Bora's eyes. "I've been going it alone for a long time. I forgot what it means to be a team. From here on out, I'm an open book."

Bora smiled. It was much broader and more authentic than the one she had shared earlier with Rick. "If Rick forgives you, then I forgive you," she said. Rick nodded, prompting Bora to step forward and open her arms to Devlin. He cautiously walked toward her and surrendered himself to her embrace. "How's that jaw?" she asked.

Devlin grimaced. "I was just about to call your pharmacy," he chuckled. "Let 'em know that an employee has been popping 'roids at work."

Even as he joked, Devlin looked quite uncomfortable in Bora's embrace. It occurred to Rick that, while chummy, Devlin never seemed the overtly affectionate type. As a rescue attempt, Rick cleared his throat. "Alright you two lovebirds, break it up," he said. "Don't we have work to do?"

"Not really," stated Bora with a shrug. "You slept through it all, Rip van Drinkle. House is salted, all the doorways and windows have horseshoes." She raised an eyebrow and looked back at Devlin. "Unless you have something else for us to do, Dev?"

"Think y'all're good for now," he said, taking a step back. "Just rest up. We should be safe, but there's no telling what the next few days have in store. *I'm* the one who's got homework."

"How so?" wondered Rick.

"Y'all ever read *The Lord of the Rings*?"

"Saw the movies," Bora admitted.

"Remember when Gandalf goes to research the One Ring for nearly two decades?" explained Devlin, rubbing the back of his neck.

Rick and Bora nodded vaguely. "That's me the next few days. While I lied about where I got the diary, I did end up visitin' my friend in Asheville. He loaded me up with a whole mess o' books. They're all in my trunk. Gotta go through 'em, see if I can't find some sort of ritual to shut this shit down once and for all. If I can't find nothing, I'll have to make something up."

"Does that work?" asked Rick.

"Don't worry, Rico," Devlin assured him, returning to his characteristic nonchalance. "All this stuff is bespoke, if'n you go far back enough. That reminds me—you got a laundry basket I could borrow?"

After Rick showed him where to find it, Devlin began hauling inside load after load of books, converting the second bedroom of the addition into a makeshift library. There he remained the rest of the day and into the evening. He even chose to take his dinner in the addition, so he could continue working.

As for Rick, he felt an overwhelming sense of relief. He had no idea how much he needed both Bora *and* Devlin until the two of them were at odds. As he settled in on the couch to watch television with Bora, he reflected on how much he had grown to appreciate this odd little ragtag family over the past week.

The only person missing was Edna. Her predicament still bothered him, but after a quick phone call, Rick assured himself that she would be alright. *She's simply too stubborn to let some minor setback like* blindness *get her down*, he wryly observed.

Rick took a deep breath and, to his surprise, found himself relaxing. Something intangible yet plainly recognizable had descended over the house: a sense of peace, of secure calm. It was similar to the way Rick felt when first putting on his horseshoe pendant. No need for another attack on the house to test their protections; he *knew* they worked, the way you knew how your instrument would react in your hands or that your bandmates would follow your lead. It was a point beyond mere hope, where faith met diligence.

As Rick drifted to sleep that night, his mind repeated the same phrase over and over. It was the second verse of *Angel Band*: "I know I'm near the holy ranks of friends and kindred dear; I hear the waves on Jordan's banks, the crossing must be near...."

45

Thursday, November 5, 2020

SOMETIMES IT COMES TO THAT

RICK SAT UP IN BED WITH A START. For the second night in a row, he had dreamed about Mary… and, for the second morning in a row, he was already starting to forget what she had said. Whatever it was, it felt important.

Rick swung his legs over the edge of the mattress and stared at the floor, hoping that the broad, empty expanse of beige carpet would somehow clear his mind enough to remember. *Something I didn't do?* he thought before immediately rejecting the possibility. *Something I need to do? Something I did, maybe?*

Nothing seemed quite right. The more Rick tried to remember, the more he forgot. Shrugging in defeat, he started getting ready for the day, hoping that concentrating on the mundane might jog his memory.

As he dressed, an uneasily familiar feeling settled over him. He had felt the same at the start yesterday: a sense of stasis, like all forward progress had been halted. While the house undeniably felt safer, there was nonetheless the sensation of treading water with weights tied to your ankles. He was managing to stay afloat, but the scenario was unsustainable.

As harrowing as his return to Ellijay had proven, at least he felt preoccupied when under attack. The stillness since Monday had become nerve-wracking. All they could do was wait while Devlin formulated a plan. In the meantime, a gigantic, imaginary countdown clock had set up shop in Rick's head, the numbers inevitably dwindling with each passing minute. They were running out of time, and he couldn't do anything to stop it.

Rick plodded out to the kitchen. It was empty, but the fresh pot of coffee indicated that someone else was awake. He poured himself a cup and replaced the clock with an image of Mary, alone in the forest. Her lips were moving, but her speech remained elusive.

There was a word, he remembered, taking a sip. *It started with a 'p.' 'Pierce'? 'Purchase'?*

Turning toward the patio, he found Devlin and Bora already outside, sitting in the swing, talking. While he was by no means the early riser of the group—that honor went to Bora—Rick was surprised to see Devlin so alert before noon. *I wonder what the occasion is...* he thought, stepping outside.

"There's the man of the hour!" shouted Devlin above the squeaking chains. "Pop a squat, Rickster."

Rick settled into a chalky white plastic lawn chair across the patio. Under calmer circumstances, it would have been the quintessential fall morning in Georgia. There wasn't a cloud in the sky. This emptiness not only imparted a clarity to the air—a chill so crisp it could snap—but also permitted the sun to shine down completely unhindered, even underneath the awning of the patio. The cold air and warm sunlight kept the temperature in perfect balance. The only thing remotely uncomfortable was the field itself. The sun was so bright, it was hard to look at, each blade of grass transformed into a beam of light, the trees on Red Ear a riot of fiery red and orange.

Even if he hadn't been hungover, Rick would have wished for a pair of sunglasses. "'Rickster'?," he repeated after taking another sip. "You're running out of nicknames, bud. Because if you start doing variations on 'Dick,' you're getting punched in the face again." Everyone laughed. "Why are you so chipper?" asked Rick after the chuckles subsided.

"Well, *Penis*," Devlin began, "are you as tired as I am of gettin' our asses handed to us? Being *reactive* instead of *proactive*?"

"Hell yeah," affirmed Rick. To this he silently added: *'Proactive'? Was that what Mary said?*

Bora smiled. She was curled up on the swing, leaving Devlin to do the rocking. "Dev was just telling me he's figured it out," she explained. Rick raised his eyebrows.

"Hold your horses," said Devlin, lighting a cigarette. "Ain't quite there. Still plenty to figure out."

Rick waited for Devlin to elaborate. When he failed to, Rick said nothing but instead leaned forward and opened his free hand expectantly.

"I have... *outlined*... a ritual that I think gives you the best chance of breaking the agreement," Devlin offered.

Rick was ecstatic. "Okay," he said eagerly, with all the exuberance of an addict promised a fresh hit. "C'mon, let's see it! Tell me!"

Devlin took a drag. "Still ironin' out the details," he exhaled. "Never found a perfect match for your situation, so I'm having to cobble together somethin' new."

These were not the words Rick wanted to hear. He wanted Devlin to say that he had found some ancient, arcane verse of immeasurable power.

'The spell that once bound Bubblebutt, Archduke of Hell,' or 'The charm that banished the Great Leprechaun from the Isle of Shamrock O'Darby,' Rick suggested to himself. *It doesn't have to make sense or even sound real; it just has to be something with a proven track record. Something tried and true.* Hanging his salvation on an experimental ritual fashioned out of whole cloth was far from the panacea he hoped Devlin would provide.

"So it's something you... just made up?" mumbled Rick, crestfallen.

"It's *all* made up, Ricky," Devlin retorted. "You think the Canaanites just woke up one day singing hymns to Asherah? The real power behind these things lies in the *intent*." Devlin's boots ground the swing to a halt. He stared at Rick with his mismatched eyes, looking dead serious. "Do you trust me?" he whispered.

After taking a deep breath, Rick decided that he had no other choice and said, "Yes."

"Good," Devlin said. The swing resumed its gentle swaying. "So we got the *when*—three hunnerd and sixty-six days after your daddy's death, which is Sunday—and we got the *what* and the *where*. I'll have the *how* nailed down by tonight."

It was Bora's turn to speak. "Hang on—what do you mean, 'We've got the *where*?"

"Feldspar mine, of course," Devlin replied casually, looking out toward the mountain. "Conrad Coulter never sold them holdings."

Rick was taken aback. "What, in *Spruce Pine?*"

"Think you can still find it?"

"Yeah. I mean, a lot's changed there... I'm pretty sure I drove by it on my way back from the visitation, but..." Rick saw so many holes in Devlin's plan. He had no idea where to start. "Okay, slow down. Why do we need to go *there*? Why not some place safer? We spent all day Monday protecting this place—"

"—*we* spent all day Monday protecting this place—" corrected Bora.

"—why not do it here?" pressed Rick. "Can't we just… I dunno… do another Estes session, call them out?"

"*Another* Estes session?" sneered Devlin. "After *that* bloodbath on Samhain? Even if you wanted to take that approach, ain't no way of making sure it would work. Remember: *repeatable, but not on demand.* It'd be better if we could guarantee their presence. Do you want to chance them not puttin' in an appearance on the night that their magic is most vulnerable? Might work without 'em, but I think we stand the best chance if they're present. They've been invading your *home*, Ricky. Time to turn the tables."

"Hang on," Bora objected. "You're always talking about them existing outside of time, outside of space, outside of… everything. What difference does it make where we are? Hell, they seem to love the mountain so much, let's just do it up there."

Devlin closed his eyes and pinched the bridge of his nose. "The mountain's just a staging area, Bora. Spruce Pine is ground zero for them—where the deal was sealed with Conrad, where Mary disappeared, shit, it's probably where they operated when they were dealing with Granpap… *Ricky, you gotta go home if you wanna save yourself.* If you wanna save your son." When he looked up, Devlin could tell that neither Rick nor Bora were convinced.

"Story time," Devlin announced after clearing his throat. "Spent a while in Madhya Pradesh back in the late nineties. There was this boy. Kept disappearing. Didn't seem to be nothing attached to him; just your regular run-of-the-mill teleportation, right? Eventually I helped him get it under control, but for the longest time, he was petrified."

A momentary distraction seized Rick. *'Petrified'?* he wondered. *Did Mary say, 'Petrified'?*

"Whole damn family was scared, actually," continued Devlin. "Everyone, that is, except his granpap. While everyone else ran around in hysterics, this old dude—Arjun—he just took it all in stride. So one night, I'm sitting up late with him, watching over the boy, and I ask him, 'Arj—how the hell are you keeping it together, my man?'

"He just says, 'I've been through worse.' I ask him what that is. Says it's a long story. And I say, 'Shit, we've got all night, and I love me a good story.'

"Arj tells me that a man-eater attacked his village when he was a young man. This big fuckin' tiger would slip into town every couple nights, for weeks on end, and just pluck people right outta their beds. Everyone was too terrified to do anything about it. Everyone, that is, except Arjun. After he lost a brother, he spent every night on the roof with a rifle, waiting for this sumbitch to come back.

"Lotta nights it didn't. Some nights it did. Arj even got off a few shots at the tiger, but always missed. It was too far away, too quick. This lil' game dragged on for about three weeks before Arj gets the stones to track it. Said he'll never forget how massive them pawprints was in the mud, how they seemed to get bigger the deeper he went into the forest. Finally, he finds the tiger's den. He goes inside, expecting an ambush, and finds the thing asleep. It's the clearest shot he ever had. Point blank. No chance of missing. He empties every bullet he has into the man-eater."

Devlin leaned forward, cigarette smoke coiling a wreath around his face. "*That's* why *we* have to go to the mine," he said. Devlin then ran his tongue across his teeth. "Y'know what else Arj did? He took a knife with him. Ended up skinning the fucker, walked back a hometown hero with its hide draped over his shoulder. But Arjun, he told me that ain't why he brought the knife. Nope. He looked me square in the eyes, just like I'm lookin' at you, Ricky, and said: 'The knife was for *me*. Because *sometimes it comes to that*.'"

Devlin flicked his cigarette butt out of the shadows and into the brightly lit field. Everyone sat there, wondering what to say next. A few songbirds chirped on their way past the patio, blissfully unaware of the weight of their conversation. Rick was lost in thought, though he wasn't thinking about man-eating tigers. He was thinking about salmon heading upstream.

"I understand," admitted Rick at last. "I'm ready to do what I have to. But there are still a lot of logistical issues you haven't considered. That mine's been flooded for thirty years."

"I know," Devlin responded flatly. "Gotta be another way in. Always is."

"Good luck with that. I don't think you realize how big that place is. It'll take days for us to find another entrance. We don't have that." When he said this, Devlin looked truly stumped.

"There's got to be another way," Bora interjected following a long drag on her vape. "Something we haven't thought about. Maybe... maybe we're looking at this all wrong."

Rick sat bolt upright. "What did you say?" he asked excitedly.

"Uh... 'There's something we haven't thought about'?"

"No, no, after that."

"'Maybe we're looking at this all wrong'?"

Rick collapsed in his chair. Bora's phrase had triggered his memory. Mary's words came rushing back to him. He had no idea what they meant, but they seemed worth sharing.

"Y'all may think I'm crazy," he slowly started, "and this may not be relevant at all, but... the last two nights, I've dreamed about Mary."

Devlin perked up. "Pray tell?"

"I don't remember much, but she said something to me."

"What was it?"

"I'm not sure," Rick murmured in frustration. "There was a word. 'Perceive.' And something about a wetnurse..."

"Wetnurse?" clarified Devlin. "Or midwife?"

Rick snapped his fingers. "That's it! How did you know? It was something like, 'Perceive thine holdings with midwife's gaze.'"

Devlin was on his feet and back inside so quickly that Rick barely had time to register his absence. When he dashed back through the open patio door, he held a book in his hand. "You're a goddamn genius Ricky!" he proclaimed breathlessly. "Or your sister is. Either way, I know exactly how we're gonna find our way back into the mine."

"How?" asked Bora.

Devlin didn't bother to sit. He held the book aloft like a preacher brandishing a Bible at an old-fashioned revival and began explaining himself with equal gusto. "Over the centuries, people have come up with lots of ways to see their world," he explained. "Some say you can look through hagstones, others say you can fast. Folks like me don't have to do *nothing*, you just see it all the time. Unfortunately, I can't do that no more, but I don't have to: *you* are going to find the way there, Ricky."

"How so?" wondered Rick.

"*Ointment.* It's gotta be what Mary was driving at. There's a whole class of stories where a *midwife*—just as she said—is summoned by a black rider to attend a f... *fairy* birth. She delivers the baby and, depending on the version, has to administer ointment to the child on a daily basis. One day, whether by accident or design, the midwife touches her own eye with the ointment and *voila!*"—Devlin snapped his fingers—"She sees *everything*. It strips away their glamour, allows you to cut through the bullshit. You see their world for the way it truly is."

"Like psychedelics, or something?" asked Bora skeptically. "We're going to get Rick high and send him underground?"

"That ain't *in*correct," Devlin answered.

"What could go wrong?" quipped Bora.

Devlin looked at Rick, jabbing a finger at the cover of the book. "You use what's described in here, and it'll make finding a new entrance to the mine a piece of cake."

"Where do we get this 'ointment,' exactly?" asked Bora. "Got some in your pocket, or something?"

"Gotta make it," Devlin explained.

"Neat," Rick chimed in sarcastically. "What's the recipe?"

"There were lots," answered Devlin. He began pacing back and forth, thumbing through the pages. "Real 'eye of newt' shit."

"Is it safe?" asked Rick. "Am I going to go blind?"

"Dunno," Devlin admitted, not looking up from the book. "Never tried it. Never had the need. Far sight safer'n forced suicide, though." He stopped on one of the pages. "A-ha! Let's see... Good, good... don't have that... I can substitute ragwort..." At last he looked up. "I have most of this stuff in my trunk. Hollyhock and hazel buds, four-leaf clover, broom, the usual suspects. Only a few things I need." He buried his nose back in the book. "Water from boiled eggs, that's simple enough," he rambled. "Cowslip, Edna has that out front, I clocked it when I first got here... yikes. Okay, this'll be a problem."

"What is it?" asked Bora. "What do we not have?"

"Two things, actually," said Devlin. "Time is one of 'em. Says this needs to sit in the sun for three days." He glanced out at the field.

"Looks like the weather's cooperatin', at least. But it means we'll have to put this together today or first thing tomorrow, if it's gonna be ready in time."

"What's the other thing?"

"Says here, 'Wild thyme harvested from hill slopes where the Gentry trod.'"

"No problem," Rick remarked dismissively, pointing at Red Ear Mountain. "Got your hill right there."

Devlin sat down on the swing beside Bora, looking pained. "Not exactly what they mean," he muttered.

"I mean, it's a hill, right?" argued Bora. "And we've seen lights up there."

"Naw," Devlin maintained, shaking his head. "They mean a fort."

"Fort?"

"In Ireland, there are these ancient structures, right? Hillforts, ringforts, and the like. People believe them places are where the Good Folk live."

"A fort isn't a hill," stated Rick.

"I was getting to that," Devlin scolded. "All across Europe, there are other sites. Some are natural hills. A lot are actually old burial mounds. Supposedly, the Gentry hang out there, too."

He waved his hands like he was pouring water from one invisible glass to another. "Part of how these things overlap with the human dead," he explained. "If we had more time, we'd hop on a plane overseas and get what we need. Unfortunately, we ain't got nothing quite like that around here. At least nowhere we can get our ingredients. I mean, there's burials at Etowah, but that place is so heavily managed, I can tell you there ain't no wild thyme growing on any of the mounds there. Same problem up in Franklin with Nĭkwăsĭ—there's a long history of the *Nûñnë'hĭ* there, but I'm not aware of any burials. Besides, they nuked that mound with herbicide a while back, ain't nothing growing there but grass. There's Fort Mountain just up the road, but are there any burials there? Not sure…"

"Wait," Bora said. "Are you telling me that we need to find an Indian burial ground?"

"*Mound*, not ground," corrected Devlin. "America's hotspots for paranormal activity. Here in the southeast, the Cherokee Little People legends are shockingly similar to those in Ireland—right down to their association with earthworks. Ain't as strong as in the old country, but it's there."

Bora inhaled deeply and told everyone to get quiet. Then she pulled out her phone and dialed Edna.

46

Thursday, November 5, 2020

FOXHOLE

"It's the same creek."

Devlin had already vaulted to the other side. Rick, on the other hand, stared pensively at the green slope below his feet, tongue pressed against the roof of his mouth, trying to evaluate Bora's observation.

It was a shallow stream, with mossy banks only a foot or two high. Between them, clean water tumbled leisurely over light brown sand, clumps of dead leaves, and stones sculpted smooth by the hands of time. A patch of red mud lurked a little further down the bend, thickened by days of rain. Pools gathered here and there, sitting so clear and calm that it almost looked like the minnows who called them home hovered above the sand, rather than swam beneath the surface. After finally taking in the serenity, Rick was forced to admit that the entire scene looked familiar, but he wasn't enough of an outdoorsman to say definitively.

"It probably doubled back on itself," he speculated before leaping across the water and landing on the opposite bank. He turned and held out a hand for Bora over the gap.

"Nope," she disagreed after thanking him for his help. "I don't quite have a photographic memory, but after years of painting, it's gotten pretty good. And I'm telling you: This is the same creek."

The two of them scurried after Devlin, who was already weaving back through the trees. He had almost mounted the rise up ahead.

"We've been following Edna's directions to the tee," said Rick, clutching a narrow trunk to secure his ascent. "She told us to enter at the trailhead, take the left fork of the path, and circle around to the southside of the mountain. 'You'll see a bunch of old, rusted oil drums,' she said. 'Leave the trail there, and after about two hundred yards, you'll pass over a crick.'"

"One 'crick,'" Bora reminded him. "Not two."

They reached the top of the small ridge and caught their breath. It was approaching four o'clock, and their hike had lasted long enough to push them beyond being merely winded. They were exhausted.

"Devlin!" shouted Rick to the figure forging through the tapestry of leaf litter below. "Quick break?" Devlin nodded and set down his messenger bag.

Rick and Bora took off their backpacks and sat down. While the detour to retrieve their belongings was wise—they had no idea how long it would take to find the mounds, and their backpacks held ample supplies should something go wrong—it had delayed their excursion's departure until mid-afternoon. Now, with the light shifting from white to gold and the shadows angling more with each passing minute, being caught outside after dark became a distinct possibility.

What's done is done, Rick thought, unzipping his bag and taking out his bottle of vodka. *At least I've got this.* He took a swig, followed by a little water. He offered a sip to Bora, but she declined.

"I can't believe I've known Edna over a year and she's never told me about these supposed mounds," grumbled Rick as he screwed the lid back on. "She's known you, what, a week?"

"What can I say?" grinned Bora as she rubbed her calves through her jeans. "People trust me."

"How did it even come up?"

"We had a lot of time to chat on Halloween, before the shit hit the fan," Bora explained. "She said the burial mounds were the main reason she hasn't been able to sell any of her land."

Rick thrust out his lower lip and grunted. He watched as Devlin leaned up against a tree, smoking. "Grows on you, doesn't he?" he asked.

"Yeah," Bora answered after giving it some thought. "Like... an entertaining skin tag."

For the next while, neither of them spoke. They sat there, listening to the wind trace through the branches. To their right, the face of Red Ear Mountain took on a life of its own, the trees snapping into motion like erect hairs on the side of a massive, agitated animal.

In the handful of days since the Estes session, the vibrancy of the leaves had notably progressed. Just over a week from now, their colors would be replaced with a final monochromatic wash of brown before they dropped entirely. Rick was grateful to live in the south but always felt disappointed by autumn. He loved the season, but it was all too brief down here. It only seemed to last a week or two between the oppressive summer heat and glum winter chill.

Movement caught Rick's eye. Devlin finished his cigarette, offered a quick wave, then started walking again. "Guess that's our cue," he said, throwing on his backpack and heading downhill.

The landscape afforded several minutes of even terrain, allowing everyone to catch their breath. Devlin always remained a few steps ahead, saying very little beyond the occasional urge for them to keep up. They kept waiting for the next landmark in Edna's directions to appear. They were looking for an old fence erected after a property feud between two of her distant relatives.

As they trudged onward, however, nothing changed. There was just the same expanse of forest, moderately thick, with no sign of the fence. Doubt began creeping in.

Maybe Bora's right, Rick thought, slowing to step around a cluster of roots hidden in the leaves. *Maybe we're lost. Or maybe Edna's wrong. I mean, when was the last time she was out here? A lot could have changed over the years...*

Devlin stopped atop a slight rise just ahead. Rick joined him, only to have his heart immediately sink. When Bora took her place, she stomped a foot in frustration.

"It's the same creek," she declared.

"It's the same fucking creek," conceded Rick, looking up and down its length.

"We're going around in circles."

"In a fashion," Devlin amended, speaking for the first time in a while. "If I had to hazard a guess, I'd say we're being pixie-led."

"Huh?" huffed Rick.

"More of their shenanigans," Devlin said. He swatted a bug out of his face. "They like to lead you astray, make familiar territory unfamiliar. No worries. This is a good thing. Means there's somethin' out here they don't want us to find—"

A series of staccato cries interrupted Devlin, rising from deep in the forest somewhere upstream. The voice was small and shrill, and struggled to catch its breath between the longer whines.

Bora's eyes widened. "Is that a... baby?" she asked. It was the closest match for what they were hearing.

"*That*," Devlin corrected, pointing in its general direction, "is a trap. Ignore it." The warning was difficult to heed. Deep in his bones, Rick felt an overpowering compulsion to rush in the direction of the noise. The idea of an abandoned infant on a chilly day in the woods was too much to bear.

Devlin sensed his apprehension. "Ride it out," he commanded, placing a hand on Rick's chest.

Sure enough, the sound decrescendoed. The space between each cry lengthened, then stopped entirely. There was a sniffle, then a cough. Rick thought he heard a sharper vocalization at the end, like a guffaw. Devlin removed his hand.

Bora made two fists and pounded them together, trying to dissipate her lingering anxiety. "What now?" she wondered.

Devlin slipped off his bag and sat down, legs splayed, focusing on the stream below. "There's a way out of this," he mumbled, "but for the life of me I can't remember exactly what." He reached into his pocket and pulled out his pack of cigarettes. "It'll come to me. In the meantime—as a wiser wizard once said—'I am too weary to decide... I need smoke.'" He lit up, inhaled, and rested his forearms on his knees.

Rick and Bora exchanged glances, not knowing what to do. They simply settled in beside him. By the time Devlin lit his third cigarette, Rick was fighting off full-blown panic.

If we can't get there, *what does that mean for getting* back? he thought. *What if we're stranded? Everyone's phones are either dead or dying.*

He looked at his hands. They were shaking. Rick grabbed his vodka from the backpack and took a long drink before replacing it.

Spotting him, Devlin said, "Now probably ain't the time, but... you know you're gonna have to kick that at some point, right?"

"Correct on both counts," said Rick, clenching and releasing his fists.

Devlin waited a few seconds before pursuing the topic. "Ricky, every day for you is like today. Lost. All the time. And that ain't the way stories are s'posed to go. Not the way *your* story's s'posed to go. You can't stay trapped in Mirkwood forever; you have to push through. You have to slay the dragon. That's the arc that the universe wants you to fulfill. When you fail these archetypal stories, when you violate these principles... you're defyin' something more powerful than any of us. You literally degrade the universe."

Rick was growing tired of Devlin's pseudopsychological ramblings. At best, they never made much sense; at worst, they sounded preachy. Personal growth was all well and good, but they had bigger problems right now, here in the real world. Trying to defuse the intervention, he thought back to a humorous sign he once noticed on the wall at Terry Mac's.

"I told myself I'd quit drinking, but I'm not about to listen to a drunk who talks to himself," he joked. "Now, if you don't mind, can we stop talking about me and focus on the matter at hand?"

Devlin just shook his head and took another drag on his cigarette. "You *are* the matter at hand," he mumbled.

Rick tried to formulate a suitable comeback but drew a blank. It didn't take long for his inner monologue to resume its panicked spiral.

The only person who knows where we are is Edna, he realized. *Jack and Cassie will figure it out eventually, but until then, Cassie will just think I'm on a bender. It'll take forever for them to send someone to rescue us. If I die in the woods, this curse will pass on to Jack. He'll have to go through all the same shit that I have and either be driven to suicide or live life thinking he's crazy until he passes it on to* his *son. He'll live his entire life thinking I abandoned him, like that baby in the woods. I can't....*

In one erratic motion, Rick stood, tossed on his backpack, ran downhill, and hurdled across the stream. Somewhere behind him, Devlin and Bora protested, but he didn't care. He had to find the mound, had to get the ingredients, had to find a second entrance to the mine, had to save himself and his son.

He ran. Cold air seared his lungs. Each breath carried the taste of copper. He tripped and stumbled several times, catching a face full of leaves, but this barely impeded his progress. He pressed onward, darting between the trees and up and down ridges. Each ascent was a manic struggle, each descent a barely controlled slide to the bottom. Again and again he climbed, until, several rises later, his legs gave out. Down he tumbled, hitting rocks and stumps and whirling head over heels…

... until, at last, Rick found himself face-down in the mud. He was wet and freezing, and could already pinpoint a dozen fresh bruises. Gasping for air, Rick lifted his head and tried to wipe his face clean. When he cleared his eyes, he saw a wall of green moss.

Rick was lying in the same fucking creek. He pushed himself further out of the water, but was already completely soaked from the waist up. At the moment, his physical needs overrode his worries. He gently touched his side, thinking that he might have broken a rib. Bruised, at least.

As he assessed his injuries, Rick noticed the sound of his name gradually growing louder. He was mildly amazed at how quickly Devlin and Bora had closed the distance. They struggled down to the water's edge and each grabbed an arm, lifting Rick to his feet.

"Jesus Christ!" scolded Bora, brushing a clump of leaves out of his hair. "Rick, what the hell were you thinking?" Devlin just shook his head disapprovingly.

"I'm sorry," Rick apologized. "I panicked."

"Well, now you're filthy and cold," Bora shot back between breaths. "And we're no closer to the mounds. I hope you're happy."

Rick glanced down at the mess that his clothes had become. His white t-shirt looked more like a brown and red tie-dye. The portions not buried underneath clods of mud were practically transparent from the water. The only thing to be thankful for was the fact that it was mostly his upper half that wound up in the stream. His pants were dirty, but mostly avoided getting wet.

You were *anxious,* Rick lectured himself. *Now you're anxious, dirty, wet, and hurt. Great job, Rick.* He limped out of the creek bed and sat down on the bank.

Devlin and Bora just looked down at him, breathing heavily. After a few seconds, they dispersed. Devlin steadied himself on a nearby tree, doubled over, gasping for breath. Bora sat down, then fell onto her back, gazing up at the canopy.

An idea occurred to Rick. He took off his backpack and felt around inside. The contents somehow managed to stay dry—including an old Rib Wrenches tee he packed on Halloween. Without saying a word, he took off his dirty shirt and mopped his chest as dry as he could. His horseshoe pendant was muddy as well, so he removed and cleaned it, too. He then tossed the old shirt aside and changed into the new one.

"Had a spare," he wheezed, collapsing alongside Bora. "Never let it be said OCD isn't worth something."

Bora looked at the black shirt and said, "It's inside out, dingus."

Rick didn't care. But Bora's criticism caught Devlin's attention. He straightened up, took a long look at the creek, and walked toward them. "Richard fuckin' Coulter," he said as he stared down. "Whoever said that 'God watches out for drunks and fools' must've been thinkin' of you."

Rick closed his eyes and shook his head. "For once, Devlin, I wish you'd just say what you mean," he moaned.

"You did it," Devlin said with a chuckle. "You fuckin' did it. That's the way you get outta being pixie-led."

"What?"

"You flip a piece of clothing inside out," explained Devlin. "Don't ask me how or why it works, but that's what the old stories say. What I couldn't remember." With his head, he gestured over his shoulder. "Take a gander."

Rick followed the motion and awkwardly lifted his head off the ground. To his amazement, the creek had vanished. The dip in the landscape remained, but there were no mossy banks, no trickle of water, no sand or muddy patches. Instead, there was simply a depression filled with a thick layer of leaves. Where the stream once flowed, jutting out like vertebrae from a long-lost burial, ran a length of weathered fenceposts, held together here and there by strands of rusted barbed wire.

Bora wearily rose to her feet. "I would say, 'I can't believe it,'" she said, brushing off her clothes. "But at this point, I'd be lying. I keep hoping to wake up from a coma in a hospital." She stepped forward and placed a shoe on a section of barbed wire. The metal groaned as it bent to touch the ground. "Ladies first," she joked. Rick and Devlin staggered past, and Bora fell in behind.

While the creek had been the most recognizable feature that kept reappearing, Rick realized that the entire layout of the forest had been repeating for the better part of an hour. Only now, in the midst of new surroundings, did he comprehend how much had remained the same. The trees were sparser here, allowing greater visibility. Accordingly, the three hikers spread out, covering more ground while still remaining within eyeshot.

They trudged onward for another fifteen minutes, keeping watch for anything out of the ordinary. Before they left, Devlin showed them some pictures online of what they were looking for, though he emphasized that they should be prepared for the mounds to appear quite different. Unlike those converted into well-manicured heritage sites, the earthworks on Edna's property were sure to be overgrown and might look like nothing more than inconspicuous hills covered in bushes and trees.

Rick pushed forward, becoming increasingly concerned about the return journey. He was exhausted and in pain, and he didn't know how much more he had left in him. To add insult to injury—*Literally,* he thought, feeling his aching ribs—the sun was beginning to set.

Hopefully we're not 'pixie-led' on the way back, too, he brooded while hopscotching between several logs and stumps. *I wonder if that power stick I packed still has a charge. If all our phones die, maybe we can still reach Edna, get her to guide us back. Or send help.*

To lighten his spirits, Rick began internally reciting the lyrics to Warren Zevon's *Lawyers, Guns and Money*. They eventually found their way to his lips. "… the shit has hit the fan," he half-sung, half-spoke as he neared the upper threshold of a shallow gully.

That was when Bora shouted, "I love you, Edna Durchdenwald!" Looking to his left in her direction, Rick watched Bora disappear over the top of the rise. Devlin crossed Rick's path from the right, running deeper into the woods, leaving him no choice but to pick up the pace himself.

When he emerged from the gully, Rick saw his friends not thirty yards away. They were crouching behind a low pile of stones, whispering excitedly to each other. A huddle of bushes and scrub sprouted between the rocks, no higher than Rick's chest. As he drew nearer, Rick could tell that Devlin and Bora cowered behind not just a simple pile of stones, but rather the remnants of an ancient wall. Similar stacks of rubble stretched to either side, some longer than others, before trailing off into the trees.

Beyond the ruins, a small break in the undergrowth separated them from a wild tangle of trees and flora skewering the landscape at odd angles. Beneath this cover stood a trio of hillocks in a staggered line beginning another twenty yards away. Each reached perhaps fifteen feet into the air.

Right away, Rick could tell that they were man made. The angle of their slopes was too abrupt to be natural, their tops far too flat. At the same time, Rick knew that he would have never spotted them if he hadn't been actively searching for them. The amount of vegetation provided an excellent disguise, holding up against all but the closest scrutiny, like a thick beard grown to conceal someone's identity.

Rick approached the stone wall reverently, passing underneath a series of taller trees towering above. Their branches pitched inward with enough coverage to rival a pavilion roof. The few leaves they held met rays from the sunset, piercing them like panes of stained glass and spilling red-tinted shadows across the forest floor. A monastic silence permeated the entire scene. Rick sensed the presence of something undeniably old and sacred, no less holy than the interior of a grand cathedral but far more dangerous.

Devlin looked back toward Rick and, noticing him, waved him closer with one hand while gesturing for him to crouch with the other. Rick tried to comply, but found his knees far too weak. Instead, he dropped to all fours and gently pushed through the leaf litter until he reached the pile of stones.

"Is that them?" he asked, fully aware of the answer.

Devlin held a finger to his lips, then pivoted it ninety degrees in the direction of the nearest mound. Rick's eyes followed it to the hillside. At first, he saw nothing—just a few patches of sunlight that managed to penetrate the undergrowth. Then he understood that these were not tenacious sunbeams but rather small patches of animated light, none bigger than a golf ball. Rick counted three. They slipped between the branches and brambles, passing in and out of view. Once or twice they passed in front of the vegetation, revealing themselves as the familiar luminous orbs Rick had come to dread.

"Great," said Rick as quietly as he could. "What do we do?"

"Nothing *to* do but wait," Devlin replied. "See if they go away. When they do, that's when we sneak in and hope there's some wild thyme somewhere up there."

"What am I looking for?"

"*You?*" whispered Bora in disbelief. "Are you nuts? You're the one they're—"

Rick held up a hand. "I'm *done*, Bora," he hissed sharply. "The two of you have risked yourselves enough. I'm done offloading my problems. This is *my* responsibility. Let me do this *one* thing." His demeanor softened. "Please?"

Bora started to object. She simply looked at the ground in defeat.

Devlin peered over the stones. The orbs of light continued bouncing along the hillside of the nearest mound. "Ain't flowering right now, so you wanna look for the leaves," he whispered, staring at the spheres. "Might be bluish-green, might be kinda hairy. Best way to tell is the aroma, it'll probably smell like oregano. They're creeping. Does that help? Know what that means?"

Rick nodded. Just to be sure, he fished out his phone. Although its battery was dangerously low, it still held enough charge for him to complete a quick image search online. After a few swipes, he got the general idea of what he needed to find.

"They've moved on to the next hill," Bora quietly announced.

"Good," said Devlin. "Keep waiting."

Sneaking a glance above the tumbling wall, Rick saw that the trio of orbs had indeed moved down the chain of mounds. By now, the sun was low enough to remove any lingering doubt that the spheres were a trick of the light. That bothered Rick—there was no way they'd be leaving in daylight now—but it also provided a measure of short-term comfort. The lights were much easier to see in the gathering darkness. They floated around the tree trunks of the second mound, chasing one another with a playfulness belying their true nature. Now and again one would stop and draw closer to the earth, as if examining a plant, then take off again to shoulder height.

Slowly, the orbs left the second mound for the third, bobbing off one at a time. Now, they were fifty yards away and looked like little more than pinpoints of light glowing among the trees. Rick felt like it might be enough distance if he stuck to the first hill.

"I'm going," he announced, and started heading around the corner on all fours. Bora grabbed his shirt, but Rick preempted her protests before she could say anything. "It's going to be dark soon," he whispered. "They're far enough away. I'll be okay." Realizing it was useless to hold him back, Bora opened her hand and let Rick slip around the corner.

As he did, Devlin offered one last word of encouragement. "Keep swimmin' upstream, Ricky," he said, nodding approvingly. "Keep swimmin' upstream."

Rick knew he had to move slowly but couldn't afford to stop. He gently pushed forward, trying to rattle the dead leaves as little as possible beneath his hands and knees. A few times, his hand touched a twig, and—knowing any snap might draw the orbs' attention—he gently set it aside. After a few minutes, he had reached the foot of the nearest mound. While the lights had not disappeared from their current position, none of them seemed to notice his presence either. He could only hope that they weren't making the rounds from hillside to hillside, that they wouldn't be restarting their patrol at the first mound.

Rick sat back on his heels, trying to make sense of the jumble of vegetation before him. The side of the mound was teeming with plants and smothered in dead leaves. It felt incredibly futile, like searching for the proverbial needle in a haystack. Rick spotted a possible candidate—small, green leaves, creeping—pinched a bit, and held it to his nose. No fragrant aroma, just a nondescript plant odor.

As quickly as he dared, Rick made a clockwise circle around the base of the mound, stopping to search every few feet. Most of the time, there was nothing even remotely resembling wild thyme. Doubts began to form that he would find anything. Each time his search yielded nothing, he would look back in the direction of his friends, shake his head, and continue.

Soon, he had completely circled the entire mound. He saw no other choice but to resume his slow, steady journey and head to the second.

Upon reaching his destination, Rick noticed movement by the stone wall. Bora's shadow was excitedly pointing toward the third mound. Rick looked down the line and saw that the lights had begun a slow procession back in his direction. For a second, all he wanted to do was flee back to the safety of the wall, but he restrained himself. It would only draw the lights' attention. Instead, Rick just went completely limp, literally burying his face in the leaves.

He lay like that for what felt like forever. Nothing happened. Rick cautiously tilted his head up and saw that the lights had returned to the first mound. If they spent as much time there as they did initially, Rick suspected that he had about ten minutes before the orbs descended upon his position.

He gradually raised himself back up to his hands and knees and began probing around in the darkness, grabbing anything that looked remotely like what he needed. Nothing. He started methodically circling the second mound, his search becoming more frantic. A trail of plants, yanked up by the fistful, roots and all, stretched behind him.

C'mon, c'mon, c'mon, he begged, snatching everything green. *For fuck's sake, just let me find—*

A pungent aroma hit Rick's nostrils. It was unmistakable. He dropped his nose to the ground and began sniffing like a bloodhound, searching for the source of the smell. Finally, he found it: a cluster of low, creeping plants that smelled like oregano. Rick reached out with both hands and grabbed as much as he could.

Suddenly, the hillside flared, and a shadow coalesced before Rick. It was his own. There was no need to look, nor was there any time; without a doubt, one of the orbs hovered somewhere close behind. Rick lurched to his feet and took off at top speed back in the direction of Bora and Devlin. His heart felt like a piledriver in his chest, fueled by a cocktail of adrenaline, fatigue, and dread.

Rick was about halfway to the wall when he tripped and fell to his stomach. At least that was what he initially thought. It wasn't until he started sliding backward that he fully understood the ghastly nature of his predicament. Something invisible had slammed him from behind, seized him by his pants, and started dragging him back to the mounds. No good could come from its success.

Rick kicked wildly and dug his knuckles into the dirt, refusing to surrender his hard-won harvest. None of it helped. He continued sliding backwards. Each time he resisted, the grip on his leg only tightened.

Through a whirlwind of debris, Rick caught glimpses of Bora and Devlin standing by the wall. They had abandoned all secrecy to stand fully upright. He could tell that they wanted to intervene, but he knew what they were thinking: they were helpless. The only thing they could do was watch him flail about and hope that he might somehow break free.

Ride it out, Rick reminded himself as his face scraped against the twigs. *Just ride it out—remember Jack—resist the darkness—they can hurt you, but they can't kill you—can't take you—you're wearing your—*

To his horror, something dawned on Rick. The familiar weight of his necklace was nowhere to be found. Thinking through the panic, the only thing he could deduce was that he had forgotten to replace it after falling in the creek. Now, he was vulnerable in a way he had not been in weeks.

With this new wave of terror came a fresh surge of adrenaline. Rick kicked and screamed. His fists, accustomed to beating the ground, now connected with nothing but empty space. The earth had fallen away below him. Somehow, he was suspended upside down, about five feet in the air. Five became six, six became seven, seven became eight.

He barely found the words: "Devlin!" he shouted. "My pendant! I lost my pendant!"

As bizarre and disorienting as this new position was, it allowed Rick to clearly see the scene below. The balls of light had taken up an orbit around his body, whizzing faster with each passing breath. The first mound sat somewhere beneath him to the rear, while his friends still stood behind the stone wall.

The instant Rick finished shouting, Devlin leapt over the rubble and skidded to a stop beneath him. Without a moment's hesitation, Devlin reached into his shirt collar and, with one forceful tug, snapped the leather strap of his own necklace.

Rick knew what was about to happen. He let the thyme fall from his left hand. Devlin backed up several steps for a running start, then careened forward once again. When he was directly below Rick, he jumped.

Time seemed to stop. Devlin's feet left the ground. He reached up with the hand that held the tiny horseshoe. Rick opened his fingers. For a moment—for the last time—their hands touched. Rick felt the iron, warmed by Devlin's palm, slip into his grasp. The moment it did, he closed a fist tightly around the necklace.

There was a heartbeat where Rick simultaneously felt the invisible grip on his leg release, but he remained in the air. Then, with terrifying velocity, he tumbled headfirst to the ground. Somewhere, something inside of him allowed him to turn his landing into a clumsy roll, avoiding any serious head or neck trauma.

There was not a moment to waste. Rick grabbed the other handful of thyme and rose as quickly as he could, tripping toward the stone wall. Despite how close he had come to oblivion, Bora was not looking at him. She was looking beyond him, at Devlin.

Rick vaulted over the wall. When he glanced back over the top in the direction of the mound, he saw a swirl of limbs being dragged through the leaves. It was Devlin, doing his best to claw his way back to them. Each time it looked like he might succeed, one of the lights would divebomb his head, forcing him to release his grip and bat it away. Devlin's feet reached the base of the mound, then his knees, then his waist.

Bit by bit, Devlin's invisible assailant pulled him upward through the undergrowth to the very top. His body never stopped fighting, but his face betrayed a different emotion: one of resignation or—perhaps more accurately—of expectations fulfilled. His grandfather's debt, paid in full.

The last thing Rick saw in the dim light was Devlin's hand, wrapped around a sapling, before his grip finally slipped. He dissolved into shadows amidst the trees atop the mound. Even in the weakening light, they should have been able to see him thrashing up there, but in reality, there was nothing. It was like he had been jerked into a deep, dark hole from which there was no escape.

The light orbs winked out with the slow, inevitable satisfaction of old men dozing after a large meal. A deep, profound silence settled over the forest.

Like that, Devlin Fox was gone.

47

Friday, November 6, 2020

IT ALWAYS MATTERS

Returning home took a fraction of the time needed to find the mounds. It happened so quickly, in fact, that neither Rick nor Bora could quite comprehend *how* they got home. All they knew was that they ran back in the direction they had come from, muscles aflame and eyes wet, and that each of Edna's landmarks had come and gone with comforting predictability.

Save for octogenarians and infants, their arrival back home was not late by anyone's standards. Yet both found themselves so numb, dull, and drained that they simply tumbled into their respective sleeping positions and instantly passed out without sharing a word. The comforting unconsciousness of sleep provided an excuse to ignore the consequences the day had wrought.

Chief among these was Devlin's disappearance, which left a strange hole in Rick and Bora's lives. The tear began the instant they returned home, but upon waking the next day, both of them found it had ripped into a full-fledged gash.

It wasn't a parent-shaped hole, or a sibling-shaped hole, or even the shape of a friend. In fact, Rick couldn't identify it at all, but he felt it as clearly as if the sun had stopped shining. Maybe that was it: the shape of a force of nature. A presence, often taken for granted, that sustained you nonetheless. It didn't necessarily care for you by any relational human standard—nor did you for it until you felt the vacuum left by its absence. Only then did you realize how much it met your needs simply by existing.

However, the *actual* sun *was* shining this morning, which coaxed Rick out of bed earlier than any other day this week. Even if Devlin hadn't vanished the night before, there was an overwhelming amount of work to do. After quickly showering and dressing, Rick grabbed a coffee, a Pedialyte, and an apple and headed past Bora's sleeping figure toward the addition, where Devlin's makeshift study still sat in the unfinished rear bedroom.

Many years ago, Rick had the good fortune of briefly touring the Pacific Northwest with one of his old bands. When one of the venues canceled at the last minute, everyone piled into a busted old van and headed to the nearest coast. Rick still cherished that sunset: standing on the beach, marveling at the silhouettes of the massive sea stacks jutting above the waves. The east coast had nothing remotely like those towering stone pillars.

Rick hadn't thought about that scene in years. Today, looking at dawn filtering through the windows of the addition, it was the *only* thing he could think of. Clusters of books pockmarked the smooth floor, stacked to various heights. There must have been at least a dozen piles of spines and pages rising precipitously above the gray sea of concrete below. Somewhere in those treacherous waters lay Rick's salvation.

Or so he hoped. He sat down and got to work.

He heard Bora get up around nine o'clock. Aside from a fleeting nod as she passed into the other bedroom—where Devlin's belongings still remained—she did not acknowledge Rick. That was fine with him; he had no time for idle chitchat. There were too many books left to read. Besides, the conversation would inevitably turn to Devlin, and both of them knew they'd end up parroting the same things back to each other.

There was a jangle from the other bedroom, and Bora slipped out of the addition. The front door opened, a key fob chirped, and finally a car trunk slammed. In an attempt to regain his focus, Rick stood up from the floor and shut the bedroom door.

About an hour later, there was a knock. Bora didn't wait for an answer and chose to open the door without hesitation. "Morning," she said. "How you feeling?"

Rick let the book he was holding drop to his lap. "Broken," he said, without looking at her. Each word that followed was not arrived at lightly, and long silences punctuated each. "Physically... mentally... emotionally. Sad, I think... Anxious. Not just about Sunday, but whether or not we should call the police about Devlin. Or at least try to track down his family, let them know."

"I get the feeling it will be a while before anyone notices that Dev is gone," said Bora. "Seems like he traveled light when it came to relationships, always flew under the radar. I get it, I want to do the right thing, too... but there's plenty of time for that later. None of it matters unless we can put together a plan to save you."

"Or it's the *only* thing that matters, since I'm a goner anyway."

Bora's forehead furrowed. "You haven't found anything?" she asked.

"To the contrary," said Rick, exchanging the book in his hands for a yellow sheet of paper on the floor. He handed it over to Bora. It came from a legal pad and was filled with hastily scrawled book titles and corresponding page numbers.

"Found that pretty early, tucked into"—he searched the floor before pointing at another book across the room—"that, something by a guy named Wentz."

"What is it?"

"Close as I can tell, it's what Devlin was planning on sending me into the tiger's den with. But..." Rick held up his hands and let them drop. "It's scattered across something, like, twenty books. Words, gestures, tools. I can't make sense of half of it, and what I can just sounds... fucking *goofy*."

Bora handed back the paper. "Well, it's better than nothing," she offered. "Just... use your intuition. You write lyrics, right? Tap into that. Try to stitch it together as best you can."

It wasn't a great suggestion, but it was better than anything Rick had told himself the past several hours. "How about you?" he asked. "Any luck with this so-called 'ointment'?"

"Yeah, actually," she admitted, looking mildly surprised to admit as much. "It's been pretty easy. The book that Dev brought out to the patio yesterday morning was in his room, along with his car keys. He had an entire apothecary chest in his trunk. Rick, it had *everything*. Not just the ingredients we need, but stuff I've never heard of. And stuff I've only heard about and never seen..." Rick could tell that, despite her sadness about Devlin, her inner psychonaut was jumping up and down with glee. "The street value alone... let's just say we can have the party to end all parties once this is over."

"Not my scene," he grumbled. "But you were able to make the ointment?"

"Yeah, it was simple enough. Clear instructions. It's sitting out front right now. Guess we leave it there through the weekend; hopefully the weather holds and Sunday morning counts as 'thrice days sun kissed.' Although I'll be honest, there's nothing psychoactive in there. I don't really see how it's going to do anything."

Rick couldn't quite put his finger on how he was feeling. *It's like... like a gig where you find out in the first ten minutes that the crowd isn't into it, and there's no way they'll ever be into it,* he thought. *Just going through the motions, hoping that something will make all that effort worthwhile.*

"Same thing with the ritual," sighed Rick, picking up another book. "Sounds like a bunch of nonsense. I just hope Devlin was right with all that mumbo-jumbo about belief." Rick paused, running his fingers through his hair. "Bora... part of me feels responsible for what happened to him."

"Remember what you told me about Edna," Bora reminded him after thinking for a moment. "Don't go down that road. It leads nowhere. What's done is done. It was a choice Dev made, not you. I can't help but imagine that he knew what he was doing."

Rick shrugged as Bora quietly left the doorway. For the rest of the morning, he scoured Devlin's notes, pulling out all the books they mentioned. Each time he found the correct passage, he laid it face down, open to the corresponding page. When all that was over, he was, as he suspected, left with more than twenty books to compile. He arranged them in the order they appeared on the page, then grabbed some paper of his own from the printer in his bedroom.

He didn't finish cobbling together all the passages into something remotely coherent until late in the afternoon. In the meantime, he started drinking again, hoping to coax out his inner muse through intoxication. Words were struck, then rescued, then struck again. He made alterations, picking the most flowery, arcane language he could to stitch each section together, hoping that it might enhance, rather than diminish, their efficacy. Tools and substances he couldn't identify were omitted. The ones he recognized were substituted with the next best thing he could find in the house. A crumpled heap of drafts piled up alongside the stacks of books until, at last, he transferred the final version onto a fresh sheet of paper, making sure there were no errors.

There it is, he thought at last. *My very own Frankenstein's monster. Just hope the seams don't show.* He read and reread the words, unsure if he could stifle his own disbelief to make them sound convincing. Rick had never been much of a fantasy fan, and the words staring back at him from the paper looked like they had been plucked from some quickly composed, self-published, sword and sorcery dreck.

He mumbled them aloud. They immediately sounded cheesy and hollow.

Rick only knew of one way to surmount this obstacle—the same method that had carried him through his career as a musician. *How do you get to the feldspar mine?* he thought, going about the house to gather the things he needed. *'Practice, practice, practice.'*

For the remainder of the day, Rick stayed in the addition, barely seeing Bora. First, he read the ritual silently until he found himself no longer tripping over the words. Then, line by line, he spoke each aloud, committing them to memory. Eventually, he found that his mind could wander, if ever so slightly, while accurately speaking them.

That helps a little, he thought in between repetitions. *If I can put myself on autopilot, maybe they won't sound as absurd. Maybe I'll feel them more.*

Rick continued late into the night. He even took his supper in the addition, just as Devlin had on Tuesday and Wednesday. When it seemed like he could recite the entire thing in his sleep, he began putting himself through an old technique he had learned long ago.

When Rick first started playing guitar, he suffered from intense performance anxiety. Nothing helped until his teacher started behaving erratically. He would fling music stands, shout and yell, stand on his head—anything bizarre and unpredictable to confuse Rick while he played. This, his teacher informed him, was nothing more than "adversity training." Soon enough, Rick could play through even the most dramatic distractions. After that, performing became a piece of cake.

Rick took those same lessons and applied them to the ritual. He altered his surroundings, going from room to room to enact the rite (Bora, sensing his embarrassment, kindly volunteered to wait in her car). He then stepped out into the night and did the same. He repeated the words standing, sitting, and lying down. He said them in the shower and in the complete darkness of the basement. He said them while pinching himself, while running laps around the house, while sticking his head in the freezer until it ached, while holding his hand above the stove until it burned. Finally, he hit the bottle as hard as ever, repeating the words through his drunken stupor until, at last, he passed out in bed.

On Saturday morning, November 7, 2020—the day before the ritual—the words were the first thing he said when he awoke. He lay in bed for a while, mumbling to himself. He felt as prepared as he ever would, but one last thing had to happen before returning to Spruce Pine.

After hydrating and returning to bed for several more hours to sleep off the worst of his hangover, Rick finally rose for good in the early afternoon. He tugged his phone from its charger and let it sit on his chest, thinking of what he needed to say. It took a while to find the words, but eventually he picked up his phone again and dialed his old home in Alpharetta.

Jack answered. "Hey Dad," he said. "You wanna call my phone instead?"

Rick had two reasons for ringing the landline. The first, which he wouldn't share with anyone, was that he didn't want to run the risk of appearing on a video chat. He knew how he must look after a week of drinking more than ever and getting sporadic sleep. He instead only disclosed the second reason to Jack.

"Hey Jack Attack," he said after closing his eyes and taking a deep breath. "I wanna touch base with Mom after this. Seemed easier this way."

"Cool," Jack replied casually. "Everything good with you? About finished with the house?"

Rick could have lied, but he knew—rather, he *hoped*—that Jack would visit sometime in the future and inevitably discover how little the addition had progressed. "Not really," he answered. "Still lots of supply chain issues. Can't get the stuff I need."

"I heard about that," said Jack. There was a pause on the line. "If you don't want me to come up there anytime soon, I get—"

"No, no, no," Rick interrupted. "No, I'd love for you to come up here. Next week, maybe? Might catch the last little bit of the leaves." Jack seemed to like the idea and launched into a dialogue that, under any other circumstances, would have been a run-of-the-mill catchup: what was happening in school, a new video game he enjoyed, their plans for Thanksgiving and beyond.

It was anything but standard for Rick. The knowledge that this might be their final conversation transformed each of his son's sentences into a song. Rick hung on every word, simply relishing in the sound of Jack's voice, thinking of all the years he had taken it for granted: those incessant cries as an infant, the unrelenting questions as a toddler, the exploratory wonder of a kid, Jack's brief sullenness as a tween before emerging as someone Rick could talk to for hours on end. There had never been a shortage of conversation, but there had never been enough. Now he thought ahead to all the talks they might never share.

Tears began falling on Rick's pillow. He hit the mute button as his body convulsed in full-blown sobs. It took him a minute to realize that Jack was talking, wondering where he went.

You're doing this for him, Rick remembered. *Never forget that. Either way, Jack is going to be okay.* Rick wiped his eyes and nose, cleared his throat, and hit the mute button again. "Yeah, buddy, I'm here," he murmured. In spite of his best efforts, his voice still trembled.

"Dad... Are you okay?"

"Yeah," he managed. "Just a little... under the weather. Listen, I... um... a friend of mine passed away. A fellow musician."

Another pause. "I'm sorry, Dad," consoled Jack. "Did I ever meet him?"

"No. And I didn't know him very long, either, but... something about it hit me extra hard. Has me thinking about a lot of things." Rick hesitated. There was no good segue. "You know that I love you, right?"

"Of course. I love you, too."

Rick nodded. "I want you to remember that. You've always been my favorite person. You're incredible, and smart, and brave, and handsome, and... you can do anything."

"Dad? What's up with the pep talk?"

"I just wanted to say it," Rick declared, clenching his fist to fight the tears. "And I wanted to say that... you can be so much more than I have been. So much more than I am." He took a deep, jagged breath.

"I know I've been a screwup a lot of the time. Most of the time, even."

"Dad..." began Jack. Rick had more to say, but hit the mute button again to cede the conversation to his son. He needed a chance to pull himself together.

"You're too hard on yourself, you know that?" continued Jack. "I never told you this, but... it's the main reason I never picked up music. I enjoy listening, but when it comes to playing... I see how hard you are on yourself whenever you mess up. I guess when you're a performer, it's useful to be your worst critic... but I don't think it's a good way to live."

Something resembling a chuckle and a sob escaped Rick's mouth. *He's not a boy*, he realized. *He's a man. Somehow, through all the mess, he learned something....*

Rick hit the mute button again. "I'm proud of you," he said. "With all the stuff I've put you through, I'm proud of the way you turned out. I'm sorry about how I messed up over the years."

Jack's response was immediate. "You always apologize," he offered.

"I guess," admitted Rick with a defeated chuckle. "But does that even matter?"

There was a long silence. Rick could hear his son shuffling on the other end. "Do you mean it when you say it?" asked Jack.

"Every time."

"Then it *always* matters," Jack finally answered. "You know what doesn't matter? How often you fuck up." If there ever was a time to let Jack's cursing slide, it was now. "I love you. You're Dad. You'll always be Dad, no matter what you do."

Rick began sobbing again but forgot to hit the mute button, prompting a series of concerned questions from Jack. In a year full of trials, regaining his composure in that moment was by far the most challenging. At last he stopped, muttered one final "I love you," and asked to speak to his wife.

A few seconds later, the voice on the line changed. "Rick? Are you okay?" It was the most concerned he had heard Cassandra sound all year.

"Hey lady," Rick said, forcing a smile. He switched the phone to his right hand to stare at his wedding ring, still stubbornly sitting on his left. Determination replaced sadness. "Yeah, yeah, I'm fine. Not sure what Jack told you, but a friend passed away last night. Has me all worked up."

"I'm sorry to hear that," said Cassie. "Were you close?"

Rick didn't know the answer. "Kinda," he decided. "He helped me through some tough times." Cassie remained silent. "Listen... I know that we haven't spoken about anything other than Jack in a while. I'm working on a lot right now—"

"Really?" she interjected. Her voice lowered, likely to keep their son from hearing. "I mean, I'm not mad. I'm... I'm surprised. If you've got a lot on your plate, I'm really proud of you for making time for Jack at a moment's notice last weekend."

Rick swallowed and continued. "Thanks. Like I said, I'm working on a lot right now... I told Jack it was the house but it's, uh... it's some personal stuff. I wanted you to know that I've got some challenges ahead. But for the first time I can remember, I have *genuine clarity* about... well, about everything. About how I've been acting toward everyone else, about me and you, about my dad... about myself. I... I want you to know that I was—am—always trying. Even when I seem selfish. When I get drunk, it's because I keep hoping it might make me... better. Calmer. More present. Even when it doesn't... Even when all it does is make me worse."

"Rick, I—"

"Let me finish," Rick urged. "Now I realize what's truly important to me. It's not music. It's not even you, to be honest. No offense. It's Jack. *He's* my priority. And I've been borrowing against our future together for short-term relief. I... have a lot of problems. I'll tell you the truth: I'm not sure if I can fix them. But they're coming to a head. If I *can* fix them, I'll stay in Jack's life. And if I can't, I won't be there."

"Rick," said Cassie. Her voice was a mixture of anxiety, frustration, and relief. "You know I'd never ask you to do that."

"I know. And I don't want to be out-of-the-picture, either. But I'd rather be absent than have my past ruin his future." There was another silence. "So just remember that. Whatever happens next... I'm not being selfish. There's only one question dictating everything I do moving forward: what is best for our son?"

"Rick, you're scaring me," Cassie said urgently. "Do you know how you sound right now? That won't help anything. If you want what's best for Jack, that's the furthest thing from it. *Please* tell me you're not going to hurt yourself. If you need to, you can come stay here for a while, there's always—"

"Cassie, Cassie, Cassie," said Rick. "Calm down. Bora's with me. She wouldn't let me do anything rash. That's not what I'm saying."

That's a lie, Rick corrected himself. *It might be exactly what you're saying. How's she going to react when she finds out that you did kill yourself, if it comes to that? How is she going to treat Bora?* Rick knew that he would be remembered as a coward. It would scar both his wife and son for the rest of their lives. They would never understand the true intention behind his suicide. *If it's a lie, make it the last you ever tell. And make it mean something.*

"Well, it sure as hell sounds like it," Cassie argued.

"No, I'm talking about... rehab," lied Rick. "You might not hear from me for a couple months. You know how those things go." It wasn't a great excuse, nor was it especially believable, but it might soften the blow of any possible absence.

Cassie sighed. "Promise me?"

"Promise," Rick said, wincing.

"Well, if you mean that, then I'm proud of you. And happy for you. Just don't do it for us... I think we're beyond that. Do it for yourself."

Rick nodded and bit his lower lip. "I figured, and that's fine." He looked back at his wedding band. "I'm sorry for what I've put you through."

There was another long pause. Rick was about to ask if Cassie was still there when she spoke. "I could have been better," she said slowly. "More understanding. I can't say that I wouldn't have wound up like you if I had lived your life. I knew all your baggage going into this. That's on me. Either way, I want you to know that I wouldn't trade a minute of it. We had a lot of good times together. And I'll always love the best parts of you. The parts I see in Jack."

There should have been some sense of regret, some sense of loss. Rick only felt gratitude. He glanced at the time on his phone and realized he had to start practicing and packing for tomorrow.

"Goodbye, Cassie," he said. "Either me or Bora will keep you updated."

"Sounds good," Cassie replied. "Bye, Rick."

She hung up. For the first time in years, Rick slipped off his wedding ring and set it on the bedside table.

48

Sunday, November 8, 2020

UPSTREAM

"Got everything?" shouted Bora from the driver's seat of the black Sentra. Rick stood at the trunk, rummaging through his backpack. It contained everything from their last hike—*water, granola bars, (new) extra shirt, flashlight, batteries, power stick, spare phone charger, rewetting drops, booze*—with a few additions.

The chef's knife, wrapped in a dish towel to keep it from slashing a hole in the bag, stood point-down, edge-out. It was integral to the ritual, and also his Plan B should he fail. Not the quickest way to end things, but effective. Behind the knife were a tambourine and a plastic freezer bag. Inside the latter was a stick of margarine and his wedding ring.

If we get pulled over by the cops and they search our stuff, they're going to think I'm some sort of hippie serial killer, Rick mused. *That, or an especially musical chef cheating on his wife.* He looked over the contents one final time: *water, granola bars, (new) extra shirt, flashlight, batteries, power stick, spare phone charger, rewetting drops, booze, knife, tambourine, margarine, ring.*

Rick took a long sip from his flask, touched Devlin's restrung pendant through his shirt, and hopped in the passenger's seat. The day began bright, clear, and chilly. At least they managed to leave on time. It was ten o'clock in the morning, which would put them in Spruce Pine around two in the afternoon. Not nearly as early as either of them would have liked, but the best compromise between leaving Bora's concoction in the sun and allowing enough time to search his father's mine.

"What took so long?" griped Bora.

"Old habits," Rick explained. "Got the ointment?"

Bora gestured to a glass salad dressing mixer sitting in the cupholder. Rick picked it up and examined the contents. The interior looked green and soupy. Popping the top, he took a whiff. It didn't smell altogether unpleasant. The strong oregano scent of the wild thyme overwhelmed any hint of decay. "Any idea how much we're supposed to use?"

"No clue," said Bora, cranking the car. Rick replaced the container.

"Ah, crap," he exclaimed abruptly. "I forgot one last thing. Can you pop the trunk?" Bora obliged, and Rick hopped out and ran over to the shed. After opening it and stepping inside, he emerged with something bulky in his hands, which he dropped into the trunk.

"Okay," he said, sliding back inside and shutting his door. "That's it. Ready to go."

Bora put the car in drive and headed up the dirt driveway. "What was that?" she asked, her eyebrows raising behind her sunglasses.

"Dad," replied Rick. He added nothing as they tumbled through the woods, nor did Bora feel the need to fill the silence as they pulled onto the main road. They remained quiet as they turned east on US-76.

Rick sat there, trying not to panic, but his anxiety increased with the same swiftness as the Sentra's speedometer. *Easy does it,* a voice inside him warned. *Pace yourself. If you stay anxious for four hours, you'll be too exhausted to function.* He reclined his seat a bit, which seemed to help. *At least I'm not driving,* he thought thankfully. He literally wasn't sure if he could have compelled his foot to work the pedals. Rick knew what had to be done but felt a near-tangible, invisible force pressing against him, like magnetic repulsion. *Or like swimming upstream*, he added.

"I'm surprised," Bora said at last.

"Hmm?" responded Rick.

"I would've thought you would have tossed your dad's ashes months ago. Or flushed them down the toilet. I know that's what I would've done if he had treated me the same way."

Rick leaned his elbow on the right armrest and looked at the landscape as it whizzed by. If he softened his focus enough, everything turned into an abstract painting. Four simple strips smudged across the window: brushstrokes of gray, yellow, brown, and blue formed by the shoulder of the road, the grass, the leaves, and the sky.

"Thought about it," he mumbled from behind his fingers. "Didn't want to do anything I'd regret. So I just sat on it for a while. I was waiting to know what to do with his remains. After Devlin read that diary, I realized something... my father was complicated. Not good. Maybe even mostly bad. But complicated."

"Why'd you bring the urn?"

"Now I know what to do with him," Rick said quietly. He shifted his eyes to the windshield and spotted a series of swayback slopes rising far in the distance. Scattered across each mountainside, glinting like diamonds buried in a pile of coal, were the tin roofs of several houses, catching the sunlight at just the right angle. The magical moment faded as the car continued forward and the reflections died.

Bora never asked him to elaborate. It was a long and somber trip, with very little conversation for the first ninety minutes or so. Rick had several guesses as to why. The first was the most obvious: neither of them had any idea what they were getting into, and both of them were terrified. The other reasons were a bit more nebulous.

We've known each other for decades, Rick realized. *We've been living together for over a month. We've rarely been out of each other's sight in nearly two weeks. What's left to say?* Another reason dawned on Rick. It disturbed him the most. *What meaningful conversation do you have on the way to the gallows?*

They were well into North Carolina before Bora spoke. "Mind if we talk a little business?" she asked as they crossed the border of the Nantahala National Forest. A narrower setting replaced the expansive vistas, bringing trees pressing in on Rick's side and the face of a mountain on Bora's. Small waterfalls to their left broke the monotony in the form of white slivers, irregular, fleeting reminders of beauty as they pressed onward.

"Sure," Rick said as they passed another. He took a quick moment to admire the sight. It was reassuring to see such majesty going about its business in the midst of his personal turmoil. Even if Rick's life didn't continue, the world and all its beauty would. "I have to admit, I'm not used to you being this quiet."

"I'm not used to you being this thoughtful," she countered with a smile. "If the past few weeks won't change a person, nothing will." She adjusted her grip on the steering wheel to navigate the sharper turns. "How are we getting into this place? Do we need permission or something?"

"Permission granted," said Rick. "Technically, I still own the place."

"Is there a gate?"

"Yes. One of those one-armed, rotating deals."

"Got a key?"

"No, but Randy Lael does. The family lawyer. Wanted me to come by and collect it in person, but the last thing I want is to be bombarded with questions. I reminded him that we're still in a pandemic. That seemed to change his mind. Got him to agree to leave the key behind the post. After that, it's just dirt roads." He looked around the Sentra's interior. "I'm glad you're driving, but I really wish you would have let me take my car. I have no idea what state those roads are in. Probably overgrown as hell, with plenty of potholes to boot."

"Eh, this thing's due for an alignment anyway," Bora said. "Besides... I'm just doing penance for all the times I ran away from other people's problems. After all we've been through, the least I can do is finish strong."

"I can't tell you how much that means to me," said Rick. "I'm not exaggerating. It's probably the most anyone has ever done for me."

They sat in awkward silence until they reached a straighter portion of the road, affording Bora the opportunity to glance at the glass container in the cupholder. "By the way, if that stuff works, you're going to need me," she said confidently. "I have it on good authority that I'm an *excellent* sitter."

"Good," said Rick. "Because I've never done anything like this."

"What, you mean you've never driven to an old abandoned mine to break a goblin blood oath?"

"No, I mean..." Rick gestured to the ointment. "Psychedelics. If that's what this is."

Bora risked a glance at Rick before navigating another curve. "What?" she asked. "Are you kidding me?"

"Hand to God."

Bora looked incredulous. "I *distinctly* remember a party where you were tripping balls. Shrooms, I think. Ted Bynall's birthday, junior year. You said that Jimi Hendrix stepped out of the poster on his wall and showed you a new song. You played it with Hideous Hideous. It was amazing."

Rick shook his head. "I remember that night. Well, that part, at least. I was too chicken-shit to take them. Just flushed them down the toilet and kept drinking. I was most likely bullshitting y'all."

Now it was Bora's turn to shake her head. "A travesty, Rick," she chuckled. "A goddamn travesty. You should have just told me. I would've put them to good use."

Rick looked back out the window. They were traveling parallel to a modest stream. Small, rickety bridges crossed here and there, leading to residences not that dissimilar to his house in Ellijay. "Had some good times, didn't we?" he asked wistfully.

"Many more to come," said Bora. "I've been meditating. Visualizing a positive outcome. Thought it might help, if everything Dev said is right… So with that in mind, none of this past-tense shit. We *had* good times, we *are having* good times, we *will have* good times."

"You sound like an ESL teacher," joked Rick. When their chuckles subsided, he thought about what she had said, adding, "I wouldn't blame you for disappearing after today, regardless of how it goes."

"Nope," Bora snapped good-naturedly. "We get through this alive, and you're going to see a lot more of me. Edna needs a caretaker after all. What, you think I'm just going to abandon her?"

"I could do it," offered Rick.

"I doubt you're up to the task," Bora goaded him. "Besides, I've been looking for a change. Nothing seems right back in town. Maybe I'll move up to Ellijay. Rent can't be any worse, and I mean, look at this." She waved out the windshield at the yellow tunnel of leaves. Even just a few hours north, their deaths had been arrested, if ever so slightly. The colors were beyond their peak, but still remained vibrant. "I always had a thing for landscapes. What more inspiration could an artist ask for?"

Rick could only smile and nod in agreement. It was refreshing to speak about the future in more certain terms. It broke the spell that the day's task cast over them, and their conversation continued more naturally. They talked about old times and forgotten friends. They talked about art and hope, about legacies and longing.

Something dawned on Rick. This, he thought, *this is what you talk about on the way to the gallows.*

Around 1:30, their journey took them onto US-19 East. The forest thinned a bit, and the more distant mountains came into view with greater regularity. Something inside Rick felt renewed. Even though leaving had been a priority all those years ago, these towering monoliths still felt like home. They dwarfed Red Ear Mountain.

People out west give us shit, saying these are 'hills', Rick thought, remembering tours through Colorado and California. *They might not be as tall. But they're older. The oldest.*

The Appalachians also interacted with the seasons more dramatically than their western counterparts. Each passing month brought a new expression: the barren stubble of winter, the fuzzy emergence of spring, the thick greenery of midsummer, and, now, the waning burst of fall colors, fading like a million dying stars.

As they drove, another feature began appearing on the slopes: broad swaths of barren rock, sometimes gray, often white, with the slightest tinge of yellow in the weak autumnal sun. The very bones of the Earth, exposed in gouges left behind by mankind's metallic claws. The marrow of the bedrock here was feldspar, and its extraction left an indelible mark on the landscape.

From this distance, discerning operating mines from those tapped dry was impossible. All appeared vacant. Even if they were closer, many would likely be shut down on a Sunday. They all looked dead, quiet, and ancient, like the ruins of some long-forgotten ivory city. Bleak, but resilient. There was an elegance to that.

"I could think of worse places to die," admitted Rick. "And worse last sights to see." Bora said nothing. A few minutes later, the outskirts of Spruce Pine—such as they were—began creeping in.

"You're gonna take a left up here," Rick instructed. They turned off the highway and began navigating a series of heavily wooded side roads. Even in the midst of fall, enough coverage remained overhead to plunge the interior of the car into shadows.

Rick was surprised at how well he remembered the way. He continued guiding Bora until, at last, a gravel drive formed on their right, its entrance barred by a one-armed gate shedding flecks of yellow paint. Just behind it, on the left hand side of the road, rusting and choked by vines, stood a large metal sign displaying the faded words "COULSPAR AMERICA LTD."

Bora needed no instruction. Part of the driveway was accessible enough to allow her to safely pull the Sentra off the road and in front of the gate.

"Let's see if Lael kept his word," Rick said as Bora parked. He hopped out and went around the front of the car in the direction of the single post upon which the gate arm was mounted. After a brief disappearance behind the hood, he popped back up, fumbling with something small and silvery. Rick took the key, walked to the opposite side of the road, and unlocked a padlock holding together a short length of heavy chain. The links fell to the ground with a clatter. Rick pocketed the key, swung the arm inward, and stood in the tall weeds alongside the gravel.

After Bora passed through the gate far enough, Rick closed it once again. Instead of securing the chain, he simply draped it over the gate so that it would look secure to anyone driving by. He then hopped back inside.

"Ready?" he asked.

Bora nodded and slowly started coaxing the Sentra forward. After a short incline through a cluster of trees, the road leveled, and they emerged into a wide field. A forested mountainside occupied most of their windshield. Although impossible to see from the road just a hundred feet or so back, they had apparently spent the last ten minutes winding around its base.

On either side stretched the overgrown meadow, mostly filled with tall grass and wildflowers. A few man made structures sat here and there. Of these buildings, none looked particularly safe. The ones whose roofs hadn't caved in were listing precariously, as if a strong wind might send them toppling over. Sprinkled between these were rusted shipping containers and a tall, metallic tower, its conveyor belt lashed together with kudzu.

"Mine's on the other side," Rick said, gesturing toward the peak ahead. He rarely got the chance to visit before his father shut down the operation, so he remembered very little—but he did know that much. Beyond the broadest details—the way the road curved, the presence of a large boulder here and there, the empty footprint where a structure once stood—everything else remained unrecognizable.

"Trucks would carry the ore down here for processing," he continued as the Sentra passed across the meadow and back into the forest fringing the base of the mountain. Although he never bothered learning the particulars of feldspar mining, he knew enough to provide a rough idea. "A lot of stuff was demolished or sold. Couldn't see it from the road, but there used to be a whole cluster of buildings dedicated to crushing the ore and processing it," he said, looking over his shoulder and pointing. "Lots of acid and chemicals to float off the different layers. Tailing pond, too."

Bora didn't acknowledge him as they slipped into the woods. She was too focused on not tearing her car apart. As the incline increased, the amount of gravel on the road decreased, long since washed away after years of disuse. It left behind a dirt road full of awkward bumps, dips, and stubborn new vegetation, including the occasional sapling. Bora never stopped the car to remove any, nor did she try to drive around them. She was having a hard enough time threading the endless hairpins drawing them up the mountain.

"Beautiful up here," said Bora. "Can't you develop this, retire a millionaire?"

"I wish," Rick scoffed. "US Geological Survey put the kibosh on that. Said that the mountain was unsafe. Pockets of underground gas, too many sinkholes, stuff like that. It's not worth much anymore." Bora grunted, like she suspected otherwise.

They continued up the mountain. It was tough and tedious going. In some places, the road had washed away, leaving barely enough room for the car to pass without tumbling down the mountainside. In others, they were forced to stop and remove a log obstructing their path. Luckily, none proved too heavy for their combined effort, and after about fifteen minutes, they found themselves passing onto the other side of the mountain. The forest parted, and for a moment, it felt like they might teeter over the edge into oblivion.

Bora stopped the car, allowing them to take it all in. For miles, they could see an endless array of mountains covered in trees stretching into the distance like frozen waves. There was no foliage here, however. The quarry below resembled ground zero of a nuclear detonation. Most of it was too sheer for anything to accumulate. On a handful of level terraces, piles of stones, byproducts from decades of mining, lay randomly strewn about the barren rock of the mountain.

Very little grew here, and what did was fledgling—weak bits of weed and scrub trying to eke out an existence in a white wasteland. For all their success, they might as well have been on the moon.

Rick leaned over in his seat to look across Bora and down the mountainside. "There," he said. "See it?"

Bora looked. Only one feature interrupted the monotonous landscape below: a massive hole. It was filled with the kind of water that looked like it could be smelled long before it could be seen.

"That's the entrance," said Rick. "Or at least it *was*. I always thought the mine stopped being productive, but according to what you told me, dad just let it die. Didn't take long for it to fill up after he shut off the pumps." He leaned back into a more comfortable position. "Let's head down there."

Bora eyed the inky hole below and the series of gravel switchbacks leading to it. They looked like misaligned rungs on some gigantic ladder. "You want us to go down *there*?" she asked in disbelief.

Rick shrugged. "Got a better place to start? Maybe, if we're lucky, there's a way into the mine down there. Something that isn't filled with water."

Bora gritted her teeth and began tracing her way down the roads. It seemed as if one false move would send them tumbling to their doom. The pace became glacial. By comparison, their ascent had been a drag race.

Once they were halfway down, Bora took a moment to look back at where they had started. It was dizzying. Here and there, where the forest ended, large portions of the naked ledge had sloughed off, exposing red clay underneath. It looked like a massive monster had bitten chunks out of the earth, letting its lifeblood dribble down the rock to stain the white cliffside.

Thankfully, the trip down the mountain was much more direct than the trip up and therefore passed in a fraction of the time, despite their slower pace. After several tense, white-knuckled moments, the terrain grew less hazardous, and the car was more or less on the same level as the top of the hole.

Bora slowed to a stop, noticing a wide footpath down into the pit. She thought about taking the Sentra down there but decided against it.

"It's wide enough to drive, but I wouldn't risk it," Rick said, sensing her apprehension and pointing to the trail. "Used to be all sorts of equipment and rails running along there. That'll get us as close as we can to the bottom."

Both of them cracked their doors, only to have them yanked wide open. Here, without any vegetation to slow it down, the wind was permitted to blow with full force. Bora grabbed the salad mixer. After finally winning the battle to shut their doors, the two of them retrieved their backpacks. Rick checked his one last time: *water, granola bars, (new) extra shirt, flashlight, batteries, power stick, spare phone charger, rewetting drops, booze, knife, tambourine, margarine, ring.*

After taking the urn from the trunk, Rick ran to catch up with Bora, who was already halfway to the footpath. As they went, their feet kicked up clouds of dust which were immediately dispersed by the wind.

The moment they slipped below the lip of the pit, calmness returned. The wind still whipped above their heads, but none of it found its way below. Even the water at the bottom remained calm and still, like a circular pane of glass fitted into the bedrock.

Mangled bits of metal and debris, including an old miner's helmet, littered the path. When he finally felt that the terrain held no more surprises, Rick allowed himself to take a better look at the body of water below them. As they drew nearer, it became difficult to tell up from down. The surface of the water so immaculately reflected the clouds above that it felt like he and Bora had descended into a short, rocky tunnel in the sky.

Rick recognized everything he saw—but he wasn't sure if he had ever been there before or had just seen photographs. Either way, it was just as he pictured, all these years later: an eighty-foot wide hole in the Earth, almost perfectly circular, with a few angled ledges cut along the stone sides to facilitate the passage of equipment and personnel.

The surface of the water stood twenty yards below the upper edge of the pit. Rick knew this depth was illusory. Somewhere far, far beneath the water lay several arched entrances, now completely inaccessible, to what was once a prosperous endeavor. Countless men made their living passing into those chthonic depths, chasing ever deeper after the promise of treasure beneath.

Most feldspar operations were simple open pits. In fact, this was the original intent behind creating the space in which Rick and Bora now stood. The Coulter holdings had proven so robust, however, that Conrad deemed tunneling profitable. From the bottom of the chasm, they dug outward, chiseling passages through the mountain.

Conrad's gamble paid off, but at a price. The endeavor was by no means as deep or as precarious as coal mining, but it still carried its own hazards. Somewhere below their feet, a handful of men died over the years.

I wonder if, had my father dug elsewhere, they would have survived, Rick thought, looking into the massive pool below. *Maybe these things didn't appreciate having their home invaded. It could be the reason why Mary was taken, too....*

At last, Rick and Bora walked as far as they could. The footpath simply met a dead end in the water, the chalky dirt turning dark with moisture. Now that he was at the bottom, Rick appreciated how truly lifeless the pit was. There was no wake, nor were there any signs of life bobbing along what constituted a shore. There was only a glassy reflection of the sky locked in a circle of rock.

"See, Devlin?" shouted Rick, the curved stone tossing his voice around the pit. "This is what I was talking about. There's nothing here. Nowhere to go."

"Not yet, at least," Bora said, lightly shaking the container of green liquid. "You ready to do this?"

"In a sec," said Rick. "Something I need to do first." He put down the urn to slip off his backpack. Once that was done, he picked up his father's ashes and examined the container. He had instructed Lael to provide the cheapest thing he could, short of a wooden or cardboard box. Lael sent him a receptacle covered in blue faux-marble. A cheaply made band of plastic flowers encircled the top, trying to pass off as silver. Rick found it funny at the time, knowing that a man who luxuriated in the finest things would languish in something so tacky and gaudy. Now he just felt petty.

It took Rick a few minutes to find the right thing to say. Bora, for her part, remained in patient silence, smoking her vape. Finally, Rick held up the urn at arm's length in front of his face.

"Dad," he said, his voice echoing off the stone walls, "I always thought you were selfish. I'm pretty sure you were. I always hated you for that. Now, I realize the burden that you carried. I've only gotten a taste of it over the past year... I don't know how you held on as long as you did. I wish you had told someone. Maybe we could've helped, maybe you would have changed. I hate what's happening to me... what you passed on to me... but it gave me a chance to learn part of what made you the way you were. I forgive you."

With that, he tossed his father's ashes, urn and all, into the water. They sent up a splash, bobbed for a moment, then succumbed to the pull of the deep. Once they fully disappeared, Rick added one postscript: "You were right. I was nothing, but not when you said it and not how you meant it. This past year, I've been nothing. Now... I'm something. Something good."

Bora waited until the waves from the urn reached the shore before she spoke. "Are you ready?" she asked.

"No," admitted Rick, pulling out his flask for a drink. "But it's time."

49

Sunday, November 8, 2020

STORY OF STORIES

Without another word, doctor and patient took their places, turning the open pit into a cavernous, empty operating theater made of stone. Rick reclined on his back in the dust along the footpath. The slope made his position less horizontal and more angled, comparable to resting in a dentist's chair. A bit awkward, but given their difference in height, it was the most logical approach.

Bora leaned over him. In one hand, she held a small glass eyedropper with a black rubber bulb. In the other, she gripped the salad dressing mixer. "Which contact did you take out?" asked Bora, popping the lid.

"Left," Rick answered. With no idea how he would react, it seemed wise to administer the ointment to just one eye. The last thing either of them needed was him blindly stumbling over a cliff.

"Looks like... oh, yeah, I see the difference," said Bora. She plunged the eyedropper into the liquid. "Feels like I'm back at work," she remarked, giving the bulb a quick squeeze. The dropper filled halfway with green soup. "Tell me, does this position come with a 401K?"

Bora disappeared to return the container to her backpack, which lay propped against the stone wall of the pit. For a moment, all Rick saw were the wispy fingers of some clouds reaching across a pale blue sky. Bora then popped back into view.

"Hold still," she requested. Leaning closer, Bora reached out with her free hand to pull her patient's eyelids further apart. The tip of the dropper hovered close to Rick's left eye. A viscous droplet formed on the end but stubbornly refused to fall. Once it finally did, two more dropped in rapid succession. Rick was able to keep his eye open for the first two, but by the third, he couldn't help himself. He sat up, his eyelids pressed tight, and held his fingers to his left eye.

"Fucking shit motherfucker," Rick cursed. He pressed more firmly but somehow resisted the urge to rub.

"Are you okay?" asked Bora, panicking. "Did I hit you with the tip?"

"No," Rick managed to answer. His left eye felt like the recipient of a hornet sting. "Fucking hell, I hope this gets better." He pawed around in the dirt until his hand hit his flask, then unscrewed the top with his free hand and drained the entire thing.

Bora looked bewildered. "I don't understand," she said. "Nothing in there should have hurt." She paused. With his good eye, Rick noticed that an expression of guilt had darkened her face. "Unless... maybe the LSD was too much?"

"What?!?" screamed Rick, his voice booming in angry repetition across the pit. "You're kidding, right?!?"

Bora looked sheepish. "Rick, nothing in there was going to make you see *anything*," she said defensively. "So I just... fortified it a little with some of my stash..."

"Bora, you goddamn fucking hippie!" shouted Rick. Dropping his fingers from his eye, he began blinking rapidly. The only thing it could see was a murky green sludge. "I fucking swear to God, you'd better hope I kill myself before I kill you!" He stumbled over to where his backpack sat by the water's edge. Kneeling, Rick unzipped the main compartment and pulled out his bottle of water. Even though the pain had subsided a bit, it remained excruciating.

"I'm sorry Rick," Bora apologized. She was dancing in the dust, wondering how close she could—or should—get. "I was just trying to make sure that we didn't come up here for nothing, I—"

"Shut up," Rick snapped. "Do you have any that you didn't spike? If it's not too late, maybe we can try again." He unscrewed the water bottle and, holding his left eye open like he was about to put in his contacts, brought the top as close as he could.

Rick was about to empty the entire thing when he hesitated. Something peculiar happened. While his right eye saw nothing, he thought he spotted something moving through the sickly green gloom cast over his left. He closed both eyes and opened them. The film smothering his dosed eye dissipated a bit, revealing several patches no longer blotted out by ointment. Sure enough, the movement was still there.

There was no mistaking it. Something swam in the flooded pit. And yet... his right eye saw nothing. There wasn't even a wake. The surface of the water was as glassy and smooth as it had ever been.

"Bora," he barked through her frantic apologies. "Bora... Bora! Hush for five seconds, will you?" Rick glanced back. She fell silent, but continued wringing her hands. He returned his gaze to the water. "Do you see anything out there?"

Rick sensed her scanning the scene over his shoulder. After a few seconds, she meekly chirped, "No."

Rick closed one eye at a time, alternating between the two. His right remained normal, and saw nothing out of the ordinary. His left, however, was starting to clear. The cloudy haze coating his eye gave way, bit by bit, to something remarkable. By the time it fully cleared, his vision had become a mosaic of shimmering pastels. A fuzzy haze outlined every rock and every crag, imbuing them with an ever-shifting rainbow aura.

Well, something *is working,* Rick thought. *Doesn't sting as much, either. Helluva first trip...* He waved a hand in front of his face. Just as he had always been told, a series of tracers lagged behind, exact replicas of his movement, as if in staggered slow motion. He looked beyond his hand back at the water, where a miniscule series of ripples continued reverberating out from the center.

I'm still thinking straight, he realized. *Or at least I* think *I'm thinking straight.* He closed his left eye and looked with his right. No ripples. *It's like seeing two worlds at once,* he thought. *Mine with my right... theirs with my left....*

The moment this occurred to him, Rick's left eye saw something break the surface of the water. Whatever it was, it was immense, slimy, and dark, like the upper half of a hump. Rick imagined an enormous eel tracing a vertical sine wave through the submerged mine. It dove under once more, trailing a spined, tapered tail the color and texture of an eggplant.

The sight sent Rick scuttling back on all fours until he was even with Bora. He only stopped once his back hit the sheer stone wall of the pit. "Bora, please tell me you saw that," he whispered urgently.

"No," Bora said, shaking her head. "Nothing. I've been staring out there ever since you... oh, wait. I mean... I see a little ripple, maybe. Probably just the wind, though."

"You know there isn't any wind down here," countered Rick. "There's something out there. Big. I just saw it surface."

Bora stared at Rick for a long time, hit her vape, then said, "I take it it's working, then?"

"I guess so."

"What's it look like?"

"An eel."

"No, I mean your vision."

"Like Lisa Frank threw up in my left eye."

Bora chuckled. "Sounds about right," she said. She held out a hand to help him up. When he was back on his feet, she put on her backpack, grabbed his, and held it out to him. "Shall we?"

"I guess," said Rick, blinking wildly and putting on his bag. "I'm not sure what I'm supposed to be looking for, but I don't think there's another entrance down here." He glanced around the pit. Beyond the colors, tracers, and hue, nothing else looked any different than it had on their way down. There was only the pathway, the stone circular confines, and the water, which sat freshly placid.

Rick thought about being trapped down here with whatever lived in the water and shivered. The pit was beginning to feel more like a cage, as if the walls were leaning in and might swallow them whole.

Bora started leading the way back up the trail, allowing Rick to keep a hand on her shoulder. He was grateful for the guidance. While both eyes were clear now—*My left is better than when I'm wearing a contact*, Rick noted—the visions absolutely wrecked his depth perception.

"Any idea how you'll find your way in?" asked Bora as they began their long, slow ascent. Here, closer to the top, the wind had started playing with her hair.

"No clue," he admitted. He was starting to feel lightheaded, and he fervently hoped that he would remain lucid.

Looking up into the sky, Rick watched a pair of crows fly over the pit, cawing loudly. The pair merged as one, then split again. The instant they broke apart, the image of an old, bearded man with an eyepatch flashed before Rick. It was neither internal nor external, neither in his physical eye nor his mind's eye. It occupied some space in between.

Rick stopped in his tracks and put a hand to his head. His knees buckled.

"You okay?" asked Bora, turning and grabbing him under his arm.

"I think so," he said, regaining his footing. "Just getting used to things. It's... weird."

"Well, don't get too distracted. Remember, we've got a job to do."

"What am I supposed to look for? A fucking neon sign?"

"No, just anything... out of the ordinary."

"Bora," he said as they made the final steps, "*everything's* out of the ordin—"

The instant his head popped above the edge of the pit, Rick staggered. He was overwhelmed. He grabbed hold of the stone ledge, closing his eyes and pressing his forehead against the rock. Bora intervened, supporting him and calling his name, asking if he was okay and what was happening.

He couldn't answer. It was as if every idea in the history of existence was being carried along on the wind. A thousand melodies, poems, and stories crashed against him. His ears filled with symphonies that were never written, that never *could* be written. Voices spanning the breadth of human hearing whispered words in every language, fictional and real, threatening to burst his eardrums and shatter his mind.

Rick gently tapped his forehead on the rock. Somehow, it helped. The sounds subsided, but they weren't even the most overwhelming part. The narratives were far more intrusive. There were tragedies and comedies, dramas and fantasies, set on a thousand worlds and no worlds, enacted by the whole of humanity. They penetrated his bones, sharing manifold tales told from the dawn of time until the heat death of the universe yet to come. They were all happening at once, and they were all happening inside Rick.

Finally, Bora's voice came back to him. "Rick!" she shouted between snippets of Gregorian chant and theremin music. "Rick!" Summoning some unidentified power within, he forced the sounds to recede. They were still there, but at least they were in the background.

"H-hey," Rick gasped. His eyes were still closed. "I'm... I'm okay."

"What is it?" asked Bora. "What's happening?"

"Every... everything," Rick mumbled. He shook his head, trying to clear Lou Gehrig's farewell speech from his ears. "It feels like I'm hearing everything that ever happened. Everything that didn't, too, and everything... everything anyone has ever made up."

"Can you keep going?" he heard her ask. He dared to open his eyes. Several pebbles stared back at him from the floor of the footpath. They danced and swirled a bit in his left eye but seemed otherwise manageable.

"I think so," he whispered. "No other choice." He blinked. "Helps if I keep both eyes open. My right seems to ground me a little."

"And the sounds?"

"Still there, but I'm getting used to them." Rick thought back to the grandfather clock at the house where he grew up. Whenever they came over to play, his friends always found it obnoxious, but Rick never noticed. He had become so desensitized that he never heard its incessant pendulum unless he paid deliberate attention. The noises now occupied a similar position in his mind: present but distant, only intrusive when granted permission.

Rick stood up straight and placed his hand back on Bora's shoulder. "Let's get to the car," he mumbled. He kept his eyes firmly fixed on the ground.

"Right over here," she said. The two of them shuffled up the last few feet of the footpath. As they stepped onto level ground, the wind —the *real* wind, not the imaginal hurricane Rick had just ridden out— hit them with full force. It was so strong, Rick lost his grip on Bora and stumbled a bit.

When he looked up to grab her shoulder again, he saw it. All of it.

In some ways, it was worse than the torrent he faced on the footpath. But at least it wasn't all happening at once. While the voices and narratives had layered themselves upon each other in an endless deluge, the visions seen in his left eye were solitary. It was like the world became a flipbook, where every page was different and lasted only a heartbeat.

Steampunk airships, art-deco flying saucers, black triangles, and luminous balls of light filled the sky. The barren mountainside metamorphosed into faces from every pantheon: Egyptian, Greek, Norse, Hindu, Sumerian, Mayan, Ojibwe, Yoruba, and a thousand others Rick could not identify. Across the dusty quarry, gnomes and goblins danced and played with werewolves and wild men; flocks of winged people took off and landed; ghosts and demons flitted on the wind; panthers stalked dinosaurs. Thankfully, none of them were present for long, nor did they seem to notice Rick.

There were even stranger things, too, but only insofar as how *familiar* they were—images drawn from imagination itself. Rick dared not even think of their names. The absurdity would cause too much self-doubt.

Spaceships in the shapes of Xs and Hs engaged in dogfights above. A grizzled gunslinger in a poncho fired the final shots of a showdown. Ladies in Victorian dresses fretted over the affections of their suitors. A detective, wearing a familiar deerstalker hat, smoked his pipe while standing over the body of an old, graying sea captain whose leg had been replaced with whalebone. A pierced and tattooed woman with short black hair sulked in the dirt, talking with another girl whose silver hair was buffeted by dragons' wings.

It was too much. *I've gone fucking nuts*, Rick thought as he stumbled forward, unable to weather the barrage of imagery. *Absolutely fucking batshit insane. There's no way I can do the ritual like this. I might as well kill myself now.*

He landed on the Sentra's black hood with a thud, eyes closed. The visions refused to stop, however. To the contrary, the space behind his left eyelid provided a blank canvas, and the images grew even more absurd. There was no escaping them.

Rick tried to slip off his backpack to get the knife and plunge it into his chest—a simple enough task, but his new reality rendered it impossible. Sometimes his backpack was there, sometimes it wasn't. Sometimes it was his guitar, while other times it was a fish, or a wardrobe, or the Gobi Desert.

Rick forced his eyes tighter, beating his fists against them. Bora came up and grabbed him by the wrists, trying to prevent him from hurting himself. It was no use. Again and again he battered his face, hoping that it might change *something*, might *somehow* draw him back into reality. Nothing seemed to help.

To make matters worse, the noises returned in full force. Rick felt completely disconnected from the world around him, lost amidst a kaleidoscope of unstable aural and visual stimuli. In desperation, he slipped his fingers into his ears... and, miraculously, the phantasmagoria behind his eyelids slowed. Just as the sounds had receded moments earlier, the visions became more manageable, forced to the edge of his awareness.

Somewhere, in the deepest recesses of his mind, Rick found his own voice once again. *You closed your eyes, and the noises became manageable*, the voice said. The person named Rick wiggled his fingers in his ears. *Maybe this will help with the visions...*

Rick found himself again and slowed the pace of his breaths. Once he had that under control, he hesitantly opened his eyes. His right saw the hood of the car. His left saw a pool of water, but the image remained stable for several seconds before gradually changing into the wooden deck of a frigate. It was still disorienting, but at least it wasn't overpowering anymore. Slowly, Bora's voice came to the forefront of his perception.

"Rick!" she shouted. Her arms were held tight around him, and she was crying. "Rick, please come back! Rick!"

He finally spoke, his voice sounding like it came from a million miles away. "I'm here," he said at last. "I'm here."

"Rick, what the fuck is happening? Are you alright?"

He pushed himself off the hood of the Sentra and managed to stand up again. *There's something more going on here than just acid*, he thought. *Fucking hell, Devlin. You could've made a fortune with this shit.*

"Rick? I asked how you were doing."

"You know those sounds?" asked Rick. "This is like that, except I'm *seeing* it." He stared out beyond the quarry. Colossal, tentacled giants stepped over the distant mountains, their heads obscured by the clouds. The image gave way to an emerald city shining on the horizon.

Rick finally realized where he stood. It was the Painter's Palette, the Poet's Vocabulary, the Storyteller's Campfire, the Chromatic Scale. It was the Marketplace of Ideas, Supply-Side Economics, the Public Forum, Laissez-Faire Capitalism, Communism and Fascism, Democracy and Anarchy. It was the Hero's Journey, the Akashic Record, the Morphogenetic Field, Gilgul, Samsara, the World Tree, the Three Act Structure. It was a thousand creation myths, the Cosmic Turtle, Revelation and Ragnarok, all rolled up into one overwhelming reality.

Everything and Nothing. Sorcery and Science. Magic and Mathematics. Satan and Christ, Heaven and Hell, Pantheism and Monotheism, Good and Evil, Yin and Yang, Light and Dark.

It was every contradiction you could think of, and countless others you never would. It was the Story of Stories.

"He was right," Rick whispered.

"Who?" asked Bora.

"Devlin," he said. "That's what these things are. 'The flora and fauna of the Collective Unconscious.'"

"What do you see now?" inquired Bora.

"You don't want to know. What do you see?"

Bora scoured the white expanse of the quarry, searching for something to reassure her friend. "I see our footprints," she observed. "Hang on..." Without moving from her position beside Rick, she stood on her tiptoes and moved her head back and forth to look beyond the pit. A series of immense tracks stretched out in the opposite direction. They had not walked anywhere near there. Even if they had, they were wearing shoes, and whoever—whatever—left those prints was barefoot. "Those aren't ours. And they just... end, halfway to the edge. The tracks just stop."

Rick nodded. "So *something* is here," he said. "It's not just in my head."

"Seems that way. Can you keep going?"

"I think so," said Rick. "For a minute there, it was absolutely crippling. Now it's just... mild existential terror, I guess." He alternated between his two eyes. In some ways, the emptiness of his right now seemed the more surreal of the two. "Thank God we just did one eye. Otherwise, I'd still be down in the pit, curled up in a fetal position. Any idea how long this is supposed to last?"

Bora winced. "It depends. Maybe a few hours. Maybe more."

"'More,' as in...?

"... twelve?" suggested Bora.

Rick fought off a wave of anxiety. As it arose, the pace of the images increased. *Breathe,* Rick thought. *Don't panic, just breathe.* The slideshow slowed. Each image now lasted an entire respiratory cycle, every exhalation bringing change.

"I don't want to worry you," Bora continued, "but we're in uncharted territory here. Acid usually takes a lot longer to kick in, so I have no idea when this stuff will wear off." Sensing that Rick was now stable, she relinquished her hold on him. "For all we know, it may *never* wear off."

"Fucking great," said Rick, glancing at a tall, red demon in a trench coat. The figure gave him the middle finger before flashing out of sight. "If this *does* wear off, you should try it," he said, using the frame of the car to shuffle toward the passenger's side. "If you can translate half of what I'm seeing into your art, you'll be set for life."

Rick fell inside, shut the door, and dropped his backpack at his feet. Bora climbed into the driver's seat. Here, in the stillness of the car, everything became more manageable. They sat there for a while, allowing Rick to acclimate. From time to time, the sounds would strengthen, and Rick would shut his eyes. They diminished with a comforting predictability. Sticking his fingers in his ears seemed to have the same effect on the visions when they became too powerful. It was a counterintuitive solution—*But if it works, it works*, Rick reflected.

When he finally had enough of a grasp on his new condition, Rick asked, "What now?"

"I was hoping you would tell me," admitted Bora, taking one last hit on her vape before turning on the Sentra. "Does *anything* make any sense to you right now?"

Rick's retinas reluctantly roamed from window to window. There were plenty of things to see, but none provided any clue as to what direction they should head in. At last, he turned his attention to the passenger's window and surveyed the face of the mountain. A group of dogs sat below the switchbacks, playing poker at a table with a green felt top. Above them, a Tiffany ceiling lamp hung in midair, casting a yellow glow over the scene.

The gambling canines vanished along with the table and the lamp. The image shifted to a woodsman taking aim with a bow and arrow— *Fucking Robin Hood, really?*—but the sickly glow remained. Rick lowered his window. Ignoring the Prince of Thieves, he stuck his neck outside and craned it upward. The light intensified. Looking beyond the switchbacks, he noticed that it appeared to originate on the far side of the mountain.

"I see a light," he said, rolling up his window as Robin Hood gave way to a gang of stick figures engaged in a fistfight.

"Where?"

"The other side."

"Where we started?"

"Yeah."

Bora just shook her head and started the engine. "Figures," she said as she completed her three-point turn. "At least I have some practice."

The Sentra pulled onto the road and began tracing its way back up the mountain. Rick stared at his lap the entire time. However, the constant course corrections left him feeling carsick, and by the time they reached the top and headed back around to the opposite side, he was forced to look up again. He immediately started shifting uncomfortably in his seat.

"You good?" asked Bora. "Sorry that I keep asking. You just look like you're in a state of perpetual shock."

"Uh... because I am," Rick replied.

"What is it, then?"

"We have an audience," said Rick, staring through the windshield, wide-eyed. While he realized that all forests were alive, he had never before seen anything quite like this.

A small pine sapling, still bent from the drive up, disappeared underneath the car and screamed. "How so?" pressed Bora.

"You sure you want to know?"

"Lay it on me."

Rick pursed his lips. "The trees have faces," he mumbled at last. It wasn't all he saw, but all he felt comfortable saying. Words failed to capture anything beyond that simple, surreal statement. In fact, it was the least alarming thing he could say. He chose not to tell Bora about the hordes of tiny beings swarming the forest floor, climbing the branches, and peeking out from the knot holes. Rick was surprised at how well he handled their arrival... but then again, he had seen an awful lot in the last half hour.

While the Little People's presence remained constant—they didn't flash in and out of existence or reposition themselves like his other visions—their appearance still fluctuated. Even this had its own consistency, however. In between costume changes, they always snapped back, ever so briefly, into small orbs of light before taking on a new guise.

Rick welcomed this slower, more predictable pace. Compared to the quarry, the imagery on this side of the mountain shifted less frequently. It was almost as if human beings, having left a smaller scar on the landscape here, inflicted less imaginal damage in the process. The forest remained pristine, stable, untainted by mankind's fantasies. The things darting behind the tree trunks and scuttling under the rocks weren't the product of human imagination. They were older. Far older.

'Older than we can comprehend,' Devlin's voice said to Rick. *'Older than comprehension itself, probably.'*

"Okay," Bora said slowly as she pushed the car through a deep depression in the road. "How about that light?"

Focusing past the throngs of tiny figures and down the mountainside, Rick spotted a cluster of light far below, stronger than the luminous orbs floating through the trees. At first, he panicked, thinking that the sunset had begun. He then realized it wasn't the sun but rather the source of the mysterious illumination that he had seen from the quarry. It seemed more concentrated than before, as if someone had set up dozens of multicolored stage lights.

"Getting warmer," he said. "It's coming from somewhere down there."

They continued tumbling down the mountain, saying very little. The road twisted and turned endlessly like a snake, and, like a serpent, both of them feared what waited for them at the business end. Finally, when they were three quarters of the way back to the field, Rick shouted, "Stop! Stop!"

"What is it?" asked Bora.

Rick jabbed a finger in front of her face, pointing out the window. "There," he said breathlessly. "It's coming from there." Rick knew she could see nothing. He, on the other hand, perceived a dazzling array of colors. Whatever it was, it couldn't be more obvious to him. It covered the forest's edge like a fresh oil slick shimmering on the surface of the water.

Bora stopped the car. There was no need to pull onto the shoulder of the road. Even if there had been, it didn't exist here. Bora simply parked, threw on the emergency brake, and popped the trunk. A few minutes later, they trudged across the road and into the woods.

50

Sunday, November 8, 2020

THRESHOLD

BORA TOOK STOCK OF THEIR SURROUNDINGS. There was a time when all forests looked the same to her, when only the most dramatic features would differentiate one woodland from another. Now, having spent so many recent days outdoors, she saw the terrain ahead with the studied eye of a seasoned hiker. While this mountain was much larger than Red Ear, the slope was far more gradual, with fewer gullies. Everything stretched out before them on a smooth, steady incline. Patches of light slipped past the branches above, reticulating the thick carpet of leaves. They looked like luminescent stepping stones, highlighting the way forward.

She let Rick take the lead. Soon, he was several paces ahead of her. He marched away from the road and uphill at a brisk pace, dipping in and out of shadow as he went. From time to time, he would stop and shut his eyes or plug his ears—not because he was lost, but because he was trying to ground himself.

To the contrary, Bora detected no doubt in Rick. For a man who had faced innumerable obstacles throughout his personal life, the path he now traveled seemed completely clear, his trajectory as straight and true as an arrow. Bora had never seen him so sure without a guitar in his hands.

I really hope he pulls through this, she thought, watching a squirrel scamper up a nearby trunk. *Mostly for him, but also for me.* Bora had no idea how she would handle law enforcement if Rick had to kill himself. For the past several days, she had tried to fabricate a suitable story, but none of them sounded believable. *Any way you present that hypothetical scenario, two people walk into the woods, and only one walks out,* a voice inside her warned.

Bora forced the thought from her head. *It won't come to that*, she reassured herself, pushing through a spiderweb connecting two trees.

It can't come to that. Rick is going to be okay. I believe in Devlin. I believe in the ritual, even if I don't know what it is. Above all, I believe in Rick. It had become her mantra over the past three days.

A fern reached out from its perch atop an old stump to brush Bora's leg, drawing her attention to the ground. A veritable minefield of similar obstacles stretched out before her, everything from more stumps to roots and rocks. She kept her eyes on the ground, taking care to keep her footing steady. As she did so, Bora realized how deceptive the incline actually was—it was easy enough to stroll uphill when nothing stood in her way, but this awkward game of hopscotch left her winded.

They hadn't gone far when Rick stopped again. Looking up, Bora saw that he stood in a thinner patch of forest. For the first time, he was neither closing his eyes nor plugging his ears. He was simply spinning in a slow circle, examining his surroundings.

Something immediately felt wrong. Everything felt heightened, realer than real. Bora suddenly became aware of every fiber she wore brushing against her skin. The colors of the leaves here were too vibrant, the air too crisp, and the trees too tall. Their barren branches reached up to the clouds, stretching out to their brethren but not quite touching. Far below the canopy, at the feet of these giants, vast gaps brimming with logs and dead leaves separated their trunks at near-regular intervals.

Bora finally identified what was bothering her. *This place feels... like a border,* she realized. *Between worlds. Between life and death...* The contrast was palpable. Each tree was a graveyard sentinel, drawing strength from its fallen comrades as they decayed into the earth.

When she caught up to him, Bora asked Rick, "Why'd we stop?"

Rick stopped spinning and looped his thumbs underneath the straps of his backpack. "I know this place," he whispered.

"Of course you do. You own this whole mountain."

"Yeah," acknowledged Rick. "But this place... it's different. Everywhere else, the memories are fuzzy... I distinctly remember being *here*. This exact spot."

"That was at least thirty years ago," Bora said. "A lot has probably changed since then. It wouldn't look the same at all."

"A lot *has* changed since then," agreed Rick. "I know because I see this place in my dreams all the time, and it looks exactly like it does now." He pointed up ahead to where the leaves parted, revealing a furrow in the earth crosshatched with logs. "See that?" he asked. "That's the old creek where Mary used to play. Where they found her."

Bora looked at the miniature cliffside snaking up along the length of the mountain. She couldn't see any water from here, only a six-foot-wide gap filled with darkness. It was hard to imagine any child wanting to play there. Everything looked so desolate.

"Rick," she whispered, "I'm not sure it's safe here..." Her instinct had proven correct. This was indeed a place of death and tragedy.

Without giving her a second glance, Rick pushed forward. "Of course it isn't safe," he replied, stepping toward the banks. "*Living* isn't safe. But it's where we have to go." He took off and jumped, easily clearing the gap and landing on his feet. "I wouldn't try crossing on the logs, they look like they're ready to snap in two. But it's not too bad if you take a running start."

Bora didn't follow right away. She decided to inspect her surroundings first. She walked toward the creek as close as she dared, letting the tips of her shoes dangle over the edge. Looking down, she saw a sad little trickle dribbling through the mud five feet below. There were no plants, no animals, no signs of life whatsoever.

Like I thought, Bora said to herself. *Everything's dead here.* Her focus shifted to Rick. He stood a short distance from the opposite bank, looking impatient. To Bora, something about the creek felt like a dangerous threshold, something with which one shouldn't trifle. The point of no return.

When it became apparent that Rick had no intention of coming back, Bora retraced her steps, turned, and ran as fast as she could. She hurtled toward the creek and leapt at the last possible moment. Her feet pushed against the lip of the bank, sinking at least half an inch into the soil before offering enough resistance to propel her into the air. She landed on the opposite side, chest on the ground, rear end in the air.

"Are you okay?" asked Rick, reaching down.

"Yeah," she said, taking his hand and brushing herself as clean as she could. "Just got the wind knocked out of me." She smiled, hoping it looked genuine. "Mind if we take a quick break?" she asked. Maybe Rick wouldn't sense her procrastination.

Rick looked at the ground before answering. Her bluff had failed. He was obviously frustrated. "Fine," he exhaled sharply, sitting down in the leaves and slinging off his backpack.

Bora did the same. She reached inside her bag, pulling out a small package of potato chips. The seal popped, and although it didn't quite echo, it sounded alarmingly loud in the quiet forest. Bora started munching away, then realized how rude she must seem.

"Want one?" she asked, holding out the open bag. Rick peered inside for a long time before shaking his head. He looked like he had just been offered a can of worms.

"If you could see what I see now...." he mumbled, reaching inside his own bag for his flask. After locating it, he unscrewed the top and immediately recoiled, staring at the opening.

"Mm-hmm," Bora said after swallowing another mouthful. "And how does *that* look?"

Rick resembled a finicky toddler facing a plate of vegetables. After a moment, he brought the flask to his lips, took a long drink, and shook his head in disgust. It was not the revulsion of a man who disliked alcohol; it was the shame of a man who hated himself for drinking it.

"Let's just say... now I know why they call them 'spirits,'" he said, screwing the top back on. He held the flask in his hands, unable to avert his gaze. He remained that way until Bora finished her snack, wadded up her trash, and shoved it in her pocket. Only then did Rick move. With shaking hands, he returned the flask to his bag, looking profoundly disturbed the entire time.

"Shall we?" asked Bora, standing back up. Rick said nothing. He simply continued uphill and resumed his course toward their unknowable destination.

I wonder what he really saw, Bora thought as they threaded between the trees. *Must have really bothered him. I've never seen him like that.* She thought back to all their college parties and how Rick was always the last man standing. His feats of inebriation had become legendary across campus... at least until he earned a reputation for raiding hosts' private collections.

Kegs, shots, punchbowls... they were never enough for you, were they? she asked him silently. *Always had to go for the bottle.*

Something made a noise behind her. The forest had been so quiet for so long that Bora couldn't help but be frightened. Even though she recognized it immediately, she jumped, ironically causing a ruckus far louder than what had startled her. This, in turn, caused Rick to stop and look back.

"What happened?" he asked.

"You didn't hear it?" responded Bora. "An owl hooted. Close." It was the first animal sound she had heard since they reached the creek.

"No," Rick said. "I've got too much other noise in my head. Plus, I was distracted by that." He gestured to her left. Just a short way uphill, something interrupted the leaf cover. Bora took a few steps forward, hoping for a better look but wary of drawing too near. When she realized what they were, she stopped. Ten stacks of flat stones, each about two feet high, sat in a circle. They looked like gray, jagged teeth, ready to close around a mouthful of leaves piled in the center.

"What are they?" asked Bora. "Graves?"

"Could be. They're cairns, but other than that, I'm not sure," Rick explained. "Hikers leave them sometimes. Don't remember them before, and I'm pretty sure they haven't been in any of my dreams..." He looked unsure of whether or not he should ask what he was thinking. "Are they... glowing for you?"

"No," answered Bora, mildly unsettled.

"Didn't think so," Rick said. "They look normal in my right eye, too."

"Is that where the light is coming from?"

"No," Rick emphatically replied. "It's still up ahead."

He resumed his mission, and Bora fell in line. The sense of apprehension she noted by the creek refused to abate. In fact, it seemed to grow stronger with each step. She kept dragging on her vape, hoping it might settle her nerves.

It feels like we're walking into a trap, Bora reflected. *Or at the very least heading somewhere no one ever should....*

After about ten minutes, the sensation was too much to bear. She wasn't sure what she was going to say to Rick—there was nothing to be done, and turning back obviously wasn't an option—but she had to say *something*, if for no other reason than to have her feelings acknowledged. She was about to speak up when her friend stopped once again.

"There," he announced. "That's where I'm supposed to go." After catching up with him, Bora saw what he was looking at. Directly ahead sat a small ravine, carved ages ago through the mountainside by a modest stream. Small rises in the landscape, crowned with trees, flanked either side. The sunken seclusion of the passage reminded Bora of the Roman roads she had seen during her semester abroad in Italy.

"The App-alach-ian Way," she said with a chuckle, trying to break the tension. Rick looked at her blankly. "Y'know?" she asked, seeking validation. "Like the Appian... forget about it. I have no idea how you ever graduated."

"Got a little bit on my mind, Bora," he said defensively, closing his eyes. "The voices are stronger here. Visions are, too, but I can't really afford to stifle those right now." He opened his eyes and peered down the dell. "It's like looking at a spotlight through a fishbowl," he added.

The pair cautiously headed inside. Only a short distance in, everything grew more ominous. Bora noticed her heart beating faster. She tried to convince herself that it was simply because of how steep the path had become. It did little to calm her. The incline could not explain how her feet seemed to barely brush the surface of the earth, nor could it answer why the trees began closing in on either side like a half-lowered drawbridge. It might have looked like a fishbowl to Rick, but Bora had the sense of falling down a long, straight funnel, ever-shrinking until the moment they dropped into nothingness.

"I see it, too," she said after about five minutes.

"Huh?" asked Rick. He hadn't noticed. Something was drawing him toward the end of the trail, something that blocked all other distractions.

"The trees," Bora said, nodding to the branches twisting and turning above. While a few leaves had clung here and there when they first entered the dell, they soon disappeared entirely, leaving the branches as exposed as if it were midwinter. In and of itself, that wasn't especially noteworthy. However, each branch now sported a fine, green fuzz—the telltale buds of early spring.

Rick stopped and looked to either side of the pathway, alternating between his left and right eye. "I'll be damned," he said. "Has there been a warm snap recently?"

"Not that I'm aware of," replied Bora, passing him. It was her turn to lead. "C'mon, slowpoke. The sooner we find where this leads, the sooner we can save your ass and go home."

Only a few minutes passed until the buds blossomed and matured into full-blown summer foliage. The sea of green on either side, combined with the chill that remained in the air, reminded Bora of how she always had to wear long sleeves in her father's house whenever she visited. She distinctly remembered the irony of staring outside on a blazing Independence Day, looking at everyone sweltering on the sidewalk while she wore a hoodie.

The unseasonal vegetation also had the knock-on effect of making the dell even more claustrophobic. There was simply no seeing beyond the emerald wall, which continued to narrow minute after minute. In fact, Bora fully expected the path ahead to be blocked.

Then we'll be in a pickle, she thought. *I forgot to pack my machete.* All joking aside, the only thing they had to bushwhack was Rick's chef's knife, which didn't seem especially up to the task.

She was about to express these concerns when she noticed something up ahead. To Bora's surprise, it was not a tangle of greenery but rather something large and gray. Coming to a stop, her heart sank. Not even a machete could overcome this obstacle.

"It's a dead end," Bora groaned, staring at the door-sized slab of rock before them. By all appearances, there was no way around it. Even if they somehow managed to hack their way through the leaves strangling the trail, the stone obviously extended far to either side. Bora suspected that they were looking at the bedrock of the mountain itself.

"What are you talking about?" asked Rick as he stepped up beside her. "Go ahead."

"Huh?" Bora was genuinely confused. The only opening was a vertical split in the rock, likely the source of the long-gone spring that formed the dell. If she really tried, Bora thought she could cram her fingers maybe as deep as her second knuckle. "If this is some roundabout way of telling me I've lost weight, I appreciate it," she said. "Otherwise, I have no idea what you're talking about."

Rick reached out his hand to touch the stone, alternating eyes. "Oh," he said with dawning realization. "Yeah, I see what you mean."

"And I *don't* see what *you* mean," Bora retorted. "Unless this is more of your Narnia shit." In the short time since she had administered the ointment, Rick had become even more frustrating than Devlin.

"It's more Narnia shit," replied Rick. With that, he thrust forward.

Bora was absolutely shocked. His hand disappeared—not into the cleft but into the sheer rock itself.

"What do you see now?" he asked.

"I, um... it.... Where your arm touches the wall, it just disappears," she answered animatedly. "I can't see anything beyond your wrist."

Licking his lips, Rick said, "You try it." He kept his hand buried in the rock. Bora looked at Rick, then at her right hand, and jabbed the rock fingers-first.

"Ow, fuck, shit!" she wailed, cradling her hand. "Jammed my fucking fingers. Fuck."

A look of disappointment spread over Rick's face as he removed his hand from the rock. It reappeared at the end of his arm, none the worse for wear. "Well," he mumbled, "that answers that question."

Despite it never being asked, Bora knew what he meant. "End of the road for me, big fella," she said. She had hoped to accompany him on the last leg of his journey, but that seemed impossible... unless...

"I've got plenty of ointment left!" she exclaimed. "Do you want me to dose myself?!?"

"I can't ask my designated driver to do that," Rick said with a lopsided grin. "Even though you're always higher than a giraffe's ass."

"Said the man seeing unicorns," chuckled Bora.

"Hey, I've only seen one unicorn since we got out of the car," Rick joked back. His smile faded. "In all seriousness, I have no idea what's waiting for me in there. Hell, for all I know, I might not be able to get back out again, even if Devlin's ritual works. No reason for you to risk that." He started sniffling. "Goddammit, I'm tired of crying," he said under his breath as he wiped his eyes. "Bora, you're the best friend anyone could ever ask for. But you've done enough for me. Some things you have to do alone. This is one of them."

Bora had less luck restraining her emotions. When he saw her crying, Rick couldn't help himself. He reached out, wrapping her in his arms. He didn't let go until her shoulder was soaked with his tears.

"I love you, buddy," Bora said, wiping her face.

"Love you too," replied Rick.

She took off her backpack and set it on the ground. "If you need me, I'll be right here," she declared.

"If I'm not back before midnight, you head home," Rick instructed. "Not sure how long that is from now, but it'll be too late for me at that point."

Bora waved a hand dismissively, half to reassure him and half to keep herself from lapsing back into sobs. "Won't come to that," she said, her voice wavering. "You wanna check your backpack one last time?"

"Eh," said Rick with a shrug. "I've checked it a dozen times already. If I don't have what I need, I'm fucked anyway."

Bora cracked a smile. "Just like you, to get a handle on yourself at the last minute," she said. "You ready?"

"Of course not. Part of me just wants to say 'no' to the whole thing and walk away."

"Well... A really smart woman once gave you some good advice on that, didn't she?"

Rick laughed. "I don't know how smart she was, but she was a badass."

"What did she tell you?" prodded Bora.

"Say 'no' today, hear 'no' tomorrow," Rick sighed. With that, he gave Bora one last hug and tightened the straps on his backpack. After a few deep breaths, he took one gigantic step forward.

The last thing Bora Choi saw was a slab of rock swallowing her best friend whole.

51

Sunday, November 8, 2020

UNDERGROUND

Rick immediately bumped his head on the jagged ceiling. If not for the condition of his left eye, he would have panicked. Everything about the situation was nerve-wracking enough—the visions, the performance ahead of him, the possibility of death—but being smothered in darkness would have brought him to his breaking point. That was all his right eye saw: an inky blackness thicker than any he had ever beheld in his entire life. It was so total that he could not even tell when he blinked.

His left eye, however, offered some hope. While it was still darker than a moonless midnight, a tiny pool of amber light blossomed somewhere in the distance, casting a weak radiance on the stone floor, walls, and ceiling.

Remembering his flashlight, Rick took off his backpack and felt around inside. He resisted the urge to enumerate its contents, only focusing on his search for what he needed. Finally, his hand fell on the familiar plastic cylinder. He extracted the flashlight, flicked it on, and held it in his mouth as he re-zipped his bag.

After sliding on his backpack and switching the light to his hand, he got a better sense of the space he occupied—the "real" space, as it were. The white beam revealed a low, rocky tunnel, too short to stand fully upright but tall enough to make crawling feel silly. He took a look at the jumble of stones littering the path before him. They also presented a choice: walk and twist your ankle, or crawl and batter your hands and knees.

He reached up to gingerly touch the spot where he hit his head. The moment he did, a shooting pain lanced through his scalp. He brought his hand into the light and saw that his fingers were red and tacky.

Great, thought Rick, taking the first few steps forward. *Two minutes in, and I'm already bleeding.* Eager to avoid repeating his mistake, he bent over and started shambling along, half-crouched. If he stretched out his arms, he could easily touch the rocks on either side of the corridor. They were wet to the touch, weeping water from deep underground, and soon Rick's fingers were washed clean by the blood of the mountain itself.

Each time he reached out to the walls to steady himself, Rick's flashlight would play across the ceiling, highlighting spots here and there that dripped at a steadier pace. If he relied solely on the flashlight, he would never have been permitted to continue in those moments. However, the tiny yellow dot in his left eye functioned as a beacon. It drew him in like a moth to a flame.

We all know what happens when moths get too close, Rick thought, noticing a dull ache in his lower back. Between the awkward stance and constant readjustment of his legs, his muscles—already put through the wringer in the past few weeks—began protesting anew. *Fucking hell, Rick... You get out of this alive, and you'd better start exercising.*

Once a minute or so, he would stop, rest, rub his hands together, and breathe on them, filling the small passageway with clouds. It was at least fifteen degrees colder beneath the mountain than above it, and his fingers' constant contact with the wet stone left them aching and stiff.

Every aspect of the journey was miserable, save one thing: here, underneath more than half a mile of earth, the sounds and visions that crippled him on the surface were practically non-existent. It was almost like the mountain insulated him from the madness above. The voices turned into indistinct whispers. The other noises became a low din, like a party thrown by your neighbors, while the visions had ceased entirely, save for the pinpoint of light ahead.

Finally, after about a hundred yards of delicately picking his way through the rubble, Rick's left eye accurately identified what he saw. It was firelight billowing from an ornate brazier suspended against the stone to his right. It cast an orange cone in all directions. Everything caught within this boundary appeared much more orderly than the debris field Rick saw in his right eye. It wasn't quite hand-hewn masonry, but it had an obvious sense of order and logic in how it was arranged.

Rick looked beyond the brazier and further down the passage. The torch seemed to be the first in a series of sconces affixed at regular intervals, perhaps every twenty feet or so. He shined his flashlight and closed his left eye. The beam only traveled a third as far as the string of torches before sputtering out into the gloom, turning the tunnel into a gray iris surrounded by rocky sclera.

There was no turning back now. Rick simply trudged forward, bent over, trying to ignore his discomfort. Each sconce passed in a steady rhythm, alternating between the right and left sides of the corridor. At first, Rick kept his flashlight turned on, hoping it would prevent any missteps. However, he discovered something odd: his footing was much better when the flashlight was *off*.

It's almost as if, in trying to light my way, I'm staying stuck in my own reality, thought Rick, rubbing his hands along the wall. It, too, felt much smoother in the darkness. After this realization, he used the flashlight sparingly, only flicking it on after he stopped between every other brazier to check his surroundings. In each instance, the tunnel remained as dull and featureless as ever.

Fully giving into the fantasy of his left eye, Rick noticed that the stonework appeared to change yet again. No longer did the walls and floor look like something out of a crudely-fashioned castle. The rounded curvature of the cobblestones yielded to sharper lines. Slowly, these angular slabs began jutting out in ways that defied logic, a non-Euclidian collage of points that seemed to converge on themselves, double back, and fold reality itself.

Sometimes, they thrust out from the walls like spines. Other times, triangles, hexagons, or even more elaborate polygons simply hovered in midair. Rick's first instinct was to dodge these, but when at last faced with an impassable choke point of these shapes, he discovered that he could simply walk through them unhindered.

However, the walls and ceiling remained inviolable, and Rick soon arrived at an unsettling conclusion. Just as the dell had slowly shrunken to a tiny, green pathway, the passage in the cavern had started narrowing on all sides. Stones pressed him down from the ceiling and in from the walls until, at last, he stopped and switched on his flashlight.

Blinding light filled his right eye, leaving him unable to see anything for several moments. When his vision acclimated, it was just as he feared. Sure enough, a belly crawl lay before him, its diameter no more than three or four feet wide.

I'm not a claustrophobe, Rick thought as he reluctantly lowered himself on his stomach, *but this feels real dicey.* The only thing offering any comfort was the fact that the braziers faithfully continued down the passageway, although their bottoms nearly touched the floor and their flames licked the ceiling. He approached the first with caution, afraid that the heat or smoke might overwhelm him. To his relief, he detected neither from the fixture. It offered light with no harmful side effects.

He shimmied past half a dozen of the torches, noting that, while still uncomfortably narrow, at least the slow collapse of the passage had been arrested. That helped very little in the grand scheme of things, as now Rick could add cramps to his list of ailments. Muscles in his arms and legs stiffened, then seized as he pushed onward. While agonizing on their own, these flares of pain were but a foretaste of the soreness to come once he stretched them out again.

Just when it seemed like too much, Rick's left eye spotted something on the floor ahead. The psychedelic fractals were gone. Whatever it was, it looked fuzzy and red. Rick pulled one of his arms from his side—*Goddamn, that hurts*—and reached out to touch it. To his surprise, it appeared like nothing less than a luxuriant expanse of carpet.

Grabbing a handful, Rick tugged with all his might, dragging his body forward. He wriggled ahead like a worm until his entire torso lay on the soft flooring. For a moment, he remained there, stretching his arms and working out the pain. He relaxed his neck and buried his face in the carpet. A clean, natural scent flooded his nostrils, like flowers blossoming in the springtime. Taking a deep breath, he inhaled the aroma, noticing that the sound echoed. Wherever he was, it was orders of magnitude larger than the space he had just crawled through.

Rick kept dragging himself forward until his legs were free. Ignoring their screaming muscles, he drew them further until he was finally on his knees. Then, with great effort, he stood upright and tried to get a sense of his new surroundings.

From what he could tell, he had emerged into an expansive foyer. The sconces were clustered more tightly here, confined to the left-hand side of the room. Their light revealed a wall covered in dark wood but exposed little of the ceiling. There was simply a vast expanse of darkness above.

In their own way, the walls were equally vacant. No portraits, ornamentation, or even the slightest hint of artistry were apparent. Whoever fashioned the wall—if it had any basis in reality—simply let the wood speak for itself. Each gigantic panel sported a dark, luxuriant grain spreading across the surface, which took on a life of its own in the dim light. With only a little imagination, Rick began coaxing faces, sigils, and landscapes from the mosaic of swirls and whirls.

While the left-hand side of the chamber was simple, the right-hand side remained a complete mystery. It was as black and empty as the ceiling. Curious to see what lay on the other side, Rick took a step, lifted his flashlight with his right hand, and flicked the switch.

He saw only a glimmer of wet stone before the ground fell away beneath him. Instinctively, Rick reached out and behind with his free hand. It found purchase in a rocky furrow deep enough to slip his fingers inside. His feet continued to drop, however, until his arm snapped tight and stopped his fall. His entire body wrenched around violently, sending his chest slamming into the stone face of a cliff.

Between having the wind knocked out of him and the sound of something snapping in his left arm, all Rick wanted to do was let go. He knew that wouldn't end well. In the brief moments before he fell, he realized that he had stepped off a ledge. Luckily, he had managed to hold onto his flashlight. Below him, the beam bounced off the walls of a deep pit, igniting veins of quartz before losing itself in the darkness.

There *was* no right-hand side of the foyer. There was only an empty shaft. Gritting his teeth, Rick tossed the flashlight back onto the ledge to free his right hand. He pawed at the rocks until he found a spot sturdy enough on the ledge to support his weight, then kicked at the cliffside until his shoes stopped slipping. Finally, with what little bit of strength he still possessed, he clambered his way back onto the carpet and collapsed on his back.

Definitely pulled something in my arm, he thought between gasps. *But it's okay. You're alive, and you're on solid ground now. You're safe. Calm down. Wherever you're going, you're not there yet.* He clenched his fists and noticed pain flaring in his left palm. Examining it, he spotted a deep gash in the center.

Guess that answers which hand I use, thought Rick. He didn't relish the idea of leaving here with both hands bleeding, but he knew what had to be done.

For the first time, Rick looked at where he had come from. He tilted his head to the right and saw no sign of the narrow corridor he had traveled. There was just more wood paneling.

No going back that way, Rick decided. He then looked to his left. That was when he finally noticed the door.

If the walls were austere, the door was simply decadent. It was wooden as well, but a deeper color, almost black. Carved spirals, filigrees, and scrolls framed the sides. A vertical triptych of images occupied the center, each depicting a scene rendered in the most minute detail: a lavish banquet, presided over by a queen; a landscape, whose focal point was a pitched battle unfolding before a stone fortress; a mountainside populated with deer, owls, rabbits, and foxes. At the top of the door, overseeing it all, emerged the face of a man, his visage surrounded by a wreath of oak leaves. A large knob sat to the right, polished so immaculately that, even at this distance, Rick could see himself lying on the floor.

He watched himself in the doorknob as he rose to his feet and removed his backpack. After quickly tearing off a strip from his spare shirt and wrapping his left hand, he replaced his bag, grabbed his flashlight, and slowly headed toward the door. His bandage loomed large in the reflection of the bronze handle. Even through the layers of cloth, it felt ice cold.

Rick rotated the doorknob, pulled the door open with a heavy creak, and stepped through into the light.

52

Sunday, November 8, 2020

PARLEY

AT FIRST, RICK COULDN'T SEE A THING, for completely opposite reasons. His right eye saw only darkness, his left eye only light. This forced him to rely on his other senses. Warmth spread across his chest, as if he had just stepped into the sunshine, and a gentle breeze tugged at his shirt. Songbirds called to each other somewhere in the distance.

Slowly, both eyes adjusted. They told two wildly different stories. His right eye was actually able to see everything fine without the flashlight, thanks to a dim light that filled the massive subterranean chamber. His left eye needed no illumination either, as an endless sunset held the lush landscape in perpetual thrall.

In his right eye, boulders of various dimensions lay strewn about the cavern floor, covered in dust and pebbles; in his left eye, there stood a massive circle of cigar-shaped stones on a low hill just ahead, each at least one story high, trying to grasp tufts of clouds as they rolled by. Right, pitted stone walls, dripping water smelling of sulfur; left, a vast stretch of rolling hills leading down to a river tinted red by the sun, a golden city gleaming beyond. Slick stalactites; pink sky. Jagged stalagmites; green grass and flowers in bloom.

By far, the most dramatic contrast was what populated these two spaces. The cavern held ten glowing spheres, which provided enough light for Rick to see his surroundings. On the other hand, the landscape presented these orbs as short human beings sitting at the foot of each standing stone. Their small frames made the monuments loom even larger.

Focusing on his left eye, Rick saw that each person was similarly attired. All wore tiny caps, though the colors varied. By contrast, their jackets and dresses—some were female—were all a vibrant green. They might have blended into the grass if not for bits of bright red here and there in the form of feathers and jewelry.

Rick surveyed the row of faces. Most of their eyes looked like little black buttons sewn to old, wrinkled leather. Below noses of various sizes sat their mouths, which were uniformly small. All of them stared at Rick, not uttering a word. None of them bore any expressions either, save the one closest to him.

It was a little man, just like the others, perhaps a bit lankier. The slightest hint of concern knotted his wizened face. His eyebrows steepled above a pair of mismatched eyes. One sparkled blue, the other brown.

These beings were not alone. In Rick's right eye, the spheres sluggishly orbited a large, black triangle suspended in midair halfway between the floor and ceiling. Although the orbs cast plenty of light throughout the cavern, the triangle did not reflect anything.

This arrangement was loosely mirrored in Rick's left eye. Here, the intelligence behind the dark triangle sat at the center of the standing stones. It looked far different, however. Instead of a simple shape, Rick saw a tall, lissome woman lounging on a throne. Her seat was crudely fashioned of black obsidian, inlaid with glittering jewels.

Her identity was obvious. She had burrowed into Rick's mind one week ago, though their history went back far longer. Here, in her element, she looked completely relaxed and unbothered.

Once again, Rick remarked on how handsome she was. Her features teetered on a knife's edge between feminine and masculine, the sort of face that would appeal to any suitor, regardless of their orientation. The last rays of sunset—going, going, but never gone here, it seemed—cast her in a warm, inviting glow, like a lover seen across the table during a candlelight dinner.

As before, the woman wore a white dress, as ornate as any wedding gown Rick had ever seen, if a bit less restrictive. Her hair was white, too, but much longer than Rick remembered. It stretched all the way to the ground.

The woman rested her dainty feet, unshod, on a long slab of rock serving as a table. Beyond her toes stretched a feast fit for a queen: trenchers of bread, bowls of fruit, plates of vegetables, platters holding lamb shanks and an entire roast duck. There were glass vessels as well, filled with a whole array of liquids, some identifiable, others not. One obviously contained wine, while another appeared to hold milk. Yet another was full of crystal-clear water. The decanter nearest the woman in white contained something dark, red, and viscous.

She either hadn't noticed Rick or she didn't care. He watched her pop a grape into her mouth, chew, then wash it down with a sip from a bejeweled goblet.

Even though the answer was obvious, Rick suddenly doubted he was in the right place. He glanced behind himself to see if the door was still there. It wasn't. There was only the edge of a thick, dark forest, representing an arch in the cavern he had passed through moments earlier.

After waiting a little while longer and still going unacknowledged, Rick began the short hike uphill. Soon he stood at the edge of the circle but dared not go any further without being invited inside. The small watchmen at each standing stone looked at Rick, then expectantly at their leader, then back at Rick.

The woman in white continued eating but finally spoke. "Rickard the Rake," she proclaimed in between bites of lamb. "A bold decision." Finally, she looked up at him. Rick tried not to stare into her blue eyes. "Please, have a seat," she continued, gesturing to a low boulder at the opposite end of the table.

Rick obliged and was surprised to find its rocky surface as comfortable as anything he had ever rested on. He was staring directly into the sunset, but it was not painful to look upon at all. After slipping off his backpack and setting it down on the ground to his left, he took a moment to relish the absurdity of the moment.

Everything his right eye told him now seemed like a lie. That place was cold and drab, dank and dirty. Here, it was paradise.

Somewhere, a million miles back in North Carolina, my ass is sitting underneath a mountain, he thought. *And yet here I am, at a table in fucking Neverland.* It all felt real enough. He could smell the grass and roasted meat mixing together. He could feel the wind. He could see the sunbeams intersecting the decanters, passing through their contents to paint the stone tabletop shades of vermillion and gold.

The woman in white smiled briefly, then resumed eating. "Forgive me," she mumbled through another nibble. "Where are my manners? Please, partake. We've plenty left. Wine?" Rick shook his head. "No

THEM OLD WAYS NEVER DIED

accounting for taste," she sneered. "Well, if you truly desire as much, I can fetch some of that swill you can't get enough of."

Rick finally spoke. "I've got my own, thanks."

"I know that," she replied. Her feet danced to and fro like the pendulum bar on a metronome.

Rick shifted in his seat. No time for pleasantries—it was time to end this. "I've come to—"

"Know that, too," interjected the woman in white matter-of-factly. "Exceedingly little passes beyond my attention." She lowered her feet to the ground, dropped the shank to her plate, and sat upright. Her long, thin fingers seemed to stretch seven full inches across the stone as she placed her hands flat on the table.

"Anything you'd like to know?" she asked, her expression turning from casual indifference to excitement. "I forget how surprising that must be to you folk. Tell me. Anything you want. Come now, don't be shy."

When Rick said nothing, she began offering suggestions. "How about where Susie Drummond wound up?" she proposed. "Surely you recall your first crush? Or maybe you'd like to know where you misplaced that capo three years ago? How about your mother's final thoughts? Hmmm?" The woman in white leaned forward and arched her fingers. "Do you know how Cassandra *actually* felt when she hung up the other day?"

Rick slammed his fists on the table and shouted, "Stop it!" The slab was too solid to cause any of the cutlery to jump, but it sent their audience a few inches into the air. They all exchanged glances before settling back down, crossing their legs, and resuming their expressionless vigil.

A wounded look fell over his host's face. "Oh my," she pouted. "My sincerest apologies. I was just trying to have a conversation before we got down to business. That's what happens at this point in the story, after all."

"Story?" spat Rick. "What story?"

"*Your* story, Rickard," she said, rising from her throne. She walked until she was halfway down the right-hand side of the table, then stopped to run her finger along the rim of a bowl. "Page 463. Chapter 52: *Parley*. 'At first, Rick couldn't see a thing, for completely opposite reasons...'" Her voice trailed off. "There's more. I won't bother you with it. It's somewhat dull and overlong, to be honest. What I'm trying to say, Rickard, is that your perspective... it's so... *limited.* If only you could see the way we do." She smiled. "You will, someday."

It was Rick's turn to interrupt her. "Enough nonsense!" he said. It wasn't a yell; it was a whisper, but it carried more rage than anything that had ever passed his lips. "You're nothing more than a parasite. Preying on people. Stripping away everything they love."

"I'm not sure I understand," the woman in white admitted, looking confused. "You are *so* important to us, Rickard. We enchanted your life. All your days, you have sought something greater. You tried raising a family." She snorted. "A valiant effort. When that failed, you tried crawling into a bottle... although to be fair, you were half inside already."

With long, graceful steps, the woman in white drew nearer until she was alongside Rick. A gentle breeze lifted a few errant strands of hair from her head, turning them into cords of light that waved like serpents in the sunset.

"You're right about one thing," she confessed. "We take what we please. But we also *give*, Rickard." She continued forward, circling around to his back, where she gently placed her slender hands on his shoulders. They felt even colder than the doorknob. Rick flinched but refused to look or fight.

"You haven't given me *anything*," said Rick, staring at the table. "Just more trouble."

When the woman in white spoke again, Rick could hear her smiling. "You know what they used to call us? 'People of Peace.' I always liked that one." Her hands gave his shoulders a quick, affectionate squeeze. "That's what we can offer you, Rickard. *Peace.* They've never understood you, have they? Your bandmates, your friends, your wife, your son. They have no idea what it's like to be trapped in that head of yours. They all think you're selfish, but I know what you're after. I've always known, since before you were born.

"You want *peace*. No more filing silverware in drawers. No more scribbling in your notebook or checking gear a dozen times before performances. No more divorce, no more pandemics, no more politics. No more hangovers. No more lectures about your drinking. *Peace.*"

Rick pursed his lips and shook his head. "Peace, death... Those sound too much alike," he observed.

"Don't all great artists die before their time?" the woman in white asked, letting go of his shoulders and circling around to his left side. The only sounds were distant birdsong and her long locks caressing the grass. "You can leave a legacy, Rickard. I have seen it. Not just an endless list of album credits, but a genuine *legacy*. Mingus, Monk, Coltrane... Coulter. Has a nice ring to it."

"Sounds nice, but it doesn't exist," Rick shot back.

"Not yet, it doesn't."

"I came here to get rid of you or die. Those are the only two options."

"Hardly," said the woman in white. "Rickard, like any top-tier musician, you always listen... but you rarely *hear*. Believe me, I'd love nothing more than for you to stay. I've even prepared you a seat at the table."

She gestured to the nearest edge of the stone circle. There was a deep rumble. Two of the monoliths parted, carrying their tiny stewards in opposite directions. Their shadows shifted as the circle widened in the sunlight. The ground between them didn't split open—it simply stretched like a piece of taffy until, in the newly created space, another stone appeared, rising from the earth until it stood as tall as the others. The space at its base was empty.

Rick stared at the slab of rock, then looked back at the woman in white. "That's no seat," he said. "It's a headstone."

She ignored him. "As I was saying," she continued, "you're not *hearing* me. We can be quite charitable under the proper conditions. I'm not talking about death. I'm offering a stay of execution. Enough time to forge a legacy. With our help, you will become a household name—not for that noise you made at the bar, mind you. You can play whatever you wish."

"Yeah, right," said Rick. "For how long?"

"Until the day you see fit to fulfill your obligation," she replied. "Every breath before your last, we shall be your constant companions. But not as we have been the past year. We will help you. *Guide* you. You shall have all your heart desires." She paused, then added, "Desire is the most powerful force in the universe, Rickard."

They're determined and contractually minded boogers. The words startled Rick. It was Devlin's voice, ringing in Rick's ears. The sound was so strong and clear that it seemed to come from somewhere other than memory.

Rick took a quick glance at the being with the mismatched eyes. He appeared deeply invested in their conversation.

"It can't be that easy," Rick finally responded.

"Oh, I assure you, it is," said the woman in white. She was casually rearranging a bowl of turnips, like their dialogue was at best a secondary concern.

"I choose when I kill myself? Even if I'm ninety?"

"Even if you're ninety."

"And that's it?"

"Primarily."

"Primarily?"

The woman in white let the roots fall back into the bowl and looked at Rick like he was a simpleton. "You know how things work," she said knowingly. "Debts accrue interest over time."

"'Interest,'" repeated Rick. "You sound like a record executive. What do you *really* want?" He wasn't very interested, but something inside him had to know. Maybe there was some way to live his life to the fullest before the bill came due.

The woman in white sighed dramatically. "We want *so* many things," she said with a frown. "Respect, for starters. We miss it. The rituals, the offerings... the pageantry."

"You didn't answer my question," said Rick.

"Oh, but I did. You asked the wrong thing."

"Fine. What do you want *from me*?"

"I told you," she replied. "Your debt, plus interest."

"I understand the first part. Tell me exactly what you mean by 'interest.'"

The woman in white walked the rest of the length of the table, then collapsed on her throne. She acted exhausted. "Your son, of course."

"You've got to be fucking kidding me."

"By the time you end your life, *two* lifetimes will have passed since your father swore his oath," she explained. "Strikes us as quite reasonable."

"Kiss my ass," snarled Rick.

The woman in white held up her hands defensively, sending spidery shadows creeping across the table. "No one's forcing you," she declared. "You always have free will." When she relaxed, her face turned sad and introspective. "I always envied your lot for that."

Rick placed his hands in his lap and stared at them as if he were seriously considering her offer. "Free will, you say?" he asked. As subversively as he could, Rick allowed his left hand to drop to his backpack and quietly unzipped the main pocket. "Where's Jack's free will in this whole arrangement?"

The woman in white launched into a short monologue. As she spoke, Rick reached inside and groped around for the chef's knife with his bandaged hand.

"Come now, Rickard," his host began in a sympathetic tone. "Surely, you can't be serious? We're all friends here, are we not? Can't we be honest?" She sat back in her throne, resting her hands on the armrests. "No need to lie. Have you ever *really* put the needs of your progeny before your own? All those late-night performances, the parties, the drinking. Looking over your life, I see an endless string of selfish acts only occasionally interrupted by fleeting moments of charity.

"You can't outsmart me. I've seen inside that tangled rat's nest you call a head. I *know* why you were kind in those moments. The visits, the gifts, the compliments. It was because you felt *guilty*. It was never motivated by altruism. You never believed you were doing the right thing. You just thought that it was what you *should* do.

"And do you know what, Rickard?" she concluded. "I don't blame you. Unlike your wife, unlike your son... unlike your father... *I* don't blame you. You're only human, after all."

Rick bit his lower lip and slowly nodded in agreement. "Sounds like you know me better than I know myself," he conceded. "You're probably right. I probably didn't believe I was doing the right thing." His bandaged hand tightened around the knife. It hurt, but he ignored the pain.

"You know what I *do* believe in?" he asked. *"This."*

53

Sunday, November 8, 2020

SACRIFICE

CALAMITY FOLLOWED. Rick launched from his seat, brandishing the knife. He pointed its tip at the woman in white, who rose from her throne as well. An expression of alarm and determination seized her face, but she didn't appear surprised. It was the look of someone who, faced with danger, knew that they had the situation under control… yet realized things could go wrong at any moment.

In the meantime, the sight of cold steel sent her entire court shrieking and wailing like a troop of startled apes. All of them leapt to their feet, scrambling in place before darting behind the standing stones. A majority of them vanished entirely, cowering on the opposite side. Only a few dared to peek out of their hiding places to watch Rick begin the ritual.

He spun in place, tracing the knife in a wide arc around him. The entire time, he visualized a silver beam of cleansing light firing from its tip. When he finished, Rick held the knife at arm's length, training it on the woman in white like it was a handgun.

Without lowering his eyes, he knelt down and used his other hand to pull the tambourine from his backpack. He stood upright and gave it a fierce shake. Once the echo of the tiny metallic disks faded, he began his recitation, drawing upon hours of careful practice.

"Oh, Clan Sidhe!" he boomed. "People of Peace, venerated in accordance with the ways of old; here before the creation of earth and heaven, night and day; present before the first dawn, enduring aeons after the last sunset; inhabitants of earth, water, sky, and flame; ye subjects of…"

Rick stuttered. This was by far the hardest part. *Autopilot, Rick*, he told himself. *Just like playing scales. Trust your muscle memory.*

"… ye subjects of Áine and Bodb; Aoibhill and Cliodhona; Diana and Ethal Anbual; Donn and Finnbheara; Gloriana and Gyre-Carling;

Grian and Mab; Medb and Nicnevin; Midir and Una; Oberon and Titania; ye with names unpronounceable on mortal tongues; I call thee from all corners of Elphame, an Saol Eile, Annwfyn, and Tir na nOg to ask thine audience. I bid thee, grant my request, in the name of propriety and honor ages past!"

To punctuate this command, he shook the tambourine once more and let it fall to the ground. As quickly as possible, he stooped over his backpack and retrieved the freezer bag and his bottle of vodka. He rose and tossed both on the tabletop, sending a bowl of dates tumbling over the side. The entire time, Rick managed to keep the tip of his blade directed on the woman in white, whose eyes had only grown wider.

Awkwardly, Rick stepped forward, grabbed the freezer bag with his free hand, ripped it open, and flipped it upside down. The contents spilled to the stone slab. His wedding ring tinkled and bounced, while the margarine, long since softened, simply landed with a wet splat. "With these gifts—gold, butter, spirits, and this most sacred fluid..."

Rick paused and moved the knife for the first time. Placing the blade in his right hand, he squeezed tight and jerked the handle down with his left, instantly cutting a long, clean gash in his palm. The faint sound of metal slicing flesh was more sickening than the pain, which was negligible until the bleeding started. When Rick uncurled his fingers, his right hand was awash with blood, flowing so plentifully that he couldn't even see the wound.

Stifling his revulsion, Rick slung his hand at the table, sending the excess fluid arcing across the feast. Crimson droplets flecked the margarine, his ring, and the plastic bottle. Bringing his palm to his face, Rick took a moment to examine the damage he had done. A pair of loose, parallel skin flaps were only visible for a moment before a fresh spout of blood blotted them from sight.

Rick brought his hand even closer until it touched his face. Pressing hard, he smeared it top to bottom with blood, then struggled through the pain to remember what came next.

"... this most sacred fluid; font of life; river of death and gateway to realms beyond; I offer expiation at mine own hand, humbling myself before thy mercy.

"On this, the day upon which Gwyn ap Nudd opens doorways; eighteen score and six dawns since the transfer of obligation; three decades and four years since the binding of my forefather's consent; through the door of Nudd I pass to demand, according to the powers of east and west, north and south"—using the sunset as a guide, he pointed the knife in each direction, then returned it to his host—"and all principalities of righteousness, our agreement null and void. Here no longer shall I stay, neither in thy realm nor within the confines of thy power.

"Let not the sins of the father be visited upon the son; with blood and steel I release thee and me from all obligations, to pass beyond these walls in peace and sovereignty!"

Echoes of Rick's voice rebounded across the stone circle. His heart hammered in his chest. Though his body trembled, he kept pointing the knife at the woman in white, who now covered her mouth with her hands.

Nothing happened. Rick closed his eyes. For a moment, the blood clung to his eyelids, restraining them a fraction of a second longer than usual before breaking free with a sticky snap. After taking a deep breath, he opened his eyes once more. One saw only darkness—the orbs had evacuated the cavern when he produced the knife—while the other finally saw the woman in white react.

During the time Rick's eyes were closed, she had doubled over. She gasped for air. Convulsions wracked her body. Her long, flowing hair left its place at her back to congregate around the sides of her head, obscuring her face.

Glancing around the circle, Rick noticed that the other beings still sheltered behind their stones, though curiosity had coaxed more of them to take a look. All remained terrified of his knife.

Then Rick heard it: a weak series of sobs arising from the other end of the table. The woman in white was crying. She had completely lost control of her body. Between how she crouched and how little he could see through her hair, it looked as if she was melting into the ground.

Did it work? wondered Rick. *She looks awful... I think... fuck me, it worked. I never thought it would, but it actually worked...*

Rick's glory was short-lived. As the weeping continued, he realized it didn't sound quite right. After several seconds, he finally admitted that his suspicions were true.

The woman in white wasn't sobbing. She was laughing.

His host lifted her head, tossing her hair back into place to reveal her face. A broad, open smile graced her features. Tears indeed filled her eyes—but not from disappointment. She cackled louder and louder, slapping her knee and steadying herself on the table. At last, the woman in white regained her composure.

"You... oh, my... You pronounced my name wrong," she hooted, wiping the last bit of water from her eyes. "Oh, Rickard, that was rich." She held out her hand in a pantomime of Rick wielding the knife. "'I believe in... *this*!'" said the woman in white, thrusting her arm forward.

"No, you didn't," she corrected him after sniffling and taking a deep breath. "Even if you *had* believed in it, I'm not sure it would have worked. It's not the worst I've heard—to be fair, we've existed before the laying of the firmament—but it's close. Where on Earth did you learn that utter *nonsense*?"

Rick opened his mouth. He didn't know what to say. So many emotions rose in him. Disappointment. Defeat. Confusion. Terror. Mostly, Rick felt angry.

Devlin had sent him into the tiger's den with a phony ritual. It was all bunk. There was no greater power in it, no proven track record of efficacy. Devlin had made it all up, and apparently it wasn't even that good—even if he himself had been there to speak them, the words would have *never* worked. It was Devlin Fox's last and greatest gamble. He had bet on Rick Coulter's belief, and Rick Coulter had lost everything.

Whatever miniscule amount of hope Rick held evaporated. He threw the knife onto the table. It landed with a clatter, knocking over the vodka bottle. Rick stepped forward and slumped on his boulder. He was beaten and battered in every sense of the word.

The vision seen in his right eye swelled and engulfed him. He was cold, alone, and in the dark. Ever since his argument with Jack this summer, he thought he had seen the worst life had to offer. Now, alone in a black pit underneath a mountain facing suicide, he knew what rock bottom actually looked like.

The darkness dissipated as a voice drew him back into the other reality. It was the woman in white, answering her own question.

"Oh," she said, realizing where Rick had learned the ritual. "Of course. The Fox." Rick looked up from the grass as she took a series of deliberate, measured steps down the table. When she was only a few feet from him, she folded her arms and leaned back against the rock.

"After that little display, I rescind my offer," she proclaimed, looking at Rick like he was a misbehaving child. "The time has come. Your window closes. The sun sets in your world, just as it does here. Tomorrow, the rest of your days shall be ours. But you can spare your lineage now." She nodded in the direction of the knife. "Take the weapon."

Rick reached out. He didn't grab the knife. He grabbed the vodka. For a few moments he just stared at the bottle. Then, for some reason he didn't understand, he tried to rub the blood off the plastic. He only added more.

"You do it," he said. "I'll even take off my pendant. But you do it. I can't."

"You came here of your own volition. That bauble holds no power here. Even if it did, it doesn't matter. It must be a *gift*, Rickard. You must make the ultimate sacrifice to fulfill your father's debt."

Despite knowing that she was going to say them, the words still stung. Rick had not looked up from the vodka in his hands. So much of his life was spent searching for a new bottle, finding a way to pay for it, making the time to drink it. He never realized that each time he emptied the bottle, he was actually emptying himself.

"Go ahead," urged the woman in white. "You deserve it. One last drink. Or finish the whole thing, for all I care. Whatever helps."

Rick finally moved. Screwing off the top, he saw the same thing he had noticed earlier in the afternoon when he and Bora rested by the creek.

Opening the bottle was like releasing a genie from a lamp. Invisible yet clear as day, a cloud escaped—a true spirit in every sense of the word, an insidious force that coiled in on itself, wanting nothing more than to be consumed so it could consume. The alcohol had a life of its own. It would enter him and make him a completely different person, supplanting his true self with something alien. Something he never wanted to be.

This is the moment I die, Rick realized, bringing the bottle to his lips. *Not when I plunge the knife. Right here, right now. With each swallow, I will become someone else, bit by bit, until Rick Coulter is no more. As I drink, I lose myself.*

Rick pressed the plastic to his lips and tilted the bottle upright. What happened next was inevitable. It had unfolded countless times before. Rick was powerless, and he knew it. A cascade of clear liquid tumbled down toward him, carrying with it the hideous force that would take him over, make him say things he would never say, do things he would never do, feel things he would never feel...

An instant before the liquor kissed his lips, Rick tilted the bottle upright. The alcoholic tide receded, swaying back and forth in the bottle before settling. At the very last moment, something stopped him.

He heard voices. They were not the constant barrage experienced on the surface, however. Some he recognized as Devlin's, some he recognized as his own.

Maybe you could sacrifice your identity... something in the fabric of your soul... I don't know who I'd be if I quit drinking... Take the chance to change....

Placing the bottle back on the table, Rick let his eyes wander to the ring of stones encircling him. Only one of the creatures had returned to its confines: the little man with mismatched eyes. He stared at Rick just as before, with one notable difference. Now he wore a slight smile.

Rick looked at the bottle, then back to the woman in white. "This," he said, picking it back up.

"Come again?" asked his host. She looked confused.

"*This*," he repeated, shoving the bottle in her direction.

"You can't."

"I can," snapped Rick. "I can for my son. What was it you said? That I can't outsmart you? I don't have to. I just have to outsmart myself. You want a sacrifice? You want a life? This. *This*. This has been more important to me than anything else. If I stop this, my old life will be gone. Tell me: is this enough?"

The woman in white unfolded her arms, looking disappointed. She rubbed her face, then looked off into the sunset. "You see that?" she asked. "It just stays there, halfway past the horizon. It never moves. It's always the same. That sunset is me." She turned back around and looked at Rick. "I have prayers, you know. Never know who to send them to. Sometimes I pray to myself, sometimes to the All-Father, to Ra, to a bodhisattva, sometimes to Gitche Manitou."

She chuckled. "In my moments of weakness, I even pray to Christ Jesus." The woman in white hung her head. "Do you know what I pray for? For something to be *different*. Anything. I just want something to be unpredictable. Yet every passage of the moon heralds another dawn where I know everything that is about to unfold. *Everything*, Rickard. Do you have any idea how tedious that is?"

Rick thought back over the past year, of the endless days spent cooped up inside the house in Ellijay. "I have an inkling," he said.

"So, believe me when I say that none of this is surprising. I've known about this forever. When I first heard your proposal millennia ago, I had my doubts. I still do, now that the moment has arrived. Sobriety? Not our usual currency. Why would we accept such a pittance?"

The woman in white looked neither at the sunset nor at Rick. She fixed her gaze at the being with the mismatched eyes.

"And yet," she sighed, "here I stand and... having borne witness to your life... I understand how much that bottle means to you. I see the change ahead and how different things will be for you. How difficult they will be. How much you will suffer."

She broke into a brief moment of candor. "I'm not going to lie, it tastes *delicious*. I can't wait to watch you squirm."

"Will I make it?" asked Rick.

"I'm no fool," the woman in white said. "I will say this: *if* you pass all of your days true to your word... we will close your account. In the meantime, our influence will become far more subtle, but we shan't desist. Every morning you rise, we will be with you. You won't always recognize us, but we'll be there. Watching. Waiting. Prodding. Encouraging. We only have to convince you once. You have to resist every day."

At last, the woman in white's gaze returned to Rick. "If you fail, we will return in full force," she continued. "We shall visit upon you tenfold what you have experienced. No negotiations. You'll *wish* you had used that knife to take your life today."

Rick placed the bottle on the table and pushed it as far as he could from his grasp. "I feel sorry for you," he said. "You have no idea what you're up against. Stubbornness kept me in the bottle. Stubbornness will keep me out of it."

For the longest time, Rick and the woman in white stared at each other. It felt like the perpetual sunset: a moment locked in time, never-ending, stretching into eternity. He had just signed up for the same thing. The changes he agreed to now would last forever.

"Forever." A daunting word. He didn't know if he could do it.

He didn't know… but he *believed* he could.

And belief is the most powerful force in the universe.

EPILOGUE

Friday, April 22, 2022

NOT TODAY

FOR YEARS, THE COFFEEHOUSE HAD CLOSED EARLY. Only recently had the owners decided to expand operations past the early afternoon, offering light alcohol sales to accompany their inaugural concert series. In their excitement to expand operations, they overlooked several crucial issues, the most glaring of which was parking.

Jack Coulter slowly circled the establishment, searching for an empty space. The building holding the coffee shop had begun its life as a church—barely bigger than a chapel, really—and the parking lot had never grown to accommodate its newfound popularity. Luckily, it was far enough on the outskirts of Blue Ridge that Jack doubted anyone would mind if he parked on the grass.

The boy climbed the old stone steps, checking his watch. Traffic coming north had been awful—predictable for a Friday—but Jack still had plenty of time before the seven o'clock downbeat. He opened the door, and a tiny bell at the top jingled, announcing his arrival.

It was a lovely space, especially at this time of day when golden light came to play. Far to the back, three of the church's original stained glass windows had been preserved. In front of them, the chancel had been converted into a surprisingly accommodating stage. At the moment, it held a few chairs and music stands as well as several instruments: a drum set, a double bass, a trumpet and flugelhorn, and some familiar guitars.

Between Jack and the stage, swarms of people congregated at their tables and the counter, laughing and talking over their coffee and beer. The crowd was more or less evenly distributed, with the exception of a huddle off to one side.

Jack approached the group and immediately recognized his father's back. He was deep in discussion with several audience members.

"Rodney told me you were pretty banged up, right?" a man asked, adjusting his glasses.

"My friend still hasn't gotten the blood stains out of her car," Jack heard his father say. "Both hands torn up, a big gash on my head."

"Holy hell," said the man, shaking his head. "Where were you—I'm sorry, I don't want to—"

"It's fine, really. I've told this story a hundred times."

"Where were you again?"

"My father's old mine in North Carolina."

"What in God's name were you doing *there*?"

Jack watched his father raise and lower his hands to convey a lack of answers. "Search me," he said. "At least I was fully clothed, right? My friend picked me up and drove me back down to Dahlonega to check me into rehab. I would say it was a miserable drive, but I barely remember it."

"Wait—how did he know you were there?"

"*She*," Rick corrected. "I, uh… I still had my phone. She says I called her."

The man just nodded, obviously self-conscious about the beer he held against his abdomen. His eyes widened from behind his spectacles when he noticed Jack.

"Looks like I need to yield the floor," he said, nodding over Rick's shoulder.

Rick spun around. The moment he laid eyes on his son, his face lit up. "Jack Attack!" he exclaimed, tackling him in a big bear hug. "Glad you made it, buddy!"

"Told you I'd be here," Jack wheezed after taking a few seconds to recover. "Traffic sucked ass. It took a lot longer than I thought."

Rick beamed. "Well, I'm just glad you made it safe," he said. He stepped aside to acknowledge the man whose conversation Jack had interrupted. "Jack, I don't know if you've ever met Travis. He used to play dobro with the Rib Wrenches."

The man smiled and held out his hand. As Jack shook it, he said, "Nice to meet you. I'll let y'all catch up."

Rick placed a hand on Travis's shoulder. "Thanks for coming out tonight, brother," he said. "I think you'll enjoy it. Hey—we still on for Monday night?"

"You were serious?" asked Travis. "About getting together and just jamming? I thought maybe you were just being nice."

"Wouldn't miss it for the world," Rick replied, turning his attention back to his son. "Text me your address. See you then, Trav." Putting his arm around Jack, Rick ducked out of the conversation and led them over to a quieter portion of the room.

"How are things back home?" he inquired, lowering his voice. "How are Mom and Logan?"

"They're fine," said Jack, leaning against the wall. "I don't like him much, though."

Concern fell over Rick's face. "He's behaving himself, right?"

"Yeah, yeah. He's just..." Jack searched for the words. "He's not you. All he talks about is his fucking Lamborghini."

"Yikes," Rick said. "Don't worry. I'll always be too poor to afford one, I promise you."

The two of them laughed. Jack looked out across the audience. It was getting close to showtime, and the drummer had already taken his seat, rearranging his toys for easy access during the coming performance.

"I had no idea it would be this packed," marveled Jack.

"Me neither," Rick admitted. "Good thing, too. It'd be embarrassing to throw a release party and have no one show up."

"What's the album called again?"

"*Belief*," Rick answered with a tinge of embarrassment. "It's cheesy, I know."

"It's a concept album, right?" chuckled Jack. "They're always cheesy."

"Can't argue with that."

"What's it about?"

"Please don't make me say it out loud," Rick begged. His son shook his head and smiled expectantly. "Okay, okay... So..." Rick tried to put it as plainly as he could. "I had this friend. A real weird cat, talking nonsense all the time. But this one day, he said something that stuck with me. He said that stories always want to turn out a certain way, right? The hero always has to slay the dragon. If he doesn't, it goes against the will of the universe, or somesuch.

"Well... I got to thinking. He was right, and he was wrong. The songs on *Belief* approach that from a different angle. While everyone's got to *defeat* the dragon, you don't have to *slay* the dragon. Is this making any sense?"

"I think so," said Jack. "But how do you beat a dragon without killing it?"

"You turn your back on it," Rick replied. "You acknowledge its power, and you walk away. By not engaging in the fight... you win the fight."

"Okay, now you've lost me," confessed Jack.

Rick smiled and put his arm back around his son. "It's okay," he reassured him. "If you need to understand someday, you will. If you don't need to—even better." Rick changed the subject. "I know you've got to be tired from the drive up. Want some coffee?"

"Yeah, but I'll get it myself," offered Jack. "You need to go get ready."

"If it's any consolation, you don't have to go back tonight," Rick said. "You can stay on the couch at my apartment, or Aunt Bora has a spare bedroom. Your choice."

Jack was about to answer when the bell on the front door jangled. The low hum of the crowd amplified by a factor of five as Bora Choi and Edna Durchdenwald whirled into the coffeehouse. They were arguing about something inconsequential, and nearly everyone in the establishment looked to see what all the fuss was about.

None of the attention bothered either woman. In fact, they continued debating until Bora spotted Rick. She immediately headed in their direction.

"Hey!" she shouted once she was within a few feet. "Sorry we're late, I had this potential buyer over and he just wouldn't leave, he kept asking so many questions and looking at the same painting over and over again, and the good news is I finally sold one, but the first time he tried to pay it was declined, so he had to get on the phone with the credit card company, and then I go over to pick up Edna and she still wasn't—oh! Hi Jack! God, it's been *forever*, how you doing?!?"

"Uh... I'm, uh, fine, Bora," Jack replied, shellshocked.

"Don't mind me," came a voice from behind Bora. "Just an old bitch, legally blind, abandoned in a crowd of fuckin' strangers." Edna tapped her white cane on the wooden floor, cursing and parting the crowd like a Tarantino remake of *The Ten Commandments.*

"What's the opposite of a caregiver, Bora?" she rambled on as she met up with the group. "Neglect-giver? 'Cause you sure as shit—" She stopped and squinted through her cataracts. "Jake? Is that you?"

The young man looked embarrassed for her. "Jack, Ms. Durchdenwald," he said. "Nice to see you again."

"Y'all, I'm sorry," interjected Rick. "We can talk afterwards, but I've got to get going." He started to leave. When he was only a few steps away, someone tugged at his shirt sleeve. It was Bora.

"You okay with all this?" she asked, looking at the beers exchanging hands at the counter.

"Yeah," answered Rick. "I'm a musician. There's no way of escaping it."

"I don't know how you do it," Bora said. "If I had to work in a dispensary, I'd never stop smoking."

Rick glanced at the stage. Everyone else had taken their places except the trumpet player, who was noodling a quick warmup on the farthest corner.

"It's like... an old lover, you know?" explained Rick. "You see them, you remember the good times and why you got together in the first place... but then you remember how they put you through hell."

That seemed to satisfy Bora. She then asked, "What about our friends? Any of them in the audience tonight?"

A quick scan of the crowd revealed no familiar faces. At least none of the ones Bora was suggesting.

"Don't think so," said Rick. "They usually show up when I'm alone. Having friends around seems to keep them at bay," he explained with a smile.

Bora responded in kind. "Alright, then," she said. "Go get 'em."

Released from her grip, Rick took the stage and began putting the finishing touches on his setup. A few minutes later, the performance began, starting with the title track of the new album. From the very first notes, everyone was spellbound. Rick was thrilled but unsurprised. He had felt the same way when he first heard that melody all those years ago.

The first set continued as a mixture of selections from *Belief* and some of Rick's favorites: *A Child is Born, There Will Never Be Another You,* and *Confirmation,* among others. When it was his turn to take a solo on *Black Orpheus,* Rick forgot the condition of his right hand and tried some of his old tricks. His fingers faltered, and he retreated to simpler shapes.

The knife wound inflicted back in 2020 had never quite healed right. At least now, two years later, the pain had finally subsided. Rick's hand just never felt as nimble as it once did. It was a small price to pay for his new lease on life. While he always felt a little disappointed at not being able to play like he used to, Rick embraced the challenge of inventing figures simple enough to execute while remaining compelling.

The combo closed the set with something a little less traditional: a jazz cover of *Colon Response* by the Shit Bees. The tune was still garbage, but with enough chord substitutions thrown underneath, it at least became harmonically interesting. Jack could barely contain his excitement.

As they entered the final reprise, Rick thought about the unlikely scene the coffeehouse presented. Certainly, it had come at a price, but everything worked out. Not the life he wanted, but the life he desperately needed.

Rick waved to the crowd, announced a quick intermission, and headed to the counter for a coffee. Along the way, he acknowledged as many compliments as he could but yearned for a break from all the commotion. Cradling the warm paper cup in his hands, he weaved through the crowd and ducked out the back door for a little fresh air.

He expected to find at least one of his bandmates there. Instead, he was alone except for a few flies buzzing around the dumpster. *Ah, the musician's natural habitat,* Rick thought, taking a sip of his coffee.

Although it was already spring, he could feel the temperature dropping with the sunset. He stared out across the small field behind the coffeehouse, thinking about laughter filling that space years ago, when the building was still a church: potlucks, baptisms, small festivals raising funds for a new roof. He thought of all the children escaping into the woods beyond the meadow's borders, of their parents' voices calling to them, full of discipline and a mild undercurrent of concern. Of the way they would tromp back to the church, feet muddy and hair full of twigs.

The final bit of the sun sank behind the treetops like a scuttled battleship. Its last surviving rays launched yellow liferafts across the field. They washed up against Rick's feet and glinted. Something sat at the edge of the blacktop. Something he hadn't noticed before.

Rick took a few steps forward and crouched down. There, sitting perfectly upright in the midst of pebbles, a nail, and a discarded candy bar wrapper, was a small plastic mini-bottle.

Someone brown baggin' it at the coffeehouse, he thought to himself. *I know the feeling. A menu only offering beer and wine might as well not have any alcohol at all.*

He reached out to collect the trash. When his hand hit the mini-bottle, it was much heavier than it should have been. Turning the tiny container over in his hands, he noticed that the seal remained intact. It was still full. It was filled with vodka.

Not just any vodka, Rick observed, noticing the label. *This is my vodka.* A familiar compulsion seized him. *It would be so easy,* he thought. *No one would know. I could just pop the lid off this coffee, pour it in, and finish the gig...*

Rick heard something. At first, he thought it was one of the guys in the band warming up, playing the album's title track. He then realized that it didn't sound like any of the instruments on stage. Moreover, the melody was too clear. It came from out here. From across the field.

Looking up and towards the direction of the sound, Rick saw two different scenes. It had gotten easier the past few years, living in different worlds, but sometimes he couldn't hold the visions at bay—especially in moments of weakness.

Rick's left eye spotted something. It was a row of ten diminutive figures standing in a line by the forest's edge, their heads barely visible above the tall grass. None of them moved.

His right eye saw nothing but a few pinpoints of light wandering between the trees. Anyone standing alongside Rick could have easily mistaken them for flashlights, or even headlights reflecting from a road somewhere beyond the forest.

After blinking a few times, Rick turned his attention back to the bottle. It felt so heavy, so full of potential. He wanted nothing more than for it to be empty. He thought back to the figures standing by the woods. It was entirely too far to see their faces, but he felt an overwhelming sense of anticipation from them, like sports fans awaiting a winning goal from the home team. All of them were rooting against him... except, Rick knew, for one sole dissenter.

Two years into overtime, thought Rick. *It may last another two or another ten. Might last another month, another week, or another day.* He gripped the mini-bottle tighter and glared at the distant spectators. *You want me to fumble, don't you?*

Rick Coulter didn't fumble. He passed.

With all his might, he pulled back his arm and lobbed the bottle as hard as he could into the field. It traced a broad arc against the orange sky, its trajectory sending it deep into the weeds, so distant that Rick couldn't even hear it hit the ground. The shapes and lights vanished.

"Not today, bastards," he whispered to the now-vacant field. "Not today."

About the author

In addition to writing, Joshua Cutchin is a published composer and maintains an active performing and recording schedule as a tuba player based out of Atlanta, Georgia. He has appeared on dozens of programs including *Coast to Coast AM*, and is regularly invited to speak at paranormal conferences about his books. Joshua contributed to Robbie Graham's 2017 essay collection *UFOs: Reframing the Debate*, as well as David Weatherly's 2018 collection *Wood Knocks: Vol. 3*. Cutchin has also appeared on the hit History Channel television show *Ancient Aliens*. He is a recurring guest on *Where Did the Road Go?*, and maintains an online presence at JoshuaCutchin.com.

Them Old Ways Never Died is his first work of fiction.

Other Books by Joshua Cutchin

A Trojan Feast:
The Food and Drink Offerings of Aliens, Faeries, and Sasquatch (2015)

The Brimstone Deceit:
An In-Depth Examination of Supernatural Scents, Otherworldly Odors, and Monstrous Miasmas (2016)

Thieves in the Night:
A Brief History of Supernatural Child Abductions (2018)

Fairy Films:
Wee Folk on the Big Screen (2023, editor and contributor)

Ecology of Souls:
A New Mythology of Death & the Paranormal (2022)

- ~ Volume One
- ~ Volume Two
- ~ Companion

With co-author, Timothy Renner

Where the Footprints End:
High Strangeness and the Bigfoot Phenomenon (2020)

- ~ Volume One: *Folklore*
- ~ Volume Two: *Evidence*

Printed in Great Britain
by Amazon